ANNE BUSTARD

EGMONT
Publishing
New York

EGMONT

We bring stories to life

First published by Egmont Publishing, 2015
443 Park Avenue South, Suite 806
New York, NY 10016

1 3 5 7 9 8 6 4 2

www.egmontusa.com
www.annebustard.com

Library of Congress Cataloging-in-Publication Data
Bustard, Anne, 1951– author.

Anywhere but paradise / Anne Bustard.
pages cm
Summary: In 1960 twelve-year-old Peggy Sue and her family move to the island of Oahu, and she is finding it anything but paradise, because from the first day at school she is bullied and made fun of by the Hawaiian children, and she is worried sick about her beloved cat, who is in mandatory quarantine—and then the tsunami hits Hilo where her parents have gone on business.
ISBN 978-1-60684-585-1 (hardcover)
1. Middle schools—Hawaii--Juvenile fiction. 2. Bullying—Juvenile fiction. 3. Ethnic relations—Juvenile fiction. 4. Friendship—Juvenile fiction. 5. Tsunamis—Hawaii—Hilo—Juvenile fiction. 6. Hawaii—History—1959—Juvenile fiction. [1. Middle schools--Fiction. 2. Schools—Fiction. 3. Bullying—Fiction. 4. Ethnic relations—Fiction. 5. Friendship—Fiction. 6. Tsunamis—Fiction. 7. Hawaii—History—1959—Fiction.] I. Title.

PZ7.1.B89An 2015
813.54
[Fic]—dc23

2014034620

Printed in the United States of America

To Leilehua, a forever friend

Jail

BEST I CAN FIGURE, Hanu, Oahu, is almost four thousand miles from home.

And my cat, my sweet Howdy, hasn't purred in days. Hasn't since we arrived all the way from Gladiola, Texas.

I can't say I blame him, seeing as he's locked up in animal quarantine jail with all the other cat and dog newcomers.

Sitting with him on this wooden bench inside his chain-link pen with a tin roof, taking in breath after breath of smelly disinfectant makes my eyes sting. Twisting my head, I can barely see the tops of the coconut trees swaying in the gray sky.

One thing's for sure—Howdy doesn't have rabies.

But no one believes a twelve-year-old girl.

When you're twelve, a lot of folks don't listen to you. Like jailers. Like parents.

When you're twelve, you don't have a choice about where you live.

Good-bye Again

FOOTSTEPS HURRY toward us. Howdy's paws clasp both of my shoulders.

"Closing time," says the animal quarantine officer. "You can come back tomorrow."

Not when you live on the other side of the island. Not when Daddy has to drive the car to work tomorrow. Not when the only reason you got to come today was because tomorrow is your first day at a new school. And you promised seeing Howdy would clear up your two-day-old stomachache.

I pick Howdy off my shoulders, look into his pretty greens, and give his nose a kiss. I hold him like a baby and he nuzzles his head into my side.

"Peggy Sue," says Mama as she moves toward me with determination. "Say your good-byes."

"He's lonely," I say. Howdy stirs his hind legs. I shift him to my lap and scratch behind his ears. Somewhere inside him, I know he wants to purr. But right now he just can't.

"He's lucky," says Mama. "Lucky he got to come."

Mama's changed. Before our plans to move and the packing and the good-byes and her headaches, Mama knew. She knew that Howdy has always needed me close.

But for some reason, Mama didn't think Howdy should come all this way on account of his age, which is ten. She wasn't certain we could visit regularly, seeing as we'd live a ways away. She wasn't convinced we should spend the money. But Daddy and I had no doubt.

"I can see you need my help letting go," Mama says, tucking both sides of her wavy brown hair behind her ears. "Let's not prolong this." And just like that, she reaches for my cat.

"No," I say.

I let go. But I don't mean to.

Howdy's eyes open extra wide and he tries to meow, but no sound comes. His silent cry is the most pitiful thing of all. It is a sad so deep it can't find its way out.

Howdy dangles in front of me.

"You're hurting him," I say.

Mama holds him at arm's length like he is a suitcase of smelly clothes.

"This isn't easy for me, either."

"Love you," I say to my gray tabby. "I'll be back this weekend."

The officer nods.

Mama plops Howdy on the wooden bench and brushes cat hair from her navy skirt. Howdy slinks underneath the bench, cowering.

The door squeals shut and the officer clamps down the lever on Howdy's cell. His release date, July 29, 1960, is stamped on the small white card in the pocket at the front of his cage.

Right next door lives a young calico named Tinkerbell. She'll leave a month before Howdy. Tink must still be out for a bath or something, because she's not there.

Dogs bark all around the station. I'm sure they're saying, "I want my family; let me out; take me home." I am worried sick for Howdy. He is very afraid of dogs.

It's our fifth day here. One hundred fifteen more days until he's free?

Hang on, Howdy.

Hang on.

Hanu Intermediate

SHE POPS OUT OF NOWHERE.

"Move it, *haole,*" says the girl wearing a bold red-and-white muumuu dress. And a big old scowl. Her long dark hair is almost to her waist.

My arm scrapes against the prickly bricks beside the counselor's office.

I know that word. It was on the list Daddy made for me just before we moved. I've heard it plenty of times since we arrived.

The girl called me white.

She said it like it was dirty.

My face heats up and my mouth opens. But no words come out. I don't understand. Why is she acting so ugly?

"I got places to go," says the girl. But she just stands there and stares, hands on her hips. "Say you're sorry."

I clutch my binder and sack lunch. I don't want

trouble. Not with her. Not with anyone. Today. Or any day. "I'm Peggy Sue Bennett and I apologize if I was standing in your way."

The girl nods, so I guess I said it right.

"But you didn't have to push," I say under my breath.

The girl's deep brown eyes fire up. She heard me? Read my mind?

"Something wrong with you, haole? You talk funny. You're skinny tall."

Not that tall. Same as her. But she's sturdier.

"You wear funny clothes, too."

I wasn't dressed like anyone else at Hanu Intermediate, that's for sure. Here, girls wear cotton dresses or short muumuus.

Before we came, I'd only seen one muumuu in real life. And that was years ago. The mayor's wife showed off her billowy, egg-yolk-yellow-and-white muumuu at a school assembly after she and her husband took a Hawaiian vacation. It was long. Since arriving, I've already observed that these dresses come in other shapes, styles, and prints.

And that no one wears saddle shoes and bobby socks to this school. At least some have ponytails, like me.

The counselor's door opens onto the outside walkway, and Mrs. Taniguchi, the woman in charge of my class schedule, pokes her head out. Her soft pink manicured fingernails match her pencil skirt. "Kiki, I asked you to come fifteen minutes before the first bell. You're late."

"It's her fault," says the girl, tossing her head in my direction.

Kiki. What I wouldn't give for a Texas twister to swoop her right up and carry her away. Far, far away. Or me.

Mrs. Taniguchi sighs. "Good morning, Peggy Sue. Let me get your paperwork." She puts her arm around Kiki's shoulders and leads her into her office.

Kiki whips around just before the door closes and mouths *Stupid haole.*

On second thought, how about a tidal wave instead of a twister? But there is no whoosh of wind. No crash of waves.

I blink hard.

What did I expect? That I'd be given a flower lei and a smile like when we arrived at the airport?

I look out onto the school courtyard surrounded by one- and two-story cinder-block buildings. Kids stand in groups under the few scrawny coconut trees, talking, laughing, kicking up the red dirt.

I count. Twice.

Eighteen haoles out of maybe one hundred.

One Chance

MRS. TANIGUCHI EMERGES a few minutes later with my schedule. "Your homeroom is B-26," she says, and gives me directions.

"Thank you, ma'am."

"Have a good day and let me know if you need anything. And, Peggy Sue, we're informal here; you don't have to call me ma'am."

I stifle my next thank-you and nod instead as she slips back into her office.

The opening bell rings loud and long. Kids holler see-ya-laters and set out for the classrooms. Some speed, juggling towers of books and poster boards lined with charts and diagrams. Some poke along, teasing out last bits of conversation. Some move halfway between zip and drag.

Back home, I was a pokey one. Gabfests with friends happened only outside of class. On Wednesday mornings, my best friend, Cindy, and I hoisted the flags at the front of the school. Afterward, we'd configure the longest possible route to homeroom.

Today is Wednesday. And I'll be pokey for a different reason. Here, I'm in no hurry to be the new kid.

After the crowd thins, I head down the covered sidewalk toward the cafeteria building and turn left. I look up. In the small gap between the cafeteria and the next buildings I see dark gray clouds pinch the corners of the green mountain range in the distance. I can't see the ocean, but I feel its breeze pushing me forward.

I plod along. Four two-story rectangular buildings with outside walkways open onto patches of shared grass. As far as I can see, banks of tan metal lockers front the classrooms on either side of the buildings. A few stragglers click locks and spin dials one last time. At the very end, I find room 26.

The door is closed, but through the open louvered windows above the lockers, I can hear a pencil sharpener grind, and I catch the rise and fall of voices settling in. I take a deep breath, turn the knob, and step inside.

The room silences.

My eyes glom on to my black-and-white saddle shoes. One lace is undone.

"Welcome, Miss Bennett," says a man's voice.

I look up at the teacher stepping toward me. His flattop haircut glistens like Daddy's. His crisp, short-sleeved white shirt looks store-bought new. "I'm Mr. Nakamoto."

I try to smile, but my upper lip sticks to my teeth. Papers shuffle, whispers rise.

I glance around the room. B-26 doesn't look much different from the classrooms back home. Same kind of desks. Same blackboard. Bulletin boards with maps and facts. Even the same framed photo of President Eisenhower. But there are also portraits of other folks I don't know. I take a closer look. They are royalty: I count seven kings and a queen.

"You'll need this after a few classes," says Mr. Nakamoto, handing me a lock with a number on the back and a combination tag attached. "You're in my last period for Hawaiian history. I'll give you your materials then."

"Thank you," I say.

Mr. Nakamoto turns to the class. "Attention." Kids sit up straighter than straight, eyes forward, mouths closed. "Meet Miss Peggy Sue Bennett, from Gladiola, Texas."

A sea of questioning faces study me. They're probably asking: Why would anyone transfer at the end of the year, and in the middle of the week, no less? Does she have a tremor or something, because that paper in her hand is quivering something fierce? Will this outsider make it? Will she last?

"Miss Bennett, would you like to say hello?" asks Mr. Nakamoto.

Mama's parting words after breakfast swirl in my head—"You only have one chance to make a first impression, so do good."

"Hi, y'all." I wave.

The class erupts into laughter and my face heats up for the second time this morning. Maybe I shouldn't have spoken. Maybe I shouldn't have waved.

"There's a seat in the back," says Mr. Nakamoto.

I hurry down the row by the windows, focused on the floor.

"For those of you just waking up," Mr. Nakamoto says as chalk marks punctuate the blackboard, "it is April sixth. Including today, that makes thirty-seven school days left."

The class whoops and hollers.

"And it would behoove you to remember the change in the bus schedule. . . ."

I slink into an empty chair, stack my belongings on the desk, and retie my shoe.

The boy on my left, with a wavy strand of black hair in the middle of his forehead, watches me.

I sit up and clasp my lock.

"Rehearsals for the May Day ceremony . . ." continues Mr. Nakamoto.

"Hey, Texas," whispers my new neighbor. "Do you have a horse?"

"I have a cat. A cat named Howdy."

The boy shrugs, looking disappointed. His eyes brighten. "How about an oil well?"

I shake my head and the boy snaps his fingers. "Oooh, junk."

Seems like I can't please anyone today.

Two girls up ahead pass notes and stifle giggles as Mr. Nakamoto's announcements march on.

Without looking at the numbers on my lock, I spin the dial this way and that, listening to the whir. It's the closest sound to a purr I've heard in days, so I keep spinning.

In Gladiola, it's lunchtime now. In Gladiola, one table in the junior high cafeteria is chatting and laughing as they fold gum wrappers for the chain whose length will surely grow to *Guinness Book of Records* status. In Gladiola, there's an empty seat beside Cindy at that table.

Out the window, the mountain range with its various shades of green is in shadow, with just a thread of light. Two thin lines of white water stream down the folds in its face.

Second Chances

"I HOPE YOU'RE a good seamstress. Or a quick learner," says Mrs. Barsdale, the first-period home ec teacher. She must use a can of hair spray on her helmet-shaped blond bob. It doesn't move as she searches for her roll book under stacks of fabric samples and whatnots on her desk. "We're already two weeks into our sewing module," she explains while I stand next to her desk.

Grams helped me make my skirt and blouse, but I don't tell her that.

"Mrs. Barsdale," a girl calls, and waves from the front row. "I need help."

"As you can see," Mrs. Barsdale says, not looking up, "I am busy."

"You always are," mumbles the girl. She keeps her arm raised, props her other elbow on the edge of the sewing machine table, and rests her head in her hand.

Two others already have their hands up. One group visits next to the supply cabinets while another chats around a sewing machine. Some girls unfold pattern directions and read; a few thread needles. One machine *zzztZzzzztZzzzts* away.

Eventually, Mrs. Barsdale pulls a thin brown book from a tangle of measuring tapes and assorted notions. "Are you in seventh or eighth?"

I remember the counselor had said this class has both. "Seventh," I say. I study her angular face and the beauty mark above her upper lip.

"Tall for your age," she muses and print-writes my name at the bottom of a page.

I slouch a tad. Back home, I'm smack-dab in the middle of my class heightwise. Here, I'm tall.

"This way," she says, and steers me toward the pattern books lying on a slanted tabletop at the back of the room.

No introductions. Good. I just want to blend in.

"Mrs. Barsdale," girls call out, waving their hands as we pass by. "Please help me next." "Then me." "And me."

The teacher doesn't answer.

"Find a simple dress you'd like to make and I'll bring you the supply list," she tells me.

I choose a stool, face the backs of my classmates, and turn page after page after page, shutting out the world around me.

"You again?" says a voice behind me. "You following me, haole?"

"Not on purpose," I say, spinning around.

"Kiki," hollers the teacher from across the room. "Get to work."

I blow a puff of air toward my bangs and return to the pages. But I don't hear her walk away.

Two quick steps. A hand shoots out. *Thwack.* The thick catalog in front of me slams shut.

I pull my fingers back, but not fast enough.

"Hey," I say, and shake my hand, trying to get rid of the sting.

Kiki grins, tosses back her long waterfall hair, and walks away. A few girls turn; their faces offer pity.

Sewing gives you second chances. I like that. If you don't get it right the first time or the second or the third, it's okay. You can rip out the stitches and begin again.

When the bell rings, I am out the door before anyone else.

It's only the end of my first class and I already want to start over.

Zigzag Day

DOWNSTAIRS CLASS. Upstairs class. Upstairs. Down. Down.

Add in three building changes, one wrong-way detour, and that was my morning.

I shift my binder and heap of books from one hip to another and step away from the crowds surging over walkways and grass toward the cafeteria. It's lunchtime. Behind me, dark clouds still cling to the mountaintops. Ahead and toward the ocean, the sky is lighter by a few degrees.

When the sidewalk empties, I speed toward my locker. I haven't made it there yet. Book spines jab into my skin. Red marks my arms from their weight.

A teacher with a whistle around his neck whips around the next corner and hustles toward me. "Where's your hall pass?"

"I don't have one, I—"

"This area's off-limits until the bell," he says in a don't-mess-with-me way.

I make a U-turn and slog toward lunch.

Inside the cafeteria, unfamiliar spicy smells fill the noisy, steamy space. I stand close to the door and scan for a seat at the end of a table. Any table. No one really looks at me, though a few give side-ways glances. I'm late and there's no room that I can tell.

I set my books beside me on the rough concrete outside the cafeteria and choke down my baloney sandwich.

After PE, I'm back in Mr. Nakamoto's homeroom for Hawaiian history. Last period.

I cram a few books and my three-ring binder into the wire holder under my desk and stack the overflow on the floor. I have a clear view all the way to Kealoha Drive, the main street through Hanu's downtown.

"Class will commence," says Mr. Nakamoto.

I fix my eyes on the front of the room.

"Sixty-seven years ago, Queen Liliuokalani was dethroned by the haoles," he says.

There is that word again.

But the two other haole girls and three boys in the room don't flinch.

Mr. Nakamoto didn't say it ugly. But it did sound like he thinks they made a mistake.

I study the photograph of the queen above the blackboard. I think I see kindness in her eyes.

Apparently, the haoles imprisoned her, too, which makes me feel even sorrier for her.

Beef

AFTER THE DISMISSAL BELL, I track down my locker—bottom row, center. I pile up my books close by and work the combination on my lock. Everyone clears out, including the teachers. There's a faculty meeting in the library.

Five more tries and the lock still won't budge.

A flash of red and white at the water fountain catches my eye. Kiki. But she isn't looking my way. I squat down. Listen. Hear nothing.

"Haole," Kiki whispers in my ear.

My shoulders jump. "Look," I say staring up, "I said I was sorry about this morning. Let's move on, okay?"

"Haole, you like beef?" she asks.

Is there a right answer? "It's okay," I say, standing. "But I like chicken better."

"What did I tell you," she says to the two girls

beside her, bent over with laughter. "She needs to be educated."

"So educate her," says the girl in yellow.

"I'm asking you to fight," says Kiki, glowering, showing me a fist.

I pull in a sharp breath.

"Didn't catch your answer," says Kiki, cupping her ear.

"No," I say a little too loudly.

"No?" she asks, circling me.

I stand rock-still.

"No?" she asks again. "That's it?"

"No, thank you?" I say, my voice unsteady.

"The haole's trying to be funny," Kiki says to her friends. "But we know she's chicken."

"Bawk. Bawk. Bawk," sounds the girl in yellow. Kiki and the other girl join in. *"Bawk. Bawk. Bawk,"* they chant.

Their words push me against the wall of metal. A lock jabs my right hip. I wince.

"How long have you been here?" asks Kiki.

"Five and a half days."

"Told you she's a fresh-off-the-boat haole," Kiki says, holding a hand out to her friends. "Pay up."

"Tomorrow," they say. "Promise."

Kiki sneers, turns back to me, and smiles extra big. "I'll go easy on you, FOB. We won't fight today. There's a special day for that. It's the last day of school. Kill Haole Day. I'll keep reminding you so you don't forget." Kiki narrows her eyes and moves closer. No smile. "Don't even think about telling," she says, "or I'll introduce you to even more of my friends."

"You are, you are . . ." I try to think of the word—"mahalo." I want to make sure she understands I know a thing or two. Understands what I think about her. *Mahalo* is on all the garbage cans at the airport—I am sure it means *trash*.

"Mahalo?" Kiki cackles. "The new haole's trying to talk Hawaiian? You heard her," she says, and pokes her friend in yellow in the shoulder. "She said 'thank you.' She thanked me for inviting her to fight."

Thank you. Why didn't I keep my mouth shut?

"I hurt from too much laughing," says Kiki. "Let's hele."

I don't know what that means yet, but I hope it means they are leaving.

It must. They back away slowly. Pointing. Chanting. Then run off.

I take in big gulps of air. Try to catch my breath. Like I am the one running. I slump down, hug my knees, and bury my face in my arms.

My body is one big shiver.

She hates me and she doesn't even know me. She hates me so much she wants to fight? I can't change the color of my skin.

Kill Haole Day.

I already feel dead.

The Dog

I CAN'T, I won't stay at school another second.

I snatch my mound of books and scurry toward our tiny house near the beach a few blocks away.

The books chafe against my already sore arms. Only when I stop to shift the heaviness from one arm to another do I take in front yards of green, chock-full of fragrant pink and yellow and white and red flowers. And kids racing their bikes down the middle of the curvy street. We forget to say hello.

Up until this move, I've hardly had anything really bad ever happen to me.

Except once.

Last year right after Christmas, a stray dog started coming around Russell Weber's house.

The afternoon I rode by on my bike, it took chase. It surprised me more than anything, running alongside me, barking, baring its teeth. I sped up, but I hit a rock and fell off.

It growled.

I screamed.

It knew I was afraid.

It charged.

And bit me. On my leg. Bit me good.

Then it ran off. Nobody ever found it, which meant they couldn't test it for rabies.

They give you a passel of rabies shots, all in the stomach.

They hurt bad. Real bad, no matter how hard I squeezed Mama's hand.

When the long needle plunged in, thousands of angry bees attacked.

Stinging.

Deep.

Deeper.

Fourteen shots in fourteen days.

After each one, Mama always offered to take me for a Dr Pepper float at the soda fountain or fix me a special meal. But it didn't begin to make up for it.

For my sorrows, Grams and I made the pleated skirt I'm wearing now. Grandpa painted a picture of spring wildflowers just for me. Every day, Cindy bought me my favorite chewing gum with yellow wrappers.

Howdy curled up even closer beside me each night.

Kiki is like that dog.

Knows I'm afraid.

And she bites.

Come September

I CLOMP UP THE STEPS of our green-and-white wood-frame rental. It came furnished. Our belongings are on the way. On either side of the front door, red hibiscus flowers bloom the same color as the roof.

"How was school?" Mama asks as soon as I walk in.

She's on the couch in the living-dining room wearing sunglasses. A surefire sign that one of her sick headaches is fixing to brew and she might take to her bed. She's had more than her fair share of late.

I plunk my books on the rattan coffee table in front of her and fake a smile. "School was"—I pause—"very educational."

"I'm glad to hear that."

Mama is good at asking questions. An expert, actually. Before she married, she taught high school English.

But I don't want to talk about my day. Not to

her. Not now. I don't want Mama to take to her bed because of me. Or march up to school and make a fuss. I may not like school, but I can make it until the end of the year. As of tomorrow, thirty-six more days. I can last thirty-six days.

Because come September, I won't be here. Not if I can help it.

This morning Mrs. Taniguchi asked me what I needed.

Now I know: a one-way ticket back home.

And of course Howdy, who should be napping in the sunbeam on the braided rug on the floor beneath me right now.

Sooner than soon, I'll shuffle cards for canasta every afternoon with Grams, watch trains roll by the station with Grandpa, and play Ping-Pong with Cindy, just like we planned. Howdy and I will live at 127 Main Street, Gladiola, Texas. Not 808 Hanu Road, Hanu, Hawaii.

I've had enough of paradise, thank you very much. I can't wait to leave.

"Mama, I need some fabric and a few sewing supplies for home ec," I say before the next question comes.

"Sewing ought to make you feel right at home," she

says, rubbing her temples. "Let's go later, just before supper."

"Sure, Mama. That'd be fine."

"And maybe you could hose off the front window later, too."

It's one of my daily chores. Living near the water, salt spray clouds the windows with a thin, sticky film. It makes it hard to see outside. Blasting the window with the hose would only make Mama's head worse.

"Okay, I better start my homework, then. My first hula lesson is in an hour."

"I like your initiative," says Mama.

"Oh, and how about a raise in my allowance?" I ask it casual-like so as not to create suspicion. It'll take a heap of money to fund my trip. I know without asking that my parents won't just hand it over. Mama's already said our grocery and gas money doesn't stretch as far here, and that I had to choose between surfing lessons and hula. "Mama, you always up the amount when I start school," I say. "And this is a new start."

"Nice try, Peggy Sue. But next year isn't that far away."

Exactly.

Just because Mama won't fund me doesn't mean

others won't. Hanu's small, but surely some folks will pay good money for my help. Pay for something they need. Pay for something so routine I'll have a steady income. Something like . . . I skedaddle into my room to make flyers for my first new business venture: Peggy Sue's Window-Washing Service.

Hula, Here i Come

I SETTLE ONTO my temporary army surplus bed with squeaky springs. With my binder paper and crayons, I compose my window-washing business advertisement.

Hawaiian music floats through my window from next door. A steel guitar and ukulele pluck and strum the sunny melody. A bass joins in. I can't catch all the words, but I hear *aloha*. The voices echo, mirroring a bright, cloudless day. I lift my chin, slow my breathing, and picture the light.

Sometimes a song sounds like a question, sometimes it sounds like an exclamation point, sometimes like a dot-dot-dot-to-be-continued story. This one sounds like an answer or at least the beginning of one.

The song takes me back to Saturday. We saw the Kodak Hula Show, just steps from the sand on Waikiki Beach. We perched on the top row of the bleachers in the squinty sunshine. The grassy area below was roped off for the performance, and just beyond, surfers navigated the sparkling blue the best they could. The breeze stirred the salty air with suntan lotion and flowers. I wore my still-fresh flower lei. Tourists clicked cameras all around. It was our second day here. And I sat inside a perfect-picture postcard.

Dancers in green leaf skirts, red tops, and yellow plumeria leis shook matching feather gourds in unison to a quick-moving song. Then, wearing long muumuus, they swayed ever so gracefully to more stories. I could have watched for hours.

Right then and there, I decided hula was for me. I wanted to dance just like them.

Turns out, it was meant to be.

Mrs. Halani lives next door and she gives lessons. Daddy knew her and Mr. Halani from when he was stationed here during World War II. They have a son in high school and a daughter my age. But I haven't met the girl yet on account of her chicken pox. It seemed like it took forever for my own itchy red spots to go away last year.

On Sunday, Mrs. Halani told me she's been teaching for more than fifteen years. She said her students are as young as four and as old as seventy-two. She said she could teach anyone to hula.

I figure that includes me. For as long as I'm here.

My First Lesson

THE CLASS LINES UP in three straight rows. I choose a spot in the back and curl my toes into the woven mat.

We face Mrs. Halani at the front of her garage-turned-studio. Red and yellow feather gourds, bamboo sticks, and smooth black stones fill the shelves behind her. To my left and right are floor-to-ceiling mirrors.

Our willowy, tall teacher wears her dark hair stylishly short. A pink plumeria blossom is bobby-pinned behind her left ear, and a gold bracelet with black letters decorates one wrist.

I stand beside a girl whose hair flows below her waist. She smiles.

There might be a girl from my homeroom in the front row, but I'm not sure. There's a pink ribbon in her hair, but she's not in school clothes.

Mrs. Halani begins to sing about lovely hula hands.

Thank goodness it's in English with just a smidgen of Hawaiian, so I can mostly understand. Her voice is high and soft and sweet. Her body dips and sways as her arms and hands tell a story about aloha, love. But it's different from the one I heard a little while ago. When she sings the mushy part, we try to act nonchalant, but a few laughs spurt out.

"Now repeat after me," Mrs. Halani says, and begins again.

I take in the song, raise my arms, and move my feet. I am a bird.

I bump into the girl next to me. "Sorry," I whisper.

"Remember to smile," says Mrs. Halani.

I picture myself onstage at the Gladiola Rec Center. I am the wind.

My elbow pokes the girl's ear. "Sorry, again."

The song ends and the girl rubs her shoulder. "Make that sorry times three," I say.

"You'll catch on," she says.

"Peggy Sue," says Mrs. Halani. "Let's focus on your footwork the next time through. We'll get to the hands later."

Practice. All I need to do is practice.

All day every day.

Like an Olympian.

After class, Mrs. Halani lets me post one of my flyers in her studio. "Saving for something special?" she asks.

"Just summer extras," I say. I keep it short, hoping she won't ask me anything else.

"You're very smart," she says. "It's always good to put a little aside."

Older girls prance in for the next class and I scoot out. I plaster the neighborhood with a dozen ads. The sky is still dark up by the mountain range, but here by the water, it's only partly cloudy.

Washed Out

"I MIGHT NOT BE UP for a trip to the store for your sewing supplies after all," says Mama when I return from posting my window-washing ads. She's still on the couch. Her sunglasses perch atop her head and her eyes read tired.

"I can go by myself," I say. The store is a fifteen-minute walk away. "Mrs. Barsdale recommended Fujimoto's Five-and-Dime, and I know exactly where it is."

"That might be for the best," says Mama. "Take my wallet and an umbrella. It's been threatening all day."

I risk it and leave the umbrella. The sun flickers behind clouds as I retrace my route to school, cut across the practice fields, and skip over to Kealoha Drive. The main business section is one long block with a few side streets. Fujimoto's Five-and-Dime is at the end. The sky grows darker and heavier.

On this side of the street, the stores stand alone. I walk close in, avoiding cars parked almost to their doors. Seascapes on easels front the art gallery window. Pink coral earrings, strands of pearls, and bracelets of jade rest on black velvet at the jewelry store. A fat drop of water lands on my shoulder, another on my shoe. The five-and-dime closes soon and I want to get back in case it pours.

I'm in and out in fifteen.

I stand under the store's entryway and watch the raindrops fall closer together. I stuff my bag of purchases under my blouse and lunge into the drippy wet. By the time I charge across the fields at school, the rain is steady. Mud splatters up the back of my legs with each step. My shoes are in soggy ruin.

I bet it's raining at the quarantine station, too. Howdy doesn't take to stormy weather. As soon as rain comes, he slinks under a bed or behind a chair. I hope his kennel doesn't leak. I hope tonight his bench will do.

• ❁ •

We eat supper as soon as I finish showering.

And I tell my parents all about my new business.

"You'll be flooded with calls," says Daddy.

I hope. But the phone hasn't rung yet.

"Mama, did I miss any while I was out?"

"No," she says, rubbing her temples. "Not a one."

After dessert, I stack the plates on the counter and reach for the receiver on the wall phone across the teeny kitchen. Maybe the line is dead. But before the phone reaches my ear, I hear the monotone. Quicker than quick, I return it to its cradle so callers won't get a busy signal and give up.

Of course. The rain. The rain washed all of my words away.

Ocean or Train?

IT'S STILL DARK.

Dawn won't come for hours.

Slowly, I stretch my legs so as not to disturb my cat.

Then I remember: Howdy's not there.

I shiver in the coolness, pull up my covers, hug my pillow, and listen.

In the stillness, I hear shushing sounds like the soft inhale and the louder, stronger exhale of the trains that pass through Gladiola while we sleep.

But this isn't Gladiola. This isn't a train.

It's the ocean.

If it weren't for other houses and trees, I could see the big blue from here. Hanu Road winds next to the beach, with occasional side streets angling to the water. If I could walk a straight line, the beach is across the road and eight houses away. Down a ways to the left, a beach park with coconut trees and tall,

tall, ironwood trees with long needles and thimble-size pinecones stand just yards from the water.

I close my eyes and pretend I hear a train. That I'm home.

Sharing

"AN INDUSTRIOUS START," says Mrs. Barsdale, the home ec teacher, the next morning at school. Her hair doesn't appear to have strayed one strand since yesterday. She inspects my fabric pieces at a huge table in the back of the room. "Though I always check my students' work before they cut."

I wrinkle my eyebrows. I must've missed hearing her say that. I stayed up late specifically to cut out the pattern.

"But it looks like you did well." Mrs. Barsdale reaches into her lab coat pocket, pulls out a scrap of paper and a pencil, and scribbles something.

"Oh, no!" someone hollers from the front of the room.

"Excuse me, I'll be right back," Mrs. Barsdale says, and hurries toward the girls congregating around a machine by the door. "Class," she yells. "Sit down. Be quiet. Work." She takes a breath and adds, "Eighth graders, I expect you to lead by example."

A girl in line for the ironing boards near the windows might be the same one from homeroom and hula. There's a pink ribbon in her hair.

Sewing machines drone. Hands wave every which way, but Mrs. Barsdale doesn't seem to notice.

"We share machines," the teacher says when she returns, and motions me toward the front of the room.

My eyes dart around the space. Every machine has two girls. Except one. Grams always says bad things happen in threes. It's only my second day of school, and I am already over my limit.

"Have you met Kiki Kahana?" Mrs. Barsdale asks.

"I have," I say.

Kiki rubs her hands together and smiles all sticky sweet.

Of all the girls, I have to partner with her?

"Let Peggy Sue take the next turn," says the teacher. "She is even further behind than you." Mrs. Barsdale looks at the clock. "Switch places," she hollers.

"Piggy Sue, Piggy Sue," whisper-sings Kiki as I sew. Over and over and over again.

I'd give anything not to be me right now. Not to be haole.

I don't talk. I try not to listen. I sew.

Maybe if I ignore her, she'll stop.

But she doesn't.

"You know Madame Pele, right?" she says a minute later.

No, not personally. But I've heard of the volcano goddess. "Yes," I say.

"Don't take pork over the Pali or she will send trouble your way. Bad trouble."

My shoulders squirm without my consent. Another threat? Or is she joshing? This girl won't quit needling me.

I purse my lips and press the foot pedal harder.

I wish I could talk to a friend about Kiki. Ask about Kill Haole Day. But I don't have a friend. Even if I did, everyone knows people keep secrets sometimes. Sometimes they don't.

Two girls sharing the machine next to us pop over. "My grandmother told me, never take bananas with you on a boat," says one.

"Or let your chopsticks stand in a full rice bowl," says the other.

Both bring bad luck. I sew in a seam and stop. But I don't look up.

"And don't," says Kiki, "pick a lehua flower unless you want it to rain."

"My cousins tested it out once," says a girl. "Not a cloud in the sky. Sixty-four minutes after picking—*boom*—rain."

"This is not a social hour, girls," says Mrs. Barsdale, clapping her hands. "Work, work, work."

The girls return to their seats.

I'm spooked. Which I'm sure is their point.

Kiki starts to sing again.

And I count the days until summer.

Hawaiian History Again

"I'M PASSING OUT A REVIEW sheet for your upcoming test," says Mr. Nakamoto at the end of class that afternoon.

I notice right off it's not one sheet, it's three or four stapled together.

I glance down the first page: *King Kalakaua the Merrie Monarch, Bayonet Constitution of 1887, "Hawaii Pono'ī," Missionary Party, Iolani Palace, John Owen Dominis, Committee of Safety.*

"But the test isn't until next Thursday," says the boy in front of me.

"Mr. Aquino," says Mr. Nakamoto, "I can see my magnanimous gesture escapes your consciousness. As I've said prior to every quiz, it would behoove you to study some each day rather than cram the night before. This aid," he says, holding the papers as high as a torch, "is a gift."

The boy sighs extra loud. Even though no one else makes a sound, the looks on our faces tell the same story—we're sighing on the inside.

Mr. Nakamoto is still talking, and I tune back in. ". . . we'll end our year with a unit on statehood and look at our first months as the fiftieth star."

Statehood? All I know is the date, August 21, last year. Gladiola held a party at the rec center to celebrate and the whole town showed up wearing red, white, and blue. Cindy and I handed out plastic leis. We drank Hawaiian punch, ate cake with coconut icing, and entered a hula hoop contest, which I lost to my friend. Before we left, we sang to Daddy, because it was his birthday, too.

Here, I imagine, there was an even bigger party. Parades with folks on floats covered in flowers, riders on horseback draped in leis. Bands playing patriotic songs for crowds gathered up and down the streets, cheering, waving flags. Important speeches by the governor and other dignitaries. Boats clustered along the shoreline, some spraying plumes of water, making rainbows. Honking horns. Hula dancing and music. And later, fireworks that reached for the stars.

But after only two days in Mr. Nakamoto's class, I

can already tell that at the end of the unit, he will give us another test instead of a party.

• ✿ •

As soon as I'm in from school, I'm out again.

The water from the garden hose beats *bat-a-bat-a* against the front window of the house. I move in time with the music next door.

Just one more day of school and I'll see Howdy. I hope he and Tinkerbell have become good friends.

I zoom back inside, make more posters for my window-washing business, and circulate them around the neighborhood once more.

It's only partly cloudy. No rain.

Extra Credit

"THIS WAS SUPPOSED TO take you over a week," Mrs. Barsdale says Friday morning while standing beside the sewing machine. She taps the beauty mark above her upper lip.

My darts are in and pressed, shoulders stitched together, and front facings basted.

It's hard for me to tell from the sound of her voice if being ahead is a good thing or not.

"So I'd like you to help Kiki."

"What?" says Kiki. "I don't need help from her. I don't need help from the haole."

"Truth be told, I'm terrible at putting in zippers. And there's so much more to do. The back facings, the hem, handwork . . ."

Mrs. Barsdale picks up a pin from the floor and sticks it into the red pincushion attached to her wrist. "I am prepared to offer you extra credit, Peggy Sue."

That sounds good, but I know it really means nothing.

"Haoles helping haoles," says Kiki.

"Typical," murmurs the girl at the machine next to us.

"Kiki, I'm trying to help you. It's the perfect solution. We discussed your academic problems in the counselor's office. You promised you'd raise your grades. You need help. This girl is an accomplished seamstress. You're akamai, Kiki. Act like it. Act smart."

"She can help me," says the girl to my left.

"Or me," says another.

"No," says Kiki, glaring right at me. "She's mine."

"It's settled, then," says Mrs. Barsdale, walking away.

"I can't wait to leave this stupid school," Kiki says. "Next year, high school will be so much better."

So she's an eighth grader.

"Stupid haole," says Kiki.

"What have I done?"

"Plenty. You're all the same; you're all related to Captain Cook. Diseased."

Diseased?

"You come over here and tell us what to do. How to live. You are not the boss of me."

"I—"

"Stop bothering me. Stop talking."

Fine, I mouth, and adjust my ponytail. That, I think, is the smart thing to do.

Hula Practice

PRACTICE TAKES TIME and this afternoon I have nothing but. I haven't gotten any phone calls for work. No sense washing our windows today. It's raining. Again. Raining so hard I can't hear the music next door.

The wind gusts outside and the hula papers on my dresser scatter to the floor. The small gray-and-white cat figurine Cindy gave me as a going-away gift tumps over on the bamboo tray.

I shut the windows before more damage is done, right the cat, and collect the pages from Mrs. Halani. They hold the words for each song, with the English translation as needed, and instructions for the movements.

I should dance each hula three times, she said.

A portable hi-fi came with the house. Mama bought me the hula records I need.

So I will dance.

I place a record on the turntable and begin.

And as soon as I do, I make a mistake. So I start again.

And again.

I want to dance all the way through the song without goofing up. Just once.

"Seems like I kept hearing the same section of music over and over," says Mama as I grab cheese and crackers a while later. "Is that record player on the fritz?"

No, I am.

Howdy

FINALLY, IT'S SATURDAY.

"I'm here, Howdy," I say as the quarantine officer unlocks the door to my cat's kennel and Daddy and I slip in.

Howdy has smushed himself up against the corner of his cell under the wooden bench.

"I'm sorry I couldn't come sooner," I say as I lie belly-down on the cold concrete and glimpse my cat in shadow. I can't read his eyes. "I can stay for two whole hours today," I say and reach out to pet him. "And tomorrow, too."

Howdy lays back his ears, opens his mouth, and hisses.

"Howdy," I cry, pulling back my hand. "It's me, Peggy Sue. You know, the one who loves you. The one who misses you. The one who wishes more than anything else that you didn't have to live here."

Howdy closes his mouth, but his ears stay in their I-don't-trust-you position.

"Howdy will be all right, Peggy Sue," says Daddy. He stretches out his long legs and settles on the bench with his paperwork. "He's a Bennett. And you brought him his favorite food." Daddy hands me the aluminum foil with a few pieces of leftover chicken I saved from dinner last night.

I lie on my side and place a piece of meat halfway between my cat and me. Howdy sniffs the air, but doesn't budge.

I brought extra chicken for Tinkerbell, too, but all I see is an empty cage next door. Maybe it's her checkup time.

I wiggle closer to Howdy and reach for him again. *Whop*. Howdy's paw hits my fingers. "Ouch," I cry, and rub my hand.

"No fighting, you two," says Daddy.

"Not funny," I say.

"Just give him a little more breathing room."

So I do. I scoot back, but my eyes never leave him. "Everything is going to be okay, Howdy. I promise."

• ✿ •

"Time to pick up your mother from the beauty parlor," says Daddy way too soon.

"That cat's got some pounds on him," says the officer as we step out of Howdy's cage. "He'll probably lose a few. Most do. At least the ones that make it."

"What do you mean?" I ask.

I look into Tinkerbell's pen. That's when I notice. No bowl of water. No bowl of food. No pan of litter. No small white card on the cage.

"Y'all were supposed to take care of her," I cry.

I squeeze my eyes shut, as if that will block out the truth. Tinkerbell was leaving four weeks before Howdy.

"We did our best," says the officer.

I open my eyes and pull away from the cage.

Poor Tink. I am sure she died of a broken heart.

"Oh, Howdy," I say. "You've got to be strong."

I trudge out of the building after Daddy, my insides tight and twisty. The waterfront just across the way mirrors the dark gray sky.

• ❁ •

On the drive back over the Pali Highway, I close my eyes and count.

Less than a day until I see Howdy again.

Then it'll be one hundred and ten more days until he is released. Unless of course I can break him out sooner.

Thirty-four more days of school.

Forty more hours until I have to see *her*.

And I don't know how many more days until Howdy and I leave this awful island and head home to Gladiola, Texas. Truth be told, anywhere sounds better today. Anywhere but paradise.

Night-Blooming Cereus

BEFORE BED, Daddy sticks his head into my room. "I've kept forgetting to show y'all something in the yard," he says. "Your mama just said she'll take a rain check, but I'm hoping you'll come out back."

The TV blares from the front room. That's Mama. She doesn't like to miss her favorites.

"Sure, Daddy."

We find the flashlight in the kitchen drawer. I scamper down the back steps and tiptoe onto the cool grass. No stepping on any bufos, brownish warty toads, for me. No petting them, either. Daddy had said it's best not to tangle with them. Though they're mostly harmless to us, these critters are poisonous. Cats tend to ignore them, but sometimes dogs can't resist. I'm not taking any chances.

Daddy strides ahead, tall, confident. I hop gingerly across the lawn, between plumeria trees with their skinny branches and long narrow leaves. I take in deep breaths of their sweet-smelling clusters and make my way to the monkeypod tree in the back corner where Daddy stands.

"This is one of the reasons I chose this house to rent," he says, giving its enormous trunk a pat. "That and of course the Halanis. This tree is probably older than me."

Starlight twinkles through its big branches and umbrella-shaped top.

"Shine the light up the trunk until you see something," says Daddy.

"Like what?"

"Go on. You'll know it when you see it."

I move the light up, up, up. And stop. Scraggly legs of a plant cling to the trunk. It doesn't look like it belongs. Instead, it looks like something I might come across in a pasture outside Gladiola. The leaves are flat, spiny, bumpy, green, and a little wider than a ruler. Like a cactus, though not like one I've ever seen.

"It's a night-blooming cereus," Daddy says.

"I don't see any flowers."

"It'll bloom when it's ready, kitten, and only in the dark."

I kind of like that. It will bloom in secret, as if it doesn't want anyone to notice. As if it doesn't want the attention of the bright light. Only people who look carefully will see.

I shine the beam back on the plant.

Not even a bud.

Sunday at the Beach

MAMA PREPS FOR SUNDAY dinner in our tiny kitchen. "Thanks, but no thanks," she said when I offered assistance. "This space is best for one." Daddy's out front, trimming hedges and visiting with Mr. Halani. We won't eat until one o'clock.

So I am fixing to work on my tan. I won't stick out so much with one.

I scamper to the ocean side of Hanu Road and race walk down the grassy shoulder. My beach bag bumps against my hip. I pass driveways and a bunch of side streets until I find the street to the park.

Tall ironwood trees with long, weepy needles and teeny tiny pinecones line the road. The breeze kicks up and I see the shimmering blue water in the distance. I take in the salty air and quicken my pace. Big white puffy clouds decorate the bluest of blue sky.

I'll stay until dinnertime. Then, after we eat, we'll drive over to see Howdy.

I sprint across the beach park grass and step into the soft, sugary sand. Here, the beach is long and broad. Sparkles of light dance off the clear blue-green water. Ribbons of turquoise, emerald, teal, and navy color its surface. Halfway to the horizon, a line of waves breaks on the reef. To the far left and right, small islands host untold numbers of birds. I cross the sand to the warm water's edge and let the lacy ocean shush over my feet.

The beach park is filling up, but not too much. I settle in between a family and a couple with cameras taking photos of each other on their beach towels. I inspect my two-piece suit. I made it right before we moved. It's orange with white polka dots and ruffles, just like one I saw in a magazine.

I slather on the baby oil and hope for the best. I'll use the system Cindy's older sister swears by. She should know. She sunned every day over spring break and came back to school the tannest girl at Gladiola High. Her foolproof method? Apply oil and turn from one side to the other every thirty minutes. Like roasting chicken on a skewer. Done.

I prop myself up on my beach towel and pop a piece of spearmint green deliciousness in the shape of a leaf into my mouth. Candy is an important part of sunning.

I gaze at the ocean. If I squint hard enough, I

can imagine this wide-open space is the land around Gladiola. This time of year, pastures of green overflow with happy shades of blue, orange, yellow, pink, and white wildflowers. And all you see is land and sky for forever.

A fly wants to become my best friend.

"Shoo," I tell it, and it wings away on the gentle breeze.

Slather and turn.

Thirty minutes. The family next to me is at the water's edge, with buckets and shovels. The girl about my age helps the younger ones fill their pails with sand. The couple next to me reads. My bag of candy is now empty. I open a pack of my favorite gum, and my mouth juices around a stick of its chewy sweetness.

I wonder if Cindy has found the key chain we won with the ticket we shared at the fall carnival at school. We put keys to both of our houses on it. She took it home first. I forgot about it until I opened my bedside drawer a few weeks later and there it was. I didn't say a word. I hid the key chain under her bed days later. She never said a thing. Next thing I knew, it was behind a pillow on my window seat. Back and forth it went. Before I left, I tucked it in a boot deep inside her closet.

Slather.

Turn.

One hour.

I pull out a postcard from my beach bag to send to Grams and Grandpa. A colorful fish on the front eyes me. "Hum-you-hum . . . ?" The letters of its name blur together. Twelve letters in the Hawaiian alphabet. And this little fish with twenty-one in its name is swimming circles around me.

Slather.

Turn.

Ouch.

I pop up and rush to the edge of the ocean where foam swirls around my feet. I tiptoe forward until I'm knee-deep and splash water over my arms and shoulders. Cooling, cooling off.

"You're red," hollers the older girl being buried up to her neck by her family.

"But I've been here less than two hours."

"That's probably long enough," says her mom as she adds a shovel of sand on top of her daughter's stomach.

"Are you sure?"

"Positive."

This I know: It's going to take a lot longer than this to become a new me.

Fire

DADDY WORKS for the agriculture department. He studies invasive species and knows a heap about sugarcane production.

They burn the fields. On purpose. To make an easier and more productive harvest. Somehow it doesn't ruin the stalks. Then they collect the cane.

We took the extra-long way back to the house after the hula show last weekend and passed by a burning field.

Yellow and red flames reached for the sky. Gray smoke billowed up and up. The wind carried it across the blue, hiding long sections. The smell was thick, heavy.

I am like sugarcane. I am on fire.

• ✿ •

My skin is tight. Itchy. Cindy's older sister looked bronzy beautiful after all her sunning. I look like the inside of a hot dog—pinky red.

Mama sits beside me on my bed, applies cold compresses, and rubs in handful after handful of lotion. I wince as she smooths another layer of cream back and forth across my shoulders.

"Your daddy and I think you need to stay put this afternoon," she says.

"Mama, no," I say, turning to meet her eyes. "I've got to see Howdy. He needs me. I don't want what happened to Tink—"

"I know you're disappointed."

"Mama, please. I promised. I don't think Howdy recognized me yesterday. If I don't see him today, he's going to forget me."

"That cat surely knows you. He's just going through an adjustment period," she says, covering my red arms with white.

Daddy enters, bearing a tall glass of water with extra ice, just like I like it. "Tell you what," he says. "How about if I check in on Howdy tomorrow?"

Daddy knew I'd be worried. "Thank you," I say.

"You look all tuckered out, Peggy Sue," says Mama. "Let me fix you a plate and then you can take a nice long nap."

Warm smells from Mama's smothered chicken permeate our house. Usually, that starts my mouth watering. But not today. All that candy has turned in my stomach. "I'm still full from breakfast."

I lay on top of my bed. Mama covers me with an extra sheet and tiptoes out of the room. I'll just rest for a few minutes. Then she'll see that I'm good to go and we'll visit Howdy after all.

But I sleep until Mama wakes me for supper and more lotion. I sip water and eat a few bites of chicken and fruit salad.

At midnight, her cold compresses warm against my skin.

"I hurt everywhere, Mama. Even my ears."

"I'm so sorry, Peggy Sue, but it's going to be okay. Unfortunately, it may get worse before it gets better."

Still Burning

I'M SWEAT-STUCK to the backseat of the car idling in front of school Monday morning and all prickly on the inside.

"You'll feel better if you socialize," says Mama.

Only if I were in Gladiola.

Before breakfast, I heard her tell Daddy that I can't stay at the house all day by myself. She's going to the doctor and a newcomers' club meeting.

"Go get 'em, tiger," Daddy says. "I won't forget to tell Howdy you said hi."

"Thank you."

More sweat collects at the back of my legs, travels to my ankles, and sneaks under my arches. I am a living puddle.

I'm delaying the pain. Fast or slow, it hurts to move. I should get out now, get it over with.

"Bye," I say, propel myself forward, and release the

suction from my back *riiip-pop*. I grit my teeth, swing my legs out the door, and stand. I think I still have all my skin.

Even though I'm wearing my lightest, softest outfit—an old pink seersucker sundress—it feels like soggy sandpaper against my skin. I'm both hot and cold.

Everyone cringes when they see me walk up.

Laughs.

Okay, just one girl laughs.

"Leper," she says.

Sour Pineapple

"LISTEN TO THIS," says Kiki to the girls at the machine next to us at the beginning of class. She slides her chair closer. "This haole's mother was yelling at the grocery man yesterday when she was picking out a pineapple. I knew it was her because she was tall and had a funny kind of accent like hers."

My face grows hotter.

Mama had fixed a fruit salad with oranges, cherries, and marshmallows last night. Usually, she added pineapple. It might have been her.

"Plus," says Kiki, "the grocer called her Mrs. Bennett. I'm telling you, she was giving the guy a hard time. She was really huhu."

It was her, all right.

If Kiki's trying to embarrass me, it's working.

"Um, Kiki," I say.

"Don't interrupt me, haole leper," she says, and

turns her back to me. "The lady held a pine in her hand and said, 'You told me this was ripe. I cut into it at home and look. It's practically white and very sour.' Everybody in that part of the store turned their grocery carts around to get out of her way. The produce guy was turning red."

"Was she wearing sunglasses?" I ask.

Kiki whips her head around. "No, and I told you," she says, "stop interrupting. I'm getting to the good part about me."

Kiki tugs on the bottom of her blouse and returns to her friends. "I know him, the grocer," she says. "He walks his dog on the beach. So I've got to say something, defend the guy. So I tell her *she's* the sour one."

"You said that? To her face?"

"Yep." She glances back and smiles. "What do you think about that, haole?"

I blow out a stream of air and look straight at Kiki. "Sometimes it's true." Like today.

I see the surprise in Kiki's eyes.

I turn to my pattern directions to figure out what I'm supposed to do next.

If only I had directions for her.

Word Problems

LATER, IN MATH, we tackle word problems. But I already have plenty of my own:

Likelike is pronounced "leakay-leakay," not "like-like."

Hilo is "hee-low," not "high-low."

Kaneohe is "kah-nay-oh-hay."

Pau is "pow," not "pa-you."

Aina is "eye-na," not "a-in-ah."

Kalanianaole is a blur of letters and sounds.

And I still can't figure *humuhumunukunukuapuaa*.

• ✿ •

That evening, Daddy honks the car horn twice as he pulls up to the house. I bolt out the door. "Howdy's in tip-top shape," he says before I can even ask. "Though he did let me know I was a poor substitute for you."

“Thanks, Daddy,” I say, and kiss him on the cheek. “I trust you to tell me the unvarnished truth.”

“Always,” he says, and grabs his briefcase from the backseat. “I just passed one of your flyers on a telephone pole. How’s my favorite entrepreneur?”

“Broke.”

“But not for long.”

“Daddy, don’t you get tired of being positive all the time?” I ask as we move toward the house.

“It beats worrying, kitten.”

I sigh. Deeply.

I wouldn’t know.

Detention

WHEN I GET to home ec the next morning, Mrs. Barsdale and Kiki are finishing up a conversation. Kiki turns, muttering, and stomps back to our sewing machine.

I scoot my chair out of her way.

"Haoles never listen. Never say sorry. Never say thank you," she says as she threads the machine.

"Typical," says the girl sewing next to us.

Kiki studies the page of instructions, balls it up, and tosses it at me. I wince as it scratches my sunburned arm and lands on the floor. I let it be.

For the next fifteen minutes, Kiki sews in darts, pops up for water, and talks to the girls beside us.

She rethreads the machine at least five times because the tension is too tight. Not to mention her darts are on the outside.

I am silent.

"Look what you made me do, leper," she shouts as she holds up her dress. "You should have stopped me." Her eyes narrow. "See you in detention," she says, and rushes away from me.

My stomach catches. "No, wait," I say, following.

"Is there a problem?" asks Mrs. Barsdale.

Kiki holds out her dress. "This," she says. "And her." Kiki steers Mrs. Barsdale out of my hearing.

I should have known better. I did nothing while Kiki made those mistakes.

Mrs. Barsdale and Kiki return. Our teacher takes the dress from her. "Peggy Sue, this kind of oversight won't earn you any extra credit today. Please help Kiki correct her error."

"I will. Which should mean I won't have detention either."

"Detention?" asks Mrs. Barsdale.

"Gotcha," says Kiki, and jabs me in the chest. "Gotcha good."

"What is going on here?" asks Mrs. Barsdale.

"I need air," I say, before barreling out of the room. And a smarter brain. I don't go far. I slump against the lockers outside the door for the rest of class. No one comes looking for me. When the bell rings, I rush in, grab my stuff, and leave.

Only two more days of her this week. Good Friday can't come soon enough.

That night, I tiptoe out back, plant my feet in the dewy coolness, and stare up at that cacti that's hanging on for its life.

Are you going to bloom?

Show me.

Shut Out

LIKE ALWAYS, I sit by myself at lunch the next day and eat my baloney sandwich. Only now, I'm in the cafeteria, smushed between a wall and a girl who is talking to everyone else. I don't listen in. I think about Gladiola. I wonder how long that gum-wrapper chain is now. I wonder if Grams made fresh tomato sandwiches for lunch. I wonder what colors Grandpa is mixing today for his next oil painting—sapphire, mint, tangerine—and who will clean his brushes?

• ✿ •

The house is silent and all the curtains are drawn when I trudge in from school. I find a note on the dining room table under a new bottle of lotion:

TV dinners in the freezer.
Mama

I guess the new doctor didn't help.

I know the drill—do not disturb.

I reach for the lotion and pour gobs into my hands. I smear the cool goodness onto my skin until I look like a ghost.

Then, I retreat to my room and study a little for Mr. Nakamoto's test tomorrow.

But it's harder to concentrate without a cat on my lap. So I slip into the kitchen, grab a banana and the extra house key, and head next door for hula.

But I'm back in two seconds. I write a note and stick it under Mama's door:

Hope you feel better soon.
Peggy Sue

Hula

I TAKE A SEAT on the bench lining the back wall of Mrs. Halani's studio and rock my feet on the woven mat.

Pairs of girls enter, their voices filled with laughter. Tammy, the girl from my homeroom, bounces in, donning another pink hair ribbon. A girl I don't know, at least I don't think I do, prances beside her. "Snow," Tammy says, and throws her arms in the air. Her charm bracelet jingles happiness. "I can't wait."

"I've never seen snow," says the other.

I stand and move closer, but still hang back. Tammy turns around.

"We're moving next month," she tells me. "My parents are taking my brother and me out of school early and we won't even have to finish on the mainland."

"I can tell you're excited," I say. Tammy hasn't just hit the double jackpot—leaving and no school to make up—she's hit the triple: no Kill Haole Day either.

Other girls crowd around her. "Tammy, we're going to miss you sooooo much."

"You guys can visit anytime. Our house will have a guest bedroom. . . ."

I fade back onto the bench. Her still-ringing bracelet reminds me of Cindy's. I gave her a four-leaf clover charm before I left.

A few minutes later, a girl with short brown hair and a big smile rushes in, says hello to everyone, and plops beside me. Her dark eyes twinkle.

"Hi, I'm Malina, Mrs. Halani's daughter."

"Peggy Sue," I say. "Nice to meet you."

Malina's a younger, smaller version of her mom, with an inked outline of an empty heart on the back of her right hand.

She shows me her arms. No chicken pox.

"Glad you're not cooped up anymore," I say.

"Glad you're the new neighbor," she says. "The last ones didn't have any kids." She studies my arms. "Your sunburn looks terrible, by the way."

"I'll survive," I say, though it still doesn't feel like it.

"Time to begin," says Mrs. Halani. Her muumuu is powder blue and white. "We have a new dance to learn."

"You may not want to stand next to me," I tell

Malina as we take our positions on the woven mat. "Last week was kind of a disaster."

"No worry, beef curry."

Just in case, even when Mrs. Halani tells us to add arm movements, I still dance only with my feet.

During a break, Malina points to my old flyer next to the door. "Trying to earn extra money?"

"As much as possible," I say.

"Me, too. I'm thinking about starting a dog-walking service."

"That's a great idea." But one I'll shy away from for sure. The memory of that bite is still too fresh. And, besides, I don't really know dogs.

"I want to go to Paris someday," says Malina. "Want to come?"

"How about right after class?"

She laughs.

It turns out Malina is in Mr. Nakamoto's homeroom and history class, but for some reason, we have different lunch schedules.

"Transferring in late is hard," she says. "We're all stuck in our ways like cement."

I nod.

"But you'll be okay," says Malina. "There's always a crack."

I want to believe her.

Where There's Smoke

THE NEXT AFTERNOON, the bulletin boards in Mr. Nakamoto's class are shrouded in black. Class hasn't started, but it's before-a-church-service quiet. Pages flip, flip, flip in textbooks like program bulletins; lips whisper names and dates like prayers.

"When you finish," says Mr. Nakamoto as he hands out the tests one by one, "open a book and read."

It's fill-in-the-blanks and short-answer essays. I pray for real that Mr. Nakamoto doesn't take off points for wrong spelling of names and places, pray that I remember enough.

Before class is over, I turn in my answers and ask to be excused.

At the end of the hall, I push on the girls' bathroom door, but it barely moves. I push again. Harder. This time, it swings open and I stumble in. The lights are off and the only light comes filtered from a frosted bank of louvers just below the ceiling that are closed tight.

I stand still until my eyes adjust. The small space, hazy with smoke, is lined with girls. Some lean against the stall doors, some against the sinks.

"Well, look who's here," says Kiki.

"Is this the haole we're going to fight with you?" asks a girl beside her.

"If she squeals," Kiki says.

I hold my breath. My eyes water like crazy. *Cough*. Breathe. *Cough*. *Cough*. "Is this a private meeting?" I finally ask.

"This is a public school, haole. So this is a public restroom."

Kiki grins wide and long.

I should do something. I should say something, I should. But what? What will stop her?

If I ever even think about thinking about telling anyone about Kiki and Kill Haole Day, all I have to do is remember this.

I cross my legs.

"You gotta go, haole, or what?" someone says.

"I can wait," I say, and back out into the light.

"Could've fooled me," someone shouts after the door closes.

Thirty-one more days. That was the number on the blackboard this morning. Thirty-one.

I find another bathroom. Barely in time.

Walking with Malina

FORGET HOW I DID on the test; all I can think about is Kiki.

But it creeps me out to even say her name as I pour out my home ec trials to Malina after school. So I don't.

"Mrs. Barsdale is so unfair," Malina says as we stroll toward our houses. "You should be in my class with Mrs. Leong. She's nice."

I hoped she might understand. But it won't make the bigger problem disappear. If Malina were Cindy, I'd say more. Ask advice. But I'd best handle Kill Haole Day myself. I can't afford for it to get worse. And I don't want Malina to know I'm scared.

"What's the girl's name?" says Malina, picking up a pinkish-red plumeria flower from the ground.

"Kiki. She's an eighth grader," I say as I stop under the shade of the tree.

"Are you sure?" she says, and takes in the scent of the flower.

"I'm positive."

Malina's lips form an O and she goes silent. She shakes her head. "Stay away from her."

If only I could.

Boyfriends

"DO YOU HAVE A BOYFRIEND?" Malina asks, changing the topic. She puts the flower behind her right ear and we take up walking again.

"I just got here, remember?" The sun hits my eyes, and I raise my hand to block the glare.

"I take that as a no. Did you have one in Texas?"

"A boy named Jake asked me to the homecoming dance, but we're just friends. I had a crush on my lab partner, Harry. I think he liked me, too, but once he heard about my move, he backed off. How about you?"

"I'm unattached for the moment." She points to the outline of an empty heart on her hand. "Ronald Lee and I just broke up. My former best friend stole him away."

"That's terrible. I'm so sorry."

"Me, too. Before him, there was Douglas and

before him Keoke. No one lasts long, so I keep moving on. I might go with Sam or Kimo next. What do you think?"

"I should know how to advise you about boys," I say. "My Grams used to be a matchmaker. A cousin of mine inherited her skills, but I don't think I did."

"Neat-o. Maybe they'll come out for a visit."

"Maybe," I say.

By the time we get to Malina's house, I know everything about her former boyfriends, future boyfriends, and for that matter, the majority of the boys in our homeroom. She makes all of them sound pretty keen. I just wish more of them were as tall as or taller than me like most of the boys back home.

Music from her mom's studio fills the courtyard, where we sit down. Purple bougainvillea blossoms cascade over clay pots on either side of the doorway into the house. Malina pulls out the *Top Teen* magazine and lays it on the wrought iron tabletop. Elvis Presley is on the cover.

We take the "Are You in Love?" quiz. I love Elvis, I do. But I'm as likely to get together with him today as I am with Harry back home. However, I know enough about him to answer some of the questions, so why not? Do you share favorite foods? Yes. Milk shakes.

Do you share favorite songs? Yes. His. Do you share favorite hobbies? Kind of. I want to learn karate, so I say yes. My score is five out of ten. The advice from the quiz—*Keep trying.*

Malina scores ten and receives an enthusiastic *You're in Love!* confirmation.

"So now what?" I ask.

Malina whips out her math book with its office-envelope-brown paper cover and a pen. "I need to practice writing Mrs. Kimo Nahoa, of course, and fill in my heart."

And so she does.

Cindy

MY FIRST THOUGHT when I wake up is—*Today is Cindy's birthday*. My second—*I've been here two whole weeks and Howdy has one hundred five days to go*. My third—*It's Good Friday, so I don't have school. I do not have to see Kiki.*

I mailed Cindy a card early so she'd get it in time. And before I left Gladiola, I bought her a gift and gave it to her mom to set out today. A bottle of nail polish in her favorite color—hot pink.

I helped Cindy plan her first boy-girl party. A costume party. Cindy's going as Gidget, the California surfer girl. Harry told me he'll go as John Wayne. I would've dressed like Dorothy from *The Wizard of Oz*. The cookout should start just about now.

"I know you miss her," says Mama at the breakfast table, when I remind her what day it is. "You two were so close, I thought you might hear from her by now."

Me, too.

"Speaking of missing," says Mama. "I can't find the extra back-door key."

"It'll turn up," says Daddy.

Yes, it will. Only not around here. Yesterday, I sent it to my best friend.

Friday Morning Lemonade

RIGHT AFTER BREAKFAST, Malina and I set up a card table and chairs next to the street. In an hour, her family is taking off for a campout over the three-day Easter weekend. Malina's transistor radio crackles out a tune about lonely boys.

Our LUSCIOUS LEMONADE and PARIS OR BUST! signs will surely lure in buyers. Guaranteed. A red balloon tied to a leg of the table spins in the wind. The sunny sun glints above the treetops.

"Lemonade. Luscious lemonade," we shout at the handful of cars that whiz by.

"Maybe we're out too early or maybe we're already too late or maybe we're charging too much."

"No, no, and no," says Malina. "It's a holiday. Folks are in a good mood. There's nothing more they'd rather do than help two ambitious girls realize their dreams."

So we wait.

And wait some more.

"You know why I like Kimo?" Malina asks.

"Tell me."

"He looks like Fabian, even if he doesn't sing like him. He draws super neat and is vice president of our class."

"All great qualities."

A strong gust flaps our Paris sign in front of the card table. One taped corner pulls up and the sign swings down.

"Do you know people in Paris take their dogs to restaurants and feed them right off their plates?" Malina says as we fix the sign.

"I do now."

"If they are small, they sit on their lap, or on a chair. And they don't sneak food to them either. They order it off the menu."

Malina tells me her mom is allergic to dogs. More than anything else, she would like to have one. But all of hers are stuffed.

With the sign secure, we again stand and wave at any and all passing cars.

I talk about Howdy. "Mostly, he's the silent type," I tell Malina. "So when he speaks, I know it's important. He loves canned pumpkin, which Grams and

I discovered early on when we made pie. I call him my alarm cat because he wakes me every morning by touching my face with his whiskers."

"He sounds wonderful. I can't wait to meet him."

If she does, it won't be until he's sprung. I explain the jailhouse rule: You have to be over eighteen or family in order to visit.

"No problem. We could be hanai family."

I know I must look puzzled because I am, and because Malina keeps talking.

"Your family could adopt me. Unofficially, of course. It's an old Hawaiian way."

"So we'd be twins, only different."

Malina's brother, David, walks up smiling. He's movie star handsome, tall, with broad shoulders. Dimples. "Hey, sis; hey, haole girl. How's it going?"

The way he says "haole girl" is playful, like a nickname instead of something mean.

"You're our first customer," I say.

David sets the two big empty glasses that he's holding in his hands on our table. "I'll take one for my girlfriend, Teresa, too."

"That'll be . . ." says Malina as she pours the lemonade, "a whole lot of money."

"Nah," says David. "You owe me a bundle, remember?"

"I'm telling Mom," says Malina.

"Tell," says David, and walks away.

"He's so aggravating, especially because he can talk my parents into anything."

Like Grandpa sweet-talking Grams into serving him another piece of her award-winning pecan pie. And Cindy writing an apology poem to her parents and getting ungrounded after her April Fools' joke last year. She convinced her younger brother that she'd just seen a bona fide UFO. By recess, the whole school thought it was gospel. Kids either fled home in a panic, lined up for the cot in the school nurse's office, or refused to return to classes for fear of missing out on a might-never-see-again phenomenon.

"You are so lucky you don't have a big brother," Malina says.

Maybe this is true.

"So, what do you want to do on our trip?" Malina asks.

"Whatever you want," I say. "I'm curious, why Paris?"

"It's the city of love."

But of course.

"Besides, my great-grandfather was French."

"Keen."

"*Oui.* And since I'm French-Portuguese-Hawaiian by my mom and Chinese-Hawaiian by my dad, China and Portugal are on my list, too."

"So I could add England and Scotland and Wales to mine."

A boy hollers from a car that drives by. "Cheapskate," Malina yells. "That was Douglas," she says, plopping back down in the metal chair. "I'm glad I broke up with him. Though he is cute."

She's right about that.

A family Malina knows from her church pulls over in their station wagon. Four boys wiggle in the backseat. Malina gives them all lemonade for free.

The good news? The mom gives Malina a babysitting job.

We celebrate Malina's good fortune by drinking the rest of the lemonade ourselves.

She's going to make it to Paris. For sure.

Underwater View

THIS MUST BE what it feels like to fly. Weightless. Free.

It's late afternoon and I'm facedown in the clear, salty smooth ocean with my snorkel and mask. My arms and legs stretch out like an X as I take in the wonders between the rippled sandy floor and me. With the gently rocking motion of the water, I float in the keyhole-shaped space between the coral heads.

This makes up for the water I swallowed figuring out the snorkel. All the mask adjustments before I plugged the leak. The spit I had to spread inside the mask to stop the lens from fogging. And the shorts and a long-sleeved shirt of Mama's I'm in instead of my swimsuit, to cover up as much of my skin as possible.

In and around the coral—fish: a bright yellow one no bigger than my hand, with a black-and-white tail; a school dressed in broad black and white stripes with thin pennants of white trailing from the tops of their heads; a mostly yellow fish with markings like a raccoon around its eyes; an all-yellow as long and wide as a wooden ruler; a green fish with a red stripe along the side and red lines running perpendicular; and a bluish-black fish rimmed in white, with a teardrop of orange red near the tail.

I wonder if any of them are the humuhumunukunukuapuaa—however you say it—fishes.

"That's enough sun for you today," says Daddy, tapping me on my shoulder. I forgot he was even here.

I lift my head—"Just one more look?"—and return my face to the water.

A turtle. I'm this close to a turtle. I motion so Daddy won't miss this. The turtle's flippers, like wings, guide his path. He seems in no hurry, like Grams and Grandpa on a lazy afternoon drive.

After we have a last look, Daddy and I approach the shore, where a family stands shoulder to shoulder in the shallows, donning snorkeling gear. "Don't put your fingers in any holes in the reef," says the mom.

"We know, we know," says a girl. "Eels bite."

Jeepers! Good thing I didn't get curious.

A wave swells at the shoreline and knocks me down. I rise, sputtering. More salty water. Not my taste.

Under the shade of the coconut tree, Mama chats with a tourist couple setting up beach mats and towels next to ours.

"Where are y'all from?" the woman asks Mama as Daddy and I approach.

"Here," Daddy says.

"Texas," I say at the same time.

That's home.

Howdy Time

SATURDAY AFTERNOON, Howdy refuses to come out from under the bench no matter how much I beg. So I lie on my stomach at the edge of his hiding place. The concrete cools my still-tender skin.

"What a good boy," I say as my hand inches closer and closer. His tail flicks back and forth. But no bopping of my hand. No hissing at my face. Howdy is still scared. About everything. But I'm sure he is happy I've come.

I scratch his favorite spot just behind his ears. I move my hand down his back. His fur feels different. Thinner? I turn over my hand and look. My palm is furry. "Daddy, something's wrong," I say.

"Looks to me like Howdy is shedding his Texas coat in order to grow his Hawaii one."

I am not convinced.

I reach for my cat with the still-swishing tail and

rub under his chin. “One hundred four more days after today,” I say. And then I lower my voice, “But I hope we’ll fly home sooner.”

Maybe Howdy isn’t convinced either. He is still purr-less.

Pele

AFTER OUR VISIT TO HOWDY, we stop at the Golden Plum to eat. Steaming plates of Chinese food arrive at our table in short order. Daddy's boss took him here for lunch this week, and ever since, he's wanted Mama and me to come. White paper lanterns hang from the ceiling. A red-and-gold dragon eyes me from the wall.

"Your hair looks nice, Mama," I say as I spoon rice onto my plate. It's fuller and curlier. Unlike mine, which is as straight as Daddy's.

"Thank you, Peggy Sue. My hair is frizzier in this climate."

"You always look beautiful, Virginia," says Daddy. "Both of you do."

Mama and I trade in our chopsticks for forks after the first few bites. But Daddy uses them the whole way through on account of all that practice he had when he served here during the war.

Afterward, we head up the valley and over the mountain to the house in Hanu.

No other cars are on the road. No lights. Not even the moon. It is hidden behind the clouds. Mama dozes.

A gust of wind moves our car to the left. The radio goes to static and Daddy turns it off. The temperature drops and the rain pings against the window.

The bag full of white cartons of leftovers on the floorboard warms my calves. I breathe in the spicy smell of egg fu yung, beef tomato, sweet and sour pork, and some kind of noodles.

I sit up with a start—pork!

I grab the bag, rustle through the cartons, and sniff. No, not that one.

"Still hungry, kitten?" asks Daddy.

"No, sir," I say, looking up to see the lights of the tunnel ahead. I've got to hurry.

On the third try, pineapple hits my nose.

I roll down my window as fast as I can, hold on to the container, and toss out the sweet and sour pork. Then I collapse back into the seat.

"Peggy Sue," says Mama, waking up. "What on earth?"

A droplet of sticky sauce plops on my leg and I reach to wipe it off.

"Don't tell me you just threw out perfectly good food?" she asks.

Obviously, Mama doesn't know.

"Some kids at school warned me," I say. "It's against Madame Pele's rules to carry pork over the Pali. If you do, your car might break down or something else bad will happen. Pele, the mean, angry goddess of the volcano, says so."

My daddy's shoulders bounce with laughter, but no sound comes out.

"Mercy," says Mama, shaking her head.

I exhale. Loudly.

On the other side of the mountain, Daddy flips the radio back on and sings about leaving his heart in San Francisco. Mama leans her head against the window again and closes her eyes.

Five songs later, we pull into the grassy driveway of our rental house. Daddy looks at me in the rearview mirror and winks. "Safe and sound, thanks to you, kitten."

"You're welcome," I say, and hop out of the car. Even if they don't believe, I know I did the right thing.

Easter

AFTER WE EAT the scrumptious hot cross buns Mama made for breakfast, she sets out the egg timer for a holiday call to Grams and Grandpa. "Long distance is expensive," she says.

We'll take turns until the sand runs through the glass. I'm up first.

"Dancing last weekend was a hoot and a holler," says Grandpa. "Only stepped on your grandma's toes twice." Most Saturday nights, they swung to jazzy country music with their friends at the Gladiola Rec Center.

I thank Grams for my Easter dress and ask them to tell Cindy I said hi.

I know she's missing me as much as I miss her.

Mama taps me on my shoulder. "Love you," I say to my grandparents, with a big old lump in my throat, and pass along the phone.

Mama's been cooking and baking since before sunup, even though I set our table for only three this year. The house smells like strawberry cake, scalloped potato casserole, and ham. "A feast," says Daddy.

But all I can think about is home—a table full of relatives for Easter dinner, dessert-serving duty with my cousins, then Parcheesi and checkers and Password.

And my cat without a purr.

Not Native

DADDY AND I stand underneath the monkeypod tree and stare up at the night-blooming cereus that night after dark.

"It's not native to the islands," says Daddy. "But it's learned to adapt."

"It's not blooming," I say. "Are you sure it's going to?"

"It's changing on the inside, kitten."

"Well, it sure is taking its sweet time."

"You can't rush it."

"Is something wrong with it?"

"Not a thing. It'll bloom."

Maybe.

Thinking About Tomorrow

MUFFLED OCEAN SOUNDS seep through my bedroom windows as I ready for sleep.

Tomorrow is a school day. Tomorrow I'll see her.

I've yet to find the needed directions on how to deal with Kiki.

Sassing her on day one, ignoring her on others, and withholding help last week hasn't worked.

Maybe I should try the opposite.

Charm.

Like Grams. Like Cindy. Like David.

It couldn't hurt to try.

Sweet-Talking Monday

IT'S APRIL 18, there are thirty more school days, and I'm smiling.

"Kiki, it's so good to see you today," I say as she sits next to me. Machines whir around us like bees, a box of straight pins skitter-scatters across the floor, and five girls swarm to the rescue. "I was hoping you'd be here," I say.

Kiki stares at me.

"How can I help you?" I ask.

She's speechless.

So I keep going. I hand Kiki the pattern instructions. "Please tell me what we need to do next?"

Two girls nearby exchange raised eyebrows. Kiki throws the paper down.

The girls shake their heads and get back to work.

"Well, let me see," I say, picking up the directions. "I'd say the best thing is to pin in the zipper. Here, let me get it started for you and then, if you'd like, you can take over. Or not. Whatever you think is best."

Still, no words.

"You have great taste in fabric, you know." Turquoise daisylike flowers with white centers, and white ones with turquoise centers, spring from a solid navy background. "These colors will look really cool on you."

"Leper girl, there's a colony on Molokai for you."

My skin is still pinky raw in places where I've peeled. I don't need her to tell me that. I'm living in it. I got a little more sun at Hanauma Bay, but it was worth it. Anyway, I can't let her throw me off track.

"Kiki, you are too funny."

Her eyes narrow.

"I meant funny in a good way, of course. Truth be told, I had no idea you had such a good sense of humor. Now, you just enjoy the class and I'll do all the work today. Really, I insist."

I pour on the sweetness as thick as I can.

"Is this a trap?"

"Trap?"

"I know you. I know your kind. First you say nice things, buttering front and back because you want something in return. Next thing you know, you'll want to be friends. Pheew! What a joke. You haoles stink inside and out. I couldn't show my face if I were friends with you. I'm not taking your bait. Take, take, take. Jobs. Land. That's all you do."

Bait? Trap? Putting it that way sounds bad. Really bad. My insides turn tight and twisty.

Kiki's right. I want something. I want her to leave me alone.

She may not be the best student in the class, but it's not because she isn't smart.

• ✿ •

Like always, first thing, when I get back to the house, I check the mailbox.

Nothing for me.

I ask Mama if I've had any calls.

Zero.

Mama looks a little piqued. She doesn't ask about my day. So I don't say. I delay the window washing until later.

Instead, I conjure up a new business. It's so green around here, surely weeds are in supply. I make HIRE-A-WEEDER flyers. It's a desperate act. I hate to weed.

Holoku

MUUMUUS OF EVERY SHAPE and color hang on a clothesline across one of the mirrored hula studio walls Wednesday afternoon.

"These are samples of all the recital costumes," says Malina. "Mom chose them to match the style of each particular dance."

"Recital? Dancing? As in onstage? But today's only my third lesson."

"No worry, beef curry. You'll be ready by June."

"This one looks like my grandma's nightgown." It's a long, loose-fitting dress with a high ruffled collar and ruffles at the wrists. The small cotton plaid is navy and white.

"That's an old-style muumuu called a *holoku*," says Malina. "Way back, the missionaries liked them because it covered women up. We'll wear it for one of our dances."

"Good. Maybe it'll cover up some of my mistakes."

Malina laughs and turns serious. "Did you know missionaries helped ban hula?"

"No, that's awful."

"Yep. They thought dancing was sinful."

"Oh," I say. "A few folks back home still think like that."

"Last century, our ancestors kept hula alive for over fifty years until King Kalakaua brought it back."

"Thank goodness."

Tammy and her bracelet jingle up. "If I was going to be here, I'd want to wear this holoku," she says.

The long orange satin fitted muumuu she points to is gorgeous. How could it have the same name?

It looks like the one the soloist wore at the hula show for a regal slow dance.

That dancer was the best of the best. She did not trip or tangle in the smooth fabric. She was extra graceful. When she danced, her muumuu with the train in the back swished ever so softly, like the gentle trade winds.

I will not be wearing that kind of holoku for this recital. Maybe ever.

"Only ten more days on the island for me," says Tammy. She's beaming.

No recital, no school, no Kill Haole Day.

Some people are just luckier than others, I guess. But Grams always says we need to make our own luck. I'm trying, that's for sure.

Mrs. Halani lets me add my HIRE-A-WEEDER flyer to my WINDOW-WASHING SERVICE notice by the door. Still, no calls.

Rock Fever

THE NEXT AFTERNOON, Mrs. Halani invites my parents and me for supper.

I think Mama will say no since it's a school night, but she surprises me.

Mrs. Halani makes teriyaki chicken and rice.

Mama brings an apple-spice cake, the recipe courtesy of her newcomers group.

Everyone talks at once.

"I reserved tables and chairs today for Tutu's retirement luau in a few weeks," says Mr. Halani.

"My grandmother," Malina explains. "She manages a doctors' office."

"The food will be ono," says David, rubbing his stomach.

"We're counting on you and your assistant to perform your best magic tricks," says Mrs. Halani. "But promise you won't saw anyone in half."

David grins. "Okay, okay."

I hear Mr. Halani ask, "Remember that party we all went to on the North Shore back in '44, Robert?"

"I remember the fire dancers," Daddy says.

"It was my first date with Alfred," says Mrs. Halani, taking Mr. Halani's hand. "You two talked those dancers into handing over their torches and paddled out on surfboards with them."

My dad the daredevil? Picturing fiery torches reminds me of the newspaper photos of lava spewing from the volcano on the Big Island. The volcano makes me think of Madame Pele. Madame Pele . . . "I heard you shouldn't take pork over the Pali," I add to the mix.

"I wouldn't cross Madame Pele," says David.

"Do you hear that, Mama?" I ask, but she is talking with Mrs. Halani.

"Taking rocks from her volcanoes will bring you bad luck, too," says David.

"I'm listening," I say, and inch my chair closer.

"After a friend's friend brought some back from the Big Island, his girlfriend broke up with him, his camera busted, and he flunked two tests. But as soon as he sent the rocks back, his luck changed."

"No kidding?" I ask.

"I don't joke about Pele," David says. "The post

office over there gets loads of returned rocks. Anyway, Pele isn't always mean, especially if you do something nice for her."

"Like what?"

"Around the volcano area, sometimes she appears at people's houses as an old woman with a white dog. If she asks you for food or drink, give her something and nothing bad will happen. I've also heard if you give her a ride, good luck can come your way."

"I'll remember that," I say, and turn to Mama.

"I hear you're going to volunteer at the school, Virginia," says Mrs. Halani.

That's the first I've heard of it.

"I'm thinking about it," says Mama. "I'm trying to fill up my time."

I hadn't really thought about what Mama does when Daddy and I aren't around. In Gladiola, she never lacked for things to do.

"You can do my homework," I say.

"And mine," say Malina and David at the same time.

"Think again, kids," says Mr. Halani.

Afterward, Malina and I clear the dishes. "I hope Kimo and I go to a party as fun as my parents' someday," she says.

"I hope so, too."

The dads move into the kitchen to do the washing. Scrape. Stack. Rinse. Wash. Dry.

As I carry in the salt- and pepper shakers, I hear Mr. Halani ask my dad, "Does Virginia have rock fever?"

I freeze. What's rock fever? Whatever it is, it sounds bad.

I tiptoe back into the family room before they spot me, and listen behind the door.

Something metal-like clatters to the floor, and I squeak. "No harm done," hollers Daddy.

"Anyone can get it," Mr. Halani continues. "But remember, it's known to hit some malihini wives particularly hard. Guys have transferred their families back to the mainland because of it."

I know he's talking about folks new to the islands. Daddy says, "I'm hopeful Virginia will pull through. I don't want to alarm Peggy Sue, so I'd appreciate if you'd keep it on the QT."

"Will do."

"And thanks for asking Malina to befriend Peggy Sue. They seem to have hit it off."

I'm a project?

"Peggy Sue?"

I turn and find Mama. Give her a big hug.

"What did I do to deserve this?" she asks.

There are two kinds of families—huggers and non-huggers.

We're non.

At least Mama.

"I just want you to feel better."

"I feel fine."

I don't believe her.

The Halanis are all huggers.

We leave a few minutes later. They all hug us when we say our good-nights. Except when I say good-bye to Malina, I don't hug back or look her in the eyes.

Consumed

IT'S HARD TO SLEEP when all you can think about is rock fever. And about someone who is forced to be your friend.

I dream about rocks.

I stand at the edge of an enormous crater.

Heat, and steam as dense as felt, rises from the burbling floor.

Below, the only remaining shelf of blackened lava collapses, consumed by the cauldron.

Whoosh-WHOOSH! Molten lava spews skyward, flinging fire higher than the rim.

The pit swallows the fountain of thick red liquid.

Beside me, Mama picks up a sharp black rock.

She opens her palm to show it to me.

It turns red-hot, like lava.

"I have a fever," she says.

"I know," I say. "I know."

Information, Please

DADDY HAD AN EARLY MEETING, too early to drop me at school, so I'm walking. Wispy clouds hover above the mountains as if they can't decide if they're going to band together or disappear.

"Peggy Sue," someone hollers.

My body tightens, remembering what I overheard. I turn around in slow motion.

"Hey," says Malina, catching up.

"Hi, you're walking, too?" I say as normal as possible.

"David's old junker wouldn't start, so he got a ride with friends and there wasn't room. I'm so glad you're here. I need your advice."

"Uh-huh."

"Can you slow down just a bit?"

"Sorry. Sure, I'll try."

My eyes are fixed on the clouds. The one in the middle is joining the two on either side.

“Should I sit next to Kimo at lunch today? Or is it too soon? What if there’s no space?”

“I don’t know.”

“Are you always this quiet in the morning?”

“I guess.”

“Peggy Sue, is everything okay?”

“Last night,” I say, slowing to a stop. I tap my knuckles above my upper lip.

“Go on,” Malina says, and stops, too.

I dig my fist into my chin and blink at the red dirt.

“How bad can it be?” asks Malina.

I drop my hand and look up. “Last night I heard my dad thank your dad for making you be my friend,” I say in one long rushed breath.

Malina’s eyes widen. “Okay, wait. You’re thinking the worst here. My parents asked me to make you feel welcome, that’s all. It took me two seconds to realize I wanted to be your friend.”

My hand unclenches. “Oh.”

“You’re not my extra credit.”

Seeing her, hearing her, I know she’s telling the truth. “I do tend to think the worst first.”

“My dad’s a worrier, too,” she says. “Mom says that’s what makes him a good policeman. He can think really far ahead in an emergency, and because of that, he's prevented terrible things from happening."

"You're trying to make me feel better."

"So we're okay, right?"

"Yes, but there's one more thing." The wisps above the mountains have melded together, forming one continuous line. I ask her about rock fever.

"Sometimes new people get it," Malina says. "It's like the island's too small for them or something, and they want to go back to the mainland."

"Oh," I say.

It's not just Mama. I have it, too.

The Sign

TEN MINUTES BEFORE the end of home ec class, Mrs. Barsdale hollers, "Clean up." Her hair is shorter and orangey at the roots.

We crowd around the closet to stuff our projects into the already full shelves.

"Avalanche," yells Tammy up front.

We stumble back, dodging each other and the fabric pieces, patterns, and sewing baskets that spill across the floor.

Then we stream forward to the rescue.

I pick up an errant pincushion that looks like a tomato that met a porcupine. "See you around, haole," says Kiki, and pats my back.

But not until Monday.

Twenty-six school days until the end of school. Twenty-six.

As I leave, a girl says, "Haole."

Then another.

On my way to my next class, a boy passes me. "Haole," he says.

Two more. Kids snicker.

My face is burning hot. I speed up and don't stop until I flop into my seat in science. Paper crinkles behind me. I twist around and tear the sign from my back.

Haole.

I crumple it into the tiniest ball I can make it into.

Twenty-six days. Twenty-six too many.

54

THAT AFTERNOON, Mr. Nakamoto passes back our tests facedown. "Some of you studied more than others," he says.

So we spend the whole class time reviewing the answers.

Queen Liliuokalani was overthrown by haoles who wanted to control the Hawaii sugar trade.

President Cleveland told the overthrowers they broke the law. But they didn't listen.

To date, no one has ever apologized.

The queen tried unsuccessfully to restore her kingdom.

The overthrowers imprisoned her for eight months.

The queen wrote the famous song "Aloha 'Oe."

Her brother was King Kalakaua.

She married a haole.

I didn't remember most of this from the study guide.

Or a bunch of other stuff, including how to spell the Hawaiian names.

Which is why I got a 54 on my quiz.

• ✿ •

"You've always been a strong student," Mama says after school.

"This just proves I shouldn't be here."

"Don't be so quick to judge." Mama takes off her sunglasses. Her eyes are puffy.

"Allergies," she says. *No*, I think, *rock fever*.

Mama fixes TV dinners for supper.

The phone finally rings. A job, I just know I have a job.

Wrong number.

Before I turn in, Daddy and I walk out back and look at the night-blooming cereus.

It doesn't look like anything has changed.

Something wet and heavy plops on my foot. "Eee-www!" I scream and flick my ankle.

Daddy's flashlight catches a bufo hopping away.

"Leave me alone," I say, and scurry back inside.

Visiting Howdy

SATURDAY AFTERNOON, Howdy bathes himself on top of the wooden bench.

"Daddy," I say. "He looks different."

"Do you think?" Daddy asks as I lift the handle and open the cage door.

Howdy stops licking and looks at me. Slowly, I walk to the bench and sit, placing a small paper bag beside me. "How's my favorite cat?" I ask, and scooch toward him. I reach under his white chin and rub my finger back and forth. He shakes his head, but doesn't run. "It's good to see you," I say, and pet him from head to tail. Like last time, hair sticks to my fingers. Not a little. A lot. "You okay?"

He meows.

I don't know if he means yes or no.

I wrap my arms around him and lift him onto my lap.

"Daddy," I say, hugging my cat. "He's lighter."

I look at his food bowl. Almost full.

I remember what one quarantine officer said.

I remember Tinkerbell.

"Snack time, Howdy," I say, and reach for the bag with two last bites of my tuna and potato chip sandwich inside.

Howdy sniffs and turns his nose away.

"Please, Howdy," I say.

"Everyone has off days," says Daddy, rubbing the top of Howdy's head. "Even cats. He's going to be okay."

"I don't know what I'd do if . . ." I say, and kiss my purr-less friend.

I pull a piece of string out of my pocket and wave it in front of Howdy's face. He's always loved to bat and chase string.

But not today.

Just before we leave, Mr. Santos, a quarantine officer, stands at the door. "May I come in, folks?" he asks. His bald head is shiny and his smile bright.

"Sure," I say.

"How's the big boy today?" Mr. Santos asks.

Howdy doesn't answer. But Daddy does. "Doing great."

I know he says that to make me feel better. I press my lips together.

"Howdy and I are buddies," Mr. Santos says, and reaches over to scratch behind my cat's ears. Howdy leans in. "He listens to all my stories. Laughs in all the right places."

"Laughs?"

"With his eyes."

Now Daddy and I are the ones laughing.

"Thanks for coming by," Daddy says, and shakes Mr. Santos's hand.

"Yes," I say. "Most of all, thanks for being his friend."

"Catch you later," Mr. Santos says, and steps out of the cage.

"Love you, Howdy," I say as I give him one last pet. "I'll be back tomorrow. Then there'll be ninety-seven days to go. I'm trying my best," I say into his fur. "But I know it's not good enough. Please be okay. Please."

Daddy and I walk out to overcast skies. Whitecaps top the water nearby.

The sun wants to shine, but somehow it just can't break through. We've had showers on and off for days. Rain makes weeds grow. Why don't folks call?

First Real Job

I KNOW EXACTLY what Grams is up to right now. It's past noon on Wednesday in Gladiola, and twelve ladies will have gathered with their sewing baskets and stitchery at someone's house. Grams calls it her lunchtime sewing circle. Grandpa calls it information central. The ladies talk and eat more than they sew or needlepoint.

Here in home ec, I have the sewing machine to myself. This is the third day Kiki hasn't shown up. I figured she had the chicken pox, but before school, I could have sworn I saw her in the courtyard. So I keep one eye on the door.

She never comes.

During Hawaiian history, Malina invites me to babysit with her right after hula today. Which goes to show that life can change for the better in an instant.

• ✿ •

The Silva family lives five doors down from Malina and she's sat with the boys before. We arrive on time. And after quick introductions, the parents take off.

In the living room, dozens of little army soldiers line up on either side of the masking-tape border.

"Cross it and you're dead," hollers Kevin as he and his older brother, Kenneth, stare down their two younger siblings.

I don't have a good feeling about this.

"Ready. Aim. Fire," Kevin hollers. "Attack. Attack."

Sounds of gunfire and explosions fill the air. The war is on full volume.

Malina sits in a recliner reading a *National Geographic* article about Paris. I back up and take a seat on the couch. Basically, the older boys are clobbering the younger.

"I think the first thing we have to do when we get to Paris is go to the top of this," says Malina, holding up the magazine page with a photo of the Eiffel Tower.

"But of course," I say with a fakey French accent, and quickly cross my fingers behind my back.

"Whoa, take it easy, y'all," I say as the older boys topple the younger ones.

No response.

"It's getting a little loud in here," I say.

It gets louder.

I wave my arms.

Nothing happens.

Malina looks up from her magazine, raises a whistle to her mouth, and blows.

The war goes silent.

"Attention," she commands just like Mr. Nakamoto, and the boys salute.

"Troops need sustenance," she says, opens her straw bag, and hands each boy a chocolate bar.

I am watching a pro. And I am way out of my league.

The boys inhale their snack and start again. When the battle gets loud enough to be heard in Honolulu, Malina blows her whistle again. She sends the troops around the room four times. Once, they are told to do twenty-five jumping jacks. Once, they have to be silent for a whole minute. And last, they have inspection before chow time.

After supper, sponge baths instead of regular baths commence since water is rationed on the frontlines, and then we do a competition to see who can build the sturdiest fort.

"We want a spooky story," they chant as we tuck them into bed.

"Not until you're older," says Malina. "Remember what happened last time?"

She turns to me, mouths *Madame Pele,* and pantomimes screaming and crying and not sleeping.

"But we're older now," says Kermit. "That was last week."

• ✿ •

"I'm exhausted," I say, collapsing on the couch after Malina's not scary story. "And all I did was watch."

"It just takes practice," says Malina.

"Like years," I say. I don't have that much time.

Malina plunks down beside me, her hands on her knees. "Ask me," she says.

"Ask you what?"

"About Kimo."

"Have you been withholding information? Tell me, hurry."

"Well," says Malina, leaning in, "Tammy said Phyllis said Melissa said Lani said she heard Kimo say my name at lunch."

"There you go. Just wait. He's sure to make a move soon."

"I know. I'm so excited. I just don't know how much longer I can wait."

"Waiting for what you want is hard."

When Malina gets paid, she hands me some of her money. I finger it, and think about Howdy, about going home to Texas. "This belongs to you," I say, returning the bills. "I wasn't a babysitter or even an assistant."

"Don't be silly," she says, giving it back. "It was so much better having you there. If you don't want to use it for Paris, you could buy Howdy some toys."

"Thank you, Malina." I smile. "Maybe I'll do both."

Lei Making

ONCE MALINA FINISHES HELPING her mom with laundry after school the next day, she bounces over. "Ready?"

"Ready," I say. "Malina's going to teach me how to make a lei," I tell Mama.

"Have fun, girls."

We pick and soak dozens and dozens of plumeria blossoms from our yards and the neighbors'. Then, it's time for the next step. Malina hands me the longest needle I've ever seen and a strand of dental floss. "Stronger than thread," she says.

Sitting here side by side reminds me of sitting next to Kiki. Only Malina doesn't care that I'm haole.

She shows me how to make a double lei. "It'll be fuller and fancier," she says.

When we finish, I inspect mine. Since making it was

kind of like sewing, I thought mine would look perfect, like Malina's. A stem shows here and there. A few petals are bruised, a few missing.

Well, at least it smells good.

Bud

WHEN THE STARS APPEAR, I dance outside to check on the night-blooming cereus. Even though the plant is way, way up there, I think I see a bud. It is wrapped in green and about the size of an egg, only flatter. I've been here almost one whole month. Something is starting to grow.

Lei Day

SCHOOL SMELLS LIKE HEAVEN.

According to Malina, today is like a holiday. We're celebrating May Day, even if technically it isn't until Sunday.

Plumeria, orchid, carnation, and I don't know what else are draped around shoulders, circle heads, or both. Kids stream by in Hawaiian print muumuus and aloha shirts.

"Close your eyes," says Malina as we walk up to the entrance.

"But I want to see everything."

"Here, hang on to my arm," she says. "We'll be there in a sec."

It's better not to argue.

"Coming through," says Malina as I shuffle beside her. "Now look."

Across the courtyard, a wooden stage, draped in

white, yellow, red, and pink plumeria, fronts the bank of classroom windows. Two wicker chairs with backs shaped like fans sit in the center with wooden classroom chairs lined up on either side. Poles topped with red and yellow papier-mâché cylinders stand at either end of the stage. Strings of yellow plumeria hang from the ceilings of the walkways that encircle the courtyard. Pink plumeria blossoms wrap around the trunks of the coconut trees.

"It's like a movie," I say.

"Just wait for the assembly."

After homeroom, the whole school crowds into the courtyard. We spill over the walkways and onto the basketball court to the far left of the stage. Malina and I wiggle our way toward the right side and sit on the grass. "This'll give us the best view," she says.

I spot Tammy a few kids over. This is her last day. She and her friends are trading addresses, promising to write, and dreaming of visiting snow. Will that ever be me?

Mr. Kam, the principal, welcomes us to Lei Day.

"As is our custom," he says, "let us sing our former national anthem."

Everyone stands. A soft breeze stirs. The warm sun rises behind us. Some place a hand over their heart.

I send Malina a questioning look. "'Hawaii Pono'i,'" she says. "In Hawaiian."

Mr. Kam lowers the mike to his side and begins. All around me, voices join his. Harmonious, strong, proud. Faces tender, earnest, resilient. Chill bumps cover my arms. The last note fades. No one speaks. We listen to the song's memory—to the echo—as the birds reply.

Mr. Kam turns the program over to Steven Hamakua, the eighth-grade class president and MC. "Representing the Big Island of Hawaii," says Steven, "we welcome Princess Sylvia Okubo and Prince Kimo Nahoa."

We all clap. Sylvia wears a long red satin holoku. Kimo, in black pants, a white shirt, and a red sash around his waist, walks barefoot across the stage, arm in arm with Sylvia. They stand in front of the last chairs on the left and wave.

I wave back.

"I read," says Malina, "that if you feel a little spark when you see someone you like, it's a good sign. And I just felt one." She strokes the K+M written on her hand.

"Y'all would make a cute couple," I say.

"And now, representing the island of Maui, we

welcome a princess who is continuing a family tradition of being in the Lei Day court: Kiki Kahana and . . ."

Is that the Kiki I know? Her hair is up in a twist. Her holoku of pink satin has an extra-long train. She wears a nervous smile, like she doesn't believe she is onstage. It makes her look softer. Instead of waving like the others, she holds up her thumb and pinkie on her right hand and shakes it back and forth.

The crowd hollers and does the hand sign right back.

It is Kiki. She must have been at rehearsals all week. "Who chose her?" I ask.

"We voted by grade before you came. It's a popularity contest." Malina wrinkles her nose. "I heard a rumor that the girls running against her dropped out."

"Do you think she had something to do with that?"

"I think she wanted it really bad."

"Look, it's Connie from hula," I say as the next couple appears.

Island after island, pairs parade across the stage. After the last representatives, those of Niihau, are presented, the royal court sits and the entertainment begins.

I recognize a hula song. It's on the flip side of one of my records.

Kiki dances it as beautifully as Mrs. Halani. She sings to the music. Her eyes follow her hands. Her knees are soft. She smiles.

I wish this Kiki would come to school every day.

Half-Full or Half-Empty?

IT'S SUNDAY AFTERNOON and Howdy lies in a thin beam of sunlight on the floor next to his door.

"Hi, sweet boy," I say, and reach my fingers through the wire to scratch the top of his head.

Howdy stands, stretches, and rubs his whiskers against his cage.

"Back up just a smidgen," I say as I lift the handle and open his door. I pick Howdy right up, sit on the bench, and set him on my lap. There's less cat hair in my hands, less on my clothes.

"See that," says Daddy. "A half-empty bowl."

I lean back against the cage. "Why, compared to last week, Howdy, you're almost a member of the clean-plate club. When you wake up tomorrow, you'll have eighty-nine days left. You can do this. Keep up the good work."

Daddy settles in beside us with a book about positive thinking.

Except for petting Howdy, I don't move for two whole hours.

It almost doesn't matter that he doesn't purr.

• ✿ •

When I get home, I send a postcard to Cindy with a photo of a lei stand. I recognize plumeria, orchid, carnation, tuberose, and pikake flowers. Only two I don't know.

Civil Defense Announcement

"CLASS," says Mr. Nakamoto, "it would behoove you to listen."

On Monday morning, May 2, the number twenty is on the board. Mr. Nakamoto shakes the announcement paper in his hand and raps the empty desk at the front of the room. I wonder if it snows in Colorado in May. I hope for Tammy's sake it does.

Malina stretches her arms up and wiggles three fingers. Before I can stop, a laugh spurts out. It is the third time in ten minutes that Mr. Nakamoto has said "behoove." His record in homeroom is four. Today it might be broken.

"Miss Bennett, a comment?"

"No," I say, and cover my eyes so I won't look at Malina and laugh again.

"The civil defense will conduct a test today, Miss Bennett. I mention this for your benefit."

"Yes, sir," I say.

We'd hear the siren loud and clear. That I know for sure. An enormous two-headed megaphone perches on top of a tall, skinny pole near the street in front of the school. It looks just like the one in Gladiola.

"Thank you," I say. "I know about the duck-and-cover drill."

"Excellent. But if it is a tidal wave?"

"Swim?" I say.

The class cracks up.

Mr. Nakamoto clears his throat extra loud and everyone snaps to.

"In the event of a tidal wave," he says, "we will move to higher ground."

I turn to Malina for an explanation after class. "We march up to the hillside until the all-clear. It's like a big party, only we have to stand in straight lines."

"Got it," I say.

"I don't care what drill we do," says Malina, "I just hope I'll end up near Kimo."

"I hope so, too."

• ✿ •

Kiki ignores me in home ec.

Everyone, and I mean everyone, keeps coming up to her and telling her how boss she looked on the May

Day stage. They say her hand sign was the coolest. They say she was the best dancer in the whole program.

Maybe this is what the last day of school will look like. Maybe everyone will crowd around her to say good-bye. Maybe Kiki will forget I'm even here.

Kiki really was the best dancer. If I tell her, will she think it's a trap?

In the Event of an Emergency

"TEN, NINE, EIGHT, SEVEN . . ." the boy next to me in math counts down the seconds on the clock.

"*WaaaaAAAHHHHH,*" wails the siren.

I cover my ears and wish I were with Howdy. He doesn't cotton to loud noises. I'm sure all the dogs around him are howling, which will only make things worse. If I were there, I'd tell him the commotion would end soon.

"Duck and cover," hollers Miss Liu. For a teeny woman, she sure has a giant voice.

In Gladiola, we'd move to an interior hallway, crouch with our backs to the wall, and cover our necks with our arms. Here, we'll stay put, but protected.

The desks in this room are older, wooden, heavier. Each sits two people. My desk partner and three other boys get dibs on the teacher's weighty desk. Another boy and I push mine toward the windows. "You're Peggy Sue, right?"

"Uh-huh," I say over the squeaks and grunts around us.

"The one with the window-washing and weeding businesses?"

"That's me."

"Thanks for nothing."

I stop pushing. "What? Why?"

"My dad saw your signs and now I'm doing the work for free. Do me a favor. Let me and my friends know if you have any more great ideas, so we can destroy your signs."

I pick at the neck of my blouse to get some air. "Sorry," I say. "I was just trying . . ."

"Save it," he says, and gives the desk one last push. It slams into another one and he disappears underneath.

"Take your positions below," yells Miss Liu.

We kneel, tuck, and cover our necks with our arms.

I'm squished between a boy and a girl.

Someone forgot to shower after PE.

Someone wears the same kind of cologne as Daddy, only four times as much.

I smell bubble gum, too.

It's warm under here. Drippy warm.

"I'm suffocating," someone says.

"I'm dying."

I'm mortified. I have even more people mad that I exist than I thought.

"Quiet," shouts Miss Liu.

Someone fake-snores.

My right foot is asleep. I hope Malina got a spot next to Kimo.

"All clear," says the teacher after way too long.

Crawling out, I bonk my head.

The whole drill takes twenty-five minutes. I don't mind missing math.

Except Miss Liu gives us extra homework.

Civil Defense Meal

APPARENTLY, AFTER THE SIREN, Mama hurried to the stores and stocked up.

Which is why the coat closet is now full of cans of beans, spaghetti, corn, jugs of water, extra blankets, a new flashlight, and a first aid kit.

For supper, Daddy and I heat up some emergency cans of spaghetti and green beans because Mama is in bed with a headache.

"Your school phoned today," he says. "The counselor called it your final-month checkup. It seems your grades aren't what they should be. I know you are spending time with Malina, practicing hula, writing letters, and putting in a lot of effort finding a job."

"They called you at work?"

"They tried the house, but your mama must have been shopping."

"I want to dance well at the recital, and Malina and I are saving for Paris."

"That's wonderful, but your first job is schoolwork, okay?"

"Sure, Daddy, sure."

Let's Make a Deal

"TAKE YOUR SEATS QUICKLY," says Mrs. Barsdale at the start of class the next morning. "I'm coming by to check everyone's progress."

Kiki and I watch as she inspects every inch of Kiki's blue flowered dress, checking for straight seams, even stitches, offending bumps and puckers. "The facings are off-kilter here and here," she says. "And the zipper is crooked."

Mrs. Barsdale doesn't miss a stitch. On my lime-green print dress either. But I get a better report. "I'm expecting greatness, girls," she says. "From both of you."

"Hear that?" Kiki says, and bumps my shoulder. "Greatness."

That sets my foot to jiggling. "I heard," I say as Mrs. Barsdale and her beauty mark bustle away.

Because of guest speakers, a film on Parisian couture, and a written test, we have only nine more class periods to complete our projects. I could just flat-out finish her dress. Then two out of the three of us would be happy. Or maybe, just maybe, there's a way all three of us can be.

"Kiki," I say.

"Extra-credit girl."

"You know what you said about me trying to trick you earlier?"

"Of course."

"Well, I was."

"Typical," says the girl next to us.

I pretend I don't hear. My foot jiggles faster.

"And I want to say that I'm sorry about that."

Kiki looks like she doesn't believe me.

"So now I want to be completely honest. I want to make a deal. You were busy all last week with May Day, so you're a little behind."

Actually, a lot. "I'll make your dress if you won't fight me."

"That's an interesting proposal, Piggy Sue."

"Is that a yes?"

"No."

"No?"

"It's a maybe."

A maybe. Everyone knows a maybe is a hundred

times better than a no. A maybe can turn into a yes.

"I'll take maybe," I say.

"Deal," says Kiki, handing me her dress.

My foot stills.

Daddy would call this the path of least resistance. Like the mountain water that irrigates the sugarcane. Wooden flumes carry it down to the fields—gravity in motion.

I'm leaving. Eventually. What do I care? This will make at least one problem go away. And I can make it happen.

It's win-win-win.

Kiki gets to start summer vacation while she's still in school. Mrs. Barsdale will be happy. I'll get what I want—peace.

Almost four more weeks of school. Surviving is important.

At any cost.

"Don't just sit there," says Kiki, "get busy."

I sew.

Kiki socializes.

We don't switch seats at the machine halfway through class. I keep working on Kiki's dress.

Later, as Mrs. Barsdale winds her way toward our side of the room, Kiki threads a needle and holds it over a facing as if she's going to stitch it down on my dress.

Kiki should be an actress.

Me, too.

We are faking out Mrs. Barsdale.

Best of all, I'm yards closer to a yes.

• ✿ •

We repeat our great performance the next day.

With identical results.

A Way Out

A MOM TALKS with Mrs. Halani at the front of the studio before class Wednesday afternoon. A partially made granny-style holoku is draped over her arm. Her voice is growing louder and louder.

"My mom hates to sew," says a girl standing next to Malina and me.

She looks familiar, but she's not in our hula class. "She says the pattern is too hard and that I'll have to wear something different instead." The girl studies the assortment of footwear just inside the door. This is a no-shoes space. Malina and I exchange glances.

"Are you thinking what I'm thinking?" I say.

"Paris?" asks Malina.

"Paris," I say. Only I mean the one in Texas.

"I can sew," I say. "I made what I'm wearing." I spin, and my bluepinkwhite skirt blurs around me.

The girl grabs my arm mid-twirl. "Mom, Mom,"

she says, and pulls me over to her.

"Name the price," says the mom after eyeing my skirt and blouse.

I look to Mrs. Halani. She says a number. Higher than what I am thinking.

"It'll be worth it," the mom says, and quickly hands me the materials.

The girl, Sylvia Okubo, turns to me. "Thanks, I owe you one."

"Believe me," I say, "you're doing me a huge favor."

"Peggy Sue," says Mrs. Halani, "once the word gets out, you're going to have more business than you know what to do with. Remember, you can always say no."

Never. I'll never say that word.

"In fact," Mrs. Halani says, "my niece needs all of her costumes made. I'll talk to my sister and set it up if that's okay."

"One of her costumes is extra special," says Malina. "Mom picks one student each year to dance the last dance with her."

Things are looking up everywhere. At school. Here. I've got a business—a sewing business!

Class Time

"EVERYONE FACE THE MIRROR to your right," says Mrs. Halani. I noticed her necklace when we talked sewing. It's a choker of polished black kukui nuts the size of walnuts and coordinates perfectly with her brown-and-black tapa print muumuu. "Spread out so you can see yourself," she says. "No hiding."

I curl my toes under. I don't mind dancing in front of my dresser mirror with only my porcelain cat watching, but I dislike dancing in class, where these girls will see all of my mistakes. So I think about dancing for Grams and Grandpa and Cindy instead.

"Make sure your elbows don't sag," says Mrs. Halani. "And most importantly, smile."

Malina is in the first row and gives me a big grin in the mirror.

"Beginning positions," says Mrs. Halani.

I bend my knees, put my hands on my hips, and

make sure my feet are slightly apart. Mrs. Halani taps a brown gourd. I bend my right elbow and raise it to chest height. My left arm goes straight out to the side at my shoulder.

Mrs. Halani chants in Hawaiian about the beauty of the island of Kauai. I imagine the blooming ginger along the banks of the streams, the barking sand, and valleys green from rain.

I peek in the mirror as I move my feet and smile at my class.

Everyone smiles back.

I keep going.

And trip.

Kimo + Malina?

"I HAVE TO TELL YOU something important," says Malina as we leave class. Her face is solemn.

"I'm listening."

"I called Kimo last night."

"And?"

"He answered."

"And?"

"I hung up."

"Why?"

"Nerves. But I called right back. Only then, his sister picked up, and before I could even ask for him, she said, 'Charlene, stop calling my brother.' "

"Who's Charlene?"

"A cute, popular girl in my PE class."

I look at her hand. The heart is empty. And I hadn't noticed.

"Don't worry, Malina. He'll come around."

I hope.

• ✿ •

I write another postcard to Cindy, who for some reason still hasn't written. Surely she hasn't broken her arm or hand. She did break a finger in fourth grade when she hit the tetherball with one finger instead of her whole hand.

This postcard shows hula dancers wearing skirts made of green ti leaves and holding signs that spell out A-L-O-H-A.

Satin

THE FOLLOWING AFTERNOON, I learn that satin doesn't cut the same as cotton and wool.

It may be shiny and smooth, but that is just an illusion.

Scissors slip on satin.

Cutting places you don't want cut.

It frays.

It is unforgiving.

Sweat marks show on satin.

Which is why I am fixing to go to the fabric department at Fujimoto's Five-and-Dime. I need more. I need to try again.

Sewing may give you second chances. But cutting does not.

"It's the price of doing business," Mama says as I grab my purse.

I'll have to spend my own money. I can't charge

Mrs. Halani's sister for my mistake. I have to pay for it. Which means no profit.

I pray it's like the first pancake—the test pancake: it tastes the same as all the others, but it never looks as pretty. And now that I've made the mistake, it won't happen again—the next time will be better.

Like hula, sewing a holoku is harder than it looks.

Holdout

HOWDY JUMPS UP right beside me as soon as I sit on the bench on Saturday.

"This is day thirty-seven, Howdy. Eighty-three more to go."

Or less, I pray.

I check out Howdy's food bowl. Almost empty!

I swing a toy mouse in front of Howdy's eyes. "I bought this just for you."

Howdy rubs his face against my hand. First one side, then the other.

"You're welcome," I say, and twirl the mouse before his nose.

But Howdy doesn't pay that toy any mind. At all. He kneads his front paws into my lap. I put aside the mouse and hug my soft, warm kitty. But not too tight.

And then, and then . . . *Purrrrrrrrrrrrrrrrrrrrrr!*

"Why, you big old holdout, you," I say.
"He sounds great to me," says Daddy.
"The best," I say. "Thank you, Howdy."

Clothesline

AS I RETURN to my room Sunday night after supper, I pause at the doorway.

Four muumuus in various states hang by clothespins on twine stretching across the front of my bedroom window. A small slip of paper with a name is attached by a safety pin to each one.

Two more mothers have already dropped off patterns and materials. Two others promised they would come by before the end of next week, which means eight muumuus so far.

The recital is in four weeks.

Solid pinks, bright oranges, turquoises, yellows. Hawaiian prints—blue and white hibiscus, brown and white and black tapa prints with tikis, red and yellow and navy and green bird of paradise.

My room is as colorful as a coral reef.

Counting Maybes

TODAY IS MONDAY, May 16. Ten days left of school. Five classes until our sewing projects are due. And only three periods left to get them done.

Every day since our agreement, I've asked Kiki for her answer. So far, she's said:

Maybe. Maybe. Maybe.

Maybe. Maybe. Maybe. Maybe. Maybe.

"Hold still, please," I ask her toward the end of class. I'm measuring and pinning the hem of her daisy dress. Everything about it suits her—the color, the style, the fit.

She peers into the full-length mirror, turns, fusses with her hair.

"Looking good, girls," Mrs. Barsdale says as she dashes by.

"I'd swear it's store-bought," says a girl waiting her turn.

"Wanna trade?" asks another.

"No," says Kiki, trying her best to look nonchalant. But her high-beam bright eyes give her away.

We've got a deal. I just know it.

After the bell, I ask for an answer.

"Maybe," she says.

Again? She can't say maybe forever.

Due Date

ON FRIDAY, home ec buzzes from the get-go. Kiki's dress is done, but I inspect it one more time just in case. Kiki is at my shoulder, inspecting, too. "Stray thread," she says, pointing to a side seam.

I clip it. "Anything else?"

She keeps looking, but says no more.

"It's all yours, then," I say, much relieved.

A clothes rack for our projects is parked beside the teacher's desk. Kiki waltzes over to the rack, grabs a hanger, and turns in her finished dress. "I did it, Mrs. Barsdale," she says.

"I had no doubt," says the teacher.

Could have fooled me.

I jump up as soon as Kiki comes back.

"So what do you think now?" I ask. My stomach flutters. I am sure her answer will be yes. Sure we have a deal. Sure there will be no fight.

"I'm still thinking," she says.

And I'm scowling. No. That is not the right answer. "I thought—"

"You thought wrong, haole. I have another week to decide."

She's playing me. Like Howdy with a toy mouse. He tears out the eyes. Rips off the tail. Bites off the felt ears. Extracts the bell with claws and teeth. Until the toy mouse is stripped of all its senses, and its insides are on the outside.

I had a win-win-win plan.

But now I'm the only one with something left to lose.

I'm caught in the maybe-middle. For five more school days.

I've got to be positive. Keep up the hope. Her answer can't be "no deal."

It just can't.

Luau Prep

I WASN'T EXPECTING to see a whole pig in the Halanis' backyard pit after school.

Especially one with an apple in its mouth.

But I've got to say, he smells smoky sweet delicious.

"Tutu will have the best retirement luau on the island, haole girl," David says. Sweat trickles down his dimpled cheeks.

His father squints at him.

"I mean the whole state," David says.

"That's better," Mr. Halani says, and laughs. "Peggy Sue, it'll be a night to remember."

And a good night for me to forget. Forget about school for a few hours.

The Halanis rented long tables and folding chairs for Tutu's party and set them up in their front yard. Malina and I are in charge of decorations. For the past two days, we've strung rows and rows of plumeria blossoms that we collected from all over the neighborhood. Now we lay them down the center of each table covered with white butcher paper.

Malina hasn't mentioned Kimo in a couple of days, and the heart on her hand hasn't been filled in. So I ask.

"I'm so down I can't talk about it," she says. "He ate lunch with Charlene yesterday and today."

"Maybe they're working on a school project together."

"I would know," says Malina.

She's right. She would.

"Come on," she says. "Only two more tables to fix up."

Countdown. One hour to go.

Dog

AS SOON AS the party starts, a brown medium-size dog with a red ribbon tied around its neck bounds over to us. I scoot behind Malina. "It's okay," she says. "This is Kahuna. He's an honored guest," and she pets him on top of his head.

"Kahuna, sit," says Malina, and the dog obeys. "Meet Peggy Sue." Kahuna holds up a paw. "You'll hurt his feelings if you don't shake it."

So I do. The dog seems friendly. "Nice to meet you," I say.

"Kahuuuuuuna," someone calls. And with that the dog takes off.

I wish I could call for Howdy and he'd come running. Leaving Howdy last weekend was as hard as ever. Especially because he was purring.

"Don't move," says Malina. "I'll go get us some punch."

I watch. And wait.

I'm almost on my own at this party, which is kind of fun. Daddy had to pick up a man flying in from the mainland for work and take him to his hotel. Of course Mama went, too. They said that they'd drop in when they got home.

A woman in a tapa print muumuu talks to a man about Tutu's trip and who's who at the party. "I hear new tenants moved in," she says, and points to where I live. "A shame they're haoles."

Her ugly words hit me, hit me hard. Like an unexpected wave.

"I wonder whose job he stole," says the man.

"He works in ag," she says as they stroll away. "At least this time his boss didn't take away yours."

The pair fades into the party, but their words still roar like pounding surf in my ears.

Mr. Halani was right. This'll be a night I don't forget. But I want to. I want to forget what they said. To pretend I didn't hear them. Pretend everything is all right.

Malina returns with a fruit punch so sweet it makes my mouth pucker. "Lilikoi," she says.

I push away the couple's comments and breathe in the music. A Hawaiian trio—bass, ukulele, and steel guitar—play and sing. Strings of twinkling lights hang in the tent, and the delicious smells of flowers and food fill the air. Tutu sits at the head table and greets her guests. She is covered up to her chin with leis. It looks like May Day all over again. Gifts overflow the card table.

In a little while, Mr. Halani hollers for everyone to gather around. A minister gives a blessing in Hawaiian, which sounds as pretty as a song.

Tutu blows kisses to her guests. "Enjoy," she says, and points the way to the food.

Malina and I get our plates and sit down at a table up front. "Isn't this ono?" she asks, licking her fingers.

"Delicious," I say as I begin taking another bite of the pineapple. My Hawaiian vocabulary is growing, though the only word I understood of the minister's Hawaiian blessing earlier was *amene*.

Malina and I scooch over our chairs to make room for another guest. I sweep the crowd. It's elbow to elbow at all the tables. Laughs float across the still air. Malina chatters with a lady next to her.

It seems like everyone knows everyone else. I move a piece of pork from one side of my plate to the other. Avoid the poi. And remember. Somewhere in the crowd is a couple who doesn't want me on the island. I wish my parents would hurry up and get here.

Not too much later, Mr. Halani stands. "And

now for more entertainment. First up, Tutu's favorite grandson."

Everyone laughs. "She only has one," says Malina, rolling her eyes.

"Presenting my son, David the Magnificent, and his lovely assistant, Teresa."

David does card tricks, pulls a stuffed pig out of a hat, and finds quarters behind the ears of people in the crowd.

"Malina and Peggy Sue, you're next," says Mr. Halani.

The trio begins to sing.

"No, not me," I say.

"Come on," Malina says, and pulls me out of my seat.

"Please, no."

"'Lovely Hula Hands,'" says Mr. Halani, and the crowd claps.

I stare at the crowd.

My mouth is dry.

I pretend-dance like a tourist at a hula show.

Someone laughs. Really loud.

I am not a dancer. I am a failure.

Cousins

"THANK YOU, GIRLS," says Mr. Halani. "And now let's give a warm welcome to Hanu's Kamehameha Day Parade's favorite dog, Kahuna, and her owner, my niece, Kiki."

Kiki?

Kahuna races from behind the house and runs in circles before the head table as people stand and clap. I can't see the dog through the people until everyone settles back down. Kahuna sits at attention on the grass. Beside him is a girl. A girl in a long pink satin muumuu.

"She's your cousin?" I blurt out.

Malina puts a finger to her lips and nods.

Cousin? With the girl who might beat me up? Why didn't she tell me? Is this a game and I'm the bet?

"Kahuna, speak," says Kiki.

The dog barks and the audience claps. Kahuna spins around and around.

I lean over my half-eaten plate of food. "What else don't I know?"

Malina wrinkles her brow.

The crowd quiets. "Kahuna, sing," says Kiki. The dog howls.

"You could have told me. You should have told me."

I don't give Malina a chance to answer.

I leap up and race next door.

Calling Home

I DIAL THE OPERATOR.

I won't talk long.

"Collect?" the operator asks when she comes on the line.

My grip tightens on the phone. "No, bill us station-to-station," I say. I'll use my own money.

"One moment, please," she says and my hand on the receiver relaxes.

After some silence and a few clicks, a ring. I know it well. A second ring. I picture Grams's cheery kitchen with a pitcher of tea and a plate of iced sugar cookies on the table. A third ring. A fourth. Where are they?

Finally, a groggy hello.

"Grandpa, it's me, Peggy Sue."

"Well, I'll be. Is it really you?" I hear him say, "Melba, I think it's Peggy Sue. The connection is a little scratchy." Then back to me, "Is everything all right?"

"Yes. No. I wanted to hear your voice." Which comes through loud and clear on my end.

"You gave us a scare. It's nearing midnight."

"I can't believe I forgot all about the time difference."

"Best wake-up call I've ever had," says Grandpa. "Here, let me give you to your grandmother. But speak up now; there's some static on the line."

I launch with tonight's disaster. "I thought, I thought Malina Halani was my friend. But she isn't. Her cousin is a girl named Kiki. But no one told me. And Kiki, Kiki is a girl at school. She laughed when I danced at the party. No one wants me here, Grams. No one at all. I miss you. . . ."

"You're wound up tight as thread on a bobbin," says Grams when I take a breath. "Change can take time, sweet pea."

"I'm running out of time, Grams."

"Now, how's your mama?"

"Still fighting headaches."

"Give her our love. And of course your daddy, too."

I forgot to set the egg timer, but we haven't talked that long.

"Wait, Grams. Please. There's more."

"Oh, sweet pea, this connection is a fright. I didn't

hear everything you said before and I'm drowsy. You just be yourself and everything will work out."

Being me is the problem.

"Your grandpa wants to say good-bye."

"No, don't go yet. Grams, I want to come home."

"Take good care now. Love you," she says. "Here's your grandpa."

"Tell your parents we'll talk to them the next time," he says, and hangs up.

I put the phone back in its cradle. Talking to them reminds me of what I left. How far away I am from getting back.

The front door opens and Mama and Daddy come in holding hands.

"There's our girl," says Daddy. "We saw you dash away just as we walked up to the party, so we only stayed a minute. Had enough fun for one night?"

"Yes, sir," I say. "I'm tired." And I cover up my pretend yawn.

Big Island

"THE OFFICE IS SENDING ME to the Big Island for a few days," Daddy says as he sits in the easy chair next to the couch. "I'm taking your mama."

I perk right up, wait for the next words. The ones that will fix everything. The ones that include me.

"I wish you could come with us, Peggy Sue," Mama says.

"But I can," I say, and sit on the edge of the couch. I'm jumpy excited inside.

"You've got school."

"I can miss, Mama. And I thought you were going to do some volunteer work."

"Peggy Sue," says Mama. "We talked about this, Robert," she says, turning to Daddy. "She needs to bring up her grades."

"You are a little behind," he says.

"Not in home ec," I counter.

"Peggy Sue," says Mama. "You've got hula lessons,

an upcoming recital, and all that sewing to do, too."

"But—" I begin.

"While it's a business trip for me," says Daddy, "I hope it'll be a little vacation for your mama. She's worked so hard on the move and deserves a rest."

I do, too!

"We've made arrangements for you to stay with the Halanis," says Mama.

"What? No. Can't Grams and Grandpa come?" I am not staying with the Halanis. Not now that I know Malina and I aren't really friends.

"Oh, Peggy Sue," Mama says.

"You know my parents don't travel by air," says Daddy.

"They'll make an exception for me. Did you even ask?"

Daddy has taken Mama on other business trips. I've always stayed with Grams and Grandpa. There's no set bedtime and I watch as much TV as I want. They take me out to the soda fountain. We go to the bowling alley and the picture show. If it's Saturday night, we mosey over to the fish fry at the volunteer fire station. And later to the Gladiola Rec Center, where there's a band and most everyone dances Western swing until we collapse.

The phone rings and Mama gets up.

"Hi, Malina. We're in the middle of a family discussion. . . . Yes, we've just told Peggy Sue, too. Can she call you back? . . . Okay, good. Thank you. Bye now."

"How long?" I ask.

"A week," says Mama.

"A week? You're leaving me with strangers for a week?" With a girl who hasn't told me the truth? Whose cousin hates me? "When are you leaving?"

"The day after tomorrow."

"Wait one more week. Please. Then I'll be out of school and I can go, too. I want to see the volcano that's erupting. Don't deprive me of a once-in-a-lifetime real live educational experience."

"Robert," says Mama, rubbing her temples.

"We're booked at a hotel next to the bay in Hilo," says Daddy. "The volcano's miles away. We may not get to it this trip. Don't worry, kitten. There'll be a next time."

No, there won't. There won't be a next time. Because I won't be here.

"Go!" I shout. "Go, and I hope you never come back!"

Blooming?

LATER, DADDY comes to my room with the flashlight and asks me to check on the night-blooming cereus with him.

"No," I say.

"I'm here when you want to talk, kitten," he says.

I answer with silence. Daddy stands there a while and then leaves. I hear the back door open and his footfalls on the steps. He stays outside for a really long time.

The party next door winds down. Good-byes and thank yous and best wishes carry across the night. Car doors open and close. Engines start. Lights flash against my bedroom walls. And then there is darkness.

After a time, I go outside and stand silent beneath the scraggly plant rooted to the tree. A dog barks on and on. The trade winds whip the palm fronds nearby. Someone smashes note after note on a drum set.

My insides still churn. Rolling over and over like waves that surge onto the beach.

I stare at the sturdy tree trunk, noticing a deep gash near its base.

Tha-wamp! The ground quivers, zinging reverberations to the top of my head. I gasp and jump back. A coconut rolls within inches of me.

Another gust of wind hits, sending the palm fronds into panicky, jerky movements. It's dangerous out here.

But I have to know.

I flick on the flashlight and shine it up the tree. The flower still isn't blooming.

And I flee to the house.

Tangled

SATURDAY MORNING is blustery. If this house had shutters like our house in Gladiola, one would surely come unhinged. Here, the curtains in my bedroom won't settle. They keep puffing up.

I press the foot pedal on the sewing machine and feed the orange cotton fabric beneath the bobbling needle.

At breakfast I thought about talking to Daddy. Until he told me I wouldn't see Howdy today. He has to work with the out-of-town person from the office. Mama has to pack.

Two whole weeks between Howdy visits? And no drop-bys from Daddy this week either. Howdy will surely think we've abandoned him. That no one loves him. Maybe he'll lose his purr again.

I speed up the machine and it jams. I yank out the material and check the underside. It is a tangled mess of thread.

The phone rings. Once. Twice. Three times. "Peggy Sue, it's Malina," says Mama.

"I'll call her back."

I don't want to talk to her.

Talking to Daddy

"TIME TO CALL it a night, kitten," says Daddy over the *zzzzZzzzzZzzzt* of the sewing machine.

I let up on the pedal, and the machine stops. "Daddy," I say, turning, "I think Mama and me have rock fever. I should go home."

There. I've spilled it.

"What kind of nonsense . . . ?" Daddy asks. He puts his hands gently on my shoulders.

"I feel it, Daddy. Right here." I point to my heart.

Daddy's shoulders sag. "I'm sorry, Peggy Sue. You know I want you to love it here."

"I don't know how much longer I can last."

I twist an end of fabric into a long, tight, skinny roll.

"I know moving hasn't been easy for you. But you should try and focus on the good."

"You don't get it, Daddy! I don't want to stay. I

have a plan. I want to go back to Texas and live with Grams and Grandpa. I'm earning good money from sewing. If you buy me a ticket now, I'll pay you back the rest someday."

"We'd be lost without you, kitten," says Daddy, his voice soft and low. "You are our daughter and we want you with us. Please, don't talk this way again."

I look down at my mangled fabric and blink real hard.

Talking with Malina

MAMA AND DADDY load their suitcases into the car Sunday morning. "Have fun," I say, slam the trunk, and turn my back to them.

I glare at the mountains in the distance, capped with clouds of gray. Daddy starts the car, honks twice, and pulls away.

Without a wave I stomp across the grass to the Halanis' with my own suitcase. Their car hesitates at the end of the drive as I plow through the hedge. I beat back the branches, but they win. I've got scratches now.

"Brownies in twenty minutes," says Mrs. Halani when she meets me at the door.

The chocolatey goodness smells divine, but I'm in no mood. "Thanks," I say, and trudge up the stairs. I recognize the peppy song that Malina's singing to—it's an Elvis oldie about a hound dog.

I hesitate outside her open door. "I'm here," I say as the song ends. It's a statement, not a greeting.

"Oh, hi," says Malina. She's propped up on her bed with a pillow, surrounded by her stuffed dog collection. A *Top Teen* magazine rests in her lap. "I've made space in the closet and emptied out my top dresser drawer."

Neither of us looks the other in the eyes.

"Thanks," I say, and cross the room. I open up my suitcase on her extra bed and start to unpack my few belongings. Malina reads.

The DJ on the radio spins another Elvis favorite and the song fills up the uncomfortable space.

I perch on the edge of the twin bed across from Malina a few minutes later. "I should have called you," I say.

She reaches to turn down the volume on the radio on her nightstand.

"I tried twice," she says. "I wanted to apologize."

"I know. But I was too hurt to talk. I just," I say and look right at her, "I just don't understand why you didn't tell me about Kiki in the first place. It feels like I'm always the last to know around here."

Malina twists her mouth. "I'm really sorry. You deserve an explanation."

"I thought we were friends."

"We were. I mean we are. If you still want to be." Malina reaches for a stuffed Dalmatian and gives it a hug. "I wanted you to like me. So I didn't tell you I was related to her."

"Oh," I say, tipping back. "So you two weren't secretly plotting against me?"

"Of course not," she says, and tosses the dog at me. I catch it with one hand. "You really do go to the worst-case scenario first, don't you? I didn't tell you because I didn't want you to think Kiki and I were the same."

I lean toward her. "Well, you both are good dancers and like dogs."

"Very funny. Seriously, I was trying to protect you when I told you to stay away from her, just like I protect myself. We're not close at all."

"We shouldn't let her ruin our friendship."

"Not another second," says Malina, and we shake on it.

Big Wave

I'M WINNING.

"Park Place!" says Malina as I land on the ritzy Monopoly property that night. "Lucky you."

The Halanis' phone rings. "Kimo?" Malina squeals and leaps right up. Maybe it is.

"Dad, telephone," she says, then plops back down with a sigh.

"Uh-huh . . . Okay . . . Got it . . ." Mr. Halani says, and hangs up without a good-bye. He calls Mrs. Halani into the kitchen and they talk so low we can't make out the words.

Malina shrugs. "Parents, always a mystery."

How true.

When they finally return to the living room, Mr. Halani wears his police uniform, and Mrs. Halani has her car keys in her hand.

"What's up?" asks Malina.

But before they can answer, the loud wail begins.

It's the siren.

And this I know—it's the wrong time of day for an emergency test. This is real.

"Tidal wave alert," says Mr. Halani.

My throat tightens and I dive toward Tutu's blue afghan on the couch. We'll have to leave.

"Let's turn on the radio," says Malina. She hops up and I follow her into the kitchen.

> *This morning, at approximately nine a.m. Hawaiian Standard Time, a major earthquake happened off the coast of Chile. Reports indicate a tidal wave is heading across the Pacific. All persons in low-lying areas must evacuate. The first wave is estimated to reach Oahu at twelve thirty a.m. Hawaiian Standard Time, the island of Hawaii, at midnight . . .*

"Mama. Daddy," I say, wrapping the afghan around my shoulders. They are in Hilo now. At a hotel next to the bay. "Howdy." The quarantine station is beside the water.

We're all in danger.

I want my family.

Together and safe.

Gone

LIKE MAMA WITH her closet of supplies, Malina's family is prepared for the alert. The Halanis act like they are in control of the situation. But my heart hasn't gotten the message. It is in a race. It wants to leave. Now.

"I'm going on duty," says Mr. Halani. "I'll check in later."

He hugs and kisses us all. "Don't you worry, Peggy Sue, it's usually a false alarm. But we have to go through the motions. Make sure everyone is safe. The hotel will take good care of your parents. I can guarantee one thing—it's going to be a long night."

I do not find that a comfort.

I picture Howdy crouched under the bench. And Daddy holding Mama's hand. Be safe. Please be safe.

The siren blares a second time and Mrs. Halani walks out the door to get Tutu. She'll be back for us soon. David is at Teresa's, and since her family lives well above sea level, they'll stay put.

Malina and I fill up a grocery bag with potato chips, cookies, cheese, and apples, and grab pillows and blankets. By the time the third siren ends, we call our job done.

"I should get a few things from my house. You know, in case—"

Whoosh! The back door flies open. I scream.

Kiki rushes in.

"He's gone!" she yells.

"Who?" asks Malina.

"Kahuna." Kiki's voice cracks. "Help me find him. Hurry."

My heart pounds even harder with her command.

"Slow down," says Malina. "Tell us what happened."

"Maybe he'll come home," I say.

Grandpa told me that when he was a boy, he had a dog that went missing once. His family looked and looked for that dog for days. "Just wasn't ready to be found," he said. Two weeks later, the dog turned up, wagging his tail and asking for supper.

Kiki glares at me. "You don't know nothing, haole. Kahuna hates sirens. When they go off, he hides. I called and called and he didn't come." Her voice catches again. She swallows. "We're wasting time. Let's go."

Kahuna

"KAHUUUUUUUUUNA," we yell as we run single file on the grassy shoulder of Hanu Road. "Kahuuuuuuuuuna." But another blast of the siren drowns our calls.

My foot catches on a rock at the base of a tree and down I go.

"Peggy Sue?" calls a passenger stopped in traffic.

I pop up and brush myself off. "Mrs. Silva. Hi." It's the family Malina and I babysat for. The dad's driving, and Kevin and his brothers are playing rock-paper-scissors in the backseat.

"Kahuna is missing."

"The trick dog?" she asks.

"Yes."

"We'll keep our eyes open," she says, and the car moves ahead.

I start running again.

"We should have left a note for Mom," says

Malina when I catch up with her and Kiki at a cross street.

"Too late now," says Kiki.

Malina looks at her watch. "She'll be back with Tutu in about fifteen more minutes. Let's divide up and search until then and meet back at the house."

We scatter in three different directions—Kiki will take off toward her house in case he returns. Malina will check the neighborhood on the mountain side of the street. I will look on the beach side.

"Go!" Kiki yells.

"Kahuuuuuuna. Kahuuuuuuna." Our voices echo and then fade as we run in opposite directions.

I scurry across Hanu Road and down a dead-end street toward the beach. The siren wails yet again, but it's fainter here.

I've only seen the dog once. What if I don't recognize him? What if I find him and he won't come? What if he growls at me? Or tries to bite?

I wish we hadn't split up.

I glance at my watch. Thirteen minutes. I can look for thirteen minutes.

I take a few more steps and stop. As afraid as I am of dogs, this is my chance to change everything with Kiki.

I want to find her dog. I have to find her dog.

On the Beach

THERE'S NOT A CAR in any driveway. Or a person anywhere. But every house on the dead-end has porch lights blazing to welcome their owners' return. That helps. If Kahuna is here, I'll find him.

A few houses don't have fences, so I peek in their backyards.

No dog.

I reach the beach access, a narrow path between houses that leads to the water.

I know what Howdy would do. He'd hunker down under my bed, or if he were outside, he'd scoot under the house or up a tree. But a dog? Maybe with all the commotion, he's headed to the beach for some peace and quiet.

A big orange-and-white cat darts across the sandy path. I jump. "You scared me." The cat keeps going, climbs the fence, and disappears. "Be safe," I call.

“Kaaaahuuuuuna. Come here, boy.” I clap my hands.

I make my way onto the beach. Alone. A sliver of a moon hangs over the smooth water. It is hard to believe that a big wave is coming. But like Mr. Halani said, maybe it won’t.

My eyes adjust to the darkness. The sand is hardest next to the water. I take off, calling, calling Kahuna’s name.

But I can’t keep it up. I stop to catch my breath and let the warm water swirl and splash around my ankles. I sink a little lower into the soft sand.

The beach is empty.

I start up again, running, calling. A stabbing pain on my side stops me short. I’ve had a side stitch before. It’ll go away. Eventually. But it will slow me down.

I don’t know exactly where I am. It’s not like I’m lost. All I need is a beach path. It will lead me to Hanu Road. I can figure it out from there.

I check my watch. My time is up. I should already be back at the Halanis’.

I clutch my side and walk as fast as I can, calling, calling for the dog.

I spot a beach access and take a shortcut, through waist-high plants at the edge of someone’s property. I cut across their wet lawn, which I’m guessing has just been watered, and head for the path.

My legs are bags of sand.

I reach the paved lanai next to the house, with its table and chairs, and take a seat. Palms swoosh overhead. The house is dark. The little bit of moon has disappeared behind the clouds.

I push back, stand, and take two steps.

My left foot slams into something hard. Another chair? My right foot tangles in something coiled. I twist and turn, but the cold, wet something won't let go. A snake?

I throw out my arms to steady myself, but I tip to the right and fall. My hip-shoulder-head slam against the concrete.

A flash of light.

Everything goes black.

Stranger

I WAKE TO JANGLING.

Someone with hot, bad breath rubs wet sand across my cheeks.

"Kahuna?"

No. The dog is white.

I hold statue still.

It licks again.

Please don't bite me. Please don't bite. Please don't.

The dog is not growling. Good. This is good. He does not look like he's going to attack. Even better. But you never know.

A red something catches my eye. A muumuu. Someone else is here.

Clap. Clap.

The dog turns and sits beside the dress.

I look up. An old lady with white hair flowing past her waist holds a garden hose. I move my legs. Freely.

The hose. I tangled with the hose. Not a big fat snake. Right. This isn't Texas.

"A tidal wave is coming," I say, sitting up real slow. Sudden movements may provoke the dog. Not to mention make my pounding head worse. "You and your dog need to get to higher ground."

She nods.

"I'm looking for a dog. A dog named Kahuna."

The old woman raises her hand and points toward the water.

A dog sits at the edge of the rise, looking out.

It's him. I know it's him.

"Kahuna," I say. "Come here, Kahuna." I turn to ask the old woman, "How did you—?"

But she and her dog are gone.

Good Dog

I CALL AND CALL AND CALL. The dog turns and looks at me. I call again. I'd go after him, but I can't get up just yet.

Finally, finally, Kahuna comes.

"Good dog," I say.

He sniffs my hand.

"Kiki sent me." My voice shakes.

Kahuna wags his tail.

"Wagging is good, right?"

Kahuna barks.

"I'll take that as a yes."

Steadying myself with the dog and the table, I rise.

Slowly, Kahuna and I make our way up the sandy path toward the street. I place my hand on fences and walls that line the way to keep upright.

My head is full of drums beating louder and longer with each step.

Maybe this is how Mama feels sometimes.

Mama. Daddy. Howdy. Be safe. Please be safe.

I stop every once in a while, lean against a fence, and start again.

Kahuna never leaves me.

Bufo

WHEN WE FINALLY reach the street, I sit on a big piece of lava rock in someone's front yard. Palms rustle overhead, a gecko chirps. The soft *pa-boom* of the waves in the near distance fills my ears.

"Go ahead, I'll be okay," I say.

Kahuna licks my hand and settles down beside me.

"Just so you know," I say, petting his head, "if I ever had a dog, I'd want one just like you."

Headlights from a car beam down the street. The blue light on top of its roof means it's the police. "We're safe now, Kahuna. Safe."

I stand and wave with both arms like I'm on a drowning ship.

The car picks up speed and stops next to us.

Mr. Halani steps out.

"You okay?" he asks.

My stomach rolls and I hold up one hand and cover my mouth with the other.

"You've got a nasty cut on your shoulder," Mr. Halani says, and takes my elbow. "I'll get Charlotte to drive you to the hospital."

I sway. Mr. Halani holds me steady.

"I see you found the dog. Good detective work."

Kahuna wags his tail as he roots his nose around the base of the large lava rock I'd sat on.

"Time to go, Kahuna," I say.

But he doesn't pay any attention.

Mr. Halani whistles. Kahuna lifts his head and lowers it again. Nuzzles his nose in the grass.

A bufo hop hop hops away. Kahuna pounces.

"No," I shout. If bitten, bufos squirt a poisonous liquid.

Kahuna turns. Two small legs of a bufo protrude from his mouth. He growls.

"Kahuna," I say. "Drop it."

The dog backs up, shakes his head from side to side, and growls some more.

"This isn't a game, Kahuna," I say.

"Kahuna, speak," says Mr. Halani.

Kahuna opens his mouth and the toad flops to the ground. Out comes a garbled bark.

"Good dog," I say, and step toward him.

Kahuna's eyes are extra big and his mouth foams.

White globs of bubbles ooze out, extend toward the ground, and plop on the grass.

"We need to take him to a vet," I say.

"My responsibility is to humans first," says Mr. Halani, stepping between the dog and me. "I can come back later."

"No, please," I say, grabbing his arm. "We have to save him."

Mr. Halani looks me straight in the eyes. "It may be too late."

"Don't say that," I cry. "It's not too late. It can't be."

"We've got one vet in Hanu, Peggy Sue, and I happen to know where he lives. He's evacuating like the rest of us."

I crouch down and open my arms. "Kahuna, come. Please. Please. Come."

The growls grow deeper.

He turns and runs.

Hospital

THOUGH THE TIDAL WAVE didn't hit Hanu, it did strike my mind.

Washed some stuff away. Rearranged others.

But I cannot forget:

Kiki's screams.

Bright lights in the emergency room.

Me telling the Halanis about the lady and her dog.

Mrs. Halani saying, "You hit your head pretty hard, Peggy Sue."

Tutu saying, "It could have been her."

"Who?" I ask. "Who?"

"Pele," says Malina.

Questions, lots of questions: How many fingers am I holding up? Who is the president of the United States? Do you know where you are?

My questions: about Mama and Daddy. About

Hilo. About Howdy. About Kahuna.

But no one answers.

Six stitches.

I didn't feel a thing.

The Radio

I JERK AWAKE.

Mama? Daddy? Howdy? Kahuna?

Where are y'all?

Malina's curtains are closed, but it's daytime. Her bed is made, but all of the stuffed dogs on her bed—gone.

The clock reads ten minutes after eight.

A note from Mrs. Halani is taped to the nightstand:

8 a.m. Good morning, Peggy Sue. Mr. Santos called to say Howdy is purring louder than ever. I'm in the studio if you need me.
Love, Mrs. H.

What about my parents? What about Kahuna?

I swing my legs over the side of the bed and my stomach lurches. I have a whopper of a headache. But I force myself to stand.

I have to find my parents. Have to find the dog.

I wobble down to the kitchen, still wearing my clothes from the day before.

Ukulele music comes from the studio. I bet Mrs. Halani is practicing her dance for the recital.

I reach the kitchen and lean against the refrigerator. The radio murmurs. The newsman says "Hilo" and I listen in:

> *. . . buildings torn off their foundations, a boat sitting on a railroad track, mangled cars, piles of wood and rubble . . .*

"Mama? Daddy?"

My whole body shakes.

I cross my arms and hold myself tight. I turn, stumble out the back door and down to the beach.

Next to the water, the shiny blue-green water, I stand. Shivering. My head throbs as I squint in the bright light. The water slips in and out, in and out.

I picture it.

The wave.

The gigantic wave.

What if Mama and Daddy are gone? Gone forever? I remember my wish. I remember what I said—that

I hoped they'd never come back. I remember that I didn't say good-bye.

I cover my face. I am so sorry. I didn't mean what I said. I'm sorry that I am prickly. I'm sorry I am a terrible daughter. I messed up with Kahuna, too. Lost the dog. Lost my chance to get on Kiki's good side.

I squeeze my eyes and imagine the wave. An enormous rushing wall of water, hurling toward me. Roaring. Like hundreds of trains. Foaming. Blocking the horizon. And before I can run, or even scream, it hits me, swallows me whole and sweeps me away. It is cold and dark here. The wave pushes me forward. Turns me sideways, upside down. Holds me under. Forever. And then, and then . . . spits me up. I cough, call for help, but no one is around to hear me. The water slaps my face and I swallow the salty sea. My eyes burn. I grab for the top of a coconut tree as I rush by. And miss. The waves don't stop coming. Won't stop. They are big. Bigger. Strong. I am pulled under again. I can't, can't breathe.

And then I do. Air. I gulp it in, sink to my knees. "Please be alive. All of you. Please."

When I look up, the ocean in front of me is glassy. Calm. Two surfers, straddling their boards, wait for waves that will rise only in their imaginations.

I scan the beach. It's empty. No people. No dogs.

I stand, half-wet, and walk away.

Beauty

I STARE at the mountain range as I plod back from the beach to the Halanis'. Like an accordion, its deep green folds divide the island.

Light green fills in the crevices.

Up close you can see vines hanging from the trees.

After a heavy rain, waterfalls stream down its faces.

A rainbow arcs across the sky. Sometimes even a double.

This side, the windward side, is greener, wetter, lush.

It looks like paradise.

I wish it were.

Kapakahi

I PICK UP THE PHONE in our kitchen. Drops of ocean pool beneath me on the floor as I dial the operator. "The Naniloa Hotel in Hilo, please," I say. "On the water."

"I'm sorry, all of the circuits for the Big Island are busy. I could contact you when one becomes available."

I give her the Halanis' number. "Could you call Texas?"

"That might be easier," she says. "Let me try."

She patches the call together through another operator.

"Let's not panic, Peggy Sue," says Grams. At least that's what I think she's saying. There is static on the line at my end this time.

"But, Grams, everything is kapakahi."

"Is what?"

"All mixed up. All because of me."

"Sweetie, what on earth are you talking about?"

"I've done something bad. Really bad. It's all my fault. It's my fault they're missing."

"What kind of talk is this?"

"It's what I wished," I say. "I wished Mama and Daddy would never come back. And now it's happened."

"Oh, sweet pea."

"I'm sorry. I didn't mean it. Not forever."

"Of course you didn't. Now listen to me, Peggy Sue. This may come as a surprise, but you don't have that much power."

I grab a tissue and blow my nose. I twist the phone cord around my finger.

"You are strong, Peggy Sue. Strong enough to weather this. You've got to remember, after the rain comes the rainbow."

I take a deep breath.

"We have faith your parents are going to come through."

"Grams, I'm scared."

"I know, sweet pea, I know."

Back at the Halanis', I leave a note on the kitchen table about the operator who's going to call. Then I change into my pajamas, crawl into bed, and bury myself under the covers.

Mama and Daddy and me belong together.

We do. Please come back. Please.

Distractions

I HEAR MRS. HALANI tiptoe in. She taps me gently on my shoulder.

"Peggy Sue, it's time to sit up for a while."

I smell toast and peek from under the blanket. A tray rests on Malina's bed. "Where are my parents?"

"Mr. Halani has a buddy on the police force in Hilo who is doing everything he can to track them down," she says. "I've been calling the hotel, but I haven't gotten through. I saw your note. You must have, too."

I nod.

"We'll have good news soon."

She sounds confident. Sure.

I toss back the covers and sit up. "Has Mr. Halani found Kahuna? He told me that he'd look for him."

Mrs. Halani shakes her head.

"I found Kahuna, or rather he found me. If it happened once, it can happen again. I want to look for him. I want to do something."

"The best thing you can do right now is get better. Believe me, there are lots of people searching for that dog." She hands me the plate of toast. "Eat."

Afterward, we troop downstairs for a game of hearts. Mrs. Halani shuffles and deals. "You go first," she says.

While we play, Mrs. Halani tells me stories of growing up here—sliding down a muddy slope on a big leaf, hiking in the mountains, bopping her sister over the head with shampoo ginger flowers to release its sudsy goo, and learning hula from her grandmother who danced for the queen. She talks so I don't have to.

I ask her about the queen.

"She was a woman of great strength and aloha," she says.

After two games, we're tied.

"I know what you're doing," I say. "Distracting me."

"Is it working?" Mrs. Halani asks, and smooths back my hair.

"A little," I say.

"Good."

"Will you call Hilo again?"

"Of course."

She does. But all the lines are still tied up.

Be Okay

"HEY, SLEEPYHEAD," says Malina, nudging me gently in the arm later that afternoon.

I wave with one finger.

"Do you want to hear about school? Only four more days."

After all this, I've lost count.

I signal thumbs-up and Malina springs over to her bed and sits. She hands me a get-well card signed by everyone in homeroom. And my porcelain Howdy from Cindy, which she must have brought from next door.

"Tell everyone I said thanks," I say. I turn on my side and hold the cat loosely in my hand. "How's Kimo?"

"Of course I still like him, but I need to be realistic. He didn't talk to me this morning. So I sat with Sam at lunch." I gaze at her hand. The heart, though empty, is there. She must still have hope.

"Everyone's jazzed because it's the last week," she says. "And most kids didn't get a lot of sleep last night. You're not going to believe this—we don't have any homework. Not even in Mr. Nakamoto's class and . . ."

Listening takes a lot of energy and I fade in and out. My head hurts something fierce.

I think about Mama and Daddy. Be okay. Please. You've got to be okay.

Kahuna, too.

The cat slips out of my hand, shattering into I don't know how many pieces on the floor.

The tears come. And I can't stop them. Salty waves wash down my face.

"Peggy Sue, I'm sorry all this has happened," says Malina.

"I want my parents. I want Kahuna to be okay."

Malina's eyes grow wide. "Let me get my mom."

They are keeping something from me. Otherwise, Malina would have told me good news by now. Or she would have said, "No worry, beef curry."

Mrs. Halani rushes in from her class.

"Where are they?"

"We still don't know yet," Mrs. Halani says.

Maybe, maybe they are alive. Maybe they're floating in the ocean, waiting to be rescued. Maybe they're in the hospital getting well.

"Kahuna?"

"No news." Mrs. Halani puts her hands on either side of my face. "Would you like to talk to the school counselor? She called when you were sleeping and asked about you."

"I want to see Howdy."

"I promise," she says, and kisses me on the top of my head. "As soon as you get your strength back, we'll go. You need to get up again. The doctor doesn't want you sleeping all day." Mrs. Halani reaches into her pocket. "I meant to hand this to you earlier. Before they left, your parents asked me to give this to you while they were gone."

On the front of the postcard is a photo of a fiery volcano. On the back, these words:

ALOHA, PEGGY SUE!
WE MISS YOU.
DON'T WORRY, IF WE VISIT PELE'S HOME,
WE WON'T GET BURNED.
Mama AND DADDY

Daddy's handwriting, but Mama signed her name.

I sink into the bed and trace their words again and again.

Headlines

NOT TOO MUCH LATER, I slip into the bathroom and stare into the mirror. My hair hangs limp at my shoulders. It looks like someone has smudged charcoal under my eyes. They are sad. So sad. I barely recognize myself. I pick up the rubber band that Malina must have left on the basin and pull my hair into a ponytail.

"You in there?" Malina asks after knocking softly.

"Uh-huh."

"How about ten minutes of Monopoly?"

"Be right out," I say. I open the door and we begin making our way downstairs.

Thunk.

My grip tightens on the handrail. I place the sound. The paperboy's aim was on target—the Halanis' front door.

Malina scampers outside, and I settle in next to the game board. Malina tosses the loosely rolled paper onto her dad's recliner and joins me around the coffee table.

"I believe it's my turn," she says, and picks up the dice from the game we started last night, the night the sirens bellowed.

Malina rolls a four, picks up her token, and travels around the board.

Mr. and Mrs. Halani enter through the back door. Mr. Halani must have just gotten off work, because he's still in his uniform. They take seats on the couch. Their faces are neutral, like the doctor in the emergency room.

Malina and I exchange a look. Something's up.

"We wanted to tell you that we have a bit of news from the Hilo police," says Mr. Halani.

I clutch the side of the coffee table and rise to my knees.

"They've found your parents' rental car."

My grip tightens. "Where?" I ask before he even has a chance to say.

"On the street, but they weren't inside."

"Was there a note or anything?" asks Malina. I can tell she's trying to be helpful.

Mr. Halani shakes his head.

"Where are they?" I cry.

"Right now, we only know where they're not. They're not in the hotel, car, or hospital."

"Mama's not a very good swimmer," I say.

"Peggy Sue," Mrs. Halani says, and kneels beside me. "They'll be found."

But she doesn't add "safe and sound."

And Malina doesn't say "no worry, beef curry."

"I don't feel so good," I say, hobbling up. "Time for ginger ale."

I pass by Mr. Halani's chair, glance in the seat, then grab hold of the back to steady myself.

Big, bold, black headlines declare Hilo a disaster. Two dozen or more folks are dead. Over twenty are missing.

Malina races over and snatches the paper away. But I rip it out of her hand, hold it overhead, and open the front page.

Photos of deserted streets thick with mud, boulders, and lumber. Telephone poles all catawampus. Where a building once stood, ruins. A car with busted windows askew on top of all the muck. Is it Mama and Daddy's?

It looks like someone crammed Hilo into a Mason jar topped with filthy water, shook it to death, and smashed it into the ground.

How did anyone survive?

I clutch my stomach, run to the nearest bathroom, and heave.

Mrs. Halani helps me upstairs and I fall back into bed.

Dinner Sounds

SLURPING CHICKEN and rice soup: me.
Screechy knife cutting pork chop: David.
Chewing carrot and raisin salad: Malina.
Clearing throat: Mr. Halani.
Humming a slow song: Mrs. Halani.
Silence: Radio. TV. Phone.

The Call

SOMEONE CALLS MY NAME.

I open my eyes. Malina stands over me. The room is daylight bright, but it's dark outside. "The phone. Hurry. It's for you."

My heart ticks up and I bolt out of bed.

"I can't believe you didn't hear it ringing," says Malina as we tear down the stairs.

"What time is it?"

"After midnight."

"Here she is," says Mrs. Halani. Her eyes shimmer as she hands me the phone.

"Hello."

"Peggy . . ." The person on the other end is crying.

"Mama? Mama, is that you?"

"Yes, yes, Peggy Sue, it's me. Your daddy's right here, too. How's our girl? And our cat?"

"You're okay? I miss you."

"We're okay. We miss you, too. It's so good to hear your voice. We finally got through once, earlier today, but no one answered."

I must have been asleep or at the beach.

"When are you coming home?"

"Tomorrow afternoon. It's the first flight we could get. We can't wait to see you. We'll all visit Howdy."

"That sounds great, Mama. Really great."

We talk a little more. A lot actually.

The Naniloa Hotel evacuated all the guests and transported them to another hotel.

I tell them Mr. Santos called to say Howdy is still purring.

I don't mention my stitches.

When I hang up, realization sinks in—my horrible wish didn't come true.

About Kahuna

I SCRAMBLE DOWNSTAIRS Tuesday morning as soon as I wake up. It's just after eight, but I slept so hard again that I didn't hear Malina leave for school.

Mrs. Halani sits at the dining room table with index cards spread out before her. *Hula O Maki* reads one. *Po La'i La'i*, another. Dances for the recital.

"I didn't dream that phone call, did I?"

"It was real," she says, and reaches out her hand. I take it and squeeze it tight. "Your parents are okay."

"They're coming back this afternoon," I say, my eyes filling.

"Before you know it," she says as she moves a strand of hair behind my ear. "Now, tell me how your head is today."

"Much better." Which is true.

"I'm so glad to hear that. The doctor will be, too.

Remember, you've got an appointment this morning. Why don't you take a quick bath and then I'll fix you breakfast?"

"Has Kahuna come home?"

"I'm afraid not," says Mrs. Halani. "And he probably won't."

My eyes fill in an instant. "I wanted to save him."

"Of course you did," Mrs. Halani says. "But it wasn't your fault."

"If only I'd made Mr. Halani find the vet right then and there."

Tears overflow and plop on my nightgown.

Mrs. Halani lifts my chin and looks me in the eyes. Hers eyes are tender. "Kahuna was a good dog, Peggy Sue. Mr. Halani did what he thought was right. He's made sure folks know Kahuna's last whereabouts. No one has found him. We have to let Kahuna go."

"I don't want Kiki to be mad at me."

Mrs. Halani moves her hand to my shoulder. "Kiki made a mistake."

I tilt my head.

"She wasn't supposed to let him out. Everyone is sorry and upset and sad. It was a tragic accident. We can't change the past. We can only take it from here."

"I want to see her."

"Are you sure?" asks Mrs. Halani.

"Positive," I say. "This morning."

"Then I'll make the call."

After the doctor declares me fit for school but excused for PE, we drive to Kiki's house. She didn't go to school today either.

With Mrs. Halani beside me, I knock on the door of the small, white wood-frame house. Right away it opens.

Whoa. It's the woman from the luau who wore the tapa print muumuu. The one who was sorry my family moved in next door. The one whose husband got passed over by a haole.

"Hello, Pua," says Mrs. Halani.

Kiki's mother looks directly at me. Her eyes narrow. "So you're the haole troublemaker."

Chills prickle my shoulder blades.

"Enough," says Mrs. Halani.

"Kiki's not here," she says. "She's looking for her dog."

"I am very, very sorry about Kahuna," I say. "I feel awful that he's still missing. Kahuna was"—my throat starts to close—"Kahuna is a very special dog. I know Kiki misses him very much. I've tried to look, too. I hope he's still out there and will come home soon."

I'm not ready to give up on him. Miracles happen.

"He's her best friend, you know," says Kiki's mom.

I lower my head. I know how Kiki feels about Kahuna. I do. He is as special as Howdy. I take a deep breath and look up. "Will you please tell Kiki what I said?"

"Okay."

Maybe Kiki will understand. Maybe she won't hate me even more.

Mrs. Halani puts her arm around me and leads me back to the car.

Reunion

AT THREE O'CLOCK, Malina and I sit on my front steps and wait. Wait for my parents to return. There's not a cloud, gray or white, in view.

"Now I'm positive you saw Pele Sunday night," says Malina.

"How can you be so sure?"

"She was old, had long white hair and a white dog."

"Yes, but—"

"You said you warned her about the wave."

"Yes, but—"

"That's helping, right?"

"I guess."

"And now your parents are safe, so she helped you back. Right?"

"Yes." I remember David saying that Madame Pele had a heart.

"Did she look like a beggar, wear old clothes?" Malina asks.

"I'm not sure. I don't remember."

"No worry. Last question. What color was her muumuu?"

"Red. I do remember that. It was red."

"If it was red or white, it was her, then. Definitely her."

I guess it's possible.

• ✿ •

A horn honks twice and our blue station wagon rolls into the drive. I jump to my feet and hold a WELCOME BACK poster above my head.

Daddy and Mama wave out the windows.

"They're here," we shout, so Mrs. Halani will come, too.

Before Daddy turns off the engine, Mama is out of the car with her arms open wide.

I drop the poster and run.

We squeeze each other until we almost pop. Then Daddy, too.

"I'm so glad you're back," I say.

"We love you," says Mama.

"I love you, too," I say.

"Welcome back," say Mrs. Halani and Malina, holding a bowl of mangoes and papayas for us.

"Thank you," Mama says. "We're just here for a minute. We need to drive Peggy Sue to see our cat. Only sixty-six more days."

Mama has been counting, too.

• ✿ •

We pass Howdy from arms to arms to arms and back again. We all agree that he feels like he's gained weight.

He never stops purring.

On our way out, I ask Mr. Santos where they took the animals when the sirens sounded. He looks to Daddy.

"She needs to hear the truth. Unvarnished."

"They weren't evacuated," Mr. Santos says.

I press my hand to my forehead. I can't imagine . . . Actually, I can.

If the wave had hit the quarantine station, I wouldn't have Howdy.

I never, ever want that siren to blow for real again.

Lava Rocks

AT HOME, I watch Mama unpack. "I brought you a gift," she says. "Something you can't find just anywhere."

Mama opens her hand. Four small black lava rocks lay in her palm. "They're from the volcano."

"Oh, Mama. You made it there after all. Thank you."

She looks pleased.

It's best not to hurt her feelings, so I don't explain.

"I also picked up a few other things," she says, handing me a bag. "And a stuffed dog for Malina as a thank-you gift for having you."

"She'll like that."

Afterward, I sit at the dining room table, write a letter, and set the lumpy envelope out for tomorrow's mail. Thanks to David, I know what to do.

Dear Madame Pele,

My mama is a malihini, a newcomer, just like me. And she doesn't know your rules. I do. Well, at least some of them anyway. I am very, very sorry that she took these rocks from your volcano. I am returning them so nothing bad will happen to her or our family. Or maybe I should say nothing more. Thank you for understanding. I hope you are having a very nice day.

Aloha,

Peggy Sue

PS I think you and your dog might have helped me on the beach the other night. I didn't get a chance to thank you. Mahalo, Madame Pele. Mahalo.

Being Safe

MY PARENTS ARE SAFE. Howdy is safe. Maybe Kahuna is, too. I've tried to talk to Kiki. The doctor says my head is okay. I feel better. Really. I can't live like this forever. This is the last week of school.

I'm tired of being scared. Tired of worrying. In fact, I don't think I have any more worry left in me. I'm tired of always thinking the worst. I'm going to be positive. Think the best.

I'm going to school tomorrow.

Hana Hou!

"I'M SO GLAD your parents are okay," kids say in homeroom the following morning.

"Did you really see Pele?"

I look at Malina. She shrugs.

In home ec, Kiki is absent. I imagine she's still looking for her dog. I wish her the best.

Instead of my afternoon PE class, I'm in the library shelving a slew of biographies and books about the solar system and World War II. A piano concerto plays on the radio as the librarian and her volunteer tussle with overdue notices.

"*WaaaaAAHHHH.*" The alert sirens wail.

"No!" I cry as my heart races. "Not again."

"Let's not panic," says the librarian, turning up the volume on the radio. I rush to her desk so I won't miss a word.

An announcer breaks in. Another earthquake shook Chile. We must evacuate.

I sink to my knees. Mama and Daddy will find higher ground. But Howdy? He's trapped in his cage. Alone. And what about everyone else? So many have already died.

Malina barrels in. "She's with me," she tells the librarian in an official-sounding voice. The two move away and speak in hushed tones.

Then Malina joins me on the floor. "It's probably a dud. But we need to leave now."

I know.

"Hana hou!" she says. "One more time."

We catch up to her math class plodding single file toward the hill.

She talk, talk, talks about everything. Nothing. Some teachers tell her to hush.

"Special case," she says, and ignores them.

I don't really listen. I can't stop remembering the last time the sirens sounded.

• ✿ •

The all-clear comes about two and a half hours later.

Howdy's safe. We're all safe.

As soon as I get home, I hug Mama. Hug her hard. For the second day in a row.

I skip hula so we can be together.

"You've done a great job sewing, Peggy Sue," she says when I show her my work. "But I know the recital is coming up and you may be behind. I'm not as good a seamstress as your grandmother, but my handwork isn't bad."

"This one's ready to hem," I say, and give her a purple-and-white shorty muumuu. "And don't worry, Grams always says quilters make mistakes on purpose. Nothing is ever perfect."

Telling

KIKI WAS A NO-SHOW for home ec Thursday morning as well. As far as I know, Kahuna is still MIA. Which means there's a chance she won't be at school tomorrow either. Of course I want her dog back. But I would be so relieved if she didn't show up.

"One more day," sings Malina after school. We're in her bedroom to practice hula.

"Um, can I ask you something?"

"Anything," she says, sorting through her records to find the right ones.

I pick at a cuticle. I know that Kiki had told me not to say anything. Or else. Now I'm sure that Kiki won't find out about Malina. Malina's true blue. And I want to know more.

"I've been wondering about Kill Haole Day."

"Who told you?"

"Guess."

"It's a dumb tradition at our school. Some eighth-grade locals beat up kids for fun. They think they're so tough."

"Why?"

"I'm not saying they're right or anything, but from the beginning, haoles have changed Hawaii, our aina—our land, our lives."

"And not always for the good."

"It makes me sad sometimes."

"So I guess some kids are so mad that on the last day of school, they pick a fight."

"Yep," she says, waving a record. "No worry, beef curry. We'll stick together."

"You'd do that for me?"

"Of course. Now, come on, let's practice."

She starts the music and we dance.

"Any chance you'll help me sew later?" I ask after one hula. Even with Mama's assistance, I'm way behind. "I'll donate to your Paris fund."

"You're on."

Malina comes over to my house. We sew. Malina stays for supper. And we sew some more.

"Time for me to go," Malina says. It's almost eight thirty. "You need to come, too. My mom says that she has a little something for us."

"Autograph books," we say, as Mrs. Halani hands each of us one. "Thank you."

Mine is light pink with *Autographs* written in loopy cursive in dark pink across the cover. *Autograph Hound* is written inside a dachshund on Malina's.

"I'm going to ask all of my old boyfriends to sign," she says.

"That's very magnanimous of you," I say.

"I know," she says.

Last Day of School

IT'S A HALANI TRADITION for Malina to be driven to school by her dad on the last day, and I'm her lucky guest. No siren. Instead, the radio blasts songs from Malina's favorite station.

We're surrounded as soon as we step out of the car. "Peggy Sue, sign my autograph book. Peggy Sue, over here. Please sign."

I don't know most of the kids, but I sign anyway. And ask for their signatures, too. I don't see Kiki.

Mrs. Taniguchi catches me on my way to homeroom. "I wanted to thank you for something," she says. Her skirt and shoes are the same shade of fern green.

"Me?" I have no idea what that could be.

"I understand that you helped Kiki Kahana with a sewing project. That was very kind of you."

Kind? Not really. "About that," I say.

"Coming," she says, signaling to someone behind me. "I'm sorry, Peggy Sue, Mr. Kam is sending an SOS. I've got to go." She flits away before I can tell her more.

There's an awards assembly first period.

No home ec.

This is my lucky day.

• ✿ •

After lunch, one of Kiki's friends bumps me in the walkway and keeps going. No big deal. Everyone is in a hurry to get out of here.

So am I. Just two more periods to go. The outside corridor is jammed.

When I leave the library, I turn the corner and head for Hawaiian history, my last class of the year.

Boom!

I collide with . . . I look down . . . Kiki. On the ground.

"Oh, no," I say. "I'm so sorry." She scowls back at me, and my shoulders stiffen. I have to make sure she got my message. That she knows how I feel about Kahuna. "I hope," I say, "that your mom told you. I'm sorry about Kahuna, too."

Kiki bounds up, her eyes boring into mine. "Today is my day," she says. "*Bwak. Bwak.*"

No more maybes.

That is her answer.

No deal.

My luck just ran out.

Help!

I FLY DOWN the hallway to class.

"Whoa there, Texas," says Kimo as I plow into him going into our room.

"Sorry, Hawaii," I say, and rush inside.

Where is Malina? Where is my friend?

Not here.

The bell rings and everyone takes a seat. Mr. Nakamoto stands beside a stack of papers on his desk.

Malina enters smiling and points to her autograph book. "Steven Hamakua, the eighth-grade class president, asked to sign," she says as she takes her seat. "Of course I couldn't turn him down."

"Malina, Malina," I urgent-whisper to her. "We have to talk. Right now."

"What's up?"

"Miss Bennett," says Mr. Nakamoto. "Your undivided attention, please."

Malina covers her mouth and whispers, "Just a sec."

"Today, we will review our old exams," Mr. Nakamoto says. "And I will excuse you one row at a time to clean out your lockers."

"No fair," says Glenn.

"Mr. Aquino," says Mr. Nakamoto. "After all I've taught you this year, if this is the first time you realize that, I have finally succeeded."

I tap Kimo's desk across from me. "Change places?"

Mr. Nakamoto picks up the papers and we make the switch. "Row one."

As Kimo walks toward the door, Mr. Nakamoto puts out his arm to block him. "Mr. Nahoa, return to your seat until I call your row." He peers down my new row. "Miss Bennett, to your locker."

"Busted," says Glenn.

I join my classmates in the hall.

The way I see it, I have three choices when the bell rings.

I can run. I can hide. I can fight.

Briiiiiiiing

I RUN.

Under the Flags

"WAIT," calls Malina as I charge away from Mr. Nakamoto's door.

Not a chance.

I run as hard and as fast as I can. Ahead in the courtyard, a haole boy is shoved to the ground. I run. Faster.

"Fight. Fight," someone yells, and the boy and his attacker are surrounded.

A sharp whistle blows.

A teacher to the rescue.

I speed past the cafeteria, through the tunnel-like entrance and into the light. I clutch my autograph book, report card, and papers.

Kiki stands under the flagpole.

Waiting.

She lifts her arm and points right at me. Arms link through my elbows and propel me toward her.

"Let go," I scream, kicking a girl's leg beside me. Arms tighten around mine.

I twist back. Kids pour out of the school, headed our way.

Not a teacher in sight.

Ahead and next to the street, buses idle, waiting for riders. A radio blares over shouts about summer vacation.

A circle has formed around Kiki but parts as I am forced forward, forced into the center. Then, just like that, it closes. The arms holding me let go and melt into the crowd. I am a few feet away from her. Nowhere to go.

Kiki grabs my autograph book. My report card and papers fall to the ground. "It says here," she shouts, opening my book, "Texas is two good to be four-gotten."

Kimo wrote that.

Kiki swings around. "I ask you people, is that true?"

"No," they shout.

I hug my arms across my chest.

"It says here this haole's no ka oi."

Malina's words say I am the best.

"No," shouts the crowd.

Kiki smiles at me, awash in their fervor. She rips

pages out of my book, throws them down, and grinds them into the red dirt.

"Yes," chants the crowd.

Why did I have to move here? Why did I have to come to this school? Why did I have to meet her? She's been nothing but mean—teasing, taunting, threatening, laughing, maybe, maybe, maybe-ing me.

I hate, hate, hate her.

Kiki tears more pages into smaller and smaller pieces, lifts her hands to the sky, and tosses the papers as high as she can. The pink rain falls.

I charge.

And trip.

And fall. Fall on the scraps of pink.

Kiki throws her head back and laughs.

The crowd joins in.

My hands, my knees—scraped raw.

I hug my knees to my chest and lower my head. My first fight. Over. Over before it even began. And I lost.

"We don't want you here," says Kiki. "Take. Take. Take. Go back to where you came from, haole dog killer."

I'm trying. I'm trying so hard.

"Kiki, that's enough."

I look up. It's Malina.

"Maybe Kahuna is still alive," she says. "I hope so.

If you hadn't let him out, none of this would have happened. Or blame my dad, not her."

"Ooooo," whisper some in the crowd.

"Haoles aren't your enemies, Kiki. Hate is," says Malina.

Hearing Malina say that, say those words about hating—she doesn't know it, but I hate, too. I am just like Kiki.

"I feel sorry for you," says Malina. "These islands are big enough for all of us. We are the Aloha State."

The state of love.

"Today's just for fun," says someone in the crowd. "You know, tradition."

"Does Peggy Sue look like she's having fun?" asks Malina.

"I should go now," I say, picking myself up. I keep my eyes on the ground and walk away. No one stops me.

"What are you afraid of, Kiki?" I hear Malina say. "That if you got to know Peggy Sue, you'd like her?"

"You crack me up, cousin," says Kiki.

"I wish I could say the same about you," says Malina. Then, "Peggy Sue, wait up," she calls after me as I keep walking.

Cindy

I YANK OPEN the mailbox beside the driveway. It's stuffed. I tug at a magazine in the middle to unclog the jam. Bills and letters spill out.

Trying to catch them is like catching water with your bare hands—you'll only get a few drops.

"This one's for you," says Malina.

I recognize the handwriting.

"It's from Cindy," I say, and sink to the grass. Finally.

I tear open the envelope and read:

Aloha, Peggy Sue!

Sorry I haven't written! You know how crazy it gets at the end of the school year!

Thanks for all of your postcards. Wish I could be there for your first hula recital.

There's a new girl, Edna Peabody? It turns out she's really nice.

Now I have someone to split a Dr Pepper float with at the soda fountain. She likes to play Ping-Pong too. I'm going to visit my grandma in Granger this summer. Edna's aunt and uncle live there, so we're going together. Isn't that the best?

Have fun surfing and sunning and hulaing (is that a word?)!

Yours truly,

D (which Edna started calling me and it's stuck!)

PS I took the key you sent me to the owners of your old house, but when they tried it out, it didn't fit. Sorry!

PPS The gum chain is so long now that it wraps around the whole outside of school!!

I smush the letter and toss it in the hedge behind me.

"Bad news?" Malina asks, taking a seat on the grass.

"When I return, I don't think we'll be best friends anymore." The words slip out before I can take them back.

"You mean, like, to visit?"

"Malina, I think I need to tell you something."

Paris Confessional

"I HAVEN'T BEEN saving to go to Paris," I say. "I've been saving to go back home."

"You lied to me?" Malina's eyes widen.

"I feel really bad about that. But truth be told, I don't belong here."

Malina scrunches her eyebrows.

"It's not you," I explain. "It's Howdy's quarantine, Mama's rock fever, mine, Daddy's long work hours, a new school, Kiki, my sunburn, humuhumuwhatawhata? and all the other words I don't know and can't pronounce, the tidal wave, the hospital, Kahuna, Kill Haole Day. It's too much. And poi. It tastes terrible."

"Hey, I don't like poi either."

"Don't make me laugh. I'm serious."

"Me, too. Listen, things have been rough. Especially after school today. But you have friends."

I look at her.

"Okay, not everyone. But you can't let one person ruin your life."

I keep staring.

"Or even a few. Not everyone in Gladiola is perfect, are they?"

I don't answer.

"You haven't been here that long, Peggy Sue. Have you given Hawaii a chance? It kind of seems like you made up your mind not to like it before you even got here."

She's right. I didn't want to move in the first place.

"You could belong if you wanted to."

Her words sting. More than bees or rabies shots.

So

MALINA AND I head to my front door. From her mom's studio comes a song I know, about the town of Lahaina on the island of Maui. I hum to cover up the silence.

I need a mid-course correction. That's a term Daddy learned in the military. When something is cockeyed, it's time for an adjustment. Malina's right. I can't let a few bad things—okay, a lot of bad things—get to me. I should rise above them. I should make the best of my present situation. I should focus on the good.

My parents are home. Malina is my friend, even if she is put out with me right now. The girls in my hula class are nice. I love to dance even though I'm not that great at it. I'm earning good money sewing. Howdy is almost halfway through his quarantine. And now it's officially summer vacation. I'll be leaving sooner than later. I almost have enough for a third of a ticket.

I should try.

I should enjoy Hawaii while I'm still here.

It's true. Nothing's perfect.

Not people.

Not Hawaii.

Not me.

"Malina, I'm sorry," I say as we reach the steps to my house. "I haven't been fair to you or to Hawaii. Thank you for sticking up for me after school. It means a lot. And for saying what you just said about giving this place a chance. I'm going to try. Really try."

We climb the steps, I open the door, and we walk through.

"Can I see what everyone wrote in your autograph book?" I ask as we grab a snack.

"I thought you'd never ask," she says, and opens to the last page: "'Stay sweet, Malina. Hope to c u this summer! Kimo.'" A cool drawing fills up the rest of the space.

"See," I say, giving her a pen for her hand heart, "no worry, beef curry."

Bump

THAT NIGHT I scoot out back with a flashlight. I haven't checked on the night-blooming cereus since my parents left. I click on the light and shine it on the base of the monkeypod tree. Up, up, up goes the light, until it touches the bottom tip of the plant.

Inch by inch, I move the glow. There it is. Not a flower. But a bump. A bump the size of a small egg. A bump that will grow until it bursts through the skin and blossoms.

Man o' War

ON THE FIRST MORNING of our summer vacation, I wash the sticky sea salt off the windows of our house until they're perfectly clear.

Then, before we sew, Malina and I walk over to the beach park with a transistor radio. We don't want to miss the countdown of this week's biggest hits.

I stare at the jelly-looking sea thingy with a lopsided iridescent blue bubble and a long skinny tail while Elvis sings about being stuck like glue in love. The bubble shimmers in the sunlight.

"It's beautiful," I say to Malina, reaching down to touch the tail.

"Don't!" she hollers. "It's a man o' war."

I pull back my hand as the tide swirls at my feet.

The tail wraps around my ankle. *"Ow. Ow. Ow."* It's a bee sting times ten and I can't fling it off.

"Go deeper," says Malina.

Okay! Next time I'll know.

I hop forward and swish my foot like a whirligig. Finally, the tendril unwraps.

But the sting remains.

"Quick, rub sand on it," Malina says as I emerge from the water.

A squiggly red welt marks my ankle and leg.

I spot another man o' war a few yards away. I pick up a stick and jab it. *Pop*. "There," I say. "One less meanie in the world."

"I don't think it's dead," says Malina.

I reach down and rub sand on my leg.

"Come on," she says.

A few minutes later, my leg hangs over her bathtub as she shakes a bottle of whitish granules from the spice cabinet over my skin. "What is this?"

"Ajinomoto. It'll make the pain go away."

"But what is it?"

"Meat tenderizer."

"Yep. That's me all right. White meat."

We crack up.

Hanai Family

MALINA AND I sew the rest of the morning, break for lunch, and sew a little more. Mama helps, too. We've got a deadline. Mrs. Halani asked all my remaining customers to come to the studio for fittings Tuesday afternoon. The recital is next Saturday.

Later, Daddy, Malina, and I drop Mama off for her hair appointment and make our way to the quarantine station. Day fifty-eight, Howdy. Almost halfway.

"Mr. Santos," says Daddy as we sign the registration book. "I don't believe you've met my other daughter, Malina."

"Pleased to meet you," says Mr. Santos. "Where have you been keeping her, Robert? All this time I could have sworn Peggy Sue was an only child."

"Malina had the chicken pox," I say, which is true.

"Real bad," says Malina, scratching her arm.

"Is that right?" says Mr. Santos. "Now, girls, stand

back and let me take a good look at the both of you."

"Y'all look like you've lined up for a firing squad," says Daddy. "Smile."

So we do.

"I can tell you aren't twins," Mr. Santos says. "But I can see a family resemblance. You both have mischievous smiles."

Daddy reaches out to shake Mr. Santos's hand. "Thanks, Clifford."

"I have a hanai brother myself," he says. "Now you folks hurry up. Howdy's waiting."

Fittings

AS GIRLS TRY on their muumuus Tuesday afternoon, Mrs. Halani, Malina, Mama, and I circulate. We determine the best length and pin up each hem. It's the fitted holokus I'm most concerned about. All the others hang loose.

Kiki stands in the corner, wearing the turquoise satin holoku for her dance with Mrs. Halani. It's the first time I've seen her since the last day of school. Since the fight. She swishes back her hair. "It's too big here and here," she says. She tugs at her shoulders and points to her waist.

Kiki likes giving orders to me. Bossing me around.

I don't talk. I just do. And then she leaves. And I start to breathe again.

The little girls are the squirmiest.

"I look like the royal princess of Oahu," says one girl in yellow, beginning a twirl in front of the mirror.

"Ouch!" I say as a pin pricks me for the umpteenth time. "Hold still, please."

The scene reminds me of snorkeling in Hanauma Bay. One fish, two, three, more are this close. And then they are gone.

Last Practice

THE SONG BEGINS.

I smile.

My eyes follow my arms and hands as they wave gently to the left. My feet travel unhurriedly to the right.

And my knees bend ever so slightly as my hips sway in time with the music.

I'm dancing!

"That's the way," says Mrs. Halani. "That's exactly the way I want you to dance at the recital."

Keep Smiling

IT SMELLS LIKE LEI DAY. All of the dancers wear flowers and many in the audience do, too.

Every chair in the Hanu Intermediate cafeteria is filled. Folks stand against the cinder-block walls on one side and sit in the windowsills on the other. Most fan their faces with their programs. With all these people in here, it's warm. Real warm.

Thanks to Mama and Malina and Mrs. Halani, I finished all the costumes on time.

All of us dancers are grouped according to class on the walkway. My class wears green-and-white hibiscus-print muumuus. Bracelets of fragrant yellow plumeria blossoms encircle our wrists.

"You know these dances," Mrs. Halani tells us. "You've practiced and practiced. Your steps don't have to be perfect. Or your arms and hands. Folks are here to cheer for you—cheer you on. Listen to the music inside you. Don't think too much. Just dance. Have fun."

Malina and I nod.

"If you lose your place, don't panic. Smile, no matter what. Honor the music. Honor Hawaii. Honor yourself. This is not a contest. No one is keeping score. Folks come to watch because they love hula."

I know what she's saying. But I don't want to mess up.

The last time I performed in front of people, someone laughed. Really loudly.

"Lovely Hula Hands"

"AND NOW," says Mrs. Halani into the mike, "my Wednesday afternoon seventh-grade class will dance a hula standard, the first hula I teach to every new student, 'Lovely Hula Hands.'"

I didn't know that. She taught it to the class again just for me, then.

The thick green velvet curtain, with folds as deep and lush as the Koolau Mountain Range, opens. We stand in three straight rows onstage, just like in class.

Though now I am not in the back row. Mrs. Halani asked me to dance up front.

We're in our starting positions, arms stretched out front, hands overlapping. I look to my left and suddenly realize that I made four of the twelve costumes, including mine.

The trio, men on ukulele, guitar, and bass, strum

an intro to our song. They begin to sing. And we dance.

I don't think. I just feel.

I am the song.

Falling

RUNNING UP AND DOWN stairs sounds one way.

But falling?

Falling sounds like a thud. Or a clunk. Or an *ummphf*.

I'm heading down the backstage stairs after the dance, just as Kiki shoves up them. She tips to one side and tumbles backward.

I reach out. But it's too late.

Kiki lands on the bottom step and bounces to the concrete floor.

"My foot," she says, clutching her ankle beneath her purple-and-white muumuu.

It's at a weird angle and already puffing up like a blowfish.

"Someone get some ice," I holler.

Girls swarm around her.

Kiki flinches.

"She needs some space," I say, and wave my arms for them to back away.

Her face twists.

"You're going to be okay," I say, sitting beside her.

"How do you know?"

"You know how to fight."

"Is there a doctor in the audience?" Mrs. Halani asks from the stage.

"I saw you dance," says Kiki.

I wait for what will come next. I wait for the insult.

"Not so bad for a haole."

"You know you just gave me a compliment."

"Maybe."

A mom with a clipboard brings a towel with ice. Two men follow. One is the doctor from the emergency room.

"We'll take it from here," they say, and I find my class.

"What will Mrs. Halani do now?" we whisper.

Last Dance

AT THE END of the program, my hula class tiptoes back into the cafeteria and settles on the floor between the stage and the first row of folding chairs.

"As you know," Mrs. Halani says to the audience from the stage, "it is customary for me to choose one of my students to dance the last dance with me." Her eyes sweep the corners of the room and the floor where we sit. "This year, I asked my niece Kiki Kahana."

The audience murmurs.

"You've all heard of the show business expression 'break a leg.' It means 'good luck.' Well, this year, my niece took that saying literally."

Folks turn to one another and say: "Oh, no." "Too bad." "What a shame."

"Yet she insisted on staying for the last dance," says Mrs. Halani. "She even went so far as to suggest her replacement."

Kiki waves from her chair not too far away. Her leg is propped up on a bench. We clap and cheer.

"So I have chosen another student to take her place."

I hope, hope, hope it is Malina.

"This girl doesn't know I'm about to call her name. I'm sure she will be surprised. But she shouldn't. She is a beautiful dancer, but even more important, a beautiful person. She has reached out in friendship, in the spirit of aloha, and I couldn't be prouder."

My eyes feel wet.

"Malina Rose Halani, will you please join me onstage. It would be my honor to dance with you."

"Go," I say, pushing her forward.

People in the audience rise up, clapping.

Malina hesitates and shakes her head. "For real?" she asks.

"Of course," says Mrs. Halani as she reaches out her hand.

And so they dance.

Response

BEFORE THE LAST NOTE ENDS, everyone is on their feet. Clapping. Well, except Kiki. But I catch her eye because I am so tall. She picks up her towel of melting ice and says, "Mahalo."

"Mahalo," I say right back.

This, I think, is what aloha looks like.

Folks storm the stage as well as all of us dancers in the audience. A lei pops over my head. Another. And another. A kiss on the cheek. Two. More. From Mr. Halani. David. All the girls in my hula class.

Fragrant flowers stack up to my nose.

I'm going to hang each and every one of them on my clothesline in my bedroom.

"I'm so proud of you," says Mama.

"You are?"

"This move . . . well, you're all grown up." She gives me a hug. "We got you a lei, too."

A tuberose and pink carnation lei hangs across her wrist. "But it looks like you already have enough."

"Watch this," I say. I take off all of my leis and thread them onto my forearm.

Mama smiles, puts the flowers around my neck, and gives me a kiss.

"Thank you, Mama."

"Great job, kitten," says Daddy.

I look at the cafeteria filled with people. Smiling people. Even Kiki. Her arms drape around two big shoulders as she hops out of the building.

"Wait up," I holler, and race toward her.

Kiki stops and I give her a flower lei. "I hope you feel better real soon."

"Thanks," she says, and hobbles away.

I've been here sixty-five days, and tonight, tonight, it feels just right. Like I belong. Maybe I'll always stumble over who-moo-who-moo-new-coo-new-coo-ah-poo-ah-ah, but when I hear others say it, when I get close, it sounds like music. I could give poi another try. Someday. I wouldn't mind meeting Madame Pele again, given different circumstances. I have a friend, more than one. And so does Howdy. Most days, over the ocean, the wide-open sky is ever so blue.

Bloom

LIKE ALWAYS, when we get home, I check on the night-blooming cereus. And there it is. Blooming. And it is magnificent. I know it's open as soon as I walk under the tree. I can smell its soft, sweet scent. The large white-petaled flower is as wide as my hand. It has a yellow center cupped by small, light greenish-yellow fingerlike petals.

Weeks ago, Daddy told me these flowers aren't native to Hawaii. They have adapted. They have found a home here.

Just like me.

Home

THERE HAVE BEEN Kahuna sightings. People say they've seen him skateboarding down Hanu Road in the middle of the night like he did in the Kamehameha Day Parade. They say they've seen a dog paddling offshore, holding a coconut in his mouth just after sunset. They say they've spotted him at the beach, spinning around and around in the moonlight.

I've seen him, too. In my dreams, dancing at Tutu's party.

No one has taken down the last two flyers about his disappearance. Even though they've been tattered by the wind, and the rain has washed away the words. They are still tacked to the telephone poles at the corner of Hanu Road and Holokai Avenue.

Malina and Kimo and I went to a picture show last weekend.

I haven't seen Kiki since the recital in June. But I've

heard her cast is coming off in another week. And that she is doing volunteer work at a veterinarian's office.

Dried leis hang on the clothesline in my room. As do the beginnings of dresses and muumuus. I've got orders to sew clothes for the start of school.

I have money now. I'm going to use it for my someday ticket to Paris. Daddy says we'll vacation in Texas next summer. I've spent some of my money on fabric. Even though it's mostly what tourists do, I'm making matching aloha wear for my family. I want folks to know we belong together. Grams and Grandpa are coming for a visit before the end of the summer. They said their fear of flying isn't going to separate us. Mama has had only one headache this month.

On July Fourth, my family joined the Halanis in the crowd outside Iolani Palace. Malina and I took turns counting every one of the fifty-gun salutes.

It made me think of another number—sixty-seven—the number of years ago that the Kingdom of Hawaii was overthrown. They imprisoned the queen in the palace. No one has ever said sorry. To her or the Hawaiian people. I hope President Eisenhower will at least try.

I told Malina about the gum-wrapper chain, and we're going to make one together. And ask everyone in the eighth grade to join us, maybe even the whole island. It may take forever, but we want it to be part of a paper chain, a lei of aloha, that stretches around the world.

This is what I'm thinking as Mama, Daddy, Malina, and me stand outside the quarantine station, waiting for the doors to open.

"Mr. Santos," says Mama, waving.

He waves back and unlocks the doors.

"Go," everyone shouts.

I run, run as fast as I can.

"Howdy," I say a few moments later. "Today is the day! The one hundred twentieth day!"

I pick up my cat, hold him to the sky, and twirl. Then I take him to my heart. He curls into me and purrs.

"Come on, Howdy," I say as I walk out of his cage. "Let's go home."

GLOSSARY OF HAWAIIAN WORDS

akamai (ah-kah-MY)—smart
Hana hou! (HAH-nah-HO)—one more time
hanai (hah-NIGH)—adopted child
Hanu (HAH-new)—fictional town on windward Oahu; to breathe
haole (HOW-lay)—a Caucasian or white person; foreigner
"Hawaii Pono'ī" (hah-WHY-ee-PO-no-EE) national anthem of the Kingdom of Hawaii
hele (HEL-lay)—to move
holoku (HO-lo-kOO)—a style of Hawaiian dress
huhu (who-WHO)—angry, upset
humuhumunukunukuapuaa (who-moo-who-moo-new-coo-new-coo-AH-poo-AH-ah)—a small reef fish
Iolani (EE-oh-LAH-nee)—Iolani Palace was once used as the residence of the reigning Hawaiian royalty
Kalakaua (kah-LAH-KAH-wah)—Hawaiian monarch who reigned from 1874 to 1891
Kalanianaole (kah-LAH-nee-AH-nah-OH-lay)—a prince in the Hawaiian Kingdom
Kamehameha (kah-MAY-hah-MAY-hah)—the name of five Hawaiian kings
kapakahi (kah-pah-KAH-hee)—crooked
Koolau (KOO-oh-lou) (lou rhymes with ow)—a mountain range on Oahu
lehua (lay-WHO-ah)—vivid red flower
lilikoi (LEE-lee-koh-ee)—passionfruit
mahalo (ma-HAH-lo)—thank you
malihini (mah-lee-HEE-nee)—newcomer, tourist
Oahu (oh-AH-who)—the most populated Hawaiian island; home to Peggy Sue
Pali Highway (PAH-lee)—Oahu road windward to leeward side, cliffs
pau (pow)—finished, done
Pele (PEL-eh)—volcano goddess
pikake (pea-KAH-kay)—fragrant, delicate white flower

Diacritical marks were used sparingly to reflect Peggy Sue's experience in 1960. Mahalo to Dr. Puakea Nogelmeier for his guidance.

A NOTE FROM THE AUTHOR

My grandfather emigrated to Honolulu, Hawaii, from Liverpool, England, in 1908. My father was born in Hawaii, and so was I. Most of my growing-up years were spent on Oahu. While I no longer reside in the islands, Hawaii is as much my home, my paradise, as Texas.

This novel is a work of fiction, complete with characters and communities that live only in my imagination. But *Anywhere but Paradise* is grounded in history and events from 1960.

Hawaii was, and still is, a rabies-free state. Unless Peggy Sue's cat, Howdy, had come from Australia, New Zealand, Guam, or the British Isles, he had to prove that he was free of the disease. That year, a 120-day stay at the Animal Quarantine Station in Honolulu was required. Two hundred and eight cats were quarantined at a cost of $256 per pet. With intention, I took creative liberties with a quarantine rule, visiting hours, and the addition of a bench in Howdy's cage.

The Kodak Hula Show that Peggy Sue visits was a popular tourist destination in Waikiki for sixty-five years. In accordance with the wishes of the missionaries and her own recent conversion to Christianity, in 1830, Kaahumanu, wife of King Kamehameha I, banned public performances of the art. Hula went underground. But when King Kalakaua ascended the throne in 1883, hula became viable and visible once more. A festival today is named in his honor. About the art, the Merrie Monarch said, "Hula is the language of the heart, therefore the heartbeat of the Hawaiian people."

Peggy Sue's dad works for the state agriculture department. The acres of sugarcane fields that were prevalent on Oahu in 1960 are gone. The last sugar harvest was in 1996. Houses have sprouted in many of the empty fields.

Rock fever is real. Sometimes people who move to the islands experience intense feelings of isolation and unease. Growing up, I heard of instances where families moved back to the mainland for this very reason.

Pele, the goddess of fire, is feared, revered, and respected. She is the subject of countless stories, hula dances, and urban myths. Dismayed by visitors who took lava rocks from the Volcanoes National Park on Hawaii Island (also known as the Big Island), a park ranger once told people the consequences of their actions would result in bad luck. Countless rocks and apologies have been mailed back. Regardless of whether people believe the curse, it is against the law to remove lava, as well as disrespectful to Hawaiians to take as a souvenir.

May Day, or Lei Day, celebrations occur in schools throughout the state. Royal courts preside, dressed in colors and lei representative of their island. Everyone is encouraged to wear aloha attire and lei.

The last Hawaiian monarch, Queen Liliuokalani, was dethroned in 1893. A group of businessmen called the Committee of Safety, with the help of the U.S. Marines, overthrew her kingdom. Despite repeated appeals and attempts for the Kingdom of Hawaii to be restored, in 1898 Hawaii was annexed by the United States. A congressional resolution (Public Law 103-105), formally apologizing to the Native Hawaiian people for overthrowing the Hawaiian monarchy, was signed by President Clinton in 1993.

Hawaiian words and phrases are sprinkled into everyday conversations in the islands. The Hawaiian alphabet has no *s*, but in the 1960s, people commonly added one to make words plural. In keeping with Peggy Sue's world, I used the the *'okina*, the symbol for the letter that represents the glottal stop, sparingly. Today, it is used more universally and recognized as the thirteenth letter of the alphabet.

The 1960 Chilean earthquake was the strongest recorded quake of the twentieth century. At the time, the quake was thought to measure between 8.25–8.5 on the Richter scale. In the late 1970s, seismologists Hiroo Kanamori and Thomas C. Hanks developed a new moment magnitude scale, and the number has been adjusted to 9.5. The 1960 tsunami swept across the Pacific and accounted for death and destruction as far away as Japan. Hilo, a town on Hawaii Island that Peggy Sue's parents visit, sustained the most damage. Sixty-one people died. An anecdotal account noted that additional warning sirens sounded on Hawaii Island the week prior to the waves, though I could not confirm days or times. On Oahu, where Peggy Sue is, dozens of homes were affected by flooding, but no lives were lost. Her worries about Howdy had merit. Dogs, and I assume cats, were not evacuated from the Animal Quarantine Station on Ilalo Street. The facility has since moved and is no longer in the evacuation zone.

The tradition of bullying called Kill Haole Day lasted for decades at my intermediate school. Thanks to the new principal in the 1990s, who envisioned, embraced, and promoted change, it stopped.

Laura Lemay

SAMS

Teach Yourself Perl in 21 Days

SAMS
A Division of Macmillan Computer Publishing
201 West 103rd St., Indianapolis, Indiana 46290 USA

International Standard Book Number: 0-672-31305-7

Library of Congress Catalog Card Number: 98-84939

Printed in the United States of America

First Printing: March 1999

01 00 99 4 3 2 1

Trademarks

All terms mentioned in this book that are known to be trademarks or service marks have been appropriately capitalized. Sams cannot attest to the accuracy of this information. Use of a term in this book should not be regarded as affecting the validity of any trademark or service mark.

Warning and Disclaimer

Every effort has been made to make this book as complete and as accurate as possible, but no warranty or fitness is implied. The information provided is on an "as is" basis. The authors and the publisher shall have neither liability or responsibility to any person or entity with respect to any loss or damages arising from the information contained in this book.

Executive Editor
Mark Taber

Development Editor
Scott Meyers

Managing Editor
Lisa Wilson

Project Editor
Rebecca Mounts

Copy Editor
Fran Hatton

Indexer
Greg Pearson

Proofreaders
Kim Cofer
Gene Redding
Mary Ellen Stephenson

Technical Editors
Rafe Colburn
Chris Spurgeon
J. Eric Townsend
Ian McKallen

Interior Design
Gary Adair

Cover Design
Aren Howell

Layout Technicians
Susan Geiselman
Amy Parker

Contents at a Glance

Contents

WEEK 3 ADVANCED PERL 357

DAY 15 WORKING WITH FILES AND I/O 359

DAY 16 USING PERL FOR CGI SCRIPTING 387

About the Author

Laura Lemay is a member of the gregarious, brightly-colored species of computer book author known as *tutorialis prolificus.* Although she has been spotted writing in the wild for numerous years, more public sightings have occurred frequently since 1995, including several versions of *Sams Teach Yourself Web Publishing with HTML, Sams Teach Yourself Java in 21 Days,* and *The Official Marimba Guide to Castanet.*

When not writing books, her primary habitat is in Northern California. Should you encounter her in person, do not make any sudden movements. Further field notes may be found at `http://www.lne.com/lemay/`.

Acknowledgments

To Larry Wall, for writing Perl.

To the excellent Perl programmers who reviewed this book—J. Eric Townsend, Rafe Colburn, Chris Spurgeon, and Ian McKallen, for being so good at finding my mistakes and confusions and offering helpful suggestions for "Other Ways To Do It."

To the perl.ind conference on The WELL—ditto.

To Jeffrey P. McManus, for his help with Windows and ActiveX necromancy. Buy his books.

To all the nice folks at Macmillan for being very patient indeed during the writing of this book.

And to Eric, for everything, not the least of which was introducing me to Perl a long, long time ago.

Tell Us What You Think!

As the reader of this book, *you* are our most important critic and commentator. We value your opinion and want to know what we're doing right, what we could do better, what areas you'd like to see us publish in, and any other words of wisdom you're willing to pass our way.

As the executive editor for the Web development team at Macmillan Computer Publishing, I welcome your comments. You can fax, email, or write me directly to let me know what you did or didn't like about this book—as well as what we can do to make our books stronger.

Please note that I cannot help you with technical problems related to the topic of this book, and that due to the high volume of mail I receive, I might not be able to reply to every message.

When you write, please be sure to include this book's title and author as well as your name and phone or fax number. I will carefully review your comments and share them with the author and editors who worked on the book.

Fax: 317-817-7070

Email: `webdev@mcp.com`

Mail: Mark Taber
Executive Editor, Web Development
Macmillan Computer Publishing
201 West 103rd Street
Indianapolis, IN 46290 USA

Introduction

A long time ago at a workstation manufacturer far, far away, a young writer—me—was learning how to program sed and awk scripts on UNIX systems. This was before there was a *Sams Teach Yourself Unix,* so I learned UNIX scripting the old-fashioned, time-honored way: trial and error, sketchy online documentation, copying other people's scripts, and asking a lot of questions. Particularly asking a lot of questions. Each time I got stuck I would send email to my various UNIX-proficient friends, and each time I would get a patient reply carefully pointing out what I was doing wrong. In addition to the advice, however, nearly every email started with "You should use Perl to do that."

It seemed that no matter what I wanted to do, the answer always included "You should use Perl to do that." Eventually I got the hint, abandoned the hodgepodge of UNIX programs I was working with, and learned Perl. And now I can't imagine using anything else.

"You should use Perl to do that" could very well be the motto of the Perl language (except that it already has a number of mottoes). Perl is the duct tape of programmer tools; it may not be the best solution to any particular problem, but it's certainly capable and pretty darn useful for just about any problem. Quick to use, quick to run, quick to change, you can often hack together a solution to a problem in Perl faster than it would take a C++ IDE to start up.

And you accomplish these solutions not just on a UNIX system—Perl runs on a wide variety of platforms including Windows and Mac, and is just as useful on those GUI-centric platforms as it is on a more command-line–centric system such as UNIX. Use the Web? Perl is one of the most popular languages (and arguably the standard) for writing CGI scripts and for maintaining Web servers.

Learning Perl, however, can often be the hardest part of using Perl. Perl is a mishmash of various UNIX tools, shell scripting, C, and occasional object-oriented features. That's where *Sams Teach Yourself Perl in 21 Days* comes in. This book is a gentle but thorough introduction to the Perl language and how it can be used. If you're a beginning programmer or if you've got some background, you'll learn the basics and build on them as the book progresses. If you're an experienced programmer, you might find the first few chapters quick going, but there's plenty of content later on to challenge even a veteran. In either case, by the time you finish this book you will have a near-complete grasp of the entirety of the Perl language and how to use it.

How This Book Is Organized

This book is split into 21 lessons and three weeks. Each week covers a variety of topics, growing in complexity and building on the lessons before it.

Each lesson describes a topic and contains two or three examples that illustrate each topic. At the end of each lesson, you get a chance to apply what you've learned with quizzes and exercises (and the answers to those quizzes also appear at the end of each lesson). On the final day of each week, we'll pause for a day to explore some longer, more useful examples in Perl, to review what you've learned in the previous week and show how larger scripts can be built.

The lessons in *Sams Teach Yourself Perl in 21 Days* include the following:

Day 1, "An Introduction to Perl," is the basic background in what Perl is, what it does, how it works, and how to get started using it.

Day 2, "Working with Strings and Numbers," introduces *scalar data*, the basic building blocks in the language, and some simple operators for using them.

Day 3, "More Scalar Data and Operators," finishes up what we started on Day 2, with more detail on the various ways you can manipulate numbers and strings. You'll also get a basic introduction to input and output in this lesson.

Day 4, "Working with Lists and Arrays," shows how to create and manipulate groups of data.

Day 5, "Working with Hashes," expands on the information from the last lesson with an exploration of hashes (also called *associative arrays* or *keyed lists*).

Day 6, "Conditionals and Loops," moves from the subject of data to program flow. This lesson covers conditionals (`if` statements) and loops (`while` and `for`) as well as similar constructs.

Day 7, "Exploring a Few Longer Examples," is the first of our longer example lessons. Here, we'll look at three examples that make use of what you've learned so far.

Day 8, "Manipulating Lists and Strings," explores some of the various ways in which Perl can be used to manipulate data stored in either a list (an array or hash) or in a string. This includes searching, sorting, extracting or adding elements, or processing all the elements in some way.

Day 9, "Pattern Matching with Regular Expressions," is the first of two chapters exploring one of Perl's most powerful features, *regular expressions*, which allow you to create and match patterns of characters in data.

Day 10, "Doing More with Regular Expressions," expands on what you learned the day before with more detail about extracting and replacing data matched by patterns, as well as building more complex patterns.

Day 11, "Creating and Using Subroutines," delves into creating subroutines (sometimes called *functions* or *procedures*) to allow reusable code.

Chapter 12, "Debugging Perl," is a bit of a sideline from the description of the core language. In this lesson we'll look at the source-level debugger that can help you track down subtle problems in your code.

Chapter 13, "Scope, Modules, and Importing Code," collects several issues surrounding global and local variables, compile-time versus run-time execution, and the use of code libraries, called modules.

Chapter 14, "Exploring a Few Longer Examples," is the second of the longer example lessons.

Day 15, "Working with Files and I/O," expands on the simple input and output you've learned in the previous parts of the book. You explore working more directly with files on the computer's file system and doing more with getting input into a script and outputting data from that script.

Day 16, "Using Perl for CGI Scripting," explores how to use Perl specifically for creating Web-server–based CGI scripts.

Day 17, "Managing Files and Directories," is an extension of the lesson on file input and output; this lesson explores how to work with file systems, including navigating directory hierarchies and renaming and moving files.

Day 18, "Perl and the Operating System," explores several features of Perl that are specific to particular platforms. Much of Perl was developed for UNIX and continues to be UNIX-centric; the Windows and Mac versions of Perl have libraries that take advantage of specific features of those platforms. This lesson explores those platform-specific features.

Day 19, "Working with References," explores one of the more advanced features of Perl—the use of references, which allow more efficient data management and more complex nested data structures.

Day 20, "Odds and Ends," finishes up the book with a summary of the few features of Perl that didn't get covered in the rest of the book.

Day 21, "Exploring a Few Longer Examples," is the last of the longer example lessons.

Conventions Used in This Book

Any word or term that appears on your screen is presented in a monospaced font to mimic the way it looks on your screen:

```
it will look like this
```

Text that you should type is presented in a bold monospaced font:

`type in text that looks like this`

Placeholders for variables and expressions are presented in *`monospaced italic`* type.

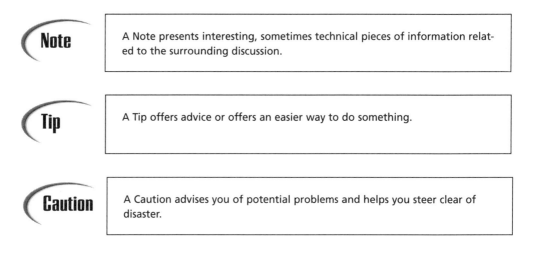

Note

A Note presents interesting, sometimes technical pieces of information related to the surrounding discussion.

Tip

A Tip offers advice or offers an easier way to do something.

A Caution advises you of potential problems and helps you steer clear of disaster.

WEEK 1

Getting Started

- An Introduction to Perl
- Working with Strings and Numbers
- More Scalar Data and Operators
- Working with Lists and Arrays
- Working with Hashes
- Conditionals and Loops
- Exploring a Few Longer Examples

WEEK 1

DAY 1

An Introduction to Perl

Greetings and welcome to *Sams Teach Yourself Perl in 21 Days*! Today, and for the next 20 days, I'll be your guide to all things Perlish. By the time you finish this book—or at least by the time you put it down—you should know enough Perl to accomplish just about anything you'd like to do and to converse intelligently with other Perl programmers.

Today we're going to start with some basic information to ease you into working with Perl. Today's lesson is kind of short, just enough to give you a little background and to get you started using Perl with some simple scripts. In particular, you'll learn

- Some background on Perl: what it is, who created it, who's working on it now.
- Why you should learn Perl (reasons besides "my boss told me to").
- Some actual Perl code, so you can get an idea for how Perl is written and run (and be prepared for the rest of this week's lessons).

And so, without further ado, let's get started. Week one, chapter one, section one—Onward!

What Is Perl and Where Did It Come From?

Perl is not a typo for *pearl*. Perl is actually an acronym. It stands for *P*ractical *E*xtraction and *R*eport *L*anguage, which is a pretty good description of what Perl does particularly well: *Extraction* for looking at files and pulling out the important parts (for example, the actual data from an HTML file, or the user or host names from a networking log file); and *report* for generating output and, well, reports, based on the information that was found. It's a *practical* language because it's much easier to write these sorts of programs in Perl than it would be in a language such as C. But no one really gets hung up on the acronym any more; Perl is just Perl.

Perl was created in 1987 by Larry Wall, who at the time was already well known in the UNIX software world for having written the freely available `patch` program as well as the Usenet newsreader `rn`. The story goes that Larry was working on a task for which the UNIX program `awk` (the popular extraction and report language of the time) wasn't powerful enough, but he realized the task would take a whole lot of work to accomplish in a language such as C. So Perl was created as a scripting language that borrows bits from various other UNIX tools and languages, such as `sed`, `grep`, `awk`, shell scripting and, yes, C. Also, as with `patch` and `rn`, Perl was released for free to the UNIX community. And the UNIX community said it was good.

For many years, Perl was the language of choice for UNIX system administrators and other UNIX programmers who needed a flexible, quick-to-program language to accomplish tasks for which a language such as C would be overkill (or take too much work), or for tasks that were too complex for shell scripting. It was because of its existing popularity as a UNIX language that Perl became popular as a Web language for creating CGI scripts—most early Web servers ran on UNIX systems. CGI (*C*ommon *G*ateway *I*nterface) allowed programs and scripts to be run on the Web server in response to forms or other input from Web pages. Perl fit neatly into that niche, and in the last couple of years as the Web and CGI have become more and more popular, the interest in the Perl language has also grown dramatically. Even as Web servers have ended up being run on systems other than UNIX, Perl moved with them and continued to be popular in this realm.

Larry Wall originally "owned" Perl and was responsible with keeping it updated and incorporating new changes. With Perl's recent surge in popularity, however, the task of maintaining Perl now falls to a close-knit group of volunteer programmers. These programmers, including Larry Wall, maintain the core Perl source, port the source to platforms other than UNIX, coordinate bug fixes, and establish the "standard" Perl release (the `Changes` file in the standard Perl distribution lists the primary *dramatis personae* of Perl). No single organization owns Perl; like the GNU tools (GNU emacs, GCC, GDB, and so on) and the Linux operating system, Perl is defined and managed on a volunteer, goodwill basis. It's also available free of charge; all you have to do is download and install it.

The current major version of Perl is Perl 5, and it is the version this book covers. All Perl releases also have minor versions with various numbers and letters, which most commonly fix bugs that were found in the original release (although some new features do creep into the minor version releases). The current UNIX and Windows version of Perl as I write this book is 5.005, with the Macintosh version at 5.004. These minor numbers may have changed by the time you read this, as work is ongoing on all the Perl ports (and at any time, there may be separate releases for less stable beta versions as well as the current "official" version). For the most part, however, the minor version is less important than making sure you have some version of Perl 5 installed.

Note

As of Perl 5.005, support for Windows was folded into the core source code for Perl (as opposed to the separate different and often incompatible ports that had been around before). If you're using Windows and an earlier version of Perl, I strongly recommend you upgrade to the newer version; the new core version fixes many bugs, synchronizes differences, and makes things a lot easier to work with.

Note

The examples in this book were written on the UNIX version of Perl, version 5.005_02, and tested using ActiveState's Perl for Windows build 508 and MacPerl 5.2.0r4 (a 5.004 port). See Appendixes C, D, and E for information on getting and installing these versions of Perl.

Why Learn Perl?

There are an enormous number of programming languages available on the market today, all of which seem to claim to be able to solve all your problems in half the time, at a quarter of the cost, and then bring about world peace, too. So why learn Perl over another one of those vaunted languages?

The best reason is that different tools are best for different tasks, and Perl is particularly good at a number of common tasks. But there are a number of other good reasons to learn and use Perl.

Perl Is Useful

How's that for a good reason? Perl is probably the language for you if any of the following profiles describes you.

- You're a system administrator looking for a general-purpose scripting language.
- You're a Web administrator with a dozen CGI programs that your Web designers want you to write.
- You're a fairly well-versed UNIX user looking to expand your knowledge.
- You're a programmer looking to quickly prototype a more complicated program.
- You just want a language that will let you hack around with stuff.

You can do real work in Perl, and you can get it done right away.

Perl Doesn't Need Any Fancy Software

To use Perl, you do not need to buy a nifty shrink-wrapped Perl program. You don't need a Perl compiler or an integrated Perl development environment. You don't need a browser that supports Perl or a computer that says "Perl Inside." All you need is one thing: the standard Perl interpreter. You can get that for free, simply by downloading it. If you've got a UNIX shell account with an ISP, you've probably already got it.

OK, there is one other thing you need: You must have a text editor in which to write your Perl scripts. One of these comes with just about every system you can run Perl on, so you're still safe.

You Can Program Perl Quickly

Perl is a scripting language, which means that your Perl scripts are just text files, and they're executed on the fly when Perl runs them. You don't have to use a compiler to convert your code to some other format like an executable or a bytecode file, as you would for a language such as C or Java. This makes Perl quicker to get running for initial programs, makes the debugging process faster, and also allows you to modify your Perl scripts quicker and easier than in C.

Note

Scripting languages are often called *interpreted languages* in Computer Science parlance. Although Perl may appear to be an interpreted language, in that its programs are scripts and the Perl interpreter runs those scripts, Perl is actually *both* a compiled and an interpreted language.

When it operates on a script, Perl reads in the whole thing, parses it for syntax, compiles it, and then executes the result. Although this gives Perl scripts the *appearance* of being interpreted, and you can modify and re-run Perl

> scripts right away as you can with an interpreted language, it also gives you some measure of control over the compilation process. Perl also runs faster than a pure interpreted language does (although not as fast as a compiled language).

Perl Is Portable

Because Perl is a scripting language, a Perl script is a Perl script is a Perl script regardless of which platform you run it on. Although there are differences in Perl on different platforms and features that work only on some platforms (I'll point those out as we run across them), in many cases moving a script from one platform to another can be done without modifying the script in any way whatsoever—without having to laboriously port to a new operating system, without even having to recompile your source code.

Perl Is Powerful

Perl was designed to be a superset of many fairly complex UNIX tools. It's also got all the features you'd expect in a high-level language (and many you wouldn't). Most everything you can do in a sophisticated language such as C, you can do in Perl, although there are, of course, tasks for which C would be better than Perl, and vice versa. You can do simple top-to-bottom scripts in Perl. You can do structured programming in Perl. You can do advanced data structures in Perl. You can do object-oriented programming in Perl. It's all there.

If Perl alone isn't good enough for you, there are also extensive archives of various tools and libraries (called *modules*) to do various common tasks in Perl. Modules to do database interaction, networking, encryption, ties to other languages—just about everything you can think of—are available in these archives. In many cases, if you think, "I need to do *X* in Perl," someone has already done *X* and put their code in the archives for you to use. Perl's cooperative nature means that there is an enormous amount of resources for you to take advantage of.

Perl Is Flexible

One of the mottoes of Perl is: "There's more than one way to do it." (This is commonly referred to by Perl folk as the acronym TMTOWTDI). Remember this phrase, because I'll be coming back to it throughout the book. The Perl language was designed around the idea that different programmers have different ways of approaching and solving problems. So instead of you having to learn how to adapt your thinking to a small set of commands and syntactical constructs (as in C or Java), the Perl language has an enormous number of constructs and shortcuts and side effects—many of which accomplish the same thing other constructs do, but in slightly different ways.

This does make Perl a very large, complex, complicated language (when I first encountered Perl as a young and idealistic programmer, my first reaction was "It's so UGLY!"). But Perl's size and depth of features also make Perl extremely flexible and fun to use. You can write a very straightforward, C-like Perl script—one that uses some of Perl's various shortcuts, while still being entire readable—or one that relies so heavily on Perl side effects and hidden features that you can make other programmers' heads explode just trying to read it (sometimes that can be a fun way to spend a quiet afternoon). It's your choice how you want to use Perl—you don't have to modify your thinking to fit the language. (These days, I still occasionally think Perl is ugly—but I also think it's really cool and fun to work in. I can't say that about C, which is a more consistent and elegant language, but seems to involve a lot more drudgery.)

Perl Is Easy to Learn

Despite the fact that Perl is a large, complex, powerful language, with lots of features and different ways of accomplishing the same tasks, Perl is not a difficult language to learn. Really. Mastering *all* of Perl can be quite daunting (and there's only a handful of people who can claim to know *every* nuance of the language). But the easy parts of Perl are very easy indeed (particularly if you've already got a programming background), and you can learn enough of Perl to do useful work very quickly. Then as you progress and become more familiar with the language, you can add more features and more shortcuts as you need them.

The Perl Community Is Out There

Perl has been developed and supported on a volunteer basis for nearly ten years now, with programmers all around the world devoting their time to evolving the language and developing the tools that can be used with it. On the one hand, this may seem like a sort of communist idea—there's no company to blame when things go wrong, no tech support number to call when you can't get it to work. On the other hand, the Perl community has provided such an enormous body of helpful libraries, mounds of documentation, and FAQ files that you can get most of your questions answered and get help when you need it. You won't really get that with C, where you usually end up buying a book or two, or seven or twenty, and then you're still on your own.

Getting Started Programming in Perl

I could go on and on about why Perl is cool and why you should use it, but then you'd get bored and go buy someone else's book. So let's put aside the background and get down to work.

To use Perl—to program in it and to run Perl scripts—you need to have Perl installed on your system. Fortunately, this isn't difficult. As I mentioned before, Perl is free for the downloading, so all you need is some time connected to the Internet to get it.

If you don't have Perl installed, or if you're not sure if you do or not, your first step is to fire up your Web browser and visit `http://www.perl.com/`. Put that URL into your bookmarks or favorites; it is the central repository of all things relating to Perl. You not only find the Perl interpreter package itself, but also the Comprehensive Perl Archive Network (CPAN), Perl news, Perl documentation, Perl conferences and contests, Perl jokes, and just about anything else you can think of.

The page at `http://www.perl.com/latest.html` has information about the latest versions of Perl for each platform. You can use that information and the instructions that come with the Perl package itself to download and install Perl on your system.

For specifics, you might also want to turn to the back of this book, to Appendixes C, D, and E, which have simple instructions for installing Perl for UNIX, Windows, and Macintosh, respectively.

Before continuing with this chapter, you should have Perl installed and working on your system.

An Example: The Ubiquitous Hello World

A long-standing tradition in the programming world is the Hello World program. When a programmer encounters a new language or a new system, the first program he is supposed to write simply prints "Hello, World!" to the screen. Far be it from me to go against tradition, so the first Perl script we'll examine in this book will do just that. In this section, you'll create and run the Hello World script, and then I'll explain what's actually going on.

Create Hello World

You'll need a text editor. Not a word processor, but a text editor. On UNIX, emacs, vi or pico is just fine; on Windows, the built-in Notepad or the shareware TextEdit or UltraEdit will work; and on the Mac, you can use SimpleText, you can use the shareware BBedit or Alpha, or you can even use the simple built-in editor MacPerl gives you. Fire it up and type in the two lines shown in Listing 1.1 (well, three if you count the blank one in the middle).

LISTING 1.1 THE `hello.pl` SCRIPT

```
1: #!/usr/bin/perl -w
2:
3: print "Hello, World!\n";
```

Don't type the numbers at the beginning of the lines in the listings throughout this book; they're just there so that I can tell you, line by line, what's going on in the script.

If you're on UNIX, you'll want to make sure you include that first line (colloquially called the "sh'bang"—or shebang—line: "sh" for the hash (or sharp) and "bang" for the exclamation point). This line tells UNIX which program to use to actually run the script. The one gotcha here is that the pathname in that line has to match the actual path to the Perl interpreter; if you installed it in `/usr/local/bin/perl` or somewhere else in your system, include that pathname there instead of the one in line 1 of Listing 1.1.

If you're on Windows or on the Mac, you don't usually need to include this first line at all. It won't really matter either way because the `#` at the start of the line is a comment, and Perl will ignore it on platforms other than UNIX. However, if you intend to write Perl programs that will eventually be run on UNIX, it is a good idea to get into the habit of including the shebang line, even if it's not entirely necessary.

Note

If you're intending to use Perl on Windows for Web CGI scripting, some servers (notably Apache) require a shebang line in your Perl scripts (albeit one with a Windows-style path starting with `C:`). Yet another reason to get into the habit.

Save that file as, say, `hello.pl`. Actually, you can call it anything you want to, with or without the `.pl` extension. If you're on Windows, you'll probably want to include the `.pl`, though; Windows prefers its programs to have extensions, and it'll make things work better overall.

Note

Don't feel like typing? All the scripts you'll be exploring in this book are also contained on the Web site for this book at `http://www.typerl.com/`, so you can use the versions there instead of laboriously typing them in. However, typing in a Perl script (and fixing the errors that inevitably occur) can help you learn how Perl scripts work, so you should probably try typing in at least these first couple of scripts.

Running Hello World

The next step is to use Perl to actually run your script.

On UNIX, you'll need to make your script executable and then simply type the name of the script on the command line like this (the bold parts are the part you actually type; the percent sign is the prompt):

```
% chmod +x hello.pl
% hello.pl
```

Note

Depending on how your execution path is set up, you might have to include the current directory when you call the script, like this:

```
% ./hello.pl
```

On Windows, bring up a DOS prompt or command prompt and type **`perl -w`** and the name of the script, as shown here:

```
C:\perl\> perl -w hello.pl
```

If you're on Windows NT and have Perl set up such that `.pl` files are associated with Perl scripts (as described in Appendix D, "Installing Perl for Windows"), then you should be able to just type the name of the script itself, as follows:

```
C:\perl\> hello.pl
```

Note

If you're on Windows 95, you'll need to use the full `perl` command each time.

In MacPerl, first choose Compiler Warnings from the Script menu, and then choose the Run Script menu item from the Script menu to run the script.

> If you're using the MPW version of MacPerl, you can run Perl from the MPW command line, and all the options I describe throughout this book will apply as if you were running the UNIX version of Perl. Throughout this book, however, I'll be focusing primarily on the standalone version of MacPerl.

On any platform, you should see the phrase "Hello, World!" printed to the screen.

What to Do if It Doesn't Work

What happens if you don't get "Hello, World!" printed to your screen? You may get a Perl error (for example, `Can't find string terminator`.) Double-check your script to make sure you typed it in correctly and that you have both opening and closing quotes. Make sure the first line starts with a hash mark (#).

If you get a `File not found` error or `Can't open perl script`, make sure you're in the same directory as your Perl script and that you're typing the filename exactly as you did when you saved the script.

If you get a `Command not found` error, make sure you have Perl installed correctly and, if you're on UNIX, make sure the path in your shebang line matches the actual path to your Perl interpreter.

If you get `Permission denied` on UNIX, make sure that you've remembered to make your script executable (use the `chmod +x` command).

If you're still having problems, and your version of Perl was installed by a system administrator, consider asking that person for help. He may have installed it wrong or be preventing you from running Perl scripts.

How Does It Work?

So, now you've got a two-line Perl script that prints the phrase "Hello, World!" to the screen. It seems simple enough, but there's some basic Perlness here that I should probably describe.

First of all, although this is one of the most simple examples of a Perl script, the idea for larger Perl scripts is the same. A Perl script is a series of statements, executed one at a time starting from the top and continuing to the bottom. (There are occasionally digressions to subroutines, bits of code executed multiple times for loops, or code from programs included from separate libraries and modules, but that's the basic idea.)

The first line in the Hello World script is a comment. You use comments to describe bits of Perl code to explain what they do, as well as to add reminders for things you have yet to do—basically, to annotate your script for any particular reason you'd like. Comments are ignored by Perl, so they're there exclusively for you and anyone else who might be reading your code. Adding comments to a script is considered good programming style, although generally you'll use fewer comments than actual code in your script.

This particular comment in Listing 1.1 is a special kind of comment on UNIX systems, but it's a comment nonetheless. Perl comments start with a hash mark (`#`), and everything from the hash until the end of the line is ignored. Perl doesn't have multiline comments; if you want to use multiple lines you'll have to start each of them with a hash.

Note

> Actually, Perl does have multiline comments, but those are used mostly for included Perl documentation (called PODs), and not for actual comments. Stick to hashes.

The second line of code (line 3 in Listing 1.1) is an example of a basic Perl statement. It's a call to the built-in function `print`, which simply prints the phrase `Hello, World!` to the screen (well, actually, to the standard output, but that's the screen in this case. More about the standard output tomorrow). The `\n` inside the quotes prints a newline character, just as it does in C; without it your script will end with the cursor still at the end of the Hello World phrase and not neatly on the next line.

Note also the semicolon at the end of the `print` statement. Most simple Perl statements end with a semicolon, so that's important—don't forget it.

More about all these concepts—statements, comments, functions, output, and so on, later on in this chapter and tomorrow in Day 2, "Working with Strings and Numbers."

A Note About Warnings

On all the various platforms on which you can run Perl, there are different ways of turning on Perl warnings. I've described all of them here:

- On UNIX, you use the `-w` option in the shebang line.
- On Windows, you use the `-w` option with the `Perl` command itself.
- On the Macintosh, you choose Compiler Warnings from the Script menu.

Turning on warnings is an extremely good idea when you're learning to write Perl scripts (and often a good idea even when you're experienced at it). Perl is very forgiving of strange and often wrong code, which can mean hours spent searching for bugs and weird results in your code. Turning on warnings helps uncover common mistakes and strange places in your code where you may have made mistakes. Get in the habit of it, and it'll save you a lot of debugging time in the long run.

Another Example: Echo

Let's do another example. Here's a script that prompts you for some input and then echoes that input to the screen, like this:

```
% echo.pl
Echo? Hi Laura
Hi Laura
%
```

On Windows NT, when you run this script, run it using Perl interpreter, like this:

```
c:\>perl -w echo.pl
```

If you try to run it using just `echo.pl`, it won't work (there's an actual `echo` command that gets in the way.

Listing 1.2 shows the contents of the `echo.pl` script:

LISTING 1.2 THE `echo.pl` SCRIPT

```
1: #!/usr/bin/perl -w
2: # echo the input to the output
3:
4: print 'Echo? ';
5: $input = <STDIN>;
6: print $input;
```

You don't have to understand all of this script right now; I'll explain all of it in lurid detail tomorrow on Day 2. But you should feel comfortable typing in and running this script and have a general idea of how it works. Here's a quick run-through of the code:

Lines 1 and 2 are both comments; the first for the shebang line, the second to explain what the script does.

Line 4 prompts you to type something. Note that unlike `"Hello World!\n"` there's no `\n` in this string. That's because you want the cursor to stay on the end of the line after you finish printing, so your prompt actually behaves like a prompt.

Line 5 reads a line of input from the keyboard and stores it in the variable called `$input`. You don't have to keep track of the characters that get typed or when the end of the line occurs; Perl reads up until the user hits Return (or Enter) and considers that the line.

Finally, Line 6 prints the value of the variable `$input` back to the screen.

A Third Example: The Cookie Monster

Oh, let's do one more example, just for fun. Back in the days of text-only computer terminals, there was a practical-joke program that floated around for a while called "the cookie monster." The cookie monster program would lock up your terminal and endlessly prompt you to "Give me a cookie" (or, "I WANT A COOKIE" or some variation), and no matter what you typed, it would always insist it wanted a cookie. The only way out of the program was to actually type **`cookie`**, something that often seemed obvious only after you had spent an hour trying to get out of the program.

Listing 1.3 shows a simple Perl version of the cookie monster program.

LISTING 1.3 THE `cookie.pl` SCRIPT

```
#!/usr/bin/perl -w
#
# Cookie Monster

$cookie = "";

while ( $cookie ne "cookie") {
  print 'Give me a cookie: ';
  chomp($cookie = <STDIN>);
}

print "Mmmm. Cookie.\n";
```

This one's slightly more complicated than either Hello World or Echo. Here's a sample of what it looks like when you run it:

```
% cookie.pl
Give me a cookie: asdf
Give me a cookie: exit
Give me a cookie: quit
Give me a cookie: stop
Give me a cookie: I mean it
Give me a cookie: @*&#@(*&@$
Give me a cookie: cookie
Mmmm.  Cookie.
%
```

> That last line is a bit of a variation on the traditional cookie monster program. Note also that this one is pretty easy to get out of; a simple Ctrl+C will break right out of it (or File->Stop Script in MacPerl). The original program was not nearly so nice. But hey, it's only Day One, we can't get that sophisticated yet.

Here's what is going on in the Cookie script, line by line:

- Line 2 and 3 are comments (you should be able to figure that out by now).
- Line 5 initializes the `$cookie` variable to be the empty string `""`.
- Line 7 is the start of a `while` loop. As long as the test inside the parentheses is true, the code inside the curly braces will be executed. Here, the test is to see if the `$cookie` variable does not contain the word `cookie`. You'll learn more about `while` and other loops on Day 6, "Conditionals and Loops."
- Line 8 prompts for the cookie. Note that there's no newline character at the end.
- Line 9 looks really weird. The `chomp` function, which you'll learn more about tomorrow, simply strips the newline (Return) character off the end of whatever it was you typed (and stored in the `$cookie` variable).

Once again, if you don't understand every line, don't panic. This is the gentle tour. All will become clear to you tomorrow.

Going Deeper

Going deeper? We've barely gone shallow! You'll find this section at the end of each lesson in this book. The idea behind "Going Deeper" is that there's stuff about Perl that I don't have the time to teach you, or additional ways of doing things (remember, "there's more than one way to do it"). The Going Deeper section will give you pointers to places where you can learn more—the online Perl documentation that comes with your Perl interpreter or the information on `http://www.perl.com/`.

Much of Perl's online documentation is in the form of *man pages* (*man* being UNIX shorthand for *manual*). Throughout this book, I'll be referring to those man pages, for example, the `perlfunc` or `perlop` man pages. If you're on a UNIX system, you can usually access these man pages using the `man` command, like this:

```
% man perlfunc
```

The contents of all the man pages are also available in *pod* format, a special form of Perl documentation that can be read on any platform or converted to plain text or HTML using conversion programs that come with Perl (*pod* stands for *p*lain *o*ld *d*ocumentation). The pod pages themselves are stored in the pod directory of your Perl distribution; you can read them on UNIX or Windows using the `perldoc` command and the name of a Perl man page, like this:

```
% perldoc perlfunc
```

If you want to know about a specific Perl function such as `print` or `chomp`, use the `-f` option to `perldoc`, as follows:

```
% perldoc -f print
```

On the Mac, all the Perl documentation is available in the Help menu for MacPerl, although you may have to guess the filenames (the `perlfunc` man page is listed under "Builtin functions," for example). MacPerl uses the Shuck application to read pod files.

Finally, all the Perl man pages are also available on the Web at `http://www.perl.com/CPAN-local/doc/manual/html/pod/`. Often, I find it easier to read and search the Perl man pages via the Web than with the `perldoc` or `man` command.

If you can't take any of this silly online stuff and you must have a paper document, one of the best ways to go deeper, in general, is in the book *Programming Perl* (Wall, Christiansen and Schwartz, O'Reilly, 1996), also known as the camel book (for the camel on its cover). The camel book is the definitive reference bible for Perl and describes Perl in almost terrifying detail—although it's also quite dense and hard to read. The goal of *Sams Teach Yourself Perl in 21 Days* is that you'll learn all the basics and the common practices, but if you do want to explore some of the more esoteric features of the language, you'll probably find *Programming Perl* an important volume to have. (My copy is quite well thumbed and scribbled in.)

Summary

Today was more of a "hello, how are you" day than a day of hard work. In this lesson, you learned a little bit about Perl history and background, why it's a fun language, and why it may be useful for you to learn. After all that background in the first half of the lesson, you got your first glimpse at what Perl scripts look like and how to get them to run on your system, including some basic information about comments, Perl statements, and how Perl programs run. At this point, you should have Perl installed on your system and ready to go—from here on, it's all code.

Q&A

Q If Perl is so easy to learn, why do I need 21 days to learn it?

A You probably don't. If you've got 21 days and nothing else to do, you can learn a whole lot of Perl—more Perl than many people who call themselves Perl programmers know. But chances are good that you can pick up just enough Perl to get by in the first week or two and ignore the harder stuff until you feel more adventurous or need to do more with the language. If you've already got a strong programming background in some other language, you can probably rip through these earlier chapters quite a bit faster than at the rate of a chapter a day. One of Perl's basic tenets is that you should be able to get your job done as quickly as possible with the least amount of work. If you can get your job done after reading only a little bit of this book, by all means go for it.

Q I have no programming background, although I've worked with HTML a lot and I know a little JavaScript. Can I learn Perl?

A I don't see why not. Although I've written this book for people who already have a small amount of programming background, if you work slowly through the book, do all the examples and exercises, and experiment on your own, you shouldn't have too much trouble. Perl's flexibility makes it a great language for learning programming. And since you already know about other Web technologies, Perl fits right in with what you already know.

Q Is the code I write called a Perl program or a Perl script?

A It depends on how nitpicky you want to get about semantics. One argument goes that compilers compile programs and interpreters interpret scripts. So you have C and Java programs (and C and Java compilers), but JavaScript or AppleScript scripts. Since Perl is essentially an interpreted language, the code you write is a Perl script and not a Perl program. Another argument is that because what you're doing is Perl programming, you're creating a program as part of that process. A third argument is that it really doesn't matter. I like that last argument, but my editor wants me to be consistent, so I'll stick to that first argument and call them scripts.

Q I typed in the Hello World one-liner and I can't get it to work! Help!

A Are you sure you have Perl installed on your system? Getting Perl installed and working is the major task to do for today. If you flip to the back of the book, to the appendixes, you'll find instructions on getting Perl installed and working on your system (assuming that you're on UNIX, Windows, or a Mac). In addition, the docs that come with your distribution can go a long way toward helping you get everything working.

Q When I double-click on my `hello.pl` script in Windows, a window comes up really quickly and then vanishes. I'm obviously doing something wrong, but what?

A You should be running these scripts from a command or DOS prompt, not from the Explorer window. Start a command-prompt window first, CD to the appropriate directory, and then type **`perl -w`** and the name of your script. Here's a simple example:

```
C:\> cd ..\scripts
C:\scripts> perl -w hello.pl
```

See the Windows Perl FAQs at `http://www.activestate.com/support/faqs/Win32` if you're still having difficulties.

Q I'm on Windows. You mention that the `#!` ("shebang") line at the start of the file is a UNIX thing. Why do I have to include it if I'm not on UNIX and don't intend to ever be on UNIX?

A You don't, if you don't expect your Perl scripts to ever need to run on UNIX (although watch out, some Web servers may require it for Perl scripting). Because the shebang line starts with a hash, it's actually a Perl comment, so it's ignored by the Windows Perl interpreter. You don't need to include it. But it's a good habit to get into, should you ever need to write Perl scripts on UNIX, or worse, convert everything you've ever written on Windows to UNIX.

Q The `hello.pl` script runs just fine, but `cookie.pl` won't run. Perl complains about "Undefined subroutine: chomp."

A Sounds like you're using Perl 4. Use the `-v` option to `perl` to find out what version you're running; you should be using Perl 5 (this book covers Perl 5; you'll run into trouble if you try to use Perl 5 features on Perl 4). Double-check your installation to make sure you're using Perl 5 for all your scripts.

Q I use the emacs editor on UNIX. Is there a `perl-mode` for emacs?

A Of course there is! Perl is a UNIX language and a popular one at that. There's a `perl-mode` that comes with both the standard GNU emacs distribution and the Perl interpreter. Depending on which version of emacs you're using and how it's set up, a `.pl` extension or a shebang line may automatically start `perl-mode` for you. Otherwise, typing **`M-X perl-mode`** will turn it on.

Q In your examples, some of your print commands use double quotes, and others use single quotes. Why?

A Good catch! There's a specific reason for that, involving whether or not you use `\n` or variable names inside the thing you're printing. You'll learn about the difference tomorrow.

Workshop

The workshop section, part of each chapter, has two parts:

- A quiz, to make sure you understood the concepts I covered in the chapter
- Exercises, so you can work with Perl on your own and gain experience actually using what you've learned

Answers to both the quiz and exercise questions are shown below.

Quiz

1. What does Perl stand for? What does it mean?
2. Who wrote Perl originally? Who maintains it now?
3. What's the most recent version of Perl?
4. What are the basic differences between compiled and interpreted languages? Which one is Perl? Why is this useful?
5. Which statement best describes Perl?
    - Perl is a small, powerful, tightly defined language with a minimum of constructs to learn and use.
    - Perl is a large, powerful, flexible language with lots of different ways of doing different things.
6. What's on the `http://www.perl.com/` Web site?
7. What does the shebang line in a Perl script do?
8. How do you create comments in Perl?
9. What are Perl warnings? How do you turn them on in your platform? Why are they useful?

Exercises

1. Try modifying the `hello.pl`, `echo.pl`, and `cookie.pl` programs in various small ways. Don't get carried away and develop an OS or anything, just try small things.

   See what kind of errors you get if you try to introduce various errors into the script (for example, try typing comments without the leading #, removing closing quote marks, or forgetting a semicolon). Become familiar with the sorts of errors that Perl complains about when you forget parts of a statement.
2. Modify the Hello World script to print the greeting twice.
3. Modify the Hello World script to print the greeting twice—on the same line.

4. **BUG BUSTER:** What's wrong with this script?

```
!/usr/bin/perl -w
print "Hello, World!\n";
```

5. **BUG BUSTER:** What's wrong with this one? (Hint: there are two errors.)

```
#!/usr/bin/perl -w
print 'Enter your name: '
# save the data $inputline = <STDIN>;
print $inputline;
```

6. (Extra Credit) Combine the Hello World and Cookie examples such that the script prompts you for your name and then says hello to you, repeatedly, until you type **goodbye**. Here's some sample output from this script:

```
Enter your name: Laura
Hello Laura!
Enter your name: Anastasia
Hello Anastasia!
Enter your name: Turok the Almighty
Hello Turok the Almighty!
Enter your name:  goodbye
hello goodbye!
%
```

Answers

Here are the answers to the workshop questions in the previous section.

Quiz Answers

1. Perl stands for Practical Extraction and Report Language. That means it's a language for extracting things from files and creating reports on those things. The *practical* part means it's a useful language for these sorts of tasks.
2. Larry Wall is the original author of Perl and continues to be intimately involved with its development. Perl is maintained and supported primarily by a group of volunteer developers.
3. The exact answer to this question will vary, depending on the version of Perl you have installed. The major current version, however, is Perl 5; on my UNIX machine, the specific version I have installed is 5.005_02.
4. Compiled languages use a compiler program to convert the program source code into machine code or bytecode. You then run that final version to execute the program. With interpreted languages, however, the source code is the final code, and the interpreter program reads the source file and executes it as is.

Perl is a combination of a compiled and an interpreted language. It behaves like an interpreted language in that it's fast to create, fast to change, and portable across different platforms; but it also compiles the source before running it and, therefore, has the speed and error-correcting features of a compiled language.

5. The second statement best describes Perl:
    - Perl is a large, powerful, flexible language with lots of different ways of doing different things.
6. The `http://www.perl.com/` Web site is the central repository of all things Perl: It's the place to look for the most recent version of Perl, the Comprehensive Perl Archive Network (tools, modules, and utilities relating to Perl), documentation, frequently asked questions, and—more information—just about anything you could want that relates to Perl.
7. The shebang line is used on UNIX to tell UNIX which program to execute for a given script. It contains the pathname to the Perl interpreter on your platform.

    On platforms other than UNIX, the shebang line looks just like a regular comment and is usually ignored.
8. Comments in Perl start with a `#`. Everything from the `#` to the end of the line is ignored.
9. Perl warnings are special diagnostic messages that can help fix common errors and point out places where you may be doing something that will result in behavior you might not expect. Beginning Perl programmers are advised to turn on warnings as you learn, to help understand how Perl behaves in different unusual situations.

    To turn on warnings in UNIX, use the `-w` option to the Perl interpreter in the shebang line.

    To turn on warnings in Windows, use the `-w` option on the Perl command line.

    To turn on warnings in MacPerl, choose Compiler Warnings from the Script menu.

Exercise Answers

1. No answers to Exercise 1.
2. Here's one way to do it:

```
#!/usr/bin/perl -w

print "Hello, World!\n";
print "Hello, World!\n";
```

3. Here's one way to do it:

```
#!/usr/bin/perl -w

print "Hello, World! Hello, World!\n";
```

4. There's a hash mark missing from the first line of that script. That line will produce an error (or, on UNIX, the script probably won't run at all).
5. There are two errors:
    - The first `print` statement is missing a semicolon at the end of the line.
    - The line just after that starts with a comment—all the text after the hash mark is considered a comment and is ignored.
6. Here's one way to do it (given what you've learned today):

```
#!/usr/bin/perl -w
#
$name = "";

while ( $name ne 'goodbye') {
  print 'Enter your name: ';
  chomp($name = <STDIN>);
  print "Hello, ";
  print $name;
  print "!\n";
}
```

WEEK 1

DAY 2

Working with Strings and Numbers

Scalar data is a fancy Perl term that means data consisting of a single thing. Numbers and strings are both forms of scalar data. In this chapter, you'll learn about scalar data, scalar variables, and various operators and functions that operate on scalar data. All these things are the basic building blocks that you will use in just about any Perl script you write.

Today's topics include

- Using numbers and strings
- Scalar variables: defining, using, and assigning values to them
- Simple arithmetic
- Comparisons and tests

Scalar Data and Scalar Variables

Perl, for the most part, has a flexible concept of data types. Unlike languages such as C or Java, which have distinct types for integers, characters, floating-point numbers, and so on (and strict rules for using and converting between types), Perl only distinguishes between two general kinds of data. The first type is *scalar data*, for single things like numbers and strings of characters; and the second is *list data*, for collective things such as arrays. The distinction is not academic; Perl has both scalar and list variables to keep track of, and different constructs in Perl may behave differently depending on whether they operate on scalar or list data. For today, however, let's keep things simple and stick to only numbers and strings and the variables that can hold them. We'll leave list data for later on in the book.

While today I'll refer exclusively to numbers and strings as scalar data, there's actually a third form: references are also a form of scalar data. But you don't need to know about references this early in your Perl education, so I'll ignore them for now. You'll learn about references much later, on Day 19, "Working with References."

Numbers

Numbers in the text of your Perl scripts can be used just about any way you'd like to type them. All of the following are valid numbers in Perl:

```
4
3.2
.23434234
5.
1_123_456
10E2
45e-4
0xbeef
012
```

Integers and floating-point numbers are both represented as you would expect; integers by whole numbers, and floating-point numbers with an integer and decimal part. Floating points less than 1 can start with the decimal itself (as in `.23434234`), or can contain a decimal with no actual decimal part (`5.`). Commas are not allowed; the underscores in `1_123_456` are an optional way of expressing a longer number so that it's more readable (they're removed from the number once it's been evaluated). You indicate exponents using an upper- or lowercase `e` and a positive or negative number (for a positive or negative exponent). Hexadecimal and octal numbers are represented by a leading `0x` or a leading `0`, respectively.

Perl does not differentiate between integers and floats, signed and unsigned, or short and long numbers. A number is simply a type of scalar data and Perl converts between number types as needed in your scripts.

Strings

It may seem somewhat odd that a string is considered a piece of scalar (singular) data, given that a string is a collection of characters and in other languages strings are actually stored in arrays. But Perl is different, and in Perl strings are simply another form of scalar data.

Strings can be represented in two ways: as zero or more characters surrounded by single quotes (`' '`) or by double-quotes (`" "`), for example:

```
'this is a string'
"this is also a string"
""
"$fahr degrees Fahrenheit is $cel degrees Celsius"
"Hello, world!\n"
```

Strings can contain any kind of ASCII data, including binary data (both high and low ASCII characters). However, text strings typically contain only low ASCII characters (regular characters, no accents or special characters). Strings also have no size limits; they can contain any amount of data, limited only by the amount of memory in your machine. Although reading the complete works of Shakespeare or a ten-megabyte UNIX kernel into a single Perl string might take a while and eat up a whole lot of memory, you could certainly do it.

There are two differences between using single-quotes and double-quotes for strings. The first is that a double-quoted string will perform *variable interpolation* on its contents, that is, any variable references inside the quotes (such as `$fahr` and `$cel` in the preceding example) will be replaced by the actual values of those variables. A string with single quotes such as `'$fahr degrees Fahrenheit is $cel degrees Celsius'` will print just like you see it here with the dollar signs and variable names in place (if you want an actual dollar sign in a double-quoted string, you'll have to backslash it: `"that apple costs \$14 dollars"`).

Note

> Variable interpolation also works with strings that contain list variables. You'll learn more about this on Day 4, "Working with Lists and Arrays."

The second difference between single and double-quoted strings is that double-quoted strings can contain the escape characters shown in Table 2.1. These will look familiar to you if you know C, but there are a number of other escapes special to Perl. In single-quoted strings, escape sequences are, for the most part, printed as typed, so `'Hello World!\n'` will print as `Hello World!\n`, instead of including a newline at the end. There are two exceptions to that rule: `\'` and `\\` will let you put quotes and backslashes, respectively, into single-quoted strings.

```
'This is Laura\'s script'            # prints This is Laura's script
'Find the input in C:\\files\\input'
# prints Find the input in C:\files\input'
```

TABLE 2.1 PERL ESCAPE CHARACTERS FOR STRINGS

Character	*Meaning*
`\n`	Newline
`\r`	Carriage return
`\t`	Tab
`\f`	Formfeed
`\b`	Backspace
`\a`	Bell
`\e`	Escape
`\0`*nn*	Octal (where *nn* are digits)
`\x`*nn*	Hexadecimal (where *nn* are `0-9`, `a-f`, or `A-F`)
`\c`*X*	Control characters, where *X* is any character (for example, `\cC` is equivalent to Control-C)
`\u`	Make next letter uppercase
`\l`	Make next letter lowercase
`\U`	Make all following letters uppercase
`\L`	Make all following letters lowercase
`\Q`	Do not match patterns (regular expressions only)
`\E`	End `\U`, `\L`, or `\Q` sequences

We'll look at `\u`, `\l`, `\U`, `\L`, and `\E` in "Going Deeper" at the end of this chapter. `\Q` will be covered as part of regular expressions on Day 9, "Pattern Matching with Regular Expressions."

Empty strings, that is, strings with no characters, are represented simply with quotes and no characters. Note that the empty string `""` is not the same as a string with a space (`" "`).

So which should you use in a Perl script, double- or single-quoted strings? It depends on what you need the string for. If you need escapes and variable interpolation, use a double-quoted string. If you've got a string with a lot of dollar signs in it (actual dollar amounts, for example), then you might use a single-quoted string instead.

Converting Between Numbers and Strings

Because both numbers and strings are scalar data, you don't have to explicitly convert between them; they're interchangeable. Depending on the context, Perl will automatically convert a string to a number or vice versa. So, for example, the string `"14"` could be added to the number 5 and you'd get the number 19 as a result.

This may sound kind of weird, at first, but it does make things like input and output very easy. Need a number entered at the keyboard? You can just read what was typed and then use it as a string. There's no need to use `scanf` or some other function to convert everything back and forth. Perl does it for you.

Perl will even attempt to do the right thing with seemingly nonsensical statements such as `"foo" + 5` or `"23skidoo" + 5`. In the former, a string without any numbers will convert to 0, and the numeric string with extra trailing characters will just lose the extra characters. However, if you use Perl warnings (via the `-w` option or by choosing Scripts->Compiler Warnings in MacPerl), Perl will complain about these sorts of operations, as well it should.

Note

There's one exception to the automatic conversion in Perl, and that's with strings that appear to contain octal and hexadecimal numbers. The `0123` and `0xabc` formats you learned about in the section on numbers apply only to the numbers you actually type into the code for your scripts (*literals* in Computer Science parlance). Input from strings or from the keyboard in octal or hex notation will remain as strings; you can convert those strings to actual numbers using the `oct` function like this:

```
$num = '0x432';
print $num;       # prints 0x432
$hexnum = oct $num;
print $hexnum;    # prints 1074 (decimal equivalent)
$num = '0123';
print (oct $num);  # prints 83
```

The `oct` function can tell from the context whether the string is an octal or hex number; you can also use the `hex` function for hex numbers only.

Scalar Variables

To store a piece of scalar data, you use a scalar variable. Scalar variables in Perl start with a dollar sign ($) and are followed by one or more alphanumeric characters or underscores, like this:

```
$i
$length
$interest_compounded_yearly
$max
$a56434
```

The rules for picking a name for your variable (any Perl variables, not just scalar variables) are:

- Variable names should start with a letter or underscore (after the initial $, of course). Other characters such as numbers or characters such as %, *, and so on are usually reserved for special Perl variables.
- After the first character, variable names can contain any other letters, numbers, or underscores.
- Variable names are sensitive to upper- and lowercase—that is, `$var` is a different variable from `$VAR` and from `$Var`.
- Variables that start with a letter or an underscore cannot be longer than 255 characters (I personally get a headache trying to imagine variable names that long, but hey, knock yourself out).

You don't have to declare or initialize variables in Perl; you can use them as you need them. Scalar variables without initial values will have the undefined value. You don't have to worry about the undefined value—it'll always show up as either an empty string or a 0 value depending on where you use them (that interchangeability feature again). You really should initialize your variables explicitly to something, however, and if you have warnings turned on in Perl, you'll get warnings that let you know when you're trying to use an undefined variable.

I'm glossing over the undefined value here. At this point, you don't have to know much about it although later on in this book (on Day 4, specifically), you'll learn more about how to test for it (using the `defined` function) or undefine a variable (using the `undef` function).

To assign a value to a variable, use an assignment operator. The most common one is the equal sign (=). This assignment operator simply assigns a value to a variable, with the variable reference on the left and the value on the right, as follows:

```
$i = 1;
```

The assignment operator returns the value of the thing assigned, and assignment expressions evaluate from right to left, so you can "cascade" assignments like this (where `$b` is assigned the value 4, and then `$a` gets the value of that expression (also 4):


```
$a = $b = 4;
```

Perl also has a number of shortcut, C-like assignment operators that I'll discuss tomorrow in "More Scalar Data and Operators."

Note

> What about global versus local variables? A variable used in the main body of a Perl script is global in scope to that script (it's available to all parts of the script). Perl allows you to create local variables inside subroutines and loops, and also allows global variable namespace management across scripts via packages, but you have to declare and use those variables in a special way to prevent them from being global. You'll learn more about local variables on Day 11, "Creating and Using Subroutines," and more about scope on Day 13, "Scope, Modules, and Importing Code."

Constructing Perl Scripts

In yesterday's lesson, I explained a little bit about what a Perl script actually looks like and how Perl executes it. Let's pause in this discussion about data to go into a little more detail about that and about the general ground rules for combining data, variables, and other operations into Perl statements, and Perl statements into Perl scripts.

Perl scripts consist of one or more statements, usually executed in order. Perl statements can be simple statements, such as variable assignment or the expressions you'll learn about later today, or they can be more complex statements like conditionals and loops, which you'll learn about on Day 6, "Conditionals and Loops." Simple statements must end with a semicolon.

Beyond that semicolon rule, Perl doesn't care a lot about whitespace (spaces, tabs, returns) as long as it can figure out what you're trying to do. You can write an entire Perl script of multiple statements on a single line (and, in fact, Perl "one-liners," executed on the command line itself, are quite common). Generally, however, Perl scripts are written on multiple lines, one statement per line, with some form of indentation to improve readability. What form of indentation style you use is up to you, although Perl programmers tend to conform to a C-like indentation style. (The `perlstyle` man page contains further suggestions for how Larry Wall prefers to format his code, and is worth a read even if you prefer a different formatting style.)

Perl statements can also contain expressions, where an expression is simply something that results in a value. `1 + 1` is an expression (that evaluates to 2). Variable assignment (`$a = 1`, for example) is an expression that evaluates to the value of the thing assigned. Perl expressions can often be used anywhere a value is expected, including inside other expressions.

Arithmetic Operators

Operators are not the most thrilling of Perl topics, but you need them to build expressions. Perl has a fairly robust set of operators for building expressions with scalars. You'll learn about some of these operators today, and most of the remainder of them tomorrow on Day 3.

We'll start with the arithmetic operators, which perform arithmetic operations on numeric data. Strings are converted to numbers as needed. Perl includes the operators shown in Table 2.2 for basic arithmetic operations, with the operands usually appearing on either side of the operator, as you'd expect:

TABLE 2.2 ARITHMETIC OPERATORS

Operator	*What It Does*	*For Example*	*Results In*
`+`	Addition	`3 + 4`	`7`
`-`	Subtraction (2 operands)	`4 - 2`	`2`
	Negation (1 operand)	`-5`	`-5`
`*`	Multiplication	`5 * 5`	`25`
`/`	Floating-point division	`15 / 4`	`3.75`
`**`	Exponent	`4**5`	`1024`
`%`	Modulus (remainder)	`15 % 4`	`3`

Little of this should be a surprise to you, although the exponent operator may be new. For exponents, the left-side operand is the base, and the right side is the exponent, so `10**3` is the same as `10E3` or 10^3.

Operator precedence for arithmetic is as you learned it in ninth grade: multiplication, division, and modulus are performed first, then addition and subtraction. However, negation (unary `-`, as it's sometimes called) has a higher precedence than multiplication, and the exponent operator has an even higher precedence than that (higher precedence means that those expressions are evaluated first). You'll learn more about operator precedence tomorrow on Day 3.

Arithmetic and Decimal Precision

All arithmetic in Perl is accomplished using floating-point numbers. Although this is convenient for doing simple math (no worrying about converting between ints and floats), there are a number of gotchas surrounding floating-point math that you may need to watch out for.

First is that the division operator always uses floating-point division. The expression `15 / 4` results in 3.75, not 3 as it would be in integer division (and what you would expect if you're coming from C). If you really want an integer result, you can use the `int` function to remove the decimal part, like this:

```
$result_as_int = int 15 / 4;  # result will be 3
```

Another side effect of floating-point division is that sometimes you end up with way more precision than you want. For example, take the simple expression:

```
print 10 / 3;
```

This expression results in the number `3.33333333333333`. This is fine if you want the number `3.33333333333333`, but not if all you want is, say, `3.33` or just `3.3`.

Perl has no built-in mathematical rounding functions, but you can use its printing functions to accomplish the same thing. The `printf` and `sprintf` functions, borrowed from C, are used to format a numerical value inside a string. The `printf` function, like `print`, prints the value to the screen, whereas `sprintf` just returns a string that you can assign to a variable or use inside some other expression. Because Perl converts happily between numbers and strings, you can use either of these functions to control rounding. For example, to print `3.33333333333` to the screen as a value with only two decimal places, use this expression:

```
printf("%.2f", 10/3);
```

The `%.2f` part of this expression is the important part; it says print a floating-point value (`f`) with 2 decimal places after the decimal point (`.2`).

To convert a value to a rounded-off equivalent inside your Perl script, without printing anything, use `sprintf` instead of `printf`:

```
$value = sprintf("%.2f", $value); # round $value to 2 decimals
```

You'll learn a little more about `printf` and `sprintf` tomorrow.

The final gotcha to note about floating-point arithmetic is in what's called a rounding-off error. Due to the way floating-point numbers are stored, sometimes very simple floating-point arithmetic may result in values that are extremely close to, but not quite, what you expect. For example, a simple operation such as `4.5 + 5.7` may actually result in the number `10.199999999999999`, rather than `10.2` as you might expect. Most of the time this isn't a problem, as Perl can keep track of the numbers internally, and `print` will cover up very small inaccuracies like this when you actually print the numbers. One particular place it will show up is if you attempt to compare the value of an expression like this to a constant—a test to see if the expression `4.5 + 5.7` is equal to 10.2 may return false. Keep this rounding-off error in mind as you work with Perl—and particularly watch out for it if you start getting results you don't expect.

An Example: Converting Fahrenheit to Celsius

With numbers, strings, and scalar variables under your belt, you can now start to write simple Perl scripts. Here's a script that prompts you for a Fahrenheit number and then converts it to Celsius. Here's what it looks like when it's run:

```
% temperature.pl
Enter a temperature in Fahrenheit: 212
212 degrees Fahrenheit is equivalent to 100 degrees Celsius
%
```

Listing 2.1 shows the Perl code for this script:

LISTING 2.1 THE `temperature.pl` SCRIPT

```
#!/usr/bin/perl -w

$fahr = 0;
$cel = 0;

print 'Enter a temperature in Fahrenheit: ';
chomp ($fahr = <STDIN>);
$cel = ($fahr - 32) * 5 / 9;
print "$fahr degrees Fahrenheit is equivalent to ";
printf("%d degrees Celsius\n", $cel);
```

This script is quite similar to the `echo.pl` script you did yesterday, but let's go over it, line by line, based on what you've learned so far today about scalars, numbers, strings, and variables.

Lines 3 and 4 initialize the variables we'll use in this script: `$fahr` for a Fahrenheit value, and `$cel` for a Celsius one. Although we could have written this script without initializing the variables, when it's done this way we have a nice list of all the variables we use in the script and what they do.

Line 6 prints the prompt. Here I used a single-quoted string because there are no variables or escapes here to worry about; just characters.

Line 7 gets a line of input from the keyboard and stores that string in the scalar variable `$fahr`. The `chomp` function pulls the newline off the response. This line is probably still kind of puzzling, but stay tuned; tomorrow you'll learn how input and the `chomp` function work.

In Line 8, all the real work takes place. Here we do the conversion calculation to the value in `$fahr`, and store the result in the scalar variable `$cel`. Note that even though the data you read from the keyboard is in string form, Perl doesn't care. You can go ahead and perform calculations on that data as if it were numbers. Of course, if you enter something non-numeric like `"philanthropic,"` Perl will squawk about it, thanks to warnings. On Day 6, you'll learn more about verifying input; for now, let's assume that all the input we get is in the form that we expect.

Note the use of the parentheses in line 8 as well. If the order in which expressions are evaluated is not what you want, you can use parentheses to group expressions so they evaluate correctly. Here we used them to make sure `32` is subtracted from the value in `$fahr` before it's multiplied by `5 / 9`. Without the parentheses, the multiplication and division would happen first.

Finally, in lines 9 and 10, we print out the result. Line 6 uses the now familiar `print` function (note that the `$fahr` variable is replaced with its actual value using Perl's automatic variable interpolation). In line 10, however, we're using the `printf` function to control how the Celsius temperature is printed out. If we used a regular print, the value of `$cel` would be a floating-point number—and could be a very large floating-point number, depending on how the calculation turned out. Using `printf` with the `%d` format, we can limit the value of Celsius to a decimal (integer) number. Note that although we have two print statements here (one `print`, one `printf`), the output appears on a single line. The first string to print did not end with `\n`, which means that the second string is printed on that same line.

You'll learn more about `print` and `printf` tomorrow on Day 3.

Operators for Tests and Comparisons

Perl's comparison operators are used to test the relationship between two numbers or two strings. You can use equality tests to see if two scalars are equal, or relational operators to see if one is "larger" than another. Finally, Perl also includes logical operators for making Boolean (true or false) comparisons. You'll commonly use the operators for tests as part of conditional and loop operations, which we'll cover on Day 6.

The Meaning of Truth

No, we're not going to digress into a philosophical discussion here, but before actually going through the operators, you do need to understand just what Perl means by the terms true and false.

First off, any scalar data can be tested for its truth value, which means that not only can you test to see if two numbers are equivalent, you can also determine if the number `4` or the string `"Thomas Jefferson"` is true. The simple rule is this: All forms of scalar data (all numbers, strings, and references) are true except for three things:

- The empty string (`""`)
- Zero (`0`)
- The undefined value (which looks like `""` or `0` most of the time anyhow)

With these rules in mind, let's move onto the actual operators.

Equality and Relational Operators

Equality operators test whether two bits of data are the same; relational operators test to see whether one value is greater than the other. For numbers, that's easy: comparison is done in numeric order. For strings, a string is considered less than another if the first one appears earlier, alphabetically, than the other (and vice versa for greater than). Character order is determined by the ASCII character set, with lowercase letters appearing earlier than uppercase letters, and spaces count. If a string is equal to another string, it must have the same exact characters from start to finish.

Perl has two sets of equality and relational operators, one for numbers and one for strings, as listed in Table 2.3. Although their names are different, they are both used the same way, with one operand on either side. All these operators return `1` for true and `""` for false.

TABLE 2.3 EQUALITY AND RELATIONSHIP OPERATORS

Test	*Numeric Operator*	*String Operator*
equals	`==`	`eq`
not equals	`!=`	`ne`
less than	`<`	`lt`
greater than	`>`	`gt`
less than or equals	`<=`	`le`
greater than or equals	`>=`	`ge`

Here are a bunch of examples of both the number and string comparisons:

```
4 < 5              # true
4 <= 4             # true
4 < 4              # false
5 < 4 + 5          # true (addition performed first)
6 < 10 > 15        # syntax error; tests cannot be combined
'5' < 8            # true; '5' converted to 5
'add' < 'adder'    # use lt for strings; this is an error under -w
'add' lt 'adder'   # true
'add' lt 'Add'     # false; upper and lower case are different
'add' eq 'add '    # false, spaces count
```

Note that none of the equality or relational expressions can be combined with other equality or relational expressions. While you can have an arithmetic expression `5 + 4 - 3`, which evaluates left to right, you cannot have an expression `6 < 10 > 15`; this will produce a syntax error in Perl because there's no way to evaluate it.

Be careful also to remember that == is the equals test, and is not to be confused with =, which is the assignment operator. The latter is an expression that can return true or false, so if you accidentally use = where you mean ==, it can be hard to track down the error.

It may seem odd to have to worry about two sets of comparison operators when Perl can convert between numbers and strings automatically. The reason there are two sets is precisely because numbers and strings can be automatically converted; you need a way of saying "no, really, compare these as numbers, I mean it."

For example, let's say there was only one set of relationship operators in Perl, as in other languages. And say you had an expression like `'5' < 100`. What does that expression evaluate to? In other languages, you wouldn't even be able to make the comparison; it'd be an invalid expression. In Perl, because numbers and strings can be converted from one to the other, this isn't invalid altogether. But there are two equally correct ways to evaluate it. If you convert the `'5'` to a number, you get `5 < 100`, which is true. If you convert `100` to a string, you get `'5' < '100'`, which is false, because in ASCII order, the character `5` appears *after* the character `1`. To avoid the ambiguity, we need two sets of operators.

Forgetting that there are two sets of comparison operators is one of the more common beginning Perl programmer mistakes (and one which can be infuriatingly difficult to figure out, given that `'this' == 'that'` converts both strings to `0` and then returns true). However, if you turn on warnings in Perl, it will let you know when you've made this mistake (yet another good reason to keep warnings turned on in all your scripts, at least until you're feeling a bit more confident in your programming ability).

Logical Operators

Logical or Boolean operators are those that test other tests and evaluate their operands based on the rules of Boolean algebra. That is, for the values of x and y:

- x AND y returns true only if both x and y are also true
- x OR y returns true if either x or y (or both) are true
- NOT x returns true if x is false, and vice versa

I've capitalized AND, OR, and NOT in the preceding list to differentiate the Boolean algebra concepts from the actual operator names. Otherwise, things can get confusing, once we start talking about how you can use && or and to deal with and, or `||` or `or` to deal with or, and/or `not` for not (I'll try to avoid talking this way for just this reason).

In Perl's usual way of making sure you've got enough syntax choices to hang yourself, Perl has not just one set of logical comparisons, but two: one borrowed from C, and one with Perl keywords. Table 2.4 shows both these sets of operators.

TABLE 2.4 LOGICAL COMPARISONS

C-Style	*Perl Style*	*What It Means*
`&&`	`and`	logical AND
`||`	`or`	logical OR
`!`	`not`	logical NOT

> **Note** There are also operators for logical XOR—`^` and `xor`—but they're not commonly used outside bit manipulations, so I haven't included them here.

The only difference between the two styles of operators is in precedence; the C-style operators appear higher up on the precedence hierarchy than the Perl-style operators. The Perl-style operators' very low precedence can help you avoid typing some parentheses, if that sort of thing annoys you. You'll probably see the C-style operators used more often in existing Perl code; the Perl-style operators are a newer feature, and programmers who are used to C are more likely to use C-style coding where they can.

Both styles of logical AND and NOT are short-circuiting, that is, if evaluating the left side of the expression will determine the overall result, then the right side of the expression is ignored entirely.

For example, let's say you had an expression like this:

```
($x < y) && ($y < $z)
```

If the expression on the left side of the `&&` is false (if `$x` is greater than `$y`), the outcome of the right side of the expression is irrelevant. No matter what the result, the whole expression is going to be false (remember, logical AND states that both sides must be true for the expression to be true). So, to save some time, a short-circuiting operator will avoid even trying to evaluate the right side of the expression if the left side is false.

Similarly, with `||`, if the left side of the expression evaluates to true, then the whole expression returns true and the right side of the expression is never evaluated.

Both forms of logical operators return false if they're false. If they're true, however, they have the side effect of returning the last value evaluated (which, because it's a non-zero or non-empty string, still counts as true). While this side effect would initially seem silly if all you care about is the true value of the expression, it does allow you to choose between several different options or function calls or anything else, like this:

```
$result = $a || $b || $c || $d;
```

In this example, Perl will walk down the list of variables, testing each one for "truth." The first one that comes out as true will halt the expression (due to short-circuiting), and the value of `$result` will be the value of the last variable that was checked.

Many Perl programmers like to use these logical tests as a sort of conditional, as in this next example, which you'll see a lot when you start looking at other people's Perl code:

```
open(FILE, 'inputfile') || die 'cannot open inputfile';
```

On the left side of the expression, `open` is used to open a file, and returns true if the file was opened successfully. On the right side, `die` is used to exit the script immediately with an error message. You only want to actually exit the script if the file couldn't be opened—that is, if `open` returns false. Because the `||` expression is short circuiting, the `die` on the right will only happen if the file couldn't be opened.

I'll come back to this on Day 6, when we cover other conditional statements in Perl (and you'll learn more about `open` on Day 15, "Working with Files and I/O").

Going Deeper

Perl is such a wide and deep language that I can't hope to explain all of it without ending up with a phonebook-sized volume. In this section, then, are the things you can do with scalar data that I haven't covered in the previous sections. Some of these things we'll explore in more detail later on in this book, but for the most part these topics are parts of the language you'll have to explore on your own.

As I mentioned yesterday, throughout this book, when I refer to the `perlop` or `perlfunc` man pages—or to any Perl man pages—you can find these pages as part of the documentation for your Perl interpreter, or on the Web at `http://www.perl.com/CPAN-local/doc/manual/html/pod/`.

Quoting Strings

The quote characters `''` and `""` in Perl may seem like immutable requirements for creating strings, but, actually, they're not. There are a number of ways you can create strings in Perl besides using single and double quotes, some of which interpolate variables, and some of which don't. For example, instead of creating the string `'Beware the ides of March'` with single quotes, you could use the `q//` operator, like this:

```
q/Beware the ides of March/
```

Don't like quotes or slashes? No problem. You can use the `q//` operator with any alphanumeric character, as long as you use the same character to begin and end the string, and start the whole thing with a `q`. The following examples are all equivalent in Perl:

```
'Beware the ides of March'

q/Beware the ides of March/

q#Beware the ides of March#

q?Beware the ides of March?
```

As with single quotes, the `q//` operator does not interpolate variables. For double quotes and variable interpolation, you can use the `qq//` operator in the same way:

```
"stored $num reminders"
qq/stored $num reminders/
qq^stored $num reminders^
```

You might want to use these formats if, for example, you have a string with lots of quotes in it that all need escaping. By substituting, say, a slash character for the quote, you can put quotes inside your strings without having to escape them.

See the `perlop` man page for details on the various quote-like operators.

Alternately, single words in lowercase without quotes that have no other meaning in Perl are interpreted as strings. Perl calls them *barewords*, and they're generally discouraged because they make scripts very hard to read, are error-prone, and you never know when a bareword you use a lot will end up being a reserved word in a future version of the language. Avoid them. If you have Perl warnings turned on, it will complain about this sort of thing.

Upper- and Lowercase Escapes

In Table 2.1, I summarized the escape characters available for interpolated (double-quoted) strings. Amongst those were escapes for upper- and lowercasing strings (`\l`, `\u`, `\L`, `\U`, and `\E`). Use these escapes to force upper- or lowercase values in strings.

The `\l` and `\u` escapes are used to make the next letter in the string lower- or uppercase. You could use `\u`, for example, to make sure the start of a sentence was capitalized. `\L` and `\U` are used to make lower- or uppercase a series of characters inside a string; they will both convert the characters that follow in the string until the end of the string or until a `\E` occurs. These escapes aren't necessarily useful in ordinary quoted strings, but they'll become useful later on when you create patterns for search-and-replace procedures.

More About Variable Interpolation in Strings

Variable interpolation is the capability for Perl to replace variable references in strings with their actual values. In some cases, however, it may be difficult for Perl to figure out where the variable ends. For example, take the following string:

```
"now reading the $valth value\n";
```

In this string, the variable to be interpolated is actually called `$val` and contains a number. But because the final string will say something like `"now reading 12th value"`, the name of the variable butts up against the `th` part and Perl looks for a variable called

`$valth` instead of `$val`. There are a number of ways around this sort of problem—not the least of which is concatenating multiple strings to form the final one. But, Perl also provides syntax to get around this problem, like this:

```
"now reading the ${val}th value\n";
```

The curly brackets in this case are simply delimiters so that Perl can figure out where the variable name starts and ends; they are not printed in the final value. Using curly brackets in this way can help get around problems in variable interpolation.

Summary

Numbers and strings everywhere! Today you learned quite a lot about scalar data. Perl uses the term *scalar data* to refer to single things, and most particularly numbers and strings. Scalar variables, which start with `$`, hold scalar data.

With scalar data in hand, you can create Perl statements, perform arithmetic, compare two values, assign values to variables, change the values of variables, and convert between numbers and strings.

The built-in functions you learned about today include these (we'll go into more detail about some of these tomorrow; see the `perlfunc` man page in Appendix A for more details about these functions):

- `print` takes a list of comma-separated values and strings to print and outputs those values to the standard output (`STDOUT`).
- `printf` takes a formatting string and any number of values, and prints those values according to the codes in the formatting string.
- `sprintf` does the same thing as `printf`, except it returns the formatted string without printing anything.
- `chomp` with a string argument removes any trailing newlines from that string and returns the number of characters it deleted.
- `int` takes a number and returns the integer part of that number (truncating any decimal part).
- `oct` takes a string and interprets it as an octal or hexadecimal number, depending on whether the string begins with `'0'` or `'0x'`.
- `hex` takes a string and interprets that string as a hexadecimal number.

Q&A

Q How do I define a variable so that it'll only contain a number?

A You can't. Perl doesn't have strong number types the way other languages do; the closest you can get is a scalar variable, and that can contain either a number or a string.

Most of the time, this will not matter; Perl will convert strings to numbers for you and vice versa.

Q But what if I end up with data in string form that isn't a number and I try to do something numeric with it?

A The default behavior is as I described in the section on "Converting Between Numbers and Strings." Strings with no numeric content will become 0. Strings that start with numbers and then contain characters will lose the characters.

If you have warnings turned on in your Perl script, then Perl will warn you when you're trying to do things to non-numeric data so you can correct the operation of your scripts before you have this problem.

If you're worried about getting non-numeric data from the user, you should be checking their input when they make it. We did some of this today; I'll show you more tricks for verifying input on Day 6 and Day 9.

Q My calculations are returning floating-point numbers with way too many numbers after the decimal point. How do I round off numbers so they only have two decimal places?

A See the section on "Arithmetic Operators," where I explain how to use `printf` and `sprintf` to do this very thing.

Q But `printf` and `sprintf` are string functions. I want to round off numbers.

A Both numbers and strings are forms of scalar data in Perl. What you can do to one, you can do to the other (in many cases). Use `printf` and `sprintf`. Really.

Workshop

The workshop provides quiz questions to help you solidify your understanding of the material covered, and exercises to give you experience in using what you've learned. Try to understand the quiz and exercise answers before you go on to tomorrow's lesson.

Quiz

1. What are the two types of data you can use in Perl?
2. What kinds of data make up scalar data?
3. What are the differences between double- and single-quoted strings?
4. Which of the following are valid scalar variables?

   `$count`

   `$11foo`

   `$_placeholder`

   `$back2thefuture`

   `$long_variable_to_hold_important_value_for_later`
5. What's the difference between the = and == operators?
6. What's the difference between a statement and an expression?
7. What does this expression evaluate to: `4 + 5 / 3**2 * 6`?
8. How do you round off numbers in Perl?
9. What are the values that Perl considers false?
10. Why are there different operators for number and string comparisons?
11. Define what a *short-circuiting* logical operator does.

Exercises

1. Modify `temp.pl` to convert Celsius back to Fahrenheit.
2. Write a program that prompts you for the width and length of a room and then prints out the square footage.
3. **BUG BUSTERS:** What's wrong with this program?

```
print 'Enter the word Foo: ';
chomp($input = <STDIN>);
if ($input = 'foo') {
   print "Thank you!\n";
} else {
   print "That's not the word foo.\n";
}
```

4. **BUG BUSTERS:** How about this version?

```
print 'Enter the word Foo: ';
chomp($input = <STDIN>);
if ($input == 'foo') {
   print "Thank you!\n";
} else {
   print "That's not the word foo.\n";
}
```

Answers

Here are the answers to the workshop questions in the previous section.

Quiz Answers

1. The two types of data you can use in Perl are scalar data, for individual things like numbers and strings, and list data, for collective things like arrays.
2. Numbers, strings, and references. Full credit if you only said numbers and strings; we haven't talked about references yet.
3. There are two differences between single- and double-quoted strings:
   - Double-quoted strings can contain any number of special character escapes; single-quoted strings can only contain `\'` and `\\`.
   - Double-quoted strings will interpolate variables inside them (that is, replace the variables with their values).
4. All of the variables in that list except for `$11foo` are valid. `$11foo` is invalid because it starts with a number (Perl does have variables that start with numbers, but they're all reserved for use by Perl).
5. The `=` operator is the assignment operator, to assign a value to a variable. The `==` operator is for testing equality between numbers.
6. A statement is a single operation in Perl. An expression is a statement that returns a value; you can often nest several expressions inside a single Perl statement.
7. `7.33333333333333`, give or take a 3 or two.
8. To round off numbers without printing them, use `sprintf`. To print numbers with less precision, use `printf`.
9. Perl has three false values: 0, the empty string `""`, and the undefined value.
10. Perl has different operators for numbers and strings because of its ability to auto-convert scalar values and the differences in handling both those values.
11. Short-circuiting operators only evaluate their right-side operands when necessary. If the value of the left-side operator determines the overall value of the expression (for example, if the left side of a `&&` operator is false), the expression will stop.

2

Exercise Answers

1. Here's one answer:

```
#!/usr/bin/perl -w

$cel = 0;
$fahr = 0;

print 'Enter a temperature in Celsius: ';
chomp ($cel = <STDIN>);
$fahr = $cel * 5 / 9 + 32;
print "$cel degrees Celsius is equivalent to ";
printf("%d degrees Fahrenheit \n", $fahr);
```

2. Here's one answer:

```
#!/usr/bin/perl -w

$width = 0;
$length = 0;
$sqft = 0;

print 'Enter the width of the room (feet): ';
chomp ($width = <STDIN>);
print 'Enter the length of the room (feet): ';
chomp ($length = <STDIN>);
$sqft = $width * $length;
print "The room is $sqft square feet.\n";
```

3. The test inside the parentheses for the `if` statement uses an assignment operator instead of an equality operator. This test will always return true.
4. This time, the test inside the parentheses has a number equality test; since this test compares strings, you need an `eq` test instead.

WEEK 1

DAY 3

More Scalar Data and Operators

Scalar data, as you learned yesterday, involves individual items such as numbers and strings. Yesterday, you learned several things you could do with scalar data; today, we'll finish up the discussion, show you more operators you can play with, and finish up with some related topics. The things you can expect to learn today are

- Various assignment operators
- String concatenation and repetition
- Operator precedence
- A short overview of input and output

Assignment Operators

Yesterday, we discussed the basic assignment operator, =, which assigns a value to a variable. One common use of assignment is an operation to change the value of a variable based on the current value of that variable, such as:

```
$inc = $inc + 100;
```

This does exactly what you'd expect; it gets the value of `$inc`, adds 100 to it, and then stores the result back into `$inc`. This sort of operation is so common that there is a shorthand assignment operator to do just that. The variable reference goes on the left side, and the amount to change it on the right, like this:

```
$inc += 100;
```

Perl supports shorthand assignments for each of the arithmetic operators, for string operators I haven't described yet, and even for `&&` and `||`. Table 3.1 shows a few of the shorthand assignment operators. Basically, just about any operator that has two operands has a shorthand assignment version, where the general rule is that

```
variable operator= expression
```

is equivalent to

```
variable = variable operator expression
```

There's only one difference between the two: in the longhand version, the variable reference is evaluated twice, whereas in the shorthand it's only evaluated once. Most of the time, this won't affect the outcome of the expression, just keep it in mind if you start getting results you don't expect.

TABLE 3.1 SOME COMMON ASSIGNMENT OPERATORS

Operator	*Example*	*Longhand Equivalent*
`+=`	`$x += 10`	`$x = $x + 10`
`-=`	`$x -= 10`	`$x = $x - 10`
`*=`	`$x *= 10`	`$x = $x * 10`
`/=`	`$x /= 10`	`$x = $x / 10`
`%=`	`$x %= 10`	`$x = $x % 10`
`**=`	`$x **= 10`	`$x = $x**10`

Increment and Decrement Operators

As in C, the ++ and -- operators are used with a variable to increment or decrement that variable by 1 (that is, to add or subtract 1). And as with C, both operators can be used either in prefix fashion (before the variable, ++$x) or in postfix (after the variable, $x++). Depending on the usage, the variable will be incremented or decremented before or after it's used.

If your reaction to that above paragraph is "Huh?", here's a wordier explanation. The ++ and -- operators are used with scalar variables to increment or decrement the value of that variable by 1, sort of an even shorter shorthand to the += or -= operators. In addition, both operators can be used before the variable reference—called prefix notation, like this:

```
++$x;
```

Or in postfix notation (after the variable), like this:

```
$x++;
```

The difference is subtle, and determines when in the process of Perl's evaluation of an expression that the variable actually gets incremented. If you used these operators as I did in those previous two examples—alone, by themselves—then there is no difference. The variable gets incremented and Perl moves on. But, if you use these operators on the right side of another variable assignment, then whether you use prefix or postfix notation can be significant. For example, let's look at this snippet of Perl code:

```
$a = 1;
$b = 1;
$a = ++$b;
```

At the end of these statements, both `$a` and `$b` will be 2. Why? The prefix notation means that `$b` will be incremented before its value is assigned to `$a`. So the order of evaluation in this expression is that `$b` is incremented to 2 first, and then that value is assigned to `$a`.

Now let's look at postfix:

```
$a = 1;
$b = 1;
$a = $b++;
```

3

In this case, $b still ends up getting incremented; its value is 2. But $a's value stays at 1. In postfix notation, the value of $b is used before it's incremented. $b evaluates to 1, that value is assigned to $a, and then $b is incremented to 2.

> To be totally, rigorously correct, my ordering of how things happen here is off. For a variable assignment, everything on the right side of the = always has to be evaluated before the assignment occurs, so in reality, $a doesn't get changed until the very last step. What actually happens is that the original value of $b is remembered by Perl, so that when Perl gets around to assigning a value to $a, it can use that actual value. But unless you're working with really complex expressions, you might as well think of it as happening before the increment.

String Concatenation and Repetition

String and text management is one of Perl's biggest strengths, and quite a lot of the examples throughout this book are going to involve working with strings—finding things in them, changing things in them, getting them from files and from the keyboard, and sending them to the screen, to files, or over a network to a Web browser. Today, we started by talking about strings in general terms.

There are just a couple more things I want to mention about strings here, however, because they fit in with today's "All Operators, All the Time" theme. Perl has two operators for using strings: `.` (dot) for string concatenation, and `x` for string repetition.

Unlike Java, which uses the + operator for both addition and for string concatenation, Perl reserves + for use with numbers; to add together two strings you use the `.` operator, like this:

```
'four score' . ' and twenty years ago';
```

This expression results in a third string containing `'four score and seven years ago.'` It does not modify either of the original strings.

You can string together multiple concatenations, and they'll result in one single long string:

```
'this, ' . 'that, ' . 'and the ' . 'other thing.'
```

The other string-related operator is the x operator (not the X operator; it must be a lowercase *x*). The x operator takes a string on one side and a number on the other (but will convert them as needed), and then creates a new string with the old string repeated the number of times given on the right. Some examples:

```
'blah' x 4;  # 'blahblahblahblah'

'*' x 3;    # '***'

10 x 5;    # '1010101010'
```

In that last example, the number 10 is converted to the string '10' and then repeated five times.

Why is this useful? Consider having to pad a screen layout to include a certain number of spaces or filler characters, where the width of that layout can vary. Or consider, perhaps, doing some kind of ASCII art where the repetition of characters can produce specific patterns (hey, this is Perl, you're allowed—no, encouraged—to do weird stuff like that). At any rate, should you ever need to repeat a string, the x operator can do it for you.

3

Operator Precedence and Associativity

Operator precedence determines which operators in a complex expression are evaluated first. *Associativity* determines how operators that have the same precedence are evaluated (where your choices are left-to-right, right-to-left, or nonassociative for those operators where order of evaluation is either not important, not guaranteed, or not even possible). Table 3.2 shows the precedence and associativity of the various operators available in Perl that you've learned about yesterday and today, with operators of a higher precedence (evaluated first) higher up in the table than those of a lower precedence (evaluated later). You'll want to fold down the corner of this page or mark it with a sticky note; this is one of those tables you'll probably refer to over and over again as you work with Perl.

You can always change the evaluation of an expression (or just make it easier to read) by enclosing it with parentheses. Expressions inside parentheses are evaluated before those outside parentheses.

Note that there are a number of operators in this table you haven't learned about yet (and some I won't cover in this book at all). I've included lesson references for those operators I do explain later on in this book.

TABLE 3.2 OPERATOR PRECEDENCE AND ASSOCIATIVITY

<table>
<tr><th>Operator</th><th>Associativity</th><th>What It Means</th></tr>
<tr><td><code>-></code></td><td>left</td><td>Dereference operator (Day 19, “Working with References”)</td></tr>
<tr><td><code>++ --</code></td><td>non</td><td>Increment and decrement</td></tr>
<tr><td><code>**</code></td><td>right</td><td>Exponent</td></tr>
<tr><td><code>! ~ \ + -</code></td><td>right</td><td>Logical not, bitwise not, reference (Day 19), unary +, unary -</td></tr>
<tr><td><code>=~ !~</code></td><td>left</td><td>Pattern matching (Day 9, “Pattern Matching with Regular Expressions”)</td></tr>
<tr><td><code>* / % x</code></td><td>left</td><td>Multiplication, division, modulus, string repeat</td></tr>
<tr><td><code>+ - .</code></td><td>left</td><td>Add, subtract, string concatenate</td></tr>
<tr><td><code><< >></code></td><td>left</td><td>Bitwise left shift and right shift</td></tr>
<tr><td><code>unary operators</code></td><td>non</td><td>Function-like operators</td></tr>
<tr><td><code>< > <= >= lt gt lt le</code></td><td>non</td><td>Tests</td></tr>
<tr><td><code>== != <=> eq ne cmp</code></td><td>non</td><td>More tests (<=> and <code>cmp</code>, Day 8, “Manipulating Lists and Strings”)</td></tr>
<tr><td><code>&</code></td><td>left</td><td>Bitwise AND</td></tr>
<tr><td><code>| ^</code></td><td>left</td><td>Bitwise OR, bitwise XOR</td></tr>
<tr><td><code>&&</code></td><td>left</td><td>C-style logical AND</td></tr>
<tr><td><code>||</code></td><td>left</td><td>C-style logical OR</td></tr>
<tr><td><code>..</code></td><td>non</td><td>Range operator (Day 4, “Working with Lists and Arrays”)</td></tr>
<tr><td><code>?:</code></td><td>right</td><td>Conditional operator (Day 6, “Conditionals and Loops”)</td></tr>
<tr><td><code>= += -= *= /=, etc.</code></td><td>right</td><td>Assignment operators</td></tr>
<tr><td><code>, =></code></td><td>left</td><td>Comma operators (Day 4)</td></tr>
<tr><td><code>list operators</code></td><td>non</td><td>list operators in list context (Day 4)</td></tr>
<tr><td><code>not</code></td><td>right</td><td>Perl logical NOT</td></tr>
<tr><td><code>and</code></td><td>left</td><td>Perl logical AND</td></tr>
<tr><td><code>or xor</code></td><td>left</td><td>Perl logical OR and XOR</td></tr>
</table>

An Example: Simple Statistics

Here's an example called `stats.pl`, which prompts you for numbers, one at a time. Once you're done entering numbers, it gives you a count of the numbers, the sum and the average. It's a rather silly kind of statistics script, but it'll demonstrate tests and variable assignment (and we'll be building on this script later on). Here's an example of what it looks like when run:

```
% stats.pl
Enter a number: 3
Enter a number: 9
Enter a number: 3
Enter a number: 7
Enter a number: 4
Enter a number: 7
Enter a number: 3
Enter a number:

Total count of numbers: 7
Total sum of numbers: 36
Average: 5.14
%
```

As with the temperature conversion example we did yesterday, I'm making the rather large assumption here that all the input you get will actually be numbers. An accidental (or intentional) string as part of the input will result in Perl warnings and potential errors. Later on in this week, you'll learn more about input validation; for the time being, let's assume we have nothing but good data to work with.

Listing 3.1 shows the code behind the statistics script.

LISTING 3.1 THE `stats.pl` SCRIPT

```
#!/usr/bin/perl -w

$input = ''; # temporary input
$count = 0; # count of numbers
$sum = 0;  # sum of numbers
$avg = 0;  # average

while () {
 print 'Enter a number: ';
  chomp ($input = <STDIN>);
```

continues

LISTING 3.1 CONTINUED

```
11:  if ($input ne '') {
12:   $count++;
13:   $sum += $input;
14:   }
15:  else { last; }
16: }
17:
18: $avg = $sum / $count;
19:
20: print "\nTotal count of numbers: $count\n";
21: print "Total sum of numbers: $sum\n";
22: printf("Average (mean): %.2f\n", $avg);
```

This script has three main sections: an initialization section, a section for getting and storing the input, and a section for computing the average and printing out the results.

Here's the initialization section (with line numbers in place):

```
3: $input = ''; # temporary input
4: $count = 0; # count of numbers
5: $sum = 0;  # sum of numbers
6: $avg = 0;  # average
```

We're using four scalar variables here, one to store the input as it comes in, one to keep track of the count of numbers, one to hold the sum and one to hold the average.

The next section is where you prompt for the data:

```
8: while () {
9:  print 'Enter a number: ';
10:  chomp ($input = <STDIN>);
11:  if ($input ne '') {
12:   $count++;
13:    $sum += $input;
14:   }
15:  else { last; }
16: }
```

This second part of the script uses a `while` loop and an `if` conditional to read the input repeatedly until we get a blank line. I still haven't discussed how these are defined in Perl (and we won't get around to it until Day 6) but if you've seen `whiles` and `ifs` before this shouldn't give you too much pause. The `while` loop has no ending test (the parentheses in line 8 are empty), which makes it an infinite loop.

Inside the body of the while, we use line 10 to grab the actual input (and I know you're still waiting to learn what chomp and <STDIN> do; it's coming up soon). Lines 11 through 15 test to make sure that the input actually contains something. Note the test in line 11, which is a string test (ne), not a number test.

If there is input to be handled, we increment the $count variable, and modify the $sum variable to add the new value that was input. With these two lines (12 and 13) we can keep a running total of the count and the sum as each new bit of input comes along, but we'll wait until the end of the loop to calculate the average.

Line 15 has the else clause of the conditional—if there was no input in the line, then we'll break out of the infinite while loop with the last keyword (you'll learn more about last when you learn about loops in Day 6).

And, finally, we finish up by calculating the average and printing the results:

```
18: $avg = $sum / $count;
19:
20: print "\nTotal count of numbers: $count\n";
21: print "Total sum of numbers: $sum\n";
22: printf("Average (mean): %.2f\n", $avg);
```

Line 18 is a straightforward calculation, and lines 20 through 22 print the count, the sum, and the average. Note the \n at the beginning of the first print statement; this will print an extra blank line before the summary. Remember that \n can appear anywhere in a string, not just at the end.

In the third summary line, you'll note we're using printf again to format the number output. This time, we used a printf format for a floating-point number that prints 2 decimal places of that value (%.2f). You get more information about printf in the next section.

Input and Output

We'll finish up today with two topics that initially might not seem to fit with everything else we've talked about concerning scalar data: handling simple input and output. I've included them here essentially for one reason: so you know what's been going on in the scripts you've been writing that read input from the keyboard and print output from the screen.

In this section we'll talk about simple input and output, and as the book progresses you'll learn more about input and output to disk files, culminating on Day 15, "Working with Files and I/O."

File Handles and Standard Input and Output

First, some terminology. In the scripts you've been looking at today and yesterday, you've used Perl code to read input from the keyboard and to write output to the screen. In reality, *the keyboard* and *the screen* aren't the best terms to use because, actually, you're reading from a source called *standard input*, and writing to a destination called *standard output*. Both of these concepts are borrowed from UNIX systems, where using pipes and filters and redirection are common, but if you're used to Windows or the Mac, the idea of a standard input or output may not make much sense.

In all cases, when you're reading data from a source, or writing data to a destination, you'll be working with what are called file handles. Most often, *file handles* refer to actual files on the disk, but there are instances where data may be coming from or going to an unnamed source, for example, from or to another program such as a Web server. To generalize data sources and destinations that are not actual files, Perl gives you built-in file handles for standard input and standard output called `STDIN` and `STDOUT` (there's also `STDERR`, for standard error, but we'll leave that for later). These two file handles happen to include (and, in fact, are most commonly used for) input from the keyboard and output from the screen.

Reading a Line from Standard Input with `<STDIN>`

In the scripts we've seen so far in this book, there's usually been a line for reading input from the keyboard that looks something like this:

```
chomp($inputline = <STDIN>);
```

You'll see that line a lot in Perl code, although often it occurs on multiple lines, something like this (the two forms are equivalent):

```
$inputline = <STDIN>;
chomp($inputline);
```

You know now that `$inputline` is a scalar variable, and that you're assigning something to it. But what?

The `STDIN` part of this line is the special built-in file handle for standard input. You don't have to do anything to open or manage this special file handle; it's there for you to use. In case you're wondering why it's in all caps, that's a Perl convention to keep from confusing file handles from other things in Perl (such as actual keywords in the language).

The angle brackets around `<STDIN>` are used to actually read input from a file handle. The `<>` characters, in fact, are often called the input operator. `<STDIN>`, therefore, means *read input from the STDIN file handle*. In this particular case, where you're assigning the

<STDIN> expression to a scalar variable, Perl will read a line from standard input and stop when it gets to a newline character (or a carriage return on the Macintosh). Unlike in C, you don't have to loop through the output and watch every character to make sure it's a newline; Perl will keep track of that for you. All you need is <STDIN> and a scalar variable to store the input line in.

Note The definition of what a line is, <STDIN> is actually determined by Perl's input record separator, which is a newline character by default. On Day 9 you'll learn how to change the input record separator. For now, just assume that the end of line character is indeed the end of a line and you'll be fine.

All this talk about input and outut brings us to the somewhat amusingly-named `chomp` function. When you read a line of input using <STDIN> and store it in a variable, you get all the input that was typed, and the newline character at the end as well. Usually, you don't want that newline character there, unless you're printing the input right back out again and it's useful for formatting. The built-in Perl `chomp` function, then, takes a string as input, and if the last character is a newline, it removes that newline. Note that `chomp` modifies the original string in place (unlike string concatenation and other string-related functions, which create entire new strings and leave the old strings alone). That's why you can call `chomp` by itself on its own line without reassigning the variable that holds that string.

Note Previous versions of Perl used a similar function for the same purpose called `chop`. If you read older Perl code, you'll see `chop` used a lot. The difference between `chomp` and `chop` is that `chop` indiscriminately removes the last character in the string, whether it's a newline or not, whereas `chomp` is safer and doesn't remove anything unless there's a newline there. Most of the time, you'll want to use `chomp` to remove a newline from input, rather than `chop`.

Writing to Standard Output with `print`

Once you get input into your Perl script with <STDIN>, or from a file or from wherever, you can use Perl statements to do just about anything you like with that input. The time comes, then, when you'll want to output some kind of data as well. You've already seen the two most common ways to do that: `print` and `printf`.

Let's start with print. The print function can take any number of arguments and prints them to the standard output (usually the screen). Up to this point we've only used one argument, but you can also give it multiple arguments, separated by commas. Multiple arguments to print, by default, will get concatenated together before they get printed:

```
print 'take THAT!';
print 1, 2, 3;     # prints '123'
$a = 4;
print 1, ' ', $a;  # prints "1 4"
print 1, " $a";    # same thing
```

I say *by default* because multiple arguments to print actually form a list, and there is a way to get Perl to print characters in between list elements. You'll learn more about this tomorrow on Day 4.

I mentioned the STDOUT file handle earlier, as the way to access the standard output. You may have noticed, however, that we've been printing data to the screen all along with print, and we've never had to refer to STDOUT. That's because Perl, to save you time and keystrokes, assumes that if you use print without an explicit file handle, you want to use standard output. In reality, the following Perl statements do exactly the same thing:

```
print "Hello World!\n" ;

print STDOUT "Hello World!\n";
```

More about the longer version of print when you learn more about file handles that are attached to actual files, on Day 15.

printf and sprintf

In addition to the plain old workhorse print, Perl also provides the printf and sprintf functions, which are most useful in Perl for formatting and printing numbers in specific ways. They work almost identically to those same functions in C, but beware: printf is much less efficient than print, so don't just assume you can use printf everywhere because you're used to it. Only use printf when you have a specific reason to do so.

As you learned yesterday, you use the printf function to print formatted numbers and strings to an output stream, such as standard output. sprintf formats a string and then just returns that new string, so it's more useful for nesting inside other expressions (in fact, printf calls sprintf to do the actual formatting).

Both printf and sprintf take two or more arguments: the first, a string containing formatting codes, and then one or more values to plug into those codes. For example, we've seen examples of `printf` that rounded off a floating-point integer to two decimal places, like this:

```
printf("Average (mean): %.2f", $avg);
```

We've seen one that rounded it to the nearest integer, like this:

```
printf("%d degrees Celsius\n", $cel);
```

Yesterday, you also saw how to use `sprintf` to round a floating-point number to two digits of precision:

```
$value = sprintf("%.2f", $value);
```

The format codes follow the same rules as the C versions (although the `*` length specifier isn't supported) and can get quite complex. A simple formatting code that you might use in Perl looks like this:

3

```
%l.px
```

The `x` part is a code referring to the type of value; in Perl you'll be most interested in the `d` formatting code for printing integers, and the `f` formatting code for printing floating-point numbers. The `l` and the `p` in the formatting code are both optional. `l` refers to the number of characters the value should take up in the final string (padded by spaces if the value as printed is less than `l`), and `p` is the number of digit precision of a floating-point number. All numbers are rounded to the appropriate precision.

Here are some typical examples of how either `sprintf` or `printf` might be used:

```
$val = 5.4349434;
printf("->%5d\n", $val);  # ->     5
printf("->%11.5f\n", $val); # ->  5.43494
printf("%d\n", $val);    # 5
printf("%.3f\n", $val);  # 5.435
printf("%.1f\n", $val);  # 5.4
```

Multiple formatting codes are interpolated left to right in the string, each formatting code replaced by an argument (there should be an equal number of formatting codes and extra arguments):

```
printf("Start value : %.2f End Value: %.2f\n", $start, $end);
```

In this example, if `$start` is `1.343` and `$end` is `5.33333`, the statement will print this:

```
Start value : 1.34 End Value: 5.33
```

If you're unfamiliar with C's `printf` formatting codes, you might want to refer to the `perlfunc` man page (or the `printf` man page) for more details.

A Note About Using Functions

Now that you've learned about the `print` and `chomp` functions, as well as had a glimpse of other functions such as `oct` and `int` and `sprintf`, this is a good time to go over how function calls work. If you've been paying careful attention, you may have noticed that I've been calling the `print` function like this:

```
print "Hello, World!\n";
```

I've also been calling `chomp` and `printf` like this:

```
chomp($input = <STDIN>);
printf("Average (mean): %.2f", $avg);
```

One form has parentheses around the arguments to the function, the other form doesn't. Which is correct? The answer is *both*. Parentheses around the arguments to a function are optional; as long as Perl can figure out what your arguments are, either form works just fine.

In this book, I've used a smattering of both. My general rule is that if a function takes one argument—`int` or `oct` being good examples—I'll leave off the parentheses. If it takes multiple arguments or if its argument is an expression (`printf`, or `chomp`), then I use parentheses. The `print` function can go either way depending on the situation.

Depending on what you're familiar with—and what looks right to you—feel free to pick your own rule for parenthesizing functions in your own scripts. I should mention, however, that the rule of parentheses being optional "as long as Perl can figure out what your arguments are," can occasionally be tricky to figure out, particularly with multiple arguments and particularly when some of them are parenthesized expressions or lists. To make it even more complex, some of Perl's built-in functions are actually operators, and have a different precedence from actual function calls (see the next section, "Going Deeper," for more information). There are rules of precedence to determine exactly how complex function calls are to be evaluated, but the safest solution, if Perl appears to be ignoring your arguments or producing weird results, is to include parentheses around all the arguments. Turning on Perl warnings will also help catch some of these problems.

Going Deeper

Had enough of strings and numbers yet? Want to learn more? No problem. This section has a number of other features to look at concerning scalar data before we forge on ahead to lists.

Operators are all discussed in the `perlop` man page; functions in the `perlfunc` man page. As I mentioned before, you can get to all these pages through the use of the `perldoc` command or on the Web at `http://www.perl.com/CPAN-local/doc/manual/html/pod/`.

Useful Number and String Functions

Perl includes quite a few built-in functions for a variety of purposes. Appendix A, "Perl Functions," contains a summary of those functions, and the `perlfunc` man page also describes them in further detail. In particular, Perl includes a number of useful functions for numbers and strings, including those summarized in Table 3.3. We'll explore some of these in more detail in forthcoming chapters; others you'll have to explore on your own.

TABLE 3.3 NUMBER AND STRING FUNCTIONS

Function	*What It Does*
`abs`	Absolute value
`atan2`	Arctangent
`chr`	The character represented by a number in the ASCII character set
`cos`	Cosine
`exp`	e to the power of (use `**` for exponentiation)
`int`	Truncate decimal part of a float
`index`	Returns the position of the first occurrence of the substring in string
`lc`	Lowercase a string
`lcfirst`	Lowercase the first character in a string
`length`	Length (number of bytes)
`log`	Logarithm
`ord`	The number of a character in the ASCII character set
`rand`	Random number
`reverse`	Reverse a scalar
`rindex`	Reverse index (starts from end of string)
`sin`	Sine
`sqrt`	Square root
`substr`	Returns a substring starting at an offset of some length
`uc`	Uppercase a string
`ucfirst`	Uppercase the first letter in a string

Bitwise Operators

Perl provides the usual set of C-like operators for twiddling bits in integers: ~, <<, >>, &, ¦, and ^, as well as assignment shortcuts for those operators. See the perlop man page for specifics.

The cmp and <=> Operators

In addition to the relational operators I described in the section on comparisons, Perl also has the <=> and cmp operators. The former is for numbers, and the latter for strings. Both return -1, 0, or 1 depending if the left operator is greater than the right, the operators are equal, or if the right operator is greater than the left, respectively. These operators are most commonly used for creating sort routines, which you'll learn more about on Day 8.

Functions and Function-Like Operators

Perl's built-in functions actually fall into two groups: functions that are functions, and operators that take one argument and masquerade as functions. The function-like operators fall in the middle of the precedence hierarchy and behave like operators in this respect (whereas function calls with parentheses always have the highest precedence). See the perlop man page under "Named Unary Operators" for a list of these functions.

Summary

Today was Part 2 of everything you ever wanted to know, and probably a whole lot you didn't, about scalar data. Today you got to look at more tables of operators, in particular operators for assigning things to variables, or changing the values of variables, and for concatenating and repeating strings. You also learned about operator precedence, which determines which operators get to go first when you have an expression with lots of them in it.

We finished up today's lesson talking about input and output, and in particular using <STDIN> to get data into a Perl script and the various print functions to print it out again. You also learned a bit about calling functions with and without parentheses around their arguments.

The built-in functions you learned about today include (see the perlfunc man page or Appendix A for more details about these functions).

- print takes a list of comma-seperated values and strings to print and outputs those values to the standard output (STDOUT).
- printf takes a formatting string and any number of values, and prints those values according to the codes in the formatting string.
- sprintf does the same thing as printf, except it returns the formatted string without printing anything.
- chomp with a string argument removes any trailing newlines from that string and returns the number of characters it deleted.
- chop is the older version of chomp; it removes the last character from the string and returns the character it removed.

Q&A

Q I want to iterate over a string and count the occurrences of the letter "t." How can I do this in Perl?

A Well, you could use a for loop and one of the string functions to work your way through the string one character at a time, but that would be a terrible amount of overkill (and expose you as a C programmer who still thinks of strings as null-terminated arrays). Perl's good with strings, and it has built-in mechanisms for finding stuff in strings so you don't have to do perverse character-by-character comparisons. You'll learn more about pattern matching on Day 9. Don't spend a lot of time iterating over strings until you read that.

Q Can I use printf just like I do in C?

A Well, you can, but you should really get used to working with print instead. The print function is more efficient, and helps cover up things like rounding-off errors in floating-point numbers. Its really a much better idea to use print for the vast majority of cases and only fall back on printf for specific reasons (like rounding).

If you do use printf, you can use all of the formatting codes you can in the C version of printf except for *.

Q Why is it important that some functions are functions and some functions are actually operators? Don't they all behave the same?

A Nope. Functions and operators behave slightly differently. Functions, for example, have a higher precedence. And arguments to an operator may be grouped based on precedence (giving you odd results) as well. In most cases, however, the difference between a function and an operator should not cause you to lay awake at night.

Workshop

The workshop provides quiz questions to help you solidify your understanding of the material covered and exercises to give you experience in using what you've learned. Try to understand the quiz and exercise answers before you go on to tomorrow's lesson.

Quiz

1. What's the difference between the postfix increment operator (`$x++`) and the prefix increment operator (`++$x`)?
2. What does operator precedence determine? How about associativity?
3. What is a file handle? Why do you need one?
4. Define standard input and output. What are they used for?
5. What does the `chomp` function do?
6. What are the differences between `print`, `printf`, and `sprintf`? When would you use each one?
7. What do the following operators do?

```
.
**
ne
||
*=
```

Exercises

1. Write a program that accepts any number of lines of any kind of input, ending with a Return or Enter (similarly to how the `stats.pl` program works). Return the number of lines that were entered.
2. **BUG BUSTER:** What's wrong with this bit of code?

```
while () {
 print 'Enter a name: ';
 chomp ($input = <INPUT>);
 if ($input ne '') {
   $names++;
}
 else { last; }
}
```

3. Write a program that accepts input as multiple words on different lines, and combines those words into a single string.
4. Write a program that takes a string and then centers it on the screen (assume an 80-character line, and that the string is less than 80 characters). Hint: the `length` function will give you the length in characters of a string.

Answers

Here are the answers to the workshop questions in the previous section.

Quiz Answers

1. The difference in prefix and postfix operators is when the variable reference is used and when its value is evaluated. Prefix operators increment the value before using it; postfix increments the variable afterward.
2. Operator precedence determines which parts of an expression are evaluated first given expressions that contain other expressions. Associativity determines the order in which operators that have the same precedence are evaluated.
3. A file handle is used to read data from or write data to a source or a destination, be it a file, the keyboard, the screen, or some other device. File handles provide a common way for Perl to handle input and output with all those things.
4. Standard input and output are generic input sources and output destinations (that is, not specifically from or to files). They are most commonly used to get input from the keyboard or to print it to the screen.
5. The `chomp` function removes the newline from the end of a string. If there is no newline on the end of the string, `chomp` does nothing.
6. The `print` function is the general way of printing output to the screen or to some other output destination. The `printf` function prints formatted strings to some output destination; `sprintf` formats a string, but then simply returns that formatted string value instead of printing it.
7. The answers are:

   `.` concatenates strings

   `**` creates exponential numbers

   `ne` "not equals" for strings

   `||` logical OR (C-style)

   `*=` Multiply and assign; same as `$x = $x * $y`

Exercise Answers

1. Here's one answer:

```
#!/usr/bin/perl -w

$input = ''; # temporary input
$lines = 0; # count of lines

while () {
 print 'Enter some text: ';
 chomp ($input = <STDIN>);
 if ($input ne '') {
   $lines++;
  }
 else { last; }
}

print "Total number of lines entered: $lines\n";
```

2. The file handle for standard input is `STDIN`, not `INPUT`.
3. Here's one answer:

```
#!/usr/bin/perl -w

$input = ''; # temporary input
$sent = ''; # final sentence;

while () {
 print 'Enter a word: ';
 chomp ($input = <STDIN>);
 if ($input ne '') {
   $sent .= $input . ' ';
  }
 else { last; }
}

print "Final sentence: $sent\n";
```

4. Here's one answer:

```
#!/usr/bin/perl -w

$input = ""; # temporary input
$space = 0; # space around
$length = 0 ; # length of string

print 'Enter some text: ';
chomp ($input = <STDIN>);
$length = length $input;
$space = int((80 - $length) / 2);
print ' ' x $space;
print $input;
print ' ' x $space . "\n";
print '*' x 80;
```

DAY 4

Working with Lists and Arrays

Days 2 and 3 dealt primarily with individual things. Today, we'll talk about groups of things, namely, lists and arrays, and the various operations you can do to manage (and mangle) them, including:

- What arrays and lists are, and the variables for storing them
- Defining and using arrays
- List and scalar context, and why context is crucial to understanding Perl
- More about `<STDIN>` and reading input into lists
- Printing lists

List Data and Variables

If scalar data is defined as being made up of individual things, then you can think of list data as a collective thing—or, more rightly, as a collection of scalar things. Just as the term *scalar data* can include both numbers and strings, the term *list data* usually refers to one of two specific things: arrays and hashes. We'll talk about arrays today and go deeper into hashes tomorrow on Day 5, "Working with Hashes."

An array is a collection of any number of scalar things. Each individual thing, or element, can be accessed by referring to the number of its position in the array (its index). Array indexes in Perl start from 0. Figure 4.1 shows an illustration of a simple array with some numbers and strings in it.

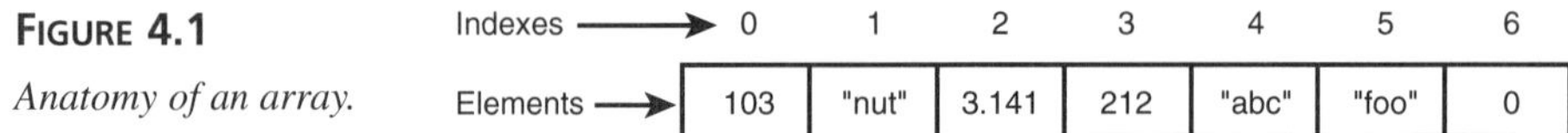

FIGURE 4.1
Anatomy of an array.

Arrays are ordered, which means they have a first element, last element, and all the elements in between in a specific order. You can change the order of elements in an array by sorting it, or iterate over the elements one at a time, from start to finish.

Arrays are stored in array variables, just like scalars are stored in scalar variables. An array variable starts with the at sign (`@`). Beyond the first character, array variables have the same rules as far as names go:

- Names can be up to 255 characters long, and can contain numbers, letters, and underscores.
- Names are case-sensitive. Upper- and lowercase characters are different.
- Array variables, unlike scalar variables, can start with a number, but can then only contain other numbers.

In addition, scalar and array variable names do not conflict with each other. The scalar variable `$x` is a different variable from the array variable `@x`.

In addition to list data being stored and accessed in an array, list data also has a raw form called, appropriately, a list. A list is simply an ordered set of elements. You can assign a list to a variable, iterate over it to print each of its elements, nest it inside another list, or use it as an argument to a function. Usually, you'll use lists to create arrays and hashes, or to pass data between a list and other lists. In many cases, you can think of lists and arrays being essentially interchangeable.

Defining and Using Lists and Arrays

The care and feeding of the wily Perl array includes defining it, assigning it to an array variable, sticking elements in and taking them out, and finding out the length (the number of elements). There are also a whole lot of things you can do to manipulate arrays and their data, but let's start with the basics.

Unlike other languages, in which arrays have to be carefully set up before you can use them, arrays in Perl magically appear as you need them and happily grow and shrink to the number of elements you have in them at any given time. They can also contain any kind of scalar data: numbers, strings, or a mix of both, and as many elements as you want, limited only by the amount of memory you have available.

Note Arrays can contain references, too, but you haven't learned about those yet. Be patient; all will become clear on Day 19, "Working with References."

Creating Lists

As I mentioned earlier, a *list* refers to a general collective set of data; an *array* can be a considered a list that has been stored in an array variable. In reality, you can use lists anywhere arrays are expected, and vice versa.

To create a list, type the initial elements, separated with commas and surrounded by parentheses. This list syntax provides raw list data that can be used to create an array or a hash depending on the kind of variable the list is assigned to. Let's look at a few array examples now and we'll cover hashes tomorrow on Day 5.

Here's an example of list syntax used to create an array called `@nums`, which has four elements:

```
@nums = (1, 2, 3, 4);
```

Lists of strings work just as easily:

```
@strings = ('parsley', 'sage', 'rosemary', 'thyme');
```

List syntax can contain any mixture of strings, numbers, scalar variables, and expressions that result in scalars, and so on:

```
@stuff = ('garbonzo', 3.145, $count, 'defenestration', 4 / 7, $a++);
```

An empty list is simply a set of empty parentheses:

```
@nothing = ();
```

You can nest lists within other lists, but those sublists are not retained in the final array; all the elements are squished together in one single array with empty sublists removed:

```
@combine = (1, 4, (6, 7, 8), (), (5, 8, 3));
# results in (1, 4, 6, 7, 8, 5, 8, 3)
```

Similarly, nesting array variables will do the same thing; all the elements in the subarrays will be concatenated into one larger list:

```
@combine2 = (@nums, @strings);
# results in (1, 2, 3, 4, 'parsley', 'sage', 'rosemary', 'thyme')

@nums = (@nums, 5); # results in  (1, 2, 3, 4, 5);
```

Say you're defining an array of one-word strings, for example, for the days of the week, or a list of names. A very common Perl trick for creating arrays of one-word strings is to use a special quoting function `qw` ("quote word"). The `qw` operator lets you avoid typing all those quote marks and commas, and may actually make the array easier to read:

```
@htmlcolors = qw(
   black white red green
   blue orange purple yellow
   aqua grey silver fuchsia
   lime maroon navy olive
);
```

Creating Lists Using the Range Operator

Want to create a list containing numbers between 1 and 1000? It'd be pretty inefficient to do it by typing all those numbers in. It'd be much easier to use a loop of some sort to stick the numbers in one at a time, but that's still kind of kludgy. (A *kludge*, by the way, is old geek-talk for a less than optimal solution to a problem. Duct tape is a popular kludgy solution for many real-world problems. Some misguided individuals would argue that Perl itself is a kludge. But we won't talk about them.)

Anyhow, given any situation where you think, "There must be an easy way to do this," chances are really good that there is an easy way to do it in Perl. In this case, what you need is the range operator (`..`). To create an array with elements from 1 to 1000, do this:

```
@lotsonums = (1 .. 1000);
```

That's it, you're done. The `@lotsonums` array now contains 1000 elements, from 1 to 1000. The range operator works by counting from the left side operand up to the right side operand by 1 (you cannot use it to count down).

The range operator also magically works for characters:

```
@alphabet = ('a' .. 'z'); # contains 26 elements for characters
```

We'll come back to the range operator on Day 6, "Conditionals and Loops," when we go over iteration.

Assignment and Lists

Up until now we've been using list syntax on the right side of assignment expression, to create a list and assign it to an array. You can also use a list of variable references on the left side of an assignment as well, and Perl will assign values to those variables based on the list on the right.

For example, take this expression:

```
($a, $b) = (1, 2);
```

There's a list on both sides of that expression, but the list on the left is still a valid place to put variables. What Perl does with this expression is assign the values in the list on the right to the variables in the list on the left, in the same order in which they appear. So `$a` will get 1, and `$b` will get 2. This is entirely equivalent to putting those values on separate lines, of course, but it is a convenient way of setting values to variables. Note that the assignments actually happen in parallel, so you can do something like this:

```
($x, $y) = ($y, $x);
```

This example swaps the values of `$x` and `$y`. Neither happens before the other, so it all works out safely.

4

The rule when you have list syntax on both sides of an assignment operator is that each variable on the left gets a value on the right. If there are more variables than values, then the extra variables will be assigned the undefined value. If there are more values than variables, the extra values will be ignored.

You can put array variables on the right, and that array will be expanded into its elements and then assigned as per list syntax:

```
($a, $b) = @nums;
```

You can even nest arrays within lists on both sides, and they will get expanded into their respective elements and assigned using the rules above—with one exception:

```
($a, @more) = (10, 11, 12, 13, 14);
```

In this example, `$a` gets `10`, and `@more` gets the list `(11, 12, 13, 14)`. Array variables on the left side of a list assignment are greedy—that is, they store all remaining members of the list on the right side of the assignment. This is important when considering an example like the following:

```
($a, @more, $b) = (10, 11, 12, 13, 14);
```

In this case, `$a` gets `10`, `@more` gets the list `(11, 12, 13, 14)`, and `$b` gets the undefined value. Because arrays eat up all the remaining values on the right, there won't be any values left for `$b` to be defined to.

Accessing Array Elements

So you have an array, perhaps with some initial elements via list syntax, or perhaps it's just an empty array you're looking to fill with values later on (based on the standard input, for example).

To access any array element, use the `[]` subscript syntax, which you may be familiar with from other languages, with the index position of the element you want to access inside the brackets:

```
$nums[4];
```

This example will give you the value of the fifth element in the `@nums` array. The following example will change that value to `10`:

```
$nums[4] = 10;
```

Stop and look at that syntax for a bit. Does it look weird to you? It should. Here, we're referring to the fifth element of an array called `@nums`, but we're using what appears to be a scalar variable. That's not a typo—that's how the syntax works. You use `@arrayname` to refer to the entire array, and `$arrayname[index]` to access or assign a value to an element inside that array.

That doesn't mean you can't use `$arrayname` to refer to a regular scalar value; `$arrayname`, `$arrayname[]`, and `@arrayname` are all different things. The best way to remember this is to remember that the elements of arrays are always scalar values, so you need a scalar variable to access them, even if they're inside an array (and Perl warnings will catch you if you forget).

Array indexes start from 0, as they do in other languages, and each index can only be a whole number (an integer, in other words). So `$arrayname[0]` refers to the first element in an array, `$arrayname[1]` refers to the second element, and so on. You don't need to use an actual number as the array index, you can use a variable reference or any other kind of expression:

```
$array[$count]; # the element at position $count;
```

What happens if you try to access an element that doesn't exist—for example, to access position 5 of a 3-element array? If you have warnings turned on in Perl, you'll get an error. Otherwise, you'll get an undefined value (`0` or `""`, depending on the context).

Growing Arrays

If you add an element beyond the last element of an array, Perl will grow the array to fit, add the element, and set the intervening elements to have the undefined value. So, for example:

```
@t = (1, 2, 3);
$t[5] = 6;
```

The array `@t`, after these two lines, will contain the elements `(1, 2, 3, undefined, undefined, 6)`. If you try to access those undefined values in the middle, Perl will give you a warning (assuming you have warnings turned on).

To avoid the warnings, and make sure you're only dealing with actual defined values, you can test for the existence of an undefined value using the `defined` function:

```
if (!defined $array[$index]) {
   print "Element $index is undefined.\n";
}
```

Alternately, you can empty an element in an array by setting it to undefined using the `undef` function:

```
if (defined $array[$index]) {
   undef($array[$index]);
}
```

4

Note that the array element that you undefined with `undef` will still be there in the array; it'll just hold the undefined value. To specifically delete an element from an array, you'll have to explicitly remove it by reconstructing the array.

The `undef` function can actually be used anywhere, inside or outside of array elements, to undefine any variable location. It can also be used without any arguments, in which case it simply returns the undefined value, for example:

```
@holeinthemiddle = (1, undef, undef, undef, 5);
```

Because of this latter use of the `undef` function, as an easy way of using an undefined value, the undefined value is commonly referred to simply as `undef` (and I'll be referring to it that way throughout the rest of this book).

Finding the End of an Array

Because arrays can be of any size in Perl, you need a way to find the end of the array, so that if you create a loop that runs over the contents of the array, the loop knows when to stop. Conveniently, Perl has syntax that gives you the index number of the last element in the array: `$#arrayname`. With the index number of the last element, you could create a simple loop that goes from index 0 to that last index. So, for example, to print the contents of an array, one element per line, you might use a construct like this one:

```
$i = 0;
while ($i <= $#array) {
   print $array[$i++], "\n";
}
```

A more common way of doing this sort of operation is to use a `for` or `foreach` loop instead of a `while` loop. But since you've only seen `while` loops up to this point, I figured I'd use another one here. We'll look at `foreach` later on in this lesson.

If you change the values of `$#arrayname`, you grow or truncate the elements of the array. Setting `$#arrayname` to a value larger than its current value sets all the intervening elements to `undef`, and setting it smaller will discard all the elements at the end of the array.

Note that the `$#arrayname` syntax is *not* the correct way to find out the length of (or number of elements in) the array. Because array indexes start from 0, the `$#array` syntax will give you *one less than the total number of elements in the array.*

Finding the Length of an Array

To get the number of elements in an array, use this statement:

```
$numelements = @arrayname;
```

Don't think about that right now, just learn it: to get the number of elements in an array, use a scalar variable and assign an array variable to it. I'll explain why this works a bit later on, in the section "List and Scalar Context."

Sorting Lists and Arrays

In other languages, if you want to sort the contents of an array, you might have to write your own sort routine. Not so in Perl; Perl has one built in. To sort an array, all you have to do is use the *`sort`* function:

```
@orderednums = sort @nums;
```

This assignment will sort the array `@nums` and then assign the new list to the `@orderednums` variable. The `@nums` array still remains unsorted.

That particular simple use of `sort` sorts the contents of `@nums` in ASCII order—that is, in string order, so 5543 will appear lower in the array than 94 (because 5 comes before 9). To sort the array in numeric order, use a special comparison in the middle:

```
@orderednums = sort { $a <=> $b } @nums;
```

The part of the sort routine determines how the array will be sorted using the comparison operator <=>. We'll go over customizing sort routines on Day 8, "Manipulating Lists and Strings," but for now you can learn that by rote: To sort an array by number, use sort with a comparison in the middle. To sort an array by ASCII strings, use the short form without the comparison.

Processing Each Element of an Array

Earlier in this section, I showed you an example of a `while` loop that processed each element of an array, from the first element to the last. A much more common way to do this—called *iterating over* the array—is to use a `foreach` loop, like this:

```
foreach $x (@list) {
   # do something to each element
}
```


The `foreach` loop executes once for each element in the list inside parentheses (here it's the `@list` array, but it could be a raw list, a range, or anything else that gives you a list as a result—for example, the *sort* function). For each element in the list, the value of that element is assigned to a scalar variable (here, `$x`), and the code inside the opening and closing brackets is executed. You could, for example, use a `foreach` loop to print each element of a list, to add them all together, or to test to see if they're undefined (`undef`).

More about `foreach` tomorrow when we talk about hashes, and on Day 6.

An Example: More Stats

Remember the script we did yesterday for simple statistics, where you entered numbers in one at a time, and the script calculated the count, sum, and average? Let's modify that script today to store the numbers that get entered into an array. Having the numbers around after the initial input means we can do more things with them, such as sorting them or finding the median (a different number from the mean).

Here's how the new version of the statistics script looks when it's run:

```
% morestats.pl
Enter a number: 4
Enter a number: 5
Enter a number: 3
(many more numbers in here that I've deleted for space)
Enter a number: 47
Enter a number: 548
Enter a number: 54
Enter a number: 5485
Enter a number:

Total count of numbers: 49
Total sum of numbers: 10430
Maximum number: 5485
Minimum number: 2
Average (mean): 212.86
Median: 45
```

There are two differences in obvious behavior between yesterday's version of the statistics script and this one:

- It calculates the maximum and minimum numbers that were entered.
- It finds the median number (the middle number in a sorted list of all the numbers).

In the code, however, there's one other significant difference between this version and the last: Here we're using an array to store the input data, rather than just discarding it (when you run the script, you still end the input with a blank line). Listing 4.1 shows the code for the new listing.

LISTING 4.1 THE `morestats.pl` SCRIPT

```
#!/usr/bin/perl -w

$input = '';  # temporary input
@nums = ();   # array of numbers;
$count = 0;   # count of numbers
$sum = 0;     # sum of numbers
$avg = 0;     # average
$med = 0;     # median

while () {
  print 'Enter a number: ';
  chomp ($input = <STDIN>);
  if ($input ne '') {
    $nums[$count] = $input;
    $count++;
    $sum += $input;
   }
  else { last; }
}
```

```
20:
21: @nums = sort { $a <=> $b } @nums;
22: $avg = $sum / $count;
23: $med = $nums[$count /2];
24:
25: print "\nTotal count of numbers: $count\n";
26: print "Total sum of numbers: $sum\n";
27: print "Minimum number: $nums[0]\n";
28: print "Maximum number: $nums[$#nums]\n";
29: printf("Average (mean): %.2f\n", $avg);
30: print "Median: $med\n";
```

The `morestats.pl` version of the statistics script has four main sections: initialization, data entry, sorting the data and calculating the statistics, and, finally, printing the results.

The initialization section, lines 3 through 7, is the same as it was in the previous script, except that we've added two variables: an array variable (`@nums`) in line 4, to store the numeric inputs, and a `$med` variable in line 8 for the median. As with the other variables, we don't have to initialize the `@nums` variable, but it looks nice and groups all our variables up at the top of the script.

Lines 10 through 19 are the new `while` loop for entering in the input. If you compare this version to the version in yesterday's lesson, you'll see that there's actually not much that's new here. We're still accepting numbers one line at a time, and still incrementing the `$count` and updating the `$sum` for each number (we're also still not watching to make sure we don't get any bad input, so make sure you only enter numbers for input). The difference is in line 14, where for each turn of the loop we put the input into a slot of the `@nums` array. The `$count` variable here can do double-duty as not only the count of items but also as the array index (note that because we use `$count` as the index before incrementing it, we're correctly starting the array from 0).

With all the input in place, we move onto line 21, where we sort the `@nums` array using the special numeric sort routine I described earlier. Note that I don't have to define the `$a` or `$b` variables—these variables are local to `sort` and are discarded as soon as the sort is complete. Line 22 calculates the average (the mean), as it did in our previous version of the script, and line 23 calculates the median value. Given a sorted set of data, the median is defined as the value in the middle (it determines the true middle value, whereas the average can be skewed if there are especially high or low values). To find the value in the middle, all we need to do is divide the `$count` variable by two, and then use that middle value as the index to the array (in the case where there are an odd number of elements, the resulting floating-point number will be truncated to an integer).

This brings us to the final summary in lines 25 through 30. Count, sum, and average as the same as before, but now we've also added maximum, minimum, and median. Maximum and minimum are easy; since our array is sorted, we don't even need to calculate anything; we can just pull the first and last elements off of the array. And since we calculated the median earlier, all we need to do is print it as we have the other values.

List and Scalar Context

Before we leave arrays behind, I'd like to pause significantly to discuss the subject of context. *Context*, in Perl, is the notion that different bits of data act differently depending on what you're trying to do with them. Context can be particularly baffling to understand, and if you're confused about context you can end up with results that seem to make absolutely no sense (or bits of other people's scripts that produce results seemingly out of nowhere). On the other hand, once you understand context in Perl, and how different operations use context, you can do very complex things very quickly, which would take several lines of code in other languages.

> If you're an experienced programmer and you've been scanning the book for the important stuff up to this point, stop it right now. Take the time to read this section carefully and make sure you understand it. Context can trip up both novice and experienced Perl programmers alike.

What Is Context?

So just what does *context* mean? Let's use an analogy from English: take the word *contract*. Define it, in 25 words or fewer.

What's the definition of the word *contract*? The correct answer is, actually, "It depends on how you use it." In the sentence, "I just signed the contract," it's a noun, and the definition of *contract* as a noun is "a legal agreement between two parties." In another sentence, "Extreme cold causes the rivets to contract," it's used as a verb, and the definition is "to become smaller in size or length." Same word, same spelling, but a different meaning (and, actually a different pronunciation) depending on whether it's used in a noun context or a verb context.

"OK," you say, "but what does this have to do with Perl?" I'm getting to that. Take the simple Perl expression `5 + 4`. What does that expression evaluate to?

"Uh, 9," you reply, wondering if there's a catch. You bet there's a catch. What if you stick that expression into a test, like this:

```
if (5 + 4) { ... )
```

Now what does `5 + 4` evaluate to? Well, it still evaluates to 9. But then, because it's being used as a test, it also evaluates to true (remember, only `0` and `""` are false). In the *context* of a test—Perl folk call it a *Boolean context*—the expression `5 + 4` evaluates to a Boolean value, not a number. The `if` construct expects a true or false value for the test, so Perl happily gives it one.

When numbers and strings are automatically converted from one to the other, they're converted based on context. In arithmetic, Perl expects numeric operands (a numeric context), so it converts any strings to numbers. The string operators, in turn, have a string context, so Perl converts numeric values to strings to satisfy the context.

Numeric, string, and Boolean contexts are all forms of the more general scalar context. For the most part, you won't have to worry a lot about differentiating between the three, as Perl can figure it out and convert it for you.

Where the complications arise is with differentiating between scalars and lists. Every operation in Perl is evaluated in either a scalar or list context. Some operations in Perl expect a scalar context, others expect lists, and you'll get errors in Perl if you try to stick the wrong kind of data where the other is expected. A third—and very common—class of operations can be evaluated in *either* a scalar or list context and may behave differently in one context than they do in the other. And, to make matters even more complex, there are no standard rules for how lists behave in a scalar context or vice versa. Each operation has its own rules, and you have to keep track of them or look them up. For every operation in Perl, then, if you're mixing lists and scalars, you should be asking yourself three questions:

- What context am I in (scalar or list)?
- What type of data am I using in that context?
- What is supposed to happen when I use that data in that context?

For the rest of this section, then, I'll discuss a few instances of when context is important. But this is definitely an area that will take further diligence on your part as you develop your skills in Perl. Keep those three questions and the Perl documentation close at hand, and you'll be fine.

Finding the Number of Elements in an Array, Revisited

You've already seen one example of how context is important. Remember how to find out the length of an array, using this line?

```
$numelements = @arrayname;
```

I told you then to just learn the rule and not worry about it. This is a classic example of where context can be confusing in Perl. The `$numelements` variable is a scalar variable, so the assignment to that variable is evaluated in a scalar context—a scalar value is expected on the right-hand side of the = (that's the answer to your first question: What context am I in? You're in a scalar context).

In the preceding example, you've put a list on the right side, in a scalar context (the answer to the second question: What kind of data am I using?). So the only remaining question is, "What's supposed to happen to a list in this context?" In this case, what happens is that the number of elements in the array `@arrayname` ends up getting assigned to the `$numelements` variable. An array variable, evaluated in a scalar assignment context, results in the number of elements in the list.

Don't think of it as converting the list to a scalar; it doesn't work that way. There's no conversion going on. The list simply behaves differently in this context than it does elsewhere.

You can use this number-of-elements feature by supplying an array variable anywhere a scalar value is expected—for example, in any of these expressions:

```
$med = $arrayname[@arrayname / 2]; # median value, remember?
$tot = @arrayname + @anotherarray + @athird;
if (@arrayname > 10) { ... }
while (@arrayname) { ... }
```

If this seems confusing or difficult to read, you can always stick to the simple assignment of a scalar on one side and an array variable on the other. Or, if you're only getting the length of the array so that you can iterate over its values, you can use `$#array` as the stopping value instead of the number of elements, and avoid the whole thing.

Context and Assignment

Assignment is probably the most common case in which context becomes important—or, at least, it's one of the places where context is easiest to explain. With the left and right side of the assignment operator, you can have contexts that match (scalar = scalar, list = list), or mismatched contexts (scalar = list, list = scalar). In this section, I'll go over some of the simple rules for how context works in assignments.

Let's start with the easy cases, where the context matches. You've already learned all of these. Scalar to scalar is an individual thing to an individual thing, with numbers and strings converted at will:

```
$x = 'foo'; # scalar variable, scalar value
```

You've also learned about list-to-list assignments, with list syntax and array variables on the left and right sides of the assignment operator, as well as nested inside other lists:

```
@nums = (10, 20, 30);
($x, $y, $z) = @nums;
($a, @nums2) = @nums;
```

Now let's look at the cases where the context doesn't match. Say you try to assign a scalar in a list context, as in either of these examples:

```
@array = 3.145;
```

```
($a, $b) = $c;
```

This one's easy! In these cases, the scalar value on the right is simply converted into a list and then assigned using list assignment rules. `@array` becomes a list of a single value, `3.145`, `$a` gets the value of `$c`, and `$b` becomes undefined.

The hardest case is dealing with assigning a list on the right to a scalar on the left. You've learned what happens when you assign an array variable to a scalar variable:

```
$numelements = @array;
```

The same thing will happen if the value on the right is a raw list:

```
$numelements = sort @array;
```

When you use actual list syntax, however, the rule is different:

```
$x = (2, 4, 8, 16);
```

In this case, the rule is that all the values in the list except the *last* one are ignored. The value of `$x` here will be 16 (this is a different rule from assigning `($x)` to that same list, where list-to-list assignment starts from the *first* element, 2, and discards unused elements).

The most important thing to remember about these contexts is that there is no general rule for how a list behaves in a scalar context—you just have to know the rules. Keep those three questions in mind and you should be fine.

Other Contexts

There are a few other contextual situations worth touching on—things that you should be aware of as you work with lists and scalars.

First, there's Boolean context, where a value is tested to see if its true or false (as in the test for an `if` or a `while`). You've already learned how a scalar value, in Boolean context, is true if it has any value except `""`, 0, or undefined.

Lists in Boolean context follow a similar rule—a list with any elements, including undefined elements, is true in a Boolean context. An empty list is false.

The second situation where context may be important is with functions. Some functions take a list as their argument, and all their arguments are combined and evaluated in that context. If you use functions with parentheses around their arguments, as you learned about yesterday, then there's no problem—you're giving the function a list of arguments. If you don't use parentheses, however, Perl will try to build a list from the arguments you give it. If those arguments contain lists or parenthesized expressions, however, Perl may get confused. Take this example with print, which is one of the functions that expects a list context:

```
print 4 + 5, 6, 'foo';
```

In this case, the arguments to print are evaluated as if they were the list `(9, 6, 'foo')`. With this case, however, the rule is different:

```
print (4 + 5), 6, 'foo';
```

Because of that parenthesized expression, Perl will assume that the `4 + 5` expression is its only argument, and become confused about what the `6` and the `'foo'` are doing hanging off the end. If you have Perl warnings turned on, it'll catch these (and complain about using constants in a void context). In this case, its best to solve the problem by parenthesizing the entire list of arguments so there's no ambiguity:

```
print ((4 + 5), 6, 'foo');
```

Most of the time, Perl can figure out whether a parentheses means a function call, an expression, or a list. And, in most of the remaining cases, Perl warnings will help you figure out what's going on where there's ambiguity. But keep the differences and context in mind as you write your Perl scripts.

The `scalar` Function

Sometimes there are times when you really want to use a list in a scalar context, but its awkward to go out of your way to create a scalar context for that operation (for example, creating a temporary scalar variable just to force the list into a scalar context). Fear not, there is a shorthand. You can always force a list to be evaluated scalar context, using the `scalar` function. For example, take the following two statements:

```
print @nums;
print scalar(@nums);
```

The `print` function evaluates its arguments in a list context (this is why you can specify multiple arguments to print seperated by commas). The first of these statements, then, expands the `@nums` array in a list context, and prints the values of that array. The second forces `@nums` to be evaluated in a scalar context which, in this case, prints the number of elements in `@nums`.

Input, Output, and Lists

We'll finish up today's lesson as we did yesterday: by talking a little more about input and output, this time with list and array context in mind. There are two topics to cover here that will help you work more with input and with files:

- Using `<STDIN>` in a list context
- Printing lists

Using `<STDIN>` in List Context

Yesterday, you learned about `<STDIN>`, and how it's used to read data from the standard input. Up to now, we've been using it like this:

```
chomp($in = <STDIN>);
```

A close look at that line shows that you're using `<STDIN>` here in a scalar context. Like many other Perl operations, the input operator `<>` behaves differently in a list context than it does in a scalar one.

If you use `<STDIN>` in a scalar context, Perl reads a line of input up until the newline character. In a list context, however, `<STDIN>` reads all the input it can get, with each line stored as a separate element in the list. It only stops when it gets to an end-of-file.

That's a rather confusing explanation, given that standard input wouldn't seem to really have an end-of-file. But it does, actually. Typing a Ctrl+D (Ctrl+Z on Windows) tells Perl "this is the end of file" for standard input. If you use `<STDIN>` in a list context, then, Perl will wait until you've entered all your data and hit Ctrl+D or Ctrl+Z, put all that data into a list, and then continue with the script.

The use of input in a list context is much more useful when you're reading input from files, and you've actually got an explicit end-of-file. Generally you'll use `<STDIN>` to read individual lines of input from the keyboard in a scalar context. But it's important to realize the difference between input in a scalar context versus input from a list context; as with many other parts of Perl, there are differences in behavior between the two.

Printing Lists

In the examples we've done in this chapter we've printed lists by using loops to examine and print each element of the list. If you just want to print the elements of a list without modifying them, however, there's an easier way: just print them using the `print` function. Given that `print` assumes its arguments are in list context, this makes it easy.

Well, sort of easy. Here's a simple list from 1 to 9:

```
@list = (1..9);
```

If you print this list with just the `print` function, you'll end up with this:

```
123456789
```

You won't even get a newline character at the end. By default, by printing a list, all the values of the list are concatenated together.

What if you want to print them with spaces in between them? You could use a loop to do that. But there is an easier way. You can use variable interpolation for the list variable. You may remember yesterday we talked about variable interpolation inside strings, where given a string `"this is string $count"`, the `$count` variable would be replaced with its actual value. Variable interpolation also happens with array and hash variables—the contents of the array or hash are simply printed in order, separated by a space. For example, if you include the `@list` variable inside quotes, with a newline character:

```
print "@list\n";
```

These lines will result in the list being printed with spaces in between the elements, with a newline at the end. Variable interpolation with list variables makes it easy to print out the contents of a list without resorting to loops. Note, however, that this does mean if you want to use the `@` character inside a double-quoted string, you'll often need to backslash it to prevent Perl from searching for an array that doesn't exist (and then complaining that it doesn't't). Perl warnings will let you know if you're making this mistake.

> **Note**
>
> Another way to control the printing of lists is to set special global Perl variables for the output field separator and output record separator. More about these special variables in "Going Deeper."

Going Deeper

We've covered a lot in this lesson, but there's still more about arrays and hashes I haven't discussed (really!). This section summarizes some of the features of lists, arrays, and hashes that I haven't covered in the body of this lesson. Feel free to explore these parts of Perl on your own.

Negative Array Indexes

In the array access expression `$array[index]`, usually the index will be the position of the element in the array, starting from 0. You can also use negative array subscripts, like this:

```
$array[-1];
```

Negative array subscripts will count back from the end of the array—so an index of `-1` refers to the last index in the array (same as `$#array`), `-2` refers to the second to last index, and so on. You can also assign to those positions, although it might be a better idea to use syntax that's more explicit and easier to read in that instance.

More About Ranges

Earlier in this lesson, we used the range operator `..` to create a list of numeric elements. Ranges also have several features I didn't mention in that section. For example, you can use ranges with characters, and the range will generate a list of all the characters in the ASCII character set between the operands. For example, the range `'a' .. 'z'` results in a list of 26 characters from a to z.

You can also use this behavior in various magical ways, combining numbers and letters or multiple letters, and the range will happily oblige with values between the upper and lower values.

The range operator can also be used in a scalar context, and returns a Boolean value, which may be useful in some loops or in emulating `awk` or `sed`-like behavior. See the `perlop` man page under Range Operator for more information.

`chomp` and `chop` on Lists

The `chomp` and `chop` functions, to remove newlines or characters from the end of strings, also work with lists as their arguments. On lists, they work through each element in the list and remove the newline or the last character from each element. This could be useful for removing all the newline characters from input you read from a file into a list.

See the `perlfunc` man page for more information on `chomp` and `chop`.

Output Field, Record, and List Separators

Part of Perl's built-in library is a set of global variables that can be used to modify Perl's behavior in many situations. You'll learn about many of these variables as this book progresses, or you can see the `perlvar` man page for a list of all of them.

Relevant to the discussion today are the output-field, output-record, and list-separator variables. These three global variables can be set to change the default way that Perl prints lists. Table 4.1 defines these variables.

TABLE 4.1 OUTPUT GLOBAL VARIABLES

Variable Name	*What It Does*
`$,`	Output field separator; the characters to print in between list elements. Empty by default.
`$\`	Output record separator; the characters to print at the end of a list. Empty by default.
`$"`	Same as the output field separator, except only for list variables interpolated inside strings. A single space by default.

As you learned in the section "Printing Lists," when you print a bare list, Perl will concatenate all the values in the list together:

```
print (1,2,3);  # prints "123";
```

In reality, Perl actually prints the elements of the list with the value of the output field separator between the elements and the output record separator at the end. Since both those variable are empty by default, you get the behavior shown above. You could set those variables to get different printing behavior:

```
$, = '*';
$\ = "\n";
print (1,2,3);  # prints "1*2*3\n"
```

The list field separator is the same as the output field separator, but only when you use a list variable inside a string. By default the list field separator contains a string—and that's the default printing behavior for list variables interpolated into strings. Change the list field separator to change the printing behavior for array and hash variables inside strings.

Void Context

In addition to list, scalar, and Boolean context, Perl also has a void context, which is defined as simply a place where Perl doesn't expect anything. You'll most likely see this in warnings and errors where you included something where Perl didn't expect it—"unexpected constant in void context," for example.

Summary

Today was list day. As you learned today, a list is just a bunch of scalars, separated by commas and surrounded by parentheses. Assign it to an array variable `@array`, and you can then get at the individual elements of that array using array access notation `$array[index]`. You also learned about finding the last index in the array (`$#array`), and the number of elements in the array (`$elements = @array`). We finished up that section with a couple of notes on list syntax and assignment, which allows you to assign variables to values in parallel in lists on either side of an assignment expression.

After arrays, we tackled context, which allows Perl to evaluate different things differently in either scalar or list context. You learned the three questions for figuring out context: what context is expected in an expression, what data have you given it, and what is that data supposed to do in that context.

4

Finally, we finished up with more information about simple input and output using lists. Tomorrow, we'll complete your basic list education by talking about hashes. (Actually, way up on Day 19, we'll get into more advanced data structures, so we're not completely done with lists yet, but lists, arrays, and hashes will get you quite a lot for your Perl repertoire.)

The built-in functions you learned about today (see the `perlfunc` man page or Appendix A for more details about these functions) include:

- `qw` takes a list of strings, separated by spaces, and returns a list of individual string elements. `qw` allows you to avoid typing a lot of quote marks and commas when you have a long list of strings to define.
- `defined` takes a variable or list location and returns true if that location has a value other than the undefined value.
- `undef` takes a variable or list location and assigns it to the undefined variable. With no arguments, `undef` simply returns the undefined variable, which means it can be used to refer to that value.

- `sort` takes a list as an argument and sorts that list in ASCII order, returning the sorted list. Sort in numeric order with the statement `{ $a <=> $b }` just before the list.
- `scalar` evaluates a list in a scalar context.

Q&A

Q What's the difference between the undefined value and `undef`?

A Not a whole lot. The undefined value is what gets put in variables or in array or hash value locations when there isn't an actual value—if you use one without initializing it, or if you add elements to an array past the boundaries of that array. If you want to explicitly use the undefined value, for example, to undefine a variable or to include that value in an array, you use the `undef` function. Because of the close relationship between the undefined value and `undef`, it's very common to see `undef` used to mean the undefined value (as in "the last three elements of that array are `undef`"). In real code, if you use `undef` anywhere you want an undefined value, you won't go wrong.

Q I want to create an array of arrays.

A You can't do that. Well, not right now. To create arrays of arrays, or arrays of hashes, or any kind of nested data structures, you need to use references. You won't learn about references for a while yet, so just sit tight for now. We'll cover references in Chapter 19.

Q Augh! I don't understand list and scalar context. If different operations can do different things, and there are no rules for how lists and scalars behave in each other's contexts, doesn't that mean I have to remember what every operation does for every context?

A Uh, well, yes. No. Well, kind of. If list versus scalar context is totally abhorrent to you, in any given script, you can usually avoid most of the more esoteric instances of context, remember how to use the few that are important (getting the length of an array, for example), and look up the rest when something doesn't work right.

If you end up having to read other people's Perl code, however, chances are good you'll end up needing to keep context in mind and watch out for sneaky contexts.

Q I want to find the number of elements in a list, so I did `"length @array..."`

A Hold it right there! The `length` function is a fine function—for strings and numbers. To find the number of elements in a list, you should be using the array variable in a scalar context: `$numelements = @array`.

Q How do I search an array for a specific element?

A One way would be to iterate over the array using a `foreach` or `while` loop, and test each element of that array in turn. Perl also has a function called `grep` (after the UNIX search command) that will do this for you. You'll learn more about `grep` on Day 8.

Workshop

The workshop provides quiz questions to help you solidify your understanding of the material covered and exercises to give you experience in using what you've learned. Try to understand the quiz and exercise answers before you go on to tomorrow's lesson.

Quiz

1. Define the differences between lists and arrays.
2. What does each of these variables refer to?

```
$foo
@foo
$foo[1]
@foo[1,2,3]
```

3. What's the result of this list:

```
@list = (1, (), (4, 3), $foo, ((), 10, 5 + 4), (), (''));
```

4. What are the results of the following Perl statements? Why does each expression evaluate to the result it does?

```
($x, $y, $z) = ('a', 'b');
($u, @more, $v) = (1 .. 10);
$nums[4] = (1, 2, 3);  # @nums previously contained (10,9,8)
undef $nums[4];
$nums[$#nums];
$foo = @nums;
@more = 4;
```

5. What's the rule for converting a list into a scalar?
6. How do you sort an array?
7. What's the difference between using `<STDIN>` in a scalar context and using it in a list context? Why is this important?

Exercises

1. Write a script that prompts the user for two numbers and then creates an array of numbers between the lower and higher bound (make sure the user can enter either the lower or higher number first).
2. Write a script that prompts you for two arrays and then creates a third array that contains only the elements present in the first two (the intersection of those arrays).
3. **BUG BUSTER:** What's wrong with this script? (Hint: there may be more than one error!)

```
print 'Enter list of numbers: ';
chomp($in = <STDIN>);
@nums = split(" ", $in);

@sorted = sort @nums;
print "Numbers: @sorted\n";

$totalnums = $#nums;
print "Total number of numbers: $totalnums\n";
```

Answers

Here are the answers to the workshop questions in the previous section.

Quiz Answers

1. A list is simply a collection of scalar elements. An array is an ordered list indexed by position.
2. The answers are:

   `$foo` is a scalar variable

   `@foo` is an array variable

   `$foo[1]` is the second element in the array `@foo`
3. The result of the list is: `(1, 4, 3, $foo, 10, 9, '')`. Actually, `$foo` will be expanded into whatever the value of `$foo` actually is.
4. The answers are:

   a. `$x` gets `'a'`, `$y` gets `'b'`, `$z` gets undefined. Assignment to lists on the left side happens in parallel, each value on the right assigned to each variable on the left.

b. `$u` gets 1, `@more` gets `(2,3,4,5,6,7,8,9,10)`, `$v` gets undefined. Array variables on the left side of a list assignment eat up all remaining values on the right.

c. `$nums[4]` gets 3. Assignment of list syntax to a scalar assigns only the last value in the list and ignores all the previous values.

   If the previous value of `@nums` was `(10,9,8)`, the new value of `@nums` is `(10,9,8,undef,3)`. Assigning a raw list to a scalar ignores all but the last value in the list.

d. `$nums[4]` will be set to the undefined value (it was previously 3).

e. `$nums[$#nums]` refers to the value at the last index in the list.

f. `$foo` gets the number of elements in the `@nums` array.

g. The 4 will be "promoted" to a list, and `@more` will be the list of one element: `(4)`.

5. Trick question! There is no rule for converting a list into a scalar. You can't even convert a list into a scalar. Lists behave differently in a scalar context depending on how you use them.

6. Sort an array using the sort function:

   ```
   @sorted = sort @array;
   ```

7. Using `<STDIN>` in a scalar context reads one line of input up until the user hits Return and stores it in a scalar variable. Using `<STDIN>` in a list context reads all the lines of input in the standard input up until end-of-file, and stores each line as a separate element in the list. The difference is important because it changes the way your program behaves and how you get input into that program.

4

Exercise Answers

1. Here's one answer:

   ```
   #!/usr/bin/perl -w

   $one = 0;
   $two = 0;

   print 'Enter a range boundary: ';
   chomp ($one = <STDIN>);
   print 'Enter the other range boundary: ';
   chomp ($two = <STDIN>);
   if ($one < $two) {
       @array = ($one .. $two);
   } else {
       @array = ($two .. $one);
   }
   ```

2. Here's one answer that makes use of `foreach` loops:

```
#!/usr/bin/perl -w

$in = '' ; # tempoary input
@array1 = (); # first arry
@array2 = (); # second arry
@final = ();  # intersection

print 'Enter the first array: ';
chomp($in = <STDIN>);
@array1 = split(' ', $in);
print 'Enter the second array: ';
chomp($in = <STDIN>);
@array2 = split(' ', $in);

foreach $el (@array1) {
    foreach $el2 (@array2) {
        if (defined $el2 && $el eq $el2) {
            $final[$#final+1] = $el;
            undef $el2;
            last;
        }
    }
}

print "@final\n";
```

Instead of the line that assigns `$el` to the last element in the array, you could also use the push function to do the same thing (which is a little easier to read):

```
push @final $el;
```

3. Trick question! There is only one error in the line where `$totalnums = $#nums`. The assumption here is that `$#nums` contains the total number of elements, which it doesn't (it contains the highest index, which is one less than the total number of elements). Use `$totalnums = @nums` instead, or `$totalnums = $#nums+1`.

WEEK 1

DAY 5

Working with Hashes

Arrays and lists provide a basic way of grouping together scalars, but they're pretty basic as far as data structures go. Perl provides a second form of list data (or a third, if you count raw lists) called hashes. In many situations—depending on the data you've got and what you want to do with it—hashes are better than arrays for storing and accessing data.

Today, then, we'll cover hashes. You'll learn all about:

- How hashes are different from arrays
- Defining hashes
- Accessing hash elements
- Hashes and context
- One more additional topic: using `split` to split a string into a list (or hash)

Hashes Versus Arrays and Lists

You learned yesterday that a list is a collection of scalars, and that an array is an ordered list, indexed by element. A hash is also a way of expressing a collection of data, but the way the data is stored is different.

A hash is an unordered collection of pairs of scalars, keys, and values, where the keys and the values can be any kind of scalar data (see Figure 5.1). You access an element (a value) in a hash by referring to the key. Neither the keys or the values are in any kind of order; you cannot refer to the first or last element in a hash, nor can you numerically iterate over the elements in that hash (although you can get a list of the hash's keys, of its values, or of both in pairs, and access all of the hash's elements that way by iterating over those values using a loop). Hashes are more useful than arrays in many ways, most typically because its easier to keep track of elements in named slots (keys in hashes) rather than by numbers (indexes in arrays).

FIGURE 5.1
Hashes.

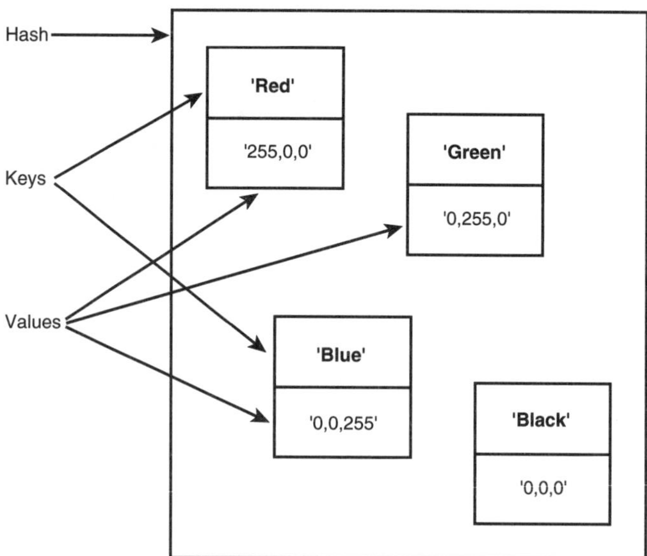

Note

Hashes are sometimes called associative arrays, which is actually a better description of what they do (the keys are associated with their values). In fact, associative arrays are the original name for hashes, but today's Perl programmers prefer to call them by the much shorter and less awkward name hash.

As with arrays, hashes have their own variables with their own symbol at the beginning. Hash variables start with a percent (`%`), and follow all the same rules as array variables do. As with all variables, the hash variable `%x` is a different thing than the array variable `@x` or the scalar variable `%x`.

Hashes

Arrays and hashes can be created and used in many of the same ways. Hashes, however, do have some peculiarities and extra features that result from the way data is stored in a hash. For example, when you put data into a hash, you'll have to keep track of two scalars for each element (the key and the value). And, because hashes are unordered, you'll have to do extra work to extract sorted values from the hash. In addition, hashes perform differently than arrays in a scalar context. Read on to learn about all these things.

List Syntax and Hashes

List syntax—enclosing the elements of a list inside parentheses, separated by commas—works to create a hash just as well as it does an array. All you have to do is list your values inside parentheses, and then stick a hash variable on the left side of the assignment, rather than array variable, like this:

```
%pairs = ('red', 255, 'green', 150, 'blue', 0);
```

With an array variable, this would end up being an array of six elements. With a hash variable (`%pairs`), the elements are added to hash in pairs, with the first element a key and the second its value, the third element the second key, and the fourth element its value, and so on down the line. If there are an odd number of values, the last value will be ignored.

With this kind of formatting, it's sort of difficult to figure out at a glance what parts of the list are the keys and which are the values. (It only gets worse the larger the list you're initializing the hash with.) Many Perl programmers format list syntax for hashes like this, with the keys and values on their own lines:

```
%temps = (
   'Boston', 32,
   'New York', 24,
   'Miami', 78,
   'Portland', 45,
    # and so on...
);
```

Even better than that formatting is the => operator, which behaves exactly the same way to the comma, but makes it easier to see the link between the keys and the values. So that first example up there with the colors would look like this:

```
%pairs = ('red'=>255, 'green'=>150, 'blue'=>0);
```

And the second, with the cities:

```
%temps = (
    'Boston' => 32,
    'New York' => 24,
    'Miami' => 78,
    'Portland' => 45,
     # and so on...
};
```

One other shortcut you can use for hashes: Perl expects the key part of each hash element to be a string. Because it has to be a string, Perl will let you leave off the quotes to save yourself some typing:

```
%pairs = (red=>255, green=>150, blue=>0);
```

If the key contains a space, however, you'll have to leave the quotes in place (Perl isn't *that* smart). As with lists, `()` assigned to a hash variable creates an empty hash:

```
%hash = ();  # no keys or values
```

Converting Between Arrays, Lists, and Hashes

A second way to create a hash is to use an array or a list for its initial elements. Because both hashes and arrays use lists as their raw form, you can copy them back and forth between each other with no problems:

```
@stuff = ('one', 1, 'two', 2);
%pairsostuff = @stuff;
```

In this example, assigning the array `@stuff` to the hash `$pairsostuff` causes the array elements to be expanded into a list, and then paired off into two key/value pairs in the hash. It behaves just the same as if you had typed all the elements in list syntax. Watch out for those odd-numbered elements, however; they'll be ignored in the final hash (Perl warnings will let you know if this is happening).

What about converting a hash back into a list? Here's an example where you're assigning a hash to an array:

```
@stuff = %pairsostuff;
```

When you put a hash on the right side of a list assignment, or in fact use it in any situation where a raw list is expected, Perl will "unwind" the hash into its component elements (key, value, key, value, and so on). The expanded list is then assigned to the array `@stuff`.

There is a catch to this nifty unwinding behavior: because hashes are not ordered, the key/value pairs you get out of a hash will not necessarily be in the same order you put them in, or in any kind of sorted order. Hash elements are stored in an internal format that makes them very fast to access, and are unwound in that internal order. If you must create a list from a hash in a certain order, you'll have to build a loop to extract them in a specific order (more about this later).

Accessing Hash Elements

To get at or assign a value to a hash, you need to know the name of the key. Unlike arrays, which just have bare values in a numeric order, hashes have key value pairs. Once you know the key, however you can then use curly brackets (`{}`) to refer to a hash value:

```
print $temps{'Portland'};
$temps{'Portland'} = 50;
```

Note that this syntax is similar to the array access syntax `$array[]`—you use an scalar variable `$` to get at a scalar value inside a hash, and curly brackets surrounding the key name, as opposed to brackets. The thing inside the brackets should be a string (here we used a single-quoted string), although Perl will convert numbers to strings for you. Also, if the key only contains a single word, you can leave off the quotes and Perl will know what you mean:

```
$temps{Portland} = 50; # same as $temps{'Portland');
```

5

As with arrays, the variable name in the hash access syntax doesn't interfere with scalar variables of the same name. All of the following refer to different things, even though the variable name is the same:

```
$name          # a scalar

@name          # an entire array

%name          # an entire hash

$name[$index]   # a scalar value contained in the array name at $index

$name{key}    # a scalar value contained in the hash name at the key 'key'
```

Also, as with arrays (sensing the trend, here?), you can assign values to individual hash elements using that same element-access syntax with an assignment statement. If you assign a value to a key that does not exist, that key/value pair is automatically created for you.

Deleting Hash Elements

With this element-access syntax, you can add, modify, and access any element of a hash. But what about getting rid of elements if you don't need them anymore? For that, Perl provides the `delete` function. This function takes a reference to a hash element (commonly just the hash access expression like `$hashname{'key'}`) and deletes both that key and value, returning the value that was deleted. So, for example, to move an element from one hash to another (deleting it from one hash and adding it to another), you could use syntax something like this:

```
$hash2{$key} = delete $hash{$key};
```

You can also test to see if a particular key/value pair exists in a hash using the `exists` function. The `exists` function tests to see if a given hash value exists in a hash and returns the value if it does (note that the value attached to that key could very well be undefined; `exists` only tests for the actual existence of that key). Use `exists` like this:

```
if (exists $hashname{$key})  { $hashname{$key}++; }
```

This particular statement tests to see if the value at the key `$key` exists, and if it does, it increments the value at that key (assuming, of course, that the value is a number).

Processing All the Values in a Hash

Say you wanted to loop over all the values in an array or list, testing each one for some feature and then doing something to that value if the test was true. To do this with an array, you'd start at element 0 and keep repeating the process until you get to the final element in the list (or use a `foreach` loop). But how do you do that for hashes? There's no order, and the keys can be made up of any kind of scalar value. What you need is a way of extracting some information out of the hash that you can then use to process that hash.

The most commonly used answer to this problem is one of two functions: `keys` and `values`. These functions both take a hash as an argument, and then return, respectively, a list of the keys in the hash, or a list of values in the hash. With that list, you use `foreach` or another loop to process each element of the hash without worrying about missing any.

So, for example, let's say you had a hash containing a list of temperatures indexed by city name (as we had in a previous example in this section) and you wanted to print a list of those cities and temperatures, in alphabetical order. You could use `keys` to get a list of all the keys, `sort` to sort those keys, and then a `foreach` loop to print the value of each of those keys, like this:

```
foreach $city (sort keys %temps) {
    print "$city: $temps{$city} degrees\n";
}
```

This loop works by working through the list of elements and assigning each one to the `$city` variable in turn (or any variable you pick). You can then use that variable in the body of the loop to refer to the current element.

Hashes and Context

Let's return to context and go over how hashes behave in the various contexts. For the most part, hashes behave just like lists, and the same rules apply, with a couple of wrinkles.

You've seen how to create a hash from list syntax, where the hash will match keys to pairs, like this:

```
%pairs = (red=>255, green=>150, blue=>0);
```

In the reverse case, where you use a hash where a list is expected, the hash will unwind back into its component parts (in some undetermined order), and then follows the same rules for any list.

```
@colors = %pairs;       # results in an array of all elements
($x, $y, $z) = %pairs; # first three elements of unwound hash assigned to
                         vars,
                        # remaining elements ignored
print %pairs;           # prints unwound hash elements concatenated together
```

5

In all these instances, if you use a hash in a list context—for example, on the right side of an assignment—then the hash will be "unwound" back into individual items, and then the list behaves as it does in any list or scalar context. The one peculiar case is this one:

```
$x = %pairs;
```

At first glance, this would seem to be the hash equivalent of the way to get the number of elements out of an array (`$x = @array`). However, Perl behaves differently with this one than it does with arrays—the result of `$x` will end up being a description of the internal state of the hash table, which in 99% of cases is probably not what you want. To get the number of elements (key/value pairs) in a hash, use the `keys` function and then assign it to a scalar variable instead:

```
$x = keys %pairs;
```

The `keys` function returns a list of the keys in the hash, which is then evaluated in a scalar context, and gives the number of elements.

Curious about just what I mean by "a description of the internal state of the hash?" OK, then. The result of assigning a hash variable in a scalar context gives you two numbers, separated by a slash. The second number is the amount of slots that have been allocated for the internal hash table (often called "buckets"), and the first number is the number of slots actually used by the data. You could use this to figure out how efficient a hash table is: A hash description of 4/100 would mean that the hash is using only 4 buckets out of the 100 allocated: bad news for the efficiency of your script. Later on in this book, on Day 19, "Working with References," we'll go over building advanced data structures so you can work around inefficiencies that may occur in Perl's built-in data structures.

An Example: Frequencies in the Statistics Program

Let's modify our statistics script again, this time to add a feature that keeps track of the number of times each number appears in the input data. We'll use this feature to print out a histogram of the frequencies of each bit of data. Here's an example of what that histogram will look like (other than the histogram, the output the script produces is the same as it was before, so I'm not going to duplicate that here):

```
Frequency of Values:
1  | *****
2  | *************
3  | *******************
4  | ****************
5  | ***********
6  | ****
43 | *
62 | *
```

To keep track of each number's frequency in our script, we use a hash, with the keys being the actual numbers in the data and the values being the number of times that number occurs. The histogram part then loops over that hash and prints out a graphical representation of the number of times the data occurs. Easy!

Listing 5.1 shows the Perl code for our new script.

LISTING 5.1 stillmorestats.pl

```
1: #!/usr/bin/perl -w
2:
3: $input = '';  # temporary input
4: @nums = ();   # array of numbers;
5: %freq = ();   # hash of number frequencies
6: $count = 0;   # count of numbers
7: $sum = 0;     # sum of numbers
8: $avg = 0;     # average
9: $med = 0;     # median
10: $maxspace = 0;# max space for histogram
11:
12: while () {
13:   print 'Enter a number: ';
14:   chomp ($input = <STDIN>);
15:   if ($input ne '') {
16:     $nums[$count] = $input;
17:     $freq{$input}++;
18:     $count++;
19:     $sum += $input;
20:    }
21:   else { last; }
22: }
23:
24: @nums = sort { $a <=> $b } @nums;
25: $avg = $sum / $count;
26: $med = $nums[$count /2];
27:
28: print "\nTotal count of numbers: $count\n";
29: print "Total sum of numbers: $sum\n";
30: print "Minimum number: $nums[0]\n";
31: print "Maximum number: $nums[$#nums]\n";
32: printf("Average (mean): %.2f\n", $avg);
33: print "Median: $med\n\n";
34: print "Frequency of Values:\n";
35:
36: $maxspace = (length $nums[$#nums]) + 1;
37:
38: foreach $key (sort { $a <=> $b } keys %freq) {
39:   print $key;
40:   print ' ' x ($maxspace - length $key);
41:   print '¦ ', '*' x $freq{$key}, "\n";
42: }
```

This script hasn't changed much from the previous one; the only changes are in lines 5, 10, 17, and the section at the end in lines 36 through 42. You might look over those lines now to see how they fit into the rest of the script that we've already written.

Lines 5 and 10 are easy; these are just new variables that we'll use later on in the script: the `%freq` hash, which will store the frequency of the data; and `$maxspace`, which will hold a temporary space variable for formatting the histogram (more about this when we go over how the histogram is built).

Line 17 is much more interesting. This line is inside the loop where we're reading the input; the line before this one is where we add the current input to the array of values. In line 17, what we're doing is looking up the input number as a key in the frequencies hash, and then incrementing the value referred to by that key by 1 (using the ++ operator).

The key is the number itself, and the value is the number of times that number appears in the data. If the number that was input doesn't yet appear in the hash, then this line will add it and increment the value to `1`. Each time after that, it then just keeps incrementing the frequency as the same number appears in the data.

At the end of the input loop, then, you'll end up with a hash that contains, as keys, all the unique values in the data set, and as values, the number of times each unique value appears. All that's left now is to print out a histogram of that data.

Instead of going over lines 36 through 42 line by line as I've done in past examples, I'd like to show you how I built this loop when I wrote the script itself, so you can see my thinking in how this loop came out. This will actually give you a better idea of why I did what I did.

My first pass at this loop was just an attempt to get the values to print in the right order. I started with a `foreach` loop not unlike the one I described in "Processing All the Values in a Hash" earlier in this lesson:

```
foreach $key (sort { $a <=> $b } keys %freq) {
  print "Key: $key Value: $freq{$key}\n";
}
```

In this loop, I use `foreach` to loop over each key in the hash. The order in which the elements are presented, however, is controlled by the list in parentheses on the first line. The `keys %freq` part extracts all the keys from the hash, `sort` sorts them (remember, `sort` by default sorts in ASCII order, adding `$a <=> $b` forces a numeric sort). This results in the hash being processed in order from lowest key to highest.

Inside the loop, then, all I have to do is print the keys and the values. For some simple data, then, I get output like this:

```
Key: 2 Value: 4
Key: 3 Value: 5
Key: 4 Value: 3
Key: 5 Value: 1
```

That's a good printout of the values of the %freq hash, but it's not a histogram. My second pass changes the print statement to use the fabulous string repetition operator (x) to print out the appropriate number of asterisks for the frequency of numbers:

```
foreach $key (sort { $a <=> $b } keys %freq) {
  print '$key ¦', '*' x $freq{$key}, "\n";
}
```

This is closer; it produces output like this:

```
2 ¦ ****
3 ¦ *****
4 ¦ ***
5 ¦ *
```

The problem comes when the input data is larger than 9. Depending on the number of characters in the key, the formatting of the histogram can get really screwed up. Here's what that the histogram looked like when I accidentally input a four-digit number in the middle of my 1 and 2 digit numbers:

```
2 ¦ ****
3 ¦ *****
4 ¦ ***
5 ¦ *
13 ¦ **
24 ¦ *
45 ¦ ***
2345 ¦ *
```

So the secret here is to make sure there are the appropriate number of spaces before the pipe character (|) to make sure the asterisks in the histogram line up. I did this with the length function, which returns the number of characters (bytes, actually) in a scalar value.

We start by finding out the maximum amount of space we'll need to allow for. I got that number from the largest value in the data set, and I added 1 to it to pad a space at the end:

```
$maxspace = (length $nums[$#nums]) + 1;
```

Then, inside the loop, we can modify the print statements to print the appropriate number of spaces (using the string repetition operator again) to pad out the smaller numbers to the largest number's width. After the padding I can then just go ahead and print the rest of the histogram:

```
foreach $key (sort { $a <=> $b } keys %freq) {
  print $key;                             # print the key
  print ' ' x ($maxspace - length $key);  # pad to largest width
  print '¦ ', '*' x $freq{$key}, "\n";    # print the stars
}
```

This last version of the histogram is the version I ended up with in Listing 5.1.

> The way I did the formatting here is kind of a hack, and I don't recommend this method for anything more substantial than the few characters we're dealing with in this example. Perl has a set of procedures specifically for formatting data (remember, it's the Practical Extraction and *Report* Language), with which it's much easier to construct formatted reports. In this age of HTML, Perl formatting isn't as commonaly used, but you get a taste of it in Day 20, "Odds and Ends" as we finish up this book.

Extracting Data into Arrays or Hashes Using the `split` Function

When you read input from the keyboard, often that data is in a convenient form so that you can just assign that value to a variable and then do whatever else you want to with it. But a lot of the input you'll deal with—particularly from files—is not often in a form that's so easy to process. What if the input you're getting has ten numbers per line? What if there's one part in the middle of the line you're interested in, but you don't care about the rest of it?

Usually, the input you get will be in some sort of raw form, and then it's your job to extract and save the things you're interested in. Fortunately, Perl makes this very easy. A built-in function, called `split`, takes a string as input and then splits it into a list for you.

You can split a string on any character or set of characters in your input data, or even on more sophisticated patterns. For today, however, we'll look at the easiest case: splitting a string into a list where whitespace (spaces or tabs) separates each element.

To call `split` in this way, use two arguments: a string of one character, and the string you want to split. The `split` function will return a list, so usually you'll want to assign the list to something (like an array). For example, here's Perl code to split the string of numbers in the first line into an array of numbers:

```
$stringofnums = '34 23 56 34 78 38 90';
@nums = split(' ', $stringofnums);
```

There! Now you've got an array of numbers (in `@nums`) that you can play around with to your heart's content.

Another Example: Alphabetical Lists of Names

To finish up this lesson, let's put together hashes and `split` into a simple example that reads a list of names, puts those names into a hash keyed by last name, and then prints out the list in alphabetical order, last name first. Here's an example of what it looks like:

```
Enter a name (first and last): Umberto Eco
Enter a name (first and last): Isaac Asimov
Enter a name (first and last): Fyodor Dostoyevski
Enter a name (first and last): Albert Camus
Enter a name (first and last): Bram Stoker
Enter a name (first and last): George Orwell
Enter a name (first and last):
Asimov, Isaac
Camus, Albert
Dostoyevski, Fyodor
Eco, Umberto
Orwell, George
Stoker, Bram
```

Listing 5.2 shows our short little script to read and adjust the data.

LISTING 5.2 THE `names.pl` SCRIPT

```
#!/usr/bin/perl -w

$in = '';       # temporary input
%names = ();    # hash of names
$fn = '';       # temp firstname
$ln = '';       # temp lastname

while () {
    print 'Enter a name (first and last): ';
    chomp($in = <STDIN>);
    if ($in ne '') {
        ($fn, $ln) = split(' ', $in);
        $names{$ln} = $fn;
    }
    else { last; }
}

foreach $lastname (sort keys %names) {
    print "$lastname, $names{$lastname}\n";
}
```

This script has three basic sections: initialize the variables, read in the data, and print it back out again. I'll skip the initialization part, since that should be obvious by now.

Lines 8 through 16 read in the data in a way that should look familiar from the statistics script, using a `while` loop, an `if` to test for an empty entry, and `<STDIN>` in a scalar context. Unlike `stats`, where we put the elements into an array, in line 12 we use `split` to separate the name input into two temporary scalar variables, `$fn` and `$ln`; and then in line 13, we add that first and last name pair to the `$names` hash, with the last name as the key.

With the hash all set up with the data, we can go ahead and print it. Again, you've seen this syntax before, most recently in the histogram example previously in this lesson. Here, we're sorting the keys in alphabetical order, so we can use the simpler form of sort here. And, finally, the `print` statement in line 18 uses the `$lastname` variable (which contains the current key) and the hash lookup for that key to print out the first and last names.

If you're puzzled by parts of this example—particularly the `sort` function or the loops, just try to understand the other parts and learn the loops by rote. Tomorrow, in Day 6, "Conditionals and Loops," you'll learn much more about `while` and `foreach` and be able to understand these examples a lot better.

Going Deeper

Hashes have a lot of similarities to arrays and lists, so there actually isn't that much deeper we need to go for this lesson. There is one other function for use with hashes that may be useful: `each`.

The `keys` function takes a hash as an argument and returns a list of the hash's keys. The `values` function does the same thing with the values in the hash. The `each` function does both: with a hash as an argument, it returns a list of two elements—the first a key and the second a value. Calling `each` multiple times works through all the hash's elements. As with all hash elements, the order of the pairs you get out of the hash are in some undetermined order. After all the elements have been exhausted, `each` returns an empty list `()`.

Summary

Today, we completed your background in list data with a discussion of hashes, which are similar to arrays and lists except that they arrange data into keys and values as opposed to simply storing elements in a numeric order. You learned about the hash variable `%hash`, and how to look up a value using hash access `$hash{'key'}`. You also learned how to delete keys from the hash, and how to process each element of a hash using a `foreach` loop and the `keys` function.

The built-in functions you learned about today include (see the `perlfunc` man page or Appendix A for more details about these functions):

- `exists` takes a hash key and returns true if the hash key exists (the corresponding value may be undefined (`undef`)).
- `delete` takes a hash key as an argument and deletes that key and value from the hash. Unlike `undef`, which undefines a value in a hash or an array but preserves the location, `delete` removes the key/value pair altogether.
- `keys` takes a hash and returns a list of all the keys in that hash.
- `values` takes a hash and returns a list of all the values in that hash.
- `split` with two string arguments splits the second string into a list of elements, where the character in the first string is the character to split on. With a third argument—a number—`split` will create only that number of elements.

Q&A

Q All these different variable characters! How can I keep them straight?

A The more you use them, the easier it'll be to remember which one is used where. If it helps, you can think of the scalar variable character `$` as a dollar sign—dollars are numbers and are scalar. The at sign (`@`) is a sort of A character—A stands for array. And the percent sign (`%`) for hashes has a slash with two dots—one dot for the key, and one for the value. In array and hash element accesses and slices, think of what you want the result of the expression to be: If you want a single element, use `$`. If you want a slice (a list), use `@`.

Q Hashes are just plain associative arrays, aren't they? They aren't actual hash tables?

A Hashes are indeed sometimes called associative arrays, and were called that in previous versions of Perl (the term *hashes* became popular because *associative arrays* was kind of unwieldy to say and too many characters to type. Or so Perl programmers thought). They're called *hashes*, as opposed to *keyed lists* or *associative arrays*, because internally they are indeed implemented as real hash tables and have all the speed advantages of a hash table over a more basic keyed collection, particularly for really huge collections.

Q All the examples you showed for hashes used a key to loop up a value. Is there any way to look up a key from a value?

A Nope. Well, there isn't a function to do it. You could use a `foreach` loop with the keys to a hash, and then test for the value you were looking for and get the key that way. But keep in mind that different keys can have the same value, so there isn't the same correspondence between a value and its key as there is the key to its value.

Workshop

The workshop provides quiz questions to help you solidify your understanding of the material covered and exercises to give you experience in using what you've learned. Try to understand the quiz and exercise answers before you go on to tomorrow's lesson.

Quiz

1. Define the differences between lists, arrays, and hashes.
2. What do each of these variables refer to?

```
$foo
@foo
%foo
$foo{'key'}
```

3. What are the results of the following Perl statements? Why does each expression evaluate to the result it does?

```
%stuff = qw(1 one 2 two 3 three 4 four);
@nums = %stuff
$foo = %stuff;
```

4. What happens if you use a hash in a list context? In a scalar context?
5. How do you sort a hash?
6. Define the differences between the `keys`, `values`, and `each` functions.
7. What's `split` good for?

Exercises

1. Modify stats so that the user can enter numbers all on one line.
2. Write a script that prompts you for a sentence, and tells you the number of characters in the sentence, the number of words, and prints the sentence in reverse word order (Hint: use the `length`, `split`, and `reverse` functions).

3. Modify the `names.pl` script to accept (and handle) names with middle names or initials (for example, Percy Bysshe Shelley or William S. Burroughs).

Answers

Here are the answers to the workshop questions in the previous section.

Quiz Answers

1. A list is just a collection of scalars; an array is an ordered list, indexed by position; and a hash is an unordered list of key/value pairs, indexed by the keys.
2. The answers are:

   `$foo` is a scalar variable

   `@foo` is an array variable

   `%foo` is a hash variable

   `$foo{'key'}` is a the value that matches `'key'` in the hash `%foo`.
3. The answers are:
   a. The `%stuff` hash gets four key/value pairs: `1/one`, `2/two`, `3/three`, and `4/four`. The `qw` function adds quotes around each element.
   b. `@nums` gets the unwound version of the key/value pairs in `%stuff` (key, value, key, value, and so on).
   c. `$foo` contains a code referring to the internal state of the hash.
4. Using a hash in a list context "unwinds" the hash into its component keys and values in some internal order. In a scalar context, the hash returns two numbers indicating the internal structure of the hash.
5. You can't sort a hash, because a hash is unordered. You can, however, sort its keys and then perform some operation on each key in the resulting list.
6. The `keys` function gives you a list of all the keys in the hash; the `values` function does the same thing with the values. The `each` function returns a list of a key/value pair in the hash; calling each multiple times eventually gives you all the elements in that hash.
7. `split` breaks a string up into two or more elements in a list. `split` is commonly used when the input you get isn't a single thing that can be assigned directly to a variable. Input from files is frequently in such a format.

Exercise Answers

1. The only difference between the old `stats.pl` program and the one for this exercise is in the input loop. Here's an example of how you might replace the first `while` loop with a call to `split`:

```
print 'Enter your numbers, all on one line, separated by spaces: ';
chomp ($input = <STDIN>);
@nums = split(' ', $input);
$count = @nums;
foreach $num (@nums) {
    $freq{$num}++;
    $sum += $num;
}
```

2. Here's one answer:

```
#!/usr/bin/perl -w
#
# phrase stats

$in = '' ; # tempoary input
@sent = (); # sentence
$words = 0; # num words
@reversed = 90; # reversed version

print 'Enter a sentence: ';
chomp($in = <STDIN>);
print 'Number of characters in the sentence: ';
print length $in;

@sent = split(' ', $in);
$words = @sent;
print "\nNumber of words in the sentence: $words\n";

@reversed = reverse @sent;
print "Reversed version: \n";
print "@reversed\n";
```

3. Here's one answer:

```
#!/usr/bin/perl -w

$in = '';       # temporary input
%names = ();    # hash of names
@raw = ();      # raw words
$fn = '';       # first name

while () {
    print 'Enter a name (first and last): ';
    chomp($in = <STDIN>);
    if ($in ne '') {
```

```
            @raw = split(' ', $in);
            if ($#raw == 1) {  # regular case
                $names{$raw[1]} = $raw[0];
            } else {  # build a first name
                $fn = '';
                $i = 0;
                while($i < $#raw) {
                    $fn .= $raw[$i++] . ' ';
                }
                $names{$raw[$#raw]} = $fn;
            }
        }
            else { last; }
}

foreach $lastname (sort keys %names) {
    print "$lastname, $names{$lastname}\n";
}
```

WEEK 1

DAY 6

Conditionals and Loops

You use conditionals and loops to control the execution of blocks of statements in your Perl script. Without these structures, your script would run from top to bottom, executing each statement in turn until it got to the end. No testing to see if a value is true and then branching to a different bit of code; no repeating the execution of a block of statements a number of times. Scripts would be very boring indeed without these constructs.

In this lesson, we'll go over the various conditional and loop constructs you have to work with, including

- An introduction to block statements
- The `if` and `if...else`, `if...elsif`, and `unless...` conditionals
- The `while`, `do...while`, and `until` loops
- The `for` and `foreach` loops
- Controlling loops with `next`, `last`, `redo`, and labels
- Using `$_` (the default variable) as a shortcut for many operations
- Reading input from files with `<>`

Complex Statements and Blocks

Conditionals and loops are sometimes called *complex statements*. That's because instead of being a single statement like `$x = 5` or `$array[5] = "fifth"` ending with a semicolon, conditionals and loops tend to be more, well, complex. Probably the biggest difference between simple and complex statements, however, is that the latter operate on chunks of Perl code called *blocks*.

A block is, simply, a group of any Perl statements surrounded by curly brackets ({}). Inside the block, you can include other statements, other blocks, or anything that can appear outside the block. As with statements in a script, too, the statements inside the block are executed in order. For example:

```
while (test) { # start of block
   statement;
   statement;
   if (test) { #start of if block
      statement;
   }
   # ... more statements
}
```

Blocks that are used outside the context of a conditional or a loop are called *bare blocks*, and the statements inside it execute only once. Bare blocks have several uses, particularly when they're labeled, but for now we'll focus on blocks that are attached to complex statements.

One other feature of blocks is that the last statement in the block doesn't require a semicolon. However, it's probably a good idea to get used to using it anyhow; if you add other statements to that block later on, Perl will complain that you forgot the semicolon.

Conditionals

Conditionals are used to execute different bits of code based on the value of a given test. If the test is true, a block of code is executed; if the test is false, either execution continues on to the next part of the script, or a different block of code is executed. Unlike loops, each block is executed only once.

`if`, `if...else`, and `if...elsif`

The most common form of conditional is the `if`, and its variant forms `if...else` and `if...elsif`. The `if` statement looks like this:

```
if ( test ) {
   # statements
}
```

The *test* is any expression, evaluated in a Boolean scalar context for its truth value. Remember that everything except `""`, `0`, and `undef` is considered true. If the *test* is true, the block is executed. If it's false, nothing happens and execution continues onto the next statement in the script.

Note that unlike in C or Java, the block after the *test* (and, in the next two forms, after the `else` and the `elsif`) is required, even if you only have one statement inside that block. You must always include the curly brackets. Note, however, that they don't have to be on different lines, as I showed here; you can format the brackets in any style you prefer.

To execute a different block if the *test* is false, use `if...else`:

```
if ( test ) {
   # statements to execute if test is true
} else {
   # statements to execute if test is false
}
```

A common operation in all languages with `if...else`-like constructs is that there are multiple nested `if`'s and multiple `else`'s, like this:

```
if ( test1 ) {
   # statements1
} else {
   if ( test2 ) {
      # statements2
   } else {
      if ( test3 ) {
         # statements 3
      } else {
         # and so on...
      }
```

To save a few keystrokes, or to avoid large amounts of indentation, Perl provides a third form of `if` conditional, the `elsif`, to compress these sorts of operations:

```
if ( test1) {
   # statements1
} elsif ( test2 ) {
   # statements2
} elsif ( test3 ) {
   # statements3
} else {
   # else statements
}
```

Note that if the test part of the first `elsif` evaluates to true, then the remaining `elsifs` are skipped (just as they would be if you had nested `if...else` statements).

6

What about switch or case statements? Perl doesn't have syntax for switch, per se (it's probably the only instance you'll find where Perl doesn't provide a syntax to do something you can do in another language). However, there are various ways to use existing Perl constructs to build switch-like constructs. We'll go over a couple of these in "Going Deeper," at the end of this lesson.

unless

The unless statement is sort of the reverse of an if. It came about because sometimes an operation is only supposed to occur if a test is false—which means in a standard if...else statement, all the good stuff would go into the else, like this:

```
if ( test ) {
   # do nothing
} else {
   # the good stuff
}
```

That's not really the most optimal way to look at an if. You could, of course, just negate the test, and then switch the blocks and leave off the else—and that's what you'd have to do, in other languages. This is a classic case of having to change your thinking to fit the syntax. Perl would prefer that you think the way you want to think, so it gives you alternative syntax. If you want to perform an operation based a test being false, just use unless instead:

```
unless ( test ) {
   # the good stuff
}
```

With the unless here, the statements inside the block are only evaluated if the test is false ("unless this is true, do that"). If it's true, execution happily moves onto the next statement. You can also add an else to an unless, if you like (but you can't have an elsif).

Conditional Operator ?...:

Some conditionals are so short that it seems silly to waste all those brackets and words on them. Sometimes, too, it makes sense to embed a conditional inside another expression (something you can't do with an if or an unless, since they don't return values). That's what the conditional operator does. Like if...else, it has a test, something to do if the test is true, and something to do if the test is false:

```
test ? true_thing : false_thing;
```

Here, the test is evaluated for truth, just as with an `if`, and if the test if is true, the *`true_thing`* expression is evaluated (and a value returned), otherwise, *`false_thing`* is evaluated and returned. Unlike `if` and `unless`, *`true_thing`* and *`false_thing`* are single expressions, not blocks. So, for example, a quick implementation of a `max` function (to find the maximum of two values) might look like this:

```
$max = $x > $y ? $x : $y;
```

This expression tests to see if the value of `$x` is larger than that of `$y`, and if so, it returns `$x`, and if the value of `$x` is less than or equal to `$y` it returns `$y`. The return value is then assigned to the `$max` variable. That same operation, as an `if...else`, would look like this:

```
if ($x > $y) {
   $max = $x;
} else {
   $max = $y;
}
```

The conditional operator is sometimes called the *ternary* operator, because it has three operands (unary operators have one, binary operators have two; therefore, a ternary operator has three).

Using Logical Operators as Conditionals

Back on Day 2, "Working with Strings and Numbers," you learned about Perl's logical operators `&&`, `||`, `and`, and `or`, and I mentioned at that time you can construct conditional statements with them. Let's re-examine those operators here so you can get a feel for how this works. Take the following expression:

```
$val = $this || $that;
```

To understand how this expression works, you have to remember two features of logical expressions: short-circuiting, and the fact that logicals return the value of the last thing they evaluated. So, in this case, the left side of the `||` is evaluated for its truth value. One of three things happens:

6

- If the value of `$this` is anything other than `0` or `""`, it's considered true. Because the `||` operator short-circuits, this means the entire expression exits without even looking at `$that`. It also returns the last thing it did evaluate—the value of `$this`, which then gets assigned to the variable `$val`.
- If the value of `$this` is `0` or `""`, it's considered false. Perl then evaluates `$that`, and if `$that` is true, then the expression exits with a truth value and returns the thing that it evaluated last—`$that`.

- If both `$this` and `$that` are false, the entire expression returns false, and `$val` gets a `0` or `""` value.

You could, of course, use the `or` operator in place of the `||`. Either one would work.

Using an `if...else` expression, you could write that expression like this:

```
if ($this) { $val = $this; }
else {$val = $that; }
```

Using a conditional operator, you could write it like this:

```
$val = $this ? $this : $that
```

But both of those take more space and are sort of complex to figure out—or at least more complex than the logical expression, which reads sort of like English: this or that. There, you're done.

As I mentioned on Day 2, probably the most common place you'll see logicals used as conditionals is when you open files, like this:

```
open(FILE, "filename) or die "Can't open\n";
```

But that's a topic for another day (Day 15, "Working with Files and I/O," to be exact).

`while` Loops

The various `if` statements in Perl are all used to control execution by branching to different parts of a script. The second way to control execution is through the use of a loop, where the same block of Perl statements are executed repeatedly, stopping only when some condition is met. Perl has two general sets of loops, both of which do roughly the same thing: `while` loops, which loop until a condition is met, and `for` loops, which loop a certain number of times. Generally, `while`s can be rewritten to emulate `for`s, and vice versa, but conceptually each one seems to lend itself to specific situations better than the other.

We'll start with the `while` loops, of which Perl has three: `while`, `do...while`, and `until`.

`while`

The basic form of the loop in Perl is the `while`, which takes a test and block, like this:

```
while ( test ) {
   # statements to loop
}
```

In the while loop, the test is evaluated, and if it's true, then the statements inside the block are executed. At the end of the block, the test is evaluated again, and if it's still true, then the block is executed again. This process repeats until the test returns false. For example, here's the while loop from the cookie script you saw on Day 1, "An Introduction to Perl":

```
while ( $cookie ne "cookie") {
  print "Give me a cookie: ";
  chomp($cookie = <STDIN>);
}
```

Here, the prompt and input will repeat until the input actually matches the string "cookie". You could read this statement as "while the value of $cookie doesn't equal the string 'cookie', do these things."

Here's another example from Day 4, "Working with Lists and Arrays," that loops through an array using an temporary variable $i as the array index:

```
$i = 0;
while ($i <= $#array) {
   print $array[$i++], "\n";
}
```

In this case, the test is whether $i is less than the largest index of the @nums array. Inside the block, we print the current array element, and increment $i such that the loop will only repeat a certain number of times: while $i is less than or equal to the largest index in @array, actually.

Remember as you write your while loops that something has to happen inside the loop to bring the state of the loop closer to exiting. If you forget to increment $i, $i will never reach a point where the test is true, and the loop will never exit.

Loops that don't exit are called infinite loops, and sometimes they're useful to use intentionally. A while loop without a test, for example, is an intentional infinite loop. You've seen these in a number of the examples we've done so far. This one's from the various statistics scripts:

```
while () {
  print "Enter a number: ";
  chomp ($input = <STDIN>);
  if ($input ne "") {
     # ... do stuff
   }
  else { last; }
}
```

This loop will read a line of input from the standard input at each pass of the loop and will never exit based on a test—there is no test. But we do test the input in an `if` conditional, and if the `$input` doesn't match our test (if it's not not-equal to the empty string), then the `last` keyword will forcibly break the loop and go onto the next part of the script. The last part is a form of loop control statement, and there are three of them: `last`, `next`, and `redo`. You'll learn about these later on in this chapter, in the section, "Controlling Loops."

I could have rewritten this loop such that the `while` had a real test, and exited at the appropriate time. For this particular type of example, I found it easier to construct it this way. Perl doesn't enforce a specific kind of mindset for creating loops or conditionals; you can construct your script in the best way based on how you see the problem.

`until`

Just as the reverse of an `if` is an `unless`, the reverse of a `while` is an `until`. `until` looks just like a `while`, with a test and a block:

```
until ( test ) {
   #  statements
}
```

The only difference is in the test—in a `while`, the loop executes as long as a test is true. In an `until`, it executes as long as the test is false—"until this test is true, do this stuff." Otherwise, they both behave the same.

`do`

A third form of `while` loop is called the `do`. With both `while` and `until`, the test is evaluated before the block is executed—so, actually, if the test ends up being false (or true for `unless`), then the block won't get executed and the loop might never do anything. Sometimes you want to execute some block of statements and then try the test afterwards. That's where `do` comes in. `do` loops are formed differently from `while` and `until` loops; unlike the former, they do require semicolons at the end of the statement. `do` loops look like this:

```
do {
   # block to loop
} while (test);
```

Or, with `until`, same idea:

```
do {
   # ...
} until (test);
```

With either of these statements, the statements inside the block are always executed before the test is evaluated. Even if the test returns false (for `while`) or true (for `until`), the block of statements will get executed at least once.

One important thing to note about the `do`: `do` in this case is actually a function call pretending to be a loop (that's why you need the semicolon). In most basic cases, it'll perform just like a loop, but if you want to use loop controls inside it (such as `last` or `next`), or include a label, you'll have to use either `while` or `until` instead. More about loop controls and labels later on, and you'll learn more about `do` on Day 13, "Scope, Modules, and Importing Code."

An Example: Pick a Number

In this example, we'll play a sort of game where Perl prompts you for a number, picks a random number between 1 and your number, and then has you try to guess which number it's picked, like this:

```
% picknum.pl
Enter top number: 50
Pick a number between 1 and 50: 25
Too high!
Pick a number between 1 and 50: 10
Too low!
Pick a number between 1 and 50: 17
Too high!
Pick a number between 1 and 50: 13
Too high!
Pick a number between 1 and 50: 12
Correct!
Congratulations!  It took you 5 guesses to pick the right number.
%
```

This script makes use of two infinite `while` loops and a number of `if` tests, as well as the `rand` function to pick the number. Listing 6.1 shows the voluminous code.

LISTING 6.1 THE `picknum.pl` SCRIPT

```
#!/usr/bin/perl -w

$top = 0;  # topmost number
$num = 0;  # random number
$count = 0; # number of guesses
$guess = ""; # actual guess

```

continues

LISTING 6.1 CONTINUED

```
8:  while () {
9:      print 'Enter top number: ';
10:     chomp($top = <STDIN>);
11:     if ($top == 0 || $top eq '0') {
12:         print "That's not a good number.\n";
13:     }
14:     else { last; }
15: }
16:
17: srand;
18: $num = int(rand $top) + 1;
19:
20: while () {
21:     print "Pick a number between 1 and $top: ";
22:     chomp($guess = <STDIN>);
23:     if ($guess == 0 || $guess eq '0') {
24:         print "That's not a good number.\n";
25:     } elsif ($guess < $num) {
26:         print "Too low!\n";
27:         $count++;
28:     } elsif ($guess > $num) {
29:         print "Too high!\n";
30:         $count++;
31:     } else {
32:         print "\a\aCorrect!  \n";
33:         $count++;
34:         last;
35:     }
36: }
37: print "Congratulations!  It took you $count guesses";
38: print " to pick the right number.\n";
```

We've got four parts to this script: initialization, picking the top number, picking the secret number, and then the guessing process. I'll skip the initialization this time around in the theory that you know how to assign scalar variables by now.

Lines 8 through 15 are the loop for picking the highest number the secret number could be. This is an infinite `while` loop, like you've seen before, but the test here in line 11 is to make sure you're actually entering a number greater than 0. Keep in mind that when Perl converts strings to numbers, if it can't find any numeric data in the string it converts that string to 0. So this test will catch both a 0 and any other non-numeric input that might get entered. (Although, given that we have warnings turned on for this example, entering a string at the prompt will produce complaints from Perl in addition to triggering the "not a number" warning. Once you learn about pattern matching, we'll see a better way of doing this that doesn't trigger warnings.)

At any rate, once we actually have a non-zero number, in lines 17 and 18 we generate the secret number between 0 and the top using the `srand` and `rand` built-in functions. The `srand` function, with no arguments, is used to seed the random-number generator with the current time, so that we'll get different numbers each time we run the script (otherwise it would be a very boring game indeed). The `rand` function generates a random number between 0 and an argument, here, our `$top`. We'll truncate that number to an integer, add 1 to it to make sure we don't have zeros and that occasionally a number will be the same as the top, and store that number in `$num` for safekeeping.

Lines 20 through 34 keep track of the guesses. Here we test for three things using nested `if...elsif` statements:

- To make sure the guess is a number greater than 0 (line 23), in which case we print a warning.
- To see if the guess is less than the secret number, in which case we print, "Too low!"
- To see if the guess is greater than the secret number, in which case we print, "Too high!"

If the guess is neither too low nor too high and is a valid number, then it must be the right number, so we beep twice (that's what the `\a` escape is for), and Perl prints a congratulatory message, and exits.

As the user is guessing the numbers, we also keep track of the number of guesses with a `$count` variable. We only want to count a guess if it's a valid number, however, so we only increment `$count` in the three valid number cases. `$count` then gets printed at the end as part of the congratulatory message.

Iteration with `for` Loops

`while` loops provide a general way to repeat a block of code—that block will just keep executing until some test is met. A second form of loop, the `for` loop, is a slightly different approach to the same problem. With `for` loops, the loop is executed a specific number of times, and then stops. This is sometimes called iteration, because of the focus on the number of loops as opposed to the more vague "loop until false" that the `while` provides.

In reality, you could write a `while` loop to do iteration, or a `for` loop to do the same thing as a `while`. But some tasks lend themselves better to one form or another, and so we have multiple kinds of loops.

Perl provides two `for` loops: a general C-like `for` loop, and a `foreach` loop, borrowed from shell scripting, that allows for a block to be repeated for each element in a list.

for

The `for` loop in Perl is the same as it is in C. Using an index or counter variable (commonly just called `$i` or `$j`), you start from some value, change the value of that variable some number of times, and then stop when a condition is met. With each turn of the loop, a block of statements is executed:

```
for ( init; test; change ) {
   # statements
}
```

In this syntax example, *`init`* is an expression to initialize the counter; the *`test`* is an expression for when to stop iterating, and *`change`* is an expression to change the counter for each pass of the loop. At the first pass of the loop, the counter is initialized, the test is tested, and if the test is true, the block is executed. At the second pass, the change expression is evaluated, the test is tested again, and if it's still false, the block is executed again. The loop continues on like that, with the change and the test for each pass, until the test is true.

So, for example, to loop five times you might use a `for` loop like this:

```
for ( $i = 1; $i <= 5; $i++) {
   print "loop $i\n";
}
```

The snippet of code produces this output:

```
loop 1
loop 2
loop 3
loop 4
loop 5
```

You could, of course, have written this loop as a `while`:

```
$i = 1;
while ($i <= 5) {
   print "loop $i\n";
   $i++;
}
```

The two loops would both loop five times, but it might take some searching in the `while` to figure that out. The `for` loop puts it all up front—where to start, where to stop, and the steps to take in between. Some problems work better this way—for example, working through all the elements in an array. A `while` loop would work just fine, but a `for` loop just seems more appropriate.

You can leave off the initialization, the test, the change, or all three, in the top part of the `for`. Don't forget to include the semicolons, however. So, to create an infinite `for` loop, you might do something like this:

```
for ($i = 0; ; $i++) {
   # statements
}
```

Or just this:

```
for (;;) {
   # statements
}
```

The first one initializes the counter and just increments it each time; the second doesn't even use a counter, it just loops. You'll need to do something inside these loops to break out of them when an appropriate condition is met.

Want to use multiple counters? You can do that, too, by separating the counter expressions with commas:

```
for ($i=0, $j=1; $i < 10, j$ < $total; $i++, $j++ ) {
   # statements
}
```

In this case, the `for` loop will exit if either of the tests returns false.

foreach

The `for` loop works best when you have a specific ending point that you can test for—for example, a topmost index in an array or a specific number. A shorthand version of `for`, `foreach`, doesn't need a numeric counter; `foreach` takes a list as an argument and performs a set of operations for as many elements as there are in the list.

You've already seen `foreach` as used to iterate over lists and over the keys in a hash. Here are the specifics of how it's used: The `foreach` loop takes a list as an argument—for example, a range, or a list of keys in a hash—and executes a block of statements for each element in the list. It also takes a temporary variable that gets assigned to each element in the list in turn.

Here's a simple equivalent of the `for` loop we did earlier that printed the number of the counter 5 times:

```
foreach $loop (1 .. 5) {
   print "loop $loop\n";
}
```

Here the range operator `..` creates a list of numbers 1 to 5, and the `foreach` loop works through that list, assigning each number to the `$loop` variable.

`foreach` loops work exceptionally well for iterating over actual lists, for example, to print out the keys and values of a hash, as you learned yesterday:

```
foreach $key (sort keys %hashname) {
   print "Key: $key Value: $hashname{$key}\n";
}
```

You'll note that I haven't initialized the `$key` variable here (or the `$loop` variable, earlier). That's because the variable after the `foreach` and before the list is a local variable to the loop—if it doesn't exist prior to the loop, it'll stop existing after the loop. If it does exist prior to the loop, the `foreach` will just use it as a temporary variable, and then restore its original value once you're done looping. You can think of the `foreach` variable as a sort of scratch variable used solely to store elements, and gets thrown away once the loop's done.

Controlling Loops

With both `while` and `for` loops, the tests at the top are there to stop the loop once some sort of condition has been reached. And, in many loops, it'll be the test that stops the loop. Once you start working with more complex loops, however, or play with infinite loops as I have in some of the previous examples we've looked at, chances are good there will be some point in the middle of a loop block where you might want to stop looping, stop executing, or somehow control the actual execution of the loop itself. That's where loop controls come in.

Loop controls are simple constructs that are used to change the flow of execution of a loop. You've already seen two of them: `next` and `last`, to restart the loop and to break out of it altogether. In addition, Perl also provides a `redo` control and labels for loops that control which loop to break out of with the other keywords.

Note

As I mentioned up in the section on the do loop, you cannot use any loop controls inside do loops, or label those loops. Rewrite the loop to use `while`, `until`, `for`, or `foreach` instead.

last, next, and redo

The `last`, `next`, and `redo` keywords are the simplest of loop controls; when one of these occurs inside a `while` or a `for`, Perl will interrupt the normal execution of the loop in some way.

You can use all three of these keywords by themselves, in which case they refer to the innermost loop, or they can be used with labels to refer to specific loops (more about labels later). Here's what happens with each keyword:

- `last` causes the loop to stop looping immediately (like `break` in C). Execution continues onto the next part of the script.
- `next` stops the execution of the current iteration of the loop, goes back to the top, and starts the next iteration with the test. It's like `continue` in C. The `next` keyword is a convenient way of skipping the code in the rest of the block if some condition was met.
- `redo` stops execution of the current loop iteration and goes back to the top again. The difference between `redo` and `next` is that `next` restarts the loop by reevaluating the test (and executing the increment, for `for` loops); `redo` just restarts the block from the top without evaluating or incrementing anything. You could think of it as the difference between restarting the current iteration or going on to the next one, which, actually, is exactly what it does.

So, for example, let's reexamine that `while` loop in the number picker game:

```
while () {
    print 'Enter the number you want to spell: ';
    chomp($num = <STDIN>);
    if ($num gt "9" ) { # test for strings
        print "No strings.  1 through 9 please..\n";
        next;
    }
    if ($num > 9) { # numbers w/more than 1 digit
        print "Too big. 1 through 9 please.\n";
        next;
    }
    if ($num < 0) { # negative numbers
        print "No negative numbers.  1 through 9 please.\n";
        next;
    }
    last;
}
```

6

Because the while loop in this example is an infinite loop, we have to use some sort of loop control expression to break out of it when some condition has been met—in this case, when a number that was actually a single-digit number was entered. In this block, the number entered is tested for three different conditions: if its a string, if it's greater than 9, or if it's a negative number. In each of those if statements, if the number meets that criteria, we use next to immediately skip over the rest of the code in the block and go back up to the top of the loop (if there was a test in that while loop, we'd have evaluated it again at that point). If the number entered ends up passing all three tests, then that number is acceptable and we can break out of the loop using last.

Loop controls are generally only necessary where you're checking for some condition that would interrupt the normal flow of the loop or, in this case, to break out of an infinite loop.

Labeling Loops

Loop controls, by themselves, exit out of the closest enclosing loop. Sometimes, however, you might have a situation with multiple nested loops, where some condition might occur that would cause you to want to exit out of multiple loops, or to jump around with multiple nested loops. For just this reason, you can label loops and then use last, next, and redo to jump to those outer loops.

Labels appear at the start of a loop, and are conventionally in all caps. This convention keeps them from getting confused with Perl keywords. Use a colon to separate the label name from the loop:

```
LABEL: while (test) {
   #...
}
```

Then, inside the loop, use last, next, or redo with the name of the label:

```
LABEL: while (test) {
   #...
   while (test2) {
      # ...
      if (test) {
         last LABEL;
      }
   }
}
```

The labels can be anything you want to call them, with two exceptions: BEGIN and END are reserved labels that are used for package construction and deconstruction. You won't learn about creating packages in this book, although you'll learn some about what a package is on Day 13. The perlmod man page provides further information on packages and modules if you're feeling like getting into advanced Perl concepts.

Here's a simple example without labels. The outer `while` loop tests to see if the variable `$exit` is not equal to the string `'n'`; the inner `while` loop is an infinite loop.

```
while ($exit ne 'n') {
   while () {
        print 'Enter the number: ';
        chomp($num = <STDIN>);
        if ($num eq '0' ) { # test for strings
            print "No strings.  0 through 9 please..\n";
            next;
        }
        # more tests
        last;
    }
    print 'Try another number (y/n)?: ';
    chomp ($exit = <STDIN>);
}
```

In this example, the `next` and the `last` command in that inner loop will exit the nearest enclosing loop—the infinite loop where you're entering the number. They will not exit out of the outer loop. The only thing that will exit the outer loop is if `$exit` gets set to `'n'` at the end of the outer loop (those last two lines prompt for the appropriate answer).

Say you wanted to add behavior to this simple script such that if you typed `exit` anywhere Perl would exit all the loops and end the script, you might label the outer loop like this:

```
OUTER: while ($exit ne 'n') {
   # etc.
}
```

Then, inside both the outer and inner loops, you'd use `last` with the name of the label, like this:

```
OUTER: while ($exit ne 'n') {
   while () {
        print 'Enter the number you want to spell: ';
        chomp($num = <STDIN>);
        if ($num eq "exit" ) { # quit!  exit!  gone!
           last OUTER;
        }
        # etc.
    }
 #  more...
}
```

6

In this case, if the user typed exit at the 'Enter the number' prompt, the last command breaks out all the way to the loop labeled OUTER which, in this case, is the outer loop.

Note that the label applies to the loop itself, and not to a specific position in the script (in fact, given a label jumps outside a loop, it actually goes to the next line past that labeled loop, not to the loop itself). Don't think of labeled loops as gotos (if you know what a goto is); think of them more as handles attached to the loop to which you can jump.

Using the $_ (Default) Variable

Congratulations! You now know (just about) everything you need to know about loops in Perl (and anything else you're curious about, you can find out in "Going Deeper.") Because we've got some space left in this lesson, I'm going to finish up with two general topics that we'll use quite a lot throughout the rest of this book: the special $_ variable, and the syntax for reading input from files on the Perl command line.

Let's start with the $_ variable. This is a special variable in Perl that you can think of as being a default placeholder for scalar values. Lots of different constructs in Perl will use the $_ if you don't give them a specific scalar variable to deal with; this has the advantage of making your scripts shorter and more efficient—but sometimes it can make them more confusing to read.

One use of the $_ variable is in foreach. Remember that the foreach loop takes a temporary variable in which each element of the list is stored. If you leave off that temporary variable, Perl will use $_ instead. Then, inside the body of the foreach, you can refer to $_ to get to that value:

```
foreach (sort keys %hash) {
   print "Key: $_ Value: $hash{$_}\n";
}
```

Many functions will also use the value of $_ if you don't give them any arguments—print and chomp being prime examples. So, for example, if you see what appears to be a bare print in someone's script, like this:

```
print;
```

Then mentally add the $_ on the end of it:

```
print $_;
```

We'll look more at the $_ variable in the next section and quite a lot more on Day 9, "Pattern Matching with Regular Expressions."

Input from Files with `while` Loops and <>

Over the last three days, you've seen a number of examples that read input from the keyboard using `<STDIN>`. You've also used the standard input file handle in both a scalar and list context, so at this point you should be doing pretty well at figuring out the difference between input in a scalar context (line by line) and input in a list context (read until end-of-file).

Getting input from the keyboard, however, is pretty tedious for any amount of input more than a few lines. That statistics script we worked on yesterday proves it—entering more than a couple of numbers into the script takes a long time, and if we want to just add to the existing data, we have to reenter all of it each time.

Ideally, then, we'd store the data in a separate file and then read it in each time the script executes. There are actually two ways to do this in Perl: one way is to open and read a specific file from inside your script. I've actually reserved an entire lesson for that, which you'll work through on Day 15. There is a quicker and easier way, however, to get data from any random file into your Perl script, which takes advantage of the Perl command line. That's the technique I'm going to teach you today.

The core of this technique involves the Perl input operator (<>). You've been using that operator with `<STDIN>` to get input from the keyboard using the `STDIN` file handle. When you use <> without a file handle, however, Perl will get its input from the files you specify on the command line. <> means, effectively, "take all the filenames specified on the command line, open them all, concatenate them all together, and then read them in as if they were one file."

> **Note**
>
> Technically, Perl gets the filenames to open and read from a special array called `@ARGV`, which contains the filenames or other values specified on the command line. You could, in fact, set the contents of @ARGV yourself. But for now, assume @ARGV contains, and <> operates on, the filenames from the command line. More about @ARGV on Day 15.

Here's an example that will read the input files indicated on the command line, line by line, and print each line in turn:

```
while (defined($input = <>)) {
   print "$input";
}
```

Say you saved that script in a file called `echofile.pl`. You'd then call it on the command line with the name of the file echo, like this:

```
% echofile.pl afile.txt
```

If you wanted to echo multiple files, just stick all the filenames on the command line:

```
% echofile.pl afile.txt anotherfile.txt filethree.txt
```

Perl will happily open all those files and read each one in turn.

> **Note** If you're using MacPerl, chances are good you don't have a command line and you're feeling somewhat confused. But fear not, you can do the same thing by saving your Perl script as a "droplet." There's a menu in the Save dialog that lets you do this (click on the Type menu to see it). Once you save your script as a droplet, you can then drag and drop your files on to your script icon, and MacPerl will launch and read those files into the script.

Let's look at that `while` loop from the inside out so you can figure out what's going on here. The `$in = <>` part will look familiar; that's similar to reading a line from `<STDIN>` in scalar context. And you may remember from yesterday that the `defined` function returns true or false whether or not its argument is defined (that is, doesn't contain the undefined value). Here, however, `defined` is used to halt the loop when we get to the end of the file—for each line we'll get a valid value up until the end of the file—then `<>` returns undefined, `$in` gets undefined as well, and that triggers the defined function to return false and the `while` loop to stop.

> **Note** Actually, you don't technically need the `defined` part. Perl will figure out where the end of the file is and stop reading automatically. If you have Perl warnings turned on, however, then it will complain that you haven't explicitly tested for the end of the file. You can avoid both the warnings and the call to `defined` using `$_` as your input variable.

Like `<STDIN>`, the empty angle brackets can be used in either a scalar or a list context. In scalar context, they will read the input files line-by-line (where the end of a line is a newline character, or a carriage return on the Mac); in a list context, each line of the file (or of multiple files) will be an element in the list.

An even shorter version of that `echofiles` script is one that takes advantage of the `$_` variable. You can use `$_` to replace the `$in` variable we used in this script, and then dispense with the temporary variable and the `defined` function altogether, like this:

```
while (<>) {
   print;
}
```

In this case, the `while` loop will read the input files line-by-line, setting the value of the `$_` variable to each line in turn, and stop when <> is undefined without you having to test for it or suffer with the warnings. You can actually use this mechanism with any input source: `<STDIN>` or a regular file handle, and it'll work.

Note, however, that it's the `while` loop that knows enough to assign each line to `$_` in turn and to test for the end of file—not the <> characters. You cannot, for example, do `chomp(<>)`; that function call will not save the current line into `$_`. Only the `while` loop will do that.

This mechanism for getting data into a Perl script is extremely common; in fact, many Perl scripts will have these loops right up at the top of the script to read the input files into an array or hash.

Here's another example of using <> and the `$_` variable in place of getting input from the standard input: yesterday, we worked through a script that prompted the user for a set of names, and then stored those names in array. The input loop for that script looked like this:

```
while () {
    print 'Enter a name (first and last): ';
    chomp($in = <STDIN>);
    if ($in ne "") {
        ($fn, $ln) = split(' ', $in);
        $names{$ln} = $fn;
    }
    else { last; }
}
```

To read those names from an input file, first we'll replace the prompt, the call to `<STDIN>` and the test for blank input:

```
while (defined($in = <>)) {
    chomp($in);
    ($fn, $ln) = split(" ", $in);
    $names{$ln} = $fn;
}
```

Then, we could shorten that further to use the default `$_` variable:

```
while (<>) {
    chomp;
    ($fn, $ln) = split(' ');
    $names{$ln} = $fn;
}
```

Here, the `$_` variable is used to store the input from the file in the `while` loop test; `chomp` uses it to remove the newline, and `split` uses it as well to have something to split. You'll find these sorts of shortcuts very common in Perl scripts.

We could shorten the split even further by leaving off the space argument; split assumes it will break the string in `$_` on whitespace without any arguments:

```
($fn, $ln) = split;
```

Going Deeper

As with the previous lessons, I still haven't told you everything you might want to know about conditionals and loops. In this section I'll summarize some of these other features. Feel free to explore these features of the Perl language on your own.

Conditional and Loop Modifiers

The conditionals and loops you learned about in today's lesson are all complex statements—they operate blocks of other statements, and don't require a semicolon at the end of the line. However, Perl also includes a set of modifiers to simple statements that can be used to form conditional and loop-like expressions. Sometimes these modifiers can provide shorter versions of simple conditionals and loops; other times they can help you express the logic of a statement you're trying to create in Perl that doesn't quite fit into the traditional conditionals or loops.

Each of the modifiers follows a simple statement, just before the semicolon. There are four of them, which mimic the more complex versions: `if`, `unless`, `while`, and `until`. Here are some examples:

```
print "$value" if ($value < 10);
$z = $x / $y if ($y > 0);
$i++ while ($i < 10);
print $value until ($value++ > $maxvalue)
```

In the conditional case, the front part of the statement will only execute if the test is true (or, with `unless`, if it's false). With the `while` and `until` loops, the statement will repeat until the test is false (or true, in the case of `until`).

Note that loops created with `while` and `until` modifiers are not the same as regular `while` and `until` loops; you cannot control them with loop control statements like `next` or `last`, nor can you label them.

The `do` loops you learned about earlier in this lesson are actually forms of loop modifiers. `do` is actually a function that executes a block of code, and you can use `while` and `until` to repeat that block of code some number of times based on a test (you'll learn more about `do` on Day 13). This is why you cannot use loop controls in `do` loops either.

Using `continue` Blocks

The `continue` block is an optional block of statements after a loop that gets executed if the block finished executing, or if the loop was interrupted using `next`. The `continue` block is not executed if the loop was interrupted using `last` or `redo`. After the `continue` block is executed, Perl continues on with the next iteration of the loop.

You might use a `continue` block to collect code that would otherwise be repeated for several different loop-exit situations, to change variables in those situations, or do some kind of cleaning up from an error that resulted in the loop exiting in the first place. It looks like this (where the `while` loop here could be a `for` or a `foreach`; any loop will do):

```
while ( test ) {
   # statements
   if (anothertest) {
      # error!
      next;  # skip down to continue
   }
   # more staements
} continue {
   # cleaup code from error
   # after this is done, go back to top of loop
}
```

Note Note that `continue` in Perl is not the same as `continue` in C; the latter is called next in Perl.

Constructing switch or case Statements

Perl, remarkably, does not have syntax for an explicit `switch` statement. A *switch*, sometimes known as a `case` depending on your favorite language, is a construct that lets you test a value and get a result in a much more compact, often more efficient, and easier-to-read manner than a whole lot of nested `if`s. That whole section of the numberspeller script that matched numbers to strings would have worked a whole lot better as a switch.

However, with labeled blocks, `do` loops, and logical expressions, you can build something that looks at least a little bit like a switch. Add pattern matching to it, and you get a Perl-like `switch` that works pretty well (I'll come back to switches tomorrow after you've learned about pattern matching).

For example, here's a simple switch-like thing in Perl:

```
SWITCH: {
   $a eq "one" && do {
                       $a = 1;
                       last SWITCH;
                     };
   $a eq "two" && do {
                       $a = 2;
                       last SWITCH;
                     };
   $a eq "three" && do {
                       $a = 3;
                       last SWITCH;
                       };
# and so on
}
```

On Day 9, you'll learn a way to make that even shorter with patterns.

goto

Yes, Perl does support the much-maligned `goto`. You can use `goto` in one of three ways:

- `goto label`, where label is a labeled position somewhere in your script.
- `goto expression`, where the expression will result in a label to be determined dynamically.
- `goto &name`, which isn't really a `goto`; it's used for performing magic during the autoloading of subroutines in packages.

See the `perlsyn` man page for further details on `goto`.

Summary

Conditionals and loops are the switches and dials of your Perl script. Without them, you can get stuff done, but it'll be the same stuff each time and your script will turn out pretty dull. Conditionals and loops allow you to make decisions and change what your script does based on different input or different situations. They're so important you had to actually start learning about them two days ago in the examples before we even got to this lesson.

Conditional statements are those that branch to different blocks of Perl code depending on whether a test is true or false. You learned about the `if`, the `if...else`, and the `if...elsif` constructs for building conditionals, as well as the conditional operator `?..:`, which can be nested in other expressions, and the use of the logical operators (`&&`, `||`, `and`, and `or`) as conditionals.

Next, we moved onto loops: specifically the `while` loops, which repeat a block of statements an unidentified number of times based on a test. There are three loops we covered here: `while`, `until`, `do...while`, and `do...until`.

The second kind of loop is the `for` loop, which also repeats a block of statements, but emphasizes the number of times aspect of the loop much more. You learned about the `for` loop, with its C-like counter syntax, and the `foreach` loop for working through elements in a list.

You then learned about loop controls, which allow you to stop executing a block and skip to some part of a loop: `next`, `last`, and `redo`, as well as using labels to control jumping around inside nested loops.

And finally, we ended this lesson as we did the previous two: with more notes about input, including using the <> syntax to read from files and using the `$_` variable as a shortcut in many popular operations.

After this lesson, the learned the core of the Perl language, and we'll explore some longer examples tomorrow to finish up the week. But don't stop now—next week's lessons will introduce you to some of the most powerful and exciting features of Perl, including various ways of processing lists and pattern matching.

The functions you learned about in this lesson include

- `do`, a function that behaves like loop with a `while` or `until` at the end of it.
- `rand` generates a random number between 0 and its argument.
- `srand` seeds the random number generator used by rand. Without an argument, `srand` uses the time as the seed.

Q&A

Q It seems to me that `for` loops could be written as `while` loops, and vice versa.

A Yup, they sure could. If you wanted to strip all the constructs out of Perl that duplicate the behavior of other constructs, this could be one place where either one or the other would work. But there are just some problems that are more easily thought of as number-of-times loops, as opposed to repeat-until-done loops. And being able to code the way you think is one of Perl's best features. Besides, even C and Java, which are both relatively small languages, have both a `while` and a `for`.

Q I tried to use `continue` to break out of a loop, and Perl spewed errors at me. What did I do wrong?

A You forgot that `continue` isn't used to break out of a loop in Perl (or you skipped that section). The equivalent of `continue` in Perl is `next`. Use `continue` as an optional block of statements to execute at the end of a block (see "Going Deeper").

Q I looked at your two examples of reading input from files, one that uses `$_` and one that doesn't. The former one is shorter, yes, but it's really hard to figure out what's going on if you don't know which operations are using `$_`. I think it's worth a few extra characters if a script is more readable that way.

A That's definitely one philosophy to follow, and there are many Perl programmers that follow that philosophy. And using the `$_` variable willy-nilly to shorten a script can definitely make it much harder to read. But in some cases—reading input from `<>` being one of them—the use of `$_` provides a common idiom in the language that once you get used to seems reasonable and easy to understand. If you have to read or modify other people's Perl scripts, chances are good you'll run into mysterious `$_` behavior at some point.

Be aware of `$_`, use it where it's most appropriate, or avoid it if you feel it hurts readability. That's your choice.

Workshop

The workshop provides quiz questions to help you solidify your understanding of the material covered and exercises to give you experience in using what you've learned. Try to understand the quiz and exercise answers before you go on to tomorrow's lesson.

Quiz

1. What is a block? What can you put inside a block?
2. What's the difference between an `if` and an `unless`?

3. What makes a `while` loop stop looping?
4. Why are `do` loops different from `while` or `until` loops?
5. What are the three parts of the part of the `for` loop in parentheses, and what do they do?
6. Define the differences between `next`, `last`, and `redo`.
7. Name three situations in which the `$_` variable can be used.
8. How does <> differ from `<STDIN>`?

Exercises

1. Write a script that prompts you for two numbers. Test to make sure that neither number is negative, and that the second is not zero. If both numbers meet each of those requirements, divide the first by the second and print the result.
2. **BUG BUSTER:** What's wrong with this script (Hint: there may be more than one error)?

```
if ($val == 4) then { print $val; }
elseif ($val > 4) { print "more than 4"; }
```

3. **BUG BUSTER:** What's wrong with this script (Hint: there may be more than one error)?

```
for ($i = 0, $i < $max, $i++) {
   $vals[$i] = "";
}
```

4. **BUG BUSTER:** How about this one?

```
while ($i < $max) {
   $vals[$i] = 0;
}
```

5. Rewrite the `names.pl` script to read from a file of names (actually, if you did the exercise yesterday to modify `names.pl` to handle middle names, rewrite that one instead).

Answers

Here are the answers to the workshop questions in the previous section.

Quiz Answers

1. A block is a group of other Perl statements (which can include other blocks) surrounded by curly brackets ({}). Blocks are most commonly used in conjunction with conditionals and loops, but can also be used on their own (bare blocks).

2. The difference between an if and an unless is in the test: an if statement executes its block if the test returns true; unless executes a block if the test returns false.
3. The while loop stops looping when its test returns false.
4. do loops are different from while or until loops in several ways. First, their blocks are executed before their tests, which allows you to execute statements at least once (for while and until, the block may not execute at all). Secondly, because the do loop is not actually really a loop (it's a function with a modifier), you cannot use loop controls inside it like last or next.
5. The three parts of the for loop in parentheses are:
   - A loop counter initialization expression such as $i = 0;
   - A test to determine how many times the loop will iterate, for example $i < $max.
   - An increment expression to bring the loop counter closer to the test, for example, $i++.
6. next, last, and redo are all loop control expressions. next will stop executing the current block and start the loop at the top, including executing the test in a for or a while loop. redo is the same as next, except it restarts the block from the first statement in that block without executing the loop control test. last exits the loop altogether without retesting or reexecuting anything.
7. Here's a number of situations that default to the $_ if a variable isn't indicated:
   - while (<>) will read each line into $_ separately.
   - chomp will remove the newline from $_;
   - print will print $_
   - foreach will use $_ as the temporary variable
8. <> is used to input the contents of files specified on the command line (and as stored in @ARGV). <STDIN> is used to input data from standard input (usually the keyboard).

Exercise Answers

1. Here's one answer:

```
#!/usr/bin/perl -w

$num1 = 0;
$num2 = 0;
```

```
while () {
    print 'Enter a number: ';
    chomp($num1 = <STDIN>);
    print 'Enter another number: ';
    chomp($num2 = <STDIN>);

    if ($num1 < 0 || $num2 < 0) {
        print "No negative numbers!\n";
        next;
    } elsif ( $num2 == 0) {
        print "Second number cannot be 0!\n";
        next;
    } else { last; }
}

print "The result of dividing $num1 by $num2 is ";
printf("%.2f\n", $num1 / $num2 );
```

2. There's only one error: `elseif` is not a valid Perl keyword; use `elsif` instead.
3. The expressions inside the `for` control expression should be separated with semi-colons, not commas.
4. Syntactically, that loop is correct, but there's no way it'll ever exit—there's no increment for `$i` inside the body of the loop.
5. Here's one answer:

```
#!/usr/bin/perl -w

%names = ();    # hash of names
@raw = ();      # raw words
$fn = "";       # first name

while (<>) {
    chomp;
    @raw = split(" ", $_);
    if ($#raw == 1) {  # regular case
        $names{$raw[1]} = $raw[0];
    } else {  # build a first name
        $fn = "";
        for ($i = 0; $i < $#raw; $i++) {
            $fn .= $raw[$i] . " ";
        }
        $names{$raw[$#raw]} = $fn;
    }
}

foreach $lastname (sort keys %names) {
    print "$lastname, $names{$lastname}\n";
}
```

DAY 7

Exploring a Few Longer Examples

To finish up the week, let's take this day to explore some more examples that make use of the techniques you've learned so far. We won't spend a lot of time on background in this lesson, nor will you have any quizzes or exercises to work through at the end. Consider this a brief pause to look at more bits of code in further detail. We'll have three of these example lessons, one after each six or so lessons, to cement what you've learned.

Today we'll look at three Perl scripts:

- A new version of `stats.pl` with a more complex histogram
- A script to spell numbers
- A script to convert text files into simple Web pages

Statistics with a Better Histogram

Here's yet another version of the statistics program we've been working with throughout the last week. Day 5's version of the statistics program included a horizontal histogram that looked like this:

```
Frequency of Values:
1    | *****
2    | *************
3    | *******************
4    | ****************
5    | ***********
6    | ****
43   | *
62   | *
```

For this version, we'll print a vertical histogram that looks like this:

```
        *
        *
        *
        *
        *
        *  *
        *  *  *
        *  *  *           *     *     *
        *  *  *     *  *  *     *     *
     *  *  *  *     *  *  *     *     *
     *  *  *  *     *  *  *     *     *
  *  *  *  *  *  *  *  *  *     *     *  *
  *  *  *  *  *  *  *  *  *  *  *  *  *  *  *  *
-------------------------------------------------
  1  2  3  4  5  6  7  8  9 12 23 25 34 37 39 42
```

This form of histogram is actually much harder to produce than a horizontal histogram; this version uses two nested `for` loops and some careful counting for it to come out the right way.

There's one other change to this version of `stats.pl`: it gets its data from a file, rather than making you enter in all the data at a prompt. As with all the scripts that read data from a file, you need to specify a data file for this script to use on the command line, as follows:

```
% statsfinal.pl data.txt
```

The data file, here called `data.txt`, has each of the numbers on individual lines. First, let's look closely at the two parts of this script that are different from the last version: the part that reads in the data file, and the part that prints the histogram.

Listing 7.1 shows the script for our final statistics script. Given how much we've been working with this script up to this point, it should look familiar to you. The parts to concentrate on are the input loop in lines 14 through 21, and the code to generate the new histogram in lines 36 through 49.

LISTING 7.1 THE `statsfinal.pl` SCRIPT

```
1:  #!/usr/bin/perl -w
2:
3:  $input = "";  # temporary input
4:  @nums = ();   # array of numbers;
5:  %freq = ();   # hash of number frequencies
6:  $maxfreq = 0; # maximum frequency
7:  $count = 0;   # count of numbers
8:  $sum = 0;     # sum of numbers
9:  $avg = 0;     # average
10: $med = 0;     # median
11: @keys = ();   # temp keys
12: $totalspace = 0; # total space across histogram
13:
14: while (defined ($input = <>)) {
15:     chomp ($input);
16:     $nums[$count] = $input;
17:     $freq{$input}++;
18:     if ($maxfreq < $freq{$input}) { $maxfreq = $freq{$input} }
19:     $count++;
20:     $sum += $input;
21: }
22: @nums = sort { $a <=> $b } @nums;
23:
24: $avg = $sum / $count;
25: $med = $nums[$count /2];
26:
27: print "\nTotal count of numbers: $count\n";
28: print "Total sum of numbers: $sum\n";
29: print "Minimum number: $nums[0]\n";
30: print "Maximum number: $nums[$#nums]\n";
31: printf("Average (mean): %.2f\n", $avg);
32: print "Median: $med\n\n";
33:
34: @keys = sort { $a <=> $b } keys %freq;
35:
36: for ($i = $maxfreq; $i > 0; $i--) {
37:     foreach $num (@keys) {
38:         $space = (length $num);
39:         if ($freq{$num} >= $i) {
40:             print( (" " x $space) . "*");
```

continues

LISTING 7.1 CONTINUED

```
41:         } else {
42:             print " " x (($space) + 1);
43:         }
44:         if ($i == $maxfreq) { $totalspace += $space + 1; }
45:     }
46:     print "\n";
47: }
48: print "-" x $totalspace;
49: print "\n @keys\n";
```

Because you've seen the boilerplate code for reading data from files using <>, nothing in lines 14 through 21 should be too much of a surprise. Note that we read each line (that is, each number) into the `$input` variable, and then use that value throughout the block.

Why not use `$_`? We could have done that here, but a lot of the statements in this block need an actual variable reference (they don't default to `$_`). Using `$_` for that reference would have made things only slightly smaller, but would have decreased the readability of the example, and in this case, it was a better idea to err on the side of readability.

A point to remember throughout this book as I explain more and more strange and obscure bits of Perl—just because Perl uses a particular feature doesn't mean you have to use it. Consider the tradeoffs between creating very small code that no one except a Perl wizard can decipher, versus longer, maybe less efficient, but more readable code. Consider it particularly well done if someone else can read your Perl code further down the line.

Anyhow, other than reading the input from a file instead of standard input, much of the `while` block is the same as it was in yesterday's version of this script. The one other difference is the addition in line 18 to calculate the `$maxfreq` value. This value is the maximum frequency of any number—that is, the number of times the most frequent number appears in the data set. We'll use this value later on to determine the overall height of the histogram. Here, all we do is compare the current maximum frequency to the current frequency, and change `$maxfreq` if the new one is larger.

Further down in the script, after we've sorted and summed and printed, we get to the histogram part of the script, in the daunting set of loops in lines 36 through 49.

Building a horizontal histogram like we did yesterday is much easier than building one vertically. With the horizontal histogram, you can just loop through the keys in the `%freq` hash and print out the appropriate number of asterisks (plus some minor formatting). For the vertical histogram, we need to keep track of the overall layout much more closely, as each line we draw doesn't have any direct relationship to any specific key or value in the hash. Also, we still must keep track of the spaces for formatting.

We'll keep track of the histogram using two loops. The outer loop, a `for` loop, controls the number of lines to print; that is, the overall height from top to bottom. The second loop is a `foreach` loop that moves from left to right within each line, printing either an asterisk or a space. With two nested loops (the `for` and the `foreach`), we can go from left to right and line to line, with both the height and the width of the histogram determined by the actual values in the data.

First, we extract a sorted list of keys out the `%freq` hash in line 34. This is mostly for convenience and to make the `for` loops coming up at least a little less complex.

Line 36 starts our outer `for` loop. The overall height of the histogram is determined by the most frequent value in the data set. Here's where we make use of that `$maxfreq` variable we calculated when the data is read in. This outer `for` loop starts at the maximum frequency and works down to 0, printing as many lines as it takes.

The inner loop prints each line, looping over the values in the data set (the keys from the `%freq` data set). For each line, we print either a space or a *, depending on whether or not the given value's frequency should start showing up on the current line. We also keep track of formatting, to add more space for those values that have multiple digits (the spacing for a value of 333 will be different than that for 1).

Line by line, starting at line 38 here's what we're doing:

- In line 38, we calculate the space this column will need, based on the number of digits in the current value.
- Lines 39 and 40 print a `*` if the `*` is warranted. The test here is to see if the current value we're looking at is as frequent as our vertical position in the histogram (frequency greater or equal to the current value of `$i`). This way, at the start of the histogram we'll get fewer asterisks, and as we progress downward and `$i` gets lower, more values will need asterisks. Note that the `print` statement in line 40 prints both the asterisk and enough spaces to space it out to the correct width.
- If there's no * to be printed in this line, we print the right amount of filler space: space for the column, plus one extra.

- Line 44 is a puzzler. What's this here for? This line is here to calculate the total width of the histogram, overall, based on the lengths of all the digits in the data set with spaces in between them all. We'll need this in line 48 when we print a divider line, but since we're already in the midst of a loop here, I figured I'd get this calculation now instead of waiting until then. What this loop does is if `$i` is equal to `$maxfreq`—that is, if we're on the very first line of the outer `for` loop—the loop adds the current amount of space to the `$totalspace` variable to get the maximum width.
- And finally, in line 46, when we're done with a line of data, we print a newline to restart the next line at the appropriate spot.

With the columns of the histogram printed, all we've got left are the labels on the bottom. Here we'll print an appropriate number of hyphens to mimic a horizontal line (using the value we calculated for `$totalspace`), and then print the set of keys, interpolated inside a string, which prints all the elements in `@keys` with spaces between them.

Complicated nested loops such as this are particularly hard to follow, and sometimes a description like the one I just gave you isn't enough. If you're still really bewildered about how this example worked, consider working through it step by step, loop by loop, making sure you understand the current values of all the variables and how they relate to each other.

A Number Speller

This second example isn't particularly useful for the real world, but does show some more complex uses of `if`s, `while`s, and various tests. This script asks you to enter a single-digit number (and has the usual verification tests to make sure you have indeed entered a single-digit number), and then it spells out that number for you—in other words, 2 is two, 5 is five, and so on. Then it asks you if you want to enter another number, and if so, it repeats the process. Here's an example:

```
% numspeller.pl
Enter the number you want to spell: foo
No strings.  0 through 9 please..
Enter the number you want to spell: 45
Too big. 0 through 9 please.
Enter the number you want to spell: 6
Number 6 is six
Try another number (y/n)?: foo
y or n, please
Try another number (y/n)?: y
Enter the number you want to spell: 3
Number 3 is three
Try another number (y/n)?: n
```

Listing 7.2 shows the full code.

LISTING 7.2 THE `numspeller.pl` SCRIPT

```
#!/usr/bin/perl -w
# numberspeller:  prints out word approximations of numbers
# simple version, only does single-digits

$num = 0;     # raw number
$exit = "";  # whether or not to exit the program.

while ($exit ne "n") {

    while () {
        print 'Enter the number you want to spell: ';
        chomp($num = <STDIN>);
        if ($num gt "9" ) { # test for strings
            print "No strings.  0 through 9 please..\n";
            next;
        }
        if ($num > 9) { # numbers w/more than 1 digit
            print "Too big. 0 through 9 please.\n";
            next;
        }
        if ($num < 0) { # negative numbers
            print "No negative numbers.  0 through 9 please.\n";
            next;
        }
        last;
    }

    print "Number $num is ";
    if ($num == 1) { print 'one'; }
    elsif ($num == 2) { print 'two'; }
    elsif ($num == 3) { print 'three'; }
    elsif ($num == 4) { print 'four'; }
    elsif ($num == 5) { print 'five'; }
    elsif ($num == 6) { print 'six'; }
    elsif ($num == 7) { print 'seven'; }
    elsif ($num == 8) { print 'eight'; }
    elsif ($num == 9) { print 'nine'; }
    elsif ($num == 0) { print 'zero'; }
    print "\n";

```

continues

LISTING 7.2 CONTINUED

```
41:     while () {
42:         print 'Try another number (y/n)?: ';
43:         chomp ($exit = <STDIN>);
44:         $exit = lc $exit;
45:         if ($exit ne 'y' && $exit ne 'n') {
46:             print "y or n, please\n";
47:         }
48:         else { last; }
49:     }
50: }
```

`While`s within `while`s, and `if`s after `if`s. Let's start from the outer loop, and work inward. The first `while` loop, in line 8, includes the bulk of the entire script in its block. That's because the entire script will repeat, or not, based on the yes/no prompt at the end. At the start, however, we need to run it at least once, so the test in line 8 will return true (note that we carefully initialized the `$exit` variable so that it would).

The second `while` loop, lines 10 through 26, tests our input through the use of three `if`s. The first one checks to make sure you haven't typed any strings (any characters greater than 9 in the ASCII character set are strings); the second one makes sure you haven't typed a number greater than 9 (this version of the script only tests for single-digit numbers); and the third tests for negative numbers. If any of these three tests are true, we use the `next` keyword, which skips the rest of the block and goes back up to the test for the nearest enclosing loop—which in this case is still that infinite `while` loop that started in 10. If the input meets all three criteria—it's not a string, and it's in between 0 and 9, then we call `last`, which breaks out of the nearest `while` loop and goes onto the next statement in the block.

That next statement is line 28, where we print the introductory message and then jump right into a set of nested `if`s that connect the actual numbers to the strings that they match. This section (lines 29 through 38) would be a prime candidate for a `switch` statement, if for no other reason than to cut down on all that repetitive typing (thank the programmer gods for copy-and-paste). We'll look at this chunk of code again when I talk about switches.

Once our number is printed, we can do it all over again if we'd like, thanks to the final `while` loop in lines 41 through 49. This one prompts for a `y` or an `n` character in response to the "Try another number" prompt. Note the call to the `lc` function in line 44—if the user types a capital Y or a capital N, we'll still accept that input because the `lc` function will lowercase it before we actually test. That line saves us some extra tests in the body of the `while`.

You'll notice that this chunk of code doesn't actually determine what to do if the reply is `y` or `n`; all it does is verify that it is indeed `y` or `n`. That's because this code doesn't need to do anything. Once `$exit` has the appropriate value, the outer `while` loop ends, and we return right back up to the top again to that test in the first `while`. If the reply was `n`, that test returns false and the script exits. Otherwise, we start the body of that outer `while` again, and continue on until the user gets bored and types `n` later on to exit the script.

Text-to-HTML Converter Script

Let's finish up with a slightly more useful script: `webbuild.pl` takes a simple text file as an argument, prompts you for some basic values, and then spits out an HTML version of your text file. It's not a very sophisticated HTML generator—it won't handle embedded boldface or other formatting, it doesn't handle links or images; really, it does little other than stick paragraph tags in the right place, let you specify the foreground and background colors, and give you a simple heading and a link to your email address. But it does give you a basic HTML template to work from.

How It Works

In addition to simply converting text input to HTML, the `webbuild.pl` script prompts you for several other values, including:

- The title of the page (<TITLE>...</TITLE> in HTML)
- Background and text colors (here I've limited it to the built-in colors supported by HTML, and we'll verify the input to make sure that it's one of those colors). This part also includes some rudimentary online help as well.
- An initial heading (<H1>...</H1> in HTML)
- An email address, which will be inserted as a link at the bottom of the final HTML page

Here's what running the `webbuild.pl` script would produce with the some given prompts and output:

```
% webbuild.pl janeeyre.txt
Enter the title to use for your web page: Charlotte Bronte, Jane Eyre,
Chapter One
Enter the background color (? for options): ?
One of:
white, black, red, green, blue,
orange, purple, yellow, aqua, gray,
silver, fuchsia, lime, maroon, navy,
olive, or Return for none
Enter the backgroundcolor (? for options): white
```

```
Enter the text color (? for options): black
Enter a heading: Chapter One
Enter your email address: lemay@lne.com
*******************************
<HTML>
<HEAD>
<TITLE>Charlotte Bronte, Jane Eyre, Chapter One</TITLE>
</HEAD>
<BODY BGCOLOR="white" TEXT="black">
<H1>Chapter One</H1>
<P>
There was no possibility of taking a walk that day. We had been
wandering, indeed, in the leafless shrubbery an hour in the morning;
....more text deleted for space...
something lighter, franker, more natural, as it were- she really
must exclude me from privileges intended only for contented, happy,
little children.'
<HR>
<ADDRESS><A HREF="mailto:lemay@lne.com">lemay@lne.com</A></ADDRESS>
</BODY>
</HTML>
```

The resulting HTML file, as output above, could then be copied and pasted into a text editor, saved, and loaded into a Web browser to see the result (Figure 7.1 shows that result).

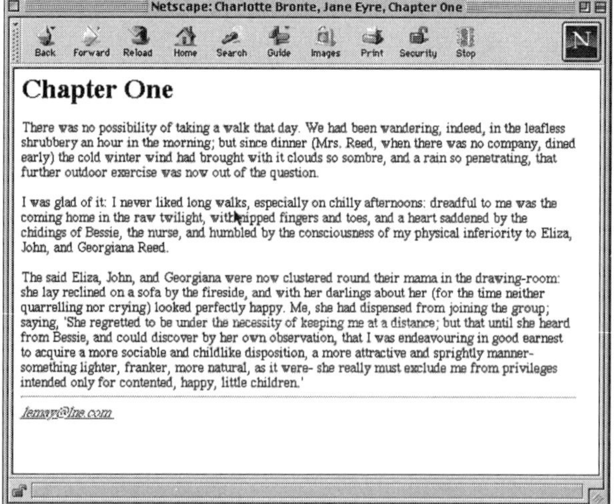

FIGURE 7.1

The result of the `webbuild.pl` *script.*

Later on in this book (on Day 15, "Working with Files and I/O," specifically), I'll show you a way to output the data to a file, rather than to the screen.

The Input File

One note about the text file you give to `webbuild.pl` to convert: The script assumes the data you give it is a file of paragraphs, with each paragraph separated by a blank line. For example, here's the content of the file `janeeyre.txt`, which I used for the example output:

```
There was no possibility of taking a walk that day. We had been
wandering, indeed, in the leafless shrubbery an hour in the morning;
but since dinner (Mrs. Reed, when there was no company, dined early)
the cold winter wind had brought with it clouds so sombre, and a
rain so penetrating, that further outdoor exercise was now out of
the question.

I was glad of it: I never liked long walks, especially on chilly
afternoons: dreadful to me was the coming home in the raw twilight,
with nipped fingers and toes, and a heart saddened by the chidings
of Bessie, the nurse, and humbled by the consciousness of my
physical inferiority to Eliza, John, and Georgiana Reed.

The said Eliza, John, and Georgiana were now clustered round
their mama in the drawing-room: she lay reclined on a sofa by the
fireside, and with her darlings about her (for the time neither
```

The Script

Listing 7.3 shows the code for our script.

LISTING 7.3 WEBBUILD.PL

```
#!/usr/bin/perl -w
#
# webbuild:  simple text-file conversion to HTML
# *very* simple.  Assumes no funky characters, embedded
# links or boldface, etc.  Blank spaces == paragraph
# breaks.

$title = '';                        # <TITLE>
$bgcolor = '';                      # BGCOLOR
$text = '';                         # TEXT
$head = '';                         # main heading
$mail = '';                         # email address

print "Enter the title to use for your web page: ";
chomp($title = <STDIN>);

```

continues

LISTING 7.3 CONTINUED

```
foreach $color ('background', 'text') {
    $in = '';                       # temporary input
    while () {
        print "Enter the $color color (? for options): ";
        chomp($in = <STDIN>);
        $in = lc $in;

        if ($in eq '?') {           # print help
            print "One of: \nwhite, black, red, green, blue,\n";
            print "orange, purple, yellow, aqua, gray,\n";
            print "silver, fuchsia, lime, maroon, navy,\n";
            print "olive, or Return for none\n";
            next;
        } elsif ($in eq '' or
                 $in eq 'white' or
                 $in eq 'black' or
                 $in eq 'red' or
                 $in eq 'blue' or
                 $in eq 'green' or
                 $in eq 'orange' or
                 $in eq 'purple' or
                 $in eq 'yellow' or
                 $in eq 'aqua' or
                 $in eq 'gray' or
                 $in eq 'silver' or
                 $in eq 'fuchsia' or
                 $in eq 'lime' or
                 $in eq 'maroon' or
                 $in eq 'navy' or
                 $in eq 'olive') { last; }
        else {
            print "that's not a color.\n";
        }
    }

    if ($color eq 'background') {
        $bgcolor = $in;
    } else {
        $text = $in;
    }
}

print "Enter a heading: ";
chomp($head = <STDIN>);

print "Enter your email address: ";
chomp($mail = <STDIN>);
```

```
64:
65: print '*' x 30;
66:
67: print "\n<HTML>\n<HEAD>\n<TITLE>$title</TITLE>\n";
68: print "</HEAD>\n<BODY";
69: if ($bgcolor ne '') { print qq( BGCOLOR="$bgcolor"); }
70: if ($text ne '') { print qq( TEXT="$text"); }
71: print ">\n";
72: print "<H1>$head</H1>\n<P>";
73:
74: while (<>) {
75:     if ($_ eq "\n") {
76:         print "<p>\n";
77:     } else {
78:         print $_;
79:     }
80: }
81:
82: print qq(<HR>\n<ADDRESS><A HREF="mailto:$mail">$mail</A></ADDRESS>\n);
83: print "</BODY>\n</HTML>\n";
```

There's little that's overly complex, syntax-wise, in this script; it doesn't even use any arrays or hashes (it doesn't need to; there's nothing that really needs storing or processing here). Just a lot of loops and tests.

There are at least a few points to be made about why I organized the script the way I did, so we can't end this lesson quite yet. Let's start with the large `foreach` loop starting in line 17.

This loop handles the prompt for both the background and text colors. Because both of these prompts behave in exactly the same way, I didn't want to have to repeat the same code for each one (particularly given that there's a really huge `if` test in lines 30 through 46). Later on, you'll learn how to put this kind of repetitive code into a subroutine, and then just call the subroutine twice. But for now, because we know a lot about loops at this point, and nothing about subroutines, I opted for a sneaky `foreach` loop.

The loop will run twice, once for the string `'background'` and once for the string `'text'`. We'll use these strings for the prompts, and later on to make sure the right value gets assigned to the right variable (`$bgcolor` or `$text`).

Inside the `foreach` loop, we have another loop, an infinite `while` loop, which will repeat each prompt until we get acceptable input (input verification is always a good programming practice). At the prompt, the user has three choices: enter one of the sixteen built-in colors, hit Return (or Enter) to use the default colors, or type `?` for a list of the choices.

The tests in lines 24 through 58 process each of these choices. First, `?`. In response to a question mark, all we have to do is print a helpful message, and then use `next` to drop down to the next iteration of the `while` loop (that is, redisplay the prompt and wait for more data).

The next test (starting in line 30) makes sure we have correct input: either a Return, in which case the input is empty (line 30); or one of the sixteen built-in colors. Note that the tests all test lowercase colors, which would seem overly limiting if the user typed `BLACK` or `Black` or some other odd-combination of upper- and lowercase. But fear not; in line 22, we used the `lc` function to lowercase the input, which combines all those case issues into one (but conveniently doesn't affect input of `?`).

If the input matches any of those seventeen cases, we call `last` in line 46 to drop out of the `while` loop (keep in mind that `next` and `last`, minus the presence of labels, refer to the nearest enclosing loop—to the `while`, not to the `foreach`). If the input doesn't match, we drop to the final else case in line 47, print an error message, and restart the `while` loop.

The final test in the `foreach` loop determines whether we have a value for the background color or for the text color, and assigns that value to the appropriate variable.

The final part of the script, starting in line 67 and continuing on to the end, prints the top part of our HTML file, reads in and converts the text file indicated on the command line to HTML, and finishes up with the last part of the HTML file. Note the tests in line 69 and 70; if there are no values for `$bgcolor` or `$text`, we'll leave off those attributes to the HTML `<BODY>` tag altogether. (A simpler version would be just to leave them there, as `BGCOLOR=""` or `TEXT=""`, but that doesn't look as nice in the output.)

You'll note also the use of the `qq` function. You learned about `qq` in passing way back on Day 2, "Working with Strings and Numbers," in the "Going Deeper" section. The `qq` function is a way of creating a double-quoted string without actually using any double-quotes. I used it here because if I had actually used double-quotes, I would have had to backslash the double-quotes in the string itself. I think it looks better like this.

Lines 74 through 80 read in the input file (using `<>`), and then simply print it all back out again, inserting paragraph tags at the appropriate spots (that is, where there are blank lines). A more robust version of this script would watch for things like embedded special characters (accents, bullets, and so on) and replace them with the appropriate HTML codes—but that's a task done much easier with pattern matching, so we'll leave it for later.

All that's left is to print the final email link (using an HTML `mailto` URL and link tags) and finish up the HTML file.

Summary

Often, programming books give you a lot of wordy background, but don't include enough actual code examples for how to do stuff. While I won't claim that this book shirks on the wordy background (you may snicker now), this lesson—and the two others to come on Day 14 and Day 21—will offer you some longer bits of code that make use of the techniques you've learned in the previous lessons, put them all together, and maybe even accomplish some sort of useful task (although I'm not certain how often you're going to need to spell a number).

In today's lesson, we explored three scripts: one, a revision of the familiar `stats` script, printed a sophisticated histogram using `for` loops and some careful measuring. The second, a number speller, used a large amount of tests to print a result. And the third, `webbuild`, took an input file from the command line and data from the keyboard and converted the contents of the file into something else—in this case, a Web page.

Congratulations on completing the first week of this three-week book. During this week, you've picked up a hefty chunk of the language. From this point on, we'll be building on what you've already learned. Onward to Week 2!

Week 2

Doing More

- Manipulating Lists and Strings
- Pattern Matching with Regular Expressions
- Doing More with Regular Expressions
- Creating and Using Subroutines
- Debugging Perl
- Scope, Modules, and Importing Code
- Exploring a Few Longer Examples

WEEK 2

DAY 8

Manipulating Lists and Strings

We'll start Week 2 with a bit of a hodgepodge of things; in today's lesson, we'll look more closely at lists, arrays, hashes, and strings and the sorts of things you can do to manipulate the data they contain. A lot of what you'll learn about today uses many of Perl's built-in functions, but these functions are useful to have in your repertoire as you learn more about the language itself.

Today we'll explore

- Creating array and hash slices (smaller portions of other arrays and hashes)
- Sorting lists
- Searching lists
- Modifying list contents
- Processing all the elements of a list
- Various string manipulations: `reverse`, finding substrings, extracting substrings

Array and Hash Slices

In addition to all the operations you learned about on Days 4 and 5 for playing with arrays and hashes, Perl also has a mechanism for copying some subset of elements from the collection. That's called a slice—a subset of an array or a hash that is, in turn, another array or hash.

You take a slice of an array similarly to how you access one element: using brackets. However, there are two significant differences between a slice and a single element. Here are a few lines of Perl code that show the syntax for slices:

```
@array = (1,2,3,4,5);
$one = $array[0];      # $one is 1
@slice = @array[0,1,2];  # @slice is (1,2,3)
```

See the differences? In the element access expression `$array[0]`, you use a `$` to refer to the array variable, and a single index number inside the brackets. The result, stored in `$one`, is a single scalar variable. With the slice notation, you use an at sign (`@`) for the array variable, and a list of indexes inside the brackets. With this notation, you end up with a list of three elements in `@slice`.

You can put any expression inside the brackets for a slice, as long as it's a list of indexes. Range operators work exceptionally well here for taking a slice of consecutive numbers:

```
@lowers = @nums[1..100];
```

Note that a very common Perl mistake is to use an array slice with a single index, when what you wanted was a single element:

```
$single = @array[5];
```

This notation won't produce what you're looking for. Here, you're extracting a list of one element from the array `@array`, and then trying to evaluate that list in a scalar context. If you have warnings turned on in your script, Perl will let you know if you're making this mistake.

Hash slices work similarly to array slices, but require different notation:

```
%hashslice = @hash{'this', 'that', 'other'};
```

Note that for a hash slice, the keys you want to extract go into curly brackets, like individual hash keys, but you still use an array variable symbol even though it's a hash. That's because the resulting slice will be a list of the keys and values (in the right order: key, value, key, value, and so on). You can then just assign that slice to a hash variable and turn it into a hash once again. Don't do this:

```
%hashslice = %hash{'this', 'that', 'other'};
```

That'll give you an error (even if you don't have warnings turned on). The rule is, if you want a scalar out of an array or hash, use `$` (scalar notation). If you want a slice, use `@` (array notation).

Sorting Lists

You've already seen how to sort a list, for example, the keys in a hash, using the `sort` function:

```
@keys = sort keys %hash;
```

By default, the `sort` function sorts a list in ASCII order. To sort a list of numbers in numeric order, use `sort` with an extra expression just before the list to be sorted:

```
@keys = sort { $a <=> $b } keys %hash;
```

What does that bit in the middle with the <=> operator do? What are `$a` and `$b` for? Up until now, I asked you to just learn that line by heart; here's where I'll explain what all that means.

The extra bit between curly brackets in the `sort` determines how the list is to be sorted, by describing what happens when one element is greater than, less than, or equal to another. Given two arguments (`$a` and `$b`), the expression inside the block should return an integer less than 0 (if the first argument is less than the second), an integer greater than 0 (if the first argument is greater), or 0 (if the two arguments are equal).

Perl, conveniently, has two operators that do just this, making it easy for you to write simple `sort` routines. Why two operators? For the same reason there are two sets of equality and relational operators: one for strings (`cmp`), and one for numbers (<=>).

The `cmp` operator works on strings, comparing two arguments and returning -1, 0, or 1 depending on whether the first operand is less than, equal to, or greater than the second. You could write `cmp` the long way something like this:

```
$result = '';
if ($a lt $b ) { $result = -1; }
elsif ($a gt $b { $result = 1; }
else { $result = 0; }
```

The <=> operator, sometimes called the spaceship operator for its appearance, does exactly the same comparison, only for numbers.

Which brings us to the `$a` and `$b` part of the `sort` routine. The `$a` and `$b` variables are temporary to the sort (you don't have to declare them, and they go away once the sort's done), and contain elements in the list you're sorting. If you were going to write your own `sort` routine inside the block, you would use `$a` and `$b` to refer to the two elements that need to be compared each time.

Because $a and $b are special to the sort routine, and refer to two elements in the list, be careful about using variables named $a and $b in your scripts, or of changing the values of $a and $b inside your sort routine. Weird and unexpected results can occur.

The default `sort` routine uses the `cmp` operator to compare values (which is why it sorts in ASCII order). Using `{ $a <=> $b }` compares the values with a numeric comparison, which sorts those values in numeric order.

By default these `sort` routines have sorted lists in ascending order. To sort in the reverse order, simply reverse `$a` and `$b`:

```
@keys = sort { $b <=> $a } keys %hash;
```

You can print a hash, sorted by keys, using a `sort` routine and a `foreach` loop. If you want to do the same thing with the values in the hash, however, things can get a little complicated. If all you need are the values, you can just use the `values` function to get a list of those values and then sort it. But by doing that you lose access to the original keys; there's no way to associate a raw value back to its key. You can, however, sort the keys in value order, and then print out both the key and its value, like this:

```
foreach $key (sort {$things{$a} cmp $things{$b}} keys %things) {
   print "$key, $things{$key}\n";
}
```

Here, the `sort` routine, instead of using raw keys for the values of `$a` and `$b`, sorts the values associated with the keys (`$things{$a}` and `$things{b}`) instead. The resulting list, which we iterate over using `foreach`, is a list of the keys in the hash sorted by value.

Searching

Sorting's easy; there's a function for it. Searching a list for a particular element—or for a part of an element—isn't quite so straightforward. Searching is one of those things where there is definitely more than one way to do it. Given a list of strings and a search string, you could, for example, simply iterate over the list with a `foreach` loop and test each element against the string, like this:

```
chomp($key = <STDIN>);  # thing to look for
foreach $el (@strings) {
   if ($key eq $el) {
      $found = 1;
   }
}
```

If the thing you were searching for can be a substring of an element in the list, you could use the `index` function to search for the substring in the string. The `index` function returns the position of the substring in the string, if it's found, and -1 otherwise (remember that string positions, like arrays, start from 0):

```
foreach $el (@strings) {
   if ((index $el, $key) >= 0) {   # -1 means not found
      $found = 1;
   }
}
```

A more efficient (and potentially more powerful) version of the substring tests would be to use patterns, which you'll learn more about tomorrow (don't worry about this syntax right now):

```
foreach $el (@strings) {
   if ($el =~ /$key/) {
      $found = 1;
   }
}
```

Despite the differences with the test, all of these examples use a number of lines of code. To make things even more efficient, number-of-characters-wise, we can use Perl's built-in `grep` function. Named after the UNIX tool of the same name, `grep` is used specifically for searching for things in lists. As with many other Perl features, however, `grep` behaves differently when used either in a list or a scalar context.

In list context, `grep` is used to extract all the elements of a list for which an expression or test is true, and return a new list of those elements. So, for example, here's an example of `grep` that will extract all the elements of the list `@nums` that are greater than 100:

```
@large = grep { $_ > 100 } @nums;
```

Note the use of our friend, the `$_` default variable. The `grep` function works by taking each element in the list and assigning it to `$_`, and then evaluating the expression inside the brackets. If the expression is true, that list element "matches" the search and is added to the final list. Otherwise, `grep` moves onto the next element in the `@nums` list until it gets to the end.

You can use any expression you want to inside the brackets. The expression you use, however, should be a test that returns true or false, so that `grep` can build the new list on that criteria.

An alternate way to use `grep` is with a pattern built using a regular expression. We'll learn all about regular expressions tomorrow and the next day, but I'll include an example here (and in the example that follows this section), just to give you a taste:

```
@exes = grep /x/, @words;
```

Instead of a test inside of curly brackets, as with the previous examples, this example uses a pattern. The characters inside the slashes (here, just the character x) are the search pattern; in this case, grep will find all the elements in the @words array that contain the letter x, and store those words in the @exes array. You can also use a variable inside the search pattern:

```
print "Search for? ";
chomp($key = <STDIN>);
@exes = grep /$key/, @words;
```

The pattern inside the slashes can be any number of characters, and grep will search for that set of characters in any element in the list. So, for example, a pattern of /the/ will match any elements that contain the letters the (which includes the word "the" as well as the words "there" or "other"). As you'll learn tomorrow, the pattern can also contain a number of special characters to build much more sophisticated search criteria. Don't forget the comma after the pattern; unlike the syntax with an expression inside brackets, the comma is required after the pattern.

In scalar context, grep behaves much the same way as in list context, except that instead of returning a list of all the elements that matched, grep returns the number of elements that matched (0 means no matches).

The grep function works best with lists or arrays, but there's nothing stopping you from using it with hashes, as long as you write your test correctly. For example, this bit of code uses grep to find all the hash keys for which *either* the key or its associated value is larger than 100:

```
@largekeys = grep { $_ > 100 or $numhash{$_} > 100 } keys %numhash;
```

An Example: More Names

On Day 5, "Working with Hashes," we had a simple example that read in names (first and last) and then split those names into a hash of names keyed by the last name. On Day 6, "Conditionals and Loops," both in the body of the lesson and in the exercises, we used the <> operator to read those names into a hash from an external file. Let's extend the names script here so that it doesn't just read the names into a hash, it also does something with those names. This version of the names script, morenames.pl, adds a large while loop that gives you a list of four options:

- Sort and print the names list by last name
- Sort and print the names list by first name
- Search for first or last name (exact match)
- Quit

If you choose any of the options to search or sort the list, the program repeats and allows you to choose another option. The fourth option exits the program. Here's a transcript of how the program might look when run:

```
$ morenames.pl names.txt

1. Sort names by last name
2. Sort names by first name
3. Search for a name
4. Quit

Choose a number: 1
Adams, Douglas
Alexander, Lloyd
Alighieri, Dante
Asimov, Isaac
other names deleted for space

1. Sort names by last name
2. Sort names by first name
3. Search for a name
4. Quit

Choose a number: 2
Albert Camus
Aldous Huxley
Angela Carter
Anne Rice
Anne McCaffrey
Anthony Burgess
other names deleted for space

1. Sort names by last name
2. Sort names by first name
3. Search for a name
4. Quit

Choose a number: 3
Search for what? Will
Names matched:
   William S.  Burroughs
   William Shakespeare

1. Sort names by last name
2. Sort names by first name
3. Search for a name
4. Quit

Choose a number: 4
$
```

Listing 8.1 shows the code for our sorting and searching script:

LISTING 8.1 morenames.pl

```
#!/usr/bin/perl -w

%names = ();                    # hash of names
@raw = ();                      # raw words
$fn = "";                       # first name
$exit = 1;                      # exit program?
$in = '';                       # temporary in
@keys = ();                     # temporary keys
@n = ();                                # temporary name
$search = '';                   # thing to search for

while (<>) {
    chomp;
    @raw = split(" ", $_);
    if ($#raw == 1) {  # regular case
        $names{$raw[1]} = $raw[0];
    } else {  # build a first name
        $fn = "";
        for ($i = 0; $i < $#raw; $i++) {
            $fn .= $raw[$i] . " ";
        }
        $names{$raw[$#raw]} = $fn;
    }
}

while ($exit) {

    print "\n1. Sort names by last name\n";
    print "2. Sort names by first name\n";
    print "3. Search for a name\n";
    print "4. Quit\n\n";
    print "Choose a number: ";

    chomp($in = <STDIN>);

    if ($in eq '1') {           # sort and print by last name

        foreach $name (sort keys %names) {
            print "$name, $names{$name}\n";
        }

    } elsif ($in eq '2') {      # sort and print by first name

        @keys = sort { $names{$a} cmp $names{$b} } keys %names;
        foreach $name (@keys) {
            print "$names{$name} $name\n";
```

```
47:         }
48:
49:     } elsif ($in eq '3') {      # find a name (1 or more)
50:
51:         print "Search for what? ";
52:         chomp($search = <STDIN>);
53:
54:         while (@n = each %names) {
55:             if (grep /$search/, @n) {
56:                 $keys[++$#keys] = $n[0];
57:             }
58:         }
59:
60:         if (@keys) {
61:             print "Names matched: \n";
62:             foreach $name (sort @keys) {
63:                 print "   $names{$name} $name\n";
64:             }
65:         } else {
66:             print "None found.\n";
67:         }
68:
69:         @keys = ();  # undefine @keys for next search
70:    } elsif ($in eq '4') {      # quit
71:       $exit = 0;
72:    } else {
73:       print "Not a good answer.  1 to 4 please.\n";
74:    }
75: }
```

The basic framework of this script is the large `while` loop that manages the choices, from 1 to 4. After printing the choices and prompting for one, the `while` loop contains a set of statements to test for each answer. If the answer was not 1, 2, 3, or 4 (and we test for the string versions of these numbers, so that an errant letter won't produce warnings), the final `else` in line 71 will handle that and repeat from the top.

The framework itself is just a bunch of tests and not worth describing in detail. What happens at each option is much more interesting. The two sorting options (options 1 and 2, starting in lines 36 and 42, respectively) each use different forms of the `sort` function you've learned about previously in this lesson. The first option, to search for something in the names, uses `grep` to find it.

Let's look at the two sorting options first. Our names hash is keyed by last name, so sorting the list by last name is easy. In fact, the `foreach` loop in lines 38 through 40 is the same `foreach` loop we used for previous versions of this example.

Sorting by first name, the second option involves sorting the hash by the values, which is more difficult. Fortunately, I just showed you how to do this in the section on sorting, so you can use the technique I showed you there in lines 44 through 47. Build a temporary list of the keys with a `sort` routine that compares the values and then to use those keys to print out the names in the right order.

Which brings us to the search. We'll start in lines 51 and 52 by prompting for the search key, storing it in the `$search` variable.

At first glance, you may think doing this search is easy—just use the `grep` function with the characters the user entered as the pattern. But the catch here is that we're searching a hash, and there are both keys and values to keep track of.

If all we wanted to search was the last names, we could just use the keys function to extract the keys and search them, like this:

```
@matches = grep /$search/, keys %names;
```

To get at the values, we could use a `foreach` loop to loop through the keys and then test the pattern against both the key and the value in turn. And there would be nothing wrong with that approach. But in this particular example, I wanted to use `grep`, so I took what might look like a rather unusual approach (I prefer to think of it as a *creative* approach): I used the `each` function, which you learned about on Day 5, which gives you a list of a key/value pair. With that list, you can then use `grep`, and if it matches, store the key for printing later.

That's what I'm doing in lines 54 through 58. Let's look at those lines more closely:

```
54: while (@n = each %names) {
55:     if (grep /$search/, @n) {
56:         $keys[++$#keys] = $n[0];
57:     }
58: }
```

The `each` function gives you a two-element list of a key and a value from the hash. Calling `each` multiple times eventually works its way through all the keys and values in the hash. So, in line 54, this `while` loop will iterate as many times as there are key/value pairs in the hash, assigning each pair to the list in `@n`. When there are no more pairs to examine, `@n` will get the empty list `()` and the `while` will stop.

Inside the `while` loop, we use an `if` test and `grep` to test for the search pattern in our simple key/value list. Here we're using `grep` in a scalar context, so if `grep` finds anything, it'll return a non-zero number, and the `if` test will be true. Otherwise, it'll return 0 and we'll skip to the next iteration of the `while`.

Line 56 is where we store the key if grep was able to find something that matched the search pattern, by simply appending the key to the end of the @keys array. This line is one of those examples of convoluted Perl, so let's look at it more closely:

```
$keys[++$#keys] = $n[0];
```

Remember that @n contains two elements, a key and a value. At this point in the script, either the key or the value have matched, so we'll store the key in the @keys array (storing the key will give us access to the value, so we don't have to worry about that). $n[0] gives us that matched key.

Next step is to assign that value to the end of the @keys array. Remember that $#keys gives us the highest index position in the array, so ++$#keys refers to the position just after that last one. Note that the increment is done in prefix notation, so we can increment that element before we assign anything to it. We can then use that new highest index position as the position in which to assign the key.

Whew! This line is one of those examples where you can cram a whole lot of information into a single line, and unless you understand each and every character, it'll take a while to decipher it. Fortunately, if this sort of syntax makes your head spin, there's a much easier way to add an element onto the end of a list, using the push function, which we'll look at later on in this lesson.

After the list of matched keys has been built, all that's left is to print them. In this case, we'll test first to see if @keys has any elements (line 60), and if so, the script sorts and prints them. Otherwise, it prints a helpful message (line 66).

Modifying List Elements

You can always add and remove list, array, and hash elements using the methods I described on Days 4 and 5. But sometimes, in some situations, the standard ways of adding and removing elements from lists can be awkward, hard to read, or inefficient. To help with modifying lists, Perl provides a number of built-in functions, including:

- push and pop: add and remove list elements from the end of a list.
- shift and unshift: add and remove list elements from the start of a list.
- splice: add or remove elements anywhere in a list.

push and pop

The push and pop functions allow you to add or remove elements from the end of a list, that is, it affects the highest index positions of that list. Both push and pop will be familiar functions if you've ever worked with stacks, where the notion is that the first element in is the first element out. If you haven't dealt with stacks before, envision one of those spring-loaded plate dispensers you sometimes see in cafeterias. You add plates to the dispenser (push them onto the stack), but the top plate is always the one you use first (pop them off of the stack). So it is with `push` and `pop` and arrays: pushing adds an element to the end of the list, and popping removes that same element.

The `push` function takes two arguments: a list to be modified, and a list of elements to be added. The original list is modified in place, and `push` returns the number of elements in the newly modified list. So, for example, in `morenames.pl` from the previous section, we used this ugly bit of code to add a key to the `@keys` array:

```
$keys[++$#keys] = $n[0];
```

That same bit could be written with `push` like this:

```
push @keys, $n[0];
```

Fewer characters, yes, and also conceptually easier to figure out. Note that the second argument here is a scalar (which is then converted to a list of one element), but the second argument can itself be a list, which lets you combine multiple lists easily like this:

```
push @final, @list1;
```

The `pop` function does the reverse of `push`; it removes the last element from the list or array. The `pop` function takes one argument (the list to change), removes the last element, and returns that element:

```
$last = pop @array;
```

As with `push`, the list is modified in place and will have one less element after the `pop`. A convoluted way of moving elements from one array to another might look like this:

```
while (@old) {
   push @new, pop @old;
}
```

Note that with this bit of code the new array will be in the reverse order, since the last element is the first to get pushed onto the new array. A better way of reversing a list is to use the `reverse` function instead, and a better way of moving one list to another is simply to use assignment. You could, however, use this mechanism to modify each element as it gets passed from one element to the other:

```
while (@old) {
   push @new, 2 * pop @old;
}
```

shift and unshift

If push and pop add or remove elements from the end of the list, wouldn't it be nice to have functions that add or remove elements from the *beginning* of the list. No problem! shift and unshift do just that, shifting all elements one position up or down (or, as is more commonly envisioned with shift and unshift, left and right). As with push and pop, the list is modified in place.

The shift function takes a single argument, a list, and removes the first element from that list, moving all the remaining elements down (left) one position. It returns the element it removed. So, for example, this bit of code moves elements from one array to another, but this example doesn't reverse the list in the process:

```
 while (@old) {
   push @new, shift @old;
}
```

The unshift function is the beginning-of-list equivalent to push. It takes two arguments: the list to modify and the list to add. The new list contains the added elements and then the old elements in the list, shifted as many places upward as there were elements added. The unshift function returns the number of elements in the new list:

```
$numusers = unshift @users, @newusers;
```

splice

Push and pop modify the elements at the end of a list, shift and unshift do the same thing at the beginning. The splice function, however, is a much more general-purpose way to add, remove, or replace elements at any position inside the list. Splice takes up to four arguments:

- The array to be modified
- The point (position, or offset) in that array to add or remove elements after
- The number of elements to remove or replace. If this argument isn't included, splice will change every element from the offset forward.
- The list of elements to add to the array, if any.

Let's start with removing elements from an array using splice. For each of these examples, let's assume a list of ten elements, 0 to 9:

```
@nums = 0 .. 9;
```

To remove elements 5, 6, and 7, you would use an offset of 5 and a length of 3. There's no list argument, since we're not adding anything:

```
splice(@nums, 5, 3);  # results in (0,1,2,3,4,8,9)
```

To remove all elements from position 5 to the end of the list, leave off the length argument.

```
splice(@nums, 5);  # results in (0,1,2,3,4)
```

To replace elements, add a list of the elements to replace to the `splice`. For example, to replace elements 5, 6, and 7 with the elements `"five"`, `"six"`, and `"seven"`, use this code:

```
splice(@nums, 5, 3, qw(five six seven)); # results in (0,1,2,3,4,
                                         # "five","six","seven",8,9)
```

Perl doesn't care whether you're removing the same number of elements as you're adding; it'll just add the elements in the list at the position given by the offset, and move all the other elements out of the way (or shrink the array to fit). So, for example, here's a call to `splice` to delete elements 5, 6 and 7, and add the word `"missing"` in their place:

```
splice(@nums, 5, 3, "missing"); # results in (0,1,2,3,4,"missing",8,9);
```

The new array, in that latter case, will contain only eight elements.

To add elements to the array without also removing elements, use 0 for the length. For example, here's a call to `splice` that adds a couple numbers after element 5:

```
splice(@nums, 5, 0, (5.1, 5.2, 5.3));
# results in  (0,1,2,3,4,5,5.1,5.2,5.3,6.7.8.9)
```

The `splice` function, as with the other list modification functions, modifies the list it's working on in place. It also returns a list of the elements it removed. You can use this latter feature to break up a list into several parts. For example, let's say you had a list of some number of elements, `@rawlist`, that you want broken up into two lists, `@list1` and `@list2`. The first element in `@rawlist` is the number of elements that should be in `@list1`; the second final list will then contain any remaining elements. You might use code similar to this, where the first line extracts the appropriate elements from `@rawlist` and stores them in `@list1`, the second removes the first element (the number of elements) from `@rawlist`, and the third stores the remaining elements in `@list2`.

```
@list1 = splice(@rawlist, 1, $rawlist[0]);
shift @rawlist;
@list2 = @rawlist;
```

Other Ways to Mess with Lists

But wait, that's not all. I've got a couple more functions that are useful for modifying and playing with lists: `reverse`, `join`, and `map`.

reverse

The reverse function takes each element of a list and turns it blue. Just kidding. reverse, as you might expect, reverses the order of the elements in the list:

```
@otherway = reverse @list;
```

Note that if you're sorting a list, or moving elements around using shift, unshift, push, or pop, you can use those methods to create reversed lists without having to reverse them using reverse (try to avoid moving array elements around more than you have to).

The reverse function also works with scalars, in which case it reverses the order of characters in a scalar. We'll come back to this in "Manipulating Strings," later in this chapter.

join

The split function splits a string into several list elements. The join function does just the reverse: it combines list elements into a string, with any character (or characters) you want in between them. So, for example, if you had split a line of numbers into a list using this split command:

```
@list = split(' ', "1 2 3 4 5 6 7 8 9 10");
```

then you could put them back into a string, with each number separated by a space, like this:

```
$string = join(' ',@list);
```

Or, you could separate each element with plus signs like this:

```
$string = join('+',@list);
```

Or with no characters at all:

```
$string = join('',@list);
```

map

Earlier, you learned about grep, which is used to extract elements from a list for which an expression or pattern returns true. The map function operates in a similar way, except that instead of selecting particular elements from a list, map executes a given expression or block on each element in a list and then collects the results of each expression into a new list.

For example, let's say you had a list of numbers, 1 to 10, and you wanted to build a list of the squares of all those numbers. You could use a foreach loop and push, like this:

```
foreach $num (1 .. 10) {
   push @squares, (@num**2);
}
```

The same operation in map might look like this:

```
@num = (1..10);
@squares = map { $_**2 } @num;
```

Like grep, map takes each element in the list and assigns it to $_. Then, also like grep, it evaluates the expression. Unlike grep, it stores the result of that expression into the new list, regardless of whether it evaluates to true or not. Depending on how you write the expression, however, you can pass anything you want to the new list, including nothing, some value other than the original list item in $_, or even multiple items. Consider map to be a filter for each of the list items, in which the result of the filter can be anything you want it to be.

The "filter" part of the map can be either a single expression or a block. If you're using a single expression, the value that gets returned at each turn of the map is simply the result of that expression. If you're using a block, the return value is the last expression that gets evaluated inside that block—so make sure you have an expression at the end that returns the value you're looking for. For example, here's a call to map that takes a list of numbers. It replaces any negative numbers with zero, and replaces all incidences of the number 5 with two numbers: 3 and 2. I've also formatted this version of map so that it's easier to read; there's no requirement for the code in either map or grep to be all on one line:

```
@final = map {
    if ($_ < 0) {
        0;
    } elsif ($_ == 5) {
        (3,2);
    } else { $_; }
} @nums;
```

This "last thing evaluated" behavior is actually a general rule for how blocks behave. You'll learn more about it when we get to subroutines on Day 11, "Creating and Using Subroutines."

Manipulating Strings

In the bulk of this lesson, we've explored ways you can manipulate lists and list contents with various built-in functions. Perl also has several useful functions for manipulating strings as well (and I summarized a number of these on Day 2). In this section, let's cover a few of these functions, including reverse, index, rindex, and substr.

Each of these functions is used to modify strings. In many cases, it may be easier or more efficient to modify strings using other mechanisms—concatenating them using the dot (`.`) operator, building them with variable values using variable interpolation, or searching and extracting substrings with patterns (as you'll learn in the next few days). But in many cases, these functions may be conceptually easier to use, particularly if you're used to similar string-manipulation functions from other languages.

reverse

You've already seen the `reverse` function, as used with lists, which reverses the order of elements in the list. `Reverse`, when used in a scalar context, behaves differently: it reverses all the characters in the number or string.

Note

> With a single string like "To be or not to be" or "antidisestablishmentarianism," you'll end up with new strings that simply have all the characters reversed. Note, however, that if the strings you're reversing have newlines at the end, that the reversed strings will have those newlines at the beginning of the string (creating somewhat puzzling results). If you don't want the newline to be reversed, don't forget to `chomp` it first.

The different behaviors of `reverse` in list and scalar context can sometimes be confusing. Take, for example, this bit of code:

```
foreach $string (@list) {
   push @reversed, reverse $string;
}
```

Offhand, that bit of code looks like it takes all the string elements in the `@list` array, reverses each one, and then pushes the result onto the `@reversed` array. But if you run that code, the contents of `@reversed` appear to be exactly the same as the contents of `@list`. Why? The `push` function takes a list as its second argument, so `reverse` is called in a list context, not a scalar context. The string in `$string` is then interpreted as a list of one element, which, when reversed, still contains the one element. The characters inside that element aren't even touched. To fix this, all you need is the `scalar` function:

```
foreach $string (@list) {
   push @reversed, scalar (reverse $string);
}
```

index and rindex

The `index` and `rindex` functions are used to find substrings inside other strings. Given two strings (one to look in and one to search for), they return the position of the second string inside the first, or -1 if the substring was not found. Positions are marked between characters, with 0 at the start of the string. So, for example, you could create a grep-like bit of code with `index` or `rindex` like this:

```
foreach $str (@list) {
   if ((index $str, $key) != -1) {
      push @final, $str;
}
```

The difference between `index` and `rindex` is in where the function starts looking. The `index` function begins from the start of the string and finds the position of the first occurrence of that string; `rindex` starts from the end of the string and finds the position of the last occurrence of that string.

Both `index` and `rindex` can take an optional third argument, indicating the position inside the string to start looking for the substring. So, for example, if you had already found a match using one call to `index`, you could call `index` again and start looking where you left off.

substr

The `substr` function is shorthand for substring, and can be used to extract characters from or add characters to a string—although it's most common usage is to extract substrings of other strings. The `substr` takes up to three arguments:

- The string to act on
- The position (offset) of the start of the substring to extract or replace. You can use a negative number as the opposite, in which case `substr` counts positions from the end of the string.
- The length of the substring to extract or replace. If the length isn't included, `substr` will change the substring from the offset to the end of the string.

The `substr` function returns the characters it removed (it does *not* modify the original string). So, for example, to extract characters 5 through 8 in the string `$longstring` and store them in `$newstr`, use this line:

```
$newstr = substr($longstring, 5, 3);
```

To create a new string that replaces characters or adds characters to another string, use the `substr` function on the left side of an assignment. The string you use on the right can be larger or smaller than the string you replace; Perl doesn't care:

```
substr($longstring, 5, 3) = "parthenogenesis";
```

If you wanted to search for and replace a substring everywhere in another string, you might use a `while` loop, `index`, and `substr` like this:

```
$str = "This is a test string.  The string we want to change.";
$pos = 0;
$key = 'i';
$repl = "*";

while ($pos < (length $str) and $pos != -1) {
    $pos = index($str, $key, $pos);

    if ($pos != -1 ) {
        substr($str,$pos,length $key) = $repl;
        $pos++;
    }
}
```

Don't become overly attached to this code, however; there are a number of ways to do this sort of operation using much less code. In particular, Perl's regular expressions allow you to compress that entire loop into one line:

```
$str =~ s/$key/$repl/g;
```

Going Deeper

In this lesson, I've shown you how to use many of the more popular functions for modifying or mangling lists and strings. And, in turn, I've only described the more common uses of these functions. If you're interested in more detail about any of these functions, or about any functions I haven't described in this book, see Appendix A or the `perlfunc` man page.

Some of the functions in this chapter have features I didn't talk about, mostly because they involve things you haven't learned yet. For example, the sorting routine for the `sort` function (the part inside the curly brackets) can be replaced with an actual subroutine name, which allows you to use that subroutine in many different places and to write quite sophisticated `sort` routines indeed.

The `pop` and `shift` functions, in turn, can also be used with no arguments. What list they affect depends on where in your script they're used: `pop` and `shift` with no arguments in the main body of the script pops or shifts the `@ARGV` array (containing the arguments to the script); `pop` and `shift` inside a subroutine affect the `@_` argument list to that subroutine (which you'll learn about once we get to Day 11.

Summary

Learning the Perl language involves learning much more than just the syntax of the core language; the built-in functions provide a lot of the cooler functionality and the power of Perl scripts. While many of the functions accomplish things in the language that can be better done some other way, others are useful to at least have around for specific cases. The functions you've learned about in this lesson are like that; most everything you've learned here can be done in some other way, although sometimes that other way might be longer, less efficient, or harder to figure out.

Today, then, you learned about the various functions you can use to modify lists and strings, and the ways to use these functions to accomplish simple tasks. You also learned about array and hash slices, which, while they aren't actually functions, give you a method for extracting elements out of a list or hash.

The functions you've learned about today include:

- `sort`, for sorting lists
- `grep`, for extracting list elements that match a criteria such as a pattern
- `push` and `pop`, for adding or removing list elements to the end of a list
- `shift` and `unshift`, for adding and removing list elements to the beginning of a list
- `splice`, for adding, removing, or replacing elements from anywhere in a list
- `reverse`, to reverse the order of elements in the list, or, in scalar context, for reversing the order of the characters in a string
- `join`, the reverse of `split`, for combining list elements into a string with one or more characters between them
- `map`, for performing some operation on each element of a list and building a new list of the results
- `index` and `rindex`, for finding the position of a given string in another string
- `substr`, for removing, adding, or replacing one string with another

Q&A

Q Most of the functions you described in this lesson seem to work only with lists. Can I use them with hashes as well?

A Hashes and lists are interchangeable in the sense that a hash will be unwound into its component parts when used as a list, and then the elements will be paired up into keys and values when the list becomes a hash again. So technically, yes, you can use many of these functions with hashes. The result, however, may not be what you expect and may not be very useful. For example, the `pop` function on a hash will unwind the hash into a list and then `pop` off the last item in that list (the last key in the hash)—but since you don't know what order the hash's keys will appear in, the result is unpredictable at best. Better to use hash slices or the `delete` function to modify hashes, or use these functions on lists of the keys or values.

Q I'm trying to use `reverse` on a list of strings. They're not reversing; it's like I never called the function.

A Are you sure you're using the `reverse` function on a string, and not on a list of one element? A list of one element is still a list, and the `reverse` function will happily `reverse` that list for you—giving you the same string you put into it. Make sure you're calling `reverse` in a scalar context, and if you're not, change the context with a different bit of code or with the `scalar` function.

Q In a previous lesson, you described the `$"` variable, which is used to set the separator character for list elements. It shows up when you interpolate a list inside a string. How is the `join` function different from this technique?

A If you're looking at the end result, it's not. Both will provide a way of "flattening" a list into a string with some character in between each of the list elements. The `join` function, however, is more efficient for this purpose because the string in question doesn't have to be interpolated for variables before it's expanded.

Workshop

The workshop provides quiz questions to help you solidify your understanding of the material covered and exercises to give you experience in using what you've learned. Try to understand the quiz and exercise answers before you go on to tomorrow's lesson.

Quiz

1. What is a slice? How does a slice affect the original list?
2. What are the `$a` and `$b` variables used for in `sort` routines?
3. What do the `<=>` and `cmp` operators do? What is the difference between them?
4. The `grep` function takes an expression or a block as its first argument. What is this block used for?
5. How can you use `splice` to add elements to an array? Replace two elements with a list of four elements?
6. How can you return a value from the block in `map`?

Exercises

1. Rewrite the following expressions using `splice`:

```
push @list, 1;
push @list, (2,3,4);
$list[5] = "foo";
shift @list;
```

2. **BUG BUSTERS:** What's wrong with this code (HINT: There may be multiple errors)?

```
while ($i <= $#list) {
   $str = @novel[$i++];
   push @final, reverse $str;
}
```

3. **BUG BUSTERS:** How about this code?

```
while ($pos < (length $str) and $pos != -1) {
    $pos = index($str, $key, $pos);

    if ($pos != -1 ) {
        $count++;
    }
}
```

4. Write a version of this expression using a `foreach` loop and `push`:

```
@list2 = grep {$_ < 5 } @list;
```

5. Write a script that prompts you for a string and a character and then returns the number of times that character occurs in the string. Use the `index` function.
6. Rewrite the script in Excercise 5 without using `index` (or patterns, if you already know something of patterns). HINT: Try using `grep`.

Answers

Here are the answers to the workshop questions in the previous section.

Quiz Answers

1. A slice is some subset of the elements in an array or hash. Slices do not affect the original list; they copy the sliced elements into the new list. Compare with elements extracted using `splice`, where the original array or list is permanently changed.
2. The `$a` and `$b` variables in a `sort` routine are local to that routine and refer to two list elements being compared. Use `$a` and `$b` to write your `sort` routines to do what you want.

3. The <=> and `cmp` operators take two operands and return -1 if the first is less than the second, 0 if the two are equal, and 1 if the first is larger than the second. While this behavior may not seem overly useful in ordinary use, these operators work exceptionally well for `sort` routines, which need exactly that kind of output to sort the elements in a list.

   The difference between <=> and `cmp` is the same as the difference between == and `eq`; the former is used for numbers, the latter for strings.

4. The expression or block as an argument to `grep` is used as a test to determine whether a particular list element (as stored in `$_`) will be saved in the final list `grep` returns. If the expression or block returns true, the list element is saved.

5. Add elements to an array with `splice` by using a length argument (the third argument) of 0. This will remove no elements, and add the new elements at the position specified by the offset:

   ```
   splice(@array, 0, 0, (1,2,3,4); # add (1,2,3,4) at the start of the
   array
   ```

   To replace two items with four items, use 2 as the length argument, and the items to add as a list:

   ```
   splice(@array, 0, 2, (1,2,3,4); # remove first two elements and
   replace with (1,2,3,4)
   ```

6. To return a value from the block of expressions in `map`, make sure the last thing to be evaluated in the block is the thing you want to return (and therefore to be passed onto the new list).

Exercise Answers

1. Here are the answers:

   ```
   splice(@list, $#list+1, 0, 1);
   splice(@list, $#list+1, 0, (2,3,4));
   splice(@list, 5, 1, "foo");
   splice(@list, 0, 1);
   ```

2. There are multiple bugs and conceptual errors in this snippet of code. The first is in the second line; the array access expression here is actually an array `splice`, so you'll end up with an array of one element instead of an actual string. Perl warnings will catch this one.

   But even if you fix that error, the string will not be reversed, because in the third line `reverse` is being called in a list context, so the string is interpreted as a list of one element. Use the `scalar` function to create a scalar context for `reverse`.

3. At some point inside the loop, you have to increment the current position. Otherwise, the loop will continue to find the same substring at the same position, over and over again, and turn into an infinite loop.
4. Here's one answer:

```
foreach (@list) {
   if ($_ < 5) {
       push @list2, $_;
   }
}
```

5. Here's one answer:

```
#!/usr/bin/perl -w

$str = '';
$key = '';
$pos = 0;
$count = 0;

print "Enter the string to search: ";
chomp($str = <STDIN>);
print "Enter the character to count: ";
chomp($key = <STDIN>);

while ($pos < (length $str) and $pos != -1) {
    $pos = index($str, $key, $pos);

    if ($pos != -1 ) {
        $count++;
        $pos++;
    }
}

print "$key appears in the string $count times.\n";
```

6. Here's one answer:

```
#!/usr/bin/perl -w

$str = '';
$key = '';
$pos = 0;
$count = 0;

print "Enter the string to search: ";
chomp($str = <STDIN>);
print "Enter the character to count: ";
chomp($key = <STDIN>);
```

```
@chars = split('',$str);
$count = grep {$_ eq $key} @chars;

print "$key appears in the string $count times.\n";
```

The sneaky part about this example is the line that uses `split` to convert the string into a list of characters. Once you have a list, then using `grep` is easy.

WEEK 2

DAY 9

Pattern Matching with Regular Expressions

After learning everything you've learned so far, you may think you've got a pretty good foundation in programming Perl, since you'd already be a good way through most of the concepts many other languages entail. But if you put down this book today and did nothing else with Perl beyond what I've already taught you, you'd miss one of the most powerful and flexible aspects of Perl—that of pattern matching using a technique called regular expressions. Pattern matching is more than just searching for some set of characters in your data; it's a way of looking at data and processing that data in a manner that can be incredibly efficient and amazingly easy to program. Learning Perl without learning regular expressions is like trying to understand snowboarding without ever encountering snow. In other words, don't stop now—you're just getting to the good part!

Today, we'll dive deep into regular expressions, why they're useful, how they're built, and how they work. Tomorrow we'll continue the discussion and cover more advanced uses of regular expressions. Today, specifically, you'll learn how to:

- Understand pattern matching and regular expressions and why you'll find them useful
- Build simple regular expressions with single-character searches and pattern-matching operators
- Match groups of characters
- Match multiple instances of characters
- Use patterns in tests and loops

The Whys and Wherefores of Pattern Matching

Pattern matching is the technique of searching a string containing text or binary data for some set of characters based on a specific search pattern. When you search for a string of characters in a file using the Find command in your word processor, or when you use a search engine to look for something on the Web, you're using a simple version of pattern matching: your criteria is "find these characters." In those environments, you can often customize your criteria in particular ways, for example, to search for this or that, to search for this or that but not the other thing, to search for whole words only, or to search only for those words that are 12 points and underlined. Pattern matching in Perl, however, can be even more complicated than that. Using Perl, you can define an incredibly specific set of search criteria, and do it in an incredibly small amount of space using a pattern-definition mini-language called *regular expressions.*

Perl's regular expressions, often called just *regexes* or *REs*, borrow from the regular expressions used in many UNIX tools, such as `grep(1)` and `sed(1)`. As with many other features Perl has borrowed from other places, however, Perl includes slight changes and lots of added capabilities. If you're used to using regular expressions, you'll be able to pick up Perl's regular expressions fairly easily, since most of the same rules apply (although there are some gotchas to be aware of, particularly if you've used sophisticated regular expressions in the past).

Note

> The term *regular expressions* may seem sort of nonsensical. They don't really seem to be expressions, nor is it easy to figure out what's regular about them. Don't get hung up on the term itself; *regular expression* is a term borrowed from mathematics that refers to the actual language with which you write patterns for pattern matching in Perl.

I used the example of the search engine and the Find command earlier to describe the sorts of things that pattern matching can do. It's important for you not to get hung up on thinking that pattern matching is only good for plain old searching. The sorts of things regular expressions can do in Perl include

- Making sure your user has entered the data you're looking for—input validation
- Verifying that input is in the right specific format, for example, that email addresses have the right components
- Extracting parts of a file that match a specific criteria (for example, you could extract the headings from a file to build a table of contents, or extract all the links in and HTML file)
- Splitting a string into elements based on different separator fields (and often, complex nested separator fields)
- Finding irregularities in a set of data—multiple spaces that don't belong there, duplicated words, errors in formatting
- Counting the number of occurrences of a pattern in a string
- Searching and replacing—find a string that matches a pattern and replace it with some other string

This is only a partial list, of course—you can apply Perl's regular expressions to all kinds of tasks. Generally, if there's a task for which you'd want to iterate over a string or over your data in another language, that task is probably better solved in Perl using regular expressions. Many of the operations you learned about yesterday for finding bits of strings can be better done with patterns.

Pattern Matching Operators and Expressions

To use pattern matching in Perl, you figure out what you want to find, you write a regular expression to find it, and then you stick that pattern in a situation where the result of finding (or not finding) that pattern makes sense. As with other aspects of Perl, where you put a pattern and what context you use it in determines how that pattern is used.

We'll start with a fairly simple case—patterns in a Boolean scalar context, where if a string contains the pattern, the expression returns true.

To construct patterns in this way, you use two operators: the regular expression operator m// and the pattern-match operator =~, like this:

```
if ($string =~ m/foo/) {
   # do something...
}
```

What that test inside the if says is that if the string contained in $string contains the pattern foo, return true. Note that the =~ operator is not an assignment operator, even though it looks like one. =~ is used exclusively for pattern matching, and means, effectively, "find the pattern on the right somewhere in the string on the left." You'll sometimes find =~ called the *binding* operator.

The pattern itself is contained between the slashes in m//. This particular pattern is one of the simplest patterns you can create—it's just three specific characters in sequence (you'll learn more about what constitutes a match and what doesn't later on). The pattern could just as easily be m/.*\d+/ or m/^[+-]?\d+\.?\d*$/ or some other seemingly incomprehensible set of characters (don't panic yet; you'll learn how to decipher those patterns soon).

For these sorts of patterns, the m is optional and can be left off the pattern itself (and usually is). In addition, you can leave off the variable and the =~ if you want to search the contents of the default variable $_. Commonly in Perl, you'll see shorthand pattern matching like this one:

```
if (/^\d+/) { # ...
```

Which is equivalent to

```
if ($_ =~ m/^\d+/)  { # ...
```

You already learned a simple case of this yesterday with the grep function, which can use patterns to find a bit of a string inside the $_ list element:

```
@foothings = grep /foo/, @strings;
```

That line, in turn, is equivalent to this long form:

```
@foothings = grep { $_ =~ /foo/ } @strings;
```

As we work through today's lesson, you'll learn different ways of using patterns in different contexts and for different reasons. Much of the work of learning pattern matching, however, involves actually learning the regular expression syntax to build patterns, so let's stick with this one situation for now.

Simple Patterns

We'll start with some of the most simple and basic patterns you can create: patterns that match specific sequences of characters, patterns that match only at specific places in a string, or combining patterns using what's called alternation.

Character Sequences

One of the simplest patterns is just a sequence of characters you want to match, like this:

```
/foo/
/this or that/
/   /
/Laura/
/patterns that match specific sequences/
```

All of these patterns will match if the data contains those characters in that order. All the characters must match, including spaces. The word `or` in the second pattern doesn't have any special significance (it's not a logical `or`); that pattern will only match if the data contains the string `this or that` somewhere inside it.

Note that characters in patterns can be matched anywhere in a string. Word boundaries are not relevant for these patterns—the pattern `/if/` will match in the string `"if wishes were horses"` and in the string `"there is no difference"`. The pattern `/if /`, however, because it contains a space, will only match in the first string where the characters `i`, `f`, and the one space occur in that order.

Upper- and lowercase are relevant for characters: `/kazoo/` will only match `kazoo` and not `Kazoo` or `KAZOO`. To make a particular search case-insensitive, you can use the `i` option after the pattern itself (the `i` indictes *ignore case*), like this:

```
/kazoo/i # search for any upper and lowercase versions
```

Alternately, you can also create patterns that will search for either upper- or lowercase letters, as you'll learn about in the next section.

You can include most alphanumeric characters in patterns, including string escapes for binary data (octal and hex escapes). There are a number of characters that you cannot match without escaping them. These characters are called metacharacters and refer to bits of the pattern language and not to the literal character.

These are the metacharacters to watch out for in patterns:

```
^    $
.    +
?    *
{    (
)    \
/    |
[
```

If you want to actually match a metacharacter in a string—for example, search for an actual question mark—you can escape it using a backslash, just as you would in a regular string:

```
/\?/  # matches question mark
```

Matching at Word or Line Boundaries

When you create a pattern to match a sequence of characters, those characters can appear anywhere inside the string and the pattern will still match. But sometimes you want a pattern to match those characters only if they occur at a specific place—for example, match `/if/` only when it's a whole word, or `/kazoo/` only if it occurs at the start of the line (that is, the beginning of the string).

I'm making an assumption here that the data you're searching is a line of input, where the line is a single string with no embedded newline characters. Given that assumption, the terms *string*, *line*, and *data* are effectively interchangeable. Tomorrow, we'll talk about how patterns deal with newlines.

To match a pattern at a specific position, you use pattern anchors. To anchor a pattern at the start of the string, use `^`:

```
/^Kazoo/  # match only if Kazoo occurs at the start of the line
```

To match at the end of the string, use `$`:

```
/end$/  # match only if end occurs at the end of the line
```

Once again, think of the pattern as a sequence of things in which each part of the pattern must match the data you're applying it to. The pattern matching routines in Perl actually begin searching at a position just before the first character, which will match `^`. Then it moves to each character in turn until the end of the line, where `$` matches. If there's a newline at the end of the string, the position marked by `$` is just before that newline character.

So, for example, let's see what happens when you try to match the pattern `/^foo/` to the string `"to be or not to be"` (which, obviously, won't match, but let's try it anyhow). Perl starts at the beginning of the line, which matches the `^` character. That part of the pattern is true. It then tests the first character. The pattern wants to see an `f` there, but it got a `t` instead, so the pattern stops and returns false.

What happens if you try to apply the pattern to the string `"fob"`? The match will get farther—it'll match the start of the line, the `f` and the `o`, but then fail at the `b`. And keep in mind that `/^foo/` will not match in the string `" foo"`—the `foo` is not at the very start of the line where the pattern expects it to be. It will only match when all four parts of the pattern match the string.

Some interesting but potentially tricky uses of `^` and `$`—can you guess what these patterns will match?

```
/^/
/^1$/
/^$/
```

The first pattern matches any strings that have a start of the line. It would be very weird strings indeed that didn't have the start of a line, so this pattern will match any string data whatsoever, even the empty string.

The second one wants to find the start of the line, the numeral `1`, and then the end of the line. So it'll only match if the string contains `1` and only `1`—it won't match `"123"` or `"foo 1"` or even `"1 "`.

The third pattern will match only if the start of the line is immediately followed by the end of the line—that is, if there is no actual data. This pattern will only match an empty line. Keep in mind that because `$` occurs just before the newline character, this last pattern will match both `""` and `"\n"`.

Another boundary to match is a word boundary—where a word boundary is considered the position between a word character (a letter, number, or underscore) and some other character such as whitespace or punctuation. A word boundary is indicated using a `\b` escape. So `/\bif\b/` will match only when the whole word `if` exists in the string—but not when the characters `i` and `f` appear in the middle of a word (as in "difference."). You can use `\b` to refer to both the start and end of a word; `/\bif/`, for example, will match in both `"if I were king"` and `"that result is iffy"`, and even in `"As if!"`, but not in `"bomb the aquifer"` or `"the serif is obtuse"`.

You can also search for a pattern not in a word boundary using the `\B` escape. With this, `/\Bif/` will match only when the characters `i` and `f` occur inside a word and *not* at the start of a word.

Matching Alternatives

Sometimes, when you're building a pattern, you may want to search for more than one pattern in the same string and then test based on whether all the patterns were found, or perhaps any of the set of patterns was found. You could, of course, do this with the regular Perl logical expressions for Boolean AND (`&&` or `and`) and OR (`||` or `or`) with multiple pattern-matching expressions, something like this:

```
if (($in =~ /this/) || ($in =~ /that/)) { ...
```

Then, if the string contains `/this/` or if it contains `/that/`, the whole test will return true.

In the case of an OR search (match this pattern or that pattern—either one will work), however, there is a regular expression metacharacter you can use: the pipe character (`|`). So, for example, the long `if` test in that example could just be written as:

```
if ($in =~ /this|that/) { ...
```

Using the `|` character inside a pattern is officially known as *alternation* because it allows you to match alternate patterns. A true value for the pattern occurs if any of the alternatives match.

Any anchoring characters you use with an alternation character apply only to the pattern on the same side of the pipe. So, for example, the pattern `/^this|that/` means "`this` at the start of the line" or "`that` anywhere," and not "either `this` or `that` at the start of a line." If you wanted the latter form you could use `/^this|^that/`, but a better way is to group your patterns using parentheses:

```
/^(this|that)/
```

For this pattern, Perl first matches the start of the line, and then tries and matches all the characters in `this`. If it can't match `this`, it'll then back up to the start of the line and try to match `that`. For a pattern line `/^this|that/`, it'll first try and match everything on the left side of the pipe (start of line, followed by `this`), and if it can't do that, it'll back up and search the entire string for `that`.

An even better version would be to group only the things that are different between the two patterns, not just the `^` to match the beginning of the line, but also the `th` characters, like this:

```
/^th(is|at)/
```

This last version means that Perl won't even try the alternation unless `th` has already been matched at the start of the line, and then there will be a minimum of backing up to match the pattern. With regular expressions, the less work Perl has to do to match something, the better.

You can use grouping for any kinds of alternation within a pattern. For example, `/(1st|2nd|3rd|4th) time/` will match `"1st time"`, `"2nd time"`, and so on—as long as the data contains one of the alternations inside the parentheses and the string `" time"` (note the space).

Matching Groups of Characters

So far, so good? The regular expressions we've been building so far shouldn't strike you as being that complex, particularly if you look at each pattern in the way that Perl looks at it, character by character and alternate by alternate, taking grouping into effect. Now we're going to start looking at some of the shortcuts that regular expressions provide for describing and grouping various kinds of characters.

Character Classes

Say you had a string, and you wanted to match one of five words in that string: `pet`, `get`, `met`, `set`, and `bet`. You could do this:

```
/pet|get|met|set|bet/
```

That would work. Perl would search through the whole string for `pet`, then search through the whole string for `get`, then do the same thing for `met`, and so on. A shorter way—both for number of characters for you to type and for Perl—would be to group characters so that we don't duplicate the `et` part each time:

```
/(p|g|m|s|b)et/
```

In this case, Perl searches through the entire string for `p`, `g`, `m`, `s`, or `b`, and if it finds one of those, it'll try to match `et` just after it. Much more efficient!

This sort of pattern—where you have lots of alternates of single characters, is such a common case that there's regular expression syntax for it. The set of alternating characters is called a *character class*, and you enclose it inside brackets. So, for example, that same pet/get/met pattern would look like this using a character class:

```
/[pgmsb]et/
```

That's a savings of at least a couple of characters, and it's even slightly easier to read. Perl will do the same thing as the alternation character, in this case: it'll look for any of the characters inside the character class before testing any of the characters outside it.

The rules for the characters that can appear inside a character class are different from those that can appear outside of one—most of the metacharacters become plain ordinary characters inside a character class (the exception being a right-bracket, which needs to be escaped for obvious reasons, a caret (^), which can't appear first, or a hyphen, which has a special meaning inside a character class). So, for example, a pattern to match on punctuation at the end of a sentence (punctuation after a word boundary and before two spaces) might look like this:

```
/\b[.!?]  /
```

Whereas `.` and `?` have special meanings outside the character class, here they're plain old characters.

Ranges

What if you wanted to match, say, all the lowercase characters `a` through `f` (as you might in a hexadecimal number, for example). You could do:

```
/[abcdef]/
```

Looks like a job for a range, doesn't it? You can do ranges inside character classes, but you don't use the range operator `..` that you learned about on Day 4. Regular expressions use a hyphen for ranges instead (which is why you have to backslash it if you actually want to match a hyphen). So, for example, lowercase `a` through `f` looks like this:

```
/[a-f]/
```

You can use any range of numbers or characters, as in `/[0-9]/`, `/[a-z]/` or `/[A-Z]/`. You can even combine them: `/[0-9a-z]/` will match the same thing as `/[0123456789abcdefghijklmnopqrstuvwxyz]/`.

Negated Character Classes

Brackets define a class of characters to match in a pattern. You can also define a set of characters *not* to match using negated character classes—just make sure the first character in your character class is a caret (^). So, for example, to match anything that isn't an `A` or a `B`, use:

```
/[^AB]/
```

Note that the caret inside a character class is not the same as the caret outside one. The former is used to create a negated character class, and the latter is used to mean the beginning of a line.

If you want to actually search for the caret character inside a character class, you're welcome to—just make sure it's not the first character or escape it (it might be best just to escape it either way to cut down on the rules you have to keep track of):

```
/[\^?.%]/   # search for ^, ?, ., %
```

You most likely end up using a lot of negated character classes in your regular expressions, so keep this syntax in mind. Note one subtlety: negated character classes don't negate the entire value of the pattern. If `/[12]/` means "return true if the data contains 1 or 2," `/[^12]/` does not mean "return true if the data *doesn't* contain 1 or 2." If that were the case, you'd get a match even if the string in question was empty. What negated character classes really mean is "match any character that's not these characters." There must be at least one actual character to match for a negated character class to work.

Special Classes

If character class ranges are still too much for you to type, there are also special character classes (and negated character classes) that have their own escape codes. You'll see these a lot in regular expressions, particularly those that match numbers in specific formats. Note that these special codes don't need to be enclosed between brackets; you can use them all by themselves to refer to that class of characters.

Table 9.1 shows the list of special character class codes:

TABLE 9.1 CHARACTER CLASS CODES

Code	*Equivalent Character Class*	*What It Means*
`\d`	`[0-9]`	Any digit
`\D`	`[^0-9]`	Any character not a digit
`\w`	`[0-9a-zA-z_]`	Any "word character"
`\W`	`[^0-9a-zA-z_]`	Any character not a word character
`\s`	`[ \t\n\r\f]`	whitespace (space, tab, newline, carriage return, form feed)
`\S`	`[^ \t\n\r\f]`	Any non-whitespace character

Word characters (`\w` and `\W`) is a bit mystifying—why is an underscore considered a word character, but punctuation isn't? In reality, word characters have little to do with words, but are the valid characters you can use in variable names: numbers, letters, and underscores. Any other characters are not considered word characters.

You can use these character codes anywhere you need a specific type of character. For example, the `\d` code to refers to any digit. With `\d`, you could create patterns that match any three digits `/\d\d\d/`, or, perhaps, any three digits, a dash, and any four digits, to represent a phone number such as 555-1212: `/\d\d\d-\d\d\d\d/`. All this repetition isn't necessarily the best way to go, however, as you'll learn in a bit when we cover quantifiers.

Matching Any Character with . (dot)

The broadest possible character class you can get is to match based on any character whatsoever. For that, you'd use the dot character (.). So, for example, the following pattern will match lines that contain one character and one character only:

```
/^.$/
```

You'll use the dot more often in patterns with quantifiers (which you'll learn about next), but the dot can be used to indicate fields of a certain width, for example:

```
/^..:/
```

This pattern will match only if the line starts with two characters and a colon.

More about the dot operator after we pause for an example.

An Example: Optimizing `numspeller`

Remember the `numspeller` script from yesterday? This was the script that took a single-digit number and converted it into a word. You may remember when I described the `numspeller` script that I mentioned it was easier to write using regular expressions. So, now that you know something of regular expressions, let's rewrite the script to use regular expressions instead of all those `if` statements.

And, while we're at it, why don't we revise the part of number speller that verifies the input. We can do a lot more in terms of input validation with regular expressions, to the point of absurdity. In fact, we'll approach absurdity with the input validation in this script. This version tests for a number of things that could be entered and replies with various comments (many of them sarcastic):

```
% numspeller2.pl
Enter the number you want to spell(0-9): foo
You can't fool me.  There are letters in there.
Enter the number you want to spell(0-9): 45foo
You can't fool me.  There are letters in there.
Enter the number you want to spell(0-9): ###
huh?  That *really* doesn't look like a number
Enter the number you want to spell(0-9): -45
That's a negative number.  Positive only, please!
Enter the number you want to spell(0-9): 789
Too big!  0 through 9, please.
Enter the number you want to spell(0-9): 4
Thanks!
Number 4 is four
Try another number (y/n)?: x
y or n, please
```

```
Try another number (y/n)?: n
%
```

Instead of showing you this script and then working through it line by line, let's go in the reverse direction: I'm going to show you sections from both the old and new versions of `numspeller`, explain them, and then at the end, I'll list the whole thing so you can get the big picture.

Let's start with the loop that accepts a number as input. This is what the loop looked like in the old version of `numspeller`:

```
while () {
    print 'Enter the number you want to spell: ';
    chomp($num = <STDIN>);
    if ($num gt "9" ) { # test for strings
        print "No strings.  0 through 9 please..\n";
        next;
    }
    if ($num > 9) { # numbers w/more than 1 digit
        print "Too big. 0 through 9 please.\n";
        next;
    }
    if ($num < 0) { # negative numbers
        print "No negative numbers.  0 through 9 please.\n";
        next;
    }
    last;
}
```

We can easily replace the three tests in this loop with regular expressions that make more sense—and we can also test for more sophisticated kinds of things. Our new loop will test for three major groups of things:

- Whether the input contains a single digit and only a single digit (in which case we're done).
- Whether the input contains any characters other than numbers.
- Whether the number is larger than 9.

That second test can then be broken into sub-tests for things like alphabetic characters, negative numbers (starting with `-`), floating-point numbers (with a decimal point), or totally bizarre characters. Here's the new version of our loop, which also makes use of the $_ variable to save us some typing in the pattern matching tests:

```
1: while () {
2:     print 'Enter the number you want to spell(0-9): ';
3:     chomp($_ = <STDIN>);
4:     if (/^\d$/) {  # correct input
5:         print "Thanks!\n";
6:         last;
7:     } elsif (/^$/) {
8:         print "You didn't enter anything.\n";
9:     } elsif (/\D/) { # nonnummbers
10:        if (/[a-zA-z]/) { # letters
11:            print "You can't fool me.  There are letters in there.\n";
12:        } elsif (/^-\d/) { # negative numbers
13:            print "That's a negative number.  Positive only,
               please!\n";
14:        } elsif (/\./) { # decimals
15:            print "That looks like it could be a floating-point
               number.\n";
16:            print "I can't spell a floating-point number.  Try
               again.\n";
17:        } elsif (/[\W_]/) {  # other chars
18:            print "huh?  That *really* doesn't look like a number\n";
19:        }
20:    } elsif ($_ > 9) {
21:        print "Too big!  0 through 9, please.\n";
22:    }
23: }
```

Let's look at those regular expressions, line by line, so you know what's getting matched here:

- Line 4: `/^\d$/` This pattern matches input with a single digit, and only a single digit—that is, it matches exactly the input we want to match. I stuck it up here at the top because if the user does enter the right value, we don't want to spend a lot of time cycling through all the options to figure out that they were right. This way, given this very specific match, if we get the correct input we can exit right out of the loop with `last`.
- Line 7: `/^$/` As you learned in the section on matching at boundaries, this pattern matches an empty line—which is just what you get here if you hit return at the prompt without entering anything.
- Line 9: `/\D/` This character code means "any characters other than numbers." If you type anything at the prompt that isn't a number—a mixture of numbers and letters, all letters, or with characters like `-`, `.`, or $—this pattern will match. This branches into a number of sub-tests for the specific non-number characters that got entered.

- Line 10: `/[a-zA-z]/` These character class ranges look for actual characters from the alphabet. I didn't use the `\w` code here because that would have included the underscore, and I want to group the underscore into the any-other-character test instead.
- Line 12: `/^-\d/` Here we're testing for a dash at the start of the line, immediately followed by a digit. This is the test for negative numbers.
- Line 14: `/\./` Input containing a decimal point is probably a floating-point number. Note here that because `.` is a metacharacter for the pattern, we have to escape it to match an actual dot.
- Line 17: `/[\W_]` Here we use a character class of two things: any character that's not a word character (0-9, a-z, A-Z), or the underscore. This is the catch-all for all other characters that might have been entered.
- Line 20: `No pattern here` This line catches input that is a number (so it won't get caught by most of the previous tests), but is a number with more than one digit. Here we'll just test the value to see if it's bigger than 9 to catch those cases. There is actually a pattern than will match this, but you haven't learned it yet. This test works just as well.

The next part of the old `numspeller` script was a set of `if...elsif` loops that compared the input value to a number string. Using regular expressions, the default variable `$_`, and logical expressions used as conditionals, we can reduce the nested `ifs` that looked like this:

```
if ($num == 1) { print 'one'; }
    elsif ($num == 2) { print 'two'; }
    elsif ($num == 3) { print 'three'; }
    elsif ($num == 4) { print 'four'; }
    # ... other numbers removed for space
}
```

into a set of logicals that looks like this:

```
/1/ && print 'one';
/2/ && print 'two';
/3/ && print 'three';
/4/ && print 'four';
# ... and so on
```

Cool, eh? It's almost switch-like, and, arguably, easier to read.

Finally, we'll rewrite our little yes-or-no loop to repeat the entire script. The old version looked like this:

```
while () {
    print 'Try another number (y/n)?: ';
    chomp ($exit = <STDIN>);
    $exit = lc $exit;
    if ($exit ne 'y' && $exit ne 'n') {
        print "y or n, please\n";
    }
    else { last; }
}
```

There's actually nothing terribly wrong with this version, but since this is the pattern matching lesson, let's use pattern matching here, too:

```
while () {
        print 'Try another number (y/n)?: ';
        chomp ($exit = <STDIN>);
        $exit = lc $exit;
        if ($exit =~ /^[yn]/) {
            last;
        }
        else {
            print "y or n, please\n";
        }
    }
```

Note the differences between this loop and the input loop. In the input loop, we stored the input in the `$_` variable, so we could just put the pattern into the test itself. Here we're matching against the string in the `$exit` variable, so we have to use the `=~` operator instead. In the pattern itself, we test to see if what was typed was either `y` or `n` (Y and N will get converted to lowercase with the `lc` function), and if so, exit the loop and return to the outer loop, which repeats the script if necessary.

In this example, I've used quite a few regular expressions, many of them gratuitous. It's worth mentioning at this point that you shouldn't necessarily use regular expressions everywhere simply because they're cool. The Perl regular expression engine is really powerful for really powerful things, but there is some overhead in terms of efficiency if you use it for simple things. Simple tests and `if` statements will often execute faster than regular expressions. If you're concerned about the efficiency of your code, keep that in mind.

Listing 9.1 shows the full code for the new version of `numspeller.pl`:

LISTING 9.1 THE numspeller2.pl SCRIPT

```
#!/usr/bin/perl -w
# numberspeller:  prints out word approximations of numbers
# simple version, only does single-digits

$exit = "";  # whether or not to exit the script.

while ($exit ne "n") {

    while () {
        print 'Enter the number you want to spell(0-9): ';
        chomp($_ = <STDIN>);
        if (/^\d$/) {
            print "Thanks!\n";
            last;
        } elsif (/^$/) {
            print "You didn't enter anything.\n";
        } elsif (/\D/) {        # nonnummbers
            if (/[a-zA-z]/) { # letters
                print "You can't fool me.  There are letters in there.\n";
            } elsif (/^-\d/) { # negative numbers
                print "That's a negative number.  Postive only,
                please!\n";
            } elsif (/\./) { # decimals
                print "That looks like it could be a floating-point
                number.\n";
                print "I can't spell a floating-point number.  Try
                again.\n";
            } elsif (/[\W_]/) {  # other chars
                print "huh?  That *really* doesn't look like a number\n";
            }
        } elsif ($_ > 9) {
            print "Too big!  0 through 9, please.\n";
        }
    }

    print "Number $_ is ";
    /1/ && print 'one';
    /2/ && print 'two';
    /3/ && print 'three';
    /4/ && print 'four';
    /5/ && print 'five';
    /6/ && print 'six';
    /7/ && print 'seven';
    /8/ && print 'eight';
    /9/ && print 'nine';
    /0/ && print 'zero';
    print "\n";
```

continues

LISTING 9.1 CONTINUED

```
        while () {
            print 'Try another number (y/n)?: ';
            chomp ($exit = <STDIN>);
            $exit = lc $exit;
            if ($exit =~ /^[yn]/) {
                last;
            }
            else {
                print "y or n, please\n";
            }
        }
    }
```

Matching Multiple Instances of Characters

Ready for more? The second group of regular expression syntax to explore is that of quantifiers. Whereas the patterns you've seen up to now refer to individual things or groups of individual things, quantifiers allow you to indicate multiple instances of things—or potentially no things. These regular expression metacharacters are called quantifiers, since they indicate some quantity of characters or groups of characters in the pattern you're looking for.

Perl's regular expressions include three quantifier metacharacters: `?`, `*`, and `+`. Each refers to some multiple of the character or group that appears just before it in the pattern.

Optional Characters with `?`

Let's start with `?`, which matches a sequence that may or may not have the character immediately preceding it (that is, it matches zero or one instance of that character). So, for example, take this pattern:

```
/be?ar/
```

The question mark in that pattern refers to the character preceding it (`e`). This pattern would match with the string `"step up to the bar"` and with the string `"grin and bear it"`—because both `bar` and `bear` will match this pattern. The string you're searching must have the `b`, the `a`, and the `r`, but the `e` is optional.

Once again, think in terms of how the string is processed. The `b` is matched first. Then the next character is tested. If it's an `e`, no problem, we move on to the next character both in the string and in the pattern (the `a`). If it's not an `e`, that's still no problem; we move on to the next character in the pattern to see if it matches instead.

You can create groups of optional characters with parentheses:

```
/bamboo(zle)?/
```

The parentheses make that whole group of characters (`zle`) optional—this pattern will match both `bamboo` or `bamboozle`. The thing just before the `?` is the optional thing, be it a single character or a group.

Note

> Why bother creating a pattern like this? It would seem that the (`zle`) part of this pattern is irrelevant, and that just plain `/bamboo/` would work just as well, with fewer characters. In these easy cases, where we're just trying to find out whether something matches, yes or no, it doesn't matter. Tomorrow, when you learn how to extract the thing that matched and create more complex patterns, the distinction will be more important.

You can also use character classes with `?`:

```
/thing \d?/
```

This pattern will match the strings `"thing 1"`, `"thing 9"`, and so on, but will also match `"thing "` (note the space). Any character in the character class can appear either zero or one times for the pattern to match.

Matching Multiple Characters with *

A second form of multiplier is the `*`, which works similarly to the `?` except that `*` allows zero or any number of the preceding character to appear—not just zero or one instance as `?` does. Take this pattern:

```
/xy*z/
```

In this pattern, the x and the z are required, but the y can appear any number of times including not at all. This pattern will match `xyz`, `xyyz`, `xyyyyyyyyyyyyyyyz`, or just plain old `xz` without the y.

As with `?`, you can use groups or character classes before the `*`. One use of `*` is to use it with the dot character—which means that any number of any characters could appear at that position:

```
/this.*/
```

This pattern matches the strings `"thisthat"`, `"this is not my sweater. The blue one with the flowers is mine"`, or even just `"this"`—remember, the character at the end doesn't have to exist for there to be a match.

A common mistake is to forget that * stands for "zero or more instances," and to use it like this:

```
if (/^[0-9]*$/) {
    # contains numbers
}
```

The intent here is to create a pattern that matches only if the input contains numbers and only numbers. And this pattern will indeed match `"7"`, `"1540"`, `"15443"`, and so on. But it'll also match the empty string—because the `*` means that no numbers whatsoever will also produce a match. Usually, when you want to require something to appear at least once, you want to use `+` instead of `*`.

Note also that "match zero or more numbers," as that example would imply, does not mean that it will match *any* string that happens to have zero numbers—it won't match the string `"lederhosen"`, for example. Matching zero or more numbers does not imply any other matches; if you want it to match characters rather than numbers, you'll need to include those characters in the pattern. With regular expressions, you have to be very specific about what you want to match.

Requiring at Least One Instance with +

The `+` metacharacter works identically to `*`, with one significant difference; instead of allowing zero or more instances of the given character or group, `+` requires that character or group to appear at least once ("one or more instances."). So given a pattern like the one we used for `*`:

```
/xy+z/
```

This pattern will match `xyz`, `xyyz`, `xyyyyyyyyyyz`, but it will not match `xz`. The `y` must appear at least once.

As with `*` and `?`, you can use groups and character classes with `+`.

Restricting the Number of Instances

For both `*` and `+` the given character or group can appear any number of times—there is no upper limit (characters with `?` can appear only once). But what if you want to match a specific number of instances? What if the pattern you're looking for does require a lower or upper limit, and any more or less than that won't match? You can use the optional curly bracket metacharacters to set limits on the quantity, like this:

```
/\d{1,4} /
```

This pattern matches if the data includes one digit, two digits, three digits, or four digits, any of them followed by a space; it won't match any more digits than that, nor will it match if there aren't any digits whatsoever. The first number inside the brackets is the minimum number of instances to match; the second is the maximum. Or you can match an exact number by just including the number itself:

```
/a{5}b/
```

This pattern will only match if it can find five 'a's in a row followed by one b—no more, no less. It's exactly equivalent to /aaaaab/. A less specific use of {} for an exact number of instances might be something like this:


```
/\$\d+\.\d{2}/
```

Can you work through this pattern and figure out what it matches? It uses a number of escaped characters, so it might be confusing. First, it matches a dollar sign (\$), then one or more decimals (\d+), then it matches a decimal point (.), and finally, it matches only if that pattern is followed by two decimals and no more. Put it all together and this pattern matches monetary input—$45.23 would match just fine, as would $0.45 or $15.00, but $.45 and $34.2 would not. This pattern requires at least one number on the left side of the decimal, and a maximum of two numbers on the right.

Back to the curly brackets. You can set a lower bound on the match, but not an upper bound, by leaving off the maximum number but keeping the comma:

```
/ba{4,}t/
```

This pattern matches b, at least four or more instances of the letter a, and then t. Three instances of a in a row won't match, but twenty will.

Note that you could represent +, * and ? in curly bracket format:

```
/x{0,1}/  # same as /x?/
/x{0,}/   # same as /x*/
/x{1,}/   # same as /x+/
```

More About Building Patterns

We started this lesson with a basic overview of how to use patterns in your Perl scripts using an if test and the =~ operator—or, if you're searching in $_, you can leave off the =~ part altogether. Now that you know something of constructing patterns with regular expression syntax, let's return to Perl, and look at some different ways of using patterns in your Perl scripts, including interpolating variables into patterns and using patterns in loops.

Patterns and Variables

In all the examples so far, we've used patterns as hard-coded sets of characters in the test of a Perl script. But what if you want to match different things based on some sort of input? How do you change the search pattern on the fly?

Easy. Patterns, like quotes, can contain variables, and the value of the variable is substituted into the pattern:

```
$pattern = "^\d{3}$";
if (/$pattern/) { ...
```

The variable in question can contain a string with any kind of pattern, including metacharacters. You can use this technique to combine patterns in different ways, or to search for patterns based on input. For example, here's a simple script that prompts you for both a pattern and some data to search, and then returns true or false if there's a match:

```
#!/usr/bin/perl -w

print 'Enter the pattern: ';
chomp($pat = <STDIN>);

print 'Enter the string: ';
chomp($in = <STDIN>);

if ($in =~ /$pat/) { print "true\n"; }
else { print "false\n"; }
```

You may find this script (or one like it) useful yourself, as you learn more about regular expressions.

Patterns and Loops

One way of using patterns in Perl scripts is to use them as tests, as we have up to this point. In this context (a scalar Boolean context), they evaluate to true or false based on whether the pattern matches the data. Another way to use a pattern is as the test in a loop, with the `/g` option at the end of the pattern, like this:

```
while (/pattern/g) {
  # loop
}
```

The `/g` option is used to match all the patterns in the given string (here, `$_`, but you can use the `=~` operator to match somewhere else). In the case of an `if` test, the `/g` option won't matter, the test will return true at the first match it finds. In the case of `while` (or a `for` loop), however, the `/g` will cause the test to return true each time the pattern occurs in the string—and the statements in the block will execute that number of times as well.

We're still talking about using patterns in a scalar context, here; the /g just causes interesting things to happen in loops. We'll get to using patterns in list context tomorrow.

Another Example: Counting

Here's an example of a script that makes use of that patterns-in-loops feature I just mentioned to work through a file (or any numbers of files) and count the incidences of some pattern in that file. With this script you could, for example, count the number of times your name occurs in a file, or find out how many hits to your Web site came from America Online (`aol.com`). I ran it on a draft of this lesson and found that I've used the word *pattern* 184 times so far.

Listing 9.2 shows this simple script:

Listing 9.2 `count.pl`

```
#!/usr/bin/perl -w

$pat = ""; # thing to search for
$count = 0; # number of times it occurs

print 'Search for what? ';
chomp($pat = <STDIN>);
while (<>) {
    while (/$pat/g) {
        $count++;
    }
}

print "Found /$pat/ $count times.\n";
```

As with all the scripts we've built that cycle through files using <>, you'll have to call this one on the command line with the name of a file:

```
% count.pl logfile
Search for what? aol.com
Found /aol.com/ 3456 times.
%
```

Nothing in Listing 9.2 should look overly surprising, although there are a few points to note. Remember that using `while` with the file input characters (<>) sets each line of input to the default variable `$_`. Since patterns will also match with that value by default, we don't need a temporary variable to hold each line of input. The first `while` loop (line 8), then, reads each line from the input files. The second `while` loop searches that single line of input repeatedly and increments `$count` each time it finds the pattern in each line. This way, we can get the total number of instances of the given pattern, both inside each line and for all the lines in the input.

One other important thing to note about this script: if you have it search for a phrase instead of a single word—for example, find all instances of both a first and last name—then there is a possibility that that phrase could fall across multiple lines. This script will miss those instances, since neither line will completely match the pattern. Tomorrow, you'll learn how to search for a pattern that can fall on multiple lines.

Pattern Precedence

Back in Day 2, "Working with Strings and Numbers," you may remember we had a little chart that showed the precedence of the various operators, and allowed you to figure out which parts of an expression would evaluate first in a larger expression. Metacharacters in patterns have the same sort of precedence rules, so you can figure out which characters or groups of characters those metacharacters refer to. Table 9.2 shows that precedence, where characters closer to the top of the table group tighter than those lower down.

TABLE 9.2 PATTERN METACHARACTER PRECEDENCE

Character	*Meaning*
`( )`	Grouping and memory
`? + * { }`	Quantifiers
`x \x $ ^ (?= ) (?!)`	Characters, anchors, look-ahead
`¦`	Alternation

As with expressions, you can group characters with `()` to force them to be evaluated as a sequence.

You haven't learned about all these metacharacters yet. Tomorrow, we'll explore more of them.

Going Deeper

In this lesson, I've given you the basics of regular expressions so you can get started, and tomorrow you'll learn even more uses of regular expressions. For more information about any of these things, the `perlre` man page can be quite enlightening. For this section, let's look at a few other features I haven't discussed elsewhere in this lesson.

More Uses of Patterns

At the start of this lesson, you learned about the =~ for matching patterns to scalar variables other than $_. In addition to =~, you can also use `!~`, like this:

```
$thing !~ = /pattern/;
```

`!~` is the logical not version of =~; in other words, it will return true only if the pattern is NOT found in `$thing`.

Another useful function for patterns is the `pos` function, which works similarly to the `index` function, except with patterns. You can use the this function to find out the exact position inside the pattern where a match was made using `m//g`, or to start a pattern-match at a specific position in a string. The `pos` function takes a scalar value (often a variable) as an argument, and returns the offset of the character *after* the last character of the match. For example:

```
$find = "123 345 456 346";
while ($find =~ /3/g) {
   @positions = (@positions, pos $find);
}
```

This code snippet builds an array of all the positions inside the string `$find` where the number 3 appears (3, 5, 13) in this case.

For more information on the `pos` function, see the `perlfunc` man page.

Pattern Delimiters and Escapes

All the patterns we've seen so far began and ended with slashes, with everything in between the characters or metacharacters to match. The slashes are themselves metacharacters, which means that if you want to actually search for a slash, you must backslash it. This can be problematic for patterns that actually contain lots of slashes—for example, UNIX pathnames, which are all separated by slashes. You can easily end up with a pattern that looks something like this:

```
/\/usr(\/local)*\/bin\//;
```

That's rather difficult to read (more so than many other regular expressions). Fortunately, Perl has a way around this: you don't have to use `//` to surround a pattern—you can use any non-alphanumeric character you want to. The only catch is that if you use a different character you must include the m on the m// expression (you can also replace the delimiters for substitution, but you have to use the s/// for that anyhow). You'll also have to escape uses of those delimiters inside the pattern itself. For example, the above expression could be written like this:

```
m%/usr(/local)*/bin/%;
```

Alternately, if you're creating a search pattern for a number of non-alphanumeric characters that are also pattern metacharacters, you may end up blackslashing an awful lot of those characters, making the pattern difficult to read. Using the \Q escape you can essentially turn off pattern processing for a set of characters, and the use \E to turn them back on again. For example, if you were searching for a pattern containing the characters {(^*)} (for whatever reason), this pattern would search for those literal characters:

```
/\Q{(^*)}\E/;
```

Using \Q to turn off pattern processing is also useful for variable interpolation inside patterns, to prevent unusual results in search pattern input:

```
/From:\s*\Q$from\E/;
```

Summary

Pattern matching and regular expressions are, arguably, Perl's most powerful feature. Whereas other languages may provide regular expression libraries or functions, pattern matching is intrinsic to Perl's operation and tightly bound to many other aspects of the language. Perl without regular expressions is just another funny-looking language. Perl with regular expressions is incredibly useful.

Today you learned all about patterns: building them, using them, saving bits of them, and putting them together with other parts of Perl. You learned about the various metacharacters you can use inside regular expressions: metacharacters for anchoring a pattern (^, $, \B, \b), for creating a character class ([] and [^]), for alternating between different patterns (¦) and for matching multiples of characters (+, *, ?).

With that language for creating patterns, you can then apply those patterns to strings using the m// expression. By default, patterns affect the string stored in the $_ variable, unless you use the =~ operator to apply the pattern to any variable.

Tomorrow, we'll expand on what you've learned here, building on the patterns you've already learned with additional patterns and more and better ways to use those patterns.

Q&A

Q What's the difference between `m//` and just `//`?

A Nothing, really. The `m` is optional, unless you're using a different character for the pattern delimiter. They both do the same thing.

Q Alternation produces a logical OR situation in the pattern. How do I do a logical AND?

A The easiest way is simply to use multiple patterns and the `&&` or `and` operators, like this:

```
/pat1/ && /pat2/;
```

If you know the order in which the two patterns will appear, you can just do something like this:

```
/pat1.*pat2/
```

Q I've got a pattern that searches for numbers: `/\d*/`. It matches for numbers, all right, but it also matches for all other strings. What am I doing wrong?

A You're using `*` when you mean `+`. Remember that `*` means "zero or more instances." That means if your string has no numbers whatsoever, it'll still match—you've got zero instances. `+` is used for at least one instance.

Workshop

The workshop provides quiz questions to help you solidify your understanding of the material covered and exercises to give you experience in using what you've learned. Try to understand the quiz and exercise answers before you go on to tomorrow's lesson.

Quiz

1. Define the terms *pattern matching* and *regular expressions.*
2. What sorts of tasks is pattern matching useful for? Name three.
3. What do each of the following patterns do?

```
/ice\s*cream/
/\d\d\d/
/^\d+$/
/ab?c[,.:]d/
/xy|yz+/
/[\d\s]{2,3}/
/"[^"]"/
```

4. Assume that $_ contains the value `123 kazoo kazoo 456`. What is the result of the following expressions?

```
if (/kaz/) {  # true or false?
while (/kaz/g) {  # what happens?
if (/^\d+/) {  # true or false?
if (/^\d?\s/) {  # true or false?
if (//d{4}/) {  # true or false?
```

Exercises

1. Write patterns to match the following things:
   - First words in a sentence (that is, words with initial capital letters following some kind of punctuation and white space)
   - Percentages (any decimals followed by a percent sign)
   - Any number (with or without a decimal point, positive or negative)
2. **BUG BUSTER**: What's wrong with this code?

```
print 'Enter a string: ';
chomp($input = <STDIN>);
print 'Search for what? ';
chomp($pat = <STDIN>);

if (/$pat/) {
   # pattern found, handle it
}
```

3. **BUG BUSTER**: How about this one?

```
print 'Search for what? ';
chomp($pat = <STDIN>);
while (<>) {
    while (/$pat/) {
        $count++;
    }
}
```

4. Yesterday, we created a script called `morenames.pl` that let you sort a list of names and search for different parts. The searching part used a rather convoluted mechanism of `each` and `grep` to find the pattern. Rewrite that part of the script to use patterns instead.

Answers

Here are the answers to the workshop questions in the previous section.

Quiz Answers

1. *Pattern matching* is the concept on Perl of writing a pattern which is then applied to a string or a set of data. *Regular expressions* are the language you use to write patterns.

2. There are many uses of pattern matching—you are limited only by your imagination. A few of them include
   a. Input validation
   b. Counting the number of things in a string
   c. Extracting data from a string based on certain criteria
   d. Splitting a string into different elements
   e. Replacing a specific pattern with some other string
   f. Finding regular (or irregular) patterns in a data set

3. The answers are as follows:
   a. This pattern matches the characters `ice` and `cream`, separated by zero or more whitespace characters.
   b. This pattern matches three digits in a row.
   c. This pattern matches one or more digits on a line by themselves with no other characters or whitespace.
   d. This pattern matches with an `a`, an optional `b`, a `c`, a comma, period, or colon, and a `d`. `ac.d` will match, as will `acb,d`, but not `abcd`.
   e. This pattern will match either `xy` or `y` with one or more `z`s.
   f. This pattern will match either a digit or a whitespace character appearing at least two but no more than three times.
   g. This pattern matches all the characters between opening and closing quotes.
4. The answers are
   a. True
   b. The loop repeats for every instance of `kaz` in the string (twice, in this case).
   c. True. The pattern matches one or more digits at the start of a line.
   d. False. This pattern matches 0 or one digits at the start of the line, followed by whitespace. It doesn't match the three digits we have in this string.
   e. False. This pattern matches four digits in a row; we have only three digits here.

Exercise Answers

1. As with all Perl, there are different ways of doing different things. Here are some possible solutions:

```
/[.!?"]\s+[A-Z]\w+\b/

/d+%/
/[+-]\d+\.?\d+/
/([a-zA-z]{3})\s*\1/
```

2. There's a mismatch between where the pattern is trying to match and where the actual data is. The pattern in the `if` statement is trying to match the pattern against `$_`, but as per the second line, the actual input is in `$input`. Use this `if` test instead:

   ```
   if ($input =~ /$pat/) {
   ```

3. This one's sneaky, because there's nothing syntactically wrong with this statement. The second `while` loop, the one with the pattern in it, will look for the pattern in `$_`, which is correct. But the test is a simple true and false test: Does that pattern exist? The first line that has that pattern in it will register as true, and then `$count` will get incremented. But then the test will occur again, and it'll still be true, and the counter will get incremented again and again, infinitely. There's nothing here to stop the loop from iterating.

   The `/g` option to the pattern in that `while` loop is what sets up the special case where the `while` loop will loop only as many times as the pattern was matched in the string and then stop. If you're using patterns inside loops, don't forget the `/g`.

4. The only parts that need to change are the lines that build the `@keys` array (the ones that use `grep` to search for the pattern). Here we'll use a `foreach` loop and a test in both the key and value. We'll also add the `/i` option to make it case insensitive, and also reset the `@keys` list to the empty list so that it doesn't build up between searches. Here's the new version of option 3:

   ```
   } elsif ($in eq '3') {        # find a name (1 or more)

      print "Search for what? ";
      chomp($search = <STDIN>);

      @keys = ();
      foreach (keys %names) {
          if (/$search/i or $names{$_} =~ /$search/i) {
              push @keys, $_;
          }
      }

      if (@keys) {
          print "Names matched: \n";
          foreach $name (sort @keys) {
              print "   $names{$name} $name\n";
          }
      } else {
          print "None found.\n";
      }
   }
   ```

WEEK 2

DAY 10

Doing More with Regular Expressions

Yesterday, we explored the basics of regular expressions, and you learned about the basic metacharacters and the ways you can use them to find patterns in strings. Today, in part two of our regular expression saga, we'll build on that background and explore other more complex ways in which regular expressions can be used. The things you'll learn about today include

- Extracting what was matched by a regular expression
- Notes on using patterns in scalar and list context
- Using patterns for search and replace
- More about using the `split` function
- Matching patterns over multiple lines

Extracting Matches

Using patterns in a Boolean scalar context, as tests for conditionals or loops, you can find out whether or not your pattern will match some part of a string. You only get one of two answers to that question: yes or no. Although this is useful for validating input, or for collating instances of patterns in a string, it's only half the story. Yes or no are fine answers, but even more useful is the ability to find out exactly what bit of data matched the pattern, and then reuse that data later on in the pattern, or to build a list of all the matches that were found.

Whether the thing you match with a pattern is useful or not, of course, depends on the pattern. If your pattern is `/abc/`, the thing that pattern matches is `abc`, and you knew that ahead of time. If, however, your pattern is something like `/\+.*/` (find a `+`, then any number of characters), then the thing that gets matched could be any set of characters—anything in your data that happens to occur after a `+` sign. Being able to get at the actual thing that gets matches is an important feature of regular expressions.

Perl has a number of ways to access matches, and different uses for those matches once you've got them. When you've got a match, you can refer back to that match later on in the pattern, save that match into a scalar variable, or collect a list of all the matches. We'll do all of those things in this section.

Using Parentheses for Backreferences

Yesterday, I showed you how to use parentheses to group together bits of a pattern, and also pointed out how you can use parentheses to change the precedence of how a pattern is matched. The third and most important use of parentheses is to save a match, and then refer back to that match later on to build a much more complex regular expression. This mechanism of saving matches is often called using *backreferences* in regular expression parlance.

Here's an example. Say you were looking for lines that begin and end with the same word. You don't care what the word is, just that they begin and end with the same one. You could do this with two pattern tests, a loop, and a couple `if`s. But a better way to do it is to test for the first word at the start of the line, save that value, and then test for that same word at the end of the line. Here's how you would do that:

```
/^(\S+)\s.*\1$/
```

Let's break it down character by character. The first character is a caret (`^`), which refers to the start of a line. Next is a parenthesis, which starts a pattern we will save for later. `\S` is a non-whitespace character, and `\S+` refers to one or more non-whitespace characters. The closing parenthesis ends the part that will be saved. With me so far? That pattern inside the parentheses will look for some set of characters followed by whitespace at the start of the line.

Moving on, we have a single whitespace character (`\s`), zero or more characters of any type (.*), `\1`, and then an end-of-line ($). What's `\1`? That's a reference to the thing we matched in the parentheses; `\1` says "put the thing you found in the first set of parentheses here." So whatever we matched inside those parentheses will then appear later on in the pattern—and therefore must appear at the end of the line for the entire pattern to return true. All parts of the pattern must be true, not just the one inside parentheses.

So, for example, let's say you had a line like this one:

```
"Perl is the best language for quick scripting.
If you want to get your job done, use Perl."
```


(OK, that's two lines. Pretend it's a single line inside a variable like `$_`). Will this match the preceding pattern, to test for the same word at the beginning and end of the line? Let's see. The pattern first tests for the beginning of the line, then any non-whitespace characters, ending with a single whitespace character. What we have: the word `Perl` and the space matches just fine (note, however, that the final whitespace character occurs outside the parentheses, so it won't get saved). The next part of the pattern (.+) will suck up any intervening characters to the end of the line, and then we'll look for a whitespace character and another instance of what we matched earlier. Remember, `\1` becomes the match, so we'll match the word `Perl`. After matching `Perl` the pattern next wants the end of the line with $—but no! We're not at the end of the line! We've got a period there! And because of that punctuation, the entire pattern will return false.

We could fix that, of course. You could include punctuation by changing the pattern to look like this:

```
/^(\S+)\s.+\s\1[.!?"]$/
```

The most important part, however, is the fact that `\1` refers to the thing that matched in parentheses. The pattern will only be successful if the thing that matched in the parentheses also appears at the same place in the string where you have the `\1` reference to that match.

You may be wondering about the significance of `\1`. It's called `\1` because there's only one pattern saved in parentheses. You can have any number of saved matches in a pattern, all surrounded by parentheses, and refer to each one to using `\1`, `\2`, `\3`, and so on, with the numbers matching up left to right. The numbers are assigned based on the *opening* parenthesis—which means that you don't have to end one saved match before starting another one. You can nest the patterns to match, and the numbers will refer to the thing matched by each one.

Be careful with parentheses—whether you use them as groups for changing precedence or you use them for saving matches—Perl will still save the values. You can prevent a parenthesized match from being saved using the special form `(?:pattern)` instead of just `(pattern)`. More about this in "Going Deeper."

Saved Match Variables

Backreferences allow you to refer to a match in a subpattern in that same pattern. There's also a way to refer to those subpatterns outside the pattern. In addition to backreferences referred to by `\1`, `\2`, and so on, Perl will assign scalar variables `$1`, `$2`, and so on to the values matched by those subpatterns. This mechanism can be incredibly useful for extracting bits out of strings or out of data. For example, here's a bit that pulls the first word out of a string:

```
if (/^(\S+)\s/) {
   print "first word: $1\n";
}
```

Here, if Perl can match the pattern (if it can find the start of the line and some number of non-whitespace characters followed by a whitespace character), then it'll print `first word:` and the match that it found. If the data doesn't have a first word (for example, if it's an empty string, or if there is no whitespace whatsoever in the string), then nothing will get printed because the test will return false. Remember, the whole pattern has to match for the pattern to return true, not just the part in parentheses.

One other important note about the match variables: their values are local to the block, read-only, and very transient. The next time you try to match anything, their original values will disappear. Those values will also vanish once a block ends. In other words, if you want to keep the values of these variables to use them later on, or if you want to change the values of those variables, you should save them off to some other variable or put them in a list. Match variables are for temporary storage only.

Matches and Context

Up until now, we've seen patterns used only in scalar context, primarily in a Boolean test. The two rules for using patterns in a scalar Boolean context are:

- A test like `/abc/` will return 1 (true) if the pattern was found in the given string (`$_` if no variable, or `=~` for anything else) and false otherwise. Most useful in conditionals.
- A `/g` option after the pattern allows iteration over the string; the pattern will return 1 (true) each time the pattern is matched and then false at the end of the string. Most useful in `while` loops.

In both these instances, parentheses inside the pattern will fill the match variables $1, $2, $3, and so on, and you can then use those values inside the conditional and loop block or up until the next pattern match.

If you use a pattern in a list context, the rules are different (surprise, surprise):

- A pattern containing parenthesized subpatterns to save will return a list of the first subpatterns that matched ($1, $2, $3, and so on, as well as the individual variables themselves). If there are no parenthesized patterns in the pattern, the list (1) is returned (that's a list of one element: the number 1).
- A /g option after the pattern returns a list of all the subpatterns that matched throughout the string.
- If the pattern doesn't match at all, the result is an empty list ().

Since patterns in list context return matches as a list, you could use patterns to split your data into elements. Here's another way of splitting a first and last name into their component parts:

```
($fn, $ln) = /^(\w+)\s+(\S+)$/;
```

A Note About Greed

On Day 2, "Working with Strings and Numbers," we had a short discussion about truth, and now we're going to talk about greed. Perhaps later on in the book we can discuss justice and envy.

Humor aside, one tricky feature of extracting patterns has to do with how the quantifier metacharacters behave in respect to what they match. The metacharacters +, *, ?, and {} are called greedy metacharacters, because given a chance, they will match as many characters as they can up to and including all the characters up to the end the line.

Normal behavior for a pattern is that if a match is to be returned (that is, if the pattern is being used in a list context), it'll return the first match it finds. Take, for example, this expression:

```
@x = /(\d\d\d)/;
```

Now say the data contained in $_ looks like this:

```
3443 32 784 234 123 78932
```

The @x array ends up being a list of one element, the first three digits, which in this case is (344). The pattern always stops at the first possible match.

The *, ?, and {} quantifiers, however, change the rule. For example, let's use that same data, and try to match this pattern:

```
/(\d*)/;
```

Since * is defined as "zero or more of the preceding character," you may think that the pattern will stop once it satisfies that condition—that is, once it's read a single appropriate character, which in the case of our number data would return (3). While that number satisfies the pattern, the * is a greedy quantifier, which means it will keep matching characters until it stops being able to. The result of matching that pattern with the string of numbers is (3443)—the * quantifier here kept sucking up numbers until it hit the space. Space isn't a number, so that's as far as it could go.

Here's an even more problematic example:

```
/'(.*)'/
```

At first glance, this pattern would appear to match (and fill $1) with characters in between quotes. However, if you tried this pattern on this string:

```
"She said, 'I don't want to eat that bug,'  and then she hit me."
```

Because the `.*` sequence is greedy, it'll match and return all the characters between the single-quotes (`I don't want to eat that bug`) and then continue to match all the rest of the characters all the way to the end of the line. Then, because it didn't get to match the quote mark, Perl will keep backing up and trying different characters until it finds the quote mark. You'll get the result you expect, but Perl will spend a lot of time backtracking in order to find it. And, to make things even worse, if you've got multiple quotes in the string, when Perl backtracks, it'll match the first one it finds. Take this string:

```
"'I despise you,' she said, throwing a pot at me. 'I wish you were dead.'"
```

Trying to match that same pattern to this string, $1 will end up containing this string:

```
I despise you,' she said, throwing a pot at me.  'I wish you were dead.
```

Assuming you were originally trying to match the contents of the first quote with that pattern (just the words `I despise you`), that's definitely not what you wanted.

Quantifiers initially appear to be a clever way of filling the space between two patterns. Because of their greedy behavior, however, in many cases they are totally inappropriate for that use, and you'll get frustrated trying to get them to work in that way. The better solution—both for making sure you only match what you want and to keep Perl from spinning its wheels spending a lot of time backtracking on the string—is to use a negated character class instead of a quantifier. Instead of thinking of the problem as "all the characters in between the opening and closing quotes," think of that problem as "an opening quote, then some number of characters that aren't a quote, then the closing quote." Implementing that pattern in a regular expression looks like this:

```
/"([^"]+)"/
```

It's a few more characters, and a little more difficult to sort out, but this pattern is guaranteed to return the characters in between quotes, not to greedily eat all he characters past the closing quote, and not to require any backtracking. Keep that rule in mind: if you want to match a pattern in between delimiters, use a negated character class with the ending delimiter inside the brackets.

A second, less efficient way to avoid the greedy behavior of the `+`,`*`,`?`, and `{}` metacharacters is to use special non-greedy ("lazy") versions of those metacharacters: `+?`,`*?`,`??`, and `{}?`. We'll look at these in "Going Deeper."

10

Using Patterns for Search and Replace

One of the niftiest uses of regular expressions involves not just searching for a pattern or extracting matches into lists or variables or whatever, but also replacing that pattern with some other string. This is equivalent to a search-and-replace in your favorite word processor or editor—only with all the power and flexibility that regular expressions give you.

To search for a pattern and then replace it with some other pattern, use this syntax:

```
s/pattern/replacement/
```

For this syntax the `pattern` is some form of regular expression; `replacement` is the string that will replace the match. A missing replacement will delete the match from the string. For example:

```
s/\s+/ /   # replace one or more whitespace characters with a single space
```

As with regular patterns, this syntax will search and replace the string in `$_` by default. Use the `=~` operator to search a different location.

The search and replace syntax, as shown, will replace only the first match, and return 1. With the `/g` option (g stands for global) on the end, Perl will replace all instances of the pattern in the string with the replacement:

```
s/--/[md]/g # replace two dashes -- with an em dash code [md]
```

Also, as with regular patterns, you can use the `/i` option at the end to perform a case-insensitive search (although the replacement will not match case, so be careful):

```
s/a/b/gi;  # replace [Aa] with b, globally
```

Feel free to use parentheses and match variables inside search and replace patterns; they work just fine here:

```
s/^(\S+\b)/=$1=/g  # put = signs around first word
s//^(\S+)(\s.*)(\S+)$/$3 $2 $1/ # swap first and last words
```

> Fans of sed will think that it's better to use \1 and \2 and so on in the replacement part of the search and replace. While this will work in Perl (basically by Perl replacing those references with variables for you), you should really get out of the habit—officially, in Perl, the replacement part of the s/// expression is a plain old double-quoted string, and \1 means a different thing in that context.

More About split

Remember the split function, from Day 5, "Working with Hashes"? We were using split to divide up names into first name and last name lists, like this:

```
($fn, $ln) = split(" ", $in);
```

At the time, I explained that using split with a space in quotes was actually a special case that would only work on data in which fields were separated by whitespace. To use split for data separated by any other characters, or needing any kind of sophisticated processing to find the elements, you'll use split with a regular expression as the pattern to match on:

```
($fn, $ln) = split(/s+/, $in);    # split on whitespace
@nums = split(//, $num);          # split 123 into (1,2,3)
@fields = split(/\s*,\s*/, $in); # split comma-separated fields,
                                  # with or without whitespace around the comma
```

The first example here, which splits on one or more whitespace characters, is equivalent to the behavior of split with a quoted space, and also equivalent to using split without any pattern whatsoever (the quoted space syntax is borrowed from the UNIX tool awk, which has that same string-splitting behavior).

You can also tell split to limit the number of chunks to split the data into using a number as the third argument:

```
($ln, $fn, $data{$ln}) = split(/,/ $in, 3);
```

This example would be useful for data that might look like this:

```
Jones,Tom,brown,blue,64,32
```

That `split` command will split the data around a comma into a last name, a first name, and everything else, for a total of three elements. The assignment will put the last and first names into scalar variables, and "everything else" into a hash keyed by last name.

Normally, the parts of the string that are stored in the final list don't include anything matched by the pattern. If you include parentheses in the pattern, however, then anything matched in the pattern inside those parentheses will *also* be included in the final list, with each match its own list element. So, for example, say you had a string like this one:

```
1:34:96:54:0
```

Splitting on the colon (with a pattern of `/:/`) will give you a list of everything that doesn't match the comma. But a pattern of `/(:)/` will give you a list that looks like this, splitting on both things not included in the pattern and things that match the parenthesized parts of the pattern:

```
1, ':', 34, ':', 96, ':', 54, ':', 0
```


Between `split` and regular pattern matching, you should be able to extract data out of strings just about any way you want to. Use patterns and backreferences to extract the things you want, and `split` to break the string up into its elements based on the parts you *don't* want. With the right sets of patterns and understanding the format of the input data, you should be able to handle data in most any format with only a few simple lines of code—something that would be much more difficult to do in a language like C.

Matching Patterns over Multiple Lines

Up to this point we've been assuming that all the pattern matching you've been doing is for individual lines (strings), read from a file or from the keyboard. The assumption, then, is that the string you'll be searching has no embedded line feeds or carriage returns, and that the anchors for beginning and end of line refer to the beginning and end of the string itself. For the `while (<>)` code we've been writing up to this point, that's a sensible assumption to make.

Quite often, however, you may want to match a pattern across lines, particularly if the input you're working with is composed of sentences and paragraphs, where the line boundaries are arbitrary based on the current test formatting. If you want to, for example, search for all instances of the term "Exegetic Frobulator 5000" in a Web page, then you want to be able to find the phrases that cross line boundaries as well as the ones that exist in total in each logical line.

To do this, then, you have to do two things. First, you have to modify your input routines such that they will read all the input into a single string, rather than process it line by line. That'll give you one enormous string with newline or carriage return characters in place. Secondly, depending on the pattern you're working with, you may have to tell Perl to manage newlines in different ways.

Storing Multiple Lines of Input

You can read your entire input into a single string in a number of ways. You could use `<>` in a list context, like this:

```
@input = <>;
```

That particular line could potentially be dangerous, however, if your input is very, very large, it could suck up all the available memory in your system trying to read all that input into memory. There's also no way to get it to stop in the middle. A less aggressive approach for reading paragraph-based data in particular is to set the special `$/` variable. If you set `$/` to a null string (`$/ = "";`), then Perl will read a paragraph of text, including newlines, and stop when it gets to two or more newlines in a row (the assumption here is that your input data has one or more empty lines between paragraphs):

```
$/ = "";
while (<>) {   # read a para, not a line
   # $_ will contain the entire paragraph, not just a line
}
```

A third way to read multiple lines into a single string is to use nested `while`s and append lines to an input string until you reach a certain delimiter. For strictly coded HTML files, for example, a paragraph ends with a `</P>` tag, so you could read all the input up until that point:

```
while (<>) {
   if (/(.*)<\/P>/) {
      $in.=$1
   } else {
      $in.=$_
   }
}
```

Handling Input with Newlines

Once you've got multiline input in a string to be searched, be it stored in `$_` or in a scalar variable, you can go ahead and search that data for patterns across multiple lines. There are several things to be aware of regarding pattern matches with embedded newlines:

- The \s character class includes newlines and carriage returns as whitespace, so a pattern like /George\s+Washington/ will match with no problem regardless of whether the words George Washington are on a single line or on separate lines.
- The ^ and $ anchoring characters refer to beginning of string or end of string—not to embedded newlines. If you want to treat ^ and $ as beginning and end of line in a string that contains multiple lines, you can use the /m option.
- The dot (.) metacharacter will NOT match newlines by default. You can change this behavior using the /s option.

That last point is the tricky one. Take this pattern, which uses the .* quantifier to extract all of a line after an initial From: heading:

```
/From: (.*)/
```


That pattern will search for the characters From:, and then fill $1 with the rest of the line. Normally, with a string that ends at the end of the line, this would work fine. If the string goes onto multiple lines, however, this pattern will match only up to the first newline (\n). The dot character, by default, does not match newlines.

You could get around this by changing the pattern to be one or more words or whitespace, avoiding the use of the dot altogether, but that's a lot of extra work. What you want is the /s option at the end of your pattern, which tells Perl to allow the dot to include \n as a character. Using /s does not change any other pattern-matching behavior—^ and $ continue to behave as beginning and end of string, respectively.

If your regular expression contains the ^ or $ characters, you may want to treat strings differently if they stretch over multiple lines. By default, ^ and $ refer to the beginning and end of the string, and ignore newlines altogether. If you use the /m option, however, ^ will refer to either the beginning of a string *or* the beginning of a line (the position just after a \n), and $ will refer to the end of the string or the end of the line (the position just before the \n). In other words, if your string contains four lines of text, ^ will match four times, and similarly for $. Here's an example:

```
while (/^(\w}/mg) {
   print "$1\n";
}
```

This while loop prints the first word of each line in $_, regardless of whether the input contains a single line or multiple lines.

If you use the /m option, and you really do want to test for the beginning or end of the string, ^ and $ will no longer work for you in that respect. But fear not, Perl provides \A and \Z to refer to the beginning and end of the string, regardless of the state of /m.

You can use both the `/s` and `/m` options together, of course, and they will co-exist happily. Just keep in mind that `/s` affects how the dot behaves, and `/m` affects `^` and `$`, and you should be fine. Beyond that, embedded newlines in strings are no problem for pattern matching.

A Summary of Options and Escapes

Throughout this lesson, I've been mentioning various options you can use with patterns, as well as a number of the special escapes that you can use inside patterns as well.

Table 10.1 shows the options you can tag onto the end of the pattern-matching expression (`m//` or just `//`) as well as those that can be used with the substitution expression (`s///`).

I haven't described all of these options in this lesson. You'll learn about some of these in "Going Deeper," but you may also want to check out the `perlre` man page for more information on any options that look interesting.

TABLE 10.1 PATTERN MATCHING AND SUBSTITUTION OPTIONS

Option	*Use*
`g`	Match all occurrences (not just once)
`i`	Match both upper- and lowercase
`m`	Use `^` and `$` for newlines
`o`	Interpolate pattern once (for better efficiency)
`s`	Dot (`.`) includes newlines
`x`	Extend regular expressions (can include comments and whitespace)
`e`	Evaluate replacement as a Perl expression (`s///` substitution only)

Table 10.2 contains the special escapes that can be used inside regular expressions, in addition to the usual string escapes like `\t` and `\n`, and backslashes used to turn metacharacters into regular characters.

TABLE 10.2 PATTERN MATCHING ESCAPES

Escape	*Use*
`\A`	Beginning of string
`\Z`	End of string
`\w`	Word character
`\W`	Non-word character
`\b`	Word boundary
`\B`	Non-word boundary
`\s`	Whitespace character
`\S`	Non-whitespace character
`\d`	Digit
`\D`	Non-digit
`\Q`	Escape all special characters
`\E`	End `\Q` sequence

An Example: Image Extractor

Let's finish up with an example of a pretty hefty regular expression (two of them, actually) used inside a Perl script. This script takes an HTML file as input, ranges over the file and looks for embedded images (using the `<IMG>` tag in HTML). It then prints a list of the images in that page, printing a list of the various attributes of that image (its location, width or height, text alternative, and so on). The output of the script will look something like this:

```
---------------
Image:  title.gif
   HSPACE: 4
   VPSACE: 4
   ALT: *
---------------
Image: smbullet.gif
   ALT: *
---------------
Image:  rib_bar_wh.gif
   BORDER: 0
   HSPACE: 4
   WIDTH; 50
   HEIGHT: 50
   ALT: --
```

If you're not familiar with HTML, the `<IMG>` tag which can be embedded anywhere inside an HTML file, looks something like this:

```
<IMG SRC="imgfile.gif" WIDTH=50 HEIGHT=75 ALT="penguins">
```

There are a couple of tricky things about this tag, however, that make this task more difficult than it would initially appear: The tag itself can appear in upper- or lowercase, and it can be spread over multiple lines. The attributes (the key/value pairs after the `IMG` part) can also be in any case, have space around the equals sign, and may or may not be quoted. The values can have spaces (but must be quoted if they are). Only one attribute is required—the `SRC` attribute—but there are a number of other attributes, and any of them can appear in any order.

All these choices make for a much more complex regular expression than just grabbing everything between the opening and closing tags. In fact, for this particular script I've split up the task into two regular expressions: one to find and extract the `IMG` tag out of the file, and one to extract and parse each individual attribute.

Listing 10.1 shows the code for this script. Try looking it over now to get a feel for how it works, but don't worry too much about grasping the pattern right now.

LISTING 10.1 THE `img.pl` SCRIPT

```
#!/usr/bin/perl -w

$/ = "";     # paragraph input mode
$raw = "";   # raw attributes
%atts = ();  # attributes

while (<>) {
    while (/<IMG\s([^>]+)>/ig ) {
        $raw = $1;
        while ($raw =~ /([^ =]+)\s*=\s*("([^"]+)"|[^\s]+\s*)/ig) {
           if (defined $3) {
              $atts{ uc($1) } = $3;
           } else { $atts{ uc($1)} = $2; }
        }
        if ($raw =~ /ISMAP/i) {
            $atts{'ISMAP'}= "Yes";
        }

        print '-' x 15;
        print "\nImage:  $atts{'SRC'}\n";
```

```
21:        foreach $key ("WIDTH", "HEIGHT",
22:                      "BORDER", "VSPACE", "HSPACE",
23:                      "ALIGN", "ALT", "LOWSRC", "ISMAP") {
24:            if (exists($atts{$key})) {
25:               $atts{$key} =~ s/[\s]*\n/ /g;
26:               print "   $key: $atts{$key}\n";
27:            }
28:        }
29:        %atts = ();
30:    }
31: }
```


This script has two main sections: a section to extract the data from the input, and a section to print out a report of what we found.

The first section uses a number of nested while loops to range over the HTML file: line 7 to loop over all the input, line 8 to find each instance of the image tag in the input, and line 10 to loop over each attribute in the <IMG> tag and store it into a hash called %atts, keyed by attribute name.

With the %atts hash built, all we have to do is print out the values. Because I wanted them printed in a specific order, with the foreach loop in line 21 I indicated the keys I wanted to find in a specific order.

But the focus of this script is the regular expressions in lines 8 and 10, so let's look at those two patterns in detail. Line 8 looks like this:

```
while (/<IMG\s+([^>]+)>/igs) {
```

Working through that regular expression, character to character, we look for the characters <IMG (the opening part of the tag), one or more whitespace characters, and then one or more characters that aren't >. We end up the pattern with the actual > character that indicates the end of the tag.

Note the parentheses around the "one or more characters that aren't >" part—that's the part we're interested in (which contains the attributes for the image), and that's the part of this pattern that will be extracted and saved for later use inside the body of this loop.

Note also the options at the end of the pattern: /i for a case-insensitive search (searching for both <img...> and <IMG...>), and /g for a global search (we'll get one pass of the while loop for each instance of <IMG in the loop). Note that we don't explicitly need to include /s or /m to worry about searching over line boundaries—HTML requires line breaks only on whitespace, and our pattern uses \s for all whitespace, so we're safe in that respect. We'll have no problem with tags that stretch over multiple lines.

Inside the body of that loop, we can save the attribute list into the `$raw` variable (line 9). We have to do this because the values of `$1`, `$2`, `$3`, and so on are all transient—they'll get reset at the next pattern match. That brings us to line 10 and the truly gnarly regular expression we've got there:

```
while ($raw =~ /([^ =]+)\s*=\s*("([^"]+)"¦[^\s]+\s*)/ig) {
```

There are four important parts of this regular expression, which I've outlined in Figure 10.1.

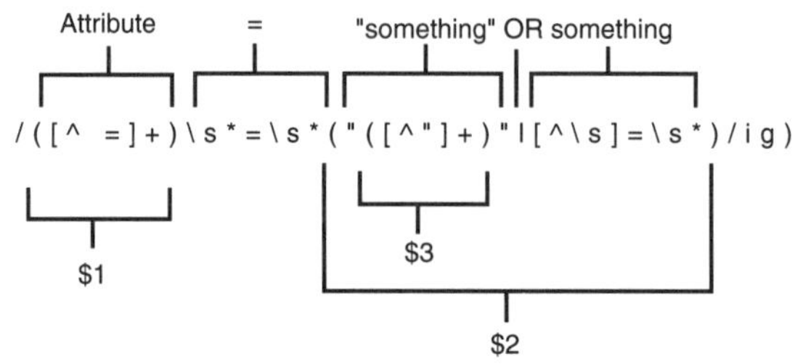

FIGURE 10.1
Regular expression parts for `img.pl`.

The parts are further explained as follows:

- The attribute name, some set of characters that are neither a space nor an equals sign. We'll save this off into `$1`.
- An equals sign with optional whitespace on either side of it.
- One of two value formats: This first one is a quote mark, followed by some number of characters, followed by another quote mark. This covers the quoted attributes (for example, `ALT="some alternative text"`).
- Some number of non-whitespace characters followed by optional whitespace. This covers the non-quoted value case (`HEIGHT=100`).

Note the placement of parentheses for the values, and remember the rule for match variables: The numbers are assigned based on the opening parentheses. So `$2` ends up being the complete value, but `$3` will be the value minus the quotes—if the value had quotes in the first place.

We cover either case in lines 11 through 14, where we test to see if `$3` is set. If it is, our value has quotes, and we'll store the non-quoted part into the `%atts` hash. If `$3` isn't defined, then our value isn't quoted, and we can store `$2` into `%atts` instead. Note here we also use the `uc` function to put our attribute names in uppercase before storing them.

Lines 15 through 17 cover a special case for the `<IMG>` tag—the `ISMAP` attribute doesn't take a value and indicates whether the image is an imagemap (that is, you can click on different areas on the image and get different results). This form of imagemaps isn't commonly used in HTML any more (it's been superseded by another tag), but we'll include it here to be complete. We have to make this one a special case because it won't get matched by the expression in line 10.

So after all those loops and patterns, we end up with a hash that stores all the attributes of the `<IMG>` tag we found. All that's left is to print those values. The loop in line 21 loops through all possible values for the `<IMG>` tag, in the order that they'll be printed out. But each `<IMG>` we find in the file can have a subset of those attributes—all of them are optional, except for `SRC`, so we have to test in line 24 to make sure the attribute actually exists before printing it. The `exists` function tests a hash to see if a key exists and returns true or false.

One other unusual line is line 25, where we do a quick search and replace of the value. This is to cover the case where the attribute might have been split over several lines—that value will have an embedded newline character, and we don't want that to be printed out in the final table. This little regular expression will look for optional whitespace followed by a newline character, and then replace it with a single space.

And finally, in line 29 we clear the attributes hash for the next go-around and the next `<IMG>` tag.

This script, while short, shows the sort of task for which Perl works exceptionally well: finding sophisticated patterns in text and then printing them back out again in sophisticated reports. This same task in C would most likely take much longer than 30 lines to code.

Hints for Building Regular Expressions

Depending on the complexity of your data or what you need to do with it, formulating a regular expression can either be very easy or need several iterations to get right. Here are some hints to help you get along with patterns:

- Know your data. Try to get a feel for the different ways that your pattern can appear, and to come up with a set of consistent rules before starting to write your pattern.
- Use multiple regular expressions if you need to. Sometimes it's easier to break the task into several smaller chunks than trying to get everything done at once.
- Don't forget `split`. Some tasks work better using `split` (removing everything except for a pattern) than they do with plain matches. And vice versa.

- Use parentheses to extract what you need (and only what you need). If you don't need the quote marks in a match, put the parentheses inside the quotation marks. Only save what you want, and you'll save yourself time removing the parts you don't want later on.
- Use negated character classes instead of quantifiers. Remember that quantifiers like `.*` are greedy, will eat up all the characters to the end of the line, and make your life miserable trying to get things to work right, not to mention making a lot more work for Perl. Avoid these constructs where a negated character class will work better.
- Remember that `*` and `?` refer to "zero or more" and "zero or one" characters. This means that if the character doesn't exist at all the pattern may still match. If your pattern requires at least one instance of a character, use `+` instead of `*` or `?`.
- Don't forget alternation. The pipe (`|`) character can come in handy for very complex patterns that may have several alternative complex cases to work with.
- Consider not using a regular expression at all for the task you're trying to accomplish. Regular expressions are incredibly powerful but there is some performance hit to using them, particularly for easy things like simple tests.
- Don't obsess. Regular expressions can be incredibly powerful but can also drive a person absolutely screamingly insane when they don't work. If a regular expression just doesn't seem to be working, stop, take a break, try to think about it in a different way.

Going Deeper

Regular expressions are one of those things that you could write a whole book about and still not cover the extent to which they can be used. In today's and yesterday's lessons, I've given you the basics of how to build and how to use regular expressions in your own programs. There's still many more features I haven't discussed, however, including many more metacharacters and regular expression forms specific to Perl. In this section I'll give you an overview of some of these other forms.

For more information about any aspect of regular expressions in Perl, the `perlre` man page can be quite enlightening. If you find yourself enjoying working with regular expressions overly much, consider the book *Mastering Regular Expressions* (Friedl, O'Reilly & Associates), which covers regular expressions of all kinds, Perl and otherwise, in an amazing amount of detail.

More Metacharacters

The metacharacters I described in yesterday's and today's lessons are most of the basic set of characters you can find in most regular expression flavors (not just those in Perl). Perl includes a number of extra metacharacters that provide different ways of creating complex patterns (or of processing the patterns that match).

The first of these are non-greedy versions of the quantifiers `*`, `+`,`?`, and `{}`. As you learned throughout the lesson, these quantifiers are greedy—they'll match any characters far beyond what you expect, sometimes to the detriment of figuring out how the pattern actually works. Perl also provides a second set of quantifiers which are non-greedy (sometimes called lazy quantifiers): `*?`, `+?`, `??`, and `{}?`. These quantifiers match the minimal number of characters needed to match the pattern, rather than the maximum like the regular quantifiers. This can be useful in some situations, but don't forget to use negated character classes when necessary. The lazy quantifiers are less efficient than a negated character class and can result in unexpected results.

The `(?:`*`pattern`*`)` construct is a variant on the use of parentheses to group patterns and save the results in the match variables `$1`, `$2`, `$3`, and so on. You can use parentheses to group an expression, but the result will get saved whether you want it to be or not. Using `(?:`*`pattern`*`)` instead, the expression will be grouped and evaluated as a unit, but the result will not be saved. It provides a slight performance advantage over regular parentheses where you don't care about the result.

The `(?o)` construct lets you nest pattern-matching options inside the pattern itself, for example, to make only some parts of the expression case-insensitive. The `o` part of the construct can be any valid pattern-matching option.

Look-ahead is a feature in Perl's regular expressions that allows Perl to peek ahead in a string and see if a pattern will match without changing the position in the string or adding anything to the parenthetical part of the pattern. It's sort of like saying "if the next part of this pattern contains X, then this part matches" without actually going anywhere. Use `(?=`*`pattern`*`)` to create a positive-lookahead pattern (if *`pattern`* matches in future bits of the string, then the previous part of the pattern also matches). The reverse is a negative-lookahead pattern, `(?!`*`pattern`*`)`, and works only if the *`pattern`* cannot match anything.

Special Variables

In addition to the match variables `$1`, `$2`, and so on, Perl also includes the variables `$'`, `$&`, and `` $` ``, which provide context for the text matches by the pattern. `$'` refers to the text leading up to the match, `$&` is the text that was matched, and `` $` `` is the text after the match (note the backquote; that's a different character from quote `'`). Unlike the transient match variables, these variables will hold their values until the next successful match and regardless of whether or not the original string was changed. Using any of these variables is a significant performance hit, so consider avoiding them when at all possible.

The $+ variable indicates the highest number of match variables that were defined; for example, if both $1 and $2 were filled, but not $3, $+ will be set to 2.

Options

You've learned about most of the options available to Perl regular expressions (both m// and s///) throughout the body of this lesson. Two that I have not touched on are /x, for extended regular expressions, and /o, to avoid repeatedly compiling the same regular expression over and over again.

The /x option allows you to add whitespace and comments to a regular expression, for better readability. Normally if you add spaces to a pattern, those spaces are considered part of the pattern itself. The /x option ignores all spaces and newlines, as well as allowing comments on individual lines of the regular expression. So, for example, that regular expression in our <IMG> extractor script, which looked like this in the script:

```
while ($raw =~ /([^ =]+)\s*=\s*("([^"]+)"|[^\s]+\s*)/ig) {
```

Might be rewritten to look like this:

```
while ($raw =~ /([^ =]+)      # find the attribute name
                \s*=\s*       # find the equals, with or without whitespace
                ("([^"]+)"|   # find and extract quoted values
                [^\s]+\s*)    # or find non-quoted values
                /igx) {
```

The use of extended regular expressions can help quite a bit to improve the readability of a regular expression.

And, finally the /o option is used to optimize how Perl compiles and reads a regular expression interpolated via a scalar variable. Take the following code snippet:

```
while (<>) {
   if (/$pattern/) {
     ...
   }
}
```

In this snippet, the pattern stored in $pattern is interpolated and compiled into a real pattern that Perl can understand. The problem is that because this pattern is inside a while loop, that same process will occur each and every time the loop comes around. By including the /o at the end of the pattern, you're telling Perl the pattern won't change, and so it'll compile it once and reuse the same pattern each time:

```
if (/$pattern/o) {   # compile once
```

For information on all these metacharacters, variables, and options, see the `perlre` man page.

Summary

In today's lesson, you learned more about using regular expressions, building on the basics you learned about yesterday. Today, we talked about extracting matches from a pattern-matching operation using parentheses, and using backreferences and match variables to save matches and refer back to them later on.

As part of that discussion, you also learned about pattern matching in different contexts (scalar contexts return true or false, lists return lists of matches), about the greedy behavior of the quantifier metacharacters, and more about the `split` function. If you made it this far, through both these lessons, you now know enough about regular expressions to match just about any pattern in any set of data.

Q&A

Q I've got a bit of code that uses a two-step process to extract something out of a string. The first pattern puts a substring into `$1`, and then the second pattern searches `$1` for a different pattern. The second pattern never matches, and printing `$1` shows that it's empty. But if it was empty, the second pattern shouldn't have even been tried in the first place. What's going on here?

A It sounds like you're trying something like this:

```
if ($string =~ /some long pattern with a (subpattern) in it/) {
   if ($1 =~ /some second pattern/) {
      # process second pattern
   }
}
```

Unfortunately, you can't do that. The `$1` variable (or any other variable) is incredibly temporary. Each time you use a regular expression, Perl resets all the match variables. So, for this particular example, the first line does match and fills `$1` with the contents of the parentheses. However, the minute you try another pattern-match (in the second line), the value of `$1` disappears, which means that second pattern can never match.

The secret here is simply to make sure you put the values of any match variables somewhere else if you want to use them again. In this particular case, just adding a temporary variable and searching it instead will work just fine:

```
if ($string =~ /some long pattern with a (subpattern) in it/) {
   $tmp = $1;
```

```
        if ($tmp =~ /some second pattern/) {
            # process second pattern
        }
    }
```

Q I've seen some scripts that set a `$*` variable to 1 to do multiline matching, similarly to the way you described the `/m` option. What's `$*`, and should I be using it?

A In earlier versions of Perl, you set the `$*` to tell Perl to change the meaning of `^` and `$`. In current versions of Perl, you should be using `/m` instead; `$*` is only there for backward compatibility.

Workshop

The workshop provides quiz questions to help you solidify your understanding of the material covered and exercises to give you experience in using what you've learned. Try to understand the quiz and exercise answers before you go on to tomorrow's lesson.

Quiz

1. Assume that `$_` contains `123 kazoo kazoo 456`. What is the result of the following expressions?

```
@matches = /(\b[^\d]+)\b/g;
@matches = /\b[^\d]+\b/;
s/\d{3}/xxx/;
s/\d{3}/xxx/g;
$matches = s/\d{3}/xxx/g;
if (/\d+(.*)\d+/) { print $1;}
@matches = split(/z/);
@matches = split(" ",$_ 3);
```

2. What is the rule for how backreferences and match variables are numbered?
3. How long do the values of match variables stay around?
4. How can you stop the greedy behavior of the quantifiers `+` and `*`?
5. What do the following options do?

```
/g
/i
/o
/s
```

Exercises

1. **BUG BUSTER:** What's wrong with this bit of code?

```
while (<>) {
   $input =~ /pat\s/path /;
}
```

2. **BUG BUSTER:** What's wrong with this bit of code?

```
@matches = /\b[^\d]+\b/;
```

3. Write a script to find duplicated words ("the the" or "any any") in its input and replace them with one instance of that same word. Watch out for words duplicated over multiple lines.
4. Write a script to expand acronyms in its input (for example, to replace the letters "HTML" with "HTML (Hypertext Markup Language)." Use the following acronyms and meanings to replace:

```
HTML (Hypertext Markup Language)
ICBM (InterContinental Ballistic Missile)
EEPROM (Electrically-erasable programmable read-only memory)
SCUBA (self-contained underwater breathing apparatus)
FAQ (Frequently Asked Questions)
```

5. Modify the `img.pl` script to extract and report about links instead of images. HINT: Links look something like this:

```
<A HREF="url_to_link_to">test to underline for the link</A>
```

   Links can also contain attributes for `NAME`, `REL`, `REV`, `TARGET`, and `TITLE`.

   Make sure you report on both the contents of the link tag and the text between the opening and closing tags.

10

Answers

Here are the answers to the workshop questions in the previous section.

Quiz Answers

1. The answers are

   a. `("kazoo", "kazoo")`

   b. `(1)` (A pattern in a list context without parenthesized parts of the pattern or with `/g` will return `(1)` if the pattern matched.)

   c. The string will be changed to `"xxx kazoo kazoo 456"`

   d. The string will be changed to `"xxx kazoo kazoo xxx"`

e. The `$matches` variable will be set to 2 (the number of changes made)

f. `"kazoo kazoo 45"` (watch out for those greedy quantifiers)

g. `("123 ka", "oo ka" "oo 456")`

h. `("123", "kazoo", "kazoo 456")`

2. Backreferences and match variables are numbered based on opening parentheses. Parenthesized patterns can be nested inside each other.
3. Match variables are extremely transient; their values stay set only until the next pattern match or until the end of a block.
4. Two ways: The best way is to avoid using greedy quantifiers with the dot (.) character and use negated character classes instead; the other way is to use the non-greedy versions of those quantifiers (`+?` and `*?`).
5. The answers are:

a. The `/g` option means "global"; it applies the pattern to the entire string (as opposed to stopping after the first match). Different things happen depending on context.

b. The `/i` option creates a case-insensitive search. Upper- and lowercase letters become irrelevant.

c. The `/o` option means "compile the pattern only once." It's most useful for optimizations on patterns with embedded variables.

d. The `/s` option allows the dot (.) character to match newlines.

Exercise Answers

1. There are two parts to that pattern (a pattern and a replacement), but no leading `s`. The fixed version looks like this:

```
while (<>) {
   $input =~ s/pat\s/path /;
}
```

2. Trick question! There's nothing actually wrong with that bit of code, although it probably doesn't do what you expect. A pattern in a list context without parenthesized subpatterns will result in the value (1) if the pattern matches. To save a list of the matches, you need to include parentheses somewhere in the patter.

3. Here's one version:

```
#!/usr/bin/perl -w
#
# Exercise 10.43  find duplicated words, regardless of line breaks
# this version finds both upper and lower case, but doesn't handle
# punctuation or more than two instances of the same word.

$/ = "";  # paragraph input mode

while (<>) {
  s/\b(\w+)\s+\1\b/$1/ig;
  print;
}
```

4. Here's one version:

```
#!/usr/bin/perl -w

%acs = (
        "HTML" => "Hypertext Markup Language",
        "ICBM" => "InterContinental Ballistic Missile",
        "EEPROM" => "Electrically-erasable programmable read-only
        memory",
        "SCUBA" => "self-contained underwater breathing apparatus",
        "FAQ" => "Frequently Asked Questions",
        );

while (<>) {
    foreach $key (keys %acs) {
        s/$key/$key ($acs{$key})/gi;
    }
    print;
}
```

5. Here's one solution:

```
#!/usr/bin/perl -w
# find and extract links
# doesn't handle link text with embedded HTML

$/ = "";      # paragraph input mode
$raw = "";    # raw attributes
$linktext = ""; # link text
%atts = ();   # attributes
```

```
while (<>) {
    while (/<A\s([^>]+)>([^<]+)<\/A>/ig) {
        $raw = $1;
        $linktext = $2;
        $linktext =~ s/[\s]*\n/ /g;
        while ($raw =~ /([^\s=]+)\s*=\s*("([^"]+)"¦[^\s]+\s*)/ig) {
           if (defined $3) {
              $atts{ uc($1) } = $3;
           } else { $atts{ uc($1)} = $2; }
        }
        print '-' x 15;
        print "\nLink text: $linktext\n";
        foreach $key ("HREF", "NAME", "TITLE",
                      "REL", "REV", "TARGET") {
             if (exists($atts{$key})) {
                $atts{$key} =~ s/[\s]*\n/ /g;
                print "   $key: $atts{$key}\n";
             }
        }
        %atts = ();
    }
}
```

DAY 11

Creating and Using Subroutines

We'll finish up your knowledge of the core of the Perl language today with a discussion of subroutines, functions, and local variables. With subroutines you can collect bits of commonly used code into a single operation, and then perform that operation at different times in your script—the same way you use the built-in Perl functions.

The specific things you'll learn about include

- The differences between user-defined subroutines and Perl's standard functions
- How to define and call simple subroutines
- Using variables local to subroutine definitions
- Returning values from subroutines
- Passing arguments to subroutines
- Using subroutines in different contexts

Subroutines Versus Functions

A function, in general, is a chunk of code that performs some operation on some form of data. You call, or invoke, a function by naming it and giving it arguments somewhere in your Perl script. Perl then transfers execution to the function definition, performs the operations in that function, and then returns to where the execution left off when the function is done. This is true of any kind of function.

In previous lessons, we've been working a lot with Perl's built-in functions such as `print`, `sort`, `keys`, `chomp`, and so on. These are functions that are defined by the standard Perl library that you can use anywhere in your Perl programs. Another set of functions are available to you using additional Perl modules or libraries, written by other Perl programmers, that you load in at the start of your script—you'll learn more about these on Day 13, "Scope, Modules and Importing Code."

A third set of functions are those that you define yourself using a subroutine definition in Perl. In common practice, the terms *function* and *subroutine* are entirely equivalent—some programmers will call subroutines *user-defined functions* to differentiate them from the built-in set; in other contexts, there's no distinction to be made. Throughout this lesson, and throughout this book, I'll refer to the functions that you define in your own programs (or modules, later on), as subroutines, and those that you get elsewhere—from the standard Perl distribution or from optional modules—as functions.

Why would you need a subroutine? Any time you're reusing more than a few lines of code in your Perl scripts, that's a good reason to put that code into a subroutine. You could also use subroutines to portion different parts of your script into chunks, perhaps to split up a complex problem into easier bites, or because it's more readable to refer to a certain operation by name (`remove_newlines`, say, or `find_max`) than simply to include the code itself. Creating a script as a set of subroutines also makes it easier to isolate programming problems: you can write and test and debug a single subroutine by itself, and be assured when you integrate that subroutine into your larger script that that subroutine will behave as you expect. Whether or not you use subroutines for different problems in your Perl scripts is a matter of programming style; use subroutines any time it will make your life easier as a programmer or your scripts easier to read and understand.

Defining and Calling Basic Subroutines

The most basic subroutine is one that takes no arguments, uses no local variables, and returns no value. Although this kind of subroutine may not seem terribly useful, it's a good place to start learning about subroutines. So, we'll start with that kind of subroutine in this section and build from there. In this section, you learn the drill for defining and calling subroutines in your Perl scripts.

An Example of a Subroutine

Let's take a really simple example of a subroutine. Remember the temperature script from Day 2, "Working with Strings and Numbers," which prompted you for a temperature in Fahrenheit and then converted that temperature to Celsius? We included the actual calculation right in the middle of the script, but it could have been included in a subroutine, like this:

```
#!/usr/bin/perl -w

print 'Enter a temperature in Farenheight: ';
chomp ($fahr = <STDIN>);
&f2c;
print "$fahr degrees Fahrenheight is equivalent to ";
printf("%d degrees Celsius\n", $cel);

sub f2c {
    $cel = ($fahr - 32) * 5 / 9;
}
```


Look over that example carefully, and see how the subroutine works. Perl executes the script line by line starting from the first line, as it always does, but when it gets to a reference to a subroutine (here, `&f2c()`), it switches execution to the subroutine definition (the last couple of lines in the script), executes the block there, and then returns to where it left off. In this case, that means that after the temperature is read from the keyboard, Perl switches to the `&f2c()` subroutine to convert the value to a Celsius value, and then prints out the value it found.

Note

By saying *switches execution,* I don't mean Perl actually jumps to that specific line of the script. Perl actually loads in the entire script first and keeps track of all subroutine definitions before the script actually begins running, so it actually does just switch execution to the subroutine definition and switch back afterward.

Defining Subroutines

From this simple example, you can probably infer the basic syntax for a subroutine definition:

```
sub subroutinename {
   statements;
   ...
}
```

A subroutine definition starts with the word `sub`, followed by the name of the subroutine, followed by a block. The block, as with the blocks you used with conditionals and loops, is a set of Perl statements surrounded by curly brackets (`{}`). Here's an example:

```
sub getnumber {
   print 'Enter a number: ';
   chomp($number = <STDIN>);
}
```

As with all other named things in Perl that start with odd characters, subroutine names can be made up of any number of alphanumeric characters and underscores. Upper- and lowercase are different from each other, and subroutine names do not conflict with any other scalar, array, or hash variable names.

Subroutine definitions can appear at the start of your script, at the end, somewhere in the middle, or even inside other blocks. Anywhere a regular statement can appear, you can stick a subroutine definition. Generally, however, to make your programs easier to read and to understand, you should group them together either at the start or end of your script.

Calling Subroutines

The most basic way to call a subroutine (or, to use the technical term, to *invoke* a subroutine) is with an ampersand (`&`) followed the name of the subroutine, followed by parentheses `()`:

```
&f2c();  # convert Fahrenheit to Celsius
&getnumber();
```

Arguments you want to pass to the subroutine are included inside the parentheses, but we'll get to that later (in "Passing Values into Subroutines").

The ampersand (`&`) is entirely optional in this case; you can call your subroutines with or without it. Some programmers find it preferable to include the ampersand because it makes it easier to differentiate between the built-in functions and those that they define themselves (or import from modules), but if you end up reading other people's Perl code, you'll see the non-ampersand version quite a bit. I'll be using the ampersand syntax throughout the examples in this book to call subroutines.

You don't have to call a subroutine from the main body of your script; you can call a subroutine from inside another subroutine, and another subroutine from inside that one. In fact, you can go as deep into subroutine calls as you want to—unlike other languages, there are no limits (other than your system memory) to how deeply you can nest subroutine calls. There are issues with nested subroutine calls concerning arguments and local variable scope, but we'll get to those soon enough.

Note

> The one place where the & is not optional is if you are referring to the subroutine indirectly, rather than calling it; for example, if you were using `defined` to find out if the subroutine had been defined or not.
>
> Also, in some cases the parentheses are also optional (specifically, when the subroutine has been predefined with a declaration earlier in the script or in an imported module). You'll learn more about declaring subroutines in "Going Deeper"; in this lesson I'll use the parentheses in each case to prevent confusion.

An Example: Son of Stats

Just for kicks, I took the final version of the statistics script we've been working with throughout this week, and "subroutinified" it. I broke the script up into its component parts, and put each of them into a subroutine. The actual body of the script, then, does nothing but call individual subroutines. There's no change in behavior to the script itself; just in how it's organized. Listing 11.1 shows the result.

Listing 11.1 The `statssubbed.pl` Script

```
#!/usr/bin/perl -w

&initvars();
&getinput();
&printresults();

sub initvars {
    $input = "";   # temporary input
    @nums = ();    # array of numbers;
    %freq = ();    # hash of number frequencies
    $maxfreq = 0;  # maximum frequency
    $count = 0;    # count of numbers
    $sum = 0;      # sum of numbers
    $avg = 0;      # average
    $med = 0;      # median
    @keys = ();    # temp keys
    $totalspace = 0; # total space across histogram
}

sub getinput {
    while (defined ($input = <>)) {
        chomp ($input);
        $nums[$count] = $input;
        $freq{$input}++;
```

continues

LISTING 11.1 CONTINUED

```
25:         if ($maxfreq < $freq{$input}) { $maxfreq = $freq{$input} }
26:         $count++;
27:         $sum += $input;
28:     }
29:
30: }
31:
32: sub printresults {
33:     @nums = sort { $a <=> $b } @nums;
34:
35:     $avg = $sum / $count;
36:     $med = $nums[$count /2];
37:
38:     print "\nTotal count of numbers: $count\n";
39:     print "Total sum of numbers: $sum\n";
40:     print "Minimum number: $nums[0]\n";
41:     print "Maximum number: $nums[$#nums]\n";
42:     printf("Average (mean): %.2f\n", $avg);
43:     print "Median: $med\n\n";
44:     &printhist();
45: }
46:
47: sub printhist {
48:     @keys = sort { $a <=> $b } keys %freq;
49:
50:     for ($i = $maxfreq; $i > 0; $i—) {
51:         foreach $num (@keys) {
52:             $space = (length $num);
53:             if ($freq{$num} >= $i) {
54:                 print( (" " x $space) . "*");
55:             } else {
56:                 print " " x (($space) + 1);
57:             }
58:             if ($i == $maxfreq) { $totalspace += $space + 1; }
59:         }
60:         print "\n";
61:     }
62:     print "-" x $totalspace;
63:     print "\n @keys\n";
64: }
```

Because this version of the stats script doesn't do anything functionally different from the one before it, there are only a couple things to note here:

- The only part of this script that doesn't live inside a subroutine definition is lines 3 through 5, which call subroutines to initialize variables, to get the input from a file of numbers, and to calculate the results.

- You may note that there are four subroutine definitions in this script, but only three subroutine calls at the top of the script. That's because the `&printresults()` subroutine calls the `&printhist()` subroutine at the end of its block.

Returning Values from Subroutines

Calling a subroutine by itself on one line is one way of splitting the execution of a script to a subroutine, but more useful is a subroutine that returns a value. With return values, you can nest subroutine calls inside expressions, use them as arguments to other subroutines, or as parts of other Perl statements (depending on whether the return value is appropriate, of course).

By default, the return value of a Perl script is the last thing that was evaluated in the block that defines the subroutine. So, for example, here's a short Perl script to read in two numbers and add them together:

```
$sum = &sumnums();
print "Result: $sum\n";

sub sumnums {
    print 'Enter a number: ';
    chomp($num1 = <STDIN>);
    print 'Enter another number: ';
    chomp($num2 = <STDIN>);
    $num1 + $num2;
}
```


The fact that subroutines can return values is important for the first line in that example; the value of the `$sum` variable will only be set as a result of the `&sumnum()` subroutine being called. Inside the subroutine, the last line where the two numbers `$num1` and `$num2` are added together is the value that is returned from the subroutine, the value that gets assigned to `$sum`, and the value that gets printed as the result.

The catch to this behavior is that although the last statement in the block is often the return value for the subroutine, that's not always the case. Remember that the rule is that the last thing evaluated is the return value for the subroutine—and that may not be the last statement in the block. With loops such as `while` loops or `for` loops, the last thing evaluated may be the test. Or with loop controls, it may be the loop control itself.

Because the return value of a subroutine isn't always readily apparent, it's a much better idea to create a subroutine that explicitly returns a value using `return`. `return`, which is actually a function, takes any expression as an argument and returns the value of that expression. So the last line of that `&sumnums()` subroutine might look like this:

```
return $num1 + $num2;
```

Want to return multiple values from a subroutine? No problem. Just put them in a list and return them that way (and then, in the main part of your script that called the subroutine in the first place, make sure you deal with that returned list in some way). For example, this snippet calls a subroutine that processes an array of values. That subroutine returns a list of three values which can then be assigned (using list assignments in parallel) to the variables `$max`, `$min`, and `$count`.

```
($max, $min, $count) = &process(@foo);
# ...
sub foo {
    # ...
   return ($value1, $value2, $value3);
}
```

What if you want to pass two or more discrete lists of elements out of a subroutine? That you can't do. The `return` function with a list argument flattens all sublists, expands all hashes, and returns a single list of elements. If you want discrete arrays or lists on the outside of a subroutine, you'll need to figure out a way of splitting that list into its component lists after the subroutine is done. This is not a problem specific to return values; Perl also uses this single-list method of getting arguments into a subroutine as well (more about that later).

Using Local Variables in Subroutines

Structuring a Perl script to use subroutines that refer to the same global variables as the code outside the subroutines is essentially an exercise in code formatting. The subroutines in this case don't give you much intrinsic value in terms of efficiency or effective script design. Subroutines are much better designed and used as self-contained units that have their own variables and that deal only with data passed to that subroutine through arguments and passed back through return values. This makes them easier to manage, easier to reuse, and easier to debug. We'll work toward that goal as this lesson progresses, but we'll start here with a discussion of local variables.

The vast majority of the variables we've been looking at up to this point—scalar, list, and array variables—have been global variables, that is, they're available to all parts of the script, and continue to exist as long as the script runs. We've seen a few minor exceptions—the element variable in a `foreach` loop or the match variables in regular expressions, for example—but for the most part we've been looking solely at variables as having global scope.

Local variables, in the context of a subroutine, are variables that spring into existence when the subroutine starts running, are available solely to that subroutine, and then disappear once the subroutine is finished. Other than the fact that they're local, they look just like other variables and contain the same sorts of data.

Perl actually has two different ways of creating two different kinds of local variables. We'll cover one way (the easiest one) here, and deal with the other and the specific differences between the two on Day 13.

To create a local variable for a subroutine, use the `my` modifier before you initialize or use the variable for the first time:

```
my $x = 1;  # $x is now local
```

The `my` modifier only applies to a single variable. If you want to create multiple local variables you have to enclose them in parentheses, like this:

```
my ($a, $b, $c);   # three locals, all undefined.
```

In the preceding section we created a subroutine that prompted for two numbers and summed them. In that example the two number variables, `$num1` and `$num2`, were global variables. We can make a single-line change to make those variables local variables:


```
$sum = &sumnums();
print "Result: $sum\n";

sub sumnums {
   my ($num1, $num2);
   print 'Enter a number: ';
   chomp($num1 = <STDIN>);
   print 'Enter another number: ';
   chomp($num2 = <STDIN>);
   return $num1 + $num2;
}
```

In this version, the line `my ($num1, $sum2)` creates variables that are local to the subroutine. They are available to the subroutine as temporary placeholders for the numbers, but cease to exist outside the boundaries of that subroutine.

What happens if you create a `my` variable that has the same name as a previously used global variable? Perl has no problem with this; the new variables created by `my` will hide the global variables with the same name. Then, when the subroutine is done, the `my` variables will go away and the globals will be visible (and usable) again. Because this can often be very confusing to debug, it's generally a good idea to give your local variables different names from globals.

> You can get to the values of global variables from inside a subroutine that declares my variables of the same name by putting your code into a package and then referring to the package name and the global variable name. But I won't discuss that here; see Day 13 for details.

Here's an example that demonstrates how this works:

```
#!/usr/bin/perl -w

$value = 0;
print "before callsub, \$value is $value\n";
&callsub();
print "after callsub, \$value is $value\n";

sub callsub {
    my ($value);
    $value++;
    print "inside callsub, \$value is $value\n";
}
```

If you run this example, you'll get the following output:

```
before callsub, $value is 0
inside callsub, $value is 1
after callsub, $value is 0
```

Note here that the `my` variable `$value` is a new variable, local to the subroutine. Changing its value has no effect on the global once the subroutine is complete.

The one other catch to watch out for with `my` variables is that they are truly local to the subroutine definition itself. If you nest subroutine calls—call one subroutine from another subroutine—the `my` variables defined in the first subroutine will not be available to the second subroutine and vice versa. This is different from many other languages, where local variables "cascade" to nested subroutines. With `my` variables, you can only use them inside the same subroutine definition and nowhere else in the script.

Note

> For the computer scientists in the audience, this means that `my` variables have lexical scope, rather than dynamic scope. They only exist inside the lexical block in which they are defined. More about this later on in the lesson when we get to scope.

Passing Values into Subroutines

Once you've got local variables to store values specific to a subroutine, and return values to send data out from the subroutine, the only part of the subroutine left is getting information into it. For that you use arguments, just as you do for the built-in Perl functions.

Passing Arguments

Let's start with how arguments get passed into subroutines. Perl has an extremely loose notion of subroutine arguments. Whereas in other languages you have to be very specific when you write your subroutines to make sure you indicate how many and what type of arguments your subroutine will take, Perl doesn't care. When you call a subroutine in Perl, any and all arguments you give it are combined or expanded into a single list of values. For scalar arguments, this is no big deal:

```
&mysub(1,2,3);
```

The `&mysub()` subroutine in this case will get a list of three numeric values. Watch out for lists, though:

```
&mysub(@list, @anotherlist);
```


In this case, both `@list` and `@anotherlist` are expanded into their component values and combined into one list. It's that single list that ends up inside the body of the subroutine. Your original arrays lose their identities when passed into a subroutine.

A similar thing happens with hashes; the hash is expanded into its keys and values (following the usual hash rules), combined with any other list arguments, and passed into the subroutine as a flat list.

But what if you really want your arguments to consist of multiple arrays or hashes? Perl's argument-passing behavior doesn't make this easy, but there are a number of ways to work around it. One way is to store your arrays or hashes as globals and just refer to them in the body of your subroutines. Another way is to reconstruct the arrays inside the subroutine using a clever hack (for example, including the count of the first array as an argument to the subroutine). A third way, and arguably the best one, is to pass the arguments to the subroutine in as references, which retains the construction of the original arrays or hashes inside the subroutine. You'll learn about references later on in this book on Day 19, "Working with References."

Handling Arguments Inside Subroutines

OK, so arguments are passed into a subroutine as a single list of values. How do you then get to those arguments from inside the body of your subroutine?

The list of arguments passed to your subroutine is stored in the special local variable `@_`. You can access elements of that array, or split those values into individual values using the standard array access and assignment expressions. The `@_` variable is a local variable to the subroutine; if you set a `@_` global variable, its values are hidden inside the subroutine, and if you call another subroutine from inside a subroutine, that second subroutine will get its own version of `@_`.

Here's an example of a subroutine that adds together its two arguments (and a line of code showing how it's called):

```
&addthem(2,3);

sub addthem {
   return $_[0] + $_[1];
}
```

The two arguments to the subroutine—here `2` and `3`—are put into the list stored in the `@_` variable. Then you can just use `$_[0]` and `$_[1]` access forms to get to those values. Keep in mind that just as `$foo[0]` and `$foo` refer to different things, so are `$_[0]` and `$_` different (the first one is the first element in the argument list; the second is the special default variable).

Note that this subroutine is kind of limited ("brain-dead" might be a better term)—it only adds together its first two arguments, no matter how many you give it. Because you cannot control how many arguments you can get inside a subroutine, you have to be careful that you only call the subroutine with the right number of arguments, test the number or type of arguments you get, or write the subroutine generally enough to be able to handle multiple arguments. We might modify the above subroutine to add all its arguments together, regardless of the number, like this:

```
sub addthem {
   my $sum = 0;
   foreach $i (@_) {
      $sum += $i;
   }
   return $sum;
}
```

Note

Very recent versions of Perl (after 5.003) do actually provide a way to define a subroutine to only take specific numbers and types of arguments. Given that this feature is quite new, it's probably not something you want to rely on in your own scripts. More about subroutine prototypes in the "Going Deeper" section.

Perl doesn't have a way of explicitly naming incoming arguments, but one common trick is to split out the array of arguments into local variables as a first step, like this, where this subroutine expects three arguments:

```
sub foo {
   my($max, $min, $inc) = @_;
   ...
}
```

You can then refer to those arguments using mnemonic local variable names rather than having to keep track of their positions in the array all the time. Another (very common) way of doing this same thing is to use `shift`. Conveniently, `shift` with no arguments inside a subroutine will extract the first element from `@_` (`pop` will do the same thing to the last element):

```
sub foo {
   my $max = shift;
   my $min = shift;
   my $inc = shift;
   ...
}
```

A Note on Arguments Passed by Reference

The argument list that you get inside your subroutine via `@_` are implicit references to the values that were passed in from outside. That means that if you pass in a list of strings, and inside the body of your subroutine, modify those strings, then the strings will remain modified outside the body of the subroutine as well. As I mentioned earlier, however, arrays and hashes do not maintain their integrity inside the subroutine, nor can you modify a number. And, if you assign the argument list `@_` to a local variable, those values will all get copied and cease to be references. Because Perl's notion of pass by reference is rather vague, it's not commonly used as such; using actual references to pass in arrays or hashes of values is a much more direct way of approaching the problem.

Subroutines and Context

Argument passing, subroutine definition, return values—these are the features of function definitions in any language. But, because this is Perl, there are always wrinkles. You already saw one of those wrinkles with the fact that individual arrays and hashes lose their identities when they're passed into subroutines as arguments. Another wrinkle is the issue of context.

Given that subroutines can be called in either a scalar or list context, and that they can return either a scalar or a list, context is a relevant issue to subroutine development. Or at least it's a relevant issue to keep in mind as you use your subroutines: be careful not to call subroutines that return lists in a scalar context, unless you're aware of the result and know how lists behave in that particular context.

There are the occasions, however, when you want to write a subroutine that will behave differently based on the context in which it was called (a very Perl-like thing to do). That's where the built-in `wantarray` function comes in. You use `wantarray` to find out the context in which your subroutine was called in. `wantarray` returns true if your subroutine was called in a list context; false if it was called in a scalar context (a more proper name might be "wantlist," but it is called `wantarray` for historical reasons). So, for example, you might test for the context of your subroutine before returning a value and then do the right thing based on that context, like this:

```
sub arrayorlist {
    # blah blah
    if (wantarray()) {
        return @listhing;
    } else { return $scalarthing }
}
```

Be careful with this feature, however. Keep in mind that just as functions that do different things based on context can be confusing (and may sometimes require a check of the documentation to figure out what they do), subroutines that do different things based on context can be doubly confusing. In many cases it's better to just return an appropriate value for the subroutine itself, and then deal with that value appropriately in the statement that called the subroutine in the first place.

Another Example: Stats with a Menu

Let's modify the stats example once more in this lesson to take advantage of just about everything you've learned so far in this book. I've modified stats such that instead of reading the values, printing everything, and then exiting, the script prints a menu of operations. You have a choice of the sort of operations you want to perform on the numbers in the data set.

Unlike the `names.pl` script from Day 8, "Manipulating Lists and Strings," however, which used a large `while` loop and a number of `if` tests to handle the menu, this one uses subroutines. In addition, it moves a lot of the calculations we did in earlier versions of this script into the subroutine that actually needs those calculations so that only the work that needs to be done gets done.

Because this script is rather long, instead of showing you the whole thing and then analyzing it, I'm going to walk through each important part and show you bits of the overall code to point out what I did when I wrote this version of the stats script. At the end of this section, in Listing 11.2, I'll show you all the code.

Let's start with the main body of code in this script. Previous versions of stats used a rather large set of global variables, which we defined and initialized at the start of the script. This version uses only two: the array of numbers for the input, and a variable to keep track of whether to quit the script or not. All the other variables are `my` variables, local to the various subroutines that need them.

The script starts with a call to a subroutine called `&getinput()`. This subroutine, which we'll look at in a bit, reads in the input from the input files and stores it in the `@nums` array. This version of `&getinput()` is significantly smaller than the one we've used in previous versions of stats—this one simply reads in the numbers. It doesn't keep track of frequencies, sums, or anything else, and it uses the `$_` variable instead of a temporary input variable. It does, however, include the line that sorts the numbers in the final `@nums` array.

```
sub getinput {
    my $count = 0;
    while (<>) {
        chomp;
        $nums[$count] = $_;
        $count++;
    }
    @nums = sort { $a <=> $b } @nums;
}
```

11

After reading the input, the core of this menu-driven version of stats is a `while` loop that prints the menu and executes different subroutines based on the part of the menu that was selected. That `while` loop looks like this:

```
&getinput();
while ($choice !~ /q/i) {
    $choice = &printmenu();
  SWITCH: {
      $choice =~ /^1/ && do { &printdata(); last SWITCH; };
      $choice =~ /^2/ && do { &countsum(); last SWITCH; };
      $choice =~ /^3/ && do { &maxmin(); last SWITCH; };
      $choice =~ /^4/ && do { &meanmed(); last SWITCH; };
      $choice =~ /^5/ && do { &printhist(); last SWITCH; };
  }
}
```

Look! A switch! This is one way to accomplish a switch-like statement in Perl, using pattern matching, do statements, and a labeled loop. For each value of `$choice`, 1 to 5, this statement will call the right subroutine and then call `last` to "fall through" the labeled block. Note that the labeled block isn't a loop, but you can still use `last` to exit out of it.

The value of `$choice` gets set via the `&printmenu()` subroutine (we'll look at that one in a bit). Note that the `while` loop here keeps printing the menu and repeating operations until the value of the `&printmenu()` subroutine comes back as `q`, in which case the `while` loop stops and the script exits.

The `&printmenu()` subroutine simply prints the menu of options, accepts input, verifies it, and then returns that value:

```
sub printmenu {
    my $in = "";
    print "Please choose one (or Q to quit): \n";
    print "1. Print data set\n";
    print "2. Print count and sum of numbers\n";
    print "3. Print maximum and minimum numbers\n";
    print "4. Print mean and median numbers\n";
    print "5. Print a histogram of the frequencies.\n";
    while () {
        print "\nYour choice --> ";
        chomp($in = <STDIN>);
        if ($in =~ /^\d$/ || $in =~ /^q$/i) {
            return $in;
        } else {
            print "Not a choice.  1-5 or Q, please,\n";
        }
    }
}
```

Let's work down the list of choices that menu gives us. The first choice is simply to print out the data set, which corresponds to the `&printdata()` subroutine. `&printdata()` looks like this:

```
sub printdata {
    my $i = 1;
    print "Data Set: \n";
    foreach $num (@nums) {
        print "$num ";
        if ($i == 10) {
            print "\n";
            $i = 1;
        } else { $i++; }
    }
    print "\n\n";
}
```

This subroutine simply iterates over the array of numbers and prints them. But there's one catch: It prints them ten per line for better formatting. That's what that `$i` variable does; it simply keeps track of how many numbers have been printed and prints a newline after ten of them.

The second menu choice prints the count and sum of the data set. The `&countsum()` subroutine looks like this:

```
sub countsum {
    print "Number of elements: ", scalar(@nums), "\n";
    print "Sum of elements: ", &sumnums(), "\n\n";
}
```

This subroutine, in turn, calls the `&sumnums()` to generate a sum of all the elements:

```
sub sumnums {
    my $sum = 0;
    foreach $num  (@nums) {
        $sum += $num;
    }
    return $sum;
}
```

In previous versions of this stats script, we simply generated the sum as part of reading in the input from the file. In this example, we've postponed generating that sum until now. You could make the argument that this is less efficient—particularly since the average uses the sum as well—but it does allow us to put off some of the data processing until it's actually required.

Our third choice is the maximum and minimum values in the data set. We don't actually have to calculate these at all; because the data set is sorted, the minimum and maximum values are the first and last elements of the `@nums` array, respectively:

```
sub maxmin {
    print "Minimum number: $nums[0]\n";
    print "Maximum number: $nums[$#nums]\n\n";
}
```

Fourth choice is the mean and median values, which we can get as we did in previous stats scripts:

```
sub meanmed {
    printf("Average (mean): %.2f\n", &sumnums() / scalar(@nums));
    print "Median: $nums[@nums / 2]\n\n";
}
```

Which brings us to the last subroutine in this script, `&printhist()`, which calculates and prints the histogram of the values. As with previous versions, this part of the script is the most complex. This version, however, collects everything relating to the histogram into this one place, instead having bits of it spread all over the script. That means more local variables for this subroutine than for others, and more processing of the data that has to take place before we can print anything. But it also means that the data input isn't slowed down calculating values that won't be used until later, if at all, and there isn't a hash of the frequencies hanging around and taking up space as the script runs. Here's the `&printhist()` subroutine:

```
sub printhist {
    my %freq = ();
    my $maxfreq = 0;
    my @keys = ();
    my $space = 0;
    my $totalspace = 0;
    my $num;

    # build frequency hash, set maxfreq
    foreach $num (@nums) {
        $freq{$num}++;
        if ($maxfreq < $freq{$num}) { $maxfreq = $freq{$num} }
    }

    # print hash
    @keys = sort { $a <=> $b } keys %freq;
    for (my $i = $maxfreq; $i > 0; $i—) {
        foreach $num (@keys) {
            $space = (length $num);
            if ($freq{$num} >= $i) {
                print( (" " x $space) . "*");
            } else {
                print " " x (($space) + 1);
            }
            if ($i == $maxfreq) { $totalspace += $space + 1; }
        }
        print "\n";
    }
    print "-" x $totalspace;
    print "\n @keys\n\n";
}
```

A careful look will show that beyond collecting all the frequency processing into this one subroutine, little else has changed. Putting it into a subroutine simply makes the process and its data more selfcontained.

Listing 11.2 shows the full script (all the individual parts put together):

LISTING 11.2 THE `statsmenu.pl` SCRIPT

```
#!/usr/bin/perl -w

@nums = (); # array of numbers;
$choice = "";

# main script
&getinput();
while ($choice !~ /q/i) {
    $choice = &printmenu();
  SWITCH: {
      $choice =~ /^1/ && do { &printdata(); last SWITCH; };
      $choice =~ /^2/ && do { &countsum(); last SWITCH; };
      $choice =~ /^3/ && do { &maxmin(); last SWITCH; };
      $choice =~ /^4/ && do { &meanmed(); last SWITCH; };
      $choice =~ /^5/ && do { &printhist(); last SWITCH; };
  }
}

# read in the input from the files, sort it once its done
sub getinput {
    my $count = 0;
    while (<>) {
        chomp;
        $nums[$count] = $_;
        $count++;
    }
    @nums = sort { $a <=> $b } @nums;
}

# our happy menu to be repeated until Q
sub printmenu {
    my $in = "";
    print "Please choose one (or Q to quit): \n";
    print "1. Print data set\n";
    print "2. Print count and sum of numbers\n";
    print "3. Print maximum and minimum numbers\n";
    print "4. Print mean and median numbers\n";
    print "5. Print a histogram of the frequencies.\n";
    while () {
        print "\nYour choice --> ";
        chomp($in = <STDIN>);
        if ($in =~ /^\d$/ || $in =~ /^q$/i) {
            return $in;
        } else {
            print "Not a choice.  1-5 or Q, please,\n";
```

continues

LISTING 11.2 CONTINUED

```
        }
    }
}

# print out the data set, ten numbers per line
sub printdata {
    my $i = 1;
    print "Data Set: \n";
    foreach $num (@nums) {
        print "$num ";
        if ($i == 10) {
            print "\n";
            $i = 1;
        } else { $i++; }
    }
    print "\n\n";
}

# print the number of elements and the sum
sub countsum {
    print "Number of elements: ", scalar(@nums), "\n";
    print "Sum of elements: ", &sumnums(), "\n\n";
}

# find the sum
sub sumnums {
    my $sum = 0;
    foreach $num  (@nums) {
        $sum += $num;
    }
    return $sum;
}

# print the max and minimum values
sub maxmin {
    print "Minimum number: $nums[0]\n";
    print "Maximum number: $nums[$#nums]\n\n";
}

# print the mean and median
sub meanmed {
    printf("Average (mean): %.2f\n", &sumnums() / scalar(@nums));
    print "Median: $nums[@nums / 2]\n\n";
}

# print the histogram.  Build hash of frequencies & prints.
sub printhist {
    my %freq = ();
```

```
    my $maxfreq = 0;
    my @keys = ();
    my $space = 0;
    my $totalspace = 0;
    my $num;

    # build frequency hash, set maxfreq
    foreach $num (@nums) {
        $freq{$num}++;
        if ($maxfreq < $freq{$num}) { $maxfreq = $freq{$num} }
    }

    # print hash
    @keys = sort { $a <=> $b } keys %freq;
    for (my $i = $maxfreq; $i > 0; $i--) {
        foreach $num (@keys) {
            $space = (length $num);
            if ($freq{$num} >= $i) {
                print( (" " x $space) . "*");
            } else {
                print " " x (($space) + 1);
            }
            if ($i == $maxfreq) { $totalspace += $space + 1; }
        }
        print "\n";
    }
    print "-" x $totalspace;
    print "\n @keys\n\n";
}
```

11

Going Deeper

Subroutines are a fairly basic concept that doesn't involve a large amount of depth in Perl. Nonetheless, there are a few concepts that I neglected to discuss in this lesson, which I'll summarize here.

The definitive description of Perl subroutines, and how to define and use them, is contained in the `perlsub` man page. Because `my` is an operator, more information about it can be found in the `perlfunc` man pages (although we'll also talk more about it on Day 13). See those pages for further details on any of the concepts described in this section.

Leaving Off the Parentheses for Arguments

When you call built-in functions in Perl, you can call them with their arguments in parentheses, or leave off the parentheses if Perl can figure out where your arguments begin and end. You can actually do the same thing with subroutines, if you want to, but only if these two rules are met:

- You also call the subroutine without the leading `&` (with the leading `&` and Perl will try to use `@_` instead);
- Perl has already seen a declaration or definition of that subroutine previously in the script

Perl, for the most part, is not particular about where in a script a subroutine is defined, as opposed to where it is called (some languages require you to define a subroutine further up in the file from where you call it). Leaving off the parentheses for the arguments is the one exception.

One way to get around this is to pre-declare a subroutine at the top of your script, similarly to how you'd declare all your global variables before using them. To do this, just leave off the block part of the subroutine definition:

```
sub mysubroutine;
```

With the subroutine declared, you can then call it with arguments with or without parentheses. Don't forget to actually define that subroutine later on in your script, however.

Note that common practice amongst Perl programmers is to include the parentheses, even if it's possible to leave them off. Parentheses make your subroutines easier to read and less error-prone, so consider using this feature sparingly.

Using `@_` to Pass Arguments to Subroutines

You've seen how the `@_` variable contains the argument list to any subroutine, and is implicitly local to that that subroutine. You can, however, also use `@_` inside or outside a subroutine to redefine a set of arguments for the subroutine call.

For example, if you set `@_` to a list of elements in the main body of your Perl script, then call a pre-declared subroutine with no arguments, Perl will use the values in that array as the arguments to that subroutine. Here's a simple example:

```
@_ = ("this", "that", "other things");
&mysubroutine;   # no specific args, use @_
```

In this case, because the subroutine `&mysubroutine()` was called without ending parentheses, Perl will use the contents of `@_` as the arguments to that subroutine. This could be useful for, for example, calling ten different subroutines with all the same arguments.

This works for calling nested subroutines as well; you can use the current contents of any `@_` variable as the arguments to a nested subroutine. Note that calling a subroutine with any arguments whatsoever, including an empty set of parentheses, overrides the use of `@_`. Note also that you must have predeclared the subroutine for this to work.

Anonymous Subroutines

Anonymous subroutines are subroutines without names, and they operate sort of like pointers to functions in C. You use anonymous subroutines to create references to a subroutine, and the use Perl's references capabilities to gain access to that subroutine later on.

We'll discuss anonymous subroutines more in Day 19, "Working with References."

Using Subroutine Prototypes

Prototypes are one of those newer features that have snuck into Perl in the minor releases. Added to Perl as of version 5.003, subroutine prototypes allow your subroutines to look and behave just like regular built-in functions—that is, to determine the type of arguments they can accept rather than just stuffing them all into a list.

Subroutine prototypes only affect subroutines called without a leading `&`; you can call that same subroutine with an `&`, but the prototype will be ignored. In this way you can call a subroutine like a function or call it like a subroutine depending on your mood or for any other reason.

To declare or define a subroutine with a prototype, use one of the following:

```
sub subname (prototype);    # predeclaration
sub subname (prototype) {
   ...
}
```

The *subname* is, of course, the name of the subroutine. The prototype contains special characters referring to the number and type of arguments:

- `$` refers to a scalar variable, `@` to an array, `%` to a hash. `@` and `%` indicate list context and must appear last in the argument list (because they eat up the remaining arguments).
- Semicolons separate required arguments from optional arguments.
- Backslashed characters require arguments that start with that actual character.

So, for example, a subroutine with a prototype of `($$)` would expect two scalar variables as arguments. One with `($$;@)` would require two scalars, and have an optional list. One with `(\@)` requires a single list variable argument starting with `@`.

While subroutine prototypes may seem nifty, the fact that they are only available in newer versions of Perl may be problematic because you must be assured that the system you run your scripts on will have at least Perl 5.003 installed.

For more information on subroutine prototypes, see the `perlsub` man page.

The `caller` Function

One function I didn't mention in the body of this lesson is `caller`. The `caller` function is used to print out information about where a subroutine was called from (which can be sometimes useful for debugging). For more information, see the `perlfunc` man page.

Summary

A subroutine is a way of collecting together commonly used code or of portioning a larger script into smaller bits. Today you learned all about defining, calling, and returning values from subroutines, including delving into some of the issues of local and global variables.

Subroutines are defined using the `sub` keyword, the name of a subroutine, and a block containing the definition of the subroutine itself. Inside that block, you can define `my` variables that have a local scope to that subroutine, you can use the special `@_` to get to the arguments that were passed into the subroutine, and you can use the `return` function to return a value (or list of values) from that subroutine. If the context in which the subroutine was called is relevant, the `wantarray` function will tell you how your subroutine was called.

When you call subroutines, you use the name of the subroutine with an options `&` at the beginning, and with the arguments to the subroutine inside parentheses. Perl passes all the arguments to the subroutine as a flat array of all the values of its arguments, expanding any nested arrays and copying all the values into the local variable `@_`.

Q&A

Q How are subroutines different from functions?

A They're not; they both refer to the same conceptual things. In this lesson I simply decided to make the distinction so there would not be any confusion about calling built-in functions versus functions you define yourself.

Note that subroutines you define are, in fact, different from the built-in functions; subroutines don't control the number or type of arguments they can receive (at least, not without prototypes), and the rules of whether you can leave off the parentheses for subroutines are different. Future versions of Perl are working toward making programmer-defined subroutines and built-in subroutines closer in behavior.

Q Subroutine calls with `&` look really weird to me. Can I just leave off the `&`?

A Yes, the `&` is entirely optional. Include it or leave it off—it's your choice.

Q I want to pass two arrays into a subroutine and get two arrays out. But the two arrays get squashed into one list on the way in and on the way out. How can I keep the two arrays separate?

11

A The best way to do this is to use references, but you won't learn about those until Day 19. The other way is to modify global variables inside the subroutine, rather than passing the array data in via an argument list.

Q. But global variables are evil and bad.

A Well, that depends on who you talk to. In Perl, sometimes the best solution to a problem involves a global variable, and if you're careful (declaring globals with `my`, for example, and making sure you limit the use of those variables), you can get around the disadvantages of global variables.

Q So I can't figure it out, are Perl subroutines pass-by-value or pass-by-reference?

A They're pass-by-reference as far as the values in argument list is concerned. Change a value inside the `@_` array (for example, modify a string), and that value will change outside as well. However, multiple arrays will get squished into a single flat list, so you could consider arrays to be pass-by-value. And, if you assign the `@_` argument list to one or more local variables, those values will be copied and any changes will not be reflected outside the subroutine.

Workshop

The workshop provides quiz questions to help you solidify your understanding of the material covered and exercises to give you experience in using what you've learned. Try to understand the quiz and exercise answers before you go on to tomorrow's lesson.

Quiz

1. Name two reasons why subroutines are useful.
2. Show how to call a subroutine.
3. Show how to define a subroutine.
4. Does it matter whether or not a subroutine is defined before it's called? Where in your Perl script should subroutine definitions appear?
5. If you don't include an explicit call to `return` in your script, what value does a subroutine return?
6. Is the argument that gets returned from the subroutine with `return` a scalar or a list value?
7. In which parts of a Perl script are variables declared using `my` available?
8. What happens when you declare a `my` local variable with the same name as a global variable?
9. What happens to a hash you pass into a subroutine?
10. What is `@_` used for? Where is it available?
11. How do you name parameters in a Perl subroutine?
12. What does `wantarray` do? Why would you want to use it?

Exercises

1. Write a subroutine that does nothing but print its arguments, one argument per line, with each line numbered.
2. Write a subroutine that takes a string as an argument and returns the string in reverse order by words.
3. Write a subroutine that takes a list of numbers and squares them all, returning the list of squares. If there are elements in the string that are not numbers, delete them from the final list.
4. **BUG BUSTER:** What's wrong with this script?

```
@int = &intersection(@list1, @list2);

sub intersection {
   my (@1, @2) = @_;
```

```
    my @final = ();
    OUTER: foreach my $el1 (@one) {
       foreach my $el2 (@two) {
          if ($el1 eq $el2) {
              @final = (@final, $el1);
              next OUTER;
          }
       }
    }
    return @final;
}
```

5. **BUG BUSTER:** How about this one?

```
$numtimes = &search(@input, $key);

sub search {
   my (@in, $key) = @_;
   my $count = 0;
   foreach my $str (@in) {
       while ($str =~ /$key/og) {
           $count++;
       }
   }
   return $count;
}
```

6. Write a subroutine that, when used in a scalar context, reads in a single line of input and reverses it (character by character this time). When used in a list context, it should read multiple lines of input into a list and reverse all the lines (last line first and so on—the individual strings don't have to be reversed).
7. Take the image extractor script we wrote yesterday and turn it into a script that uses subroutines.

Answers

Here are the answers to the workshop questions in the previous section.

Quiz Answers

1. Subroutines are useful for a number of reasons:
   - They help break up a large script into smaller bits to help manage complexity.
   - Procedures in subroutines can be referred to by name to make scripts more readable.
   - Subroutines can define local variables that are more efficient, easier to manage and control than globals.

- If you use the same code repeatedly throughout your programs, you can put that code into a subroutine and then just reuse it.
- Smaller chunks of scripts can be more easily developed and debugged.

2. Call a subroutine using one of these forms:

```
&thisubroutine();     # both % and parens
&thissubroutine(1,2); # with arguments
thissubroutine(1,2);  # & is optional
```

3. Define a subroutine like this:

```
sub name {
   # body of subroutine
}
```

4. For most instances, you can call a subroutine before defining it, and vice versa. Perl is not particular about predefining subroutines.

   You can define a subroutine anywhere a regular Perl statement can go, although typically subroutines are defined in a group at the beginning or end of a Perl script.

5. Without an explicit `return`, subroutines return the last value that was evaluated in the block.
6. Trick question! `return` can be used to return either a scalar or a list, depending on what you want to return.
7. My variables are only available to code inside the nearest enclosing block and not to any nested subroutines.
8. Variables declared with `my` that have the same names as global variables will hide the value of the global. Once the subroutine or other block is finished executing, the original value of the global will be restored.
9. When you pass any list into a subroutine, it is flattened into a single list of scalar values. In the case of hashes, this means unwinding the hash into its component keys and values (the same way a hash is handled in any general list context).
10. `@_` refers to the argument list of the current subroutine. It's most commonly used inside a subroutine definition, although you can also define is as a global variable (see "Going Deeper").
11. Perl does not have formal named parameters. You can extract elements from the argument list `@_` and assign them to local variables in the body of your subroutine (although once assigned to local values, they cease to be references to the same values outside that subroutine).

12. The wantarray function allows you to find out the context in which your subroutine was called (scalar or list) to provide different behavior or return a sensible result.

Exercise Answers

1. Here's one answer:

```
sub printargs {
    my $line = 1;
    foreach my $arg (@_) {
        print "$line. $arg\n";
        $line++;
    }
}
```

2. Here's one answer:

```
sub reverstring {
    my @str = split(/\s+/, $_[0]);
    return join(" ", reverse @str);
}
```

3. Here's one answer:

```
sub squares {
    my @final = ();
    foreach my $el (@_) {
        if ($el !~ /\D+/) {
            @final = (@final, $el**2);
        }
    }
    return @final;
}
```

4. The fallacy in this script is assuming that the two lists, @list1 and @list2, will remain as two lists inside the body of the subroutine. Because Perl combines all list arguments into a single list, you cannot retain individual lists inside the body of the subroutine. Consider using globals instead.

5. The problem with this script results because of the order of the arguments. The list and scalar arguments are flattened into a single list on their way into the subroutine. The failure results with the line that assigns the local variables @in and $key to the argument list in @_; because @in is a list it will copy all the elements in @_, and leave none left for $key. By simply reversing the order of the arguments (put the key first, then the list), you'll get around this problem.

6. Here's one answer:

```
sub rev {
    my $in = "";
    if (wantarray()) {  # list context
        my @inlist = ();
        while () {
            print 'Enter input: ';
            $in = <STDIN>;
            if ($in ne "\n") {
                @inlist = ($in, @inlist); # reverse order
            }
            else { last; }
        }
        return @inlist;
    }
    else {  # scalar context
        print 'Enter input: ';
        chomp($in = <STDIN>);
        return reverse $in;
    }
}
```

7. Here's one approach:

```
#!/usr/bin/perl -w

$/ = "";     # paragraph input mode

while (<>) {
    while (/<IMG\s([^>]+)>/ig) {
        &processimg($1);
    }
}

sub processimg {
    my $raw = $_[0];
    my %atts = ();

    while ($raw =~ /([^\s=]+)\s*=\s*("([^"]+)"|[^\s]+\s*)/ig) {
        if (defined $3) {
            $atts{ uc($1) } = $3;
        } else { $atts{ uc($1)} = $2; }
    }
    if ($raw =~ /ISMAP/i) {
        $atts{'ISMAP'}= "Yes";
    }
    &printatts(%atts);
}

sub printatts {
    my %atts = @_;
```

```
    print '-' x 15;
    print "\nImage:  $atts{'SRC'}\n";
    foreach my $key ("WIDTH", "HEIGHT",
                     "BORDER", "VSPACE", "HSPACE",
                     "ALIGN", "ALT", "LOWSRC", "ISMAP") {
        if (exists($atts{$key})) {
            $atts{$key} =~ s/[\s]*\n/ /g;
            print "   $key: $atts{$key}\n";
        }
    }
}
```

DAY 12

Debugging Perl

No matter how good a programmer you are, chances are fairly high that any script over a few lines long is going to have some bugs. Some of those bugs are easy to figure out—syntax errors, infinite loops, or complaints from Perl because of `-w`. Others are much more subtle, producing incomprehensible results or no results at all.

You could figure out what's going on at each point in your script by using several `print` statements to determine the current values of variables and see if loops and conditionals are actually getting executed. But there is an easier way—particularly for larger scripts. Perl comes with a source-level debugger that lets you step through your script, watch it as it executes, and print out the various values of variables throughout the script's execution. The debugger can help you track down subtle problems in your code far quicker than `print` statements can.

In this chapter, we'll look at how to use the Perl debugger. In particular, we'll:

- Explore a quick example of how you might commonly use the debugger
- Learn how to start and run the debugger

- Trace the execution of your program
- Step through the execution of your script
- List the source in various ways
- Print out the values of variables
- Set breakpoints for halting execution at specific places

Using the Debugger: A Simple Example

Probably the best way to see how Perl's debugger works is to show you a small example of a typical use of the debugger. For this example, we'll step through the execution of a simple script that contains subroutines—the names script from Day 6, "Conditionals and Loops," which reads in a list of names, prompts you for something to search for, and returns the names that match that search key.

When you run a script with the Perl debugger turned on, you'll end up inside the debugger itself, which will look something like this:

```
% perl -d  statssubbed.pl statsdata.txt

Loading DB routines from perl5db.pl version 1.01
Emacs support available.

Enter h or `h h' for help.

main::(statssubbed.pl:3):       &initvars();
  DB<1>
```

Don't worry about starting the debugger yet; you'll see how to do this after we do this little walkthrough.

That DB<1> at the end is the debugger prompt; you'll type in various commands at this prompt. The number 1 means this is the first command; you can repeat commands by referring to the command number.

The line before the prompt shows the current line of code that Perl is about to execute, just before it runs it. The part on the left refers to the current package, name of the file, and the line number. The part on the right is the actual line of code, including any comments for that line.

To execute a line of code, use either the `s` or `n` command. The `s` command is more exhaustive; it will step into subroutines. The `n` command only steps through lines of code at the top level of your script; it'll execute subroutines silently. Once you've used either `s` or `n`, you can repeat either one by just pressing Return (or Enter) at each prompt:

```
main::(statssubbed.pl:3):         &initvars();
  DB<1> s
main::initvars(statssubbed.pl:8):               $input = "";
  DB<1>
main::initvars(statssubbed.pl:9):               @nums = ();
  DB<1>
main::initvars(statssubbed.pl:10):              %freq = ();
  DB<1>
```

Note in this example how when the script execution moves to the `&initvars()` subroutine (immediately, in the case of this script), the information on the left side of the output shows the name of that subroutine. This way, you always know where within your script you are. But in case you forget or can't place the position based on the one line, you can use the `l` command to list some lines:

```
DB<1> l
10==>        %freq = ();    # hash of number frequencies
11:          $maxfreq = 0; # maximum frequency
12:          $count = 0;    # count of numbers
13:          $sum = 0;      # sum of numbers
14:          $avg = 0;      # average
15:          $med = 0;      # median
16:          @keys = ();    # temp keys
17:          $totalspace = 0; # total space across histogram
18      }
19
```


The `l` command will list ten lines after the current line; you can also use `-` to print lines before the current line. Multiple uses of `l` and `-` will move back and forth in the script's source code. Keep in mind that this just prints the lines so you can get some context for where you are in the script—`l` and `-` don't actually execute anything.

As you step through the code, you can print out the value of any variable—any scalar, array, hash, and so on, using the `x` command. In this next example, the `&getinput()` subroutine has just read a line from the data input file, stored it in the `$input` variable, and chomped the newline off the end of it. At `DB<5>` we print the value of `$index`, and print the current values of `@nums` (the array indexes are on the left, and the actual elements on the right). Keep in mind that the line of code displayed (line 23 in the source) is displayed *before* it is run, so the value of `$input` will not yet be in `@nums`.

```
main::getinput(statssubbed.pl:21):          while (defined ($input = <>)) {
  DB<5> s
main::getinput(statssubbed.pl:22):              chomp ($input);
  DB<5>
main::getinput(statssubbed.pl:23):              $nums[$count] = $input;
  DB<5> x input
0  5
DB<6> x @nums
0  1
1  4
2  3
3  4
DB<7>
```

You can also use the `x` command to execute bits of Perl code, in the following case, to find the number of elements in `@raw`, or to show the first element:

```
DB<3> x scalar(@nums)
0  4
  DB<4> x $raw[0]
0  1
```

Stepping through the script using `n` or `s` lets you see each line in excruciating detail, but sometimes it's more detail than you want. If you're inside a subroutine, you can use the `r` command to stop stepping through that subroutine, execute the rest of it, and return to the place where that subroutine was called (which, in the case of nested subroutines, may be still another subroutine).

To stop stepping through the script at any time, use the `c` command (*c* for continue). Perl then runs the rest of the script with no intervening stops (unless you've put them into your script itself, for example, to read some input).

In addition to stepping through the execution of a script line by line, you can also control execution of your script with breakpoints. A *breakpoint* is a mark at a line of code or the beginning of a subroutine. Using `c` will run the script until the breakpoint, and then stop. At the breakpoint, you can then use `n` or `s` to step through lines of code, use `x` to print variables, or use `c` to continue to the next breakpoint.

For example, take the `statsmenu.pl` script we created yesterday, which organized the stats script into several subroutines. The `&countsum()` subroutine prints out the count and the sum of the data, calling the `&sumnums()` subroutine to get the latter value. To set a breakpoint at the `&sumnums()` subroutine, use the `b` command with the name of that subroutine, then `c` to execute the script up to that breakpoint:

```
# perl -d statsmenu.pl statsdata.txt

Loading DB routines from perl5db.pl version 1.01
Emacs support available.

Enter h or `h h' for help.

main::(statsmenu.pl:3): @nums = (); # array of numbers;
  DB<1> b sumnums
  DB<2> c
Please choose one (or Q to quit):
1. Print data set
2. Print count and sum of numbers
3. Print maximum and minimum numbers
4. Print mean and median numbers
5. Print a histogram of the frequencies.

Your choice --> 2
Number of elements: 70
main::sumnums(statsmenu.pl:72):     my $sum = 0;
  DB<2>
```

Can't remember the name of a subroutine? You can use the `S` command to print all the available subroutines. `S main` in particular will show you the subroutines you've defined (although there may be some extra Perl subroutines listed in there as well). Take a look at the following example.

```
DB<7> S main
main::BEGIN
main::countsum
main::getinput
main::maxmin
main::meanmed
main::printdata
main::printhist
main::printmenu
main::sumnums
  DB<8>
```

12

Note

> The `main` part is in reference to the `main` package, which is where all your variables and subroutines live by default. We'll explore more about packages tomorrow on Day 13, "Scope, Modules, and Importing Code."

If you want to set a breakpoint at a particular line, you can find the line using `l` to list the script, and then just use that line number with the `b` command:

```
DB<3> l
38:       print "5. Print a histogram of the frequencies.\n";
39:       while () {
40:           print "\nYour choice --> ";
41:           chomp($in = <STDIN>);
42:           if ($in =~ /^\d$/ || $in =~ /^q$/i) {
43:               return $in;
44            } else {
45:               print "Not a choice.  1-5 or Q, please,\n";
46            }
47        }
DB<3>
```

One other neat feature of the debugger is the ability to trace the execution of the script as it's running. The `s` and `n` commands step through each statement one at a time, but sometimes it's useful to see a printout of each statement as it executes even if you aren't stepping through each one. The `t` command will turn tracing on or off, toggling between the two. Here's a trace from the `&printdata()` subroutine, with a breakpoint set at the top of the `foreach` loop:

```
  DB<1> b 54
  DB<2> t
    Trace = on
  DB<2> c
Please choose one (or Q to quit):
1. Print data set
2. Print count and sum of numbers
3. Print maximum and minimum numbers
4. Print mean and median numbers
5. Print a histogram of the frequencies.

Your choice --> 1
Data Set:
1 main::printdata(statsmenu.pl:54):        foreach $num (@nums) {
DB<2> c
main::printdata(statsmenu.pl:55):              print "$num ";
1 main::printdata(statsmenu.pl:56):            if ($i == 10) {
main::printdata(statsmenu.pl:59):              } else { $i++; }
main::printdata(statsmenu.pl:54):          foreach $num (@nums) {
  DB<2>
```

Note here that tracing prints not only the script's output (note the `1` at the start of the line in the middle of the output after the `c` command), but it also prints each script line as it's being executed. If we typed `c` here again, we'd get another loop of the `foreach`, and that same output all over again.

To quit the debugger, use the q command (not quit, just q).

```
DB<18> q
%
```

With that walkthrough under your belt, you should now have a basic idea of how the debugger works. For the rest of this section, I'll show you more detail on the specific commands.

Starting and Running the Debugger

Perl's built-in debugger is run from the command line using the -d option. If you've been running your Perl scripts on UNIX or Windows NT using just the name of the script, you'll need to call Perl explicitly, with the name of the script and any filename arguments after that. In other words, if you usually call a script like this:

```
% myscript.pl names.txt
```

Call it like this for the debugger:

```
% perl -d myscript.pl names.txt
```

Alternately, if you think you'll be using the debugger a lot for a particularly gnarly script, you can add the -d option to the shebang line in the script itself:

```
#!/usr/bin/perl -wd
```

Don't forget to remove it again once you're done debugging.

To turn on the debugger in MacPerl, choose Perl Debugger from the Script menu, and then save your script and run it as usual. If you're going to use the script as a droplet (to accept files as input), don't forget the save the script as a droplet.

Note that before the debugger can run, your script has to be free of syntax errors or warnings. You'll have to fix those fatal errors before you can start debugging your script. But you'd have to do this anyway, so it shouldn't be too much of a burden.

To get help at any time as the debugger is running, use the h command, which will print out a list of possible commands. If it scrolls by too quickly you can use the |h command instead (which will pause between pages). You can also get help on any command using h with an argument; all the commands that match the argument will be printed, as shown in the following:

```
DB<3> h c
c [line¦sub]      Continue; optionally inserts a one-time-only breakpoint
                  at the specified position.
command           Execute as a perl statement in current package.
  DB<4>
```

Each debugger command has an associated number (in the preceding example, the command `h c` was command number 3). You can refer back to any previous command using an exclamation point and the command number:

```
DB<4> !3
```

You can review the last few commands using `H` and number with a minus sign in front of it:

```
  DB<13> H -3
13: H-3
12: b sumnums
11: x @nums
  DB<14>
```

To quit the debugger, use the `q` command. In addition, if the execution of your Perl script is complete, you can use `R` to restart the execution. Note that `R` may not work, depending on the environment and command-line arguments you used for that script.

Tracing Execution

Tracing allows you to see each line of your script as Perl executes it. If a line is executed multiple times, for example, as a loop, Perl will show it in the trace multiple times. For very complex scripts, this can often be more output than you need, but with breakpoints in place it may be helpful to see the actual order of execution that Perl takes through your script.

To toggle between trace modes in your Perl script, use the `t` command. If tracing is off, `t` will turn it on, and vice versa. For example, this output shows the result of executing a loop with trace turned off and with trace turned on (the breakpoint has been set at line 54, a `foreach` loop).

```
main::printdata(statsmenu.pl:54):          foreach $num (@nums) {
  DB<4> c
2 main::printdata(statsmenu.pl:54):          foreach $num (@nums) {
  DB<4> t
Trace = on
  DB<4> c
main::printdata(statsmenu.pl:55):                print "$num ";
```

```
2 main::printdata(statsmenu.pl:56):              if ($i == 10) {
main::printdata(statsmenu.pl:59):                } else { $i++; }
main::printdata(statsmenu.pl:54):            foreach $num (@nums) {
```

Turning tracing on shows you your script as it's executing. A stack trace shows you where you've already been—in the case of nested subroutines, it'll show you the subroutine that called the one you're currently executing, the one that called that subroutine, and so on, all the way back up to the top level of your script. Use the `T` command to show the stack trace, as follows:

```
  DB<4> T
@ = main::sumnums() called from file `statsmenu.pl' line 68
$ = main::countsum() called from file `statsmenu.pl' line 13
  DB<4>
```

The characters at the beginning of those lines show the context in which the subroutine was called—for example, the first line of this stack trace shows that the `&sumnums()` subroutine (the current routine) was called in a list context (the `@` at the beginning of the line indicates that), from inside the `&countsum()` routine. The `&countsum()` routine in turn was called from the main body of the script, in a scalar context (the `$` at the beginning of the line shows that).

Stepping Through the Script

To step through the code to your script one statement at a time, use either the `s` or `n` commands. Return (or Enter) will repeat the previous `s` or `n`. At each step, Perl displays the line of code it will execute next (not the one it just executed):

```
  DB<1> s
main::getinput(statsmenu.pl:25):                $nums[$count] = $_;
  DB<1>
```

12

The difference between the `s` and `n` commands is that `s` will descend into subroutine definitions. The `n` command stays at the same level, executing the subroutines without stepping through them.

To stop stepping through a subroutine, execute the remainder of that subroutine, and return to the statement where the subroutine was originally called, use the `r` command.

To stop stepping through the code altogether, use the `c` command.

Listing the Source

You can list the current source code being run, with line numbers, to get an idea of the context of the current line of code or to find a specific line at which to set a breakpoint.

To list the next ten lines of code from the current line down, use the `l` command:

```
 DB<15> l
75==>             $sum += $num;
76            }
77:           return $sum;
78        }
79
80        # print the max and minimum values
81        sub maxmin {
82:           print "Maximum number: $nums[0]\n";
83:           print "Minimum number: $nums[$#nums]\n\n";
84        }
  DB<15>
```

Additional calls of `l` will continue to show the next couple of lines. You can also use `l` with a line number to display just that line, with a range of numbers (`1-4`, for example) to display those particular lines, or with a subroutine name to list the first ten lines of that subroutine.

To back up a few lines in the display, use the `-` command. As with `l` for moving forward in the source, multiple uses of `-` will continue to move back.

The `w` command will show a window around the current line (or the line number, if you specify one): a few lines before and a few lines after. An arrow (==>) will show the current line position:

```
DB<3> w
20        # read in the input from the files, sort it once its done
21:       sub getinput {
22:           my $count = 0;
23==>         while (<>) {
24:               chomp;
25:               $nums[$count] = $_;
26:               $count++;
27            }
28:           @nums = sort { $a <=> $b } @nums;
29        }
```

To search for a particular line in the source, use the pattern matching expression. `/key/`, for example, will find the first instance of the word key. Use `?pattern?` to search backward in the file.

One last useful listing command is `S`; the `S` command will show all the subroutines available in the script. Most of those subroutines will be internal to Perl or to the debugger itself, but `S` with a package name (such as `main`) will only print those in that package, as shown here:

```
DB<20> S main
main::BEGIN
main::getpat
main::readnames
main::searchpat
```

More about packages tomorrow.

Printing Variables

Scrolling around in the source for your file is all well and good, but it helps to be able to figure out what Perl is doing while it's running your script. To print out the values of variables, use one of the following commands:

The X command will print out all the variables in the current package. Because many of these variables are special to Perl (including special variables such as @_, $_, and $1), the list can be fairly long. X with the name of a variable will print all the variables that match that name. Note that you should use just the name itself, and not include the $, @, or % character. X foo prints the values of all the variables named foo, ($foo, @foo, and %foo).

The V command is identical to X, except it takes an optional name of a package and prints the variables in that package. This won't be of much use until you start using packages, but I mention it here for completeness.

The one problem with X is that it seems to be unable to recognize local variables inside subroutines. For printing the values of local variables, or to execute small bits of Perl code that will result in values of interest, use the x command, as follows:


```
DB<3> x $input
0  'Dante Alighieri'
```

Printing arrays or hashes shows the contents of that array or hash. The output of X and V is slightly easier to read than that of x, particularly for hashes. Here's how a hash looks using X:

```
DB<4> X %names
%names = (
   'Adams' => 'Douglas'
   'Alexander' => 'Lloyd'
   'Alighieri' => 'Dante'
   'Asimov' => 'Isaac'
   'Barker' => 'Clive'
   'Bradbury' => 'Ray'
   'Bronte' => 'Emily'
)
```

Setting Breakpoints

Setting breakpoints inside a script allows you to execute the script normally, but then you can stop at a particular point (usually the point where everything begins to go wrong). You can set as many breakpoints in your script as you need to, and then use the stepping or variable-printing commands to work through the problem. Use `c` to continue execution past the breakpoint.

To set a breakpoint, use the `b` command. With the name of a subroutine, the breakpoint will be set at the first statement inside that subroutine; with a line number, the breakpoint will be set at that line number. With no argument, `b` will set a breakpoint at the current line. Breakpoints show up as a lowercase `b` in the source listings (there's one here at line 33):

```
DB<19> w 33
30      }
31
32      sub searchpat {
33:b        my $key = $_[0];
34:         my $found = 0;
35:         foreach $ln (sort keys %names) {
36==>           if ($ln =~ /$key/o || $names{$ln} =~ /$key/o) {
37:                 print "$ln, $names{$ln}\n";
38:                 $found = 1;
39              }
```

The `L` command is used to print all the breakpoints you have set at any given time, like in the following:

```
DB<22> L
namessub.pl:
 9:         my @raw = ();  # raw list of names
   break if (1)
 33:        my $key = $_[0];
   break if (1)
```

You can delete a breakpoint using either a line number or a subroutine name using the `d` command. Use `D` to delete all set breakpoints.

```
DB<22> d 9
DB<23> L
namessub.pl:
 33:        my $key = $_[0];
   break if (1)
```

Other Commands

So far, I've only shown you the commands that will help you get started with the debugger and that you're likely to use the most. In addition to the commands here, Perl also allows you to set conditional breakpoints, to change the values of variables, to perform actions at particular lines and, in fact, to enter entire Perl scripts and watch them execute interactively. As you learn more about the Perl debugger, you'll definitely want to make active use of the `h` command, and to refer to the `perldebug` man page when necessary.

One Other Thing

The debugger will help you figure out problems in your code. However, judicious use of the `-w` option can help you prevent many problems before you even start running your script (or having to resort to the debugger to figure out what's going wrong). Don't forget to use `-w` when you can.

Going Deeper

I've discussed essentially all of the most important debugger commands in this chapter, but not the complete set. If you begin using the debugger quite a lot, you might want to check the `perldebug` man page or the debugger's online help for more of the options.

Using Different Debuggers

Perl allows you to customize the behavior of the debugger, or to plug in an entirely different debugger system if you like. The `-d` switch, when used with a colon and the name of a module, will use that module as the debugger. For example, the `Devel::DProf` module, available from CPAN, provides profiling for your Perl scripts (testing how long it takes to run each subroutine, to figure out the inefficiencies in your code). Once it is installed, you can call it like this:

```
% perl -d:DProf thescript.pl
```

In addition, the `perl5db.pl` file contains the actual code for the debugger; you can copy and modify that file to change the behavior of the debugger. For more information, see the `perldbug` man page, or the documentation that comes with the `DProf` module.

Running Perl Interactively

The debugger can be used to run Perl in a sort of interactive mode to test commands and see their output right away. And you don't even need an actual script to do it. Here's a simple command that will load the debugger without a script to debug:

```
% perl -d -e1
```

Actually, you have given Perl a script to execute, a script of one character: 1. The `-e` option is used to run Perl scripts directly on the command line. We'll come back to this at the end of the book, on Day 20, "Odds and Ends."

Common Pitfalls and FAQs

Throughout the past 12 days I've tried to point out common mistakes that new Perl programmers (and even experienced programmers) make in various topics. The Perl documentation also contains a list of common pitfalls, and many many more, in the `perltraps` man page. A quick perusal of that page can provide interesting hints for solving problems in difficult code.

The Perl documentation also contains an extensive set of FAQ files (Frequently Asked Questions). Before pulling your hair out over a particular problem, check the FAQs. Start from the `perlfaq` man page and work from there.

Summary

Today you learned not so much about Perl itself, but about Perl's associated command-line debugger. You learned how to start and run the debugger, how to step through each line of your script, list the source, set breakpoints, trace the execution, and find out information about different parts of your script as they're running.

With the debugger there are few problems you can't figure out, and you can usually figure them out faster this way than trying to use `print` statements everywhere.

Q&A

Q I use emacs. Is there any way to tie the Perl debugger into emacs?

A Yup. The `cperl-mode.el` file has a ton of stuff for tying Perl into emacs. You can find this file in the standard Perl distribution in the `emacs` directory.

Q I'm used to graphical debuggers; this command-line stuff annoys me. Are there any graphical debuggers for Perl?

A If you're using the ActiveState port of Perl for Windows, ActiveState has a fabulous graphical Perl debugger available. See `http://www.activestate.com/` for more information.

Workshop

The workshop provides quiz questions to help you solidify your understanding of the material covered and exercises to give you experience in using what you've learned. Try to understand the quiz and exercise answers before you go on to tomorrow's lesson.

Quiz

1. What is a debugger for? Why is it more useful than, say, `-w` or `print`?
2. How do you start the Perl debugger?
3. Name three ways of listing bits of code inside the debugger.
4. How do you print the values of variables in the debugger?
5. How is tracing execution different from stepping through each line of code?
6. How are the `X` and `V` commands for printing variables different?

Exercises

Type in the following script:

```
#!/usr/bin/perl -w

my @foo = (2,5,3,7,4,3,4,3,2,3,9);

foreach $thing (0..10) {
    &timesit($thing, $foo[$thing]);
}

sub timesit {
    my ($num, $val) = @_;
    print "$num times $val is ", $num * $val, "\n";
}
```


Run the debugger on it. Perform the following debugger operations:

1. Turn on tracing using the `t` command. Type **`c`** to see the result.
2. Type **`R`** to restart running the script. Use `n` to step through the script. When you get inside the `foreach` loop, print the values of `$thing` a number of times.
3. Type **`R`** to restart the script again. Use `s` to step through the script. Print the values of `$num` and `$val` from inside the `×it()` subroutine. Use `r` to return from inside the `×it()` subroutine.
4. Type **`R`** to restart the script. Set a breakpoint at the `×it()` subroutine using the `b` command. Type **`L`** to view the breakpoint. Type **`c`** to run until the breakpoint is hit. Use `d` to delete the breakpoint.

5. **BUG BUSTER:** Use the debugger to find the bugs in this script:

```
#!/usr/bin/perl -w

@foo = (2,5,3,7,4,3,4,3,2,9);

while ($i < $#foo) {
    &timesit($i, $foo[$i]);
}

sub timesit {
    my ($num, $val) = @_;
    print "$num times $val is ", $num * $val, "\n";
}
```

Answers

Here are the answers to the workshop questions in the previous section.

Quiz Answers

1. The `-w` command in Perl is there to help you fix (or avoid) syntax mistakes or poor coding practices. The Perl debugger is there to help you with all other problems: arrays not getting built or not getting printed, values not getting matched, script logic not running the way you expect it to. Using `print` statements will get you some of the same effect, but it'll take longer and often be more difficult to figure out the problem. With the debugger you can also change values of variables and execute different bits of code at different times while your script is running—something you cannot do with a simple `print` statement.
2. Start the Perl debugger by running `perl` on the command line with the `-d` option followed by the name of your script and any script arguments. In MacPerl, choose Perl Debugger from the Script menu.
3. There are several ways of listing code in the debugger:
   - Use the `l` command to show succeeding chunks of code
   - Use `l` with a line number to show that line number
   - Use `l` with a range of line numbers to show those lines
   - Use `-` to show the preceding chunks of code
   - Use `w` to show a few lines before and a few lines after the current line
4. Print values of global and package variables using the `X` command with a variable name (minus the `$`, `@`, or `%`). Use the `x` command to print other variables and execute other Perl expressions (such as `$hash{'key'}`).

5. Turning on tracing shows each line of code as it's being executed, whether you are stepping through the execution or not. Stepping through the code shows each line as it's about to be executed. Stepping through code using the `n` command skips over subroutines (they get executed, but their contents are not displayed).
6. The `X` command prints the variables for the current package (`main`). The `V` command prints variables in any given package (something you'll need later on when you work with packages).
7. A breakpoint is a marker somewhere in your Perl code. When you run the code in the debugger, Perl runs until it find a breakpoint and then stops. You can then step through the code from there, print values of variables, or continue to the next time the breakpoint is hit.

Exercise Answers

1-4. There are no answers to these exercises; they demonstrate the use of the debugger.

5. There are two bugs in the script:
   - `$i` is never initialized, which means that the `×it()` subroutine will get initialization errors when it tries to print the value of `$num`.
   - `$i` is never incremented, which means it will be `0` each time and go into an infinite loop.

WEEK 2

DAY 13

Scope, Modules, and Importing Code

In today's lesson, we'll discuss issues concerning space and time (to complement our earlier discussions of truth and greed). By space, I'm referring to variable *namespace*: how variable names are managed across local and global scope, and how packages can be used to manage global variables across programs. Related to space is the ability to import code from modules into your scripts, either at compile time or runtime (thus covering the *time* part of today's lesson). Today we'll explore

- The problem with global variables and various ways of controlling those variables
- More about local variables; going beyond `my` and subroutines
- Importing and using external code with modules and pragmas
- Using modules from the standard library and from CPAN

Global Variables and Packages

Variable scope, in general, refers to the availability and existence of a variable in your script. A *global scope*, then, refers to a variable that is available to all parts of your script and exists as long as your script is running. *Local scope*, in turn, refers to a variable that has some limited scope and may pop in and out of existence depending on what part of your Perl script is currently executing.

We'll start this chapter with a look at global variables and global scope. In the next section we'll turn to local scope.

The Problem with Globals

Throughout this book, we've been using global variables (and global scope) in most of the examples, with the exception of the occasional local variable in a subroutine. There's a good reason for this: global variables are easy to create and easy to use. Any variable that is not explicitly declared with `my` (or, as you'll learn soon, `local`) automatically becomes a global variable, regardless of the context in which you use it, and is available at any point in that script.

This makes simple scripts easy to write. But as your scripts become larger and larger, the use of global variables becomes more and more problematic. There are more variables to keep track of and more variables taking up space as your script runs. Global variables that mysteriously appear deep in the body of a script can be difficult to debug—which part of the script is updating this variable at what time? Do you even remember what that global variable does?

As you develop larger scripts that use global variables, there's also a significant danger that you will accidentally use a name for a variable that already exists somewhere else in your script. While this problem can make it more difficult to debug your scripts, it's a particularly difficult problem if you have to incorporate your scripts into someone else's code, or if you want to create reusable Perl libraries. The risk of clashing variable names across multiple bodies of code becomes a very real and very painful problem.

The best way to control the potential of name clashes with promiscuous global variables is to try not to use them. Organize all your scripts in subroutines, and declare all your variables local to those subroutines. Data that needs to be shared between subroutines can be passed it from subroutine to subroutine via arguments. Many software developers argue that all programs—no matter how small, no matter how specialized the purpose, should be written this way, that the avoidance of global variables is Good Software Design.

In real life, however, everyone uses the occasional global variable, particularly in situations where every part of the script must access the same stored data in a list or other structure. Which brings us to another method for organizing and managing global variables: packages.

What's a Package?

A *package* is a way to bundle up your global variables such that they aren't really global anymore—they're only global inside a given package. In other words, each package defines its own variable name space. Packages enable you to control which global variables are available to other packages, thereby avoiding the problems of clashing variable names across different bits of code.

Chances are good you'll only need to develop your own packages if you're creating Perl modules or libraries or classes in object-oriented Perl programming—all topics that are too advanced for this book. Even if you don't develop your own, however, packages are all around you as you write and run your Perl scripts, whether you know it or not. With that in mind, having at least a passing understanding of how packages work will help you not only understand how Perl looks at variables and name spaces in your own scripts, but also how importing code from modules works as well. And it'll help in the event that your code grows to the point where it does become a library or a module later on. Learn the rules now, and it'll be that much easier later on.

How Packages and Variables Work

The core concept of the package is that every line of Perl is compiled in the current package, which can be the default package or one you define yourself. Each package has a set of variable names (called a *symbol table*) that determines whether a variable is available for Perl to use and what the value of that variable currently is. The symbol table contains all the names you could possibly use in your script—scalars, arrays, hashes, and subroutines.

If you refer to a variable name—say, `$x`—in your script, Perl will try to find that variable in the current package's symbol table. If you tell Perl to switch packages, it will look up `$x` in the new package. You can also refer to a variable by its complete package name, which tells Perl which symbol table to look in for the variable and its value. Package names contain both the name of the package, two colons, and the name of the variable. The special character indicating whether the variable is a scalar, a list, or a hash, or so on, is still included at the start of the package.

So, for example, `$main::x` would be used to refer to the scalar variable `$x` stored in the `main` package, whereas `$x` would refer to the scalar variable `$x` in the current package, which may or may not be the same variable stored in the package `main`. They have the same variable name but because they live in different packages, they have different values (or they may not exist at all in other packages).

`main` is the default package that you've been using all along, although you haven't been aware of it. When you create and use global variables in scripts that do not define an explicit package, you're actually creating variables that belong to the `main` package (you may have seen this come up in the error messages you get when you make a mistake—some of them refer to `Name main::foo used only once...`). All this time, whenever I've been referring to global variables, I've actually been slightly dishonest: global variables are actually package variables belonging to the package `main`.

Note that the existence of global variables in packages doesn't make them any less difficult to manage if you use lots of them. A hundred global variables defined in `main` are going to be just as difficult to use as a hundred global variables defined in a new package called `mypackage`. Using local variables and passing data between subroutines is still good programming practice for your own bit of the Perl world.

To create a new package, or switch between packages, use the `package` function:

```
package mypack;  # define or switch to a package other than main
```

Package definitions have a scope similar to that of local variables: package definitions inside a subroutine or block compile all the code inside that subroutine or block as part of that new package and then revert to the enclosing package. Calling `package` at the start of a script defines a new package for that entire block.

As I said earlier, you'll define your own packages most often when you're writing code libraries or modules of your own. The most important things to understand about packages are

- Every variable name and value is stored in a symbol table for the current package.
- You can refer to a variable name as either a plain variable name for the current package, or with a complete package name. This determines which symbol table Perl checks for the variable's value.
- The default package is package `main`.

Using Non-Package Global Variables

One way of creating well-mannered globals is to create packages. However, there is one other trick that is very commonly used for creating globals: declare your globals as local to your own script.

If you declare your global variables with the `my` modifier, as you do local variables inside subroutines, then those global variables won't belong to any package, not even `main`. They'll still be global to your script, and available to all parts of that script (including subroutines), but they won't conflict with any other variables inside actual packages, including those declared in package `main`. Global variables declared with `my` also have a slight performance advantage, since Perl doesn't have to access the package's symbol table each time the variable is referenced.

Because of these advantages of using non-package globals, it's recommended Perl practice to do this for all but the simplest of Perl scripts. To make use of it in your own scripts, simply include the `my` modifier when you declare your global variables, the same way you do for the locals:

```
my %names = (); # global hash for the names
```

Perl also includes a special feature to help you make sure you're using all your variables properly, as either local variables inside subroutines, or as non-package variables if they're global. Add the line `use strict` at the top of your script to turn on this feature, like this:

```
#!/usr/bin/perl -w
use strict;

my $x = '';  # OK
@foo = ();   # will cause script to exit

# remainder of your script
```

With `use strict` in place, when you run your script Perl will complain about stray global variables and exit. Technically, `use strict` will complain about any variables that are not declared with `my`, referenced using package names, or imported from elsewhere. Consider it an even stricter version of the variable warnings you get with `-w`.

There's one odd side effect of the `use strict` command worth mentioning: it will complain about the placeholder variable in a `foreach` loop, for instance, `$key` in this example:

13

```
foreach $key (keys %names) {
  ...
}
```

Technically, this is because the `foreach` variable, which is implicitly local, is actually a global variable pretending to be a local. It's still only available to the `foreach`, and behaves as if it were local, but internally it's declared differently (you'll learn about the two different kinds of local variables later on in this lesson, in "Local Variables with my and local." To fix the complaint from use strict, simply put a my in front of the variable name:

```
foreach my $key (keys %names) {
   ...
}
```

Throughout the rest of this book, all the examples will use use strict and declare global variables as my variables.

Local Scope and Variables

A local variable, as you learned on Day 11, "Creating and Using Subroutines," is one that is only available to a certain part of a script. After that part of the script is finished executing, the variable ceases to exist. Local variables also have a limited availability to other parts of a script; they may be private to just the scope in which they were defined, or they may only be available to those parts of the script that are running at the same time as the part of the script that defined the variable.

Local Variables and Local Scope

On Day 11, we looked at local variables, defined with my, inside subroutines. A subroutine defines a local scope, and the local variable is available to all the code defined inside that subroutine.

A subroutine isn't the only thing that can create a local scope, however. Any block surrounded by brackets defines a local scope, and any local variables defined within that block will cease to exist at the end of the block. This enables you to define local variables inside loops or conditionals, or even inside bare blocks, if there's some portion of code that will benefit from a new local scope.

All of the following snippets of code define a local scope. Each declaration of the variable $s is local to that enclosing block, and each $x is different from all the other versions of $x. Note, in particular, the use of a local variable in the foreach loop; here the variable is local to the entire loop, not to each iteration. $x will be incremented 5 times, as you'd expect:

```
if ($foo) {       # conditional
    my $x = 0;
    print "X in conditional: $x\n";
    $x++;
}

foreach (1..5) {  # loop
    my $x += $_;
```

```
    print "X in loop: $x\n";
}

{                   # bare block
    my $x = 0;
    print "X in bare block: $x\n";
    $x++;
}
```

One other rule of variables and scope to always keep in mind: local variables with the same name as global variables hide the values of the global variable of the same name. The value of the local variable is used throughout the current local scope, and then the original global and its original value will be restored at the end of that scope.

While this is a convenient feature, it can also be terribly confusing. Generally it's a good idea to avoid naming your locals the same name as your globals unless you've got good reasons for doing so.

Alternately, you can always refer to a global variable using its complete package name, even from inside a local scope. This technique assumes you did not use `use strict` or declare your globals with `my`:

```
$foo = 0;  # global
{
   my $foo = 1;          # local
   print "$foo\n";       # prints 1
   print "$main::foo\n";  # prints 0
}
print "$foo\n";          # prints 0
```

Local Variables with `my` and `local`

In addition to the local variables defined with `my`, there are also local variables defined with `local`. The `local` modifier is used the same way as the `my` modifier, with one or more variable names:

```
local ($x, $y);
```

13

What's the difference? The most obvious difference between `my` local variables and `local` local variables is that the scope for `local` local variables is determined by the execution of the script, not by how the code is laid out. A `my` variable is only available to the code up until the nearest enclosing block or subroutine definition; if you call another subroutine from within that one, the second subroutine won't have access to those variables. Local variables declared with `local` are available to the code inside that block and subroutine *and* to nested subroutines called from that same subroutine. That variable definition will cascade to any nested subroutines, much in the same way that global variables are available everywhere. `local` local variables are available from that subroutine and all the subroutines it calls as well.

In technical terms, `my` variables are *lexically scoped*, and `local` variables are *dynamically scoped*. But you don't have to know those terms unless you're a computer scientist or you're trying to impress other computer scientists.

I've put an example of how the scope differences between `my` and `local` variables work in the section "Going Deeper" if you're interested in looking more at `local` versus `my`. For the most part, however, local variables are best defined with `my`, and not `local`; `my` variables follow the more common definition of *local scope* in other languages and are easier to use and manage.

Using Perl Modules

Half of learning how to script Perl successfully is knowing how to write the code. The other half is knowing when NOT to write the code. Or, to be more exact, knowing when to take advantage of the built-in Perl functions or when to use libraries and modules that other people have written to make your programming life easier.

If you've got a given task to do in Perl that sounds kind of complex but that might also be something other programmers may have done in the past, chances are really good that someone else has already beat you to it. And, in the Perl tradition, that someone may very well have packaged up their code in a module or a library and made it available for public downloading. If it's a really common task, that module may even be part of the standard Perl distribution. Much of the time, all you have to do to make use of these libraries is import them into your own Perl scripts, add some code to customize them for your particular situation, and that's it. You're done.

Throughout many of the lessons in the remainder of this book, we'll be looking at a number of modules that you have available to you as part of the standard Perl distribution, as part of the distribution for your particular platform, or as downloadable files from the Comprehensive Perl Archive Network. In this section, then, you'll learn the basics: what a module is, and how to import and use modules in your own scripts.

Some Terminology

But first, some terminology. I've been bandying about the terms *function*, *library*, *module*, and *package*, and it's worth noting what all of these terms mean.

A built-in function, as I've noted before, is a function that comes with Perl and is available for you to use in your script. You don't need to do anything special to call a built-in function; you can just call it anything you want to.

A Perl *library* is a collection of Perl code intended for reuse in other scripts. Old-style Perl libraries were nothing more than this, and were used in other Perl scripts by importing them with the `require` operator. More recently, the term library has come to be equivalent to a Perl module, with old-style libraries and `require` falling out of favor. More about importing code with `require` later in this lesson.

A Perl *module* is a collection of reusable Perl code. Perl modules define their own packages, and have a set of variables defined by that package. To use a module, you import that module into your script with the `use` operator, and then you can (usually) refer to the subroutines (and, sometimes, variables) in that module as you would any other subroutines (or variables). Some modules are object-oriented, which means using them in slightly different ways, but the basic procedure is the same.

In addition, there are also *pragmas*, which are special kinds of Perl modules that affect both how Perl compiles and runs a script (whereas most Perl modules only affect its actual execution). Otherwise, they behave the same. `use strict` is an example of the use of a pragma. We'll look at pragmas later in this lesson (in "Using Pragmas").

Getting Modules

Where does one find these modules? If you have Perl, you already have a number of modules to play with and you don't need to do anything further. The *standard Perl library* is the collection of modules, pragmas, and scripts that are distributed with the standard Perl distribution. Different versions of Perl for different platforms may have a different standard library—the Windows version of Perl, for example, has a set of modules for accessing capabilities specific to Windows machines. While you have to explicitly import these modules to use them, you don't have to download them or install them.

The "Official" set of library modules is fully described in the `perlmod` man page, and includes modules for the following:

- Interfaces to databases
- Simple networking
- Language extensions, module and platform-specific development support, dynamic module and function loading
- Text processing
- Object-oriented programming

- Advanced math
- File, directory, and command-line argument handling
- Error management
- Time
- Locale (for creating international scripts)

Appendix B, "A Survey of Perl Modules," also contains some further information on many of the modules contained in the standard library.

For the Windows version of Perl, there are standard `Win32` modules for Windows extensions, including the following:

- `Win32::Process`: Creation and use of Windows processes
- `Win32::OLE`: For OLE automation
- `Win32::Registry`: Access to the Windows Registry
- `Win32::Service`: Management of Windows NT services
- `Win32::NetAdmin`: Remotely create users and groups

MacPerl includes `Mac` modules for accessing the Mac Toolbox, including AppleEvents, dialogs, files, fonts, movies, Internet Config, QuickDraw, and speech recognition (whew!). We'll explore some of the `Mac` and `Win32` modules on Day 18, "Perl and the Operating System."

In addition to the standard Perl library, there is the *Comprehensive Perl Archive Network*, otherwise known as CPAN. CPAN is a collection of Perl modules, scripts, documentation, and other tools relating to Perl. Perl programmers all over the world write modules and submit them to CPAN. To use the modules from the CPAN, you'll need to download and install those modules into your Perl distribution; sometimes you'll also need to compile them with a C compiler. Let's start in this section with using the modules you've already installed; we'll look more at CPAN later in this lesson.

Importing Modules

To gain access to the code stored in any module from your script, you *import* that module using the `use` operator and the name of that module:

```
use CGI;

use Math::BigInt;

use strict;
```

The `use` operator imports the subroutine and variable names defined and exported by that module into the current package so that you can use them as though you had defined them yourself (in other words, that module has a package, which defines a symbol table; importing that module loads that symbol table into your script's current symbol table).

Module names can take on many forms: a single name refers to a single module, for example, `CGI`, `strict`, `POSIX`, or `Env`. A name with two or more parts separated by double-colons refers to parts of larger modules (to be exact, they refer to packages defined inside other packages). So, for example, `Math::BigInt` refers to the `BigInt` part of the `Math` module, or `Win32::Process` refers to the `Process` part of the `Win32` module. Module names conventionally start with an initial capital letter.

When you use the `use` operator to import a module's code into your script, Perl searches for that module's file in a special set of directories called the `@INC` array. `@INC` is a Perl special variable that contains any directories specified on the Perl command line with the `-I` option, followed by the standard Perl library directories (`/usr/lib/perl5` and various subdirectories on UNIX, `perl\lib` on Windows, `MacPerl:lib` on Macintosh), followed by `.` (dot) to represent the current directory. The final contents of `@INC` will vary from system to system, and different versions of Perl may have different values for `@INC` by default. On my system, a Linux machine running Perl 5.005_02, the contents of `@INC` are

```
/usr/lib/perl5/5.00502/i486-linux
/usr/lib/perl5/5.00502
/usr/lib/perl5/site_perl/5.005/i486-linux
/usr/lib/perl5/site_perl/5.005
.
```

If you want to import a module that's stored in some other directory, you can use the `lib` pragma at the start of your script to indicate that directory in your script:

```
use lib '/home/mystuff/perl/lib/'
use Mymodule;
```

Perl module files have the same names as the module itself, and have the extension `.pm`. Many modules contain just plain Perl code with some extra framework to make them behave like modules, so if you're curious how they work you can go ahead and look at the code. Other modules, however, contain or make use of compiled code specific to the platform on which they run, and are not quite as educational to look at.

> **Note**
>
> These latter modules use what are called Perl extensions, sometimes called XSUBS, which enable you to tie compiled C libraries into Perl modules. Working with extensions is way too advanced for this book, but I'll provide some pointers to more information on Day 20, "Odds and Ends."

Using Modules

Using `use` enables you to import a module. Now what? Well, now you can use the code that module contains. How you actually do that depends on whether the module you're using is a plain module or an object-oriented one (you can find out from the documentation for that module whether it's object-oriented or not).

For example, take the module `Carp`, part of the standard Perl library. The `Carp` module provides the `carp`, `croak`, and `confess` subroutines for generating error messages, similarly to how the built-in functions `warn` and `die` behave. By importing the `Carp` module, the three subroutine names are imported into the current package, and you gain access to those subroutines as if they were built-in functions or subroutines you defined yourself:

```
use Carp;
open(OUT, ">outfile" || croak "Can't open outfile\n";
```

> The `carp` and `croak` subroutines, by the way, are analogous to `warn` and `die` in that they are used to print an error message (and then exit, in the case of `die` and `croak`). The difference is that if they're used inside a module, the `Carp` subroutines are better at reporting where an error occurred. In the case where a script imports a module that has a subroutine that calls `carp`, `carp` will report the package and line number of the enclosing script, not the line number inside of the module itself (which would not be very useful for debugging). We'll come back to `Carp` when we look at CGI scripts on Day 16,"Using Perl for CGI Scripting."

Some modules are object-oriented. In object-oriented programming parlance, functions and subroutines are called methods, and they're executed in a different way than normal functions. So, for modules you import that are object-oriented, you'd use special syntax to get at that code (your script itself doesn't have to also be object-oriented, so don't worry about that. You can mix and match object-oriented Perl with regular Perl). Here's an example from the CGI module (which we'll look at in more detail on Day 16):

```
use CGI;
my $x = new CGI;
my $name = $x->param("myname");
print $x->header();
print $x->start_html("Hello!");
print "<H2>Hello $name!\n";
print $x->end_html();
```

Weird-looking, isn't it? If you're familiar with object-oriented programming, what's going on here is that you're creating a new CGI object, storing the reference to that object in the `$x` variable and then calling methods using the `->` notation.

If you're not familiar with object-oriented programming, this is going to seem odd. Here's the short version:

- The line `my $x = new CGI;` creates a new CGI object and stores a reference to it in the variable `$x`. `$x` isn't a normal scalar like an array or a string; it's a reference to a special CGI *object*.
- To call subroutines defined by the module, otherwise known as a method, you use the variable holding the object, the `->` operator, and the name of the subroutine. So the line `$x->header()` calls the `header()` subroutine, defined in the object stored in `$x`.

Follow this same notation for other subroutines in that same module, and you'll be fine. We'll get back to references and object orientation later on Day 19, "Working with References."

Importing Symbols by Hand

Importing a module using `use` brings in the variables and subroutine names defined and exported by the module in question. The words *and exported* in the preceding sentence are important—some modules export all of their variables, some export only a subset, and others export none at all. With `use`, you gain access to all the code in the module, but not necessarily as if you had defined it yourself. Sometimes you'll have to do some extra work to gain access to the parts of the module you want to use.

If a module you're using doesn't export any variables or subroutine names, you'll find out soon enough—when you try and use those names, you'll get undefined errors from Perl. There are two ways to gain access to the features of that module:

- You can refer to those variables or subroutines using the full package name.
- You can import those symbols (variable or subroutine names) by hand, in the `use` statement.

With the first method, all you need to do to access a module's variables or subroutines is to add the package name to those variables or subroutines. This is especially useful if you've got variables or subroutines of the same name in your own code and you don't want those names to clash:

```
# call additup, defined in Mymodule module
$result = &Mymodule::additup(@vals);
```

```
# change value of the $total variable (defined in Mymodule)
$Mymodule::total = $result;
```

Note that if the package name itself contains two colons, you just add the whole thing before the variable name:

```
$Text::Wrap::columns = 5;
```

The second method, importing all the symbols you need, is easier if you intend to call a module's subroutines a lot in your own code; importing them means you don't have to include the package name each time. To import any name from a module into the current package, add those names to the end of the `use` command. A common way to do this is to use the `qw` function, which lets you leave off the quotes and add new symbols easily:

```
use MyModule qw(oneSub, twoSub, threeSub);
```

Note that these are symbol names, not variable names. There are no special letters before these names, and all the variables in the module with that name will be imported (the symbol `foo` will import `$foo, @foo, &foo,` and so on). To import specific variables, you can use the variable characters:

```
use MyModule qw($count);
```

Some modules are defined such that they have a set of variables that are imported by default, and a set that are only imported by request (if you look at the code, the hash `%EXPORT` commonly defines exported symbols by default; `%EXPORT_OK` defines the optional symbols). The easiest way to import both these things is to issue two calls to `use`: one for the defaults, and one for any optional symbols:

```
use Mymodule;    # import all default names
use Mymodule qw(this, that);   # import this and that as well
```

Import Tags

Some of the larger modules enable you to import only a subset of their features, for greater efficiency. These modules use what are called *import tags*. If you've got a module that uses import tags, you can find out which tags a module supports by checking the documentation of that module; alternately, the `%EXPORT_TAGS` hash in the source code will show you which tags you can use (tags are exported from the module, and imported into your code).

To import a subset of a module, add the tag to the end of the `use` statement:

```
use CGI qw(:standard);
```

Once again, `qw` is the quote word function; while you could just quote the import tag itself, this format is more commonly used and enables you easily to add more tags if you need them.

How a module behaves—if it uses import tags, or if it has variables or subroutines that must be imported by hand—is defined by the module itself, and (hopefully) documented. You might try running `perldoc` on the module to extract any online documentation the author of that module provided, or check the readme files that came with the module to make sure you're using it right.

Using Pragmas

The line `use strict` for restricting global variables to the current script is an example of a special kind of module called a pragma. A *pragma* is a module that affects how Perl behaves at both compile-time and runtime (as opposed to regular modules, which provide code for Perl just at runtime). The `strict` pragma, in particular, tells Perl to be strict in its parsing of your code, and to disallow various unsafe constructs.

The notions of *compile-time* and *runtime* may initially seem odd if you remember back to Day 1, "An Introduction to Perl," where I noted that Perl isn't a compiled language like C or Java. In those languages, you run a compiler to convert your source code into bytecode or an executable file; then you execute that new file to actually run the program. With Perl, the script is your executable. There's no intermediate compiled step.

In reality, I fibbed a little on Day 1. Perl does indeed compile its source code, just as C and Java do. But then it goes ahead and runs the result; there is no intermediate executable file hanging around.

What this means is that there are tasks that Perl does during compile-time (as the script is compiled) and tasks that happen during runtime (as the result is executing). At compile-time, Perl checks for syntax and verifies that everything it needs to run that script is available. At runtime, the script actually executes and operates on the data you give it. As you grow more advanced in your knowledge of Perl, you'll learn about different operations where *when* they happen is as important as the fact that they happen at all.

But back to pragmas. As I mentioned, a pragma is a bit of imported code that affects how Perl operates both during compile-time and runtime. Unlike most imported code in modules and libraries, which only affect a script's runtime behavior, pragmas can change the whole look and feel of your code and how Perl looks at it.

Perl has very few pragmas in its standard library (unlike modules, of which there are dozens). Pragmas are conventionally spelled in all lowercase letters, to differentiate them from modules. You use pragmas just like you do modules, with the `use` operator:

```
#!/usr/bin/perl -w
use strict;
use diagnostics;
```

Each of the pragmas can be used at the top of your script to affect the entire script. They can also be used inside a block, in which case they only change the behavior of that enclosing block. At the end of the block the normal script behavior resumes.

Some of the more useful Perl pragmas include `strict` and `diagnostics`. You can find a more complete listing of available pragmas in the `perlmod` man page under the section "Pragmatic Modules."

strict

The `strict` pragma, which you've seen already, restricts various unsafe constructs in your scripts. The `strict` pragma watches for misplaced global variables, barewords (unquoted strings with no definitions in the language or defined as subroutines), and symbolic references (which we'll look at in greater detail on Day 19). You can control only some of these unsafe constructs by including the strings `'vars'`, `'subs'`, or `'refs'` after the `use strict`, like this:

```
use strict 'vars';
```

You can turn off strictness for various blocks of code using the `no strict` command (and with optional `'vars'`, `'subs'`, and `'refs'`, if necessary). The `no strict` applies only to the end of the enclosing block (subroutine, conditional, loop, or bare block) and then Perl reverts to the usual amount of strictness.

diagnostics

The `diagnostics` pragma is used to turn on Perl verbose warnings. It works similarly to the `-w` switch; however, it can be used to limit diagnostic warnings and messages to specific parts of your script enclosed in blocks. You cannot turn off `diagnostics` at the compile phase of your script (as you can with `strict` using `no strict`), but you can control runtime warning using the `enable` and `disable` directives:

```
use diagnostics;

# various bits of code

disable diagnostics;
```

```
# code that usually produces run-time warnings
enable diagnostics;

# continue on as usual...
```

The `English` Module

The `English` module is worth mentioning specifically because, like the pragmas, it offers a way to change how Perl interprets your script, but unlike the pragmas, it operates at runtime and you can't limit its scope to a block. The `English` module is used to make Perl less terse in its built-in special variable names. While true Perl wizards can gleefully litter their scripts with variables like `$_`, `$"`, `$\`, and so on, most mere mortals have trouble keeping all but the most common special variables straight. That's where `use English` can help, by aliasing various longer variable names to the shorter versions.

For example, the variable `$,` (a dollar sign and a comma) is known as the output field separator, and it's used to separate items in `print` statements. With `use English,` you can still refer to the variable as `$,` if you like, or you can also use the names `$OUTPUT_FIELD_SEPARATOR` or `$OFS`. All three will work equally well.

You can find a list of Perl's special variables and all their names (both using the `English` module and not) in the `perlvar` man page.

An Example: Using the `Text::Wrap` Module

Here's a small example that uses a module from the standard library: the `Text:Wrap` module, which, given a very long string, will wrap that string into multiple lines of a given length, and with an optional indentation character to include for each line.

This particular example formats an input file to be 80 or so characters wide and indents it in a format familiar to you if you're used to email: it puts a > symbol at the start of each line. The file to be quoted is assumed to be broken up into multiple paragraphs with a blank line between each one. So, for example, if the input file looks like this (a single long string; the end of lines here are not actual ends of lines in the input):

13

```
The event on which this fiction is founded has been supposed, by Dr.
Darwin, and some of the physiological writers of Germany, as not of
impossible occurrence. I shall not be supposed as according the remotest
degree of serious faith to such an imagination; yet, in assuming it as the
basis of a work of fancy, I have not considered myself as merely weaving a
series of supernatural terrors. The event on which the interest of the
story depends is exempt from the disadvantages of a mere tale of spectres
```

```
or enchantment. It was recommended by the novelty of the situations which
it develops; and, however impossible as a physical fact, affords a point
of view to the imaginationfor the delineating of human passions more
comprehensive and commanding than any which theordinary relations of
existing events can yield.
```

The output will look like this:

```
> The event on which this fiction is founded has been supposed, by Dr.
> Darwin, and some of the physiological writers of Germany, as not of
> impossible occurrence. I shall not be supposed as according the remotest
> degree of serious faith to such an imagination; yet, in assuming it as
> the basis of a work of fancy, I have not considered myself as merely
> weaving a series of supernatural terrors. The event on which the interest
> of the story depends is exempt from the disadvantages of a mere tale of
> spectres or enchantment. It was recommended by the novelty of the
> situations which it develops; and, however impossible as a physical
> fact, affords a point of view to the imagination for the delineating of
> human passions more comprehensive and commanding than any which the
> ordinary relations of existing events can yield.
```

Listing 13.1 shows the code for the script to do this.

LISTING 13.1 THE `wrapit.pl` SCRIPT

```
1:  #!/usr/bin/perl -w
2:  use strict;
3:
4:  use Text::Wrap;                     # import module
5:  my $indent = "> ";                  # indent character
6:
7:  while (<>) {
8:      print wrap($indent, $indent, $_);
9 : }
```

As you can see, this is not very much code at all, and it's much easier than writing the same procedure using raw Perl code. The important parts of this script are:

- Line 4, where we import the `Text::Wrap` module.
- Line 5, which defines the indent character (here `"> "`, although it could be any set of indentation characters you want).
- Line 8, where we call the `wrap` function to actually wrap the test. The `wrap` function, defined in the `Text::Wrap` module, takes three arguments: the character to indent the first line with, the character to indent each successive line with, and the string to wrap. In this case, we wanted to indent all the lines with the same character, so we called `wrap` with `$indent` specified twice.

By default, the `Text::Wrap` function wraps to 76 characters wide. You can change this value using the `$columns` variable, although that variable is not imported from the module by default. You'll have to import that variable explicitly or use its full package name to be able to make use of it:

```
use Text::Wrap qw($columns);   # import $columns
$columns = 50;                 # set it
```

Using Modules from CPAN (The Comprehensive Perl Archive Network)

If the modules standard Perl library don't have enough capabilities—and often, they don't—there is also CPAN. The Comprehensive Perl Archive Network, as I mentioned earlier, is a massive collection of publicly available modules for Perl covering just about every topic you can imagine. Want a module to handle encrypting data? CPAN's got it. Need to send email? CPAN's got a module to do that. Want to read in and process an entire HTML file? Not a problem. No matter what it is you want to do, it's a good idea to check CPAN first to see if someone has already done it for you. There's no point in reinventing the wheel when you can use someone else's code. That's the advantage of having a Perl community to rely on.

A Note of Caution

There are two drawbacks to the CPAN modules. The first is that you have to download, build, and install modules before you can use them, which means a bit more work involved than just inserting a `use module` line in your script. Some modules may require you to compile them, which means you'll need a working C compiler installed on your computer.

The second problem with modules on CPAN is that most of them are developed for use with UNIX Perl. If you're using Windows or MacPerl, the module you want to use may not be available for that platform. This is changing as time goes on, however, and more and more modules are being developed cross-platform. Windows support, in particular, is becoming more and more widespread. There's even a special tool, PPM, for installing and managing Windows-specific CPAN modules for the ActiveState version of Perl for Windows (we'll look at PPM later in this lesson in "Installing CPAN Modules on Windows Using PPM"). If you're not sure if a particular module is available for your platform, you'll need to check the documentation for that module—or be prepared to port it yourself.

Acquiring Modules from CPAN

The CPAN modules are stored on the CPAN Web site or one of its mirrors. If you start at `http://www.perl.com/CPAN/CPAN.html` you'll find out what CPAN contains, how to get the files, and how to find out if a particular module is available on your platform. There's also a module search engine available so you can figure out quickly if there is a module to do what you want. Appendix B also contains a list of many of the modules available as of this writing (since new modules are being added all the time, you'll want to consult the online version as well).

Some modules come in bundles to reduce dependencies between different modules (there's nothing more irritating than trying to run a script, which needs one module, only to find after downloading that module that it requires another module, which then requires a third module and so on down the line). Module bundles usually start with the word `lib`—for example, the `libwww` group of modules includes a whole set of modules for handling things relating to the World Wide Web. If the module you want is contained in a bundle available on CPAN, it's usually a good idea to download the whole bundle instead of the individual module, just to be safe.

Say you've found a module that you want to use. Usually, you'll download that module, uncompress or unarchive it using the tools for your platform (usually `gzip` and `tar` for UNIX, `WinZip` for Windows, Stuffit for Mac). On UNIX many modules include a makefile to install everything in the right spots (type **`make`** to get the process started). On Windows and the Mac, if there are not specific directions for installing the files on your platform you can sometimes just copy the `.pm` module files into the appropriate spots in your Perl hierarchy. The `perlmodinstall` man page part of the 5.005 Perl installation offers many specific suggestions for getting modules decompressed and installed. The process, however, can be different for each module, so follow what the `README` files say to make sure everything is installed correctly.

Some modules have parts written in C that may require you to have a C compiler installed on your machine. If you don't have a C compiler, you may be able to use the module without these extra parts, depending on the module. Again, check the documentation that comes with the module.

If you're on UNIX, and you're installing modules that have compiled parts, make sure that the C compiler you use to compile the modules is the same compiler you used to compile Perl in the first place (with network-mounted file systems this isn't as unusual a case as it sounds). You can run into difficult-to-solve incompatibilities with modules compiled in different environments than those with which Perl was compiled.

After you're done de-archiving, building, compiling, and installing, you should have a number of files installed into the right locations in your Perl hierarchy. You might want to explore the various directories in your `@INC` array to make sure they're there.

Installing CPAN Modules on Windows Using PPM

The Perl Package Manager, or PPM, is a tool that comes with the ActiveState version of Perl for Windows that makes installing and managing CPAN modules on Windows much, much easier. With PPM, you don't have to worry whether a particular module is supported on Windows, or figure out how to compile or install it using arcane UNIX-based tools. PPM lets you install, update, and remove individual already-built modules from inside a single program.

A *package*, per the Perl Package Manager, is a collection of one or more modules and supporting files. It's different from a Perl namespace package.

To use PPM, you must be connected to the Internet. The PPM script gets its packages from a repository on the ActiveState Web site. To start PPM, simply type **ppm** from inside a command shell:

```
c:\> ppm
PPM interactive shell (0.9.5) - type 'help' for available commands
PPM>
```

At the PPM prompt, you have several choices, including

- `help`, to print a list of choices
- `search`, to show which packages you have available to install
- `query`, to show the packages you already have installed
- `install`, to install a specific package
- `verify`, to check to make sure all your packages are up to date
- `remove`, to remove a specific package

You can find out more about PPM from the PPM Web page (part of ActiveState's Perl for Windows installation), or at `http://www.activestate.com/activeperl/docs/ppm.html`.

Using Modules from CPAN

After you've got a module from CPAN installed—either through downloading and installing it yourself, through the use of PPM, or even by copying files manually to your

13

Perl installation, that module is available to your scripts. You can then import it with `use` and use its capabilities as if it were any other module. You'll need to check its documentation to see if it's a regular or object-oriented module, or to see if it uses import tags, but other than the fact that they need to be installed first, the CPAN modules typically behave the same as those in the standard library.

Going Deeper

I've covered a lot of ground in this chapter, from packages to modules to importing, to how Perl actually looks at code at various times. Much of what I've discussed in this chapter is the tip of the iceberg: packages and modules, in particular, could fill up entire books of their own, and the few paragraphs I devoted to object orientation is barely even enough to get started.

We'll go a little deeper into a few of these topics later in this book. Other topics, however, including developing your own packages and just about everything to do with creating modules, are best left to the advanced Perl programmer, and as such are outside the scope of this book. After finishing the 21 days of this course, consider exploring modules and packages with the text in the online man pages and FAQs.

There are a few topics that I can describe in this section, however, that relate more closely to the topics we've discussed in this lesson.

Typeglobs

Typeglobs is a strange name that involves being able to refer to multiple types of variables by a single name (the term *typeglob* is borrowed from UNIX, where referring to multiple files using `file.*` or some such character is called file *globbing*). Typeglobbing refers to the symbol table entries of a given package.

The typeglob expression `*foo` refers to any variable with the name `foo`—`$foo`, `@foo`, `&foo`, and so on. Normally, these variables are distinct; typeglobbing is a way of lumping them all together.

In earlier versions of Perl, typeglobbing was used to pass arrays into subroutines by reference. You could use a typeglob to alias a local variable to a global array, and then any changes you made to the local array would be reflected outside the global array, like this:

```
@foo = (1,2,3);
&removethrees(*foo);
```

```
sub removethrees {
   my *list = @_;
   foreach my $x @list {
      if ($x == 3) { undef $x }
   }
   return @list;
}
```

In this example, all the changes made to the local list in `@list` are reflected in the list `@foo`, because `@list` has been set up as an alias for `@foo`.

Typeglobs for passing arrays into subroutines have been essentially replaced by the newer reference feature; references not only enable you to pass individual arrays into subroutines by reference, but also enable you to maintain the integrity of multiple arrays. Use references instead of typeglobs for this purpose (more about references on Day 19).

One Other Difference Between `local` and `my`

The most obvious difference between variables defined with `my` and those defined with `local` is that of lexical and dynamic scope, as I noted in the body of this lesson. The other difference is how Perl manages those variables:

- `Local` local variables are actually global variables in disguise. When you create a local variable, if a global of the same name exists, Perl saves the value of that global and reinitializes the same variable (and its same location in the symbol table) to the new local value. The value of the global is restored at the end of the local variable's scope.
- `My` local variables are entirely new variables that are not stored in the symbol table. They are wholly private to the block or subroutine in which they're stored. This makes them slightly faster to use than `local` local variables, because they don't require a symbol table lookup.

Neither of these differences really change how you would use `local` or `my` in your own scripts (`local` local variables are relevant when it comes to using typeglobs, but that's a detail outside the scope of this book). In most cases, use `my` where you want a local variable and you'll do just fine.

13

An Example of `local` Versus `my`

In the section on local variables defined using either `local` or `my`, I promised an example of how this works if the difference was totally befuddling. Listing 13.2 shows a script to make things clearer (or perhaps just completely dark).

Listing 13.2 A Scope Script

```
#!/usr/bin/perl -w

$global = " global available here\n";

&subA();
print "Main script:\n";
foreach $var ($global, $mylocal, $locallocal) {
    if (defined $var) {
        print $var;
    }
}

sub subA {
    my $mylocal = " mylocal available here\n";
    local $locallocal = " local local available here\n";
    print "SubA:\n";
    foreach $var ($global, $mylocal, $locallocal) {
        if (defined $var) {
            print $var;
        }
    }
    &subB();
}

sub subB {
    print "SubB: \n";
    foreach $var ($global, $mylocal, $locallocal) {
        if (defined $var) {
            print $var;
        }
    }
}
```

This script uses three variables: `$global`, `$mylocal`, and `$locallocal`, and declares them all appropriately. For each subroutine, and then once again at the end of the script, the values of those variables are printed if they exist and if they have a proper value. Try to follow the flow of this script and predict what will get printed when.

Here's the actual output:

```
SubA:
 global available here
 mylocal available here
 local local available here
SubB:
 global available here
 local local available here
```

```
Main script:
 global available here
```

Was it what you expected? Let's work through it. This script starts at the top and calls `&SubA()`, which calls `&SubB()`, and then prints some variables. In the subroutine `&SubA()`, we declare both `$mylocal` and `$locallocal` with the `my` and `local` modifiers, respectively, in lines 14 and 15. Both those variables, plus the `$global`, will then be available inside the boundaries of that subroutine, so all three values will be printed.

In line 22, `&subA()` calls `&SubB()`, and here we just print the variables that we have available. The global will be there because global variables are available to all parts of a script. But `$mylocal` is not there—the `my` modifier makes that local variable only available to that subroutine and not to other parts of the script. The `$locallocal` variable definition, however, is available to subroutines further down than the one in which it was defined.

After `&SubB()` is finished, execution pops back up to `&subA()`, and then back up to the main part of the script where we try printing those same values again. Here only the global will be available, and only the global will get printed.

Package Initialization and Finalization with `BEGIN` and `END`

One aspect of packages worth mentioning before we move on is the subroutines `BEGIN` and `END`, which are used to initialize a script before it runs and to finalize a script after it's done running. These subroutines are most commonly used inside complex Perl libraries and modules, and as constructors and destructors for object-oriented classes.

The `BEGIN` subroutine is executed just as soon as it's found, during compile-time, before the rest of the script is parsed. Use `BEGIN` for any code that you want to run at compile-time, for example, importing symbols for module definitions that will later be exported to other code, or to include other code that is required by the module.

`END`, on the other hand, is executed as the Perl script finishes executing, both if the script executed correctly or if there was an error that caused it to execute prematurely (including `die`). Use `END` to clean up after your script. You can change the status value that is returned to the UNIX shell after your script exits using `END`, for example.

13

You can find out more about `BEGIN` and `END` in the `perlmod` man page.

Importing Code with `require`

In this lesson, I showed you how to import code from modules using the `use` function. The `use` function, in short, imports code from another source at compile-time, and imports various symbols into the current package. The `require` function, on the other hand, is used to include code from other sources at runtime (in fact, `use` is equivalent to calling `require` inside a `BEGIN` subroutine and importing that file's variables into the current namespace).

In earlier versions of Perl, `require` was used as the general-purpose import mechanism. You stuck your subroutine or global variable definitions in a separate file, and then included that file in another script using `require`, like this:

```
require 'foo.pl';
```

Perl looks for the given file to be imported in the directories stored in `@INC`. In addition, it keeps track of which files have been already imported, so it won't reimport code that's already been loaded. If the included file, however, defines its own package, then `require` will not import that package's variables into the current package (not even `main`), and you'll have to refer to those variables using the complete package name. Also, you have to be careful when you use `require`; because the `require` occurs at runtime, you must make sure the `require` happens before you actually call or use anything defined in that imported file.

This mechanism for importing code from one file to another still works just fine in current versions of Perl, and you can use it to build your own simple libraries of subroutine definitions. However, the new mechanisms of packages and modules provide better features and more control over what gets imported when. For serious library development, consider learning more about the development packages, modules, and `use`.

One other cool use of `require` is with a Perl version number, in which case if the script is being run with an earlier version of Perl, the script will immediately exit with an error. Use this mechanism for making sure the version of Perl that's being run has the features you use in your script—for example, features that only exist in Perl 5, or more advanced features that may only exist in 5.005 or higher:

```
require 5.005;
```

See the `perlfunc` man page for further information on `require`.

Summary

Today's lesson has covered a few topics that might be considered somewhat esoteric, but will become more important as the remainder of this book unfolds. The first half of this lesson discussed aspects of variables and scope, including what a global variable means when there are packages to restrict it from being truly global, and making sure your global variables are local to a script by defining them with `my`.

Then we turned to local variables, and you learned more about the use of `my` variables inside blocks and subroutines, as well as defining local variables with `local`.

Given all these choices for declaring and using different variables, it's confusing to know what's right. Among Perl programmers, there are general rules and practices that are commonly used for dealing with variables and scope:

- Don't declare raw global variables. Declare all global variables using `my`, and use `use strict` to make sure you're doing it right.
- Use `my` variables over `local` unless you have specific reasons for doing so. `Local` local variables suffer from many of the same reusability and debugging problems that global variables do, and confuse what's an otherwise clean distinction between the concepts of *local* and *global*.
- Try to avoid using local variables that have the same name as globals unless you have a good reason for doing so.

In the second half of the lesson, we looked at the `use` function, and how to use it to turn on pragmas—hints to Perl for how to compile and run your scripts—and to import and use code contained in modules either in the standard library or from CPAN. The module part of this lesson was potentially the most important thing you'll learn today; we'll be using modules throughout the rest of this book.

The functions and other commands we explored today include:

- `package`, to switch between different packages
- `my`, to define a local variable or a non-package version of a global variable
- `use strict`, to make sure you're not using any stray global variables
- `local`, another way of defining local variables (use `my` instead)
- `use`, in general, to import a pragma or module

Q&A

13

Q How is declaring global variables with `my` any advantage over using regular global variables if I'm writing self-contained scripts to do very simple things?

A If the only scripts you write are smaller, self-contained scripts, then you don't really need to use `use strict` or make sure your variables are declared using `my`. You'd use `my` globals if there was a chance for your code being incorporated into someone else's code, even accidentally. Because quite a lot of code has a chance of being used in ways contrary to how you intended it to be used, the use of `my` globals and `use strict` is considered a defensive move and good programming practice. But it is not required.

Q I'm using ActiveState's Perl for Win32. My script has `use strict` defines, but it complains about the variable inside a `foreach` definition. I declare that variable with `my` and I get another error. What am I doing wrong?

A Nothing. ActiveState's version of Win32 Perl won't let you put a `my` declaration inside the `foreach` loop. Just declare it as a `my` variable elsewhere and then use it inside the `foreach` and you'll be fine.

Q Most languages use either lexical or dynamic scope, but not both. Why does Perl confuse things and provide multiple kinds of local scopes?

A It's mostly historical. Earlier versions of Perl provided a dynamic scope for variables with the `local` operator. The `my` operator was added later to provide a more distinct lexical local scope; `local` stays around for backward compatibility with earlier scripts.

If the difference seems hopelessly confusing, just use `my` variables and assume they are private to any given subroutine, and you'll be fine.

Q I've got an older script that someone wrote that starts out with a lot of `require thislibrary.pl` lines. Should I change those to use `use` instead?

A Actually, no. The `require` operator was the old way of incorporating library code into Perl scripts, and it's likely that the library you're importing (`thislibrary.pl` in your example) isn't written as a module, and won't work well with `use`. Unless you're intending to rewrite the entire script—and potentially rewrite all the libraries as well—you can go ahead and continue to use `require`.

Q I've got a module called `Mail` which is supposed to give me access to subroutines for sending and receiving mail: `send_mail()` and `rec_mail()`. I've imported the module with `use`, but I keep getting undefined errors for those two subroutines.

A Sounds like the module doesn't explicitly import those subroutine names. You have two choices: you can import them yourself, or you can call those subroutines using the full package names:

```
use Mail;  # import defaults, if any
use Mail qw(send_mail rec_mail);  # import subroutines
send_mail();
# OR
&Mail::send_mail();  # call subroutine with full package name
```

Workshop

The workshop provides quiz questions to help you solidify your understanding of the material covered and exercises to give you experience in using what you've learned. Try to understand the quiz and exercise answers before you go on to tomorrow's lesson.

Quiz

1. What is a package? Why are packages useful?
2. How do you call a variable by its full package name?
3. Can you use `my` with global variables? Why would you want to do this?
4. What does the line `use strict` do? Why would you want to use it?
5. What are the differences between libraries, modules, packages, and pragmas?
6. What is the CPAN? Where is it?
7. What is the `@INC` array used for?
8. How do you import a module into your script? What does that give you?
9. What is an import tag and why would you use it?
10. How do you call a subroutine you've imported from a module? How do you call a subroutine from an object-oriented module?

Exercises

1. Define a subroutine that takes a single argument, a string, and builds a new string with each of the characters separated by another globally defined value (such as `":"`). Return the new string. The catch: Use the same variable name for the local variable that holds the new string and the global variable that stores the separator character. HINT: Don't use `use strict` or `my` globals.
2. **BUG BUSTER**: What's wrong with this script?
   ```
   use This:That;                  # import module
   while (<>) {
       print theother($_);
   }
   ```
3. Modify the `wrapit.pl` script to prompt you for the column width, and then wrap the input text to that width.
4. Consider the `Config` module, part of the standard Perl library. This module is used to store configuration information about the current version of Perl. Using the documentation that comes with `Config` (which you can get to via the `perldoc`

13

program, the Shuck application in MacPerl, or via the `perlmod` man page), write a script that prints out the various values available in `Config`. NOTE: The `Config` module does not automatically import any subroutine names.

Answers

Here are the answers to the workshop questions in the previous section.

Quiz Answers

1. Packages are used to, well, package sets of global variables in a single unit, such that those units can be combined without one unit's variables tromping over another's. Packages work best for scripts that are made up of lots of parts that must work in harmony, or for modules of reusable library code.
2. The full package name for any variable or subroutine consists of the variable symbol (`$` for scalars, `@` for arrays, `%` for hashes, `&` for subroutine calls), the package name, two colons, and the variable name, for example, `$AModule::avariable` or `&Amodule::asubroutine()`.
3. Declaring global variables with `my` prevents them from being declared in the `main` package, which makes them slightly more efficient for value lookup and assignment, as well as making your script more well-behaved should it ever be incorporated into a package or combined with other scripts.
4. `use strict` is a special Perl directive that makes sure all the variables in your script are local variables or assigned to a particular package. At this point in your Perl knowledge, it's most useful for catching random global variables and making sure your scripts are self-contained as far as variable declarations go.
5. Libraries are collections of Perl code intended to be reused. Libraries can use packages to manage variable names inside that library. A module is a library that uses a package and has the same filename as that package. Modules include code that allows that module to be reused easily in other scripts. A pragma is a special kind of module that affects Perl's operation during both compile-time and runtime.
6. CPAN stands for Comprehensive Perl Archive Network; it's a collection of user-contributes modules, scripts, documentation, and utilities for use by anyone programming in Perl. CPAN is available at several sites around the world; you can find a site local to you starting at `http://www.perl.com/CPAN/`.
7. The `@INC` array defines the directories in which Perl will look for modules and code imported into your scripts using `use`.

8. Import a module into your script using `use` with the name of the module and an optional list of variables or import tags. Importing a module gives you access to the variables and subroutines defined by that module.
9. An import tag defines a subset of variables and subroutines in the module to be imported into your own script. Import tags are defined by the module developer and documented in the documentation for that module.
10. Subroutines imported from modules can be called just like regular subroutines, using the name of the subroutine with parentheses surrounding any arguments.

    In object-oriented modules, you must create a new object before you can call subroutines. With a new object stored in a scalar variable, you'd then call a subroutine using the `$var->sub()` syntax, where `$var` is the name of the variable holding the object and `sub` is the name of the subroutine. Subroutines defined inside objects are called methods.

Exercise Answers

1. The secret is to use a real global, stored in the package `main`, and then refer to it by its full package name in the body of the subroutine. Note that this doesn't work with global variables defined by `my` because they do not belong to any package.

```
#!/usr/bin/perl -w

$x = ":";                # separator character (global)
print &splitit("defenestration"), "\n";

sub splitit {
    my $string = $_[0];
    my $x = '';                 # new string (global);

    $x = join $main::x, (split //,$string);
    return $x;
}
```

2. There's only one colon in that module name; modules with two names always have two colons.
3. Changing `wrapit.pl` is a simple question of modifying the `$columns` variable. This variable isn't imported into your script by default, so you'll have to explicitly import it yourself.

```
#!/usr/bin/perl -w
use strict;

use Text::Wrap;                 # import module defaults
use Text::Wrap qw($columns);    # also import $columns
```

13

```
$\ = "";                              # Paragraph mode
my $indent = "> ";                                # indent character

print 'Enter a width: ';
chomp($columns = <STDIN>);

while (<>) {
    print wrap($indent, $indent, $_);
}
```

4. The subroutine `myconfig()` will do this for you. Because this subroutine is not imported by default, you'll have to call it with its full package name (or import it explicitly):

```
#!/usr/bin/perl -w
use strict;
use Config;

print Config::myconfig();
```

DAY 14

Exploring a Few Longer Examples

To finish up the week, let's explore a couple longer, more useful examples that make use of the techniques you've learned so far in the book. We won't spend a lot of time on background in this lesson, nor will you have any quizzes or exercises to work through at the end. Consider this a brief pause to look at code in detail. We'll have three of these example lessons, one after each six or so lessons, to cement what you've learned.

Today we'll look at two longer Perl scripts:

- An address-book script that stores names an addresses in a simple text database format. Our Perl script will allow you to search for addresses in the database using simply logical AND and OR tests.
- A Web log file analyzer. This script takes the standard Web server log format (called the *common log format*) and generates various statistics about how the Web site is being used.

A Searchable Address Book (`address.pl`)

Our first script today consists of two parts:

- A simple address book file, containing names, addresses, and phone numbers
- A Perl script that prompts you for things to search for, and then prints out any matching addresses

This script makes use of just about everything you've learned so far this week: scalar and hash data, conditionals, loops, input and output, subroutines, local variables, and pattern matching. There's even a function call here and there to make things interesting. And so, without further ado, let's dive in.

How It Works

The `address.pl` script is called with a single argument: the address file, called `address.txt`. Call it on the command line as you have other Perl scripts:

```
% address.pl address.txt
```

If you're using MacPerl, save the `address.pl` script as a droplet, and then drag and drop the `address.txt` file onto the `address.pl` icon.

The first thing the address book script does is prompt you for what you want to search for:

```
Search for what? Johnson
```

The search pattern you give to `address.pl` can be in several different forms:

- Single words, such as the `Johnson` in the preceding example.
- Multiple words (`John Maggie Alice`). Any addresses that match any of those words will be printed (equivalent to an OR search).
- Multiple words separated by `AND` or `OR` (in upper- or lowercase). Boolean searches behave as logical operators do in Perl, and are tested left to right. (Note that AND searches only make sense when matched inside a single address; they will not match across multiple addresses the way OR searches will.)
- Multiple words surrounded by quotes (`"this that"`) are treated as a single search pattern. Spaces are relevant in this case.
- Pattern-matching characters are accepted and processed as regular expressions (don't include the // around the patterns).

So, for example, in my sample `address.txt` file, the search for the word `Johnson` returned this output:

```
*********************
Paul Johnson
212 345 9492
234 33rd St Apt 12C, NY, NY 10023
http://www.foo.org/users/don/paul.html
*********************
Alice Johnson
(502) 348 2387
(502) 348 2341
*********************
Mary Johnson
(408) 342 0999
(408) 323 2342
mj@asd.net
http://www.mjproductions.com
*********************
```

In generating this sample address file, I made up all names, addresses, phone numbers, and Web pages. Any similarity between this data and any persons living or dead is coincidental.

The Address File

The core of the address book (and something you'll have to generate yourself if you want to use this script) is a file of addresses in a specific format that Perl can understand. You could consider this a simple textual database, and write Perl scripts to add and delete records (addresses) to or from that database.

The format of the address book file looks like this, generically:

```
Name: Name
Phone: number
Fax: number
Address: address
Email: email address
URL: Web URL
---
```

For example:

```
Name: Paul Johnson
Phone: 212 345 9492
Address: 234 33rd St Apt 12C, NY, NY 10023
URL: http://www.foo.org/users/don/paul.html
---
```

Each record has a list of fields (Name, Phone, Fax, Address, Email, and URL, although not all of them are required) and ends with three dashes. The field names (`Name`, `Phone`, `URL`, and so on) are separated from their values with a colon and a space. The values do not have to be in any specific format. While you can include other field names in the database, and search keys will search those extra fields, those fields will be ignored in the final printed output (although if you had to have an extra field, say, for a pager number, you could always modify the script. Perl is easy that way).

You can have as many addresses in the `address.txt` file as you like; the larger the address book, the longer it will take to find matching records, as each address is checked from start to finish in turn. Unless you have four or five million friends, you probably won't notice Perl working very hard.

Inside the Script

The `address.pl` script reads in the `address.txt` file, one address at a time, and then processes the search pattern for each of those addresses. The topmost part of the script is a `while` loop that does just this, which in turn works through five other subroutines to handle more complex parts of the script.

Let's start with this topmost part of the script. At this top level, we define three global variables:

- `%rec`, which will hold the current address record, indexed by field name.
- `$search`, the search pattern you enter at the prompt.
- `$bigmatch`, whether a record was found anywhere in the address file that matched the search pattern (there are also local variables for whether the current record matches, but we'll get to those soon enough.

Step one in this outer part of the script is to prompt for the search pattern and store it in `$search`:

```
$search = &getpattern();        # prompt for pattern
```

The `&getpattern()` subroutine is the basic "read the input/chomp it/return the result" code you've seen all too often in this book so far:

```
sub getpattern {
    my $in = '';  # input
    print 'Search for what? ';
    chomp($in = <STDIN>);
    return $in;
}
```

Step two in the outer script is an infinite `while` loop that reads in a record, processes the search pattern, and prints it if it matches. That `while` loop looks like this:

```
while () {                  # range over address file
    %rec = &read_addr();
    if (%rec) {             # got a record
        &perform_search($search, %rec);
    } else {                # end of address file, finish up
        if (!$bigmatch) {
            print "Nothing found.\n";
        } else { print "*********************\n"; }
        last;               # exit, we're done
    }
}
```

Inside the `while` loop, we call `&read_addr()` to read in a record, and if a record was found, we search for it by calling `&perform_search()`. At the end of the address file, if the `$bigmatch` variable is 0, that means no matches were found, and we can print a helpful message. At any rate, at the end of the address file, we call `last` to exit from the loop and finish the script.

Reading the Address

The `&read_addr()` subroutine is used to read in an address record. Listing 14.1 shows the contents of `&read_addr()`.

Listing 14.1 The `&read_addr()` Subroutine

```
sub read_addr {
    my %curr = ();                  # current record
    my $key = '';                   # temp key
    my $val = '';                   # temp value

    while (<>) {
        chomp;
        if ($_ ne '---') {          # record seperator
            ($key, $val) = split(/: /,$_,2);
            $curr{$key} = $val;
        }
        else { last; }
    }
    return %curr;
}
```


In past examples of using a `while` loop with <>, we've read in and processed the entire file at once. This `while` loop is a little different; this one reads chunks of the file, and stops when it reaches a record separator (in this case, the string '---'). The next time the &read_addr() subroutine is called, the while loop picks up where it left off in the address file. Perl has no problem with this stopping and restarting the input, and it makes it particularly convenient for reading and processing sections of a file as we have here.

That said, what this subroutine does is read in a line. If the line is not '---', then it's the inside of a record, and that line gets split into the field name (Name:, Phone:, and so on) and the value. The call to the split function in line 9 is where this takes place; note that the 2 argument at the end of split means we'll only end up with two things overall. With the field name ($key) and the value ($val), you can start building up the hash for this address.

If the line that gets read is the end-of-record marker, then the if statement in line 8 drops to the else part in line 12, and the last command exits the loop. The result of this subroutine is a hash containing all the lines in the address, indexed by the field name.

Performing the Search

At this point in the script's execution, you have a search pattern, stored in the $search variable, and an address stored in the %rec variable. The next step is to move to the next part of our big while loop at the top of the script, where if %rec is defined (an address exists), then we call the &perform_search() subroutine to actually see if the pattern in $search can be matched to the address in %rec.

The &perform_search() subroutine is shown in Listing 14.2.

LISTING 14.2 THE &perform_search() SUBROUTINE

```
sub perform_search {
    my ($str, %rec) = @_;
    my $matched = 0;            # overall match
    my $i = 0;                  # position inside pattern
    my $thing = '';             # temporary word

    my @things = $str =~ /("[^"]+"|\S+)/g;  # split into search items

    while ($i <= $#things) {
        $thing = $things[$i];   # search item, AND or OR
        if ($thing eq 'OR' || $thing eq 'or') { # OR case
            if (!$matched) {    # no match yet, look at next thing
                $matched = &isitthere($things[$i+1], %rec);
            }
            $i += 2;            # skip OR and next thing
        }
        elsif ($thing eq 'AND' || $thing eq 'and') { # AND case
            if ($matched) {
            # got a match, need to check other side
```

```
19:                 $matched = &isitthere($things[$i+1], %rec);
20:             }
21:             $i += 2;            # skip AND and next thing
22:         }
23:         elsif (!$matched) {     # no match yet
24:             $matched = &isitthere($thing, %rec);
25:             $i++;               # next!
26:         }
27:         else { $i++; }          # $match is found, move onto next thing
28:     }
29:
30:     if ($matched) {             # all keys done, did we match?
31:         $bigmatch = 1;  # yes, we found something
32:         print_addr(%rec);       # print the record then
33:     }
34: }
```

That's one large subroutine, and quite complex, but it's not as awful as it looks. Starting from the top, then, this subroutine takes two arguments: the search pattern and the address hash. Note that since those values are stored in global variables, there's really no point to passing these along into the subroutine via arguments; we could just have referred to those global variables in the body of this subroutine. This strategy, however, makes the subroutine more self-contained in that the only data it deals with is that which it gets explicitly. You could, for example, copy and paste this subroutine into another search script without having to worry about renaming any variables.

The first real operation we do in this subroutine is in line 7, where we split the search pattern into its component parts. Remember, the search pattern can appear in many different ways, including nested quoted strings, ANDs and ORs, or just a list of keywords. Line 7 extracts each element from the search pattern and stores all the search "things" in the array `@things` (note that the regular expression has the `g` option at the end, and is evaluated in a list context—meaning the `@things` list will contain all the possible matches captured by the parentheses. What does that particular pattern match? There are two groups of patterns, separated by alternation (`|`). The first is this one:

```
"[^"]+"
```

Which, if you remember your patterns, is a double-quote, followed by one or more characters that are not a double-quote, followed by another closing quote. This pattern will match quoted strings in the search pattern such as `"John Smith"` or `"San Francisco"` and treat them as a single search element.

The second part of the pattern is simply one or more characters that are not whitespace

14

(`\S`). This part of the pattern matches any single words, such as AND or OR, or single keywords. Between these two patterns, a long complex pattern such as `"San Jose" OR "San Francisco" AND John` will break into the list `("San Jose", OR, "San Francisco", AND, John)`.

With all our search things in a list, the hard part is to work through that list, search the address when necessary, and deal with the logical expressions. This all takes place in the big `while` loop that starts in line 9, which keeps a placeholder variable `$i` for the current position in the pattern, and loops over the pattern until the end. Throughout the `while` loop, the `$matched` variable keeps track of whether any particular part of the pattern has matched the record. We start with a 0—false—for no match yet.

Inside the `while` loop, we start in line 10 by setting the variable `$thing` to the current part of the pattern we're examining, just as a shorthand. Then, there are four major tests:

- If the current thing is an OR, then we're in the middle of two tests, one of which has already occurred and returned either true or false depending on the value of `$matched`. If `$matched` was true, then the thing on the left side was a match, and there's no point to actually trying the thing on the right (yes, it's a short-circuiting OR). If the thing on the left didn't match, the `$matched` variable will be 0, and we have to test the thing on the right. That's what line 13 does; it calls the `&isitthere()` subroutine to actually search for a search pattern, giving it an argument of the right side of the OR (the next thing in the `@things` array) and the record itself (`%rec`).

  Whether there was a match or not, this test handles both the OR itself and the pattern on the right of the OR, so we can skip two elements forward in the `@things` array. Line 15 increments the `$i` counter to do just that.
- If the current thing is an AND, we trigger the test in line 17. This section operates in much the same way as the OR did, with one exception; it short-circuits in the other way. Remember, given a test `x AND y`, if `x` is false then the entire expression is false. If `x` is true, you still have to test to see if `y` is also true. That's how this test works; if the `$matched` variable is true, then the left side of the AND was true, and we call `&isitthere()` to test the right side. Otherwise, we do nothing, and in either case we just skip the AND and the right side of the AND (`$i+=2`, line 21) and move on.
- At line 23, we've covered ANDs and ORs, so the thing we're looking at must be an actual search pattern. It could be a single search pattern, or it could be one of many search patterns contained in a string. Doesn't matter; each one can be treated individually. But we only need to actually search for it if we haven't already found a match (remember, multiple searches are treated as OR tests, so if one matches

we're all set for the others). So, in line 23, if we haven't found a match, we search for that thing using `&isitthere()`.

- The final case covers a `$thing` that's an actual search key, and `$matched` is true. We don't need to actually do anything here because the match has already been made. So, increment the position in the pattern by one and restart the loop.

If you can follow all of that, you've made it through the hardest part of this script, by far. If it's still confusing you, try working through various search patterns, with single search elements, elements separated with ANDs and ORs, and patterns with multiple search keys. Watch the values of `$i` and `$matched` as the loop progresses (once you learn how to use the Perl debugger, this will be easy, but you can do it on paper by hand as well).

So what happens in the mysterious `&isitthere()` subroutine that gets called throughout that big `while` loop? That's where the actual searching takes place, given a pattern and the record. I'm not going to show you the contents of `&isitthere()` itself (you can see it in the full code printout in Listing 14.3), other than to note that it simply loops through the contents of the address hash and compares the pattern to each line using a regular expression. If it matches, the subroutine returns 1, and returns 0 if it doesn't match.

In the last part of the subroutine, all the parts of the pattern have been read, some amount of searching has taken place, and now we know whether the pattern matched the record or not. In lines 30 through 33, we test to see if a match was made, and if it was we set the `$bigmatch` variable (we found at least one address that matched), and call `&print_addr()` to print the actual address.

Printing the Record

It's all downhill from here. The last subroutine in the file is one that's only called if a match was made. The `&print_addr()` subroutine simply loops over the record hash and prints out the values to display the address record:

```
sub print_addr {
    my %record = @_;
    print "*********************\n";
    foreach my $key (qw(Name Phone Fax Address Email URL)) {
        if (defined($record{$key})) {
            print "$record{$key}\n";
        }
    }
}
```

The only interesting part of this subroutine is the list of keys in the `foreach` loop. I've listed the specific keys here in this order (and quoted them using the `qw` function) so that the output will print in a specific order. Since hashes are stored in an internal order, this way because we can print the data out in the right order. It also lets us print only the

14

lines that were actually available—the call to `defined` inside the `foreach` loop makes sure that only those fields that existed in the record get printed.

The Code

Got it? No? Sometimes seeing all the code at once can help. Listing 14.3 shows the full code for `address.pl`. If you've downloaded the source from this book's Web site at `http://www.typerl.com`, the code there has many more comments to help you figure out what's going on.

As I mentioned yesterday in the section on my variables, some versions of Perl may have difficulties with this script's use of `my` variables and `foreach` loops. To get around this problem, simply predeclare the `foreach` variable before using it, like this:

```
my $key = 0;
foreach $key (qw(Name Phone Fax Address Email URL)) { ...
```

LISTING 14.3 THE CODE FOR `address.pl`

```
#!/usr/bin/perl -w
use strict;

my $bigmatch = 0;                 # was anything found?
my %rec = ();                     # record to be searched
my $search = '';                  # thing to search for

$search = &getpattern();          # prompt for pattern

while () {                        # range over address file
    %rec = &read_addr();
    if (%rec) {         # got a record
        &perform_search($search, %rec);
    } else {            # end of address file, finish up
        if (!$bigmatch) {
            print "Nothing found.\n";
        } else { print "*********************\n"; }
        last;           # exit, we're done
    }
}

sub getpattern {
    my $in = '';  # input
    print 'Search for what? ';
```

```
    chomp($in = <STDIN>);
    return $in;
}

sub read_addr {
    my %curr = ();              # current record
    my $key = '';               # temp key
    my $val = '';               # temp value

    while (<>) {                # stop if we get to EOF
        chomp;
        if ($_ ne '---') {      # record seperator
            ($key, $val) = split(/: /,$_,2);
            $curr{$key} = $val;
        }
        else { last; }
    }
    return %curr;
}

sub perform_search {
    my ($str, %rec) = @_;
    my $matched = 0;            # overall match
    my $i = 0;                  # position inside pattern
    my $thing = '';             # temporary word

    my @things = $str =~ /("[^"]+"|\S+)/g;  # split into search items

    while ($i <= $#things) {
        $thing = $things[$i];   # search item, AND or OR
        if ($thing eq 'OR' || $thing eq 'or') { # OR case
            if (!$matched) {    # no match yet, look at next thing
                $matched = &isitthere($things[$i+1], %rec);
            }
            $i += 2;            # skip OR and next thing
        }
        elsif ($thing eq 'AND' || $thing eq 'and') { # AND case
            if ($matched) {     # got a match, need to check other side
                $matched = &isitthere($things[$i+1], %rec);
            }
            $i += 2;            # skip AND and next thing
        }
        elsif (!$matched) {     # no match yet
            $matched = &isitthere($thing, %rec);
            $i++;               # next!
        }
        else { $i++; }          # $match is found, move onto next thing
    }
```

continues

LISTING 14.3 CONTINUED

```

    if ($matched) {              # all keys done, did we match?
        $bigmatch = 1;  # yes, we found something
        print_addr(%rec);        # print the record then
    }
}

sub isitthere {                  # simple test
    my ($pat, %rec) = @_;
    foreach my $line (values %rec) {
        if ($line =~ /$pat/) {
            return 1;
        }
    }
    return 0;
}

sub print_addr {
    my %record = @_;
    print "*********************\n";
    foreach my $key (qw(Name Phone Fax Address Email URL)) {
        if (defined($record{$key})) {
            print "$record{$key}\n";
        }
    }
}
```

A Web Log Processor (`weblog.pl`)

The second example script is one that takes a log file, as generated by Web servers, and generates statistics about the information contained in that log file. Most Web servers keep files of this sort, which keep track of how many accesses ("hits") have been made to a Web site, the files that were requested, the sites that requested them, and other information.

Many log-file-analyzer programs already exist on the Web (and there are usually programs that come with the Web server), so this example isn't breaking any new ground. The statistics it generates are fairly simple, although this script could be easily modified to include just about any information that you'd like to include. It's a good starting point for processing Web logs, or a model to follow for processing log files from any other programs.

How It Works

The weblog.pl script is called with one argument: a log file. On many Web servers, these files are commonly called access_log, and follow what is known as the *common log format*. The script processes for a while (it'll print the date of the logs it's working on so you know it's still working), and then prints some results. Here's an example of the sort of output you can get (this example is from the logs on my own Web server, www.lne.com):

```
% weblog.pl access_log
Processing log....
Processing 09/Apr/1998
Processing 10/Apr/1998
Processing 11/Apr/1998
Processing 12/Apr/1998
Web log file Results:
Total Number of Hits: 55789
Total failed hits: 1803 (3.23%)
(sucessful) HTML files: 18264 (33.83%)
Number of unique hosts: 5911
Number of unique domains: 2121
Most popular files:
  /Web/index.html (2456 hits)
  /lemay/index.html (1711 hits)
  /Web/Title.gif (1685 hits)
  /Web/HTML3.2/3.2thm.gif (1669 hits)
  /Web/JavaProf/javaprof_thm.gif (1662 hits)
Most popular hosts:
  202.185.174.4 (487 hits)
  vader.integrinautics.com (440 hits)
  linea15.secsa.podernet.com.mx (437 hits)
  lobby.itmin.com (284 hits)
  pyx.net (256 hits)
Most popular domains:
  mindspring.com (3160 hits)
  aol.com (1808 hits)
  uu.net (792 hits)
  grid.net (684 hits)
  compuserve.com (565 hits)
```

This particular output shows only the top 5 files, hosts, and domains, to save space here. You can configure the script to print out any number of those statistics.

The difference between a host and a domain may not be readily apparent; a host is the full host name of the system that accessed the Web server, which may include dynamically assigned addresses and proxy servers. The host dialup124.servers.foo.com will be a different host from dialup567.servers.foo.com. The domain, on the other hand, is a larger group of hosts, usually consisting of two or three parts. `foo.com` is a domain, as is `aol.com` or `domon.co.uk`. The domain listings tend to collapse separate entries for hosts into major groups—all the hosts under `aol.com`'s purview will show up as hits from `aol.com` in the domain list.

Note also that a single hit can be an HTML page, an image, a form submission, or any other file. There are usually significantly more raw hits than there are actual page accesses. This script points those out by keeping track of HTML hits separately from the total number of hits.

What a Web Log Looks Like

Because the `weblog.pl` script processes Web log files, it helps to know what those log files look like. Web log files are stored with one hit per line, and each line in what's called common log format (common because it's common to various Web servers). Most Web servers generate their log files in this format, or can be configured to do so (many servers use a superset of the common log format with more information in it). A line in a common log format log file might look something like this (here I'm showing it to you on two lines; actually, it only appears on one in real life):

```
proxy2bh.powerup.com.au - - [03/Apr/1998:00:09:02 -0800]
"GET /lemay/ HTTP/1.0" 200 4621
```

The various elements of each line in the log file are:

- The host name accessing the server (here `proxy2bh.powerup.com.au`).
- The username of the person accessing the page, discovered through ident (a UNIX program used to identify users), or through the user signing into your site. These two parts usually show up as two dashes (`- -`) when the username cannot be determined.
- The date and time the hit was made, in square brackets.
- Inside quotes, the action for the hit (actually a Web server action): `GET` is to get a file or submit a form, `POST` is to submit a form in a different way, `HEAD` is to get header information about a file.
- After the action, the filename (or directory) that was requested, here `/lemay/`.
- The version number of the protocol, here `HTTP/1.0`.
- The return code for the hit; 200 is successful, 404 is "not found," and so on.
- The number of bytes transferred.

Not all these elements of the log file are interesting to a statistics generator script, of course, and a lot of them won't make any sense to you unless you know how Web servers work. But a few, like the host, the date, the filename, and the return code, can be extracted and processed for each line of the file.

Building the Script

The path of execution for this script is easier to follow than the one for the `address.pl` script; there are basically only two major steps—process the log and generate the statistics. We do have a number of subroutines along the way to help, however.

In fact, all of the code for this script is contained in subroutines. The body of the code consists of a bunch of global variables and two subroutine calls: `&process_log()` and `&print_results()`.

The global variables are used to store the various statistics and information about parts of the log file. Because many of these statistics are hashes, using local variables and passing around the data would become complicated. In this case, keeping the data global makes it easier to manage. The global data we keep track of includes:

- The number of hits, number of failed hits, and number of hits to HTML pages
- A hash to store the various host names and the number of times those hosts appear in the log
- A hash to do the same for the various files in the log

In addition, there are two other global variables worth mentioning:

- The `$topthings` variable stores a number indicating how many entries you want to print for the "most popular" parts of the statistics. In the example output I showed you, `$topthings` was set to 5, which gives us some nice short output. Setting it to 20 will print the top 20 files, hosts, and domains.
- The `$default` variable should be set to the default HTML file for your Web server, often called `index.html` or `Home.html`. This is the file that serves as the main file for a directory when the user doesn't ask for a specific file. Usually it's `index.html`.

These two variables determine how the script itself will behave. While we could have put these variables deep inside the program, putting them up here, right up front, lets you or someone else using your script change the overall behavior of the script in one place without having to search for the right variable to change. It's one of those "good programming practices" that make sense, no matter what programming language you're using.

14

Processing the Log

The first part of the `weblog.pl` script is the `&process_log()` subroutine, which loops over each line in the script, and stores various statistics about that line. I'm not going to show you every line of this subroutine, but I will point out the important parts. You can see the complete code in Listing 14.7 at the end of this section.

The core of the `&process_log()` subroutine is yet another `while (<>)` loop, to read each line of the input at a time. Unlike `address.pl`, this script doesn't pause anywhere; it just reads in the file from start to finish.

The first thing we do to process each line is to split the line into its component parts and store those parts in a hash keyed by the part name (`'site'`, `'file'`, and so on). There's a separate subroutine to do the splitting, called `&splitline()`. Listing 14.4 shows this subroutine.

Listing 14.4 The `&splitline()` Subroutine

```
1:  sub splitline {
2:      my $in = $_[0];
3:      my %line = ();
4:      if ($in =~ /^([^\s]+)\s              # site
5:                 ([\w-]+\s[\w-]+)\s        # users
6:                 \[([^\]]+)\]\s            # date
7:                  \"(\w+)\s                # protocol
8:                 (\/[^\s]*)\s              # file
9:                 ([^"]+)\"\s               # HTTP version
10:                (\d{3})\s                 # return code
11:                ([\d-]+)                  # bytes transferred
12:     /x) {
13:        $line{'site'} = $1;
14:        $line{'date'} = $3;
15:        $line{'file'} = $5;
16:        $line{'code'} = $7;
17:        return %line;
18:     } else { return (); }
19: }
```

The first thing that probably catches your eye about that subroutine is that enormous monster of a regular expression smack in the middle in lines 4 through 11. It's so ugly, it needs six lines! And comments! This regular expression is in a form called *extended regular expressions*; if you read the "Going Deeper" section on Day 5, "Working with Hashes," I described these there. But here's a quick review: Say you've got a particularly ugly regular expression like the one in this example (here I've put it on two lines because it doesn't fit on one line!):

```
if ($in =~ /^([^\s]+)\s([\w-]+\s[\w-]+)\s\[([^\]]+)\]\s\"(\w+)
\(\/[^\s]*)\s([^"]+)\"\s(\d{3})\s([\d-]+)/)
```

Chances are good you won't be able to make head nor tail of that expression without a lot of patient dissecting or very strong tranquilizers. And debugging it won't be much fun either. But if you put the `/x` option on the end of the expression (as we have in line 12), then you can spread that regular expression apart into sections or onto separate lines, and comment it as you would lines of Perl code. All whitespace in the pattern is ignored; if you want to match for whitespace in the text, you'll have to use `\s`. All the `/x` option does is make a regular expression easier to read and debug.

This particular `regex` assumes the common log format I described earlier. Specifically:

- Line 4 matches the site (host) name. The site always appears at the start of the line, and consists of some non-whitespace characters followed by a space (a `\s` here so that extended patterns work).
- Line 5 matches the user fields (two of them). The users consist of one or more alphanumeric characters or a dash, separated by and followed by whitespace. Note the dashes inside the character classes; dashes are not included by the `\w` class.
- Line 6 matches the date, which is one or more characters or whitespace in between brackets (`[]`).
- Line 7 matches the protocol (`GET`, `HEAD`, and so on), by starting the string with a quote and following it by one or more characters (the closing quote is after the HTTP version in line 9).
- Line 8 matches the file. It always starts with a slash (/), followed by zero or more other characters and ending with whitespace.
- Line 9 matches the HTTP version, which includes any remaining characters before the closing quote.
- Line 10 matches the return code, which is always three digits long followed by whitespace (it would be less specific to just use `\d+` here, but this is a chance to show off the use of the `{3}` pattern.
- Line 11 finishes up the patter with the number of bytes transferred, which is any number of digits. If no bytes were transferred—for example, the hit resulted in an error—this field will be a dash. The pattern covers that as well.

Each element of this regex is stored in a parenthesized expression (and a match variable), with the extra brackets or quotes removed. Once the match has occurred, we can put the various matched bits into a hash. Note that we only use half or so of the actual matches in the hash; we only need to store what we're actually going to use. But if you extend this example to include statistics on other parts of the hit, all you have to do is add lines to add those matches to the hash. You don't have to muck with the regular expression to get more information.

With the line split into its component parts, we return from the `&splitline()` subroutine back up to the main `&process_log()` routine. The next part of this subroutine checks for failed hits. If a line in the Web log didn't match the pattern—and some don't—then the `&splitline()` subroutine will return null. That's considered a failed hit, so we add it to the count of failed hits, and then skip to the end of the loop to process the next line:

```
if (!%hit) {  # malformed line in web log
   $failhits++;
    next;
}
```

The next part of the script is a convenience for the person running the script. Processing a log file of any size takes a long time, and sometimes it can be hard to tell whether Perl is still working on the log file, or if the system has hung and it's never going to return anything. This part of the script prints a processing message with the date of the lines being processed, printing a new message each time a day's hits are complete and showing Perl's progress through the file:

```
$dateshort = &getday($hit{'date'});
if ($currdate ne $dateshort) {
    print "Processing $dateshort\n";
    $currdate = $dateshort;
}
```

Here, the subroutine `&getday()` is simply a short routine that grabs the month and the day out of the date field using a pattern so they can be compared to the date being processed (I'm not going to show you `&getday()`; you can see it in the full code if you're curious). If they're different, a message is printed and the `$currdate` variable is updated.

In addition to lines in the log file that don't match the log format, also considered failed hits are those that matched the pattern, but didn't result in an actual file being returned (misspellings in URLs or files that have moved will cause these kinds of hits, for example). These hits are recorded in the log with error codes that start with 4, for example, the 404 you've probably seen on the Web. The return code was one of the things we saved from the line, so testing that is a simple pattern match:

```
if ($hit{'code'} =~ /^4/) { # 404, 403, etc. (errors)
    $failhits++;
```

The `else` part of this `if` test handles all other hits—that is, the successful ones that actually returned HTML files or images. Those hits will have return codes of 200 or 304:

```
} elsif ($hit{'code'} =~ /200|304/) {   # deal only with sucesses
```

Web servers are set up to deliver a default file, usually index.html, when a site requests a URL that ends in a directory name. This means that a request for `/web/` and a request for `/web/index.html` actually refer to the same file, but they show up as different entries in the log file, which means our script will process them as different files. To collapse directories and default files, we have a couple lines that test to see if the file requested ends with a slash, and if so, to add the default filename on the end of it. The default file, as I noted earlier, is defined by the `$default` variable:

```
if ($hit{'file'} =~ /\/$/) { # slashes map to $default
    $hit{'file'} .= $default;
}
```

With that done, now we can finish up the processing by incrementing the `$htmlhits` variable if the file is an HTML file and updating the hashes for the site and for the file:

```
if ($hit{'file'} =~ /\.html?$/) { # .htm or .html
    $htmlhits++;
}

$hosts{ $hit{'site'} }++;
$files{ $hit{'file'} }++;
```

At this point, we're now at the end of the `while` loop, and the loop starts over again with the next line in the file. The loop continues until all the lines are processed, and then we move onto the printing part of the script.

Printing the Results

The `&process_log()` subroutine processes the log file line by line, and calls the `&splitline()` and `&getday()` subroutines to help. The second part of the `weblog.pl` script is the `&print_results()` subroutine, and it has a few other subroutines to help it as well. Much of `print_results()`, however, is as it sounds: a bunch of `print` statements to print out the various statistics.

The first few lines print out the total number of hits, total number of failed hits, and total number of HTML hits. The latter are also shown as a percentage of total hits, with HTML hits a total of successful hits. We can get these values with a little math and a `printf`:

```
print "Web log file Results:\n";
print "Total Number of Hits: $totalhits\n";
print "Total failed hits: $failhits (";
printf('%.2f', $failhits / $totalhits * 100);
print "%)\n";
print "(sucessful) HTML files: $htmlhits (";
printf('%.2f', $htmlhits / ($totalhits - $failhits) * 100);
print "%)\n";
```

Next up: total number of hosts. We can get this value by extracting the keys of the `%hosts` hash into a list and then evaluate that list in a scalar context (using the `scalar` function):

```
print 'Number of unique hosts: ';
print scalar(keys %hosts);
print "\n";
```

To get the number of unique domains, we need to process the `%hosts` hash to compress the hosts into their smaller domains, and build a new hash (`%domains`) that has the new count of all the hits for each domain. We'll use a subroutine called `&getdomains()` for that, which I'll discuss in the next section; assume we've done it, that we have our domains `%hash`. We can do the same `scalar` trick with the keys to that hash to get the number of unique domains:

```
my %domains = &getdomains(keys %hosts);
print 'Number of unique domains: ';
print scalar(keys %domains);
print "\n";
```

The last three things that get printed are the most popular files, hosts, and domains. There's a subroutine to get these values as well, called `&gettop()`, which sorts each hash by its values (the number of times each thing appeared in a hit), and then builds an array of descriptive strings with the keys and values in the hash. The array will contain only the top five or ten things (or whatever the value of `$topthings` is). More about the `&gettop()` subroutine in a bit.

Each of those arrays gets printed to the output to finish up. Here's the one for files:

```
print "Most popular files: \n";
    foreach my $file (&gettop(%files)) {
        print "  $file\n";
    }
```

The `&getdomains()` Subroutine

We're not done yet. We've still got to cover the helper subroutines for printing the statistics: `&getdomains()`, to extract the domains from the `%hosts` hash and recalculate the stats, and `gettop()`, to take a hash of keys and frequencies and return the most popular elements. The `&getdomains()` subroutine is shown in Listing 14.5.

LISTING 14.5 THE `&getdomains()` SUBROUTINE

```
1:  sub getdomains {
2:      my %domains = ();
3:      my ($sd,$d,$tld);       # secondary domain, domain, top-level domain
4:      foreach my $host (@_) {
5:          my $dom = '';
6:          if($host =~ /(([^.]+)\.)?([^.]+)\.([^.]+)$/ ) {
7:              if (!defined($1)) { # only two domains (i.e. aol.com)
8:                  ($d,$tld) = ($3, $4);
9:              } else {            # a usual domain x.y.com etc
10:                 ($sd, $d, $tld) = ($2, $3, $4);
11:             }
12:             if ($tld =~ /\D+/) { # ignore raw IPs
13:                 if ($tld =~ /com|edu|net|gov|mil|org$/i) { # US TLDs
14:                     $dom = "$d.$tld";
15:                 } else { $dom = "$sd.$d.$tld"; }
16:                 $domains{$dom} += $hosts{$host};
17:             }
18:         } else { print "Malformed: $host\n"; }
19:     }
20:     return %domains;
21: }
```

This is less complex than it looks. There are a few basic assumptions I'm making here about the makeup of a host name: in particular, that each host name has a number of parts separated by periods, and that the domain consists of either the rightmost two or three parts, depending on the name itself. In this subroutine, then, we'll reduce each host into its actual domain, and then use that domain name as the index to a new hash, storing all the original hits from the full hosts into the new domain-based hash.

The core of this subroutine is the `foreach` loop starting in line 4. The argument that gets passed to this subroutine is an array of all the host names from the `%hosts` array, and we'll loop over each host name in turn to make sure we covered them all.

The first part of that `foreach` loop is the long scary-looking regular expression in line 6. All this pattern does grab the last two parts of the host name, and the last three if it can (some host names only have two parts; this regex will handle those, too). Lines 7 through 11 then check to see how many parts we got (2 or 3), and assign the variables `$sd`, `$d`, and `$tld` to those parts (`$sd` stands for secondary domain, `$d` stands for domain, and `$tld` stands for top-level domain, if you want to keep them straight).

The second part of the loop determines whether we'll use two or three parts of the host as the actual domain (and ignores any hosts made up of IP numbers rather than actual domain names in line 12). The purely arbitrary rule I used for determining whether a domain has two or three parts is this: if the top-level domain (that is, the rightmost part of the host name) is a US domain such as `.com`, `.edu`, and so on (full list in line 13), then the domain only has two parts. This covers `aol.com`, `mit.edu`, `whitehouse.gov`, and so on. If the top-level domain is anything else, it's probably a country-specific domain such as `.uk`, `.au`, `.mx`, and so on. Those domains typically use three parts to refer to a site, for example, `citygate.co.uk` or `monash.edu.au`. Two parts would not be enough granularity (`edu.au` refers to all universities in Australia, not to a specific place called `edu`).

This is what lines 13 through 15 deal with: building up the domain name from two or three parts and storing it in the string `$dom`. Once we've built the domain name, we can then use it as the key in the new hash, and bring over the hits we had for the original host in line 16. By the time the domain hash is done, all the hits in the host's hash should be accounted for in the domain's hash as well, and we can return that hash back to the `& print_results()` subroutine.

One last bit: Line 28 is a bit of error checking for this subroutine. If the pattern matching expression in 6 doesn't match, then we've got a very weird host name indeed, and we'll print a message to that effect. Generally speaking, however, that message should never be reached because a malformed host name in the log file usually means a malformed host name on the host itself, and the Internet makes that difficult to do.

The `&gettop()` Subroutine

One last subroutine to cover, and then we can put this week to bed and you can go have a beer and celebrate finishing two thirds of this book. This last subroutine, `&gettop()`, takes a hash, sorts it by value, and then trims off the top `X` elements, where `X` is determined by the `$topthings` variable. The subroutine returns an array of strings, where each string contains the key and value for the top `X` elements in form that can be easily printed by the `&print_results()` subroutine that called this one in the first place. Listing 14.6 shows this subroutine.

LISTING 14.6 THE `&gettop()` SUBROUTINE

```
sub gettop {
    my %hash = @_;
    my $i = 1;
    my @topkeys = ();
    foreach my $key (sort { $hash{$b} <=> $hash{$a} } keys %hash) {
        if ($i <= $topthings) {
            push @topkeys, "$key ($hash{$key} hits)";
            $i++;
        }
    }
    return @topkeys;
}
```

The Code

Listing 14.7 contains the complete code for the `weblog.pl` script.

> Once again, watch out for the `my` variables inside `foreach` loops in certain versions of Perl. See the note just before Listing 14.3 for details.

LISTING 14.7 THE CODE FOR `weblog.pl`

```
#!/usr/bin/perl -w
use strict;

my $default = 'index.html';     # change to be your default HTML file
my $topthings = 30;             # number of files, sites, etc to report
my $totalhits = 0;
my $failhits = 0;
my $htmlhits = 0;
my %hosts= ();
my %files = ();

&process_log();
&print_results();

sub process_log {
    my %hit = ();
    my $currdate = '';
    my $dateshort = '';
    print "Processing log....\n";
    while (<>) {
        chomp;
        %hit = splitline($_);
        $totalhits++;

        # watch out for malformed lines
        if (!%hit) {  # malformed line in web log
            $failhits++;
            next;
        }

        $dateshort = &getday($hit{'date'});
        if ($currdate ne $dateshort) {
            print "Processing $dateshort\n";
            $currdate = $dateshort;
```

continues

LISTING 14.7 CONTINUED

```
        }

        # watch 404s
        if ($hit{'code'} =~ /^4/) { # 404, 403, etc. (errors)
            $failhits++;
        # other files
        } elsif ($hit{'code'} =~ /200¦304/) {
        # deal only with sucesses
            if ($hit{'file'} =~ /\/$/) { # slashes map to $default
                $hit{'file'} .= $default;
            }

            if ($hit{'file'} =~ /\.html?$/) { # .htm or .html
                $htmlhits++;
            }

            $hosts{ $hit{'site'} }++;
            $files{ $hit{'file'} }++;
        }
    }
}

sub splitline {
    my $in = $_[0];
    my %line = ();
    if ($in =~ /^([^\s]+)\s                # site
              ([\w-]+\s[\w-]+)\s          # users
              \[([^\]]+)\]\s              # date
               \"(\w+)\s                  # protocol
              (\/[^\s]*)\s                # file
              ([^"]+)\"\s                 # HTTP version
              (\d{3})\s                   # return code
              ([\d-]+)                    # bytes transferred
    /x) {
       # we only care about some of the values
       # (every other one, coincidentally)
       $line{'site'} = $1;
       $line{'date'} = $3;
       $line{'file'} = $5;
       $line{'code'} = $7;
       return %line;
    } else { return (); }
}

sub getday {
    my $date;
    if ($_[0] =~ /([^:]+):/) {
        $date = $1;
```

```
        return $date;
    } else {
        return $_[0];
    }
}

sub print_results {
    print "Web log file Results:\n";
    print "Total Number of Hits: $totalhits\n";
    print "Total failed hits: $failhits (";
    printf('%.2f', $failhits / $totalhits * 100);
    print "%)\n";

    print "(sucessful) HTML files: $htmlhits (";
    printf('%.2f', $htmlhits / ($totalhits - $failhits) * 100);
    print "%)\n";

    print 'Number of unique hosts: ';
    print scalar(keys %hosts);
    print "\n";

    my %domains = &getdomains(keys %hosts);
    print 'Number of unique domains: ';
    print scalar(keys %domains);
    print "\n";

    print "Most popular files: \n";
    foreach my $file (&gettop(%files)) {
       print "  $file\n";
    }
    print "Most popular hosts: \n";
    foreach my $host (&gettop(%hosts)) {
       print "  $host\n";
    }

    print "Most popular domains: \n";
    foreach my $dom (&gettop(%domains)) {
       print "  $dom\n";
    }
}

sub getdomains {
    my %domains = ();
    my ($sd,$d,$tld);       # secondary domain, domain, top-level domain
    foreach my $host (@_) {
        my $dom = '';
        if($host =~ /(([^.]+)\.)?([^.]+)\.([^.]+)$/ ) {
            if (!defined($1)) { # only two domains (i.e. aol.com)
```

continues

LISTING 14.7 CONTINUED

```
                ($d,$tld) = ($3, $4);
            } else {                # a usual domain x.y.com etc
                ($sd, $d, $tld) = ($2, $3, $4);
            }
            if ($tld =~ /\D+/) { # ignore raw IPs
                if ($tld =~ /com|edu|net|gov|mil|org$/i) { # US TLDs
                    $dom = "$d.$tld";
                } else { $dom = "$sd.$d.$tld"; }
                $domains{$dom} += $hosts{$host};
            }
        } else { print "Malformed: $host\n"; }
    }
    return %domains;
}

sub gettop {
    my %hash = @_;
    my $i = 1;
    my @topkeys = ();
    foreach my $key (sort { $hash{$b} <=> $hash{$a} } keys %hash) {
        if ($i <= $topthings) {
            push @topkeys, "$key ($hash{$key} hits)";
            $i++;
        }
    }
    return @topkeys;
}
```

Summary

Often programming books give you a lot of wordy background, but don't give you enough actual code examples for how to do stuff. While I won't claim that this book shirks on the wordy background (you may snicker now), these example sections offer you some longer bits of code that accomplish real things and show how a real-world script is put together.

In today's lesson, we explored two longer scripts: a simple searchable address file, which used a text-based database of names and addresses. The script to process that file enabled you to process a reasonably complex search pattern, including nesting logical expressions and grouping words and phrases via quotes. You could extend this example to cover just about any situation that calls for a complex search over parts of a data file; for example, to filter mail messages out of a mail folder based on some criteria, or to search for specific comic books in a collection of comics. Any text file can serve as a simple database, and this script can search it as long as it's modified to handle the data in that database.

The second example was a log file analyzer that processes Web log files and prints statistics about those files. Raw Web log files tend to be sort of daunting to look at; this script provided some basic summary information about what's actually going on with the Web site. Along the way, it used some complex regular expressions and a whole lot of hashes to store the raw data. You could extend this example to generate other statistics (for example, to generate histograms of the number of hits per day or per hour, or to keep track of image or other files in addition to HTML files). Or you could modify it to cover other log files (mail logs, FTP logs, whatever logs you have lying around).

Congratulations on completing the second week of this three-week book. After this week, you've picked up a substantial part of the language, and you should be able to accomplish quite a few tasks in Perl. From this point on we'll be building on what you've already learned. Onward to Week 3!

WEEK 3

Advanced Perl

- Working with Files and I/O
- Using Perl for CGI Scripting
- Managing Files and Directories
- Perl and the Operating System
- Working with References
- Odds and Ends
- Exploring a Few Longer Examples

DAY 15

Working with Files and I/O

All throughout the first two weeks of this book, I introduced you to input and output (otherwise known as I/O) a little at a time. You've learned about standard input and output using `<STDIN>` and `print`, and about file input using the command line, the `<>` operator, and a `while` loop to automatically assign each line to the `$_` variable.

In today's lesson, we'll expand on what you already know about input and output in greater detail, as well as touch more on script argument lists and getting data and options into your script. Today, we'll explore:

- All about file handles: creating them, reading input from them, writing output to them
- Simple file tests for finding out information about a particular file
- Working with script arguments and `@ARGV`
- Using the `Getopt` module for managing switches

Input and Output with File Handles

Way back on Day 2, "Working with Strings and Numbers," you learned just a bit about file handles, as part of the information on standard input and output. At that time, I explained that `STDIN` and `STDOUT` are a special kind of file handle that refers to non–file-based input and output streams—the keyboard and the screen, for example. And, conveniently, much of what you've learned already is going to apply just as well to file handles that refer to actual files.

In this section, you'll learn how to tame the wily file handles: creating them with the `open` function, reading from them, writing or appending to them, and closing them when you're done. Along the way, we'll review what you've learned so far about input and output.

Creating File Handles with `open`

To read input from a source, or to write output to a destination, you need to use a file handle. A file handle is commonly associated with a specific file on a disk that you're reading or writing from, but it can also refer to a network connection (a socket), to a pipe (a sort of connection between standard output and standard input we'll look at on Day 18, "Perl and the Operating System"), or even to and from a specific hardware device. The file handle simply just makes all those things consistent so you can do the same things regardless of where the data is coming from or going to.

Perl provides three default file handles, two of which you've already seen: `STDIN`, `STDOUT`, and `STDERR`. The first two are for standard input and output (the keyboard and the screen, typically). `STDERR` is the standard error, and is used for error messages and other asides that aren't part of the actual script output. You'll commonly see `STDERR` messages printed to the screen just like `STDOUT`; it's only programs that specifically make use of standard output (programs on the other side of pipes in UNIX, for example) that will notice the difference.

You don't have to do anything to open or initialize these file handles; you can just go ahead and use them (as we have been throughout last week's lessons).

To read from or write to a file, you must first create a file handle for that operation with the `open` function. The `open` function opens a file for reading (input) or for writing (output), and associates a file handle name of your choosing to that file. Note that reading from and writing to a file are separate operations, and you'll need a file handle for each one.

15

The open function takes two arguments: the name of a file handle, and the file to open (which includes a special code indicating opening the file for reading or writing). Here are a few examples:

```
open(FILE, 'myfile');

open(CONFIG, '.scriptconfig');

open(LOG, '>/home/www/logfile');
```

The name of the file handle is anything you want it to be. File handles are, by convention, all uppercase, and contain letters, numbers, or underscores. Unlike variables, they must start with a letter.

The second argument is the name of the file on the disk that will be attached to your file handle. A plain filename with no path information will be read from the current directory (either the one your script is being run from, or from some other directory if you've changed it). You learn more about navigating directories on Day 17, "Managing Files and Directories."

If you're going to use pathnames other than single files, be careful—the path notation varies from platform to platform. On UNIX, paths are delineated with forward slashes, as in the last one of the preceding examples.

For Windows systems, standard DOS notation, with backslashes in between directory names, works fine as long as you use single quotes to surround the path. Remember, backslashes indicate special characters in Perl, so you may end up creating a bizarre path with no relation to reality. If you do use double-quoted string, you must escape each backslash to get the correct result.

```
open(FILE, 'c:\tempfiles\numbers');  # correct

open(FILE, "c:\tempfiles\numbers");
# eeek! contains a tab and a newline (\t, \n)

open(FILE "c:\\tempfiles\\numbers"); # correct
```

Because most modern Windows systems can handle directory pathnames with forward slashes, you might want to use those instead, for better portability to UNIX systems (if you care).

On the Mac, the directory separator is a colon, and absolute pathnames start with the disk or volume name (hard disk, CD-ROM, mounted disk, and so on). If you're concerned about portability to other systems, you'll need to make a note of it and convert your pathnames later on. A couple examples of Mac syntax:

```
open(FILE, "My Hard Disk:Perl Stuff:config");

open(BOOKMARKS, "HD:System Folder:Preferences:Netscape:Bookmarks.html");
```

In each of these cases, we've been opening a file handle for reading input into the script. This is the default. If you want to write output back to a file, you still need a file handle and you still use `open` to get it, but you use it with a special character ahead of the filename:

```
open(OUT, ">output");
```

The > character indicates that this file handle is to be opened for writing. The given file is opened and any current contents, if they exist, are deleted (you can test to see if a file exists before you open it for writing to avoid this behavior; more about file tests later on in "File Tests.")

What if you want to read input from a file, do something with it, and then write the same file back? You'll have to open two file handles: one to read in the input, and then another later on to re-open the file for writing. Reading and writing are different processes and require different file handles.

> Actually, there is a code for both reading and writing to the same file: `"+>`*`filename`*`"`. You might use this if you wanted to treat a file as a database, where instead of reading in the whole thing, you store it on disk and then read and write to that file as you read or change data. In this book, I'm going to stick with reading and writing simple text files, in which case it's less confusing and easier to manage the data if you use two separate file handles: one to read the data into memory, and one to write the data back out again.

You can also open a file for appending—where the current contents of the file are retained, and when you print to the output file handle, your output is appended to the end of that file. To do this, use the >> special characters in your call to `open`:

```
open(FILE, ">>logfile");
```

The `die` Function

The `open` function is nearly always called in conjunction with a logical `or` and a call to `die` on the other side, like this:

```
open(FILE, "thefile") or die "Can't find thefile\n";
```

The call to `die` isn't required, but it occurs so frequently in Perl code that the combination is almost boilerplate. If you don't do something like this, chances are good that if anyone else sees your code, they're going to ask you why you didn't.

"Open this file or die!" is the implied threat of this statement, and that's usually precisely what you want. The `open` command could potentially fail—for example, if you're opening the file for reading and it doesn't exist, if the disk is behaving weirdly and can't open the file, or for whatever other strange reason. Usually, you don't want your script to plow ahead if something has gone horribly wrong and it can't find anything to read. Fortunately, the `open` function returns `undef` if it could not open the file (and `1` if it could), so you can check the result and decide what to do.

Sometimes "what to do" can vary depending on the script. Commonly, however, you just want to exit the script with an error message. That's what the `die` function does: it immediately exits the entire Perl script, and prints its argument (a string message) to the `STDERR` file handle (the screen, typically).

If you put a newline character at the end of the message, Perl will print that message as it exits. If you leave off the newline, Perl will print an additional bit of information: `at script.pl line` *nn*. The `script.pl` will be the name of your script, and `line` *nn* will be the actual line number in which the `die` occurred. This can be useful for debugging your script later on.

One other clever use of `die`: The Perl special variable `$!` contains the most recent operating system error (if your OS will generate one). By putting the `$!` variable inside the string to `die`, your error message can sometimes be more helpful than just "Can't open file." For example, this version of `die`:

```
die "Can't open file: $!\n";
```

may result in the message `Can't open file: Permission denied` if the reason the file can't be opened is because the user doesn't have the right access to that file. Use of `$!` is generally a good idea if you're calling `die` in response to some sort of system error.

Although `die` is commonly used on the other side of a call to `open`, don't think it's only useful there. You can use `die` (and its non-fatal equivalent, `warn`) anywhere in your script where you want to stop executing the script (or print a warning message). See the `perlfunc` man page for more information on how to use `die` and `warn`.

Reading Input from a File Handle

So you've got a file handle. It's attached to a file you've opened for reading. To read input from a file handle, use the <> (input) operator with the name of that file handle, like this:

```
$line = <FILE>;
```

Looks familiar, right? You've been doing the same thing with `STDIN` to get a line of input from the keyboard. That's what's so cool about file handles—you use exactly the same procedures to read from a file as you do to read from the keyboard or to read from a network connection to a server. Perl doesn't care. It's exactly the same procedure, and everything you've already learned applies.

In scalar context, the input operator reads a single line of input up until the newline:

```
$line = <STDIN>;
if (<FILE>) { print "more input..." };
```

One special case of using the input operator in a scalar context is to use it inside the test of a `while` loop. This has the effect of looping through the input one line at a time, assigning each line to the `$_` variable, and stopping only when the end of the input is reached:

```
while (<FILE>) {
   # ... process each line of the file in $_
}
```

You've seen this same notation a lot with empty input operators. The empty input operators `<>` are, themselves, a special case in Perl. As you've learned, you use the empty input operators to get input from files contained on the script's command line. What Perl does for those files is open them all for you and send their contents to you in order via the `STDIN` file handle. You don't have to do anything special to handle them. Of course, you could open and read each file yourself, but the use of `<>` in a `while` loop is an extremely handy shortcut.

In list context, the input operators behave as if the entire input was being read in at once, with each line in the input assigned to an element in the list. Watch out for the input operator in a list context, as it may not always do what you expect it to. Here are some examples:

```
@input = <FILE>;   # read the entire file into @input;

$input = <FILE>;   # read the first line of file into $input

($input) = <FILE>; # read the first line of file into $input,
                   # throw the rest of FILE away (yikes!)
print <FILE>;      # print the entire contents of <FILE> to the screen
```

Writing Output to a File Handle

To write output to a file handle, you'll commonly use the `print` or `printf` functions. (There's also the `write` function, but that's used mostly with formats, which we'll touch on in Day 20, "Odds and Ends."

By default, the print (and printf) functions print to the file handle STDOUT. To print to a different file handle, for example, to write a line to a file, first open the file handle for writing, as follows:

```
open(FILE, ">$myfile") or die "Can't find $myfile\n";
```

And then use print with a file handle argument to put data into that file:

```
print FILE "$line\n";
```

The printf and sprintf functions work similarly; include the file handle to print to before the formatting string and the values as shown here:

```
printf(FILE "%d responses have been tabulated\n", $total / $count);
```

One very important part of print and printf that you need to be aware of: there is no comma between the file handle and the list of things to print. This comes under the heading of most common Perl mistakes (and will be caught if you have Perl warnings turned on). The file handle argument is entirely separate from the second argument, which is a list of elements separated by commas.

Reading and Writing Binary Files

Throughout this book, we've been reading and writing text data. But not all the files you work with in Perl are in text format; many of them may be binary files. If you're using Perl on UNIX or the Mac, the difference won't matter; UNIX and MacPerl can handle both text and binary files just fine. If you're using Windows, however, you'll get garbled results if you try to process a binary file in a normal Perl script.

Fortunately, there's an easy workaround: The binmode function takes a single file handle as an argument, and will process that file handle (read from it or write to it) in binary mode:

```
open(FILE, "myfile.exe") or die "Can't open myfile: $!\n";
binmode FILE;
while (<FILE>) { # read in binary mode...
```

Closing a File Handle

Once you're done reading from or writing to a file handle, you need to close it. Actually, you often don't have to close it yourself; when your script finishes executing, Perl closes all your file handles for you. And if you call open multiple times on the same file handle (for example, to open a file handle for writing after you're done reading from it), Perl will close that file handle automatically before opening it again. However, it's considered good programming practice to close your file handles after you're done with them; that way they won't take up any more space in your script.

To close a file handle, use the `close` function, like this:

```
close FILE;
```

An Example: Extract Subjects and Save Them

Email mailboxes are one of those formats that Perl is really good at managing: each message follows a very specific format (based on the protocol RFC822), and all are collected in a mailbox in a specific format. If you want to range over a mailbox and do something to messages that fits a specific criteria, then Perl is your language. In fact, we'll look at a filter to deal with mail when we finish up this book on Day 21, "Exploring a Few Longer Examples."

For this example, however, let's do something really simple: this script takes a mailbox as an argument on the script command line, reads in each message, extracts all the Subject lines, and writes a file called `subjects` in the same directory containing that list of subjects. If the file `subjects` already exists, this script will overwrite it (we'll learn in the next few sections how to test to see if the file exists and complain if it does).

Listing 15.1 shows the (very simple) code.

LISTING 15.1 THE `subject.pl` SCRIPT

```
1:  #!/usr/bin/perl -w
2:  use strict;
3:
4:  open(OUTFILE, ">subjects") or die "Can't open subjects file: $!\n";
5:
6:  while (<>) {
7:      if (/^Subject:/) {
8:          print OUTFILE $_;
9:      }
10: }
11: close OUTFILE;
```

A short script almost not worth pointing out as an example, you might think. But that's just the point: reading from and writing to files uses the same techniques you've used all along for standard input and output. There are two things to watch for here. First, line 4 opens the file `subjects` for writing (note the > character at the start of the filename). Second is line 8, where we print to that same `OUTFILE` file handle, rather than to standard output.

This script has no visual output, although if you run it on a file of mail and then examine the subjects file, you'll see lines like this (I ran this particular example on a file of "commercial mail," otherwise known as spam—hence the strange subjects):

```
Subject: FREE SOFTWARE TURN$ COMPUTER$ INTO CA$H MACHINE$!!
Subject: IBM 33.6 PCMCIA Modem $89.00
Subject: 48 MILLION Email Leads $195 + BONUSES
Subject: Re: E-ALERT: URGENT BUY RECOMMENDATION
Subject: Make $2,000 - $5,000 per week -NOT MLM
Subject: Email your AD to 57 MILLION People for ONLY $99
Subject: SHY?....................................
Subject: You Could Earn $100 Every Time the Phone Rings!!
```


File Tests

Opening files for reading and writing is all well and good when you know something about the files you're working with—for example, that they're all there, or that you're not about to overwrite something important. But sometimes in Perl you want to be able to do check the properties of a file before you open it, or handle a file differently depending on the various properties of that file.

Perl has a (rather large) set of tests for the various properties of files: to see if they exist, that they have data in them, that they're a certain kind of file, or they are a certain age ("1996 was a very good year for binary files, wasn't it?"). These tests all look like switches (`-e`, `-R`, `-o`, and so on), but don't confuse them with actual switches (the reason they look like this is because they're borrowed from UNIX shell scripting, and they look like that there).

Table 15.1 shows some of the more useful file tests. The `perlfunc` man page, in the entry for `-X`, contains the complete set (although you might note that not all the options are appropriate for all platforms).

Each of these tests can take a filename or a file handle as an argument; either will work (although if you're testing to see whether or not a file exists, you'll probably want to test the filename before calling `open` on it).

TABLE 15.1 FILE TESTS

Test	*What It Does*
`-d`	Is the file a directory?
`-e`	Does the file exist?
`-f`	Is the file a plain file (as opposed to a directory, or a link, or a network connection)?
`-l`	Is the file a link (UNIX only)?
`-r`	Is the file readable (by user or group on UNIX)?

continues

TABLE 15.1 CONTINUED

Test	What It Does
-s	How big is the file in bytes?
-t	Is the file handle open to STDIN (or some other tty on UNIX)?
-w	Is the file writable (by user or group on UNIX)?
-x	Is the file executable?
-z	Is the file there, but empty?
-A	How much time has elapsed, in seconds, since the file was last accessed?
-B	Is the file a binary file (as opposed to a text file)?
-M	How much time has elapsed, in seconds, since the file was last modified?
-T	Is the file a text file (as opposed to a binary file)?

Each test returns either true (`1`) or false (`""`), except for `-e`, which returns `undef` if the file doesn't exist, `-s`, which returns the number of bytes (characters) in the file, and the time operators `-M` and `-A`, which return the number of seconds since the file was modified or accessed, respectively.

So, for example, let's say you wanted to modify the `subject.pl` script such that if the `subjects` file exists, you'd prompt the user to make sure they want to overwrite it. Instead of the plain call to `open` we had, you could test to see if the file exists using, and if it does, make sure the user wants to overwrite it. Study the following code:

```
if (-e 'subjects') {
    print 'File exists.  Overwrite (Y/N)? ';
    chomp ($_ = <STDIN>);
    while (/[^yn]/i) {
        print 'Y or N, please: ';
        chomp ($_ = <STDIN>);
    }
    if (/n/i) { die "subjects file already exists; exiting.\n"; }
}
```

Here you see another use of the `die` function, this time away from the `open` function. If the user answers `n` to the overwrite question, you could simply exit the script; the `die` function is an explicit end and prints a message to that effect.

Working with @ARGV and Script Arguments

One aspect of running Perl scripts that I've sort of sidestepped over the last few days is that of dealing with command-line arguments. Yesterday we talked a bit about Perl's own switches (`-e`, `-w`, and so on), but what if you want to actually pass switches or arguments to your own scripts—how do you handle those? That's what we'll discuss in this section: script arguments in general, and handling script switches.

Anatomy of the @ARGV

When you call a Perl script with arguments beyond the name of the script, those arguments are stored in the special global list `@ARGV` (on the Mac, for droplets, `@ARGV` will be the filenames that were dropped onto the droplet). You can process this array the same way you would any other list in your Perl script. For example, here's a snippet that will just print out the arguments the script was called with, one on each line:

```
foreach my $arg (@ARGV) {
   print "$arg\n";
}
```

If your script uses a construct such as `while (<>)`, Perl will use the contents of the `@ARGV` list as the filenames to open and read (if there are no files in `@ARGV`, Perl will try to read from the standard input). Multiple files are all opened and read sequentially, as if they were all one big file.

If you want more control over the contents of the files you're reading into a script, you could examine the contents of `@ARGV` to find the filenames to open and read. Processing `@ARGV` is also useful if you're looking for a specific number of arguments—for example, one configuration file and one data file. If you just want to process the contents of any number of files, it's handy to use the `<>` shortcut. If you want to specifically have a set of arguments, and control the processing of each one, read the files from `@ARGV` and process them individually.

> **Note**
>
> Unlike C and UNIX's `argv`, Perl's `@ARGV` contains only the arguments, not the name of the script itself (`$ARGV[0]` will contain the first argument). To get the name of the script, you can use the special variable `$0` instead.

Script Switches and Fun with Getopt

One use of the script command line is to pass switches to a script. Switches are arguments that start with a dash (`-a`, `-b`, `-c`) and are usually used to control the behavior of that script. Sometimes `-s` are single letters (`-s`), sometimes they're grouped (`-abc`), and sometimes they have an associated value or argument (`-o outfile.txt`).

You can call a script with any switches you want; those switches will end up as elements of the `@ARGV` array just as any other arguments do. If you were using `<>` to process `@ARGV`, you'll want to get rid of those switches before reading any data—otherwise, Perl will assume that your `-s` switch is the name of a file. To process and remove those switches littering `@ARGV`, you *could* laboriously go through the array and figure out which elements were options, which ones were options with associated arguments, and finally end up with a list of actual filenames after you were done doing all that. Or you could use the `Getopt` module to do all that for you.

The `Getopt` module, part of the standard module library that comes with Perl, manages script switches. There are actually two modules: `Getopt::Std`, which processes single-character switches (`-a`, `-d`, `-ofile`, and so on); and `Getopt::Long`, which allows just about any kind of options, including multicharacter options (`-sde`) and GNU-style double-hyphen options (`--help`, `--size`, and so on).

In this section, I describe the `Getopt::Std` module, for handling simple options. If you want to handle more complex options via the `Getopt::Long` module, you are welcome to explore that module's documentation for yourself (see the `perlmod` manual page for details).

To use the `Getopt::Std` module, you import it in your script as you do all modules:

```
use Getopt::Std;
```

Importing `Getopt::Std` gives you two functions: `getopt` and `getopts`. These functions are used to extract the switches from your `@ARGV` array and set scalar variables in your script for each of those switches.

> The `Getopt` module does not work properly with the application version of MacPerl (as there's no easy way to get command line switches into MacPerl). See the section "Script Switches on the Macintosh" for accomplishing much the same thing using MacPerl.

getopts

Let's start with `getopts`, which defines and processes single-character switches with or without values. The `getopts` function takes a single string argument containing the single-character switches that your script will accept. Arguments that take values must be followed by a colon (:). Upper- and lowercase are significant and represent different switches. For example:

```
getopts('abc');
```

The argument here, 'abc', processes -a, -b, or -c switches, in any order, with no associated values. Those switches can be grouped: -ab or -abc will work just as well as the individual switches will. Here's another:

```
getopts('ab:c');
```

In this example, the -b switch can take a value, which must appear on the Perl command line immediately after that switch, like this:

```
% myscript.pl -b 10
```

The space after the switch itself isn't required; -b10 works as well as -b 10. You can also nest these switches as long as the value appears after the switch itself, like this:

```
% myscript.pl -acb10 # OK
% myscript.pl -abc10 # wrong
```

For each switch defined in getopts, the getopts function creates a scalar variable switch with the name $opt_x, where x is the letter of the switch (in the preceding example, getopts would create three variables for $opt_a, $opt_b, and $opt_c). The initial value of each scalar variable is 0. Then, if that switch was included in the arguments to the script (in @ARGV), getopts sets the value of its associated variable to 1. If the switch required a value, getopts assigns the value on @ARGV to the scalar variable for that option. The switch, and its associated value, are then deleted from @ARGV. After getopts finishes processing, your @ARGV will either be empty, or will contain any remaining filename arguments which you can then read with file handles or with <>.

After getopts is done, you'll end up with a variable for each switch that will either have a value of 0 (if that switch wasn't used), 1 (if that switch was used), or some value (if that switch was used with the given value). You can then test for those values and have your script perform different functions based on the switches it was called with, as shown here:

```
if ($opt_a) {  # -a was used
   ...
}
if ($opt_b) {  # -b was used
 ...
}
```

So, for example, if your script was called like this:

```
% script.pl -a
```

then getopts('abc') will set $opt_a to 1. If it was called like this:

```
% script.pl -a -R
```

then $opt_a will be set to 1, and the -R switch will be quietly deleted with no variable set. If you called it like this:

```
% script.pl -ab10
```

and called `getopts` like this:

```
getopts('ab:c');
```

then `$opt_a` will get set to `1`, and `$opt_b` will get set to `10`.

Note that if you're using `use strict` that Perl will complain about the `$opt_` variables suddenly popping into existence. You can get around this by pre-declaring those variables with `use vars`, like this:

```
use vars qw($opt_a $opt_b $opt_c);
```

Error Processing with `getopts`

Note that `getopts` reads your `@ARGV` in order, and stops processing when it gets to an element that does not start with a dash (`-`) or that isn't a value for a preceding option. This means that when you call your Perl script, you should put the options first and the bare arguments last, otherwise you may end up with unprocessed options or errors trying to read files that aren't files. You may want to write your script to make sure `@ARGV` is empty after `getopts` is done, or that its remaining arguments do not start with a dash.

The switches defined by `getopts` are expected to be the *only* switches that your script will accept. If you call a script with a switch not defined in the argument to `getopts`, `getopts` will print an error (`Unknown option`), delete that option from `@ARGV`, and return false. You can use this behavior to make sure your script is being called correctly, and exit with a message if it's not. Just put the call to `getopts` inside an `if` statement, as follows:

```
if (! getopts('ab:c')) {
   die "Usage: myscript -a -b -c file\n";
}
```

Note also that if `getopts` stops processing your switches in the middle because of an error, any switch variables that were set beforehand will still have their values, and may contain bad values. Depending on how robust you'd like your argument checking to be, you may want to check those values if `getopts` returns false (or exit altogether).

`getopt`

The `getopt` function works just like `getopts`, in that it takes a string argument with the switches, and it assigns `$opt_` variables to each of those arguments and removes them from `@ARGV` as it goes. However, `getopt` differs from `getopts` in three significant respects:

- The argument to `getopt` is a string containing the switches that must have associated values.

- getopt does not require you to define arguments without values beforehand. It allows any single-letter options, and creates an $opt_ variable for each one.
- getopt does not return a (useful) value, and does not print errors for unexpected options.

Say, for example, you have a call to getopt like this:

```
getopt('abc');
```

This function assumes that your script will be called with any of three switches, -a, -b, or -c, each one with a value. If the script is called with switches that don't have values, getopt will not complain; it happily assigns the next element in @ARGV to the variable for that switch—even if that next element is another switch or a filename that you might have wanted to read as a file. It's up to you to figure out if the values are appropriate or if the script was called with the wrong set of arguments.

Essentially, the core difference between getopt and getopts is that getopt doesn't require you to declare your options, but also makes it more difficult to handle errors. I prefer getopts for most cases, to avoid having to do a lot of value testing.

Script Switches on the Macintosh

The Mac does not have a script command line, and as such, MacPerl scripts cannot accept command-line switches the way UNIX and Windows scripts can (you can always accept filename arguments using droplets). There are several ways around this; one might be to prompt for switches at the start of your script, and set @ARGV to the result (which will let you use getopt to process those switches inside the script). Here's a snippet of code to do just that:

```
print "Enter switches: ";
chomp($in = <STDIN>);
@ARGV = split(' ', $in);
```

A more sophisticated version of those three lines that uses the MacPerl module and a dialog box is supplied as part of the MacPerl FAQ at http://www.perl.com/CPAN-local/doc/FAQs/mac/MacPerlFAQ.html:

```
if( $MacPerl::Version =~ /Application$/ ) {
        # we're running from the app
        local( $cmdLine, @args );
        $cmdLine = &MacPerl::Ask( "Enter command line options:" );
        require "shellwords.pl";
        @args = &shellwords( $cmdLine );
        unshift( @ARGV, @args );
    }
```

An even more Mac-like way of getting around command-line switches would be to use MacPerl modules to create your own dialogs such that switches are implemented as actual user interface elements. We'll look at some simple dialogs on Day 18; the MacPerl documentation has more information about simple dialogs.

Note that if you're using the MPW version of MacPerl, all of this is moot; you have a command line. Use it!

Another Example

Here's a simple example (in Listing 15.2) that processes a file in various ways depending on the switches that you use with that script.

LISTING 15.2 THE `switches.pl` SCRIPT

```
#!/usr/bin/perl -w
use strict;
use Getopt::Std;
use vars qw($opt_r $opt_l $opt_s $opt_n);

if (! getopts('rlsn')) {
    die "Usage: switches.pl -rlsn\n";
}

my @file = <>;

if ($opt_s) {
    @file = sort @file;
}

if ($opt_n) {
    @file = sort {$a <=> $b} @file;
}

if ($opt_r) {
    @file = reverse @file;
}

my $i = 1;
foreach my $line (@file) {
    if ($opt_l) {
        print "$i: $line";
        $i++;
    } else {
        print $line;
    }
}
```

This script uses single switches only, with no values (note the call to getopts in line 7; there are no colons after any of those options). Those switches are -r, to reverse the contents of the file; -s, to sort the lines of the file; -n, to sort the lines numerically; and -l, to print line numbers. You can combine options on the command line, although some multiple options don't make sense (-sn sorts the file, and then resorts it numerically).

Line 4 pre-declares our variables, so they won't suddenly spring into existence when getopts creates them (and cause use strict to complain).

The test in lines 6 through 8 makes sure the script is being called with the right options. If a stray option slipped through (for example, an -a or -x), then the script exits with a usage message.

Finally, the various if statements test for the existence of the $opt_r, $opt_l, $opt_s, and $opt_n variables, and performs different operations depending on which options were called on the command line. Any arguments that aren't switches remain in @ARGV after getopts is done, and are read into the script via the <> operator in line 10.

Going Deeper

In this lesson, I've given you the basics of I/O and managing file systems; the stuff you learn here should apply to all your basic Perl programs that need to use files and command-line arguments. On Day 17 we'll explore how to handle aspects of the file system itself. In this lesson's "Going Deeper," I'll try to point you to a number of other places to look for more information and details about advanced input and output and handling file system features.

All the built-in Perl functions, as I've noted before, are documented in the perlfunc man page. Also of some use may be the FAQ on files and formats contained in the perlfaq man page.

More About open and File Handles

A few other shortcuts and features of the open function:

You can leave off the filename to the open function if, and only if, a scalar variable with the same name as the file handle has already been set to the file to be opened. For example:

```
$FILE = "myfile.txt";
open(FILE) or die "Can't open $FILE: $!\n";
```

This can be useful for filenames that need to be opened or reopened; you can set a variable at the start of your script and then use that filename over and over again.

Contrary to what I claimed earlier in this chapter, you can open a file both for reading and writing, using the +> special character in front of the filename:

```
open(FILE, "+>thefile") or die "Can't open file: $!\n";
```

Because this can often be confusing, however, I prefer to use separate file handles and to read and write as separate operations.

Filenames that start with pipes (|) operate as if the filename was a command, and the output will be piped to that command via the command shell for your system.

For many more details about the various uses of `open`, see the `perlfunc` man page.

Various Other File-Related Functions

Table 15.2 shows several file-related built-in functions that I have not described in this lesson.

TABLE 15.2 MORE I/O FUNCTIONS

Function	*What It Does*
`eof`	Returns true if next line input will be at the end of file
`eof()`	Different function than `eof`; this version detects end of the last file for files input using <>
`lstat`	Displays information about links
`pack`	Outputs data into a binary structure
`select`	Changes the default file handle for output (commonly used with formats, see Day 20
`stat`	Prints various bits of information about a file or file handle
`truncate`	Truncates (delete the contents of) a file or file handle
`unpack`	Inputs data from a binary structure

Expert-Level I/O

The input and output techniques I've described in this chapter provide simple, line-oriented buffered input and output from and to file handles and standard input, output, and error. If you're interested in doing more low-level sophisticated forms of input and output, explore the various other I/O functions Perl provides for you, as listed in Table 15.3.

TABLE 15.3 MORE I/O FUNCTIONS

Function	*What It Does*
`fcntl`	File control (the UNIX `fctrl(2)` function).
`flock`	Lock file (UNIX `flock(2)` function).
`getc`	Get next byte.
`ioctl`	TTY control (The UNIX `ioctl(2)` system call).
`read`	Input a specific number of bytes (`fread(2)`).
`rewinddir`	Set the current (input) position to the beginning of the directory handle.
`seek`	Position the file pointer at a specific location in a file (same as `fseek()` in C).
`seekdir`	Same as `seek` for directory handles.
`select`	Make file descriptors ready for reading (same as the `select(2)` command on UNIX. Not to be confused with `select` on a file handle for setting the default file handle.
`syscall`	Call a UNIX system call (`syscall(2)`).
`sysopen`	Open a file handle with a mode and permissions.
`sysread`	Read a certain number of bytes using `read(2)`.
`syswrite`	Write a certain number of bytes to the file handle with `write(2)`.
`tell`	Return the current file pointer position.
`telldir`	Same as `tell` for directory handles.
`write`	Write a formatted record to an output file handle (see Day 20). `write` is not the opposite of `read`.

In addition, the `POSIX` module provides a number of features for handling more sophisticated I/O (but, alas, works only on UNIX). See the `perlmod` man page for more information about `POSIX`.

DBM Files

Perl provides built-in and module behavior for reading and writing files from and to Berkeley UNIX DBM (database) files. These files can be smaller and faster to deal with than flat text-based databases. For more information about DBM, see the `DB_File` module, the `tie` function, and the various `Tie` modules (`Tie::Hash`, `Tie::Scalar`, and so on).

CPAN also provides a number of modules for dealing with databases—both those you write yourself, as well as interfaces to and drivers for various commercial databases such as Oracle and Sybase. For the latter, the DBD (Database Drivers) and DBI (Database Interface) packages by the Perl Database Initiative come highly recommended.

Timestamps

Files and directories can both contain timestamps, that is, indications of when that file was created, modified, or just accessed. You can test a file for its timestamp using the `-M` (modification), `-A` (access), and `-C` (inode change, UNIX only) file tests, get more information about timestamps via the `stat` function, or change the timestamp of a file using the `utime` function. The behavior of these tests and functions may vary from platform to platform.

All times are in seconds elapsed since a certain date; that date is January 1, 1970, for UNIX and Windows and January 1, 1904, on the Macintosh. The functions `time`, `gmtime`, `localtime`, and the `Time::Local` modules may also be of interest for decoding and changing timestamps.

Summary

In this chapter, we've reviewed and expanded on all the information you've learned about input and output so far in this book, taking what you already knew about reading from standard input and writing to standard output and using those same techniques to read and write from files.

Files and file handles were the focus of the start of this chapter, and you learned about using the `open` function to open a file and create a file handle to read from or write to that file. As an adjunct to `open` you also learned about `die`, a function that exits the script and prints an error message to the standard error file handle as it goes.

In the next part of the lesson, we talked about script arguments and switches: what happens when you call a script with arguments (they get put into `@ARGV`) and what you can do to process those arguments. If those arguments includes switches, the best way to process them is with the `Getopt::Std` module, which lets you define and process switches to your script and then test for the existence of those switches using special variables.

The functions you learned about in this chapter include:

- `open`, for creating file handles
- `die`, for exiting the script with an error message
- `binmode`, for setting a file handle to binary mode
- `close`, to close a file handle
- `getopts`, part of the `Getopt` module, for declaring and processing arguments
- `getopt`, also part of the `Getopt` module, for handling arguments

Q&A

Q I'm trying to open a file for writing, but `die` keeps getting triggered and I can't figure out why. The directory is readable, the file doesn't exist—there's no reason why things should be going wrong.

A Did you remember to put the > character at the start of your filename? You need that character to tell Perl that the file is to be written to—otherwise it'll assume the file is to be read from, and if it can't find the file it won't be able to open it.

The `open` function should work most of the time; it should only fail under unusual circumstances. If it's consistently failing for you, consider double-checking your use of `open`.

Q I want to use a subroutine to open my file, and then pass the file handle around to other subroutines. But when I try this is doesn't work. Why?

A Well, you can't. You can do sneaky things with typeglobs to pass symbol names between subroutines, but that's a kludge with its own set of problems. The best way to pass file handles around is to use the `FileHandle` module, create a file handle as an object, and then pass that object between subroutines.

But, since we haven't learned much about objects, you may (for now) want to just create your file handle globally and refer to them inside subroutines instead. (We'll explore objects a bit on Day 20.)

Q I'm trying to read a simple text-based database file in Perl. I know what the format for the file is, and I know how to decode it into something I can use, but the input I'm getting is really garbled. What's going on here?

A Are you on a Windows system? Is the database file in a binary format? Use the `binmode` function to make sure Perl is reading your file handle in binary format.

Q I'm using MacPerl. I got this file of numbers from a UNIX system, and when I read it into my script, I end up with one huge string instead of an array of individual strings. MacPerl appears to be ignoring line feeds. What's going on here?

A Well, MacPerl *is* ignoring the linefeeds. This is a difference in how UNIX and Macintosh systems handle end-of-line characters. UNIX systems use `\n` (linefeed, ASCII 10), Macintoshes use `\r` (carriage return, ASCII 13). MacPerl is intended to read Macintosh files, so its idea of end of line is indeed `\r` instead of linefeed. (In case you're curious, Windows/DOS uses both.)

To get around this problem, you have one of two choices. First, most FTP and file-transfer programs these days will autoconvert the linefeeds to carriage returns for you when you move a UNIX file to a Mac. If they don't, many editors will do it. By converting the UNIX file to a Mac file, you won't have the problem.

The other solution is to change MacPerl's input record separator at the top of your script to actually be a linefeed, like this:

```
$/ = "\n";
```

Workshop

The workshop provides quiz questions to help you solidify your understanding of the material covered and exercises to give you experience in using what you've learned. Try to understand the quiz and exercise answers before you go on to tomorrow's lesson.

Quiz

1. What's a file handle? What are the `STDIN`, `STDOUT`, and `STDERR` file handles used for?
2. What are the differences between creating file handles for reading, writing, or appending?
3. What's the `die` function used for? Why should you bother using it with `open`?
4. How do you read input from a file handle? Describe how input behaves in a scalar context, in a scalar context inside a `while` loop test, and in a list context.
5. How do you send output to a file handle?
6. What do the following file tests test for?

```
-e
-x
-f
-M
-z
```

7. What is `@ARGV` used for? What does it contain?
8. What's the difference between `getopt` and `getopts`?
9. What switches do the following calls to `getopts` allow?

```
getopts('xyz:');
getopts('x:y:z');
getopts('xXy');
getopts('xyz');
getopt('xyz');
```

Exercises

1. Write a script that merges two files (specified on the command line) with their lines intertwined (one line from file 1, one line from file 2, another line from file 1, and so on). Write the resulting data to a file called `merged`.
2. Write a script that merges the two files only if the filename extensions are the same, and use that same filename extension for the final merged file. If the extensions are different, exit the script with an error message. (HINT: use regular expressions to find the filename extensions.)
3. Write a script that merges two files and takes a single option: `-o`, which bypasses the error message from the previous exercise and merges the file anyhow (the extension of the final file is up to you).
4. Write a script that takes single string argument and any of four switches, `-u`, `-s`, `-r`, and `-c`. `-u` returns the string in uppercase, `-s` removes all punctuation and whitespace (s stands for "squash"), `-r` reverses the string, and `-c` counts the number of characters. Make sure you can combine the options for different effects.
5. **BUG BUSTERS:** This script is called like this:

   ```
   myscript.pl -sz inputfile
   ```

   What's wrong with this script? (HINT: The test for `$opt_z` will not return true.)

   ```
   use strict;
   use Getopt::Std;
   use vars qw($opt_s $opt_z);
   getopt('sz');

   if ($opt_z) {
      # ...
   }
   ```

Answers

Here are the answers to the workshop questions in the previous section.

Quiz Answers

1. A file handle is used by Perl to read data from or write data to some source or destination (which could be a file, the keyboard, the screen, a network connection, or another script). The `STDIN`, `STDOUT`, and `STDERR` file handles refer to standard input, standard output, and standard error, respectively. You create file handles to any other files using the `open` function.

2. Use special characters in the filename to be opened to indicate whether that file will be opened for reading, writing, or appending. The default is to open a file for reading.
3. The `die` function exits the script gracefully with a (supposedly) helpful error message. It's most commonly used in conjunction with `open` because if something so unusual happened that the file couldn't be opened, generally you don't want your script to continue running. Good programming practice says *always* check your return values for `open` and call `die` if it didn't work.
4. Read input from a file handle using the input operator <> and the name of the file handle. In scalar context, the input operator reads one line at a time. Inside a `while` loop, it assigns each line to the `$_` variable. In a list context, all the input to end of file is read.
5. Send output to a file handle using the `print` function and the name of the file handle. Note that there is no comma between the file handle and the thing to print.
6. `-e` tests to see if the file exists.

   `-x` tests to see if the file is executable (usually only relevant on UNIX).

   `-f` tests to see if the file is a plain file (and not a directory, a link or anything else).

   `-M` tests the modification date of the file.

   `-z` tests to see if the file exists and is empty.
7. The `@ARGV` array variable stores all the arguments and switches the script was called with.
8. The `getopt` function defines switches with values, and can accept any other options. The `getopts` function declares the possible options for the script and if they have values or not. The other difference is that `getopts` returns a false value if there were errors processing the command-line switches; `getopt` doesn't return any useful value.
9. `getopts('xyz:')` allows the switches `-x`, `-y`, and `-z` with a value.

   `getopts('x:y:z')` allows `-x` and `-y`, each with values, and `-z` without a value.

   `getopts('xXy')` allows `-x` and `-X` (they are separate switches) and `-y`, none with values.

   `getopts('xyz')` allows `-x`, `-y` and `-z`, none with values.

   `getopt('xyz')` allows `-x`, `-y` and `-z`, each one with required values, as well as any other single-character switches.

Exercise Answers

1. Here's one answer:

```
#!/usr/bin/perl -w
use strict;

my ($file1, $file2) = @ARGV;

open(FILE1, $file1) or die "Can't open $file1: $!\n";
open(FILE2, $file2) or die "Can't open $file2: $!\n";
open(MERGE, ">merged") or die "Can't open merged file: $!\n";

my $line1 = <FILE1>;
my $line2 = <FILE2>;
while (defined($line1) || defined($line2)) {
    if (defined($line1)) {
        print MERGE $line1;
        $line1 = <FILE1>;
    }
    if (defined($line2)) {
        print MERGE $line2;
        $line2 = <FILE2>;
    }
}
```

2. Here's one answer:

```
#!/usr/bin/perl -w
use strict;

my ($file1, $file2) = @ARGV;
my $ext;

if ($file1 =~ /\.(\w+)$/) {
    $ext = $1;
    if ($file2 !~ /\.$ext$/) {
        die "Extensions do not match.\n";
    }
}

open(FILE1, $file1) or die "Can't open $file1: $!\n";
open(FILE2, $file2) or die "Can't open $file2: $!\n";
open(MERGE, ">merged.$ext") or die "Can't open merged file: $!\n";

my $line1 = <FILE1>;
my $line2 = <FILE2>;
while (defined($line1) || defined($line2)) {
    if (defined($line1)) {
        print MERGE $line1;
        $line1 = <FILE1>;
    }
```

```
    if (defined($line2)) {
        print MERGE $line2;
        $line2 = <FILE2>;
    }
}
```

3. Here's one answer:

```
#!/usr/bin/perl -w
use strict;
use Getopt::Std;
use vars qw($opt_o);
getopts('o');

my ($file1, $file2) = @ARGV;
my $ext;

if ($file1 =~ /\.(\w+)$/) {
    $ext = $1;
    if ($file2 !~ /\.$ext$/) {
        if (!$opt_o) {
            die "Extensions do not match.\n";
        }
    }
}

open(FILE1, $file1) or die "Can't open $file1: $!\n";
open(FILE2, $file2) or die "Can't open $file2: $!\n";
open(MERGE, ">merged.$ext") or die "Can't open merged file: $!\n";

my $line1 = <FILE1>;
my $line2 = <FILE2>;
while (defined($line1) || defined($line2)) {
    if (defined($line1)) {
        print MERGE $line1;
        $line1 = <FILE1>;
    }
    if (defined($line2)) {
        print MERGE $line2;
        $line2 = <FILE2>;
    }
}
```

4. Here's one way:

```
#!/usr/bin/perl -w
use strict;
use Getopt::Std;
use vars qw($opt_s $opt_r $opt_u $opt_c);
getopts('sruc');

my $str = $ARGV[0];

if ($opt_s) {
    $str =~ s/[\s.,;:!?'"]//g;
}

if ($opt_r) {
   $str = reverse $str;
}

if ($opt_u) {
   $str = uc $str;
}

if ($opt_c) {
   $str = length $str;
}

print "$str\n";
```

5. The script snippet uses the `getopt` function. This function (as opposed to `getopts`) assumes all the switches will have values associated with them. So when the script is called with the switch `-sz`, `getopt` assumes that you're using the `-s` switch, and that its value is `z`. The `-z` switch never registers to `getopt`. Use the `getopts` function instead to make sure both `$opt_s` and `$opt_z` are set.

WEEK 3

DAY 16

Using Perl for CGI Scripting

In recent years one of the most common uses of Perl has been for creating CGI scripts. CGI, short for the Common Gateway Interface, refers to programs and scripts that live on a Web server and run in response to input from a browser—form submissions, complex links, some image maps—just about anything that isn't a plain ordinary file involves some sort of CGI script.

Because of Perl's popularity as a CGI language, I would be remiss if I did not give you a short introduction to CGI using Perl. Today we'll use what you already know about Perl in the context of creating CGI scripts on the Web. Today, you'll learn

- Some notes about CGI, before we start
- How the CGI process works, from browser to server and back again
- Creating a short CGI script, from start to finish
- An introduction to the `CGI.pm` module
- Working with data from HTML forms

- Printing the output
- Debugging the script

Before You Start

To write CGI scripts in Perl, you'll need three things:

- A Web server that supports Perl, and an understanding of how to install CGI scripts on that server
- The `CGI.pm` module, which should have come with your Perl distribution (more about this later)
- A basic understanding of HTML

> You don't *specifically* need the `CGI.pm` module to do CGI scripting in Perl. There are other utility scripts to help you do CGI, or you could hand-write all of the underlying code yourself. But that would mean a lot of work for you, and it's much, much easier just to use `CGI.pm`. Everyone else is doing it; why not join us?

Because of the wide variety of Web servers for different platforms and the differences between them, I don't have the space to get into a discussion of getting your Web server set up for CGI. There are extensive help files on the Web, however, including

- The basic CGI documentation at `http://hoohoo.ncsa.uiuc.edu/cgi/`, which applies mostly to UNIX-based servers.
- The Perl CGI FAQ at `http://www.perl.com/CPAN-local/doc/FAQs/cgi/perl-cgi-faq.html`.
- "The Idiot's Guide to Solving CGI Problems" at `http://www.perl.com/CPAN-local/doc/FAQs/cgi/idiots-guide.html`.
- For Windows, the Perl for Win32 FAQ at `http://www.activestate.com/support/faqs/win32/` has a great deal of information about programming, setting up, and using Perl for CGI. Your Web server may also have information on writing or configuring Perl CGI scripts for that particular software package.
- For MacPerl, the `README.CGI` file in MacPerl's MacPerl CGI folder contains lots of information for getting CGI to work under Mac-based Web servers.

You should also refer to the documentation that came with your Web server. If you plan to do a lot of work with CGI, you might consider *Sams Teach Yourself CGI*

Programming in a Week by Rafe Colburn for more help and more examples beyond what I have to offer here.

If you don't have at least a passing background in HTML, much of the rest of this lesson may be difficult to follow. Again, consider boning up the multitude of HTML tutorials on the Web, or with *Sams Teach Yourself Web Publishing with HTML 4 in 21 Days*, by Laura Lemay (that's me!).

How CGI Works

Let's start with some conceptual background about CGI and how it fits into the relationship between a Web browser and a Web server.

CGI, as I've mentioned, stands for Common Gateway Interface. Common because the same process is used for many different kinds of Web servers and gateway because the scripts at one time commonly served as a gateway between the Web server itself and some larger program—for example, a database or a search engine. These days, CGI has lost much of its original precise meaning, and now refers simply to a script or program that runs in response to input from a Web browser.

There are a lot of different things you can do with a CGI script and different ways to write one. For the purposes of this lesson, we'll focus on one typical use: CGI scripts to handle data received as part of an HTML form. Figure 16.1 shows a typical flowchart for how things work when a user with a Web browser requests a form, fills it out, and submits it.

FIGURE 16.1

The CGI process.

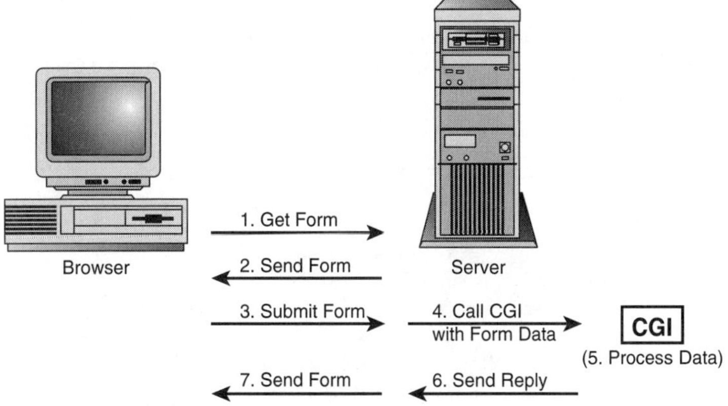

Here's what's going on at each step:

- The user, running a Web browser, requests a page with a form on it.
- The server sends the form. The form itself may be a CGI script that generates the HTML for the form, or just a plain old HTML file.
- The user fills out the form and clicks the Submit button.
- The browser packages up the form data and sends it to the Web server.
- The Web server passes the data to the CGI script.
- The CGI script decodes the data, processes it in some way, and returns a response (typically another HTML file).
- The server sends the response to the browser.

This is obviously not all that complicated, but you should understand where the CGI script fits into the process so you know where the data is coming from and where its going. This will be important later on.

Building a CGI Script, From Form to Response

The best way to learn how to code CGI is to go ahead and do it, so let's do it. In this section we'll create a really simple CGI script—the equivalent of Hello, World—using a basic HTML form, Perl for the CGI script, and the `CGI.pm` module to help put it all together. I'll give you the HTML form to work from, but we'll build up the script itself line by line.

The Form

Listing 16.1 shows the HTML code for a simple HTML form that asks you for your name. Figure 16.2 shows what this form looks like in a Web browser.

LISTING 16.1 THE `name.html` FILE

```
<HTML>
<HEAD>
<TITLE>Tell Me Your Name</TITLE>
</HEAD>
<BODY>
<FORM ACTION="/cgi-bin/name.pl">
<P>Enter your Name: <INPUT NAME="name">
<P><INPUT TYPE="SUBMIT" VALUE="Submit me!">
</FORM>
</BODY>
</HTML>
```

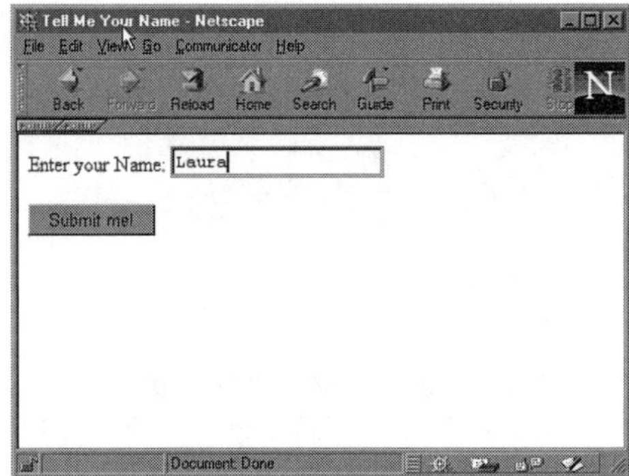

FIGURE 16.2
Hello!

There are two important parts to note about this bit of HTML:

- In line 6, the `ACTION` attribute points to the CGI script that will process this form when it's submitted to the server. Here, that script is called `name.pl`, and it's stored in the server's `cgi-bin` directory (the usual place for CGI scripts to be stored, although it may be different for your server, or you may need permission to put your scripts there). You'll need to substitute the path to your version of the script when you write it in the next section.

> Some Web servers may also require you to rename your scripts with a `.cgi` extension for those scripts to be recognized as CGI scripts. This differs from server to server, so check your documentation.

- Line 7 defines a text field form element (in the `<INPUT>` tag). Note that the `NAME` attribute gives this element a name. This will also be important when you build the CGI script for this form.

Creating the Script

Now let's create a Perl script to process the data we get back from that CGI script. Although writing a CGI script in Perl is similar in many ways to writing an ordinary command-line Perl script, there are several important differences relating to the fact that your script is called by the Web server, not by you. You won't get any command-line options or filename arguments. All the data you get into the script will come from the Web server (or you'll read it in yourself from files on the disk). The output you write will have to be in a specific format—usually HTML.

Fortunately, the `CGI.pm` module, written by Lincoln Stein and available in the current Perl distributions, is there to make CGI scripting easier and to cover up a lot of the oddities.

Let's start with the top few lines of our CGI script:

```
#!/usr/bin/perl -w
use strict;
use CGI qw(:standard);
```

The shebang line and `use strict` you already know, and the third `use CGI` line shouldn't be much of a surprise either. The `:standard` tag, as you learned on Day 13, "Scope, Modules, and Importing Code," imports a subset of the CGI module, rather than importing the whole thing. In the case of `CGI.pm`, the `:standard` tag will probably be the one you use most often.

Most CGI scripts have two main parts: the initial part reads and processes any data you got from the form or from the Web browser, and the second outputs a response, usually in HTML form. In this example, because there isn't any real processing to do, we can skip directly to the output part.

The first thing you need to output is a special header to the Web server indicating the kind of file you're sending back. If you send back an HTML file, the type is `text/html`. If you send back a plain text file, it's `text/plain`. Send back an image, and it's `image/gif`. These file types are all standardized as part of the MIME specification, and if you get into serious CGI scripting you'll need to learn at least some of these. The most common type, however, is `text/html`. `CGI.pm` provides a basic subroutine, `print_header()`, for printing out the appropriate header for that type:

```
print header();
```

After the header, all the output you print will be in HTML format. You can either print raw HTML tags or use `CGI.pm`'s Perl subroutines for generating HTML, or you can use a combination of both. Because I know HTML fairly well, I like to use the `CGI.pm` subroutines where it will save me some typing, and regular `print` statements for everything else. Here's the remainder of our simple CGI script then:

```
print start_html('Hello!');
print "<H1>Hello, ", param('name'), "!</H1>\n";
print end_html;
```

The first line calls `CGI.pm`'s `start_html()` subroutine, which prints the top part of an HTML file (the `<HTML>,<HEAD>,<TITLE>`, and `<BODY>` tags). The string argument to `start_html()` is the title of the page. There are also other arguments you can give this subroutine to set the background color, keywords, and other features of the header (more about that in the next section).

The second line is a regular `print` statement, which prints an HTML heading (<H1> tag) to say hello. In between the opening and closing tags, however, is the interesting part. The `param()` subroutine, part of `CGI.pm`, is how you get to the information that your user entered into the form. You use `param()` with the name of the form element (from the `NAME` attribute of the element's HTML tag), and it returns the value the user entered for that element. By calling `param('name')` here, we get the string the user entered into the one text field on our form, and we can use that value to generate the response.

The third line is another `CGI.pm` subroutine that simply prints out the closing bits of HTML (</BODY> and </HTML>), finishing up the response. Here's the complete script, all put together:

```
#!/usr/bin/perl -w
use strict;
use CGI qw(:standard);

print header;
print start_html('Hello!');
print "<H1>Hello, ", param('name'), "!</H1>\n";
print end_html;
```

You may have noticed that we're not doing anything special as far as output is concerned; we're just using simple `print` statements. And yet, the output doesn't go to the screen; it goes back to the browser. A CGI script is a prime example of how standard input and output don't necessarily have to be the keyboard or the screen. CGI scripts do read their input from the standard input, and output to the standard output. Except in this case the standard input and output are the Web server. You don't have to do anything special to deal with that server; the standard ways work just fine.

So what is the output? If the user entered `Fred` into the form, the output of the CGI script will look like this, with the header and the HTML data in place:

```
Content-type: text/html

<!DOCTYPE HTML PUBLIC "-//IETF//DTD HTML//EN">
<HTML><HEAD><TITLE>Hello!</TITLE>
</HEAD><BODY><H1>Hello, Fred!</H1>
</BODY></HTML>
```

That data will get passed over the standard output to the Web server, which in turn will pass it back to the Web browser that Fred is running.

Testing the Script

Before actually installing the script on your Web server, it's helpful to be able to test it to make sure you haven't made any obvious errors. Using `CGI.pm`, you can run a CGI script from the command line to test it, like this:

```
% name.pl
(offline mode: enter name=value pairs on standard input)
```

After that line, you can enter sample form input as a name=value pair. For example, for the Hello form the name is `name` and the value would be a sample name (like `Fred`), so you'd type:

```
name=Fred
```

You don't have to include quotes unless the input has spaces in it. After you've entered your name and value pairs, hit Ctrl-D (Ctrl-Z on Windows) to end the standard input. The script will then run as if it had received that input from the form, and output the result to the screen.

Alternatively, you can also enter the names and values as arguments to the script's command line:

```
% name.pl name=Fred
```

The script will then use those name=value pairs as the input, and not prompt you for more.

Once you've verified your CGI script works as you expect, the final step is to install it on your Web server. Installation might involve putting the script in a special directory called `cgi-bin`, renaming it with a `.cgi` extension, or indicating by some other method to the Web server that your script is a CGI script. (Again, this varies from server to server, so see the docs that came with your server to figure it out.) You may also need to make sure the script is executable or to give it special user permissions. And, finally, you'll need to modify the original HTML file to point to the actual location of the script.

With all that out of the way, you should then be able to bring up the HTML for the form, fill in a name, click on the Submit button, and have the CGI script give you a response. Figure 16.3 shows the response as a Web page.

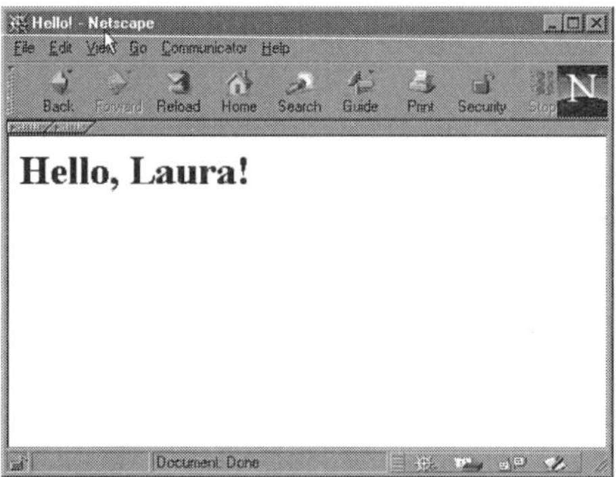

FIGURE 16.3
Hello, the response.

Developing CGI Scripts with CGI.pm

The core of any CGI script is the CGI.pm module. While you can write CGI scripts using raw Perl, or using other various CGI programs out there, CGI.pm is available as part of the Perl distribution, is well-supported and robust, runs across platforms, and gives you just about any feature you might want as you work with CGI. Working without it will make your CGI scripting life much harder.

In the preceding section, I showed you a really simple example of using CGI.pm. Let's explore the features of this module in more detail in this section, so you know the sorts of things you can do with it.

Getting CGI.pm

Chances are good if you have a current version of Perl, you've got CGI.pm bundled with it. If you're not sure, you can check the lib directory of your Perl installation to see if the module is there. If you don't have it, you can download it from the Web site at http://www.genome.wi.mit.edu/ftp/pub/software/WWW/cgi_docs.html, and it's also available as part of CPAN as well. The CGI.pm page also explains how to install it, but the short version is that all you really need to do is copy the CGI.pm file to your Perl lib directory.

In addition to CGI.pm, the CGI.pm package comes with another module called Carp. Carp goes in the CGI directory inside your Perl lib directory (if its not already there). Carp is used for printing helpful error messages to your Web server logs or to the Web browser and is invaluable for debugging CGI scripts as you get into more advanced territory (we'll look at Carp a bit later on).

Both CGI.pm and Carp.pm come with built-in documentation in POD format, which means you can type perldoc CGI to view it (in MacPerl, use the shuck application). You can also find current documentation on the Web at http://www.genome.wi.mit.edu/ftp/pub/software/WWW/cgi_docs.html.

Using CGI.pm

To use CGI.pm in your Perl scripts, you import it like you do any module. CGI.pm has several import tags you can use, including the following:

- :cgi imports features of CGI protocol itself, including param().
- :html2 imports features to help generate HTML 2 tags including start_html() and end_html().
- :form imports features for generating form elements.
- :standard imports all the features from :cgi, :html2, and :form.

- `:html3` imports features from HTML 3.0.
- `:netscape` imports features from Netscape's version of HTML.
- `:html` imports all the features from `:html2`, `:html3`, and `:netscape`.
- `:all` imports everything.

`CGI.pm` is implemented such that you can use it in an object-oriented way (using a CGI object and calling methods defined for that object), or by calling plain subroutines. If you use any of the preceding import tags, you'll have those subroutine names available to you in your script. If you just use `CGI` without any import tags, it's assumed you'll be using the object-oriented version of CGI.

Processing Form Input

The most significant feature that `CGI.pm` gives you is that it handles the CGI-encoded form input that the Web browser sends to the Web server and the server passes on to the script. This input comes from the browser in a special encoded form, sometimes on the standard input and sometimes as keyword arguments, with non-alphanumeric characters encoded in hex. If you were writing a raw CGI processor you'd have to deal with all that decoding yourself (and its not pretty). By using `CGI.pm` you can avoid all that and deal solely with the actual input values, which is what you really care about.

The input you get from a form is composed of key/value pairs, where the key is the name of the form element (as indicated by the `NAME` attribute in HTML), and the value is the actual thing the user typed, selected, or chose from the form when it was submitted. The value you actually get depends on the form element—some values are a string, as with text fields; others might be simply yes or no, as with check boxes. Pop-up menus and scrolling lists created with the HTML `<SELECT>` tag may have multiple values.

The `CGI.pm` module stores these keys and values in a parameter array. To get at them you use the `param()` subroutine. Without any arguments, `param()` returns a list of keys in the parameter array (the names of all the form elements). This is mostly useful to see whether the form was filled out in the case where the CGI script generates both the initial HTML page and the result. You could also call `param()` without any arguments if you were printing out all the keys and values on the form for debugging purposes, like this:

```
foreach $key (param()) {
   print "$key has the value ", param($key), "\n";
}
```

Note that the order of the parameters in the array is the same order in which they were sent by the browser, originally, which in many cases will be the same order in which they appear on the page. However, that behavior isn't guaranteed, so you're safest referring to each form element explicitly if you're concerned about order.

The `param()` subroutine with a form element name as an argument returns the value of that form element, or `undef` if there's no submitted value for that form element. This is probably the way you'll use `param()` most often in your own CGI scripts. The key you use as the argument to `param()` must match the name of the form elements in the HTML file exactly—to get to the value of a text field defined `<INPUT NAME="foozle">` you'd use `param('foozle')`. Most of the time you'll get a single scalar value back, but some form elements that allow multiple selections will return a list of all the possible selections. It's up to you to handle the different values you get from a form in the CGI script.

Generating HTML

The bulk of a CGI script is often taken up mostly by generating the HTML for the response. The scripts we write for handling CGI will probably have more `print` statements than any other scripts we've written so far.

To generate HTML output, you simply print lines of output to the standard output as you would any other script. You have a number of options for doing this:

- Using individual `print` statements
- Using "here" documents
- Using shortcut subroutines from `CGI.pm`

Output with `Print`

The first way is simply to use `print` with the bit of HTML to output, as you've been doing all along, like this:

```
print "<HTML><HEAD><TITLE>This is a Web page</TITLE></HEAD>\n";
print "<BODY BGCOLOR=\"white\">\n";
# and so on
```

Output with Here Documents

While `print` statements work fine, they can get somewhat unwieldy, particularly when you have a lot of print and you have to deal with nested quote marks (as with the "white" value in the preceding example). If you've got a block of HTML to print pretty much verbatim, you can use a Perl feature called a "here" document. Awkward name, but what it means is simply "print everything up to *here*." A here document looks something like this:

```
print <<EOF;
These lines will be printed
as they appear here, without the need
for fancy print statements, "escaped quotes,"
or special newline characters.  Just like this.
EOF
```

That bit of Perl code results in the following output:

```
These lines will be printed
as they appear here, without the need
for fancy print statements, "escaped quotes,"
or special newline characters.  Just like this.
```

In other words, the text outputs pretty much exactly the same way the text appears in the script. The initial `print` line in the here document determines how far to read and print before stopping, using a special code that can be either a word that has no other meaning in the language or a quoted string. Here I used `EOF`, which is a nice, short, common phrase and easy to pick out from the rest of the script.

The quotes you use around that word, if any, determine how the text inside the here document is processed. A single word, like the `EOF` we used above, allows variable interpolation as if the text inside the here document were a double-quoted string. The same is true if you use a double-quoted word (`EOF`). A single-quoted word (`EOF`) suppresses variable interpolation just as it does in a regular single-quoted string.

The end of the here document is that same word or string that started the here document, minus the quotes, on a line by itself with no leading trailing characters or whitespace. After the ending tag you can start another here document, go back to `print`, or use any other lines of Perl code that you like.

For more information on using here documents, see the `perldata` man page.

Output with `CGI.pm` Subroutines

The third way to generate HTML in a CGI script is to use `CGI.pm`'s subroutines for doing so. Most HTML tags have equivalent Perl subroutines in `CGI.pm`, and the `CGI.pm` subroutines have the advantage of letting you insert variable references (through double-quoted strings) and to generate things like form elements quickly. In addition, `CGI.pm` has the `start_html()` and `end_html()` subroutines to print the top and bottom of an HTML file, respectively. All the HTML generation subroutines return strings; you'll need to use them with a `print` to actually print them.

Some subroutines generate one-sided tags that take no arguments (`p()` and `hr()`, for example, which generate `<P>` and `<HR>` tags, respectively). Others create opening and closing tags, in which case they take one or more string arguments for the text between the opening and closing tags. You can nest subroutines inside other subroutines:

```
h1('This is a heading');        # <H1>This is a heading</H1>
b('Bold');                      # <B>Bold</B>
b('some bold and some', i('italic'));   # <B>some bold and some <I>italic</I></B>
ol(
  li('item one),
  li('item two'),
  li('item three'),
);
```


If the HTML tag takes attributes inside the tag itself, indicate those using curly brackets `{}` and the name and value of the attribute separated using => (as with hashes):

```
a({href=>"index.html", name=>"foo"}, "Home Page");
# <A HREF="index.html" NAME="foo">Home Page</A>
```

Most every HTML tag you can use in an HTML file is available as a subroutine, although different tags may be available at different times depending which group of subroutines you import in your `use CGI` line. `CGI.pm` has a particularly robust set of subroutines for generating other form elements. I won't go through all of them here; if you're interested, see the documentation for `CGI.pm`.

Debugging the Result

You've already seen, in the Hello example, one of the ways to debug your scripts before you install them by entering your CGI input as name=value pairs either on the script command line or as standard input. This mechanism can be invaluable in fixing the smaller errors that creep up as you're writing your CGI scripts. By running the script from the command line you can also use the Perl debugger to make sure your script is running right before you install it.

There comes a time, however, when you need to install the CGI script and run it in place to make sure that it's working right. Once it's installed, however, it can be difficult to debug because errors tend to get reported to the browser with unhelpful messages like `Server Error 500`, or to the error logs without any kind of identifiers or timestamps to figure out which errors are yours.

That's where the `CGI::Carp` module comes in. `CGI::Carp` comes with `CGI.pm`, although as with the latter module it should also be part of your standard Perl distribution (make sure you look for it in the CGI subdirectory of Perl's `lib` directory; there's also a regular `Carp` module that's related but not the same thing). `Carp` is used to generate error messages for CGI scripts, which can be useful for debugging those scripts. In particular, the `:fatalsToBrowser` keyword can be very useful for debugging because it prints any Perl errors in the CGI script as an HTML response, which is then displayed in response to the form submission in the browser that called the form in the first place. To echo these errors to the browser, include a `use` line at the top of your script like this:

```
use CGI::Carp qw(:fatalsToBrowser);
```

Even if you don't use `:fatalsToBrowser`, the `CGI::Carp` module provides new definitions of the `warn()` and `die()` functions (and adds the `croak()`, `carp()`, and `confess()` subroutines) such that errors are printed with sensible identifiers and appear in the errors logs for your Web server. (See the documentation for the standard `Carp` module for information on `croak()`, `carp()`, and `confess()`.) `CGI::Carp` is quite useful for debugging your CGI scripts in place.

An Example: Survey

Our Hello World example earlier may have given you a taste of how CGI scripts work, but it was too simple to be of much use. Here's a much more complex script that handles a Web-based survey. The script keeps track of all the survey for the data, handling the input from the current form and generating tables of results based on all the data submitted so far. Figure 16.4 shows our simple survey.

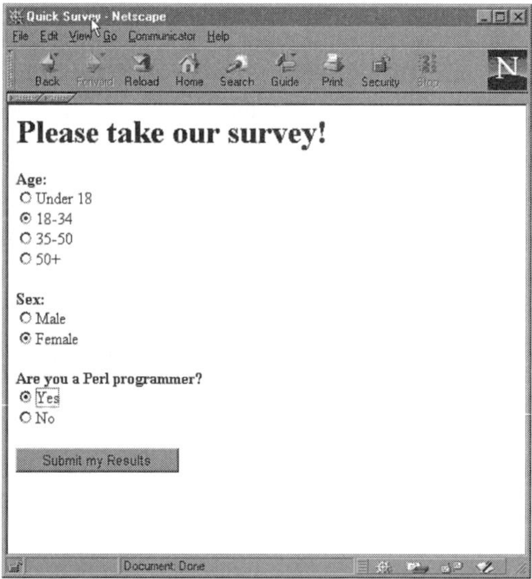

FIGURE 16.4
A simple Web survey.

After filling out the survey, the CGI script processes the input, adds it to the data already received, and generates a set of tables, shown in Figure 16.5.

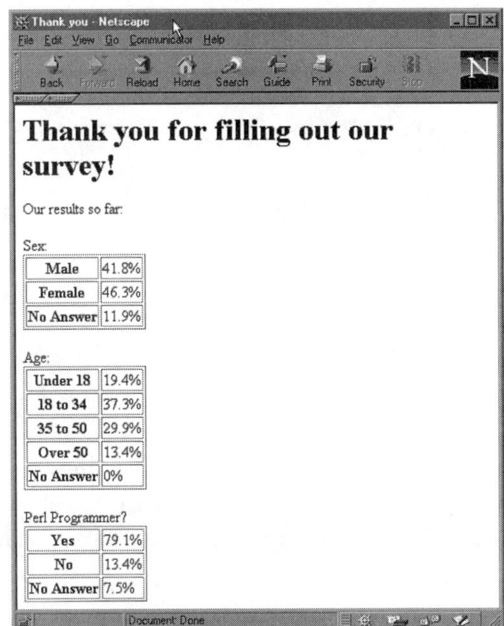

FIGURE 16.5
The Web survey results.

All the data from the survey is stored in a separate file on the Web server. You'll open, read, and write that data file as part of the CGI script to process the form.

The Form

Let's start with the HTML for the form, just to point out the values that you'll be working with in the CGI script. Listing 16.2 shows that HTML code:

LISTING 16.2 `survey.html`

```
<HTML>
<HEAD>
<TITLE>Quick Survey</TITLE>
</HEAD>
<BODY>
<H1>Please take our survey!</H1>
<FORM ACTION="/cgi-bin/survey.pl">
<P><STRONG>Age: </STRONG><BR>
<INPUT TYPE="radio" NAME="age" VALUE="under18">Under 18<BR>
<INPUT TYPE="radio" NAME="age" VALUE="18to34">18-34<BR>
<INPUT TYPE="radio" NAME="age" VALUE="35to50">35-50<BR>
<INPUT TYPE="radio" NAME="age" VALUE="50plus">50+
<P><STRONG>Sex: </STRONG><BR>
```

continues

LISTING 16.2 CONTINUED

```
<INPUT TYPE="radio" NAME="sex" VALUE="male">Male<BR>
<INPUT TYPE="radio" NAME="sex" VALUE="female">Female
<P><STRONG>Are you a Perl programmer? </STRONG><BR>
<INPUT TYPE="radio" NAME="perl" VALUE="yes">Yes<BR>
<INPUT TYPE="radio" NAME="perl" VALUE="no">No
<P><INPUT TYPE="submit" VALUE="Submit my Results">
</FORM>
</BODY>
</HTML>
```

There are only a few important things to note about this HTML code. Here, instead of a text field like we had in the last example, we're using groups of radio buttons. Note that each group has the same name (for example, all four radio buttons in the age group are named "age"). This prevents more than one radio button from being selected at one time. It also means that when you get the input from your script, only one value from each group will appear. You'll have to test for the existence of each one to find out which one was selected.

The Script

The CGI script to process this form accomplishes four main things:

- It opens and reads the survey data file into a hash.
- It processes the input from the form, adding the new data to the old data.
- It writes out the new data to the file again.
- It generates HTML for the output, containing tables generated from the current survey data.

Listing 16.3 shows the code for our CGI script, called `survey.pl`.

LISTING 16.3 THE `survey.pl` SCRIPT

```
#!/usr/bin/perl -w
use strict;
use CGI qw(:standard);

my $results = 'survey_results.txt';
my %data = ();
my $thing = '';
my $val = 0;

open(RESULTS, $results) or die "Can't open results file: $!";
while (<RESULTS>) {
```

```
    ($thing, $val) = split(' ');
    $data{$thing} = $val;
}
close(RESULTS);

# overall total
$data{total}++;

# handle age
if (!param('age')) { $data{age_na}++ }
else {
    if (param('age') eq 'under18') { $data{age_under18}++; }
    elsif (param('age') eq '18to34') { $data{age_18to34}++; }
    elsif (param('age') eq '35to50') { $data{age_35to50}++; }
    elsif (param('age') eq '50plus') { $data{age_50plus}++; }
}

# handle sex
if (!param('sex')) { $data{sex_na}++ }
else {
    if (param('sex') eq 'male') { $data{sex_m}++; }
    elsif (param('sex') eq 'female') { $data{sex_f}++; }
}

# perl
if (!param('perl')) { $data{perl_na}++ }
else {
    if (param('perl') eq 'yes') { $data{perl_y}++; }
    elsif (param('perl') eq 'no') { $data{perl_n}++; }
}

open(RESULTS, ">$results") or die "Can't write to results file: $!";
foreach $thing (keys %data) {
    print RESULTS "$thing $data{$thing}\n";
}
close(RESULTS);

print header;
print start_html('Thank you');
print <<EOF;
<H1>Thank you for filling out our survey!</H1>
<P>Our results so far:
<P>Sex:
<TABLE BORDER><TR><TH>Male</TH><TD>
EOF

print &percent('sex_m'), "</TD></TR>\n";
print "<TR><TH>Female</TH><TD>\n";
print &percent('sex_f'), "</TD></TR>\n";
print "<TR><TH>No Answer</TH><TD>\n";
```

continues

LISTING 16.3 CONTINUED

```
62: print &percent('sex_na'), "</TD></TR>\n";
63: print "</TABLE>\n";
64:
65: print "<P>Age:\n";
66: print "<TABLE BORDER><TR><TH>Under 18</TH><TD>\n";
67: print &percent('age_under18'), "</TD></TR>\n";
68: print "<TR><TH>18 to 34</TH><TD>\n";
69: print &percent('age_18to34'), "</TD></TR>\n";
70: print "<TR><TH>35 to 50</TH><TD>\n";
71: print &percent('age_35to50'), "</TD></TR>\n";
72: print "<TR><TH>Over 50</TH><TD>\n";
73: print &percent('age_50plus'), "</TD></TR>\n";
74: print "<TR><TH>No Answer</TH><TD>\n";
75: print &percent('age_na'), "</TD></TR>\n";
76: print "</TABLE>\n";
77:
78: print "<P>Perl Programmer?\n";
79: print "<TABLE BORDER><TR><TH>Yes</TH><TD>\n";
80: print &percent('perl_y'), "</TD></TR>\n";
81: print "<TR><TH>No</TH><TD>\n";
82: print &percent('perl_n'), "</TD></TR>\n";
83: print "<TR><TH>No Answer</TH><TD>\n";
84: print &percent('perl_na'), "</TD></TR>\n";
85: print "</TABLE>\n";
86:
87: print end_html;
88:
89: sub percent {
90:     if (defined $data{$_[0]}) {
91:         return sprintf("%.1f%%", $data{$_[0]} / $data{total} * 100);
92:     }
93:     else { return '0%'; }
94: }
```

I'm not going to go through this script line by line because much of this is code you've seen in a similar form before (and a whole lot of it is just `print` statements). Here are some of the important parts to note, however:

The name of the survey data file is stored in the `$results` variable in line 10. Here, that file is assumed to be in the same directory as the CGI script itself; you'll need to set the pathname to the appropriate location for your script. That file consists of a set of data keys for each choice in the survey, as well as "na" keys for no answer. Each key has a value for the number of "votes" that have been submitted. Lines 10 through 15 open and read that data file into the `%data` hash, closing it again immediately afterward.

> **Note**
>
> The results file—here, located in the same directory as the CGI script—must be writeable by the Web server. On UNIX, that means the file must have the right permissions so that the user or group ID the Web server runs under (usually `nobody`) can write to it; on Windows that means your security must also be set accordingly. If you run into "can't write to results file" errors when you run this script under a Web server (that didn't happen when you ran it with regular Perl), check your file permissions.

Lines 17 through 41 process the input from the form in groups, corresponding to each group of radio buttons in the HTML file (age, sex, and perl). Note that for each group, you have to test to see if there was no answer (in which case, there won't be a key for that group in the `param()` array `CGI.pm` gives you). If there was a vote, we'll increment the value of that key in the data hash. We also keep track of the overall total (line 16), which we'll need to calculate the percentages for the final output.

After we're done processing the data, we can write out the new data file to that same file, one data key and value per line, separated by a space. The actual order of the keys doesn't matter because they'll just be re-read by the script again into a hash. A simple `foreach` loop in lines 44 and 45 will print the new values to the results file (which we re-opened for writing in line 43).

The second half of the script prints the output to the survey so the user can get a response from the survey. Starting from line 49 we print the output starting with the header (line 49), the beginning of the HTML file (line 50), and some boilerplate HTML printed with a here document in lines 51 through 56.

Line 58 is where things start getting interesting. The rest of the HTML file consists of tables that show the current results of the survey. Much of the printing here involves the HTML code for the tables, but the final percentages are calculated using a help subroutine we defined called `&percent()`. The `&percent()` routine, defined in lines 89 through 94, generates a percent string based on the value it's given divided by the total number of responses. It also makes sure that the given data key actually has a value (if it's zero, it won't even appear in the `%data` hash). And, finally it formats the percentage with one decimal point and a percent sign using the `sprintf` function (note that because of the `sprintf` formatting codes, if you want to print an actual percent sign, you have to type it as `%%`).

Going Deeper

As I mentioned at the beginning of this lesson, I could easily go on for pages and pages and chapters and chapters about all the different aspects of CGI. Documenting all of CGI.pm itself would give us a much larger lesson than I've got here. There are a few other features of CGI.pm I'd like to mention, however. All of these features are documented in the documentation for CGI.pm (perldoc CGI will show it to you), as well as in the Web page at http://www.genome.wi.mit.edu/ftp/pub/software/WWW/cgi_docs.html.

If you need further details about CGI itself, feel free to visit the Web pages or to read the book I mentioned at the beginning of this lesson. The Usenet newsgroup comp.infosystems.www.authoring.cgi can also provide assistance in getting your CGI scripts to work on different platforms.

Using CGI Variables

When your CGI script gets called, along with the data from the browser, the Web server also provides several values in its environment that relate to the script itself, to the Web server, and to the system running the browser that submitted the form in the first place. On UNIX systems, these are environment variables that you can access from inside your Perl script using the %ENV hash. Other Web servers may have different ways of passing in these variables. However, CGI.pm provides subroutines to access these variables in a way that works across platforms and Web servers. You aren't required to use any of these subroutines in your CGI scripts, but you may find the data useful.

Table 16.1 shows the CGI variable subroutines for CGI.pm.

TABLE 16.1 CGI VARIABLE SUBROUTINES

Subroutine	*What It Gives You*
accept()	A list of MIME types the browser will accept.
auth_type()	The authentication type (usually 'basic').
path_info()	Path information encoded into the script URL (if used).
path_translated()	Same as path_info() expanded into a full pathname.
query_string()	Arguments to the CGI script tagged on to the URL.
raw_cookie()	Returns raw cookie information. Use the cookie() subroutines to manage this information.
referer()	The URL of the page that called this script (note the incorrect spelling).
remote_addr()	The IP address of the host that called this script (the browser's host).
remote_ident()	The user's ID, but only if the system is running ident (not common).

Subroutine	*What It Gives You*
`remote_host()`	The name of the host that called this script.
`remote_user()`	The name of the user that called this script (usually set only if the user has logged in using authentication).
`request_method()`	The Web server method the script was called with (for example, `GET` or `POST`).
`script_name()`	The name of the script.
`server_name()`	The host name of the Web server that called this script.
`server_software()`	The name and version of the Web server software.
`virtual_host()`	For servers that support virtual hosts, the name of the virtual host that is running this script.
`server_port()`	The network port the server is using (usually 80).
`user_agent()`	The browser name and version that called this script, for example `Mozilla/4.x (Win95)`.
`user_name()`	The name of the user who called this script (almost never set).

`POST` Versus `GET`

CGI scripts can be called by a browser in one of two forms: `POST` and `GET`. `GET` submissions encode the form elements into the URL itself; `POST` sends the form elements over the standard input. `GET` can also be used to submit a form without actually having a form—for example, you could have a link in which the URL contained the hard-coded form elements to submit.

Inside your CGI script, `CGI.pm` will process both these kinds of methods and store them in the parameters array, so you don't have to worry about which method was used to submit the script. If you really want to get the parameters from the URL, use `url_param()` instead of `param()`.

Redirection

Sometimes the result of a CGI script isn't a raw HTML file, but rather a pointer to an existing HTML file on this server or elsewhere. `CGI.pm` supports this result with the `redirect()` subroutine:

```
print redirect('http://www.anotherserver.com/anotherfile.html');
```

The redirect tells the user's browser to retrieve a specific page on the Web, rather than to display any HTML. Because a CGI script that uses redirect isn't doesn't create a new Web page, you should not combine a redirect and any HTML code in the output from a CGI script.

Cookies and File Upload

`CGI.pm` also enables you to manage cookie values and to handle files that get uploaded via the file upload feature of HTML forms. For managing cookies, see the `cookie()` subroutine in `CGI.pm`. File upload works similarly to ordinary form elements; the `param()` subroutine is used to return the filename that was entered in the form. That filename is also a filehandle that is open and which you can read lines from using the standard Perl mechanisms.

See the `CGI.pm` documentation for information on both these things.

CGI Scripts and Security

Every CGI script is a potential security hole on your Web server. A CGI script runs on your server based on input from any random person out on the Web. Depending on how carefully you write your scripts and how determined someone is, your CGI scripts could offer openings up to and including allowing malicious users to break into your system and irreparably damage it.

The best way to prevent a problem is to understand it and take steps to avoid it. A great starting point is at the World Wide Web security FAQ at `http://www.genome.wi.mit.edu/WWW/faqs/www-security-faq.html`. Perl also includes a feature, called *taint mode*, which prevents you from using nonsecure data in a way that could do harm to your system. More about taint mode on Day 20, "Odds and Ends."

Embedding Perl in Web Servers

Each time a Perl CGI script is called from a Web server, Perl is called to execute that script. For very busy Web servers, running lots and lots of CGI scripts can mean running many copies of Perl at once, and a considerable load for the machine acting as the Web server. To help with performance, many Web servers provide a mechanism for embedding the Perl interpreter inside the Web server itself, so that scripts that run on Web servers no longer run as actual CGI scripts. Instead, they run as if they were Web server libraries, reducing the overhead and startup time for each script. In many cases, you don't even have to modify your CGI scripts to get them to work under this system.

Different Web servers on different platforms provide different mechanisms for doing this. You'll need to check the documentation that comes with your Web server to see if Perl-based CGI scripts can be embedded, and if so, where to get the tools or modules to embed them.

If you're using an ISAPI-based Web server on Windows (such as IIS), you'll need the Perl for ISAPI package (sometimes called PerlIIS). This package is part of ActiveState's version of Perl for Windows and is installed with that package. You can also get it separately from ActiveState's Web site at `http://www.activestate.com`.

If you're using the open source Apache Web server, `mod_perl` is an Apache module that embeds the Perl interpreter in the Apache Web server. While the most obvious feature this gives you is better CGI performance, it also allows you access, with Perl, to all of Apache's internal extension APIs, allowing almost infinite customization of the Web server itself. Find out more about the Apache Web server at `http://www.apache.org` and from the Apache/Perl Integration Project, the developers of `mod_perl`, at `http://perl.apache.org`.

Summary

Not everything to do with Perl has to involve long and involved scripts with lots of subroutines. Sometimes the most useful things in Perl can be done using modules with a little glue code to get the result you want. CGI is a terrific example of this; the `CGI.pm` module covers up most of the gritty parts of CGI scripting and makes it easy to get the values from a form or other CGI submission and return an HTML file as the result.

Today you learned something about using Perl for CGI, including how CGI works from the browser to the server to the script and back again; how `CGI.pm` can be imported and used in your script, and how to use its various features to make your life with CGI more pleasant. We also explored a couple of CGI examples: a survey form that keeps track of the survey data in an external file, and a color-generation script that is its own form and which maintains the current form values each time the form is regenerated. I can't guarantee that this lesson has given you everything you need to create CGI scripts (because it hasn't), but hopefully it's given you a starting point from which you can work.

The subroutines you've learned about in this lesson are all part of the `CGI.pm` module, and include

- `param()` gets the parameters that were given to the CGI script, usually as part of a form submission. `param()` with no arguments returns a list of the keys (form element names) available; `param()` with a key argument returns the value for that key.
- `print header()` prints the CGI header for the output. The `print_header()` subroutine without any arguments assumes the output will be in HTML format.
- `start_html()` returns the top part of an HTML page, including the `<HTML>`, `<HEAD>`, `<TITLE>` and `<BODY>` tags. Different arguments to the `start_html()` tag will generate different values for the HTML (for example, a single string argument will set the title of the page.
- `end_html()` generates closing `</BODY>` and `</HTML>` tags for the output.

Q&A

Q I've seen a number of CGI scripts written in Perl that don't use `CGI.pm`; they use other libraries like `cgi-lib.pl`. Are those bad scripts that should be fixed?

A Not necessarily. There are a number of libraries floating around the Web for managing CGI scripts with Perl; `cgi-lib.pl` is one of the more popular ones. There's nothing wrong with using those other libraries. I chose to use `CGI.pm` for this lesson because it's become the standard for using Perl with CGI, it's a well-behaved module and follows the standard module conventions, it's object-oriented if you choose to use it that way and, most importantly, it's available as part of the standard Perl distribution. This gives it significant advantages over other libraries.

Q My CGI scripts work from the command line, but don't work when I try them from a Web page. What am I doing wrong?

A With all the different platforms and Web servers out there, there's no one single answer to this question. Is the script executable? Is the place where you put your script an "official" CGI location according to your server (usually a special `cgi-bin` directory or something like it)? Does your script have the right permissions (Web servers run CGI scripts as a special user with limited permissions)? Are you sure you even have a Web server running on your machine?

The Web sites I gave you earlier in the lesson have ideas and suggestions for debugging CGI scripts.

Q My Web site is stored on a UNIX machine. I can run CGI scripts there. But I'd like to write and debug my CGI scripts on my Windows NT machine at home so I don't have to be logged in all the time. Can I do this?

A Through the wonder of cross-platform Perl and the `CGI.pm` module, you certainly can. You'll need a Web server running on your NT system—hopefully one similar or identical to the one running on your UNIX machine—but then you can install and debug and run CGI scripts locally all you want. Watch out for differences in paths to files and differences in how different servers deal with CGI, and try to keep things simple, and you should need little work to get your scripts to run on UNIX.

Q I modified the survey file to be used with a guestbook-like script, which allows people to post comments to a Web page. But I'm having problems where if multiple people post to the Web page at once, sometimes the file gets written to before the other one is done, and the comments get lost or weird things happen. What's going on here?

A The survey example here demonstrates basic CGI scripting in the technical sense; for real production Web sites you'll need to go a little deeper (I recommend the Web sites I mentioned earlier, or another book). In particular, if you've got an external file that will potentially be written to by multiple users at once—as any CGI script might—you'll want to "lock" the file before writing to it, and then release the lock after you're done. This could be as easy as creating another temporary file, called, for example, `survey.lock`. In your script, before actually writing to the survey results file, you would:

- Check to see if the lock file exists. If it does, someone else is writing to the file. Wait a little bit (check out the `sleep` function for this) and try again.
- Once the file is free, set the lock file yourself.
- Write the data.
- Unlock the file.

Workshop

The workshop provides quiz questions to help you solidify your understanding of the material covered and exercises to give you experience in using what you've learned. Try to understand the quiz and exercise answers before you go on to tomorrow's lesson.

Quiz

1. What does CGI stand for? What's it used for?
2. What does the `CGI.pm` module give you? How do you get it and use it?
3. Why would you want to run a CGI script on the command line before trying to run it via a Web page?
4. How do you use the `param()` subroutine?
5. List three ways to print HTML code as output for your CGI script.
6. Why is a here document sometimes more useful than `print`?

Exercises

1. Write a CGI script that prints the form elements it was submitted with as a bulleted list. HINT: bulleted lists in HTML look like this:

```
<UL>
<LI>One item
<LI>Two items
<LI>Three items
</UL>
```

Another hint: `param()` without any arguments gives you a list of all the form element names the script was submitted with.

2. **BUG BUSTER**: What's wrong with this bit of script?

```
if (!param()) { $data{sex_na}++ }
else {
    if (param() eq 'male') { $data{sex_m}++; }
    elsif (param() eq 'female') { $data{sex_f}++; }
}
```

3. Write a CGI script that prints a simple HTML page (a hello world is fine) but also keeps track of how many times the page has been accessed and prints that value on the page as well.
4. Write a CGI script to implement a very simple "guestbook"-like feature that allows users to post one-line comments to a Web page. Keep track of all past postings. You can assume the existence of an HTML form with two elements: a text field called `mail` for the email address of the poster, and a text field called `comment` for comments.

Answers

Here are the answers to the workshop questions in the previous section.

Quiz Answers

1. CGI stands for Common Gateway Interface and refers to programs that run on the Web server in response to requests from a Web browser (commonly from a form on an HTML page).
2. The `CGI.pm` module provides behavior for writing, running, and debugging CGI scripts. It provides a number of subroutines for managing input to and output from those scripts as well as other utility subroutines for just about any aspect of CGI you can think of.

   The `CGI.pm` module is shipped with most current versions of Perl. If it is not already available as part of your Perl distribution, you can download and install it from the URL mentioned earlier in this lesson.

   To use the CGI module, you import it like you do any other module: with `use` and an import tag such as `:standard` or `:all`.
3. Running a CGI script from the command line is usually easier to find the smaller syntax or basic errors you might have made without you needing to install the script on the Web server, connect to the Internet, and so on. By running the script

on the command line and giving it sample data, you can test your script before actually putting it online.

4. The `param()` subroutine is used to find out the values of any form elements on the Web page that called this script. Without any arguments, `param()` returns a list of keys referring to the names of the form elements. With a key argument (a string), `param()` returns the value associated with that form element.
5. You can print HTML code using one of these methods:
   - Use regular `print` statements. Watch out for embedded quotes!
   - Here documents.
   - Various subroutines via the `CGI.pm` module.
6. Here documents provide a way to print a block of text verbatim: all newlines and quotes are printed verbatim. Here documents provide a way for you to avoid a lot of repetitive `print` statements or escaped quotation marks.

16

Exercise Answers

1. Here's one way to do it:

```
#!/usr/bin/perl -w
use strict;
use CGI qw(:standard);

my @keys = param();

print header;
print start_html('Hello!');
print "<H1>Key/Value Pairs</H1>\n";
print "<UL\n";

foreach my $name (@keys) {
    print "<LI>$name = ", param($name), "\n";
}
print "</UL>\n";

print end_html;
```

2. The `param()` subroutine is called without any arguments. In some cases—such as the one in Exercise 1—this may be exactly what you want to do. In this case, however, since the tests are looking for string values, `param()` should probably be called with some sort of string argument to extract a value from the form parameters.

3. Here's one way to do it (don't forget to create `count.txt` beforehand):

```
#!/usr/bin/perl -w
use strict;
use CGI qw(:standard);

my $countfile = 'count.txt';
my $count = '';

open(COUNT, $countfile) or die "Can't open counter file: $!";
while (<COUNT>) {
    $count = $_;
}
close(COUNT);

$count++;

open(COUNT, ">$countfile") or die "Can't write to counter file: $!";
print COUNT $count;
close(COUNT);

print header;
print start_html('Hello!');
print "<H1>Hello, World</H1>\n";
print "<P>This page has been visited $count times.\n";

print end_html;
```

4. Here's one (particularly simple) way of doing it. This script assumes a file of past comments, one per line, with the email address first.

```
#!/usr/bin/perl -w
use strict;
use CGI qw(:standard);

my $guestbook = 'guest.txt';
my $mail = '';                    # email address
my $comment = '';                 # comments

open(GUEST, $guestbook) or die "Can't open guestbook file: $!";

print header;
print start_html('Comments');
print "<H1>Comments</H1>\n";
print "<P>Comments about this Web site!\n";
print "<HR>\n";

while (<GUEST>) {
    ($mail, $comment) = split(' ',$_,2);
    if ($mail) {
        if (!$comment) { $comment = "nothing\n"; }
        else {  print "<P><B>$mail says:</B> $comment"; }
    }
}
```

```
$mail = param('mail');
$comment = param('comment');
print "<P><B>$mail says:</B> $comment\n";

open(GUEST, ">>$guestbook") or die "Can't open guestbook file: $!";
print GUEST "$mail $comment\n";

print end_html;
```

WEEK 3

DAY 17

Managing Files and Directories

On Day 15, "Working with Files and I/O," we covered dealing with reading and writing files inside a Perl script. In today's lesson, we'll look at several other aspects of managing files—in particular, dealing with various aspects of the file system itself from inside your scripts. Here's what you learn about today:

- Managing files: removing, renaming, copying, and linking them, and changing permissions
- Managing directories: navigating, creating, and removing them
- Getting the contents of directories with file "globs" (a way to indicate groups of files quickly) and using directory handles

Managing Files

In addition to simply reading from and writing to files, you can also manage them from inside Perl, just as you might from a command line or in a file manager: you can rename them, delete them, change their permissions, or create links to them. Each of these tasks makes use of several Perl built-in functions. In this section, you get an overview of each of these.

Renaming Files

To rename a file from one name to another, keeping its contents intact, use the `rename` function with two arguments: the old name of the file and the new name:

```
rename myfile, myfile.bak;
```

If a file with the same name as the new file already exists, Perl will overwrite it. If you're used to UNIX, this won't be a problem. If you're a Windows or Mac user, beware! There are no checks to make sure you're not overwriting an existing file. You might want to test to make sure that the new file doesn't exist (with one of the file tests, such as `-e`) before you rename it.

The `rename` function returns `1` or `0` (true or false) depending on whether the rename was successful or not. You (or the user running the script) must have the right file permissions to rename the file.

Creating and Following Links

The UNIX version of Perl also provides two functions for creating links between files: `link` and `symlink`, which create hard and symbolic links, respectively (similar to the UNIX command `ln(1)`). *Hard links* are used to create a file with more than one name; if you remove any of those names (including the original file), the file will continue to exist as long as there are multiple names for it. *Symbolic links* are pointers to other files; if you remove the link, the file will continue to exist, but if you remove the original file, the symbolic link will no longer point to anything useful. Some UNIX systems may not support symbolic links.

Use either the `link` or `symlink` functions with two arguments: the name of the original file to link to, and the name of the new link. Take this example:

```
link file1, file2;
```

Both functions return `1` (true) or `0` (false) depending on whether they were successful or not.

Both hard and symbolically linked files are transparent to Perl; if you use `open` with a filename that is actually a link, the original file will be opened instead. You can test to see if a given file is a symbolic link with the `-l` file test, and then follow that link to its original location with the `readlink` function:

```
if (-l $file) {  # file is a link
   $realfile = readlink $file;   # get the real file
}
```

Note that `readlink` returns the location of the real file as a relative path to the symbolic link, which means you may need to expand that path into a full path or change directories to the place where the symbolic link is to be able to use the original file's pathname. More about changing directories further on in this chapter.

Using Perl for Windows? Neither hard nor symbolic links are available in Perl for Windows. You can use the `Win32::Shortcut` module to create Windows Explorer shortcuts on Windows.

In MacPerl, hard links are not available, but symbolic links are analogous to aliases in the Finder. The `symlink` function will create a finder alias, the `-l` file test will return true if a file is an alias, and `readlink` will give you the location of the thing the alias is linked to.

Removing Files and Links

You're done with a file, you're sure you don't need it anymore. How do you get rid of it? Use the `unlink` function (despite its name, it's used to remove *both* links and files). It works much like the UNIX command `rm` or the DOS command `del`; it does not move the file to a trashcan or recycle bin like Windows or the Mac. Once the file is removed, it's really removed. Be careful or you can easily delete files you actually wanted to be there.

`unlink` takes a list argument, which can be a single file or a list of files. It returns the number of files it deleted:

```
unlink temp, config, foo;
```

Be aware that on some systems—UNIX being the most obvious one—Perl has no qualms about deleting read-only files, so watch what you're doing (the state of being read-only actually determines whether the *contents* of the file can be changed, not whether or not that filename can be moved or deleted).

The `unlink` function, when used on a hard link, will remove that link. Other hard links to the file will continue to exist. On a symbolic link, you'll remove the link, but not the original file. You can use `readlink` to follow any symbolic links. Note that removing a file that has other symbolic links to it will cause those symbolic links to point to nothing.

You cannot use `unlink` to remove directories; you'll learn how to remove directories in the section "Managing and Navigating Directories."

Other Operations

I'm going to lump a number of other file-related functions together here, because these operations tend to vary from platform to platform (or not to exist at all on Windows or

Mac). Table 17.1 shows some of the other file-management functions available on UNIX systems, all of which correspond to actual UNIX commands. If you're interested in running any of the functions listed in Table 17.1, check the documentation for your particular version of Perl to see if these functions are supported (or if the capabilities are supported through other means such as platform-specific modules).

For more information on any of these functions, see the `perlfunc` man page.

TABLE 17.1 OTHER FILE MANAGEMENT FUNCTIONS

Function	*What It Means*
`chmod`	Change the permissions for the file (read, write, execute, for world, group or owner). Windows and Mac have limited versions of this command that only accept permissions of 0666 (read and write) and 0444 (read only or locked).
`chown`	Change the owner of the file (UNIX only)
`fileno`	Return the file descriptor number for the file
`utime`	Change the timestamp for a file

For managing file permissions and attributes on Windows and Windows NT, consider the `Win32::File` and `Win32::FileSecurity` modules, which allow you to check and modify file attributes and NT user permissions.

Managing and Navigating Directories

Just as you can work with files inside Perl as you might in a shell or command line, you can also navigate around your file system and manage directories (or folders, depending on your OS loyalties). You can find out the current directory, change the current directory, list the contents of that directory or some subset of its files, and create or remove the directories themselves. This section explains some of the nuances of performing these operations with Perl.

Navigating Directories

Each Perl script has a notion of a current working directory, that is, the directory from which the script was called (if you're used to working with command-line based systems, this will be no surprise to you). On the Mac, with droplet scripts, the current working directory is the location of the droplet itself.

To change the current directory from inside a Perl script, use the `chdir` function:

```
chdir "images";
```

As with the directory names in the open function, watch out for pathnames and different systems. Relative paths, as in this example, are fine. This example changes the current working directory to the images directory, which is stored in the same directory in which the script was originally called (whew!).

Is it possible to actually find out what directory you're currently in? Yes, but it varies depending on the system on which you're running. In UNIX, the back-quote operator can execute the UNIX pwd command to find out the current directory (you'll learn more about back-quotes on Day 18, "Perl and the Operating System"):

```
$curr =`pwd`;
```

This method also works in MacPerl. On Windows, the Win32::GetCWD function will give you the current working directory. However, the best way to find out the current working directory—and the method that will work across platforms—is to use the Cwd module, part of the standard library. The Cwd module gives you a cwd function, which returns the current working directory (in fact, cwd actually executes `pwd` on UNIX, so you're safe there as well):


```
use Cwd;
$curr = cwd();
```

Listing Files

Perl provides two ways to get a list of files in a directory: the first, *file globbing*, gives you a list of specific files matching a pattern; the second method, using the opendir and readdir functions, allows you to get a complete list of all files in a directory.

File Globbing

The somewhat bizarrely named technique called file globbing lets you get a list of files in the current directory that match a certain, simple pattern. If you've used a command-line system, and you've ever listed files using a pattern such as *.txt or *foo*, then you've done file globbing (although you may not have known it was called that).

> The term *glob*, in case you haven't guessed, is borrowed from UNIX. Never use a simple word when a weird one will work just as well.

File globbing allows you to indicate a set of filenames using a *. Don't confuse file globbing with regular expressions—here, the * simply stands for any character (zero or more), and it's the only special character you can use. The result of a file glob is all the filenames in the current directory that match the pattern: *.html will return all the filenames that end with a .html extension, *foo* will return all the files with foo in their names, and so on. You could then use those filenames to perform operations on each file in turn.

Perl has two ways of creating file globs: the <> operator, which looks like the input operator but isn't, and the `glob` function.

To use the <> operator for file globs, put the pattern inside the brackets:

```
@files = <*.pl>;
```

This expression, using <> in a list context, returns a list of all the files with a `.pl` extension. If you use <> as a glob in a scalar context, you get each filename in turn, just like with input (and if you stick it inside a `while` loop, each filename will get assigned to `$_`, just like input as well).

So, for example, this snippet will print out a list of all the files in the current directory that end with a `.txt` extension:

```
while (<*.txt>) {
   print $_, "\n";
}
```

Don't confuse the <> operator for globbing with the <> operator for input—they may look the same, but they behave differently. The latter needs a file handle as an argument and reads the contents of that input file; the former returns the plain filename strings that match the pattern in the current directory.

Because it's so easy to confuse the use of <> for globbing and for input, there is also the `glob` function, which makes globbing more apparent and less open to confusion. With the `glob` function, put the file glob pattern inside quotes:

```
@files = glob "*.pl";
```

The result is the same; you end up with a list of files that end with the `.pl` extension (or one at a time, in scalar context). The latter form is preferable to the former in modern Perl scripts.

Directory Listings

The second way to get a listing of files in a directory is through directory handles, which look and behave sort of like file handles, but only apply to directories. Reading with directory handles will give you a list of all the files in a directory, including hidden files starting with a dot (which file globs won't give you), as well as `.` and `..` for the current and parent directories on UNIX and Windows (the Mac doesn't print these as actual directory elements, although you can use `:` and `::` to refer to the current and parent directories).

Just as you open and close file handles, so do you open and close directory handles using the opendir and closedir functions. The opendir function takes two arguments: the name of a directory handle—of your choosing—and the directory to print:

```
opendir(DIR, ".") or die "Can't open directory: $!\n";
```

As with the open function, you should always check the result and fail gracefully with the die function (the $! variable is helpful here as well).

The directory file handle (here DIR) follows all the same rules as a file handle in terms of naming. Directory file handles are also entirely separate from file handles—you could give both the same name and they would not conflict.

Once the file handle is open, use readdir to read from it. As with the input operator <>, readdir returns a single filename in scalar context, and a list of all the filenames in list context. So, for example, this snippet will open the current directory (the "." directory on UNIX and Windows; use ":" on Mac instead), and print a directory listing:

```
opendir(CURR, ".") or die "can't open directory: $!\n";
while (defined($file = readdir(CURR))) {
   print "$file\n";
}
```

Note that unlike the input operator <>, readdir does not assign anything automatically to the $_ variable. You can do that yourself inside the while loop or just use a temporary variable (as I've done here).

Readdir gives you a list of all the files and subdirectories in the directory. If you want to screen out specific files (hidden files, . or ..), you'll have to do that yourself with a regular expression test.

Once you're finished with the directory handle, close it using the closedir function:

```
closedir(CURR);
```

Making and Removing Directories

You can also create new directories and remove unused directories from inside Perl using the mkdir and rmdir functions.

The mkdir function takes two arguments: a directory (folder) name, and a set of permissions. On UNIX, the permissions refer to the standard permission bits from the chmod command in octal format (0 plus three numbers 0 through 7). On Windows and the Mac, the permissions argument is required but not useful; use 0777 as the permissions argument and you'll be fine:

```
mkdir temp, 0777;
```

0777 is an octal number that refers to UNIX permission bits for read, write, and execute permissions for world, group, and owner. Mac and Windows use different forms of file and directory permissions, and don't use the permissions argument to `mkdir` (although you'll need to put something in there, anyhow. 0777 is a good general purpose answer).

The `mkdir` function creates the given directory in the script's current working directory. You can create directories in different locations using full path names, by changing the current directory first, or if you want to get really fancy, check out the `File::Path` module, part of the standard library, which lets you create or remove whole subsets of directories.

To remove a directory, use `rmdir`:

```
rmdir temp;
```

The directory must be empty (contain no files) for you to be able to remove it.

An Example: Creating Links

Here's a useful example I tend to use a whole lot in real life: Given a directory full of files that are either GIF or JPEG images (that is, they have `.gif`, `.jpeg`, or `.jpg` extensions), this script will generate an HTML file, called `index.html`, which contains nothing but links to each of the files. This is a good way to get a whole lot of images up on the Web really quickly without having to spend a lot of time creating HTML files (or it at least provides a basic file you can then edit to make it read better).

The script I wrote for this task uses file handles to open and write to the index.html file, directory handles to read the contents of the current directory, and file tests and regular expressions to match the files we're actually looking for. Listing 17.1 shows the result.

INPUT **LISTING 17.1** THE `imagegen.pl` SCRIPT

```
#!/usr/bin/perl -w
use strict;
use Cwd;

open(OUT, ">index.html") or die "Can't open index file: $!\n";
&printhead();
&processfiles();
&printtail();

```

continues

LISTING 17.1 CONTINUED

```
10: sub printhead {
11:     my $curr = cwd();
12:     print OUT "<HTML>\n<HEAD>\n";
13:     print OUT "<TITLE>Image files in directory $curr</TITLE>\n";
14:     print OUT "</HEAD>\n<BODY>\n";
15:     print OUT "<H1>Image Files</H1>\n";
16:     print OUT "<P>";
17: }
18:
19: sub processfiles {
20:     opendir(CURRDIR, '.') or die "Can't open directory ($!),
        exiting.\n";
21:     my $file = "";
22:
23:     while (defined($file = readdir(CURRDIR))) {
24:         if (-f $file and $file =~ /(\.gif¦\.jpe?g)$/) {
25:             print OUT  "<A HREF=\"$file\">$file</A><BR>\n";
26:         }
27:     }
28:     closedir(CURRDIR)
29: }
30:
31: sub printtail {
32:     print OUT "</BODY></HTML>\n";
33:     close(OUT);
34: }
```


We start by opening the output file (index.html) in line 5. Note the > character, which indicates an output file handle.

The `&printhead()` subroutine, in lines 10 through 17, simply prints out the top part of an HTML file. The only tricky part is the use of the current working directory in the title of the page, which we get using the `cwd()` function (as imported from the `Cwd` module in line 3). I didn't bother using a "here" document to print out the HTML code; that would have ended up being even more lines than are already here.

The `&processfiles()` subroutine (lines 19 through 29) is where the real work goes on. Here, we open the current directory in line 20 (for the Mac, change the `"."` to `":"`), and then loop over each filename in that directory in the `while` loop in lines 23 through 26. The test in line 24 checks to see if the file is an actual file and not a directory (the `-f` test), and uses a regular expression to only operate on image files (those that have a `.gif`, `.jpg`, or `.jpeg` extension). If the current file is indeed an image file, we print out a link to that file in line 25, using the filename as the actual link text.

Note that using the filename as the link text doesn't make for very descriptive links—you could end up with a set of links that say "image1.gif," "image2.gif," "image3.gif," and so on. Not very descriptive. But it's a start; after the script runs you could edit the HTML to create more descriptive links ("nice sunset," "Easter parade," "Bill behaving foolishly," and so on).

To finish up the script we call the `&printtail()` subroutine, which simply prints the end of the HTML file and closes the output file handle.

Going Deeper

In addition to the functions I've described in this lesson and on Day 15, all of which are described in the `perlfunc` man page, there are also quite a few modules in the standard module library for managing files and file handles.

Many of these modules are simply object-oriented wrappers for the standard file operations; others are especially useful for covering up or getting around cross-platform issues. Still others simply provide convenience functions for managing files and directories.

I've mentioned a number of these modules previously in this chapter—`Getopt` and `Cwd` in particular. Table 17.2 shows the more complete list; for details on any of these modules, see the `perlmod` man page.

TABLE 17.2 FILE-RELATED MODULES

Module Name	*What It Does*
`Cwd`	Finds out the current working directory in a safe, cross-platform way
`DirHandle`	An object-oriented wrapper for manipulating directory handles
`File::Basename`	Allows you to parse file and directory pathnames in a cross-platform manner
`File::CheckTree`	Performs multiple file tests on a group of files
`File::Copy`	Copies files or file handles
`File::Find`	Similar to the UNIX find command, traverses a directory tree to find a specific file that matches a specific pattern
`File::Path`	Creates or removes multiple directories or directory trees
`FileCache`	Some systems may not let you have large numbers of files open at once; this gets around that limit
`FileHandle`	An object-oriented wrapper for manipulating file handles
`Getopt::Long`	Manages script arguments (complicated POSIX syntax)
`Getopt::Std`	Manages script arguments (simpler single-character syntax)
`SelectSaver`	Saves and restores file handles (Used with the `select` function. We'll look at `select` on Day 20, "Odds and Ends.")

Summary

No Perl script is an island. At some point, chances are good your script is going to need to peek outside at the world of the file system, particularly if your script reads and writes extensively from files. On Day 15, you learned how to read and write the contents of the files themselves; today, we covered how to handle the bigger issues of file and directory management from inside Perl scripts.

We started with files: renaming them, linking them, and moving them as you might outside your script with a command line or iconic file manager.

If you can manage files, you must be able to manage directories. And so, in the second half of this lesson, we discussed creating and removing directories, printing and changing the current working directory from inside the Perl script, and reading lists of the files inside a directory (either through the use of file globs or by reading from a directory handle.

Q&A

Q I'm trying to write a portable script that reads in a config file. I can use forward slashes in pathnames for both UNIX and Windows, but the Mac with its colon paths is really screwing things up. How can I get around this?

A You could use a test to see if you're running on a Mac, and then set up the path separator in the appropriate way (and build your file paths by appending strings together). Use the Config module to figure out what platform you're running on:

```
use Config;
if ( $Config{'osname'} =~ /^macos/i ) {
   # ... Macintosh-specific stuff goes here
}
```

Q I'm on UNIX. I was testing a script that reads from a file and then deletes it. Because I didn't want it to actually delete the file until I was done debugging the script, I removed write permission from the file. But Perl went ahead and deleted it anyhow. Why?

A Setting the permissions on a file determines whether or not you can read or write the contents of that file. The filename—and whether or not that file can be renamed, moved, or changed—is controlled by the permissions of the enclosing directory. To actually prevent Perl from deleting files, remove write permission from the directory the file is in. Or—even better—comment out your `unlink` command until you've got the rest of the script debugged.

There's a page at `http://www.perl.com/CPAN-local/doc/FMTEYEWTK/file-dir-perms` that explains how this works in excruciating detail.

Q You've described how to rename a file, how to link to one, and how to remove it. How do you copy a file?

A You could just open both the file to copy from and the file to copy to and then read lines from one and print them to the other. Or you could use back-quotes to call the system copy command (as you'll learn on Day 18). Or you could use the `File::Copy` module, which gives you a copy function for copying files or file handles from a source to a destination.

Workshop

The workshop provides quiz questions to help you solidify your understanding of the material covered and exercises to give you experience in using what you've learned. Try to understand the quiz and exercise answers before you go on to tomorrow's lesson.

Quiz

1. What's the difference between a hard link and a symbolic link? What happens if you remove the file that you've linked to with either one?
2. What's the difference between `` `pwd` `` and `cwd()`? Why would you want to use one over the other?
3. What is a file glob? Why are they useful?
4. What's the difference between a file glob of `<*>` and the list of files you get with `readdir()`?
5. What are the differences between file handles and directory handles?
6. What does the permissions argument to `mkdir` do?

Exercises

1. Write a script that reads in a list of files from the current directory and prints them in alphabetical order. If there are directories, print those names with a slash (/) following them.
2. **BUG BUSTER:** This script is supposed to remove all the files and directories from the current directory. It doesn't. Why not?

```
while (<foo*>) {
   unlink $_;
}
```

3. **BUG BUSTER:** How about this one?

```
#!/usr/bin/perl -w

opendir(DIR, '.') or die "can't open directory ($!), exiting.\n";
```

```
while (readdir(DIR)) {
  print "$_\n";
}
closedir(DIR);
```

4. Write a script that gives you a menu with five choices: create a file, rename a file, delete a file, list all files, or quit. For the choice to create a file, prompt the user for a filename and create that file (it can be empty) in the current directory. For the rename and delete operations, prompt for the old file to rename or delete; also for rename, prompt for the new name of the file and rename it. For the choice to list all files, do just that. SUGGESTION: You don't have to bother with handling directories. Extra Credit: Do error checking on all filenames to make sure you're not creating a file that already exists, or deleting/renaming a file that doesn't exist.

Answers

Here are the answers to the workshop questions in the previous section.

Quiz Answers

1. Hard links provide a way for a single file to have multiple filenames. Removing one instance of the filename—be it the original or the link—leaves all other hard links intact. The file is only actually removed when all the links to it are also removed. Symbolic links also provide a way for a single file to have multiple names, except that the original file is separate from the links. Removing the links has no effect on the file; removing the original file makes any existing links point to nothing.

   Note that only UNIX systems differentiate between hard and symbolic links, and some UNIX systems don't even have symbolic links. Aliases on the Mac or shortcuts on Windows are analogous to symbolic links.

2. The `` `pwd` `` command makes use of back quotes and the `pwd` command in UNIX. While some versions of Perl will work around this function on other systems (notably MacPerl), for a more portable version use the `Cwd` module and the `cwd()` function. Note you'll have to import `Cwd` (`use Cwd`) before you can use it.

3. A file glob is a way of getting a list of files that match a certain pattern. `*.pl`, for example, is a glob that returns all the files in a directory with a `.pl` extension. Globs are useful for grabbing and reading a set of files without having to open the file handle, read the list, and process only those files that match a pattern.

4. A file glob of `<*>` returns all the files in a directory, but it does not include hidden files, files that start with a `.`, or the `.` and `..` directories. Directory handles return all these things.

5. File handles are used to read and write the contents of files (or to the screen, or to a network connection, and so on). Directory handles are used to read lists of files from directories. Both file handles and directory handles use their own variables, and the names do not clash.

6. The argument to `mkdir` determines the permissions that directory will have. On UNIX, those permissions follow the usual format of read, write, and execute access for owner, group, and all; on Mac and Windows, the permissions argument isn't useful, but you have to include it anyway (use `0777` and everything will work fine).

Exercise Answers

1. Here's one answer:

```
#!/usr/bin/perl -w
use strict;
use Cwd;

my $curr = cwd();
opendir(CURRDIR, $curr) or die "can't open directory ($!),
exiting.\n";

my @files = readdir(CURRDIR);
closedir(CURRDIR);

foreach my $file (sort @files) {
    if (-d $file) {
        print "$file/\n";
    }
    else { print "$file\n"; }
}
```

2. The `unlink` function is only used to remove files. Use `rmdir` to remove directories. If the goal, per the description, is to remove all the files and directories in the directory, you'll need to test each filename to see if it's a file or directory and call the appropriate function.

3. The bug lies in the test for the `while` loop; the assumption here is that `readdir` inside of a `while` loop assigns the next directory entry to `$_`, the same way that reading a line of input from a file handle does. This is not true. For `readdir` you must explicitly assign the next directory entry to a variable, like this:

```
while (defined($in = readdir(DIR))) { ... }
```

4. Here's one example. Pay particular attention to the `&getfilename()` subroutine, which handles error checking to make sure the file that was entered doesn't already exist (for creating a new file) or does actually exist (renaming or deleting a file).

```
#!/usr/bin/perl -w
use strict;

my $choice = '';
my @files = &getfiles();

while ($choice !~ /q/i) {
    $choice = &printmenu();
  SWITCH: {
      $choice =~ /^1/ && do { &createfile(); last SWITCH; };
      $choice =~ /^2/ && do { &renamefile(); last SWITCH; };
      $choice =~ /^3/ && do { &deletefile(); last SWITCH; };
      $choice =~ /^4/ && do { &listfiles(); last SWITCH; };
      $choice =~ /^5/ && do { &printhist(); last SWITCH; };
  }
}

sub printmenu {
    my $in = "";
    print "Please choose one (or Q to quit): \n";
    print "1. Create a file\n";
    print "2. Rename a file\n";
    print "3. Delete a file\n";
    print "4. List all files\n";
    while () {
        print "\nYour choice --> ";
        chomp($in = <STDIN>);
        if ($in =~ /^[1234]$/ || $in =~ /^q$/i) {
            return $in;
        } else {
            print "Not a choice.  1-4 or Q, please,\n";
        }
    }
}

sub createfile {
    my $file = &getfilename(1);

    if (open(FILE, ">$file")) {
        print "File $file created.\n\n";
        @files = &getfiles();
        close(FILE);
    } else {
        warn "Cannot open $file ($!).\n";
    }
}
```

```
sub renamefile {
    my $file = &getfilename();
    my $in = '';

    print "Please enter the new filename: ";
    chomp($in = <STDIN>);

    if (rename $file,$in) {
        print "File $file renamed to $in.\n";
        @files = &getfiles();
    } else {
        warn "Cannot rename $file ($!).\n";
    }
}

sub deletefile {
    my $file = &getfilename();

    if (unlink $file) {
        print "File $file removed.\n";
        @files = &getfiles();
    } else {
        warn "Cannot delete $file ($!).\n";
    }
}

sub getfilename {
    my $in = '';

    # call with no args to make sure the file exists
    my $new = 0;

    # call with an arg to make sure the file *doesn't* exist
    if (@_) {
       $new = 1;
    }

    while (!$in) {
        print "Please enter a filename (? for list): ";
        chomp($in = <STDIN>);
        if ($in eq '?') {
            &listfiles();
            $in = '';
        } elsif ((grep /^$in$/, @files) && $new) {
            # file exists, not a new file, OK
            # file exists, new file: error
            print "File ($in) already exists.\n";
            $in = '';
```

```
        } elsif ((!grep /^$in$/, @files) && !$new) {
            # file doesn't exist, new file, OK
            # file doesn't exist, not a new file: error
            print "File ($in) not found.\n";
            $in = '';
        }
    }

    return $in;
}



sub getfiles {
    my $in = '';
    opendir(CURRDIR, '.') or die "can't open directory ($!),
    exiting.\n";
    @files = readdir(CURRDIR);
    closedir(CURRDIR);
    return @files;
}

sub listfiles {
    foreach my $file (@files) {
        if (-f $file) { print "$file\n"; }
    }
    print "\n";
}
```

WEEK 3

DAY 18

Perl and the Operating System

Throughout this book I've been focusing on those features of Perl that behave the same whether you're running your scripts on a UNIX system, under Windows, or on a Mac (or at least I've been letting you know about the differences where they exist). Fortunately, as far as the core language is concerned, there aren't too many issues surrounding writing cross-platform scripts; a hash is a hash is a hash, regardless of where you're looking at it.

There are other features of Perl, however, that are not portable. Some of these are historical—because Perl was developed for UNIX, many of its built-in features relate to features of UNIX that simply don't exist on other platforms. Other features are contained in platform-specific modules, and relate to features of those platforms (the Windows Registry or the Mac Toolbox, for example). If you're certain your scripts will only run on a single platform, you can take advantage of these features to solve platform-specific problems. Or, if you've been given a script to port from one platform to another, it'll help if you know which features are specific to which platform.

In this lesson we'll look at some of the features of Perl available to specific platforms, both in the built-in language and in some of the modules. In particular, today we'll explore:

- UNIX features such as back quotes and the `system` function
- Creating UNIX processes with `fork` and `exec`
- Functions for handling various UNIX system files
- Windows and MacPerl compatibility with UNIX features
- Using the Win32 group of modules, including the `Win32::Process` and `Win32::Registry` modules
- Creating dialog boxes in MacPerl

UNIX Features in Perl

Perl's UNIX heritage shows in many of its built-in features, which are borrowed directly from UNIX tools such as shells, or relate specifically to the management of various UNIX files. In this part of the lesson, then, we'll look at the features in Perl useful on UNIX systems, including:

- Working with environment variables
- Using the `system` function to run other programs
- Running other programs and capturing their output with backquotes
- Creating and managing new processes with `fork`, `wait`, and `exec`
- Some functions for managing UNIX user and group information

Note that with the exception of processes, many of these features may also be available in versions of Perl for other systems, with different or more limited behavior. So, even if you're working on Windows or a Mac, you might want to at least scan this section before skipping down to the part that relates to your own platform.

Environment Variables

Perl scripts, like shell scripts, inherit their environment (the current execution path, username, shell, and so on) from the shell in which they were started (or from the user ID that runs them). And, if you run other programs or spawn processes from inside your Perl script, they will get their environment from your script in turn. When you run Perl scripts from the command line, these variables may not have much interest for you. But Perl scripts run in other environments may have additional variables relating to that environment, or may have different values for those variables than what you expect. CGI scripts, for example, have a number of environment variables relating to various CGI-related features, as you learned on Day 16, "Using Perl for CGI Scripting."

Perl stores all its environment variables in a special hash called `%ENV`, where the keys are the names of the variables, and the values are those values. Environment variables are commonly in uppercase. So, for example, to print the execution path for your script, you'd use a line like this:

```
print "Path: $ENV{PATH}\n";
```

You can print out all the environment variables and values using a regular `foreach` loop:

```
foreach $key (keys %ENV) {
   print "$key -> $ENV{$key}\n";
}
```

Running UNIX Programs with system

Want to run some other UNIX command from inside a Perl script? No problem. Just use the `system` function to do it, like this:

```
system('ls');
```

In this case, `system` will simply run the `ls` command, listing the contents of the current directory to the standard output. To include options to the command you want to run, just include them inside the string argument. Anything you can type at a shell command (and that is available through the current execution path), you can include as an argument to `system`.

```
system("find t -name '*.t' -print | xargs chmod +x &");
system('ls -l *.pl');
```

If you use a double-quoted string as the argument to `system`, Perl will interpolate variables before it passes the string on to the shell:

```
system("grep $thing $file | sort | uniq >newfile.txt");
```

Note

Be very careful when passing data you have not personally verified to the shell (for example, data some user entered from the keyboard). Malicious users could give you data that, when passed through to the shell unchecked, could damage or allow unauthorized access to your system. At the very least, verify incoming data before passing it to the shell. Alternatively, a mechanism in Perl called taint mode allows you to control and manage potentially insecure ("tainted") data. See the `perlsec` man page for more information.

The return value of the `system` function is the return value of the command itself from the shell: 0 for success and 1 or greater for failure. Note that this is the reverse of the standard values Perl uses for true and false, so if you want to check for errors that might result from calling `system`, you'll want to use an `and` logical instead of an `or`:

```
system('who') and die "Cannot execute who\n";
```

When `system` runs, Perl passes the string argument to a shell (usually `/bin/sh`) to expand any shell metacharacters (for example, variables or filename globs), and that shell then executes the command. If you don't have any shell metacharacters, you can make the process more efficient by passing `system` a list of arguments, instead of a single string. The first element of the list should be the name of the command to run, and any other elements should be the various arguments to that command:

```
system("grep $thing $file");  # starts a shell
system("grep", "$thing", "$file");
# bypasses the shell, slightly more efficient
```

Perl will also make this optimization for you if your string argument is simple enough—that is, if it doesn't contain any special characters that the shell must process before actually exiting the program (for example, shell variables or filename globs).

In either case—a single string argument or a list—the `system` function will end up spawning new subprocesses to handle each of the commands in its argument. Each new process inherits its current environment variables from the values in `%ENV`, and shares its standard input, output, and error with the Perl script. Perl will wait for the command to complete before continuing on with the script (unless the command has a `&` at the end of it, which will run that command in the background, just as it would in the shell).

Don't be too quick to use the `system` function. Because `system` spawns a separate process for each of the commands it runs (and sometimes a process for the shell that runs those commands as well), all those extra processes can mean a lot of overhead for your Perl script. Usually it's better to do a task with a bit of code inside your Perl script than to spawn a UNIX shell to do the same thing. More portable, too.

Input with Backquotes

You've already seen how to get input into a script through the use of standard input and via file handles. The third way is through the use of backquotes (``), a common paradigm used in UNIX shells.

Backquotes work similarly to `system` in that they run a UNIX command inside a Perl script. The difference is in the output. Commands run with `system` simply print their output to the standard output. When you use backquotes to run a UNIX command, the output of that command is captured either as a string or as a list of strings, depending on the context in which you use the backquotes.

For example, take the `ls` command, which prints out a listing of the directory:

```
$ls = `ls`;
```

Here, the backquotes execute the `ls` command in a UNIX shell, and the output of that command (the standard output) is assigned the scalar variable `$ls`. In scalar context (as with this example), the resulting output is stored as a single string; in list context each line of output becomes a list element.

As with `system`, any command you can give to a UNIX shell you can include as a backquoted command, and that command runs in its own process, inherits its environment from `%ENV`, and shares standard input, output, and error. The contents of the backquoted string are also variable-interpolated by Perl as double-quoted strings are. The return status of the command is stored in the special variable `$?`. As with `system`, that return status is 0 if successful, or 1 or greater if it failed.

Using Processes: `fork`, `wait`, and `exec`

When you run a Perl script, it runs as its own UNIX process. For many simple scripts, one process may be all you need, particularly if your script runs mostly in a linear start-to-finish way. If you create more complex scripts, where different parts of the script need to do different things all at the same time, then you'll want to create another process and run that part of the script independently. That's what the `fork` function is used for. Once you have a new process, you can keep track of its process ID (PID), wait for it to complete, or run another program in that process. You'll learn about all of these things in this section.

Note

> Creating new processes, and managing how they behave, is the one feature of UNIX Perl that's nearly impossible to duplicate on other systems. So while creating new processes can give you a good amount of power over your Perl scripts, if your scripts are portable you'll want to avoid these features or think about how to work around them on other platforms.
>
> Threads, a new experimental feature in Perl 5.005, promise to help with the problems of porting process-based scripts across platforms. Threads offer quite a lot of the multiprocessing-like behavior of UNIX processes, while also being more lightweight and portable across all platforms. As I'm writing this, however, threads are extremely new and very experimental. We'll look at them briefly on Day 21, "Exploring a Few Longer Examples."

How Processes Work

Processes are used to run different parts of your script concurrently. When you create a new process from inside a script, that new process will run on its own, in its own memory space, until it's done or until you stop it from running. From your script you can spawn as many processes as you need, up to the limits of your system.

Why would you need multiple processes? When you want different bits of your program to run at once, or for multiple copies of your program to run at the same time. One common use for processes is for creating network-based servers, which wait for a connection from a client, and then process that connection in some way. With a server that uses a single process, once the connection comes in the server "wakes up" and processes that connection (parsing the input, looking up values in databases, returning files—whatever). But if your server is busy processing one connection and another connection arrives in the meantime, that second connection will just have to wait. If you've got a busy server you can end up with a whole queue of connections waiting for the server to finish and move on to the next connection.

If you create a server that uses processes, however, you can have a main body of the script that does nothing but wait for connections, and a second part that does nothing but process those connections. Then if the main server gets a connection, it can spawn a new process, hand off the connection to that new process, and then the parent is free to go back to listening for new connections. The second process, in turn, handles the input from that connection and then exits (dies) when it's done. It can repeat this procedure for every new connection, allowing each one to be dealt with in parallel rather than serially.

Network servers make a good example for explaining why processes are useful, but you don't need a network to use them. Any time you want to run different parts of your script in parallel, or separate some processing-intensive part of your script from the main body, processes can help you.

If you're familiar with threads in a language like Java, you may think you understand processes already. But beware. Unlike threads, any running process is completely independent of any other process. The parent and child processes run independently of each other. There is no shared memory, no shared variables, no simple way to communicate information from one process to another. To communicate between processes you'll need to set up a mechanism called inter-process communication (IPC). I don't have the space to talk about IPC in this book, but I'll give you some pointers in "Going Deeper" at the end of the lesson.

Using `fork` and `exit`

To create a new process in your Perl script, you use the `fork` function. `fork`, which takes no arguments, creates a new second process in addition to the process for the original script. Each new process is a clone of the first, with all the same values of the same variables (although it doesn't share those with the parent; they're different memory locations altogether). The child continues running the same script, in parallel, to the end, using the same environment and the same standard input and output as the parent. From the point of the `fork` onward, it's as if you had started up two copies of the same script.

Running the same identical script, however, is not usually why you create a new process. Usually you want the new process (known as the child) to execute something different from the first process (the parent). The most common way to use `fork`, then, is with an `if` conditional, which tests for the return value of the `fork` function. `fork` returns a different value depending on whether the current process is the parent or the child. In the parent, the return result is the PID (process ID) of the new process. In the child, the return result is 0 (if the `fork` didn't happen, for whatever reason, the return value is `undef`). By testing for this return value, you can run different bits of code in the child than you do in the parent.

The core boilerplate for creating processes often looks something like this:

```
if (defined($pid = fork)) {  # fork worked
   if ($pid) {               # pid is some number, this is the parent
      &parent();
   } else {                  # pid is 0.  this is the child.
      &child();
   }
} else {                     # fork didn't work, try again or fail
   die "Fork didn't work...\n";
}
```

18

In this example, the first line calls `fork` and stores the result in the variable `$pid` (the variable name `$pid` is almost universally used for process IDs, but you can call it anything you want, of course). That result can be one of three things: a process ID, 0, or `undef`. The call to `define` in that first line checks for a successful result; otherwise we drop down to the outer `else` and exit with an error.

Note

> If the `fork` doesn't occur because of some error, the current error message (or error number, depending on how you use it) will be stored in the global system variable `$!`. Because many `fork` errors tend to be transient (an overloaded system may not have new processes available at the moment, some Perl programmers test for a value of `$!` that contains the string `"No more Processes"`, wait a while, and then try `fork`ing again.

The successful result can either be 0 or some number representing the process ID (PID) of the new process; each result tells the script which process it is. Here I called two mythical subroutines, `&parent()` and `&child()` to execute different parts of the script depending on whether the script is executing as the parent or as the child.

Here's a simple example (in Listing 18.1) of a script that `forks` three child processes, printing messages from the parent and from each child. The end of the script prints the message `"End"`.

LISTING 18.1 `processes.pl`

```
#!/usr/bin/perl -w
use strict;

my $pid = undef;

foreach my $i (1..3) {
    if (defined($pid = fork)) {
        if ($pid) { #parent
            print "Parent: forked child $i ($pid)\n";
        } else {    #child
            print "Child $i: running\n";
            last;
        }
    }
}

print "End...\n";
```

The output of this script will look something like this (you may get different results on your own system:

```
% processes.pl
Parent: forked child 1 (8577)
Parent: forked child 2 (8578)
Parent: forked child 3 (8579)
End...
%
Child 1: running
End...
Child 2: running
Child 3: running
End...
End...
```

That's some weird output. All the output from each process is intermingled, and what's that extra prompt doing in the middle? Why are there four `End...` statements?

The answer to all these questions lies in how each process executes and what it prints at what time. Let's start by looking solely at what happens in the parent:

- `fork` a new process in line 7. In the parent, `$pid` gets the process ID of that new process.
- Test for a non-zero value of `$pid`, and print a message for each process that gets `fork`ed (lines 8 and 9).
- Repeat these steps two more times for each turn of the `foreach` loop.
- Print `End....`
- Exit (printing the system prompt).

All that occurs fairly rapidly, so the output from the parent happens fairly quickly. Now let's look at any of the three children, whose execution starts just after the `fork`:

- Test for the value of `$pid` in line 8. `$pid` for each of the children is 0, so the test in line 8 is false and we drop to line 10. Print the message in line 11.
- Exit the `foreach` immediately with `last`. Without a `last` here the child would go ahead and repeat the loop as many times as remain (remember, the child starts from the exact same point as the `fork` left off. It's a clone of the parent).
- Print `End....`
- Exit. No system prompt, because it was the parent that created the child.

The output from all the processes is intermingled as each one prints to the standard output. Each child process, however, does take some time to start up before it runs, which is why the output of the parent is printed and the parent exits before some of the children even start. Note also that the line that prints the `End...` is printed regardless of whether a parent or a child is running; because the child has all the same code as the parent when it runs, it will happily continue past the block that it's supposed to run and continue on.

Depending on your situation, you may not want any of this behavior. You may want the parent to exit only after the child is done, or the child to stop running when it's done with its specific block of code. Or you may want the parent to wait for one child to finish before you start up another child. All of this involves process management, which we'll explore in the next section.

Process Management with `exit` and `wait` (and Sometimes `kill`)

Starting up a child process with `fork` and then letting it run is kind of like letting an actual child of say, age 4, run wild in a public place. You'll get results, but they may not be exactly what you (or the people around you) want. That's what process control is for. Two functions, `exit` and `wait`, help you keep control of your processes.

Let's look at `exit` first. The `exit` function, most simply, stops running the current script at the point where it occurs. It's sort of like the `die` function, in that respect, except that `die` exits with a failed status (on UNIX) and prints an error message. `exit` simply ends the program with an option status argument (0 for success, 1 for failed).

`exit` is most commonly used to stop a child from executing more of the parent's code than it's supposed to. Put an `exit` at the end of the block of the child's code, and the child will run only that far and then stop. So, for example, in the little `processes.pl` script we looked at in that last section, let's replace the call to `last` with a call to `exit`, like this:

```
# ...
} else {     #child
    print "Child $i: running\n";
    exit;
}
```

With this modification, the child will print its message, and then exit altogether. It won't restart the `foreach` loop, and it also won't ever print the `End...`. The parent, which is executing the other branch of the `if`, executes the `End...` after the loop is complete. The output of this version of the script will look like this:

```
% procexit.pl
Parent: forked child 1 (11828)
Parent: forked child 2 (11829)
Parent: forked child 3 (11830)
End...
%
Child 1: running
Child 2: running
Child 3: running
```

As with the previous example, the output from the parent and the child is mingled, and the parent completes before the children do.

For further control over when each child runs and when the parent exits, use the `wait` or `waitpid` functions. Both `wait` and `waitpid` do the same thing: they cause the current process (often the parent) to stop executing until the child is finished. This prevents mingling of the output, keeps the parent from exiting too soon and, in more complicated scripts than this one, prevents your script from leaving "zombie" processes (child processes that have finished executing but are still hanging around the system taking up processing space).

The difference in `wait` and `waitpid` is that `wait` takes no arguments, and waits for any child to return. If you spawn five processes and then call `wait`, then the `wait` will return a successful result when any of the five child processes exits. The `waitpid` function, on the other hand, takes a process ID argument, and waits for that specific child process to finish (remember, the parent gets the PID of the child as the return to the `fork` function).

Both `wait` and `waitpid` return the PID of the child that exited, or `-1` if there are no child processes currently running.

Let's return once again to our process example, where we spawn three children in a `foreach` loop. For `exit` we changed the behavior of the children. Now let's change the behavior of the parent by adding a call to `wait` and another message inside the parent part of the conditional:

```
if ($pid) { #parent
  print "Parent : forked child $i ($pid)\n";
  wait;
  print "Parent: child $i ($pid) complete\n";
} else { ....
```

In the parent code for the previous example, the parent simply printed the first message, and then the `foreach` loop would repeat, spawning three children in quick succession. In this version, the child is created, the parent prints the first message and then waits for that child to complete. Then it prints the second message. Each turn of the loop occurs only after the current child is done and has exited. The output of this version of the script looks like this:

```
% procwait.pl
Parent : forked child 1 (11876)
Child 1: running
Parent: child 1 (11876) complete
Parent : forked child 2 (11877)
Child 2: running
Parent: child 2 (11877) complete
Parent : forked child 3 (11878)
Child 3: running
Parent: child 3 (11878) complete
End...
%
```

Note here that execution is very regular: Each child is forked, runs, and exits before the next process starts. And the parent stays in execution until the third child is done, exiting only at the end.

The fact that this example runs each child serially, one after the other, makes it sort of silly to have processes at all (particularly given that each process takes time to start up and takes up extra processing space on your system). Because the `wait` function is so flexible, however, you don't have to wait for the most recently spawned child to finish before spawning another one—you could spawn five processes, and then later on in your script call `wait` five times to clean up all the processes. We'll look at an example of this later on in this lesson when we explore a larger example.

There's one last function worth mentioning in reference to controlling processes: the `kill` function, which sends a kill signal to a process. To use `kill`, you'll need to know something about signals. For the sake of space I'm not going to talk about signals in this chapter, but see "Going Deeper" and the `perlfunc` man pages for a few pointers.

Running Something Else in a Process with `exec`

When you create a new process with `fork`, that process creates a clone of the current script and continues processing from there. Sometimes, however, when you create a new process, you want that process to stop what it's doing altogether and to run some other program instead. That's where `exec` comes in.

The `exec` function causes the current process to stop running the current script, and to run something else. The "something else" is usually some other program or script, given as the argument to `exec`, something like this:

```
exec("grep $who /etc/passwd");
```

The arguments to `exec` follow the same rules as with `system`; if you use a single string argument, Perl passes that argument to the shell first. With a list of arguments you can bypass the shell process. In fact, the similarities between `exec` and `system` are not coincidental—the `system` function is actually a `fork` and an `exec` put together.

Once Perl encounters an `exec`, that's the end of that script. The `exec` shifts control to the new program being `exec`'ed; no other lines in the script will be executed.

Other UNIX-Related Functions

In addition to the functions mentioned throughout this section, Perl's set of built-in functions includes a number of other process-related functions and smaller utility functions for getting information about various parts of the system. Because these functions apply specifically to UNIX system files or features, most of these functions are not available on other systems (although the developers porting Perl to those systems may attempt to create rudimentary equivalents for the behavior of these functions).

Table 18.1 shows a summary of many of these functions. For more information on any of these, see Appendix A, "Perl Functions," or the `perlfunc` man page.

TABLE 18.1 UNIX-RELATED FUNCTIONS

Function	*What It Does*
`alarm`	Send a SIGALRM signal to a process
`chroot`	Change the root directory for the current process

Function	*What It Does*
`getgrent`, `setgrent`, `endgrent`	Look up or set values from `/etc/groups`
`getgrgid`	Look up a group file entry in `/etc/groups`
`getgrnam`	Look up a group file entry by name in `/etc/groups`
`getpgrp`	Get the process group name for a process
`getppid`	Get the process ID of the parent process (if the current script is running in a child process)
`getpriority`	Return the current priority for a process, process group, or user
`getpwent`, `setpwent`, `endpwent`	Look up or set values from `/etc/passwd`
`getpwnam`	Look up a user by name in `/etc/passwd`
`getpwuid`	Look up a user by user ID (UID) in `/etc/passwd`
`setpgrp`	Set the process group for a process

Perl for Windows

Perl for Windows supports most of the core set of UNIX features, as well as a number of extensions for Win32 features. If you've installed the ActiveState version of Perl for Windows, you'll get the Win32 modules as part of that package. If you compile Perl for Windows yourself, you'll need to get the `libwin32` package from CPAN (see `http://www.perl.com/CPAN-local/modules/by-module/Win32/` for the latest version). Otherwise, the functionality is the same.

Note

Earlier versions of Perl for Windows were much less coordinated as far as which modules and features were available in which package. If you're using a version of Perl for Windows earlier than 5.005 (or ActiveState's Perl for Windows earlier than Build 500), you should upgrade to make sure you've got the newest and best version.

If you run into trouble with any of these aspects of Perl on Win32, there are a number of sources for help. The Perl for Win32 FAQ, which I've mentioned before, has a number of good starting places (find it at `/http://www.activestate.com/support/faqs/win32/`).

Compatibility with UNIX

With a few notable exceptions, most UNIX-like Perl features will work on Windows, although how they are used is different. The biggest notable exception is `fork` and its related functions, which are not supported, although you can run another program from inside a Perl script using `system`, `exec`, backquotes, of one of the Win 32 extensions (more about those later).

The `system` function, `exec`, and backquotes work on Perl for Windows. The "shell" for these commands is `cmd.exe` for Windows NT, or `command.com` for Windows 95. Commands and argument lists that you give to these commands must follow Windows conventions, including pathnames and file globbing.

Keep in mind, of course, that if you're porting a UNIX script to Windows, and that UNIX script uses UNIX utilities in `system` or backquotes, that you'll need to find the Windows equivalents of those same utilities; simply having support for `system` and backquotes is not enough.

Functions that relate to specific UNIX features (such as those listed in Table 18.1) are unlikely to work on Perl for Windows. Other functions that do not work are specialized functions I haven't bothered to mention in this book relate to interprocess communication or low-level networking. In general, most of the common Perl functions you'll use will be available in Perl for Windows. You can find a complete list of unimplemented functions in the FAQ for Perl for Win32 at `http://www.activestate.com/support/faqs/win32/` (look in the section on "Implementation Quirks").

Built-In Win32 Subroutines

The extensions to Perl for managing Windows features come in two parts: a set of built-in Win32 subroutines, and a number of additional Win32 modules for more sophisticated techniques (such as `Win32::Registry` or `Win32::Process`). The Win32 subroutines provide easy access to system information, as well as a number of smaller utility routines. If you are running Perl for Windows, you don't need to import any of the Win32 modules to use these subroutines. Table 18.2 contains a list of several of the Win32 subroutines available in Perl for Windows.

For more information on any of these subroutines, you may want to check the Perl for Win32 FAQ. I also found Philippe Le Berre's pages at `http://www.inforoute.cgs.fr/leberre1/main.htm` to be especially helpful.

TABLE 18.2 BUILT-IN WIN32 SUBROUTINES

Subroutine	*What It Does*
`Win32::DomainName`	Returns the Microsoft Network domain.
`Win32::FormatMessage` *`errorcode`*	Takes the error returned by `GetLastError`and turns it into a descriptive string.
`Win32::FsType`	The filesystem type (FAT or NTFS).
`Win32::GetCwd`	Gets the current directory.
`Win32::GetLastError`	If the last Win32 subroutine failed, this subroutine will give you the reason why (format the result of this with `FormatMessage`).
`Win32::GetNextAvailDrive`	Gets the drive letter of the next available drive, for example, `E:`.
`Win32::GetOSVersion`	Returns an array representing the OS version and number: (`$string`, `$major`, `$minor`, `$build`, `$id`), where `$string` is an arbitrary string, `$major` and `$minor` are version numbers, `$build` is the build number, and `$is` is 0 for a generic Win32, 1 for Windows 95, or 2 for Windows NT.
`Win32::GetShortPathName`	Given a long filename (`thisisareallylongfilename.textfile`), returns the 8.3 version (`THISI~1.TXT`).
`Win32::GetTickCount`	The number of ticks (milliseconds) that have elapsed since Windows was started.
`Win32::IsWin95`	True if you're on Windows 95.
`Win32::IsWinNT`	True if you're on Windows NT.
`Win32::LoginName`	The username of the user running the script.
`Win32::NodeName`	The Microsoft Network node name for the current machine.
`Win32::SetCwd` *`newdir`*	Changes the current directory.
`Win32::Sleep` *`milliseconds`*	Sleep for the given number of milliseconds.
`Win32::Spawn`	Spawn a new process (see the following section, "Win32 Processes").

18

Win32::MsgBox

The basic Win32 subroutines give you access to basic Windows features and system information from inside Perl. Installing the libwin32 modules (or using ActiveState's version of Perl for Windows) gives you access to the Win32 modules, with which you can access a lot more of the advanced Windows features. One nifty feature in the Win32 modules is the `Win32::MsgBox` subroutine, which can be used to pop up rudimentary modal dialog boxes from inside your Perl scripts. `Win32::MsgBox` takes up to three arguments: the text to put in the dialog itself, a code representing the icon in the dialog and some combination of buttons, and the text to put in the title bar of the dialog. For example, the following code will show the dialog on the left side of Figure 18.1:

```
Win32::MsgBox("I can't do that!");
```

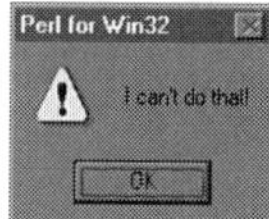

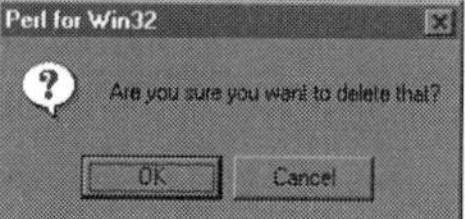

FIGURE 18.1
Dialogs.

This one shows a dialog with two buttons, OK and Cancel, and a Question icon (as shown on the right side of Figure 18.1):

```
Win32::MsgBox("Are you sure you want to delete that?", 33);
```

The second argument represents the codes for the number of buttons and the type of icon. Table 18.3 shows the choices for a number of buttons.

TABLE 18.3 BUTTON CODES

Code	*Result*
0	OK
1	OK and Cancel
2	Abort, Retry, Ignore
3	Yes, No, and Cancel
4	Yes and No
5	Retry and Cancel

Table 18.4 shows the choices for the icon.

TABLE 18.4 ICON CODES

Code	*Result*
16	Hand
32	Question (?)
48	Exclamation point (!)
64	Asterisk (*)

To get the second argument for `Win32::MsgBox`, just pick a choice from each table and add the numbers together. So an exclamation icon (48) with Yes and No buttons (4) would result in a code of 52.

The return value of `Win32::MsgBox` is based on the buttons you used in the dialog and what the user actually clicked. Table 18.5 shows the possible return values.

TABLE 18.5 BUTTON CODES

Code	*Button Clicked*
1	OK
2	Cancel
3	Abort
4	Retry
5	Ignore
6	Yes
7	No

Win32 Processes

Perl for Windows does not include support for `fork`; that function relies too heavily on UNIX behavior. However, you can start new processes that run separate programs (the equivalent for a `fork` followed by an `exec`). The easiest way to do this is to use either `system` or backquotes, or to halt the current script with an `exec`. An alternative way is the use either `Win32::Spawn` or the `Win32::Process` module.

`Win32::Spawn` is part of the basic Win32 subroutines, and lets you start up another process in a really simple way. The `Win32::Process` module, on the other hand, is more recent, more robust, uses proper module conventions, but is somewhat more difficult to understand.

To create a new process with `Win32::Spawn`, you'll need three arguments: the full pathname to the command to run in the new process, the arguments to that command (including the command name again), and a variable to hold the process ID of the new process. Here's an example that starts up Notepad on Windows NT with a temporary file in `C:\tempfile.txt`. It also traps errors:

```
my $command = "c:\\winnt\\notepad.exe";
my $args = "notepad.exe c:\\tempfile";
my $pid = 0;
```

```
Win32::Spawn($command, $args, $pid) || &error();
print "Spawned!  The new PID is $pid.";

sub error {
    my $errmsg = Win32::FormatMessage(Win32::GetLastError());
    die "Error: $errmsg\n";
}
```

One annoying side effect of `Win32::Spawn` is that the new process—in this case, Notepad—comes up minimized, so it appears as if nothing is happening. The original Perl script also continues executing (or, in this case, finishes executing) as the new process is running.

The `Win32::Process` module handles processes in a much more sensible way. However, it's more complex, and it's set up to be object-oriented, which means some slightly different syntax (but you learned the basics on Day 13, "Scope, Modules, and Importing Code," so you should be OK).

Creating a `Win32::Process` object is vaguely similar to using `Win32::Spawn`. You'll still need a command and a list or arguments, but you'll also need some other stuff. To create a `Win32::Process` object, first make sure you import `Win32::Process`:

```
use Win32::Process;
```

Then call the `Create` method to create your new process object (you'll need a variable to hold it):

```
my $command = "c:\\winnt\\notepad.exe";
my $args = "notepad.exe c:\\tempfile";
my $proc; # process object

Win32::Process::Create($process,
      $command,
      $args,
      0,
      DETACHED_PROCESS,
      '.') || &error();
```

(I've left off the definition for the error subroutine here to save space.)

The arguments to `Win32::Process` are:

- A variable to hold a reference to the new process object.
- The command to run.
- The arguments to that command.
- Whether handles are inherited (if you don't know what that means, just use 0).

- One of several options. DETACHED_PROCESS is the most popular, although CREATE_NEW_CONSOLE may also be useful.
- The temporary directory for this process.

In this case, when the new process is created, Notepad will start up maximized and edit the file in C:\tempfile. But the original Perl script will still continue right on executing.

To make the parent process wait for the child to finish executing, use the Wait method (note the capital W; this isn't the same as Perl's wait function). You'll have to call this as an object-oriented method, with the process object first:

```
$proc->Wait(INFINITE);
```

In this case, the parent process will wait indefinitely until the child finishes. You can also give Wait an argument of some number of milliseconds to wait before continuing.

In addition to Wait, the Win32::Process module also includes these methods:

- Kill, to kill the new process
- Suspend, to temporarily stop the process
- Resume, to start a suspended process
- GetPriorityClass and SetPriorityClass, to look up or change the process's priority
- GetExitCode, to find out why a process exited

You can get more information about Win32::Process from the documentation that comes with the Win32 modules, or from the online documentation at http://www.activestate.com/activeperl/docs.

Working with the Win32 Registry

The Windows Registry is a storehouse of information about your system, its configuration, and the programs installed on it. The Win32::Registry module, an object-oriented module, allows you to read from, modify, and add values to the Windows Registry from inside a Perl script.

Note

> If you're unfamiliar with the Windows Registry, chances are good you should not be playing with it from inside Perl. You can make your system unusable by mucking with the Registry and changing things that are not intended to be changed. You can use the Windows program regedit to examine and modify the Windows Registry.

The Windows Registry consists of a number of trees of keys and values. At the topmost level, the Registry contains several subtrees, including HKEY_LOCAL_MACHINE for information about the configuration of the local machine, or HKEY_CURRENT_USER for information about the currently logged-in user. Depending on whether you're running Windows NT or Windows 95, you'll have a different set of subtrees. Inside each subtree are a number of sets of keys and values, like hashes, only nested (a key can map to a whole other hash tree).

When you import the `Win32::Registry` module (with use `Win32::Registry`), you get a Registry key object for each of the topmost subtrees, for example `$HKEY_LOCAL_MACHINE`. Using the various `Win32::Registry` methods, you can open, traverse, and manage any part of the Windows Registry.

Unfortunately, to get the most use out of the `Win32::Registry` module, you need to know something of references to handle the nested-hash nature of the Registry keys. For now, Table 18.6 shows several of the `Win32::Registry` methods and their arguments; after going on to the lesson on references, you will find these to be more meaningful.

To start working with any part of the Registry, you must first use `Open` with one of the major subkey objects, like this (don't forget to use `Win32::Registry` at the top of your script):

```
use Win32::Registry;
my $reg = "SOFTWARE";
my ($regobj, @keys);
$HKEY_LOCAL_MACHINE->Open($reg,$regobj)|| die "Can't open registry\n";
```

Then you can call the various Registry methods on that new `Registry` object:

```
$regobj->GetKeys(\@keys);
$regobj->Close();
```

TABLE 18.6 `Win32::Registry` METHODS

Method	*What It Does*
`Close`	Closes the currently open key.
`Create` *`keyname`*, *`keyref`*	Creates a new key with the name *`keyname`*. *`keyref`* will contain a reference to the new key.
`DeleteKey` *`keyname`*	Deletes the key *`keyname`*.
`DeleteValue` *`valname`*	Deletes the value *`valname`*.
`GetKeys` *`listref`*	Returns a list of the keys in the current key. *`listref`* is a reference to a list.
`GetValues` *`hashref`*	Returns a hash of the keys and values in the current key. The keys in this hash are nested lists. *`hashref`* is a reference to a hash.

Method	*What It Does*
`Open` *`obj, objref`*	Opens a key. *`obj`* is the key to open, `objref` is a reference to the object that will hold that key.
`Save` *`filename`*	Saves the currently open key to *`filename`*.
`SetValue` *`keyname`*, `REG_SZ`, *`value`*	Change the value of *`keyname`* to *`value`*. The second argument must be `REG_SZ`.
`Load` *`keyname, filename`*	Imports the keys and values in *`filename`* into `keyname`.

For more information on `Win32::Registry`, the documentation that comes with the Win32 modules is helpful. You might also want to check out Phillipe Le Berre's How To Guide at `http://www.inforoute.cgs.fr/leberre1/main.htm`, which has lots of examples and notes on using `Win32::Registry`.

Other Win32 Modules

The `Win32` modules, shipped with Active State's Perl and gathered in the `libwin32` bundle, contain lots and lots of modules for handling various aspects of Windows operations—by only describing `Win32::Process` and `Win32::Registry` I've only touched the surface. And in addition to those "standard" Win32 modules, more and more are being written and included on CPAN. If you do lots of work with Windows, and intend to do more work with Perl on that platform, do look into these modules for many more features to work with. Table 18.7 contains a summary of the standard Win32 modules; see CPAN for even more.

18

TABLE 18.7 WIN32 MODULES

Module	*What It Does*
`Win32::ChangeNotify`	Provides access to Windows change-notification objects.
`Win32::EventLog`	Provides access to the Windows NT event log (Windows NT only).
`Win32::File`	Manages file attributes.
`Win32::FileSecurity`	Manages NTFS file security.
`Win32::IPC`	Inter-Process Communication: allows you to synchronize and communicate between Process, ChangeNotify, Semaphore, and Mutex.
`Win32::Mutex`	Provides access to Windows Mutex objects.
`Win32::NetAdmin`	Administers users and groups (Windows NT only).
`Win32::NetResource`	Administers system resources (printers, servers, and so on) (Windows NT only).
`Win32::Process`	Creates and manages Windows processes.
`Win32::OLE`	Provides access to OLE automation.

continues

TABLE 18.7 CONTINUED

Module	*What It Does*
`Win32::Registry`	Works with the Windows registry.
`Win32::Semaphore`	Provides access to Windows Semaphore objects.
`Win32::Service`	Allows you to administer services.
`Win32::WinError`	For handling Windows-defined (or generated) errors.

MacPerl Features

Quite a lot of Perl's features are available in MacPerl, particularly if you have MPW (Macintosh Programmer's Workbench) installed. In addition, MacPerl provides interfaces to the Macintosh Toolbox, giving you access to MacOS features via Perl—assuming you already know something of the very complex Macintosh Toolbox. But even if you don't delve into advanced Mac programming with Perl, several smaller features of MacPerl—dialogs in particular—are easy to create and use with MacPerl to provide a more Mac-like interface to your scripts.

For working with MacPerl in general, the MacPerl FAQ at `http://www.perl.com/CPAN/doc/FAQs/mac/MacPerlFAQ.html` provides lots of good information, on top of the information in the standard Perl FAQ. In addition, there is a mailing list for users and developers of MacPerl for even more information about MacPerl itself; see the FAQ for information on how to subscribe.

Compatibility with UNIX

As with the Windows versions of Perl, throughout this book I've tried to note differences in behavior in MacPerl where they exist. As with Windows, however, there are a number of features in the UNIX version of Perl which are difficult to duplicate on the Mac, and particularly so in the standalone version of MacPerl. Some compatibility issues to be aware of are

- Perl features that run external programs (`system`, `exec`, backquotes) do not work in MacPerl. If you have MPW's ToolServer installed, features like backquotes, filename globbing, and the `system` function will work with Mac-based commands. Perl can also call AppleScript, which can in turn run external programs.
- Standalone MacPerl does have some basic support for some common uses of backquotes, including `` `pwd` `` or `` `Directory` `` for the current directory and `` `stty -raw` `` and `` `stty -cooked` `` for handling raw input from the keyboard.

- MacPerl does not have support for `fork` or for UNIX-style processes. There is Mac Toolbox access to Macintosh processes via the `Mac::Processes` module, but you'll need an understanding of low-level Macintosh processes before you start.
- The notion of environment variables is not really useful in MacPerl and is only really supported for compatibility. The `%ENV` hash does exist and by default has a few basic values (as defined in the MacPerl Preferences and including the locations of MacPerl and its libraries).
- All dates and times start from 1/1/1904.
- All path names use : as the directory separator, and `:` and `::` as the equivalent to `.` and `..`.
- Functions that relate specifically to UNIX features (for example, the ones listed in Table 18.1) do not work in MacPerl. See the FAQ for a list.

Dialogs

MacPerl provides a number of simple subroutines for creating and handling simple dialog boxes from your Perl scripts. With these subroutines you can create dialogs with up to three buttons, a text box for accepting input, a dialog with a number of choices, or even the standard file dialogs.

18

To create a dialog with one or more buttons, use `MacPerl::Answer` with up to four arguments (depending on the number of buttons you'd like). The first argument is the dialog text; all arguments after that indicate button values. You can have a maximum of three buttons.

```
MacPerl::Answer("That's not a number.");  # default OK button
MacPerl::Answer("That's not a number.", "Darn");  # one button
MacPerl::Answer("Really quit?", "OK", "Cancel");  # two buttons
MacPerl::Answer("Go where?", "Left", "Right", "Up");
```

Figure 18.2 shows examples of what each of these dialogs looks like. The return values for `MacPerl::Answer` is the empty string for dialogs with a single OK button, 0 for dialogs with one button, and 0, 1, or 2 for dialogs with more than one button depending on which button was selected (buttons are numbered as they appear in the list of arguments).

To create a dialog with a text box in it, use `MacPerl::Ask` with a prompt:

```
$age = MacPerl::Ask("Please Enter your Age: ");
```

You can also give a default value for the text field:

```
$url = MacPerl::Ask("URL to check: ", "http://");
```

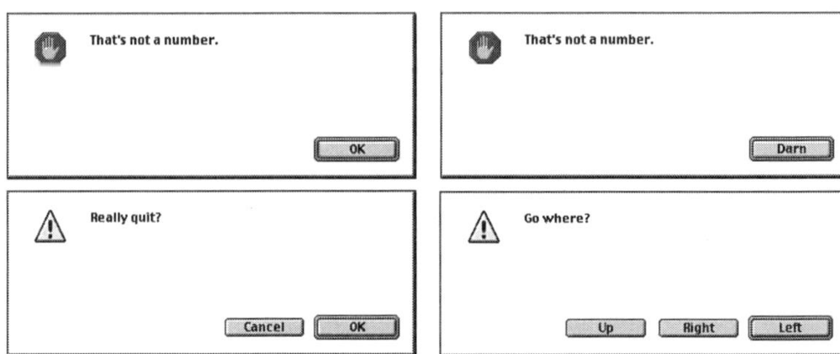

FIGURE 18.2
Dialogs in MacPerl.

`MacPerl::Ask` returns the text value the user entered, or `undef` if the dialog was canceled with no input. Figure 18.3 shows a sample:

FIGURE 18.3
Text prompts in MacPerl.

Need to give your user several choices to choose from? Use `MacPerl::Pick` with a prompt and a list of items:

```
$food = MacPerl::Pick("Please choose a food: ",
   "Pad Thai", "Burrito", "Pizza");
```

`MacPerl::Pick` returns the value of the thing chosen, or `undef` if the dialog was canceled. Figure 18.4 shows this dialog:

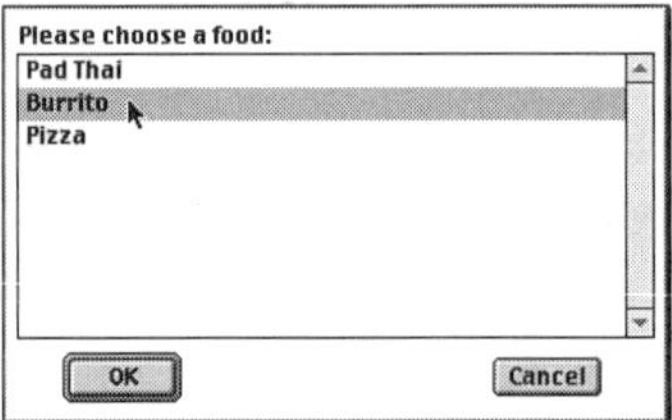

FIGURE 18.4
Choice dialogs in MacPerl.

For standard file dialogs (the dialogs that let you pick a file from the Mac file system), you'll want to include the file `StandardFile.pl` in your own scripts, which will give you an easy-to-use front end to the raw subroutine `MacPerl::Choose`. Use `require` for the `StandardFile` code:

```
require 'StandardFile.pl:
```

A The `Config` module can help you with that. The `'osname'` key in the `%Config` hash contains the platform you're running on. So, for example, to make sure you're running on Windows, you could use something like this:

```
use Config;
if ( $Config{'osname'} !~ /Win/i ) {
  die "Hey!  This is a Win32 script.  You can't run it here.\n";
}
```

Workshop

The workshop provides quiz questions to help you solidify your understanding of the material covered and exercises to give you experience in using what you've learned. Try to understand the quiz and exercise answers before you go on to tomorrow's lesson.

Quiz

1. What is `%ENV` used for? Why is it useful?
2. What's the difference between using `system` and backquotes?
3. Why would you want to use multiple processes in your Perl script?
4. What does `fork` do?
5. What's the difference between `system` and `exec`?
6. Can Win32 processes be used interchangeably with `fork`?

Exercises

1. (UNIX only) Create a script that takes a single number as an argument. `fork` that number of child processes, and make sure the parent waits for each to finish. Each process should
    - Generate a random number between 1 and 100,000.
    - Sum all the numbers between 1 and that random number.
    - Print the result.
2. (UNIX only) Modify the `img.pl` script from Day 10, "Doing More with Regular Expressions," (the one that printed information about the images in an HTML file) such that the output is emailed to you instead of displayed on the screen. HINT: This command will send a message:

    ```
    mail yourmail@yoursite.com < bodyofmessage
    ```

3. (Windows only) Create a script that takes a directory listing (using the `dir` command) and prints only the filenames, one per line (you don't have to sort them).
4. (Mac only) Create a script that prompts you for a text file (and only text files) using the standard file dialog and then opens and prints that file to the console.

Answers

Here are the answers to the workshop questions in the previous section.

Quiz Answers

1. The `%ENV` hash holds the variable names and values for the script's environment. On UNIX and Windows, the values in this hash can be useful for finding out information about the system environment (or for changing it and passing it on to other processes). On the Mac `%ENV` doesn't serve any useful purpose.
2. The `system` command runs some other program or script from inside your Perl script and sends the output to the standard output. Backquotes also run an external program, but they capture the input to a scalar or list value (depending on context).
3. Multiple processes are useful for portioning different parts of your script that may need to be run simultaneously, or for splitting up the work your script needs to do.
4. The `fork` function creates a new process, a clone of the original process. Both the new processes continue executing the script at the point where the `fork` occurred.
5. System and `exec` are strongly related; both are used to execute an external program. The difference is that `system` does a `fork` first; `exec` stops running the current script in the current process and runs the external program instead.
6. `Win32::Process` and `fork` are not interchangeable. The `fork` function ties very strongly to processes on UNIX; `Win32::Process` is more analogous to a `fork` followed immediately to an `exec`.

Exercise Answers

1. Here's one answer:

```
#!/usr/bin/perl -w
use strict;

if (@ARGV > 1) {
    die "Only one argument, please.\n";
}
 elsif ($ARGV[0] !~ /^\d+/) {
    die "Argument should be a number.\n";
}
```

```
my $pid;
my $procs = pop;

foreach my $i (1..$procs) {
    if (defined($pid = fork)) {
        if ($pid) { #parent
            print "Parent: forked child $i\n";
        } else {    #child
            srand;
            my $top = int(rand 100000);
            my $sum;
            for (1..$top) {
                $sum += $_;
            }
            print "Finished child $i:  Sum of $top is $sum\n";
            exit;
        }
    }
}

while ($procs > 0) {
    wait;
    $procs--;
}
```


2. All you need are three changes. First, create and open a temporary file:

```
my $tmp = "tempfile.$$";                    # temporary file;
open(TMP, ">$tmp") || die "Can't open temporary file $tmp\n";
```

Second, make sure all print statements write to that file:

```
if (exists($atts{$key})) {
   $atts{$key} =~ s/[\s]*\n/ /g;
   print TMP "   $key: $atts{$key}\n";
}
```

Finally, use `system` to mail the temporary file and remove it:

```
close TMP;
my $me = "youremail@yoursite.com";
system("mail $me <$tmp");
unlink $tmp
```

3. Here's one way to do it (start the `substr` function from character 44 if you're on Windows 95):

```
#!/usr/bin/perl -w
use strict;

my @list = `dir`;
```

```
foreach (@list) {
   if (/^\w/) {
      print substr($_,39);
   }
}
```

4. Here's one way to do it:

```
#!/usr/bin/perl -w
use strict;
require 'StandardFile.pl';

my $file = &StandardFile::GetFile("Choose a file for input",
    'TEXT','ttxt','ttro', "input");

open(FILE, "$file") || die "Cannot open $file\n";
while (<FILE>) { print };
```

WEEK 3

DAY 19

Working with References

For the last several chapters, we've been looking at a number of aspects of Perl that one might consider auxiliary to the core language itself—working with various functions in the standard library for managing filesystems or processes, importing code from modules and then using those modules to accomplish various tasks, or working with the Perl debugger. Today, as we reach the final few lessons in this book, we'll return to the core language with a discussion of references. References are a way of indirectly pointing to other bits of data in Perl. They allow you to manage data in more advanced and often more efficient ways than handling the data itself. In today's lesson, we'll explore these topics:

- What references are, and the advantages they give you
- Creating and using references to scalars, arrays, and hashes
- Using references in subroutines for arguments and return values
- Creating nested data structures (multidimensional arrays, arrays of hashes, and so on)

What Is a Reference?

A *reference* is a form of data in Perl that indirectly points to some other bit of data. The reference itself is a scalar, like a number or string—it can be assigned to a scalar variable, printed, added to, tested to see if it's true or false, stored in a list, or passed to a subroutine, just as numbers and strings can. In addition to its scalar-like behavior, however, the reference also refers, or points to, the location of some other bit of data. To find out what the reference points to, you *dereference* the reference—fancy terminology for essentially following the pointer to the thing it points to.

If you actually want more fancy terminology in your life, the thing the reference points to is called the *referent*. You dereference the reference to get to the referent. Me, I prefer regular words like "the thing it points to."

References in Perl are similar to pointers or references in other languages, and have the same advantages. But if you're not used to other languages, you may wonder, "What's the point? Why would you want to deal with a reference when you could deal with the data itself?" The answer is that by indirectly referring to data, you can do more advanced things with that data—for example, pass large amounts of data by reference into and out of subroutines, or create multidimensional arrays. References also allow more advanced uses of data, including creating object-oriented structures in Perl. We'll look at a number of these uses as the lesson progresses.

There's one other technical point to make before we move on to actual code: What I'm referring to in this chapter as references are known in technical Perl circles as *hard* references. Perl also has another form of reference called a *symbolic reference*. While there are perfectly good reasons for using symbolic references, hard references are more useful in general, so for the bulk of this chapter we'll stick to those. I'll talk more about symbolic references in "Going Deeper" at the end of this lesson.

The Basics: A General Overview of How to Use References

Let's look at a few simple examples of creating and using references so you can get a feel for the technique. Perl actually has a number of ways of working with references, but here we'll focus on the easiest and most popular mechanisms, and explore the others in a later section ("Other Ways of Using References").

Creating a Reference

Start with something you've seen a gazillion times before in this book: a plain old scalar variable that contains a string.

```
$str = "This is a string.";
```

This is an ordinary scalar variable, holding ordinary scalar data. There's some location in memory that stores that string, which you can get to through the `$str` variable name. If you assigned something else to `$str`, the memory location would have different contents and there would be a different value for `$str`. All this is the basic stuff you've been doing all along.

Now let's create a reference to that data. To create a reference, you need the actual memory location of the data in question (a scalar, an array, a hash, or a subroutine). To get at that memory location, you use the backslash (`\`) operator and a variable name:

```
$strref = \$str;
```

The backslash operator gets the memory location of the data stored in `$str` and creates a reference to that location. That reference then gets assigned to the scalar variable `$strref` (remember, references are a form of scalar data).

> **Note:** The backslash operator is very similar to the address (&) operator in C. Both are used to access the actual memory location of a piece of data.

19

At no point here do the actual contents of `$str`—the string `"This is a string."`—come into play. The reference doesn't care about the contents of `$str`, just its location. And `$str` remains a scalar variable containing a string; the reference's existence doesn't change anything about that either. (See Figure 19.1.)

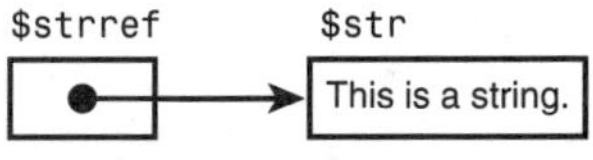

FIGURE 19.1
A variable, a string, and a reference.

This example created a reference to a string. But you can also create references to arrays, hashes, or subroutines—anything that has a memory location in Perl. For example, here's a reference to an array:

```
@array = (1..10);
$arrayref = \@array;
```

And here's one for a hash:

```
%hash = (
   'red' => '0 0 255',
   'green' => '0 255 0',
   'blue' => '255 0 0; );
$hashref = \%hash;
```

As with the reference to a scalar value, the array and hash in these examples remain arrays and hashes stored in the `@array` and `%hash` variables, respectively. And the array and hash references in `$arrayref` and `$hashref` are bits of scalar data, regardless of the data they point to. The most important thing to remember here is that the reference itself is a scalar. The thing it points to can be any kind of data.

You can also create references to subroutines. Because this is an advanced topic, and not as commonly used as references to scalars, arrays, and hashes, we'll look at references to subroutines and how they're used in this lesson's "Going Deeper" section.

Printing and Using References

So now you've created a reference with the backslash operator and stored it in a scalar variable. What do these references look like? They're scalars, and as such can be used anywhere a scalar can, and as with numbers and strings they behave differently based on context.

A reference used as a string indicates the data it refers to (a scalar, an array, a hash, and so on), and a hexadecimal number representing the internal memory location the reference points to. So, for example, if you did this:

```
print "$strref\n";
```

You'd get something like this:

```
SCALAR(0x807f61c)
```

The equivalent for `$arrayref` and `$hashref` would look like this:

```
ARRAY(0x807f664)
```

```
HASH(0x807f645)
```

Using a reference in a numeric context gives you the same hexadecimal number that you get when you use the reference in a string context, representing the memory location of the thing the reference points to. The numbers in both the string and number representations of the reference will vary depending on when you run the script and the memory that's free for Perl to use at that time. You wouldn't want to rely on those numbers; just consider that to be an internal representation of where the reference points to.

Other uses of references? You can assign them to scalar variables, as we have here, use them as list elements, or store them in arrays and hashes (although they cannot be used as hash keys—more about this later). A reference, when used as a test, will always be true. But the most typical thing you do with references is to dereference them to gain access to the data they point to.

Dereferencing References

When you dereference a reference, you get at the data that reference points to. You could also think of it as following the reference, or accessing the location the reference refers to. But the term *dereference* is what is most commonly used.

There are a number of ways to dereference a reference, but the easiest way is to substitute the reference's scalar variable where a plain variable name would be expected, like this:

```
$originalstr = $$strref;
```

Two dollar signs? Yes. A single dollar sign is just the scalar variable `$strref`, which gives you the reference itself. The double dollar sign says "give me the thing that `$strref` points to." In this case, the thing that `$strref` points to was the original string `This is a string`. You could think of two dollar signs as putting the reference—`$strref`—in place of the actual name of the variable you want to access.

To follow an array reference and gain access to the array itself, you'd do the same thing with an `@` sign instead, and the `$arrayref` goes where the name of the array would be:

```
@firstlist = @$arrayref;
```

The contents of `@firstlist` will now be that initial array we created and that `$arrayref` pointed to (actually, it'll be a copy of all the elements of that array).

Need to gain access to an actual array element from a reference? No problem. It's the same rule, just put the variable holding the reference where the name of the array would be:

```
$first = $$arrayref[0];
```

Same rule for getting the topmost index number of an array:

```
$index = $#$arrayref;
```

Hashes work similarly:

```
%newhash = %$hashref;     # copy what $hashref points to

$value = $$hashref{red};  # get the value for the key "red"

@keys = keys %$hashref;   # extract keys
```

Changing Referenced-to Data

Here's the tricky part of references: changing the data that the reference points to. Say you've got your `$strref` as before, but then you change the value of `$str` later on:

```
$str = "This is a string."
$strref = \$str;
#...
$str = "This is a different string."
```

What happens to the reference `$strref`? It continues to exist. It continues to point to that same memory location named by `$str`. If you dereference it, you'll now get the new string:

```
print "$$strref\n";   # results in "This is a different string."
```

The reference itself doesn't care about the contents of the thing it points to, just the location. You can merrily change the contents all you want—the reference will just keep pointing to that same spot. Each time you dereference it, you'll get the thing contained at that location.

Note that this is different from regular variable assignment, which copies the contents of one memory location to another. References always continue to point to the same locations, and the contents can be changed out from under that reference. Take, for example, these statements:

```
@array1 = qw(ready set go);
@array2 = @array1;
$arrayref = \@array1;
push @array1, "stop";

$, = ' ';  # set the array element delimeter
print "@array1\n";
print "@array2\n";
print "@$arrayref\n";
```

Can you guess what will get printed in each of the three print statements? The contents of `@array1` were created in the first statement and then changed in the fourth, so the printout of `@array1` will be this:

```
ready set go stop
```

`@array2` was assigned to the contents of `@array1` in the second line. With list assignment, the array on the right is expanded into its component elements, and then those elements are assigned to the array on the left. So `@array2` gets a copy of `@array1` at that time, and will print like this:

```
ready set go
```

Modifying `@array2` has no effect on `@array1`; they are now separate arrays with separate contents.

The reference to `@array1` in `$arrayref`, however, will be the same as the current contents of `@array1`, because the reference points to the same memory location as `@array1` does. Printing that dereference, then, will result in

```
ready set go stop
```

Using References with Subroutine Arguments and Return Values

So far, you've got a basic idea of how references work. There's still lots more detail to explain about creating and using references, but let's stop for a moment and do something practical. On Day 11, "Creating and Using Subroutines," when we talked about subroutines, I mentioned that lists and subroutines tend to be somewhat awkward without references. Let's revisit that topic and explore how references can make subroutine list arguments and return values much easier to manage.

Subroutine Arguments

As you already know, Perl has a very basic ability to pass arguments into and out of subroutines. All list arguments into a subroutine are flattened into a single list and stored in `@_`. Return values, as well, are returned as a single scalar or flattened list of scalars. Although this makes simple arguments easy to process, subroutines that take several lists as arguments can become problematic, as those lists lose their identities on their way into the subroutine. As I noted on Day 11, you can work around this limitation in a variety of ways, including storing lists in global array or hash variables (avoiding argument passing altogether), or passing along information about the lists themselves (such as the length) as an argument, which allows you to reconstruct the list inside the subroutine itself.

The most sensible way—and often the most efficient—to get around Perl's list-flattening behavior with subroutines is to avoid passing actual list contents into subroutines altogether. Pass in references instead, and then dereference the references inside the subroutine to get at the contents of those lists.

Here's an example, borrowed from an earlier exercise, of a subroutine that takes two arrays as arguments and returns a list of all the elements that are common between them (the intersection of the two arrays). The length of the first array is passed in as the first argument, so we can reconstruct the two arrays inside the subroutine. Here we do it with a call to splice (remember that shift inside a subroutine, with no arguments, shifts @_):

```
sub inter {
  my @first = splice(@_,0,shift);
  my @final = ();
  my ($el, $el2);

  foreach $el (@first) {
      foreach $el2 (@_) {
          if (defined $el2 && $el eq $el2) {
              push @final,$el2;
              undef $el2;
              last;
          }
      }
  }
  return @final;
}
```

We'd call this subroutine with a length and two arrays as arguments:

```
@one = (1..10);
@two = (8..15);
@three = inter(scalar(@one),@one,@two);
```

One could argue that this example isn't too awful; it's only two arrays, after all, and a splice takes care of splitting up the elements. But what if you had more than two arrays as arguments? That'd be a lot of splitting. And if any of the arrays were particularly huge, that would mean a lot of copying elements before you even started actually processing any elements. Not very efficient.

Let's rewrite that subroutine to use references. Instead of passing the actual arrays into the subroutine, pass references to those arrays. Then assign those references to variables inside the subroutine and dereference them to get the contents. Our new subroutine might look like this:

```
sub inter {
    my ($first, $second) = @_;
    my @final = ();
    my ($el, $el2);

    foreach $el (@$first) {
        foreach $el2 (@$second) {
            if (defined $el2 && $el eq $el2) {
                push @final,$el2;
                undef $el2;
                last;
```

```
12:             }
13:         }
14:     }
15:     return @final;
16: }
```

You'd call this subroutine with only two arguments, two references to arrays:

```
@one = (1..10);
$oneref = \@one;
@two = (8..14);
$tworef = \@two;
@three =  inter($oneref,$tworef);
```

There are only two differences between this subroutine and the one before it: the first line that manages the argument list (line 2), and the references to the lists inside both nested `foreach` loops (lines 6 and 7). In the reference version, we don't need to splice elements from a single argument list; the argument list only has two elements: the two scalar references. So we can replace the splice with an ordinary scalar assignment to two local variables.

With the references in hand, we move on to the `foreach` loops that test each element. Here, we don't have local arrays at all; all we have are references. To get at the array contents, we dereference the references using `@$first` and `@$second`, and access the array contents from there.

With this subroutine, each array retains its original contents and makeup. If you pass in references to hashes, those hashes remain hashes and are not flattened into lists. And there's also no copying of the list data from one place to another as there is with passing regular lists. It's more efficient and it's often easier to manage and to understand, particularly with subroutines with complex arguments.

Passing References Back from Subroutines

The converse of passing lists to subroutines is returning lists back from subroutines using the `return` operator. By default, `return` can return either a single scalar or a list, and will flatten multiple lists into a single list.

To return multiple items from a subroutine, and keep the integrity of lists and hashes, simply return references to those structures instead of the contents themselves, just as you did with passing list data into the subroutine:

```
sub foo {
   my @templist;
   my @temphash;
   #...
```

```
    my $tempref = \@templist;
    my $temphashref = \%temphash;
    return ($tempref, $temphashref);
}
```

This may initially seem wrong, given that the variables in this example, `@templist` and `%temphash`, are local variables, and will vanish after the subroutine is done executing. If the variables go away, what do the references have left to point to? The secret here is that even though the variable *name* goes away when it goes out of scope (when the subroutine finishes executing), the data it contained still exists, and the reference continues to point to it. In fact, dereferencing that reference will now be the *only* way to continue to get access to that data. This behavior affects how Perl stores and reclaims memory while your script is running; we'll look at that notion in the section "A Note About Memory and Garbage Collection."

Other Ways of Using References

Both using the backslash operator to create a reference and putting the reference where a name would be expected to dereference that reference are two common ways of creating and using references. But there are lots of other ways for doing the same things, some of which give you new and complex abilities, and others which provide more readable ways of doing the same thing. In this section, we'll look at some of the other ways to create and use references, as well as explore some of the other issues surrounding references.

Dereferencing List Reference Elements

If you've got a reference to a list, one of the more common things you'll want to do with that reference is to get access to the individual elements inside that list—to print them, to sort them, to slice them, and so on. One way to do that is to use the basic syntax you learned about at the start of this lesson, and that we used in the previous example:

```
print "Minimum number: $$ref[0]\n";
```

This particular line prints the first element of the array pointed to by the reference `$ref`. If you were going to do the same thing to a hash, you'd use hash syntax, and replace the hash name with the reference:

```
print "John's last name: $$ref{john}\n";
```

There's another way to gain access to the list and hash elements pointed to by a reference, one which in many cases (particularly with complex data structures and object-oriented objects) is slightly easier to read. Use the reference, the arrow operator (`->`), and an array subscript to gain access to list elements pointed to by references:

```
$first =  $listref->[0];
```

Note that in this expression there is only one dollar sign. This expression dereferences the list reference in the variable `$listref`, and returns the 0th element of that list. It is precisely the same as using the standard dereferencing mechanism:

```
$first = $$listref[0];
```

To use this syntax with hashes, use the hash reference, the arrow operator `->`, and the hash key in brackets:

```
$value = $hashref->{$key};
```

This form is just the same as the standard way:

```
$value = $$hashref->{$key};
```

Don't confuse the arrow operator -> with the hash pair operator =>. The former is used to dereference a reference; the latter is the same as a comma and is used to make initializing the contents of hashes easier to read.

We'll come back to this syntax in the section on "Creating Nested Data Structures with References."

References with Blocks

A third way of dereferencing references is similar to that of basic references; instead of using a reference variable name in place of a regular variable name, you use a block (inside curly brackets) in place of a regular variable name. The block, when evaluated, should return a reference. So, for example, say you had a reference to a list:

19

```
$listref = \@list;
```

You could get at the third element of that list using regular dereferencing:

```
$third = $$listref[3];
```

Or through arrow notation:

```
$third = $listref->[3];
```

Or with a block:

```
$third = ${$listref}[3];
```

To get the contents or last index of a list through a reference you might use regular dereferencing:

```
@list = @$listref;
$index = $#$listref;
```

Or a block:

```
@list = @{$listref};
$index = $#{$listref};
```

This particular block doesn't have much of a point, given that all it does is evaluate the `$listref` variable, and you could do that just as easily and with fewer characters using a regular dereference. But you could, for example, have called a subroutine inside the block that returned a reference, used an `if` conditional to choose one reference or another, or put any other expression inside that block. It doesn't have to be a simple variable.

Block dereferencing also allows you to build up some very complex dereferences for very complex structures that use those references. We'll look at this in more detail in the section on "Accessing Elements in Nested Data Structures."

The `ref` Function

Say you've got a reference stored in a scalar variable. You'd like to know what kind of data that reference actually points to, so you don't end up trying to multiply lists or get elements out of strings. Perl has a built-in function to do just that called `ref`.

The `ref` function takes a scalar for an argument. If the scalar isn't a reference, that is, if it's a string or a number, then `ref` returns a null string. Otherwise, it returns a string indicating the kind of data the reference points to. Table 19.1 shows the possible values.

TABLE 19.1 POSSIBLE RETURN VALUES OF THE `ref` FUNCTION

Return Value	*Means the Reference Points To*
REF	Another reference
SCALAR	A scalar value
ARRAY	An array
HASH	A hash
CODE	A subroutine
GLOB	A typeglob
"" (null string)	Not a reference

We'll look at references to subroutines and typeglobs in "Going Deeper."

The ref function is most commonly used to test references for their type:

```
if (ref($ref) eq "ARRAY") {
   foreach $key (@$ref) {
     #...
   }
} elsif (ref($ref eq "HASH") {
   foreach $key (keys %$ref) {
     #...
   }
}
```

A Note About Memory and Garbage Collection

One internal side effect of using references concerns the amount of memory that Perl uses up as it runs your script and creates various bits of data. Normally, when your script runs, Perl sets aside bits of memory for your data automatically, and then reclaims the memory once you're done with it. The process of reclaiming the memory—called *garbage collection*—is different from many other languages, such as C, where you must allocate and free memory on your own.

Perl uses what's called a reference-counting garbage collector. This means that for each bit of data, Perl keeps track of the number of references to that data—including the variable name that holds it. If you create a reference to that bit of data, then Perl increments the reference count by 1. If you move the reference to something else, or if a local variable that holds a bit of data disappears at the end of the block or a subroutine, Perl decrements the reference count. Once the reference count goes to 0—there are no variables referring to that data, nor any references that point to it—then Perl reclaims the memory that was held by that data.

Normally, this all works automatically and you don't have to do anything about it in your scripts. However, there is a case with references that you have to be careful about: the problem of circular references.

Take these two references:

```
sub silly {
   my ($ref1, $ref2);
   $ref1 = \$ref2;
   $ref2 = \$ref1;
   # .. do silly things
}
```

In this example, the reference in `$ref1` points to the thing `$ref2` points to, and `$ref2` points to the thing `$ref1` points to. This is called a circular reference. The difficulty here is when the subroutine is done executing, the local variable names `$ref1` and `$ref2` disappear, but the data that each one contains still has at least one reference pointing to it, so the memory those references hold cannot be reclaimed. And without the variable names, or a returned reference to one or the other of the references, you can't even get to the data inside that subroutine. It's just going to sit there. And each time that subroutine runs while your script executes, you'll end up with more and more bits of unclaimable memory until Perl takes up all the memory on your system (or your script stops executing).

Circular references are bad things. Although this particular example may seem silly and easy to catch, with complex data structures containing references pointing all over the place, it is possible to accidentally create a circular reference where you don't intend one to be. Consider "cleaning up" any references you use in blocks or subroutines (`undef` them or assign them to something like `0` or `''`) to make sure they don't become unclaimed memory.

Creating Nested Data Structures with References

Subroutines are not the only place where references come in handy. The other significant feature that becomes possible with references is complex data structures such as multidimensional arrays. In this section we'll look at constructing complex data structures with nested arrays and hashes using references and anonymous data. Later on in the lesson, in "Accessing Elements in Nested Data Structures," we'll look at getting data back out of the nested data structures you've just created.

What Is a Nested Data Structure?

Normally in Perl, lists, arrays, and hashes are flat, one dimensional, containing nothing but scalars. Combine multiple lists, and they all get squished down to a single one. Hashes are effectively just lists with a different way of organizing the data inside them. While this makes creating and using collections of data really easy, it's also quite limiting when you're trying to represent larger or more complex data sets efficiently.

Say, for example, that your data consists of information about people: first name, last name, age, height, and names of all that person's children. How would you represent this data? First and last names are easy: create a hash, keyed by last name and with the first names as the values for those keys. Heights—well, you might create a second hash, also keyed by last name, for the heights. But then there's the names of children. Perhaps a third hash, keyed by last name, with the values being strings representing the names of the children, separated by colons and then split on-the-fly when you want to use them? As you can see, once the data gets complex, you end up creating too many flat lists to keep track of it all, or creating funny workarounds with strings in order to get around the inability to store lists inside other lists.

That's where references come in. It's true a list is a flat collection of scalars. But a reference is a scalar—and a reference can point to another list. And that list, in turn, can contain references to other lists. Get it? References allow you to nest lists inside other lists, arrays inside arrays, hashes inside arrays, arrays as values for hashes, and so on. We'll call all these things—any combination of lists, arrays, and hashes—*nested data structures*.

Using Anonymous Data

Although references are crucial for creating nested data structures, there's one other thing you need to know about that will make building nested data structures easier: anonymous data. The term *anonymous* means "without a name." Anonymous data in Perl, specifically, refers to data (usually arrays and hashes, but also subroutines) that you can only access through a reference—that data does not also have an associated variable name.

> **Note**
>
> As with the last section, in this section we'll look specifically at arrays and hashes. We'll cover anonymous subroutines and the references to them in "Going Deeper" at the end of this lesson.

We've already seen anonymous data earlier in this chapter, when we created arrays inside subroutines and then returned references to those arrays. After the subroutine exits, the original local variable that held the data disappears, and the only way to get at the data is through a reference. That data is then anonymous.

Anonymous data is useful for nested data structures because if you're going to create a list of lists, then the only variable name you need is the one that holds the outside list (and you don't even really need that one). You don't need separate variables for all the data inside the lists; references will work just fine.

You could create anonymous data for nested data structures using local variables inside subroutines or blocks. In some ways, when you're filling structures with data you read from files or from standard input, it's easier to do so that way. But there's another way to create anonymous data, and that's with actual Perl syntax: brackets (`[]`) or curly brackets (`{}`).

Say you wanted to create a reference to an array. The normal way would be as we've seen it:

```
@array = ( 1..10 );
$arrayref = \@array;
```

But this isn't anonymous; the array is stored in the variable `@array`. To create that same array anonymously, you'd initialize that list inside brackets, instead of parentheses. The result is a reference, which you can then store:

```
$listref = [ 1..10 ];
```

This array is accessible through the reference. You would dereference it the way you would any array, but not through a variable name. It's anonymous data.

You can do the same thing with anonymous hashes, where curly brackets create a reference to an anonymous hash:

```
$hashref = {
   'Taylor' => 12,
   'Ashley' => 11,
   'Jason'  => 12.
   'Brendan' => 13,
}
```

Note that the elements inside the hash must still be in pairs, and will be combined into keys and values just as regular hashes are.

The brackets and curly brackets here should not be confused with the array indexes (`$array[0]`) and hash lookups (`$hash{key}`). The characters are the same so that you can remember that brackets go with arrays and curly brackets with hashes, but they do entirely different things.

Array and hash brackets construct an array or hash in memory, and then return a reference to that memory location. Anything that you can put inside an array or a hash, you can put inside anonymous array or hash brackets. That includes array and hash variables, although these two lines do *not* produce the same result:

```
$arrayref = \@array;

$arrayref = [ @array ];
```

The difference between these two is that the first reference points to the actual memory location of the `@array` variable. The second one produces a new array, copying all the elements of `@array`, and then creates a reference to that new memory location. You could consider it as simply creating a reference to a copy of `@array`. This will be an important trick to know later on when we create data structures inside loops.

Creating Data Structures with Anonymous Data

With anonymous data and references, creating nested data structures is a simple matter of putting it all together. In this section, we'll look at three kinds of nested data structures: arrays of arrays, hashes of arrays, and hashes of hashes.

Arrays of Arrays

Let's start with something simple: an array of arrays, or a *multidimensional array* (see Figure 19.2). You might use an array of arrays to create a sort of two-dimensional field such as a chessboard (where each square on the "board" has a position somewhere inside a row, and the larger array stores all the rows).

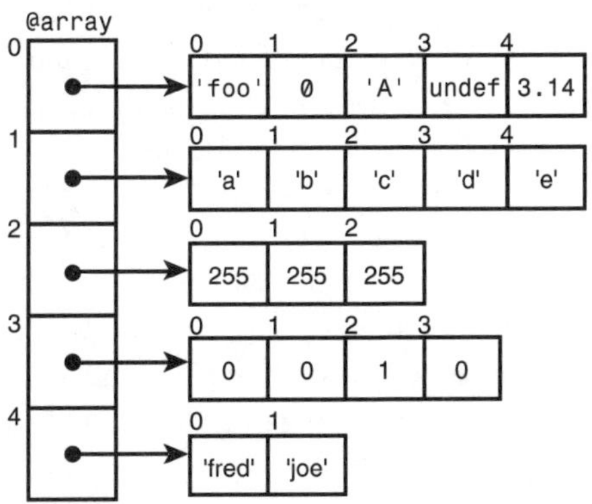

FIGURE 19.2
An array of arrays.

> **Note**
>
> If you're used to C's true multidimensional arrays, note that Perl's multidimensional arrays are more like arrays of pointers and are not truly multidimensional.

To create an array of arrays, use anonymous array syntax for the inner arrays, and regular list syntax for the outer (this array of arrays represents the red, green, and blue values for various shades of gray):

19

```
@greys = (
   [ 0, 0, 0 ],
   [ 63, 63, 63 ],
   [ 127, 127, 127 ],
   [ 191, 191, 191 ],
   [ 255, 255, 255],
);
```

Here, the arrays with the numbers are inside brackets, which creates references to those arrays. Then the larger array, inside parentheses, creates a simple array of those references. Be careful not to do this:

```
@greys = [
   [ 0, 0, 0 ],
   [ 63, 63, 63 ],
   #...
];
```

The brackets around the outer array will create a reference to an array, not a regular array. Perhaps that is what you want, but in that case you wouldn't assign it to an array variable. Use a scalar variable to hold the reference instead.

Hashes of Arrays

A hash of arrays is a nested data structure in which a hash, with normal keys, has values that are references to arrays (see Figure 19.3). You might use a hash of arrays to keep track of a list of people and their children, where the hash would be keyed by the people's names, and the values would be lists of their children's names. Or a movie theater might keep a hash of movie names and their associated show times.

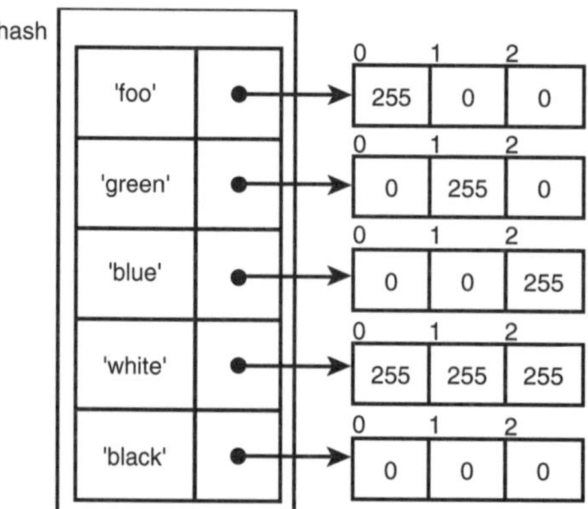

FIGURE 19.3
Hashes of arrays.

To create a hash of arrays, use hash syntax for the outer hash, normal strings as the keys, and anonymous arrays as the values (this one keeps track of a schedule of activities at a summer camp):

```
%schedule = (
   'monday' => [ 'archery', 'soccer', 'dance' ],
   'tuesday' => [ 'basketweave', 'swimming', 'canoeing' ],
   'wednesday' => [ 'nature walk', 'soccer', 'dance' ],
   'thursday' => [ 'free time', 'swimming', 'canoeing' ],
   'friday' => [ 'archery', 'soccer', 'hike' ],
);
```

Once again, watch out for the placement of brackets and parentheses. Here, the inner brackets create the anonymous arrays. The outer parentheses create a list that is then converted into a hash when it's assigned to the `%schedule` variable. Using curly brackets (`{}`) around the entire list would create a reference to an anonymous hash.

Note that in a hash of arrays, only the values can be arrays. The hash keys must be strings, and, in fact, Perl assumes they will be strings and converts anything else (numbers and references) to strings. Be careful when you build nested hashes to make sure your keys are strings.

Hashes of Hashes

How complex would you like to get? Hashes of hashes allow you to create very complex data structures. In a hash of hashes, the outer hash has regular keys and values that in turn store other hashes (see Figure 19.4). You could then look up specific keys and "subkeys" in each of the hashes. For example, a hash of hashes could collect a classroom full of children and the grades they were getting in each subject. Have the children's last names be the keys, and the values would be another hash containing, for example, first name, date of birth, and then the grades for each class.

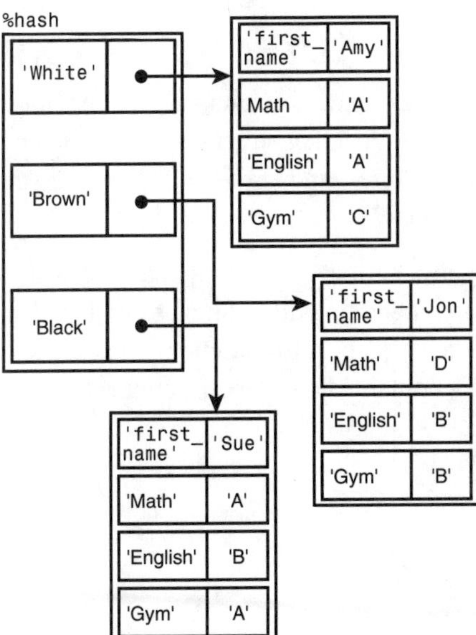

FIGURE 19.4
Hashes of hashes.

Hashes of hashes get anonymous hash syntax for the insides, and regular list syntax for the outside:

```
%people = (
   'Jones' => {
      'name' => 'Alison',
      'age' => 15,
      'pet' => 'dog',
   },
   'Smith' => {
      'name' => 'Tom',
      'age' => 18,
      'pet' => 'fish',
   },
);
```

Other Structures

I've shown you three simple and common nested data structures in this section: arrays of arrays, hashes of arrays, and hashes of hashes. But you can combine arrays and hashes with references and anonymous data in just about any way you'd like, depending on the data you're working with and the best way to organize that data. You can also nest your data further down than I did here, to create, for example, a hash of a hash in which the keys are in turn arrays, and those array elements are hashes, and so on. There's no limit to how deeply you can nest your data structures, so if it seems appropriate, go ahead and do it.

Building Data Structures with Existing Data

The examples of creating nested data structures with anonymous data work great when you already know exactly what data that structure is going to contain ahead of time. But in real life, these sorts of structures tend to get built from data that might be read in from a file or entered via the keyboard.

In that case, sometimes you'll end up combining anonymous data with references to regular variables. As long as you end up with references in the right spot, there's no harm in using whatever mechanism works best for building your data structure. For example, let's say that you had a file that contained a matrix of numbers that looked something like this:

```
3 4 2 4 2 3
5 3 2 4 5 4
7 6 3 2 8 3
3 4 7 8 3 4
```

You want to read that file into an array of arrays, with each row its own array, and a larger array to store the individual rows. You might accomplish that with a loop that looks something like this:

```
while (<>) {
   chomp;
   push @matrix, [ split ];
}
```

That loop would read each line, chomp off its newline with `chomp`, split it into elements with split, create an anonymous array of those elements with brackets, and then finally push the reference to that array onto a larger array.

You might think that this example would be more readable if we split the elements into a list first, and then stored a reference to that list instead, like this:

```
my @list = ();
while (<>) {
   chomp;
   @list = split;
   push @matrix, \@list;
}
```

But there's a big catch to this example (a catch lots of programmers make the first time they try this). Given input like the preceding matrix, with this loop you'd end up with an array of arrays that looked like this:

```
3 4 7 8 3 4
3 4 7 8 3 4
3 4 7 8 3 4
3 4 7 8 3 4
```

19

Can you guess why? The problem is with the variable name and, later, the reference to it. With each turn of the loop, although the *contents* of the variable `@list` change, the memory location stays the same. Each time you read a line, you're pushing a reference to the *same* memory location. The array you end up with is an array of four references, and each one points to exactly the same place.

One solution to this mistake—and it's a common one, so watch out for it—is to create a reference to a copy of the array's data, not to the array itself. This way, a new location is created in memory each time the loop executes, so you end up with references to different places. You can do this simply by putting anonymous array brackets around your array variable:

```
my @list = ();
while (<>) {
   chomp;
   @list = split;
```

```
   push @matrix, [ @liot ];
}
```

Watch out with hashes that you do the same thing with an anonymous hash (in this case, putting an anonymous hash into an array of hashes):

```
push @arrayofhashes, { %hash };
```

The other solution to this problem is to use a `my` variable inside the loop itself. Since the `my` variable will get created from scratch at each turn of the loop, the references will point to different bits of memory each time:

```
while (<>) {
   chomp;
   my @list = split;
   push @matrix, \@list ;
}
```

Accessing Elements in Nested Data Structures

Building nested data structures is one thing; getting elements out of them is another. With references inside arrays pointed to by other references, getting at an actual element can be a chore, particularly in complex structures. Fortunately, Perl has syntax to help.

Say you have a matrix (array of arrays) of numbers like the one we used in the last section:

```
@nums = (
   [ 3, 4, 2, 4, 2, 3 ],
   [ 5, 3, 2, 4, 5, 4 ],
   [ 7, 6, 3, 2, 8, 3 ],
   [ 3, 4, 7, 8, 3, 4 ],
);
```

Now let's say you wanted to access the fourth element of the third row. You could use standard array access to get to the third row:

```
$nums[2];
```

But that would give you a reference, not the data that reference points to (remember, you only get the data pointed to by a reference by explicitly referencing it). To dereference the reference and give you an actual element, you could do this (the fourth element of the array pointed to the reference in `$nums[2]`):

```
$nums[2]->[3];
```

Or this (`$nums[2]` gives you a reference which is dereferenced inside the block):

```
${ $nums[2] }[3];
```

Either one of these would work, but neither one is particularly readable. Perl provides a shorthand syntax for multidimensional arrays that makes this easier: using the standard arrow deferencing syntax, you can leave off the `->` characters, like this:

```
$nums[2][3];
```

That's much easier to figure out, and analogous to multidimensional array access in other languages (like C, for instance).

The situation is different if, instead of an actual array in `@nums`, all you had was a reference to an array of arrays. Then there are two references to dereference, and you'd use syntax like this (where `$numref` is the reference to the array of arrays):

```
$numref->[2][2];
```

Nested hashes of arrays and hashes of hashes work analogously, using curly brackets for the hash keys and brackets for the array indexes:

```
$hash{joe}[5]; # sixth element of array accessed
               # by the key 'joe' in the hash %hash

$hashref->{joe}[5]; # same thing, if $hashref contains a reference

$hash{Jones}{age}; # age value for the Jones record in the hash %hash

$hashref->{Jones}{age}; # same thing, $hashref is reference
```

19

If all these nested subscripts and keys are too disturbing, there's nothing wrong with creating a temporary copy of the reference to an internal array or hash, and then dereferencing that reference in a more simple way:

```
my $tempref = $nums[0]; # get reference to first row of nums
print $$tempref[5];  # print fifth element
# same as $nums[0][5]
```

Need to take a slice of a nested array? You'd use normal slice syntax for that, with the references in the appropriate spots. You'll also need to use block dereferencing in this case, and you'll end up with something ugly like this (this one extracts elements 2 through 5 in the second array in `@nums`:

```
@elements = @{ $nums[1] }[2..5];
```

Because this notation can quickly become really ugly, it may be easier to either pull references into temporary variables and take slices of those, or to create loops that extract individual elements from a nested array. If you want to take vertical slices (one element from some number of nested "rows") or rectangular slices (some number of elements across, another number of elements down), then you'll have to create a loop to do that.

Another Example: A Database of Artists and Their Works

Nested data structures work best for representing complex sets of data and allow you to do various things with that data. In this example, then, we'll look at a database of artists, some information about those artists, and their various works. To save space, we'll keep this example short. All this example does is:

- Read the artist data from a file into a complex nested data structure
- Prompt for a search string
- Given that search string, print the data for that particular artist

The data we'll look at in this example consists of an artist's first and last names, their birth and death dates, and a list of titles of their works. The artist's data is stored in an external file consisting of two lines per artist:

```
Monet,Claude,1840,1926
Woman With a Parasol:Field of Poppies:Camille at the Window:Water Lillies
```

The first line consists of the artist's personal data, separated by commas. The second line is the artist's works, separated by colons. The data file (which I've called `artists.txt`) contains a number of artists in this format.

The structure we'll read this information into is a hash of hashes with a nested array. The topmost hash is keyed by artist's last name. The extra artist data is a nested hash with the keys `FN`, `BD`, `DD` and `works`. The value of the `works` key is, in turn, an array consisting of all the titles. Figure 19.5 shows how a single record (artist) of this structure might look and where each part of the data fits into that structure.

Listing 19.1 shows the code for this simple example. Before reading down to the discussion of this code, look carefully at the lines inside the `while` loop in the `&read_input()` subroutine (lines 21 through 35), and the dereferences in the `&process()` subroutine (lines 53 and 55).

Listing 19.1 The `artists.pl` Script

```
#!/usr/bin/perl -w
use strict;

my $artdb = "artists.txt";                # name of artists database
my %artists = ();                         # hash of artists, keyed by last name

&read_input();
&process();

sub read_input {
    my $in = '';                    # temp input line
    my ($fn,$ln,$bd,$dd);           # last name, first name
                                    # date of birth, date of death
    my %artist = ();                # temp artist hash

    open(FILE, $artdb) or die "Cannot open artist's database ($artdb): $!\n";

    while () {
        # name and dates on first line
        chomp($in = <FILE>);
        if ($in) {
            ($ln,$fn,$bd,$dd) = split(',',$in);
            $artist{FN} = $fn;
            $artist{BD} = $bd;
            $artist{DD} = $dd;

            chomp($in = <FILE>); # list of works in second line
            if ($in) {
                my @works = split(':',$in);
                $artist{works} = \@works;
            } else { print "no works";}

            # add a reference to the artist hash in the bigger
            # artists hash
            $artists{$ln} = { %artist };

        } else { last; }        # end of DB
    }

}

sub process {
    my $input = '';
    my $matched = 0;

```


continues

LISTING 19.1 CONTINUED

```
46:     print "Enter an Artist's Name: ";
47:     chomp($input = <>);
48:
49:     foreach (keys %artists) {
50:         if (/$input/i  and !$matched) {
51:             $matched = 1;
52:             my $ref = $artists{$_};
53:             print "$_, $ref->{FN} $ref->{BD}-$ref->{DD}\n";
54:             my $work = '';
55:             foreach $work (@{$ref->{works}}) {
56:                 print "    $work\n";
57:             }
58:         }
59:     }
60:     if (!$matched) {
61:         print "Artist $input not found.\n";
62:     }
63: }
```

You may note that in this example I did exactly the reverse of the last example: I'm using a global variable to hold the global artists database, rather than keeping all variables local. How you organize your data and variables is your choice; in this case I'm using a global variable because the dereferences are complicated enough without adding another level of reference at the topmost level.

One other kind of odd thing I did in this example was to hard-code the name of the artists database into the script, rather than indicating the name of the database file on the command line. Once again, this is a question of programmer choice and how the script will be used; either way will work equally well (note, however, that I put the filename of the artists database right up there at the top of the script so that it can be easily changed if necessary).

Let's look first at the `&read_input()` subroutine, which reads the artists database and fills our nested data structure with that data. The way I've approached this task is to create a temporary hash for the current artist, to fill up that hash with the data, and then to put that temporary hash into the larger hash with a reference.

We start in line 18 with a loop that reads in the artists database file, two lines at a time. The loop will be exited when there's no more data (as determined by the test in line 21). We'll start with the first line of data, which contains the artist's name and date information:

```
Monet,Claude,1840,1926
```

Line 22 splits this data into its component parts, and lines 23 and 25 put that data into a temporary hash (called `%artist`, not to be confused with the larger `%artists` hash).

Line 27 reads the second line of each artist's data, the list of works:

```
Woman With a Parasol:Field of Poppies:Camille at the Window:Water Lillies
```

In line 29, we split this line into list elements, based on a ":" separator character, and then store that list into the `@works` temporary array. In line 30 we add a reference to that array to the temporary `%artist` hash with the key "works." Note that each time the `while` loop executes, we'll end up with a new `@works` temporary array (declared with `my`), so we'll avoid the problem of referencing the same memory location each time.

With the individual artist's data built, we can add that record to the larger artist's hash with the last name as the key. Line 35 does just that. Note in this instance that because we use the same `%artist` hash for each turn of the loop, we'll use an anonymous hash constructor and a copy of the `%artist` hash to make sure the reference points to a different memory location each time.

If `&read_input()` puts data into the nested hash, then `&process()` subroutine gets that data out again. Here we'll use a simple search on the artist's last name and print the matching record. The output that gets printed looks like this:

```
Enter an Artist's Name: Monet
Monet, Claude 1840-1926
   Woman With a Parasol
   Field of Poppies
   Camille at the Window
   Water Lillies
   The Artist's Garden at Giverny
```

19

The most important parts of this subroutine are the parts that dereference the references to get at the important data in lines 52 through 56. But let's back up a bit and start from line 49, the `foreach` loop. In this loop, because we don't have an actual loop variable, Perl will store each key (each artist's last name) in the `$_` variable.

Line 50 is our core test: We use a pattern-match here with the input and the current key to see if a match was made. And, because we're only interested in the first match for this example, we'll also keep track of a `$matched` variable to see if we've already found a match.

Assuming a match was indeed found, we move to line 52. Here we'll create a temporary variable to hold the reference to the artist's data record—as in the stats example, not entirely necessary, but it makes it easier to manage references this way. In this case, since `$_` holds the matched key, we can use a simple hash lookup to get the reference.

With the reference in hand, we can dereference it to gain access to the contents of the hash. In line 53 we print the basic data: the last name (`$_`), the first name (the value of the key `FN` in the hash), the date of birth (`BD`), and date of death (`DD`).

Lines 54 through 56 are used to print each of the artist's works on separate lines. The only odd part of these lines is the reference in the `foreach` loop. Let's look at that one in detail:

```
@{$ref->{works}}
```

Remember that what we have in `$ref` is a reference to a hash. The expression `$ref->{works}` dereferences that reference, and returns the value indicated by the key `works`. But that value is also a reference, this time a reference to an array. To dereference that reference, and end up with an actual array for the `foreach` loop to iterate over, you need the block syntax for dereferencing: `@{}`.

Figuring out references and how to get at the actual data you want can be a complex process. It helps to start from the outer data structure and work inward, using blocks where necessary and temporary variables where it's helpful. Examining different referencing expressions in the Perl debugger or with `print` statements can also go a long way toward helping create the right dereferences.

Going Deeper

The creation and use of references is probably one of the more complex aspects of Perl (arguably surpassed only by object-oriented programming, which we'll look at tomorrow). In today's lesson I've introduced you to the basics of references and the places where you'll most commonly use them. But as with most Perl topics, there's plenty of other features I haven't covered that relate to references, including symbolic references (a whole other form of reference), and references to subroutines, typeglobs, and filehandles.

For more information on references, check out the `perlref` man page. If you do more work with nested data structures, the man pages `perldsc` (data structures cookbook) and `perllol` (lists of lists) provide further detail and examples.

Shorthand References to Scalars

Need to create a lot of scalar references at once? Here's an easy way to do it:

```
@listofrefs = \($thing1, $thing2, $thing3, $thing4);
```

Here you'll end up with a list of references in `@listofrefs`. It's a shorthand for something doing this:

```
@listofrefs = (\$thing1, \$thing2, \$thing3, \$thing4);
```

Symbolic References

As I mentioned in passing earlier in this lesson, Perl actually defines two kinds of references: hard references and symbolic references. The references I've used throughout this lesson are hard references that are actual bits of scalar data that can be manipulated like scalars or dereferenced to get to the data they refer to.

Symbolic references are different: A symbolic reference is simply a string. If you try to dereference that string, the string is interpreted to be the name of a variable, and if that variable exists, you get the value of that variable. So, for example

```
$foo = 1;                                   # variable $foo contains 1
$symref = "foo";                            # string
$$symref = "I am a variable";               # sets the variable $foo
print "symbolic reference: $symref\n";      # results in "foo"
print "Foo: $foo\n";                        # results in "I am a variable"
print "dereferenced: $$symref\n";
# prints $foo, results in "I am a variable"
```

As you can see, you can use symbolic references as if they were real references, but they're just strings that name variables. The difference is subtle and confusing, particularly if you mix hard and symbolic references. You can accidentally dereference a string when you meant to dereference a scalar, and end up with it being difficult to debug problems. For this reason, Perl provides a `strict` pragma to restrict the use of references to hard references:

```
use strict 'refs';
```

Setting this pragma at the top of your script will prevent you from using symbolic references. You'll also get this effect if you use a regular `use strict` at the top of your script as well.

References to Typeglobs and Filehandles

Two types of references I didn't mention in the body of this lesson were references to typeglobs, which in turn allow references to filehandles. A typeglob, as I've mentioned in passing previously in this book, is a way of referring to multiple types of variables that share the same name (it holds an actual symbol table entry). Typeglobs are not as commonly used in Perl as they were in the past (they used to be how you passed references to lists into subroutines before there were references), but they do provide a mechanism for creating references to filehandles, which allows you to pass filehandles into and out of subroutines, or to create local filehandles, if you feel the need to do so.

To create a reference to a filehandle, use a typeglob with the name of the filehandle and the backslash operator (\):

```
$fh = \*MYFILE;
```

To create a local filehandle, use the `local` operator (not `my`) and a filehandle typeglob:

```
local *MYFILE;
```

See the `perldata` man page (the section on typeglobs and filehandles) for details.

References to Subroutines

Much more useful than references to filehandles are references to subroutines. Given that a subroutine's definition is stored in memory just as an array or hash is, you can create references to subroutines just as you can references to other bits of data. By dereferencing the reference to a subroutine, you call that subroutine.

References to subroutines allow you to change the definition of a subroutine on-the-fly, or to choose between several different subroutines depending on the situation. They also allow advanced features in Perl such as object-oriented programming and closures (anonymous subroutines whose local variables "stick" based on the time and scope in which they were defined, even if they're called in a different scope).

To create a reference to a subroutine, you can use the backslash operator with the name of a predefined subroutine:

```
$subref = \&mysub;
```

You can also create an anonymous subroutine by simply leaving off the name of the subroutine when you define it:

```
$subref = sub { reverse @_;};
```

Deference a subroutine using regular reference syntax or with a block. When you dereference a subroutine, you call it, so don't forget to include arguments:

```
@result = &$subref(1..10);
```

For more details on references to subroutines, and of closures, see the `perlref` man page.

Summary

The last major feature of Perl we had left to cover in this book were references, and today you got a good introduction to creating and using references in various contexts.

A reference is a bit of scalar data that points to another piece of data: another scalar, an array, a hash, or a subroutine. Because a reference is a scalar, you can pass it to subroutines, store it in variables, treat it as a string or a number, test it for its truth value, or include it inside another array. To create a reference, you can use one of two methods:

- Use the backslash operator (\) with a variable
- Use one of the anonymous constructors to create a reference to an array, a hash, or a subroutine

To gain access to the thing the reference points to, you dereference that reference. You can dereference references in one of three ways:

- Place the reference variable where a regular variable name might go, for example `$$ref`, `@$ref`, or `$$ref[0]`.
- Place a block expression (which evaluates to a reference) where a variable name might go, for example `@{$ref[0]}`.
- Use "arrow notation," particularly for references to lists (`$ref->[0]` or `$ref->{key}`). For nested arrays and hashes, you can include multiple subscripts without needing intervening arrows (`$ref->[0][4]`, or `$ref[0]{key}`).

In addition to the basics of creating and using references, we also looked at two of the most common uses of references: as subroutine arguments (for retaining the structure of arrays and hashes inside subroutines), and for creating nested data structures such as arrays of arrays and arrays of hashes. Finally, you also learned about the `ref` function, which returns a string indicating the kind of data the reference contains.

19

Congratulations! Today you've completed the bulk of the hard work of this book. Tomorrow we'll explore some of the other Perl features we haven't looked at in this chapter, and then finish up on Day 21 with some examples that make use of everything you've learned in this book.

Q&A

Q Can you create references to references?

A Sure! All you have to do is use the backslash operator to get the memory location of that reference. Keep in mind that if you create references to references, you'll need to dereference them twice to get to the data at the end of the chain.

Q I'm trying to fill an array of arrays from a bunch of data in a file. I read the data into an simple array, and the add that array to a larger array. But at the end, the whole array has nothing but the last values I added. What am I doing wrong?

A Sounds like you're doing something like this:

```
while (<>) {
    @input = split $_;
    @bigarray = \@input;
}
```

The problem is that each time you create a reference to `@input`, you're pointing to exactly the same location each time. The contents of `@input` change with each turn of the loop, but the location is the same. Each reference then points to the same location and has the value of the last thing you put in there. To get around this problem, either

- Declare your temporary input variable as a `my` variable inside the loop itself. This will create a new memory location each time.
- Use an anonymous array constructor with the `@input` variable (that is, `[ @input ]`). This will create a reference to a copy of the contents of input, creating a new memory location each time.

Q I created an array of arrays. I printed it with a simple `print "@myarray\n";`. But all I got was this:

```
ARRAY(0x807f048) ARRAY(0x808a06c) ARRAY(0x808a0cc)
```

What am I doing wrong?

A You can't use variable interpolation with arrays of arrays. What your print command is doing is printing the top-level of the array—which is essentially three references. The `ARRAY(...)` stuff is the printable string representation of those references. To print a nested array (or any nested data structure) you'll have to use one or more `foreach` loops and dereference the references yourself. Here's an example of what you're actually looking for:

```
foreach (@myarray) {
  print "( @$_ )\n";
}
```

Workshop

The workshop provides quiz questions to help you solidify your understanding of the material covered and exercises to give you experience in using what you've learned. Try to understand the quiz and exercise answers before you go on to tomorrow's lesson.

Quiz

1. What's a reference? What advantages do they give you?
2. Show two ways of creating a reference to an array.

3. Show two methods for gaining access to an element of an array through a reference.
4. What happens to a reference if you change the data that reference points to?
5. What happens when you print a reference? Add four to it? Test to see if it's true?
6. Assume you have a reference in `$ref` that can refer to a scalar, an array, a hash, or to some nested data structure. What do the following dereferences result in? (Assume the reference points to the data most appropriate for each example.)

```
$$ref;
$$ref[0];
$ref->[0];
@$ref;
$#$ref;
$ref->[0][5];
@{$ref->{key}};
```

Exercises

1. Create a subroutine that takes any arbitrary number of references to arrays, reverses each of those arrays, and returns them in the same order it received them. Be sure to test whether the references you get are indeed references to arrays.
2. **BUG BUSTER**: What's wrong with this snippet of code? (HINT: there's more than one error.)

```
%hash = {
 key => [ 1.. 10 ],
 key2 => [ 100 ..110],
};
$ref = \%hash;
foreach (keys %$ref) {
   print "$$ref{$_}\n";
}
```

19

3. Write a subroutine that takes a rectangular slice of a multidimensional array. Your subroutine should take five arguments: a reference to the array to slice, the indexes of the element to start with (row and element), and the number of rows and number of elements to slice. So, for example, if you had a reference to a multidimensional array that looked like this stored in the variable `$listref`

```
[ 3, 4, 2, 4, 2, 3 ]
[ 5, 3, 2, 4, 5, 4 ]
[ 7, 6, 3, 2, 8, 3 ]
[ 3, 4, 7, 8, 3, 4 ]
```

And if you called your subroutine (`&rect()`) to start at 0,0 and slice a 3 by 3 element square, like this:

```
&rect($listref,0,0,3,3);
```

Your result should be:

```
3 4 2
5 3 2
7 6 3
```

4. Write a simple version of the game Battleship. Use a 5×5 grid (numbers for the rows, letters for the columns), choose one "cell" at random, and then allow the user to choose a cell to hit. Print out the current state of the board, with choices marked, in between guesses. Here's a sample:

```
Enter the coordinates of your choice (eg A4): C4
Miss!  Try again.

   A B C D E
   ---------
1| 0 0 0 0 0
2| 0 0 0 0 0
3| 0 0 0 0 0
4| 0 0 X 0 0
5| 0 0 0 0 0

Enter the coordinates of your choice (eg A4): B3
Miss!  Try again.

   A B C D E
   ---------
1| 0 0 0 0 0
2| 0 0 0 0 0
3| 0 X 0 0 0
4| 0 0 X 0 0
5| 0 0 0 0 0

Enter the coordinates of your choice (eg A4): E1
Congratulations!  You sank the battleship!
```

Answers

Here are the answers to the workshop questions in the previous section.

Quiz Answers

1. A reference is a bit of scalar data that allows you to refer to some other bit of data in an indirect way. References allow you to pass subroutine arguments by reference

(retaining the structure of multiple arrays and hashes), return discrete multiple lists, as well as create and manage nested data structures such as lists of lists.

2. You can create a reference to an array using the backslash operator:

   ```
   $ref = \@array;
   ```

   Or with an anonymous array constructor:

   ```
   $ref = [ 1 ..100 ];
   ```

3. You can dereference a reference to an array to get access to its elements by substituting the reference where the array name is expected:

   ```
   $thing = $$ref[0];
   ```

   Or using arrow notation:

   ```
   $thing = $ref->[0];
   ```

4. Changing the data a reference points to has no effect on the reference itself. The reference points to that data's location in memory, not to the data itself.

5. A reference is a scalar, and will behave like a scalar in scalar context, according to these rules:

   - A reference as a string prints the type of data the reference points to (`SCALAR`, `ARRAY`, `HASH`, and so on) and a hexadecimal number representing the memory location that data is located in.
   - A reference as a number is that same memory location number. Adding four to it gets you that same number plus four (not a very meaningful number).
   - All references are true.

6. The answers are as follows:

   a. Assuming `$ref` is a reference to a scalar, returns a scalar

   b. Assuming `$ref` is a reference to an array, returns the first element of that array

   c. Same as b

   d. Assuming `$ref` is a reference to an array, returns the contents of that array (or the number of elements, in scalar context)

   e. Assuming `$ref` is a reference to an array, returns the last index in that array

   f. Assuming `$ref` is a reference to a multidimensional array, returns the sixth element in the first row

   g. Assuming `$ref` is a reference to a hash of arrays, returns the contents of the array that is the value of the key `key`

Exercise Answers

1. Here's one answer:

```
sub reverseall {
    my $listref;
    foreach $listref (@_) {
        if (ref($listref) eq 'ARRAY') {
            my @templist = reverse @$listref;
            $listref = \@templist;
        } else {
            print "$listref is not a list\n";
        }
    }
    return @_;
}
```

2. There are two errors in this snippet. The first is in the definition of the hash; the curly brackets around the hash definition ({}) produce a reference to a hash, not a regular hash. Use parentheses for that, like this:

```
%hash = (
 key => [ 1.. 10 ],
 key2 => [ 100 ..110],
);
```

The second error is in the print statement. This print will successfully dereference `$ref` and print each value in the hash, but each value is in turn a reference, and you'll end up with a printout that looks like this:

```
ARRAY(0x807f670)
ARRAY(0x807f7a8)
```

To print the actual values of those arrays, you need to dereference those references as well. You could do that with some complex dereferences like this:

```
print "@{ $$ref{$_} }\n";
```

Although judicious use of temporary references would make that easier to read:

```
my $arrayref = $$ref{$_};
print "@$arrayref\n";
```

3. Here's one answer (this one does no error-reporting for slices that are too wide or too tall for the data; it slices as much as it can):

```
sub rect {
    my $ref = shift;
    my ($c1,$c2,$width,$height) = @_;
    my @finalarray = ();
    my @slice = ();
    my $rowref;
```

```
    for (; $height > 0; $height--) { # do the rows
        my $c = $c2;
        if ($$ref[$c1]) {       # catch too-tall heights
            $rowref = $$ref[$c1];
        } else {next;}

        for (my $w = $width; $w > 0; $w--) {  # do the columns
            if ($$rowref[$c]) { # catch too-wide widths
                push @slice, $$rowref[$c];
                $c++;
            }
        }
        push @finalarray, [ @slice ];
        @slice = ();            # reset the slice for next time
        $c1++;
    }
    return \@finalarray;
}
```

4. Here's one example. The "board" is a nested array of arrays:

```
#!/usr/bin/perl -w
use strict;

my @board = (
          [ 0, 0, 0, 0, 0 ],
          [ 0, 0, 0, 0, 0 ],
          [ 0, 0, 0, 0, 0 ],
          [ 0, 0, 0, 0, 0 ],
          [ 0, 0, 0, 0, 0 ],
          );
my $hit = 0;
my @coords = &init();

while () {
    &print_board();
    my @choice = &get_coords();

    if (&compare_coords(@choice,@coords)) {
        print "Congratulations!  You sank the battleship!\n";
        last;
    } else {
        print "Miss!  Try again.\n";
        &mark_board(@choice);
    }
}

sub init {
    srand;
    my $num1 = int(rand 5);
    my $num2 = int(rand 5);
    return ($num1, $num2);
}
```

```
sub print_board {
    $, = ' ';
    print "\n   A B C D E \n";
    print "   --------- \n";
    my $i = 1;
    foreach (@board) {
        print "$i¦ @$_ \n";
        $i++;
    }
    print "\n";
}

sub get_coords {
    my ($c1, $c2);
    my $coords;
    while () {
        print "Enter the coordinates of your choice (eg A4): ";
        chomp($coords = <>);
        ($c1,$c2) = split('',$coords);
        $c1 = uc $c1;

        if ($c1 !~ /[ABCDE]/i) {
            print "Invalid letter coordinate.  A - E, please.\n";
            next;
        } elsif ($c2 !~ /[1-5]/) {
            print "Invalid number coordinate.  1- 5 please.\n";
            next;
        } else { last; }
    }
    ($c1 eq 'A') and $c1 = 0;
    ($c1 eq 'B') and $c1 = 1;
    ($c1 eq 'C') and $c1 = 2;
    ($c1 eq 'D') and $c1 = 3;
    ($c1 eq 'E') and $c1 = 4;
    $c2--;

    return ($c1, $c2);
}


sub compare_coords {
    my ($c1,$c2,$d1,$d2) = @_;
    if ($c1 == $d1 and $c2 == $d2) { return 1; }
    else { return 0; }
}

sub mark_board {
    my ($c2,$c1) = @_;
    $board[$c1][$c2] = 'X';
}
```

WEEK 3

DAY 20

Odds and Ends

As this book draws to a close, you've now learned, or at least explored, the bulk of the Perl language as it exists today. But, as with every individual subject in Perl, there are other things to do and other ways to do them that I have not had the space to explore in this book.

This lesson, then, is the "Going Deeper" for the whole book. In this lesson we'll look at a number of topics that are either too complex or too tangential to have been explored earlier. Those topics include the following:

- One-liner scripts called on the Perl command line
- An introduction to object-oriented programming in Perl
- Output formatting
- Sockets and simple networking
- POD files (Plain Old Documentation)
- Evaluating code on-the-fly
- International Perl scripts
- Checking for security holes with Perl's "taint mode"

- Using PerlScript on Windows
- Extending Perl
- Other new features of 5.005

Perl One-Liners

When you write a Perl script, much of the time you'll write it as you have throughout this book—putting the script into a file and then using the Perl interpreter to run that script. But sometimes there might be a task that's just really simple, or there might be something that you only need to do once (or very infrequently). For these kinds of tasks, it's almost a waste of time to start up an editor to write an actual script. For just this reason there are Perl one-liners.

Perl one-liners are Perl scripts that you type directly on the Perl command line. They aren't saved anywhere; if you get them wrong you'll have to type them again.

To create a Perl one-liner, use the `-e` option, followed by the script inside quotes, like this:

```
%  perl -e 'print "this is a one-liner\n";'
this is a one-liner
%
```

In Windows, you'll have to use double-quotes around the entire script and back-slash the quotes for the strings, like this:

```
C:\> perl -e "print \"this is a windows one-liner\n\";"
```

If you're using MacPerl, you don't have a command line. Don't panic! There is a Oneliner menu item under the Script menu; you can type in your Perl one-liner there, but you'll have to include the word `perl`, the `-e` option, and the script in quotes. Figure 20.1 shows an example.

FIGURE 20.1

A one-liner in MacPerl.

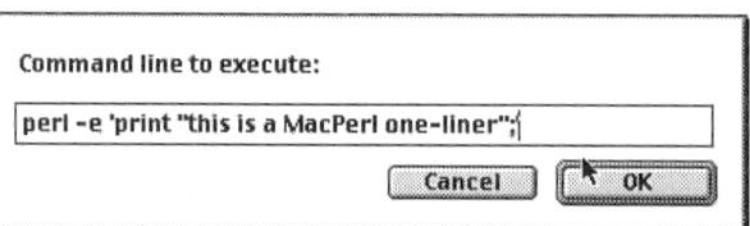

If your script contains multiple statements, put them all on the single line (in most UNIX shells, you can continue a single command onto multiple lines by putting a backslash (\) at the end of a line). Remember, Perl doesn't care much about whitespace, so you could theoretically create an incredibly complex Perl one-liner, and Perl would have no problem executing it (in fact, this is a boast you'll commonly hear from Perl programmers—"I can do that in one line!"—of course, you can do anything in Perl in one line, as long as that line is long enough).

Here are a couple Perl one-liners as examples. To reverse all the lines in a file

```
% perl -e 'print reverse <>;' filename.txt
```

To print all the lines in a file, with line numbers

```
% perl -e '$i=1;while(<>){print "$i: $_";$i++}' filename.txt
```

To remove all leading whitespace from each line in a file

```
% perl -e 'while(<>){s/^\s+//g;print;}' filename.txt
```

To print a file all in uppercase

```
% perl -e 'while(<>){print uc  $_;}'
```

Because these sorts of scripts commonly use `while` loops with <> and some form of `print`, Perl has a shortcut for that. The `-p` option allows you to omit the `while (<>)` part; It will also print `$_` for each line. So, for example, that uppercase example could be written like this instead (whether this example is better or not is up to you):

```
% perl -p -e '$_ = uc $_;' test.txt
```

This is equivalent to the code

```
while (<>) {
   $_ = uc $_;
   print;
}
```

You can also collapse the options into a single dash, as long as the `e` comes last:

```
% perl -pe '$_ = uc $_;' test.txt
```

20

Note

`-p` isn't the only Perl option designed to let you do less typing in your one-liners. The `-n` option does the same thing as `-p`, minus the `print` part (all it gives you is the `while (<>)` loop). The `-l` option, when used with either `-p` or `-n`, will automatically chomp the newlines off of each line for you and then put it back when you print the line. (Or, to be more specific, it sets the value of the `$\` variable, the output record separator, to be `$/`, the input record separator, usually a newline.) You can also give `-l` an octal argument representing the character you want to use as the output record separator.

Finally, Perl one-liners can be extremely powerful when used in conjunction with the `-i` option. For example, say you had written a novel and had it stored in a series of files ending with a `.txt` extension. You want to change all instances of the name "Steve" with the name "Fred." Here's a Perl one-liner that modifies all the original files and creates a backup copy of each:

```
% perl -p -i.bak -e 's/Steve/Fred/g' *.txt
```

The `-i` option changes your original files in place, so that the new versions will have the same filenames as the originals. The old versions of the files (the ones with Steve in them) will be saved off to filenames with the extension `.txt.bak`. This way, if you find that it wasn't Steve you wanted to change, it was Albert, you can get your original files back. Be careful when you use this Perl command—try it on a single file without modifying it, first, to make sure your one-liner works right. Otherwise you could end up moving a lot of `.bak` files back to where they belong!

Object-Oriented Programming

One of the major topics I didn't cover in this book is the use of Perl for object-oriented programming, or OOP (if this was *Sams Teach Yourself Perl in 25 and a Half Days*, we might have been able to cover it). Fortunately, Perl makes object-orientation easy by using familiar Perl features such as packages, subroutines, and references to implement an object-oriented programming environment. This way, if you know something about OOP, you can start programming right away by following only a few rules. If you don't know object-oriented programming, you've got some basic background to catch up on, but then you won't have any other major new language features of Perl to learn to be able to use OOP skills right away.

Getting Started and Learning More

If you're unfamiliar with object-oriented programming but want to do some, your best first step is to learn about the basic concepts. Object-oriented programming is simply a different way of looking at the same programming problem. Everything you've learned so far in this book about syntax and good programming practice still applies; the difference is how your whole larger script is organized and how it behaves.

The central notion behind object-oriented programming is that instead of your script being a collection of sequentially executed statements and subroutines, your script is a collection of objects that interact with each other in some predefined way. Each object has a defined appearance or state (variables) and a defined set of behaviors (subroutines, called methods in OOP parlance). Objects get this template of behavior and state from a class definition. That class definition, in turn, often automatically inherits (uses) features from one or more other classes. When you build an object-oriented script, you use Perl to create one or more of your own classes, which import and use classes and objects from other sources (usually modules). When your Perl script runs, runtime objects are created from the various classes that modify each other's variables and call each other's subroutines to produce some result at the end.

If that previous paragraph scared the living daylights out of you, don't panic. Perl makes it easy to learn about OOP slowly, to use only some features of OOP without having to learn about everything at once. And there are lots of OOP tutorials out there to help you grasp the concepts and the theory. The following are some good places to start:

- The `perltoot` (object-oriented tutorial) man page comes with Perl and offers a basic tutorial and Perl background for object oriented programming. From there, the `perlobj` (Perl Objects) and `perlbot` ("bag of tricks") man pages will fill in the gaps.
- The OO Soapbox at `http://www.progsoc.uts.edu.au/~geldridg/cpp/` offers collections of links to various bits of OOP-related information—not solely Perl-related—including some basic tutorials.
- Many books that deal with other OOP languages such as Java or C++ may offer basic OOP background chapters, if you've already got those books kicking around or if you can borrow one from a friend. I wrote one for *Sams Teach Yourself Java in 21 Days* that may be of use (you can read that chapter at `www.typerl.com`). OOP concepts can usually be applied from one language to another.

If you're still boggled, you still don't need to panic. Although OOP is considered the wave of the future by many, if you're comfortable working in plain old Perl and no one at a job is demanding that you learn OOP, there's nothing wrong with sticking to what you know. There's More Than One Way to Do It.

The Basics (for Those Who Already Know OOP)

So you know what an object is, how it relates to a class, and you're familiar with the terms instance variable, method, inheritance, constructors, destructors, and encapsulation. Let's apply that terminology to Perl.

Using Classes, Objects, and Object References

In Perl, a class is a package, and the namespace defined by the package defines the encapsulation and scope for that class. Variables defined in that package are class (static) variables; instance variables are typically created by using a reference to a hash, keyed by an instance variable name. Class and instance methods are both defined by using subroutines; the only difference between a method and a regular subroutine is that a method assumes its first argument will be a classname (for class methods) or an object reference (for instance methods).

An object reference? Indeed. This is the one bit of new Perl information you need to know to use OOP in Perl. An object in Perl is effectively a reference to some data structure (typically an anonymous empty hash) that has been specially marked so that it behaves as an object and knows to which class it belongs. To mark a thingy as an object, you use the built-in `bless` function. The `bless` function returns a reference to an object that you can then assign to a scalar variable the way you would any reference.

Typically you'll use `bless` in the constructor for your class. That constructor is simply a subroutine conventionally called new. The `bless` function takes two arguments: the thingy for which you want to create an object reference and the name of a class. A simple class definition, then, might look something like the following:

```
package MyClass;
sub new {
   my $classname = shift;
   my $self = {};
   return bless $self, $classname;
}
```

Here, the `new` class method is assumed to be called with one argument, a classname. Inside `new` we create an empty anonymous hash, `bless` it with the current classname, and return that reference. Note that this is a class method, and class methods always have the name of the class as their first argument.

You can also use `bless` with a single argument (the thingy to `bless`), and Perl will use the name of the current class for the second argument. However, because of the way Perl operates on inherited methods, using the single-argument `bless` can result in wrong results if some other class inherits your constructor. It's generally a good idea to get into the habit of using the two-argument version of `bless` and to get the classname from the argument list for the method.

To create and use an object (from this class or from any other class), you'd call the `new` method with the package (class) name. You can do it in the same file as your class definition, as long as you switch to `package main` first:

```
package main;
$obj = new MyClass;
```

The scalar variable `$obj` then contains a reference to the object defined by the class `MyClass`. Alternately, you can use an alternate syntax with `->` to call the new constructor:

```
$obj = MyClass->new();
```

The two different ways of calling `new` are exactly the same; however, if your `new` constructor requires arguments other than the classname, it's often easier to use the latter format:

```
$obj = MyClass->new(12, 240, 15);
```

To call methods defined in your new object, you'd simply dereference the object reference. The `->` syntax works particularly well here:

```
$obj->aSubroutine('foo','bar');
```

Alternately, you can use a more standard function call syntax for methods, where the classname or an object reference must be the first argument to that method:

```
aSubroutine $obj, 'foo', 'bar';
```

In this case, because the first argument is an object reference, Perl will dereference the reference for you and call the right method.

You can also call a method as if it were a function inside a package (`Myclass::aSubroutine(...)`), but don't do that unless you know what you're doing. You're subverting the OOP-ness of the class when you do that, and you lose the ability to get at a method definition available through inheritance. More about defining and calling references in the next section, "Instance Variables."

Instance Variables

When you create an object by using this example, you use an anonymous hash as the thingy to be blessed into an object. Why a hash? Because you can use that hash to store and access instance variables, and you'll get a new version of those variables each time. This is how all internal object states are stored in Perl objects.

20

Note

Some OOP languages make a distinction between instance variables and class variables (the latter is sometimes called *static* data). Perl does not have class variables per se. Although you can always create package global variables to represent class variables (and access them through normal package syntax (`$MyClass::myclassvar`), those variables are not inherited and can be accessed or changed without restriction by any user of your class. Try to work around the use of class variables by using instance variables instead.

Generally a class's instance variables are defined and initialized in the constructor for your class. In fact, you may want to pass arguments to new that represent the initial values of that class:

```
#!/usr/bin/perl -w

package Rectangle;
sub new {
   my ($classname, $w, $h) = @_;
   my $self = {};
   $self->{Width} = $w;
   $self->{Height} = $h;
   return bless $self, $classname
}
sub area {
   my $self = shift;
   return $self->{Width} * $self->{Height};
}

package main;
$sq = new Rectangle (12, 20);
print "Area: ", $sq->area(), "\n";
```

In this example, we used a class constructor that takes two extra arguments—a width and a height—with which it constructs the rectangle object, storing those values in the object's hash keyed by the strings `Width` and `Height`. We also created an `area` method that multiplies the current values of those instance variables and returns the result.

Generally, Perl's model for instance variables is that to access or modify the values of those variables, you create and use methods to do so rather than modifying those values yourself through direct assignment. This has advantages for inheritance, and some would argue provides more of a "pure" object-oriented interface to your class or object. You can, however, access instance variables by using regular dereferencing syntax:

```
# non OOPy variable access
print "Width: $sq->{Width}\n";
print "Height: $sq->{Height}\n";
```

Inheritance

Like any respectable object-oriented programming language, Perl provides class inheritance to allow classes to automatically make use of and expand on the definitions of other classes. If class B inherits behavior from class A, class A is called the superclass or base class. Class B, in turn, is called the derived class or subclass.

To indicate that a class inherits from some other class, use the special array `@ISA`. The `@ISA` array indicates in which classes to search for method definitions if a definition for a method being called does not exist in the current class. So, for example, if you had a superclass called `Feline`, a subclass called `Lion` might look like this:

```
package Lion;
@ISA = qw( Feline );
...
```

The call to `qw` here isn't really needed when a class inherits from only one superclass, but it does make it easy to add more superclasses later, for multiple inheritance:

```
package HouseCat;
@ISA = qw( Feline Pet );
...
```

When a method is invoked on a particular object and no definition of that method is found in the current class definition, Perl looks for a method definition in each of the listed superclasses, depth first, in the `@ISA` array. In other words, the method `eat`, invoked on the `HouseCat` class, would first look for a definition in `HouseCat` itself, then in `Feline`, and then in all the superclasses of `Feline`, if any, and in those classes' superclasses, before looking for that definition in `Pet`. The first definition found is the one that will be used.

Perl only provides method inheritance. For "inherited" instance variables you can use inherited constructor methods to build a single hash of instance variables, which is made up of all the superclasses instance variables plus any defined for the current class (the `perlobj` man page includes an example of this).

Defining Methods

There are three general conceptual ways to look at defining a method:

- New methods specific to the current class
- Methods that override methods defined in superclasses
- Methods that expand on or add to the behavior of a superclass's methods

Regular methods that don't make use of inheritance are defined as regular subroutines inside the class (package) definition. The only assumption you need to make concerns the first argument to that subroutine, which determines whether the method is a class or instance method.

For instance methods, the first argument is an object reference. Typically, the first thing you do in these methods is extract that reference from the argument list and store it in a scalar variable (`$self` is a very common variable name, but you can call it anything you like):

```
sub myMethod {
   my $self = shift;
...
}
```

For class methods, the first argument is simply the name of the class—just a string, nothing special. Again, generally you'll want to extract and save it in a scalar variable.

What about methods that could be class or instance methods, depending on their argument? You'll need a way to test that argument inside the body of the method to see if it's an object or a class. The `ref` function works well this way:

```
sub classOrInstance {
  my $arg = shift;
  if (ref($arg)) {
     print "Argument is an object\n";
  } else {
     print "Argument is a class name\n";
  }
}
```

Note that the `ref` function, given an object reference as an argument, returns the name of the class of which the object is an instance.

Invoking methods defined in the current class will execute that method—even if there's a method of the same name further up in the inheritance chain. This is how you define methods that override existing methods—just define it and you're done.

If you want to add to the behavior of some superclass's method rather than override it altogether, a special package called SUPER tells Perl to search for a method definition in the classes defined by `@ISA`:

```
sub calculate {
   my $self = shift;
   my $sum = $self->SUPER::calculate(); # do superclass first

   foreach (@_) {
      $sum += $_;
   }
   return $sum;
}
```

Note

One common use of SUPER is in inherited constructors (new methods). With SUPER, you can create a constructor that runs up the chain of inheritance to make sure the current object has all the instance variables and default state of those variables that it needs.

You've already seen how to create constructor methods by using `bless`; you can also create destructor methods, which are executed after all references to the object have gone away and the object is just about to be garbage collected. To create a destructor method, define a subroutine called `DESTROY` in your class:

```
sub DESTROY {
   print "Destroying object\n";
   ...
}
```

Autoloaded Methods

One nifty feature of Perl's method invocation is that of autoloaded methods. Autoloaded methods are sort of the methods of last resort—if you invoke a method on an object and Perl cannot find any existing definition for that method, it will attempt to call a method called `AUTOLOAD` instead. The package variable `$AUTOLOAD` will contain the name of the method that was called (including the original classname from which it was called); you can then use that information to do something for otherwise unknown methods. The `perlobj` man page shows a great example of using autoloaded methods as accessor methods for instance variables without having to define separate methods for each one. Here's a simple example of an autoloaded method to handle this sort of behavior:

```
package HouseCat;
@ISA = qw( Feline, Pet );

sub new {
  my $classname = shift;
  return bless {}, $classname;
}

sub AUTOLOAD {
   my ($self,$arg) = @_;
   my $name = $AUTOLOAD;

   my $iv =~ s/.*://;  # get rid of package part
   if ($arg) {  # set value
      $self->{$iv} = $arg;
      return $arg;
   } else {     # no arg, return value
      return $self->{$iv};
   }
}

package main;
my $cat = new HouseCat;
$cat->color("Grey");
print "My cat is $cat->color()\n";
```

20

In this example, the `HouseCat` class doesn't have a `color` method (and we're assuming that none of its superclasses has one either). When the `color` method is called, Perl calls `AUTOLOAD` instead. For this definition of `AUTOLOAD`, we get the name of the method that was called through the `$AUTOLOAD` variable, strip off the package name at the beginning, and then use that method name as an instance variable name. If the method was called with an argument, we'll set that instance variable; otherwise we'll just print the current value (it's up to the caller to manage undefined instance variables). You could just as easily use this `AUTOLOAD` method for any instance variable—`name`, `age`, `temperament`, `favorite_food`, and so on.

`AUTOLOAD` methods aren't technically the methods of last resort; in addition to `AUTOLOAD` there is also the `UNIVERSAL` class. `UNIVERSAL` is used as sort of a global superclass; you can define your last-resort methods there.

An Example: Using Object-Oriented Modules

Perl's sense of OOP is that much of it is optional; you can use only a little OOP, or go whole hog and OOP everything in sight if you want to. It all depends on whatever's easiest, and how much of an OOP fanatic you are.

In many cases, the easiest way to use Perl's OOP in your scripts is to make use of the various CPAN modules in an object-oriented way, but not necessarily to structure your own scripts as a set of objects. Let's re-examine the work we did on Day 16, "Using Perl for CGI Scripting," with CGI scripts and the CGI.pm module. This module is written so that its subroutines can be used as ordinary subroutines or as object-oriented methods. Let's take an exercise we did at the end of that lesson—Exercise #1, a CGI script that does nothing but print the keys and values that were submitted to it—and use the CGI module in an object-oriented way.

Listing 20.1 shows the original script.

LISTING 20.1 `pairs1.pl`

```
#!/usr/bin/perl -w
use strict;
use CGI qw(:standard);

my @keys = param();

```

```
 7: print header;
 8: print start_html('Hello!');
 9: print "<H1>Key/Value Pairs</H1>\n";
10: print "<UL\n";
11:
12: foreach my $name (@keys) {
13:     print "<LI>$name = ", param($name), "\n";
14: }
15: print "</UL>\n";
16:
17: print end_html;
```

We use four of the CGI module's subroutines in this script: `param` (lines 5 and 13), which gives us both the full list of available keys and the values of specific keys; `header` (line 7), which prints a CGI header; `start_html` (line 8), which prints the top part of an HTML file; and `end_html` (line 17), which prints the tail end of an HTML file. In this previous example, we used these subroutines as regular subroutines.

But the CGI module can also be used as an object-oriented class. Create an instance of that class, and you can use those subroutines as if they were methods (because, well, they are). All this involves is one extra line of code and some slightly different syntax for the subroutines. Listing 20.2 shows the result.

LISTING 20.2 AN OBJECT-ORIENTED `pairs1.pl`

```
#!/usr/bin/perl -w
use strict;
use CGI qw(:standard);

my $obj = CGI->new();
my @keys = $obj->param();

print $obj->header();
print $obj->start_html('Hello!');
print "<H1>Key/Value Pairs</H1>\n";
print "<UL\n";

foreach my $name (@keys) {
    print "<LI>$name = ", $obj->param($name), "\n";
}
print "</UL>\n";

print $obj->end_html();
```

See the differences? There are effectively only two:

- Line 5 is where we instantiate our CGI object and store a reference to it in the `$obj` variable. Following Perl conventions, the object constructor for the CGI class is called `new`.
- All our subroutines—`param`, `start_html`, `header`, and `end_html`—are called as object methods by using dereferencing syntax (the object, `->`, and the name of the method)

The end result? Exactly the same thing as the non-OOP version. The CGI module is written to work equally well as a regular collection of subroutines and as an object-oriented class.

Note that this example isn't a pure OOP program; we haven't created any of our own classes here. A "true" OOP script would put the bulk of the code into its own class, using the CGI module there, and then do little in the main package other than instantiate our class and call a method or two to get it running. This is one of the neat things about OOP in Perl—you can use only as much object-oriented programming as you need to. Unlike more strict OOP languages, you don't have to objectify the things that don't seem to fit into objects.

Formats

Considering that Perl is supposed to be a Practical Extraction and Report Language, you may be surprised to note that throughout this book I've given you a whole lot of the extraction part and not much on the report part. That's what formats are for: printing formatted text-based reports of the information you've previously read or processed or otherwise mucked with.

Why leave it until now, when the book is almost over? Quite a lot of the output of Perl scripts these days is in HTML format, as the result of CGI scripts, and less is in pure text-only format. If you expect to do a lot of your Perl work in CGI, HTML works as a better output language than pure text. If you are working more in plain text output, and `print` statements are kind of onerous for making sure all your output lines up properly, you'll definitely want to explore formats.

The notion of formats is that you declare a special template for how the output will look (by using the `format` function), and then you apply that template to the data (by using the `write` function and a file handle) to produce a result, with special placeholders in the template replaced by actual values from a given set of data. The template determines the location of each column of data, the widths of those columns, and how they are aligned. With special Perl variables, you can also keep track of the size of a page (in lines), headers to appear at the top of each page, and the current page number. All this together allows you to create full-page textual formatted reports with just about any kind of data with which you might be working.

You declare a template with the `format` function. Template names are like subroutine or other variable names; they have the same rules for the characters they contain, and their names do not clash with the names of any other type of variable. A `format` declaration contains a name, a set of *picture lines* defining what the format will look like, and a set of variables that determine the data that will be fit to the template. The format ends with a single period by itself on its own line. For example, a simple format to print a set of companies, stock ticker symbols, and high, low and closing prices might look something like this:

```
format STDOUT =
@<<<<<<<<<<<<<<<<<<<@||||@|||||@|||||@|||||
$name,              $sym,$high,$low, $current
.
```

Picture lines include symbols that indicate a plain single-line column (`@`) or a simple filled text column (`^`). Each column can be justified in various ways (left, center, right, numeric) with other symbols (`<`, `|`, `>`, `#`, respectively). The variables indicate the data that will be filled into the format when each line is displayed. If you use `use strict`, you'll need to predeclare those variables with `my` before you use them in a format.

To print formatted data to a file handle, use the `write` function:

```
write STDOUT;
```

Note that the name of the format must match the name of the filehandle you're writing to (although you can change that with the `FileHandle` module). Here we've used the default `STDOUT` filehandle.

Here's an example. Our data is a simple to-do list, where the records are the date the item is due, the priority of that item (1 to 5), whether it's done or not (`0` or `1`), and a text description (a string of roughly 40 characters or less. The data is stored in a file and read into an array of hashes (`@data`) by using the methods you learned about in yesterday's lesson. One of the options you'd like to do in your script is to print your to-do list, sorted by priority, in a nicely formatted fashion. Here's an example of the output:

```
 Done?  Date Due    Priority  Description
------------------------------------------------------------
   No    10/23/1998    1        Finish Chapter 21
   No    10/31/1998    1        Finish Chapter 20, do editing
   No    1/5/1999      2        Meet Fred for lunch
   Yes   12/5/1998     3        item 3
   No    1/10/1999     5        Build Pyramid
```

To print this data without using formats, you'd use a foreach loop to work through each record, build a line, and then print it to a filehandle. Without formats, however, you'd have to keep track of the spacing in your data to make sure it all lined up right. With formats, making everything line up right is much easier.

To format and print this data, first we'll define how the output will look with a `format` declaration. Actually, we'll use two `format` declarations: a simple text-only one for the header, and one for the data lines. We'll also predeclare our format variables first, to get around `use strict`:

```
my ($done, $date, $prior, $desc); # format vars;

format STDOUT_TOP =
  Done?  Date Due    Priority  Description
------------------------------------------------------------
.
format STDOUT =
  @||||  @<<<<<<<<<    @|      @<<<<<<<<<<<<<<<<<<<<<<<<<<<<<<<<<<<
  $done,  $date,     $prior,   $desc
.
```

The first `format` declaration, for `STDOUT_TOP`, is a special kind of format that defines a header for the page. Headers are defined as having the same name as the regular format (here `STDOUT`), with `_TOP` appended. You could, of course, just print this test as a regular `print` statement, but format headers have the advantage of being printed on each page of multipage output automatically. I find they also make defining the formats easier, so I like to include them anyway.

On to the more interesting format, the second one, which is our true `format` declaration. In this one, we define the width and alignment of all our columns: `Done` and `Priority` are centered (note the | characters), and `date` and `desc` are left justified (the < characters). The number of alignment characters determines how many characters to put in that column; if there are more characters in the data than characters in the column, they will be truncated.

With the formats defined, step two is to loop through the data and print it. First, we'll sort it by priority:

```
my @sorteddata = sort { $a->{'prior'} <=> $b->{'prior'} } @data;
```

Then, we'll loop through all the data and print it:

```
foreach (@sorteddata) {
    my %rec = %$_;
```

```
    if ($rec{'done'}) {
         $done = 'Yes';
    } else {
         $done = 'No';
     }
     $date = $rec{'date'};
     $prior = $rec{'prior'};
     $desc = $rec{'desc'};

     write STDOUT;
}
```

For each part of each record, you set up the temporary variables in the format to contain the data to be printed (the `%done`, `$date`, `$prior`, and `$desc` variables). For `$done`, the value is stored in the data as either a `0` or `1`. Here we'll replace it with `Yes` or `No` to make it display better.

The last step after setting all the variables is just a `write`, which will use the appropriate format to generate a line of data and move on to the next record in the line.

For more information about formats, see the `perlform` man page. You'll also want to look at the format-specific Perl variables in the `perlvar` man page for determining things like format headers or page numbers. Finally, the `FileHandle` module provides an OOP-oriented interface to filehandles and formats and provides easier access to many of Perl's capabilities for managing multiple formats and filehandles.

Sockets

Networking is something UNIX has always done well, and Perl would be remiss in not providing access to UNIX's networking features, particularly TCP and UDP sockets. Perl provides a number of built-in functions for dealing with sockets (as listed in Table 20.1), which behave similarly to their C counterparts. If you're familiar with socket-based programming, these functions should look familiar to you. You might also want to use the Socket module, which gives you access to the common structure definitions from C's socket.

Some caveats about the use of sockets in Perl, however. The first is that many of the Perl socket features are available only on UNIX; on Windows or Macintoshes you'll need to use Win32 or MacPerl equivalents, making your scripts much less portable. The second caveat is that unless you're implementing some form of non-standard networking protocol, chances are very good that there's a module that already exists to do what you want to do with sockets. There's no reason to implement any part of a Web server or Web browser; there are modules that will do that, and all you have to do is use them. We'll look at an example of the especially useful `LWP` (Library for WWW access in Perl) modules tomorrow as an example of this.

Check out the section of CPAN on Networking for modules that can handle the vast majority of networking tasks you might want to do. If those modules don't handle it, check out the `perlipc` man page for more details on using sockets, including simple client and server examples.

Table 20.1 shows the built-in functions for sockets; see the `perlfunc` man page for details on any of these functions.

TABLE 20.1 SOCKET FUNCTIONS

Function	*What It Does*
`accept`	In a network server, accepts a socket connection from a client. Same as `accept(2)`.
`bind`	Binds an address to an already-open socket filehandle. Same as `bind(2)`.
`connect`	In a network client, connects to a server that is waiting for connections. Same as `connect(2)`.
`getpeername`	Returns the socket address at the other end of a connection.
`getsockname`	Returns the socket address at this end of a connection.
`getsockopt`	Returns values of socket options.
`listen`	In a server, tells the system to listen for and queue socket connections to this socket. Same as `listen(2)`.
`recv`	Receives a message on a socket. Same as `recv(2)`.
`send`	Sends a message on a socket. Same as `send(2)`.
`setsockopt`	Sets the socket options.
`shutdown`	Closes a socket, with some control options. You could also use `close()`.
`socket`	Opens a socket and associate it with a filehandle.
`socketpair`	Opens a pair of unnamed sockets. Same as `socketpair(2)`.

POD (Plain Old Documentation) Files

POD, short for Plain Old Documentation, is a simple formatting language for creating documentation to go along with your Perl scripts or modules. Commonly, you'll embed that documentation inside your script file itself; that way you can keep both the script and the documentation together and not have to keep track of each separately (Perl will happily ignore the POD content when it executes your scripts).

To view the POD content of your script (or to view POD files containing nothing but POD content), you can use the `perldoc` script (part of the Perl distribution) to display that text on your screen, or you can use a translator to convert the POD files into something else—for example, `pod2text` for text files, `pod2html` for HTML, `pod2man` for `nroff`-formatted man pages, or `pod2latex` for LaTeX formatting. Throughout this book you've probably been using `perldoc`—and therefore POD files—to view the various bits of Perl documentation online.

POD is not a fully featured text-formatting language like `troff`, LaTeX, or even HTML. If you want to create lots of heavily formatted documentation for your scripts, you'd be better off using something else and keeping your document files separate from your scripts. But POD files generally can be read on different platforms and with different systems or can be converted to other more common formats on-the-fly.

You can find examples of POD text in just about any publicly available script or module from the Perl distribution and from CPAN. More details than those in this section can also be found in the `perldoc` man page.

Creating POD Files

POD-formatted text consists of command paragraphs and regular paragraphs. Command paragraphs describe simple formatting and some text; regular paragraphs contain actual body text. You can also embed character-formatting commands inside regular paragraphs.

Command paragraphs appear on individual lines and begin with an equal sign. Some command paragraphs have associated text, which appears just after the name of that paragraph. The end of the command paragraph is a blank line.

For headings, use the `=head1` and `=head2` command paragraphs, with the text of the heading immediately following the command. These headings are similar to the `<H1>` and `<H2>` tags in HTML or the `.SH` tag in `troff` or `nroff`.

For lists or other indented items, use the `=over`, `=item`, and `=back` commands. Use `=over` to start a list, with an optional number indicating the number of spaces to indent the list. Each list item begins with an `=item` tag, with an optional character indicating the symbol or number to mark each item (you'll have to do numbering yourself; it doesn't happen automatically). And, finally, use `=back` to undo the indent created by the `=over`.

Regular paragraphs are included as simple paragraphs, typed, with no command paragraph to indicate them. Paragraphs that start without initial whitespace are typically reformatted to fit the page width (like `<P>` in HTML); paragraphs with initial indentation are used verbatim (like `<PRE>` in HTML). All paragraphs must end with a blank line.

You can embed character-formatting codes and links in paragraphs to emphasize a particular word or to link to something else (commonly another Perl related man page like `perlfunc` or the like). The following are some of the more common character formats:

- `I<text>` will italicize the word `text`.
- `B<text>` will boldface the word `text`.
- `C<text>` uses `text` as literal code.
- `&escape;` substitutes a special character for the code escape. These are nearly identical to the HTML escape codes for accents and other special characters.
- `E<escape>` does the same thing as `&escape;`.
- `L<manpage>` will create a link (or a textual cross-reference) to a man page; for example, `L<perlfunc>` links to the `perlfunc` man page. You can also link to specific sections in the man page itself.

To embed text formatted in some other formatting language—HTML, or `troff`, for example—use the `=for`, `=begin`, and `=end` commands. Text formatted for specific formatting languages will be output unprocessed by the specific translator (for example, the `pod2html` translator will copy any formatted HTML directly to the output) and will be ignored otherwise. Use embedded formatting as a way of providing conditional formatting in specific instances.

Embedding POD in Scripts

You can either include POD-formatted text in its own file (conventionally as files ending with a `.pod` extension), or you can include them inside your script files, making them easy to change and keep updated.

To include POD text inside a script, start it with any POD command (typically `=head1`, although the `=pod` command can indicate the start of POD text as well). End all the POD text with `=cut`. This will tell Perl when to stop and restart parsing the text for actual Perl code.

While POD text is usually included as a block either at the beginning or end of a script, you can also put it anywhere inside your script, for example, to describe a subroutine's behavior next to the subroutine itself. As long as you start and end your POD text with a command paragraph and `=cut`, Perl won't have a problem with this.

To include POD text at the end of a file, and you're using an `__END__` marker (as you might be if you're creating modules), make sure you include a blank line after the `__END__`.

Evaluating Code On-the-Fly

One useful advanced feature of Perl borrowed from other languages is the ability to evaluate a string as a bit of Perl code on-the-fly at a script's runtime. This is accomplished through the use of the `eval` function, which takes a string or a block as an argument and compiles and runs that bit of Perl code as if it were typed into a file or executed by using a Perl one-liner—all inside another currently running Perl script.

Why is this useful? For a number of reasons. One use is that it allows you to build up sophisticated structures and function calls without needing extensive if-else branches: just compose the thing you want to call by appending strings together, and then call `eval` to execute that string. It also allows you to read in and execute other files of Perl code from inside a Perl script—similarly to how `use` and `require` work, but always at your script's runtime (in fact, `require` is semantically similar to `eval` with some extra features for handling where to find files and reloading those files). It also allows you to execute code on-the-fly when that's your actual intent—the Perl debugger's code execution feature uses this, for example. Or you could write an interpreter for your own language in Perl by using `eval`.

The `eval` feature of Perl is also useful for testing code before actually running it and handling any errors or unusual conditions that result from executing that code. This is a feature other languages often call exceptions. For example, if you were looking for a particular feature of Perl to see if it was available on the current system—for example, `fork`—you could try a simple example inside an `eval`, see if it works and, if so, continue on with the script and if not try something else. Exception handling with `eval` allows for more robust error-checking and handling in your scripts.

For a description of `eval`, see the `perlfunc` man page.

Creating International Perl Scripts

20

Internationalization, sometimes called I18N, is the process of generalizing a script or program so that it can by easily moved or translated into different language or dialect. Localization, L10N, is the process of taking the internationalized version of a script and making it work in a specific language. Some internationalization can be done in core Perl—extracting all the text strings that a script uses, for example, to allow those to be translated without mucking with the core code. Other things—working with character sets other than English's A to Z, using sorting (collating) systems other than simple A to Z, and formatting numbers—can be controlled through the use of Perl's local module.

For more information on using and managing Perl locales to create internationalized (or localized) scripts, see the `perllocale` man page.

Script Security with Taint Checking

Say you wrote a Perl script that was intended to be run by someone you don't know and don't necessarily trust—for example, if you're administering a multi-user UNIX machine or if your script will be used for CGI. Since you don't know the person running that script, that person could theoretically have hostile intentions and attempt to use your script to gain authorized access to your system or damage it in some way.

So what can you do to prevent a malicious user from doing any damage through your script? Careful programming can help with that—checking to make sure input doesn't include any sneaky things before passing it to a `system` function call or backquotes, for example. But sometimes it's hard to keep track of what data might be insecure, or hard to remember to make those sorts of checks. That's where taint mode can come in handy.

Taint mode is enabled with the `-T` option to Perl. (It also runs automatically if the user or group ID of the script itself is different from the user or group ID of the person running the script—for example, setuid scripts on UNIX systems.) When taint mode is enabled, Perl will watch the data that comes into your script—the environment, any command-line arguments, or data from a file handle (including standard input). If you try to use that data to affect anything outside your script, Perl will immediately exit. To actually use that data, you'll have to write your script to modify or extract specific bits of that data, thereby preventing data you don't expect from slipping through.

In other words, taint mode doesn't provide any extra security, but it does force you to write your code with an eye for security. If your scripts may end up running in an insecure environment, taint mode can help you make sure your scripts aren't glaring security holes for your system.

Find out more about taint mode and security in Perl in the `perlsec` man page. For more general issues of security and CGI, check out the WWW security FAQ at `http://www-genome.wi.mit.edu/WWW/faqs/www-security-faq.html`.

If you're particularly concerned about the security of your scripts in general, you might also want to check out Penguin, part of CPAN, which provides an environment that allows you to encrypt and digitally sign a piece of code and send it to some other site. At the destination site, Penguin decrypts and checks the trustworthiness of that code before executing it. Even then, Penguin executes the code within tightly controlled confines. You could consider Penguin similar to Java's mechanism for signing applets and then running them inside a closed, secure "sandbox." See CPAN for more details about Penguin.

PerlScript

PerlScript, part of ActiveState's Perl for Windows package, is an ActiveX scripting engine. PerlScript allows you to add Perl as a scripting language to any ActiveX scripting host—in Internet Explorer, IIS or any Web server, or Microsoft's Windows Scripting Host (WSH), for example.

Microsoft's ActiveX scripting engines natively support VBScript and JavaScript scripting engines. While those languages are adequate for many purposes, Perl can in many instances provide for features and more power. And if you're used to working with Perl, the ability to continue working in Perl rather than having to switch between languages is a nice advantage.

For the Web, PerlScript allows you to create Perl scripts embedded inside Web pages both on the client (Web browser) and the server side, in much the same way JavaScript and VBScript scripts and Active Server Pages (ASP) behave today.

PerlScript also works with the Windows Scripting Host, which allows you to control various aspects of the Windows system itself through the use of scripts (it's a replacement for old-fashioned DOS batch scripts). Currently Windows Scripting Host is only available by default with Windows 98, but you can download and install it for Windows 95 and Windows NT from `msdn.microsoft.com/scripting`.

PerlScript is installed with ActiveState's version of Perl for Windows. You can also download it as a separate component from ActiveState's Web page (but you must have a version of Perl for Windows installed before installing Perl for Windows).

For information on ActiveX scripting in general, check out `http://msdn.microsoft.com/scripting`. For information on PerlScript, see the simple documentation that comes with PerlScript at `http://www.activestate.com/activeperl/docs/perlscript.html`, or Matt Sargeant's excellent Complete Guide to PerlScript at `http://www.fastnetltd.ndirect.co.uk/Perl/Articles/PSIntro.html`.

20

Perl Extensions

A Perl extension is the ability to incorporate an external library, commonly written in C, inside a Perl script. When you create a Perl extension, you create special code that allows you to import that external library into a Perl script with `use`, just as if it were a Perl module. In fact, many of the Perl modules you'll find in the CPAN use both Perl code and Perl extensions.

To create Perl extensions, you use a language called XS, which provides the "glue" between Perl and C (Perl extensions are sometimes called XSUBs for the `XSUB` function in the XS language). You can write XS files yourself or create them from an existing C library. There are also special makefiles that need to be created or generated for everything to fit together at the end (a makefile is a script that is used to compile a project and manage the dependencies between multiple files in a project).

The Perl distribution includes a number of tools and modules to help make developing extensions easier, including tools to tie existing C libraries into Perl by generating XS files or to generate C code from XS files. In addition, the modules in the `ExtUtils` package, particularly `ExtUtils::MakeMaker` (to help generate makefiles) will be of some help.

To learn about creating Perl extensions, you'll need a general background in developing Perl modules. Start with the `perlmod` man page for that background, and then see the `perlxstut` man page for a introduction to creating extensions. You'll also want to look at `perlxs` (the XS reference manual), `h2xs` (a script to convert C header files into XS files), and `perlguts` (for Perl's internal functions). The POD files contained in the various `ExtUtils` modules provide information about how to use those modules.

New and Advanced Features in Perl 5.005

Perl 5.005 was released as this book was being written, and throughout this book I've tried to indicate differences and new parts of Perl that would be important if you're using this new version. For the vast majority of Perl features, there are few differences between the use of Perl 5.005 and earlier version of Perl 5; you shouldn't notice radical difference. If you've got Perl 5.005, however, and you feel like experimenting, there are a number of new features available in Perl 5.005. This section covers some of those new features that have not been previously mentioned in this book.

Probably the most significant change to Perl for 5.005 is the use of threading. If you remember back to Day 18, "Perl and the Operating System," when I covered the `fork` function and the use of processes, I noted that the process capabilities in the UNIX version of Perl were difficult to port to other platforms. Threading is meant to solve all that. It allows you to create multiple, concurrently running threads of execution, each of which can be stopped or started independently of any others. More importantly, threading will be supported in the Perl language across platforms, which means that the same complex multi-threaded script written for UNIX will work just as well on Windows or on the Macintosh. Perl's thread system is contained in the Thread module; you'll need to use that module to get the thread system to work. Note that threading is currently in a beta-release state—in other words, it may be buggy or hard to use, and its features are subject to change in future releases of Perl. See the POD documentation that comes with the Thread module for details.

A second significant change is the inclusion of a Perl compiler. The compiler, called `perlcc`, can convert a Perl script into C code, compile that code into a native executable, or convert/compile a Perl module into a native library. Actually, `perlcc` is a front end to a generic Perl compile back-end engine (the B and O modules) that could be used to convert or compile Perl scripts into just about anything you'd like.

Perl 5.005 also includes a new regular expression engine with some bug fixes and a few new features. You can also precompile regular expressions for better performance with the new `c` operator. See the `perlre` and `perlop` man pages in 5.005 for more information.

Going Deeper

Since this whole chapter is a larger version of the "Going Deeper" sections, there's not much left to talk about here. So instead, a reminder: If you've got problems, questions, difficulties, or just curiosity about how any part of Perl behaves—from the basic operators to regular expressions to references to modules—try the Perl documentation (man pages and POD files), and particularly the Perl FAQs—for help and more information. The camel book (*The Perl Programming Language*, which I mentioned in Day 1's "Going Deeper") can often clear up many of the smaller details of how Perl is supposed to behave. If you're still stuck, hit the Web—`www.perl.com`, `www.activestate.com` (for Windows) and many of the other Web sites I've mentioned throughout this book can offer further assistance. Beyond that, there are a number of newsgroups (like the `comp.perl` hierarchy—`comp.perl.misc`, in particular) and mailing lists where other Perl programmers hang out.

Good luck!

20

Summary

Today is the tying-up-the-loose-ends day. Today we looked at a number of extra features in Perl, the stuff that there wasn't time or space to talk about in the previous 19 lessons of this book. It's a bit of hodgepodge of stuff, including:

- Perl one-liners, simple scripts that can be run directly from a command line to accomplish basic tasks without having to create a whole script
- Object-oriented programming in Perl—a combination of references, packages, modules, and subroutines, and some extra stuff to pull it all together

- Perl formats, which allow you create templates for text-formatted reports (the "report" part of the "Practical Extraction and Report Language")
- An overview of network socket programming in Perl
- POD files, Perl's simple method for creating embedded documentation that can be formatted in various other ways (HTML, text, and so on)
- Building and evaluating code on-the-fly with `eval`
- Internationalization and localization with the locale module
- Checking for tainted data to prevent security bugs and holes in your scripts
- Using the PerlScript engine on Windows to incorporate Perl scripts into HTML Web pages or as a replacement for DOS and Windows batch files
- XSUBs, Perl extensions that allow you to connect Perl scripts to native (C-code) libraries
- A short overview of some of the more interesting features in the new Perl 5.005

Congratulations! We've only got one day left, and that one's full of examples. You've now learned enough of Perl to get quite a lot of exciting things done. Go to it! And don't forget—Perl is a collaborative effort. Make use of the modules in the CPAN. And if you write something that you think others might find useful, consider submitting it to the CPAN yourself.

Q&A

Q My one-liners don't work in MacPerl.

A Make sure in the Edit->Preferences->Scripts dialog that you have Run Scripts Opened from Finder selected. If you've chosen Edit here, your one-liners won't work ("One Liner" is itself a MacPerl script).

Q My one-liners don't work in Windows.

A Notions of quotes are different in the Windows/DOS command line than they are on UNIX. You can use both single- and double-quotes in UNIX; in Windows you can only use double-quotes. For one-liners in Windows, make sure that you surround the entire one-line script in double-quotes and that all quotes inside the actual script are back-slashed.

Q My one-liners don't work in UNIX.

A They don't? Did you type the script all on one line with no returns? Did you surround the entire script with single-quotes? Did you remember the `-e` option to Perl? If you've checked all these things, make sure the same script works if you put it into a file of its own.

Q From your description, Perl doesn't appear to support the object-oriented programming notions of public and private data. What's to stop someone from using methods in your class that you didn't intend to be part of the public API?

A Nothing. Perl's object-oriented model doesn't enforce any notion of a public or private API; it assumes that you and the programmers who use your classes will behave decently as far as the API is concerned. As the developer of a class, you should be sure to document your API and which of your methods are public (POD is good for this) and assume that if someone is using your class that they'll stick to that API. Conversely, if you're using someone else's class, you should stick to their documented public API and use internal methods or data only at your own risk and if you're sure you know what you're doing.

Q Multiple inheritance is really confusing and error-prone. Why didn't Perl use single inheritance instead?

A What, and limit the power of the language? It should be apparent at this point in the book that Perl doesn't really ever try to limit what the programmer can do. Multiple inheritance may indeed often be confusing and difficult to debug, but it's also incredibly powerful when used in conjunction with a good design (and don't forget, a good design doesn't necessarily involve inheritance). The designers of Perl would rather err on the side of having enough rope to hang yourself than not enough to tie a good knot.

Q Where on earth did the terms I18N and L10N come from?

A There are 18 letters between the I and the N in the word internationalization (and 10 between the L and N in localization). Internationalization and Localization are really long words to type. Programmers hate that.

Q Your description of Perl extensions describes how to call C code from within Perl scripts; how do I call Perl code from inside C programs?

A Check out the `perlcall` man page. You'll also need to know something of the XS language and how to construct extensions.

Workshop

The workshop provides quiz questions to help you solidify your understanding of the material covered and exercises to give you experience using what you've learned. Try to understand the quiz and exercise answers before you go on to tomorrow's lesson.

Quiz

1. What do the following Perl switches do (with regard to one liners)?

   ```
   -e
   -i
   -p
   ```

2. How are classes, methods, and instance variables represented in Perl?
3. Show two ways to call a method.
4. How are multiply-inherited superclasses searched when a method is invoked?
5. What do autoloaded methods do?
6. What are Perl formats used for? What are the two functions that make them work?
7. What is a POD file? Why use POD in your Perl scripts over some other format like HTML?
8. What does the `eval` function do? Why would you want to use it?
9. What is "taint mode" used for? How do you turn it on?
10. What's an XSUB?
11. Perl 5.005 includes capabilities for multithreading in Perl. What are threads for and why are they of benefit to Perl programmers?

Exercises

1. Write a Perl one-liner that counts all occurrences of the letter "t" in the input and prints the result.
2. Write a Perl one-liner that sums all its input (assume all the input is numeric).
3. Write a Perl one-liner that replaces all instances of three spaces with a tab and saves the result in a file of the same name.
4. **BUG BUSTER**: What's wrong with this one-liner?

   ```
   perl -p 's/t/T/q';
   ```

5. **BUG BUSTER**: How about this one (HINT: There's more than one problem)?

   ```
   perl -ne 'print 'line: ', reverse $_;';
   ```

6. (Extra Credit): Write a Perl class called `SimpleClass` that has three instance variables: `a`, `b`, and `c`. Include these methods:
   - A new constructor to create and initialize the `a`, `b`, and `c` variables.
   - Methods to print and change the values of `a`, `b`, and `c`. Implement these however you like.
   - A method to print the sum of `a`, `b`, and `c`. Be sure to test to see if `a`, `b`, and `c` contain numbers; print warnings otherwise.

Answers

Here are the answers to the workshop questions in the previous section.

Quiz Answers

1. The `-e` option runs a Perl script on the command line (a one-liner).

   The `-i` option edits files in place; that is, the result of the script will be saved back to the original file. Any file extension argument to the `-i` option will be used to save the original version of the file.

   The `-p` option surrounds the Perl one-liner with a `while (<>)` loop with a `print` statement at the end. If you want to perform some operation for each line of a file and then print it, use this command to save some typing.
2. Classes are packages in Perl; methods are subroutines that have either a classname or an object reference as their first argument. Instance variables are commonly implemented as hash elements with the name of the variable as the key.
3. You can call methods as if they were regular functions:

   ```
   method $obj,1,2,3;
   ```

   Or using dereferencing syntax:

   ```
   $obj->method(1,2,3);
   ```
4. Multiply-inherited superclasses are searched depth-first; that is, all the superclasses of the first superclass in the list (including any multiply-inherited ones, in turn) are searched before the other superclasses in the list are searched.
5. Autoloaded methods are called when a method is called that doesn't have a corresponding method definition in the current class or any of its superclasses. You can use autoloaded methods to group together common methods (like `get` and `set` variable methods) or to otherwise catch unknown method names.
6. Perl formats are used to format data in a tabular format for text output. The data will be fit automatically to the appropriate width, with each column aligned or filled based on the format you define. To create a format, you use `format` to define the format template and `write` to output the final result.
7. POD stands for Plain Old Documentation; it's a simple way of creating online-accessible documentation for your Perl scripts. POD makes a good general-purpose documentation format that can be easily extracted and converted into some other output format, like HTML or `troff`.
8. The `eval` function is used to evaluate bits of Perl code on-the-fly, during your script's runtime. You might use `eval` to incorporate other scripts into your current script or to test bits of code before actually running them for real.

9. Perl's taint mode is used to protect against errors and omissions in your Perl scripts that could result in insecure code. Insecure code, run in an insecure environment, could result in a malicious user tampering with or damaging your system. Taint mode puts all external data and settings in a special controlled environment and prevents you from accidentally using that data in a way that could be harmful. You turn on taint mode by using the `-T` option to Perl; it'll also automatically run if Perl is run in a situation where the user or group of the person running the script are different from the user or group of the script itself, for example, a CGI script running from a Web server.
10. XSUB is the colloquial name for a Perl extension; a bit of native code intended to be run from inside a Perl script. XSUB comes from a function in the XS language.
11. Multithreading allows multiple "threads" of execution to occur simultaneously in a Perl script. Perl threads are interesting not just because of the new power and flexibility that they give Perl programmers, but also because they can be used across different platforms. Previously, only UNIX's `fork` function had this sort of behavior, but using `fork` meant your scripts could not be ported to other platforms. Threads resolve that issue.

Exercise Answers

1. Here's one way to do it:

   ```
   perl -e ' while (<>){while (/t/g){$c++;}};print $c;' file.txt
   ```

2. Here's one way:

   ```
   perl -e 'while(<>){$sum+=$_;}print "$sum\n";'
   ```

3. Here's one way:

   ```
   perl -pe -i.bak 's/   /\t/g' ozy.txt
   ```

4. It's missing the `-e` option.
5. There are two problems with this example: one syntactic, one conceptual. The first is that you cannot nest single-quotes inside single quotes. Replace the inner single quotes with double-quotes.

   The second problem concerns the `reverse` function. While this one-liner might appear to print each line in reverse order by character with the word "line" at the start, keep in mind that the `reverse` function behaves differently depending on whether it's used in scalar or list context. Here, because the arguments to print are always a list or combination of lists, `reverse` is called in a list context, which reverses the order of lines in an array. The `$_` argument is then converted to a list, that list of one line is reversed and then passed onto print. In other words, nothing appears to happen.

To actually get the string to be reversed, you have to call the reverse function in a scalar context. This can be easily remedied with the scalar function:

```
perl -ne 'print 'line: ', scalar (reverse $_);'
```

Watch out for the newlines, though. Reversing a line with a newline at the end will print the newline at the beginning. An even better solution is to chomp the string, reverse it, and then print it with the newline tacked on again:

```
perl -ne 'chomp;print "line: ", scalar(reverse $_), "\n" ; '
```

Conveniently, there's a Perl option that'll let you shorten this a little bit: the -l option, which pulls the newline off input and then puts it (or any other end-of-line character you choose) back for you:

```
perl -lne 'print "line: ", scalar(reverse $_);'
```

6. Here's one way to do it (with code to test the result at the end). This version shows three different ways you might consider implementing instance variable access. Note that none of these methods is very robust; none of them check to make sure you're not trying to get or set the values of nonexistent variables (and, in fact, the generic versions will happily add an instance variable other than a, b, or c).

```
#!/usr/bin/perl -w

package SimpleClass;

sub new {
   my ($classname, $a, $b, $c) = @_;
   my $self = {};
   $self->{a} = $a;
   $self->{b} = $b;
   $self->{c} = $c;
   return bless $self, $classname;
}

# the long way
sub getA {
    my $self = shift;
    return $self->{a};
}
sub setA {
    my $self = shift;
    if (@_) {
        $self->{a} = shift;
    } else {
        warn "no argument; using undef\n";
        $self->{a} = undef;
    }
}
```

```
# a more generic way, needs more args.
sub get {
    my ($self, $var) = @_;
    if (!defined $var) {
        print "No variable!\n";
        return undef;
    } elsif (!defined $self->{$var}) {
        print "Variable not defined, or no value.\n";
        return undef;
    } else {
        return $self->{$var};
    }
}
sub set {
    my ($self, $var, $val) = @_;
    if (!defined $var or !defined $val) {
        print "Need both a variable and value argument!";
        return undef;
    } else {
        $self->{$var} = $val;
        return $val;
    }
}


# a really generic way
sub AUTOLOAD {
    my $self = shift;
    my $var = $AUTOLOAD;
    $var =~ s/.*::Σet//;
    $var = lc $var;

    if (@_) {
        $self->{$var} = shift;
        return $self->{$var};
    } else {
        return $self->{$var};
    }
}

sub sum {
   my $self = shift;
   my $sum = 0;
   foreach ('a','b','c') {
       if (!defined $self->{$_} or $self->{$_} !~ /^\d+/ ) {
           warn "Variable $_ does not contain a number.\n";
       } else { $sum += $self->{$_}; }
   }
   return $sum;
}
```

```
package main;
$obj = new SimpleClass (10,20,30);

print "A: ", $obj->getA(), "\n";
$obj->setA("foo");
print "A: ", $obj->getA(), "\n";

print "B: ", $obj->get('b'), "\n";
$obj->set('b', 'bar');
print "B: ", $obj->get('b'), "\n";

# no such method getC; will autoload
print "C: ", $obj->getC(), "\n";
$obj->setC('baz');              # ditto setC
print "C: ", $obj->getC(), "\n";

# reset
print "\nA: 10\n";
$obj = new SimpleClass (10);
print "Sum: ", $obj->sum(), "\n";
print "\nA: 10 B: 5\n";
$obj = new SimpleClass (10,5);
print "Sum: ", $obj->sum(), "\n";
print "\nA: 10 B: 5 C: 5\n";
$obj = new SimpleClass (10,5,5);
print "Sum: ", $obj->sum(), "\n";
```

WEEK 3

DAY 21

Exploring a Few Longer Examples

As with Days 7 and 14, which closed out Weeks 1 and 2 of this book, we'll close Week 3 with another chapter of examples. The two we'll cover here cover nearly every aspect of Perl you've learned over the last 20 days. If you can make it through these examples, you'll be just fine with most of the things you might be asked to do with Perl.

Today we'll look at two examples, both of which are CGI scripts:

- A customized home page generator that uses a configuration file and the HTML from a bunch of other sites to generate a Web page with the information you want on it—and only the information you want.
- A Web-based To Do list that allows you to add and remove items, mark them as done, prioritize them, and sort them in a variety of ways.

Both of these examples are longer than the ones we've looked at earlier; the latter example more than doubly so. Remember that all the examples from this book are available online at the Sams Teach Yourself Perl Web site at `http://www.typerl.com/`—please don't think you have to type in 350 lines of

Perl code yourself. Use this chapter to explore what the code does and then, if you want to experiment further, you can download the online versions.

Both of these examples run as CGI scripts. As with the CGI scripts we looked at on Day 16, "Using Perl for CGI Scripting," how these scripts are installed and used may vary from platform to platform and from Web server to Web server. Some servers may require scripts to be installed in a special directory (`cgi-bin`), to have special filename extensions (`.cgi` rather than `.pl`), or to have special permissions. You may also need to set the permissions of the configuration and data files that these scripts use. See the documentation that comes with your Web server or your system administrator for more information on installing and using CGI scripts.

A Home Page Generator (`myhomepage.pl`)

Lots of so-called "portal" Web sites these days allow you to customize their content so that you can get an entry page ("My Portal" or some such) with just the content you want, making it easy to see just what you want to see when you go to those sites. These pages are great for all the content that one site provides. I thought it would be nice to take it one step further, to have a single page just for me that had different bits of content from different sites on the Web—not just links to those pages, like a Bookmarks or Favorites list—but the content itself. Stock quotes from one site, weather or news from another, a collection of stuff from other sites, all together on one page.

That's what `myhomepage.pl` does. It makes use of the `LWP` module, which allows Perl to retrieve Web pages from sites over a network (this is one of those examples of scripts where you can use lots of modules for the bulk of the hard work and then just Perl to glue them together). For each bit of content, it retrieves the HTML for those pages, extracts the important bits, and builds a new Web page with just the interesting parts (as well as some other links that relate but that I don't necessarily need to see every day). An example of how My Homepage works is in Figure 21.1; this particular version has basic stock quotes, weather, and today's Dilbert cartoon from United Media (the Dilbert is out of sight on the page both for lack of room and for legal reasons; take my word for it, it's there).

How It Works

I could have written this script with all the Web sites and how to process them hard-coded in—grab a page for stock quotes, extract the data, write the HTML, and then repeat for the weather and the comic strip. If I wanted to add more data, more links, or new sections, I'd have to modify the script itself.

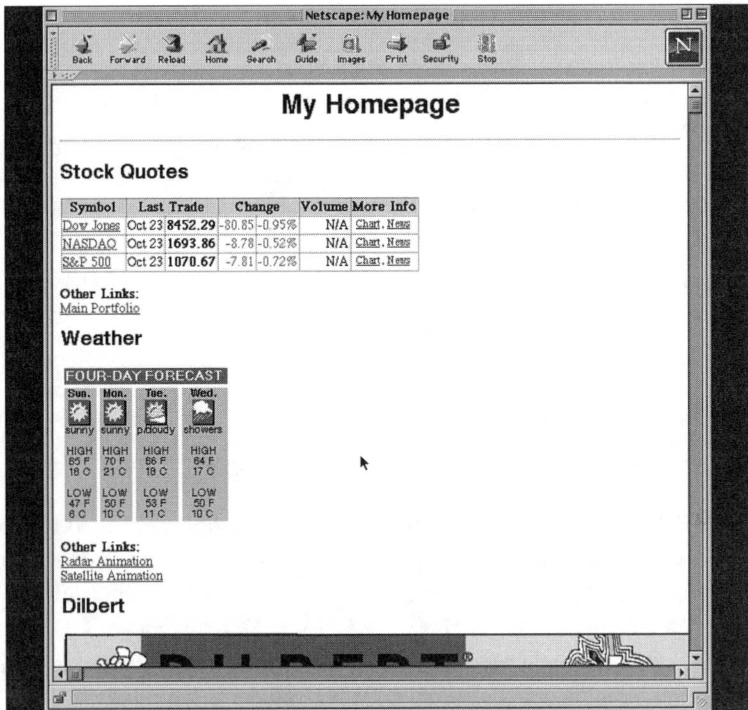

FIGURE 21.1
My Homepage, final result.

Although imminently practical, it seemed that it would be more useful if I separated the data—what to put on the home page—from the script that downloads and processes everything. This script, then, has two parts: a configuration file and a Perl script to read and process the data in the configuration file.

The configuration file is like the address book from Day 14: it's a file with several "records" separated by three dashes (---). Each record represents a section of the home page and contains four fields:

- A title, for the title of the section
- A URL, the URL that contains the content we'll need to retrieve from the Internet
- A code section, containing a block of code to extract the important parts of the Web page (commonly a whole lot of regular expressions)
- Another section, containing code for a hash of other links, where the keys are the titles of the links and the values are the URLs

Listing 21.1 shows a sample entry from the `config` file I used:

LISTING 21.1 MY HOMEPAGE CONFIGURATION FILE (SAMPLE)

```
title=Dilbert
url=http://www.unitedmedia.com/comics/dilbert/
code={
   if ($content =~ /src=\"(.*dilbert\d+.gif)\"/i) {
        print "<P><IMG SRC=\"";
        print url($1,$data{'url'})->abs->as_string, "\">\n";
    }
}
other=( 'United Media Comics' => 'http://www.unitedmedia.com/comics/',
       'San Jose Mercury news Comics' =>
           'http://comics.mercurycenter.com/comics/',
       'Tom Tommorow (mondays only)' =>
           'http://www.salonmagazine.com/comics/tomo/',
)
---
```

The script part of My Homepage is a CGI script, and you'll need to install it as you would any other CGI script. Unlike the CGI scripts we looked at on Day 14, however, this one doesn't have a form that calls it; it doesn't even deal with form parameters. It's called directly as a URL (`http://www.yoursite.com/cgi-bin/myhomepage.pl`, or some such), reads and processes the configuration file (install it somewhere the script can find it), and returns the generated HTML for the home page.

Inside the Script

You're up to your Perl by now; take a glance over the code in Listing 21.2 and get a feel for how the script runs. Pay close attention to the `&procsection()` subroutine; that's where the interesting stuff happens.

LISTING 21.2 THE CODE FOR `myhomepage.pl`

```
#!/usr/bin/perl -w
use strict;
use LWP::Simple;
use URI::URL;
use CGI qw(header start_html end_html);

my $config = 'config';

print header;
print start_html('My Homepage');
print "<H1 ALIGN=CENTER><FONT FACE=\"Helvetica,Arial\" SIZE+2>";
print "My Homepage</FONT></H1>\n";
print "<HR>\n";
```

```

open(CONFIG, $config) or &quitnow();

while () {
   my %rec = &readrec();

    if (%rec) {
        &procsection(%rec);
    } else { last; }
}

print end_html;

sub readrec {
   my %curr = ();
    my $key = '';
    my $val = '';

    while (<CONFIG>) {
       chomp;
        if ($_ ne '---' and $_ ne '') { # record seperator
           if ($_ =~ /^\#/) { next;} # comments

            ($key, $val) = split(/=/,$_,2);

            # process multiple-line entries
            if ($key eq 'code' or $key eq 'other' ) {
                my $in = '';
                while () {
                    ($in = <CONFIG>);
                    $val .= $in;
                   if ($in =~ /^[})]/) { last; }
                }
            }

            $curr{$key} = $val;
        }
        else { last; }
   }
    return %curr;
}

sub procsection {
    my %data = @_;

    print "<H2><FONT FACE=\"Helvetica,Arial\">";
    print "$data{'title'}</FONT></H2>\n";

    my $content = get($data{'url'});
    if (defined $content) {
```


continues

LISTING 21.2 CONTINUED

```
        eval $data{'code'};
    } else {
       print "<P><B>Ooops!</B> Can't get data\n";
        exit;
    }

    if (defined $data{'other'}) {
        my %others = eval $data{'other'};

        print "<P><B>Other Links:</B> <BR>\n";
        foreach (keys %others) {
            print "<A HREF=\"$others{$_}\">$_</A><BR> ";
        }
       print "\n";
    }

}

sub quitnow {
    print "<H2>Ooops! Error:</H2><P><TT> Can't open config file: $!</TT>\n";
    print "<P>Please check your installation or contact ";
    print "your system administrator\n";
    print end_html;
    die "can't open config file: $!\n";
}
```

The `myhomepage.pl` script accomplishes four main things:

- It opens the configuration script and reads a record, creating a hash for the fields in that record.
- It grabs the HTML source of the page at the given URL.
- It applies the code from the configuration file to that HTML source.
- It prints out the resulting HTML.

The script then repeats for each entry in the configuration file.

Much of this script uses things you've seen before—in fact, as a starting point for writing this script, I used the `address.pl` script from Day 14, since the configuration files for each are similar. The only two parts that are unfamiliar are the use of two modules, `LWP::Simple` and `URI::URL` (and the subroutines they supply: `get`, `url`, `abs`, and `as_string`), and the use of the `eval` function to bring the code from the configuration file into the body of the script.

The `LWP::Simple` and `URI::URL` Modules

When in doubt, use someone else's code. Or rather, instead of spending a lot of time in your scripts trying to do something complicated (like, for example, writing networking code to retrieve a file from a Web site), check the CPAN first. In this case, the `LWP` (Library for WWW access in Perl) modules were just what I needed. While I was on the CPAN, however, I downloaded the entire `libwww` package, which contains all kinds of modules for handling Web pages and Web data.

To run this script, you'll need to download these files from CPAN (see `www.perl.com` for more details) and install them on the system where you'll be running the script. Turn back to Day 13, "Scope, Modules, and Importing Code," if you need reminders on how to install and use modules in Perl.

> **Note**
>
> The `libwww` library isn't all you're going to need; there are also a bunch of other modules you'll need to install, including `libnet`, `HTML-Parser`, and a few others. The process of installing all the modules some other modules need can sometimes seem like an endless process (module A needs module B, which needs module C, and so on), but take the time to do it now; these are important and useful modules to have. The `README` file that comes with the `libwww` library tells you exactly which other modules you'll need to download and install.

The `LWP` package contains a number of modules for handling the Web and Web pages. Most of those modules are object-oriented and provide a wide variety of features; if you're interested, examine the POD documentation for those modules. For this particular script, however, all we needed was a simple way to get a Web page from a server into the script. And for that the `LWP::Simple` module worked just fine.

`LPW::Simple` is just that: an easy set of subroutines for doing simple tasks. The one we used here is the `get` subroutine, which, given a URL, contacts the Web site over the Internet, retrieves the file at that URL, and returns that file as one big string. In line 59 of our `myhomepage.pl` script we used it like this:

```
my $content = get($data{'url'});
```

That's basic enough: The `%data` hash contains the record for this section of the home page, with the URL stored in the URL key. We use that URL as the argument to the `get` subroutine and store the result in the scalar variable `$content`. Later (when we get to the section on `eval`), we'll look at how to get the important parts out of that content.

21

The other module we used in this script is the `URI::URL` module. A URI is a uniform resource identifier; it's sort of a generic version of a URL (uniform resource locator). The URL module, also object-oriented, provides various ways of creating, modifying, and analyzing URLs of all kinds. We use it in the code parts of the `config` file. Here's a line from the `config` file I showed you earlier:

```
print url($1,$data{'url'})->abs->as_string, "\">\n";
```

This bit of code actually uses three subroutines (methods, actually—remember, this is an object-oriented module): `url`, `abs`, and `as_string`. The three together are boilerplate code to convert a relative URL—the sort you find in a Web page you've just pulled off its home on a Web server—into a complete absolute URL. We use this code to make sure all the links in the bits of code we use on our home page point back to the site where they belong. See the POD documentation for the `URI:URL` man page if you're interested in more information.

> Actually, I found this code in a great document called the LWP cookbook, which comes with the LWP module. It contains lots of examples for doing common tasks with LWP. If you need to expand this script or do more with the Web and Perl, check out the cookbook to see if it contains an example of the thing you want to do.

Using `eval`

Here's the puzzle: How do you manage to generically extract important parts of an HTML file, when the important parts vary from file to file? The answer is that you don't do it generically, but you do keep it out of the main script. There's no code in `myhome-page.pl` to extract the important parts of an HTML file. All that code—usually a bunch of regular expressions—is in the configuration file next to the titles and URLs and varies, depending on the page.

So the next puzzle: how to get that code into the script itself. The first part is simply to read it out of the configuration file, and the part of the script that reads in the configuration file handles that, putting the entire code section into a single element in a hash, keyed by the string `'code'`.

The final part of the puzzle is the `eval` function, which, as I explained yesterday, takes a string and evaluates that string as if it were Perl code. In this case, our string is Perl code, so `eval` is the equivalent of copying and pasting that code at that point. The code that gets `eval`ed has access to all the variables that happened ahead of time, so we can use the `%data` hash and the `$content` string to process the HTML code and then print it.

Here's that example from the config file again; this one extracts the actual comic strip image URL (made up of the name dilbert, some string of numbers, and a .gif extension) and generates a new IMG tag in our home page (expanding the complete URL along the way).

```
code={
   if ($content =~ /src=\"(.*dilbert\d+.gif)\"/i) {
        print "<P><IMG SRC=\"";
        print url($1,$data{'url'})->abs->as_string, "\">\n";
     }
}
```

The HTML that bit of code generates looks something like this:

```
<P><IMG SRC="http://www.unitedmedia.com/comics/dilbert/archive/images/
dilbert973012490104.gif">
```

The eval function is also used for the 'other' part of the config file, which contains a hash with all the extra links. I could have formatted these keys and URLs in some other way and processed them into a hash as part of the script itself, but this way was easier. Lines 70 through 73 in the myhomepage.pl script show how the other links are evaluated and displayed on the HTML page.

Another Configuration

The sample configuration file I showed you earlier was a particularly simple one; let's work through another more complex one from the standpoint of the myhomepage.pl script. We'll focus on the procsection subroutine from myhomepage.pl, shown in Listing 21.3:

LISTING 21.3 THE procsection SUBROUTINE

```
sub procsection {
    my %data = @_;

    print "<H2><FONT FACE=\"Helvetica,Arial\">";
    print "$data{'title'}</FONT></H2>\n";

    my $content = get($data{'url'});
    if (defined $content) {
       eval $data{'code'};
    } else {
       print "<P><B>Ooops!</B> Can't get data\n";
       exit;
    }
```


continues

Listing 21.3 continued

```
14:
15:     if (defined $data{'other'}) {
16:     my %others = eval $data{'other'};
17:
18:     print "<P><B>Other Links:</B> <BR>\n";
19:     foreach (keys %others) {
20:         print "<A HREF=\"$others{$_}\">$_</A><BR> ";
21:     }
22:     print "\n";
23:     }
24: }
```

Starting from the top, we store the record hash argument in a local variable and print the top part of the section (by using the title part from the configuration file in line 5).

Line 7 goes and gets the HTML file using `LWP`'s `get` subroutine. If that was successful (lines 9 through 13), we evaluate the configuration file's code section; otherwise, we print an error and skip to the next section.

Let's look at the code from the configuration file in Listing 21.4. This is code from the weather part of the page, which pulls out a bunch of table cells in the middle of the page.

Listing 21.4 Configuration Code for Weather Section

```
{
    my $table = "<table>\n";
    while ($content =~ /(<tr.*?<\/tr>)/gis) {
        my $row = $1;
        if ($row =~ /FOUR-DAY/is) { # grab header row
            $table .= $row;
        }
        if ($row =~ /<strong>(Fri|Sat|Sun|Mon|Tue|Wed|Thu)\./is) {
            $table .= $row;
        }
    }
    $table =~ s/src="([^\"]+)"/'src="' .
          url($1,$data{'url'})->abs->as_string . '"'/eisg;
    $table =~ s/"#FF[9C]+66"/"#8FCDFF"/g; # can be #FF9966 or #FFCC66

    $table .= "</table>";
    print "$table\n";
}
```

Much of this code is regular expressions, but an idea of what we're looking for would help decipher this. Figure 21.2 shows the result we're aiming for, which includes the top row ("Four-Day Forecast") and the four long cells with the weather images and the temperatures.

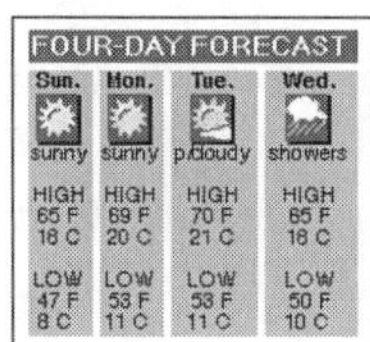

FIGURE 21.2
My Homepage, weather part.

Each of these elements is represented by table rows in the larger page, so the first regular expression in line 3 looks for table row code—text surrounded by `<TR>` and `</TR>` tags. But there's one tricky thing about this particular regular expression—it's actually a pattern you didn't learn in Days 9 and 10 (well, if you looked at "Going Deeper," you did learn it, but we didn't cover it in the body of those lessons). You'll remember that `.*` is a greedy quantifier that will happily eat up everything to the end of the row. That's a bad idea, but it's really hard to get around the use of it here, given that we need to match up to `</TD>` as a whole and not to a single character. So we use `.*?` instead, which is a special non-greedy version of the `.*` pattern—it'll match up to the first instance of `</TD>` and then stop, rather than matching everything and then trying to backtrack.

The only other parts to note about that expression in line 3 are the options: `g` for global, to allow the `while` loop to match on each one, `i` for case-insensitive searching, and `s` to let `.` match across lines (remember, the entire HTML file is in the single string stored in `$content` with embedded newlines.

If we find table rows, the next step is to look for the table rows we want. The first one is the dark-colored top row, matched in line 5 with simple characters. The second are the actual weather rows, matched using the day names in line 8, starting with a `<strong>` tag

21

and ending with a period. When we match each one, we append that matching code to the `$table` string, building up a real HTML table.

Lines 12 through 14 clean up the table we just built. Line 12 expands the URLs to the image files so that they point back to the original site by using the boilerplate URL code you learned about in the previous section. Line 14 is a bit of personalization on my part; the original background colors of the weather bars are various shades of orange; this line substitutes a blue color instead (I don't like orange).

All that's left in lines 16 and 17 is to finish up the table with a closing `</table>` tag and print the result. From here we pop back to the `myhomepage.pl` script, print the various links in the other hash, and the result is a customized Web page with only the content you want to see.

Of course, this system isn't infallible; if the source pages get redesigned or moved to other URLs, you'll have to redo your configurations. Hopefully, if you write your code generically enough, you won't have to do it that often—but that is a side effect of relying on someone else's Web pages.

A Web-Based To Do List Manager (`todolist.pl`)

Our second—and final—example is a simple To Do List application that runs on the Web called `todolist.pl`. You can add, delete, and change list items, sort by date, priority, or descriptions, and mark items as done. Figure 21.3 shows an example of the To Do list at work.

The To Do List application consists of a large table containing the To Do items. Each item has a check box indicating whether it is done or not, a priority, a due date, and a description. All the data in this table is editable through form elements; the changes are applied when the user chooses the Update button. Also affected with Update are whether or not an item is to be removed (the check boxes in the rightmost column of the table), how to sort the data (the Sort By menu just below the table), and whether or not to display done items (the Show Done check box under the table as well).

In addition to the table and the display preferences, there is also an area for adding new items to the list. By filling out the boxes in that part of the application and choosing Add Item, new items are added (and all other changes applied as well).

As with `myhomepage`, the script that runs the To Do list is a CGI script and runs directly as a URL, no initial form needed. The script generates its own content, including the forms that let you change the items in the list and how they are displayed. It's all the same script. The only other part is a data file—`listdata.txt`—which stores the To Do data, and which is read and written by the To Do script.

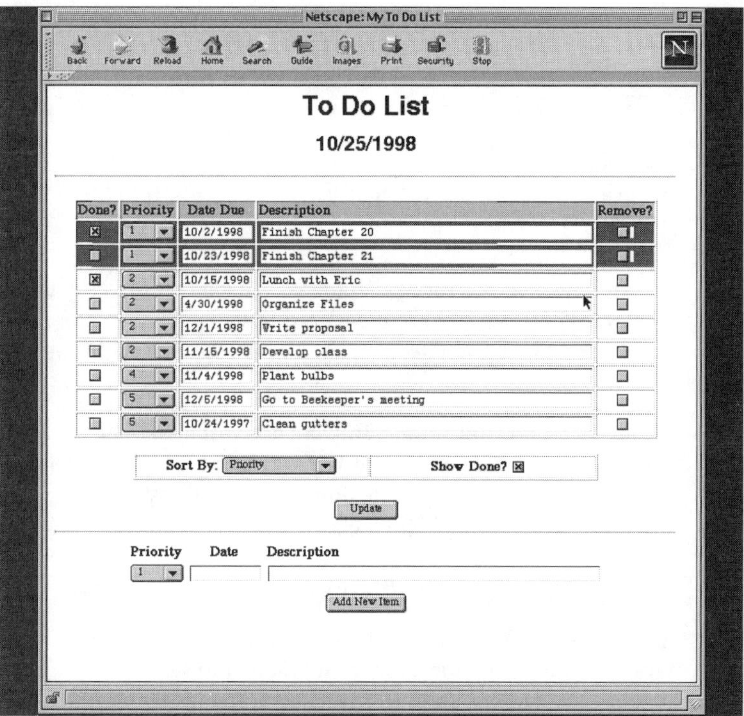

FIGURE 21.3
To Do List Web application.

This script is twice the size of anything we've looked at in this book so, as with the last example, I'm not going to go over it line by line. The complete script is at the end of this section, in Listing 21.5, and you can get it from the Web site for this book as well. In this section, I'll describe the flow and general structure of how the script works and, if you're still curious, you can check out the code for yourself.

The Data File

As with most of the examples we've looked at this week, this script has a data file that it reads and writes to that keeps track of the script's data. The data file for this script, called `listdata.txt`, stores the To Do item data. The `todolist.pl` script reads this file at each iteration and writes new data to it whenever anything is changed. It looks much like the data files you've seen previously in other examples:

```
desc=Finish Chapter 20
date=10/2/1998
prior=1
done=1
---
desc=Finish Chapter 21
date=10/23/1998
prior=1
done=0
---
desc=Lunch with Eric
date=10/15/1998
prior=2
done=1
---
```

As with the data file for My Homepage, each record is separated in the file by three dashes (`---`). Each field of the record has a key and a value, separated by an equals sign. Unlike the data for My Homepage, this one has no multiline records, just keys and values.

When the CGI script for the To Do list is installed, an initial data file must also be installed somewhere where the Web server can read (and write) it. The initial data file can be empty—the script will simply generate a Web page with no items in it—but the file must exist for the script to work.

How the Script Works

The `todolist.pl` is large but pretty straightforward. There aren't many confusing regular expressions, and the flow from function to function is fairly straightforward. In fact, much of the bulk of the script is taken up by `print` statements to generate the HTML for the To Do List and its various form elements—and customizing those elements to behave differently in different situations.

The two starting subroutines for the `todolist.pl` script are `&init()` and `&process()`. `&init()` determines the current date, calls the `&read_data()` subroutine, and prints the top part of the HTML file to be generated by the script. Let's start from there and work down.

Data Initialization with `&init()`

The initialization subroutine is responsible primarily for calling `&read_data()` to open the data file and read each of its elements into a single data structure. That data structure is an array of hashes, with each hash containing the data for each To Do item. The keys in the hash are:

- `desc`—The description of the item.
- `date`—The due date for the item. The date is of the format `MM/DD/YYYY` (this is enforced by the script).

- `prior`—The priority of the item, from 1 (highest) to 5.
- `done`—Whether or not this item is complete.

In addition to these keys, which come from the data file, each item in the list also has an ID. The ID is assigned when the data file is read, from 0 to the number of elements. The ID will be used later to keep track of the various form elements for each list item.

Process the Form and the Data with `&process()`

The `&process()` routine is where the major work of the script takes place. In this subroutine there are two main branches, based on the `param()` function from the `CGI.pm` module. Back on Day 16 you learned about `param()` and how it can be used to get the values of form elements. Another way of using `param()` is without any arguments, in which case it returns the names of all the form elements—or, if the script wasn't called with a form, `param()` returns undefined (`undef`). In the `&process()` subroutine, we take advantage of that behavior to produce two different results:

- The first time the script is called, there are no parameters, so we simply display the current To Do list (by using the `&display_all()` subroutine).
- All other times the script is called, there are potential changes to be managed, either changes to how the existing items are or changes and additions to the items. If the Update button was selected, we remove the items to be deleted (the `&remove_selected()` subroutine), update all the data (`&update_data()`), write the data back out to the file (`&write_data()`), and display it over again (`&display_all()`).

  If the Add Items button was pressed, we do all the same steps, except that between updating the data and writing it out, we call `&add_item()` to add the new To Do item to the list of items.

As all the updating and adding is happening, we're also checking for formatting errors in the dates. More about that later when we talk about updating the data and adding list items.

Displaying the Data with `&display_all()` and `&display_data()`

The largest part of the To Do List script is contained in the `&display_all()` and `&display_data()` script. These subroutines don't just generate HTML for the data; the data table is also a form, and all the elements need to be generated automatically. In addition, a lot of the HTML that gets generated is conditional on various states of the table. Priority 1 items are displayed in red, for example, and the menu for each priority is set to its current values based on the data. So rather than using an enormous "here" document for this part of the script, we need to work through line by line to generate it.

The &display_all() subroutine is the main one that gets called first. It starts the table, prints the headers, sorts the main array based on the current sort order, and then calls &display_data() inside a for loop to display each element in the To Do list. It also generates the elements below the data itself: the Sort By menu, the Show Done check box, the form elements for adding an item, and both of the buttons to submit the form. Along the way, it also prints and manages warnings if there's an error processing the date. All this involves a lot of conditional statements and prints, as well as a whole lot of lines of HTML.

The &display_data() subroutine has a similar task for each specific element of the To Do list. Each row of the table has five columns, each of which contains a form element. Each element needs a unique name, and many form elements change appearance based on the data they reflect (a check box is checked if an item is done, for example). &display_data() also handles NOT displaying some items—if the Show Done check box is not selected, it won't display any item that is marked Done—but it will generate a hidden form element with some of that item's data so that the updates work right.

As with &display_all(), this involves a lot of if statements and a lot of HTML. The result is a gigantic form with each form element attached to the item to which it refers, and which is already filled in with the current To Do list data. Change any part of that data and, when the form is submitted, those changes will make it back to the original data set.

Updating Changes with &update_data()

Speaking of updating the changes, let's move onto the &update_data() subroutine. This subroutine is called regardless of whether the user chooses the Update or Add Item button to make sure that any changes made to the script get made in either case. What &update_data() does is loop through all of the form elements on the page—each element for the list items, as well as the Sort By and Show Done form elements—and change the data or global settings to reflect the changes that were made on the Web page.

Let's focus on the data itself. Each part of the HTML form that gets generated by &display_data() has a unique name, generated from the name of the field (description, priority, and so on) and that item's ID number. By picking apart those form element names that come back when the form is submitted, we can match each name to each part of the data set, compare the values and, if they differ, update the data set with the new value. Each time the form is submitted, every single element is checked. This isn't the most efficient way to keep track of the data, but it does let us keep everything on one page.

The other thing the &update_data() subroutine does is check for bad dates in the existing data. If you tried to change a date from its normal format (10/9/1998 or something like that), `&update_data()` will catch that and report an error, which will then be displayed along with the data set when `&display_all()` is called.

Adding and Removing items with `&add_item()` and `&remove_selected()`

To remove items from the list, you select the check boxes in the Remove column for the data and choose Update. To add an item to the list, you enter its data in the form at the bottom of the page and choose Add Item. In either case, `&remove_selected()` is called; for the latter case, `&add_item()` is also called.

The `&remove_selected()` subroutine is responsible for updating the data to delete any records that have been chosen by the user to be removed. In this case, because all our data is stored in an array of references, removing those items is easy—we just build another array of references, minus the ones we want to delete, and then put that new array back in the old one's variable. Because it's an array of references, all the data referred to by those references stays put and doesn't need to be recopied or reconstructed anywhere.

The `&add_item()` subroutine is equally easy; with all the data from the form elements, all we need to do is stuff it into a hash and put a reference to that hash in the data array. We also assign this new item a new ID, one larger than the current largest ID (if intervening items are deleted, we don't try to keep track of filling in the IDs—once the data file is written, the items get new IDs when that file is read in again at the next iteration of the script).

Other Subroutines: Writing Data and Checking for Errors

All that's left are a few minor supporting subroutines: `&write_data()` to write the data back out to the `listdata.txt` file, and two subroutines to manage date formats and comparisons.

The `&write_data()` subroutine is easy; here all we do is open the `listdata.txt` file for writing and then loop over the data set to write out each of the records. Because this subroutine is called once each time the script is run and after any changes have been made to the data, we can be close to certain that the data will never get corrupted or items lost. Note here that the item IDs are not written to the data file with the rest of the data; those IDs are generated when the data is initially read and used only to keep track of form elements, so they don't need to be preserved between calls to the script.

The final two sets of subroutines relate to date management. Dates, as I mentioned earlier, are of the format `MM/DD/YYYY`. Using a single consistent format is important because it allows the list of items to be sorted by the date—which is a form of numeric sort. To convert the data format into a number that can be compared to some other number, the formatting must be correct. For this reason, whenever a date is changed in the existing data or added to a new item, its format is checked with the `&check_date()` subroutine and errors are reported if the format doesn't match up (both a large red message at the top of the Web page and by asterisks added to the wrong date itself).

Sorting the list by date happens in the `&display_all()` subroutine, if the value of the Sort By menu is Date. To convert the dates into something that can be compared against something else, we use the `Time::Local` module, a built-in module that can be used to convert various parts of a date and time into `time` format—that is, number of seconds since 1900 (the value returned by the `time` function). The `&date2time()` subroutine is used for just this purpose, to split up a correctly-formatted date into its elements and return the `time` value. The `&date2time()` subroutine also watches for dates in error format—with leading asterisks—and sorts those values to the top.

Note that because we use four-digit years in all the data for this script, we won't end up with year 2000 problems. `Time::Local` actually does a good job at figuring out whether two-digit dates belong to this epoch or to the next, but I figured it was best to err on the safe side. It may very well be the year 2000 by the time you read this.

The Code

Listing 21.5 contains the (very) complete code for the `todolist.pl` script. Start from the top and read down. The only tricky parts are those that deal with attaching the IDs to the form elements, and handling the data errors (watch for the `&check_date()` subroutine). And, as with all CGI scripts, it helps to have an understanding of HTML and of how forms and `CGI.pm` interact with each other.

LISTING 21.5 THE CODE FOR `todolist.pl`

```
#!/usr/bin/perl -w
use strict;
use CGI qw(:standard);
use CGI::Carp qw(fatalsToBrowser);
use Time::Local;

my $listdata = 'listdata.txt';  # data file
my @data = ();                  # array of hashes
my $id = 0;                     # top ID

# global default settings
my $sortby = 'prior';           # order to sort list
my $showdone = 1;               # show done items?  (1 == yes)
```

```
&init();
&process();

sub init {
    # get the current date, put in in MM/DD/YY format
    my ($day,$month,$year) = 0;
    (undef,undef,undef,$day,$month,$year) = localtime(time);
    $month++;                 # months start from 0 (yuck)
    $year += 1900;            # Perl years are years since 1900;
                              # this keeps us from getting bit by Y2K
    my $date = "$month/$day/$year";

    # open & read data file
    &read_data();

    # start HTML
    print header;
    print start_html('My To Do List');
    print "<H1 ALIGN=CENTER><FONT FACE=\"Helvetica,Arial\" SIZE+2>";
    print "To Do List</FONT></H1>\n";
    print "<H2 ALIGN=CENTER><FONT FACE=\"Helvetica,Arial\" SIZE+2>";
    print "$date</FONT></H2>\n";
    print "<HR>\n";
    print "<FORM ACTION=\"/cgi-bin/todolist.pl\" METHOD=POST>\n";
}

sub process {
    my $dateerror = 0;          # error in date format in old list
    my $newerror = 0;           # error in date format in new item

    # main switching point.  There are 2 choices:
    # no parameters, for displaying defaults
    # any parameters: update, add item if necessary, write and display
    if (!param()) {                 # first time only
        &display_all();
    } else { # handle buttons
        &remove_selected();
        $dateerror = &update_data();# update existing changes, if any

      # add items
        if (defined param('additems')) {
            $newerror = &check_date(param('newdate'));
            if (!$newerror) {
                &add_item();
            }
        }

```

continues

21

LISTING 21.5 CONTINUED

```
       &write_data();
         &display_all($dateerror,$newerror);
     }

   print end_html;
}

# read data file into array of hashes
sub read_data {
    open(DATA, $listdata) or die "Can't open data file: $!";
    my %rec = ();
    while (<DATA>) {
        chomp;
        if ($_ =~ /^\#/) { next;} # comments

        if ($_ ne '---' and $_ ne '') { # build the record
            my ($key, $val) = split(/=/,$_,2);
            $rec{$key} = $val;
        } else {                # end of record
            $rec{'id'} = $id++;
            push @data, { %rec };
            %rec = ();
        }
    }
    close(DATA);
}

# major HTML display.  This is pretty yucky.
sub display_all {
    my $olderror = shift;               # has an error occurred?
    my $newerror = shift;


    print "<TABLE BORDER WIDTH=75% ALIGN=CENTER>\n";

    if ($olderror or $newerror) {
        print "<P><FONT COLOR=\"red\"><B>Error:  Dates marked with *** ";
        print "not in right format (use MM/DD/YYYY)</B></FONT><P>\n";
    }

    print "<TR BGCOLOR=\"silver\"><TH>Done?<TH>Priority";
    print "<TH>Date Due<TH ALIGN=LEFT>Description<TH>Remove?</TR>\n";

    # determine sort type (numeric or string) based on $sortby
    my @sdata = ();

    # sort the array of hashes based on value of $sortby
```

```
    if ($sortby eq 'date') {   # special date sort
        @sdata = sort {&date2time($a->{'date'}) <=>
                        &date2time($b->{'date'})} @data;
    } else { # regular text/priority sort
        @sdata = sort {$a->{$sortby} cmp $b->{$sortby}} @data;
    }
    # print each item in order
    foreach (@sdata) {
        &display_data(%$_);     # pass in record
    }
    print "</TABLE>\n";
    # preference table, with state preserved
    print "<P><TABLE BORDER WIDTH=75% ALIGN=CENTER>\n";
    print "<TR><TD ALIGN=CENTER><B>Sort By:</B> <SELECT
    NAME=\"sortby\">\n";
    # get current val of sortby, show menu
    print "<OPTION VALUE=\"prior\"  ";
    if ($sortby eq 'prior') { print "SELECTED>"}
    else { print ">"; }
    print "Priority\n";
    print "<OPTION VALUE=\"date\" ";
    if ($sortby eq 'date') { print "SELECTED>"}
    else { print ">"; }
    print "Date\n";
    print "<OPTION VALUE=\"desc\" ";
    if ($sortby eq 'desc') { print "SELECTED>"}
    else { print ">"; }
    print "Description\n";
    print "</SELECT></TD>\n";
    # get current val of showdone, show check boxn
    print "<TD ALIGN=CENTER WIDTH=50%><B>Show Done?<B>\n";
    my $checked = '';
    if ($showdone == 1) { $checked = 'CHECKED'}
    print "<INPUT TYPE=\"checkbox\" NAME=\"showdone\"
     VALUE=\"showdone\"";
    print " $checked> </TD>\n";
    # print submit button and start of add items table
    print <<EOF;
    </TR></TABLE>
    <P><TABLE ALIGN=CENTER>
    <TR><TD ALIGN=CENTER VALIGN=CENTER>
    <INPUT TYPE="submit" VALUE="   Update   "
     NAME="update"></TD></TR>
```


continues

LISTING 21.5 CONTINUED

```
    </TABLE><HR>
    <TABLE ALIGN=CENTER>
    <TR><TH>Priority<TH>Date<TH ALIGN=LEFT>Description
EOF
    # print priority menu;
    print "<TR><TD><SELECT NAME=\"newprior\">\n";
    my $i;
    foreach $i (1..5) {          # priorities 1 to 5
        if ($newerror and param('newprior') == $i) {
            $checked = 'SELECTED';
        }
        print "<OPTION $checked>$i\n";
    }
    print "</SELECT></TD>\n";

    # print date and description cells; may be different in case of
    # errors
    my $newdate = '';
    my $newdesc = '';
    print "<TD ALIGN=CENTER><INPUT TYPE=\"text\" NAME=\"newdate\"";
    if ($newerror) {             # has an error occurred?
        $newdate = "***" . param('newdate');
       $newdesc = param('newdesc');
    }
    print "VALUE=\"$newdate\" SIZE=10></TD> \n";

    # description cell; preserve old value if error
    print "<TD><INPUT TYPE=\"text\" NAME=\"newdesc\"
     VALUE=\"$newdesc\"";
    print "SIZE=50></TD></TR></TABLE><TABLE ALIGN=CENTER>\n";

   # and finish up
    print <<EOF;
    <TR><TD ALIGN=CENTER VALIGN=CENTER>
    <INPUT TYPE="submit" VALUE="Add New Item"
     NAME="additems"></TD></TR>
    </TABLE></FORM>
EOF
}

# display each line of the data.  Data is already sorted; this just
# prints an inidividual record
sub display_data {
    my %rec = @_;                # record to print

    # don't show done items if Show Done is unchecked
    # BUT include their settings anyhow (otherwise its too
    # difficult to figure out what's shown and changed versus
    # what's hidden
```

```
    if ($showdone == 0 and $rec{'done'}) {
        print "<INPUT TYPE=\"hidden\" NAME=\"done", $rec{'id'};
        print "\">\n";
        next;
    }

    # make 1 priority items print in red
    my $bgcolor = '';   # priority items are red, all others ''
    if ($rec{'prior'} == 1) {
        $bgcolor = "BGCOLOR=\"red\"";
    }

    # Is it done or not?
    my $checked = '';           # done items are checked
    if ($rec{'done'}) {
        $checked = 'CHECKED';
    }

    print "<TR>\n";             # start row

    # done boxes
    print "<TD WIDTH=10% ALIGN=CENTER $bgcolor>";
    print "<INPUT TYPE=\"checkbox\" NAME=\"done", $rec{'id'};
    print "\" $checked></TD>\n";

    # priority menus
    print "<TD WIDTH=10% ALIGN=CENTER $bgcolor>";
    print "<SELECT NAME=\"prior", $rec{'id'}, "\">\n";
    my $select = '';
    my $i;
    foreach $i (1..5) {         # priorities 1 to 5
       if ($rec{'prior'} == $i) {
           $checked = 'SELECTED';
        }
        print "<OPTION $checked>$i\n";
        $select = '';
    }
    print "</SELECT></TD>\n";

    # dates
    print "<TD $bgcolor WIDTH=10% ALIGN=CENTER>";
    print "<INPUT TYPE=\"text\" SIZE=10 NAME=\"date", $rec{'id'}, "\" ";
    print "VALUE=\"", $rec{'date'}, "\"></TD>\n";

    # descriptions
    print "<TD $bgcolor><INPUT TYPE=\"text\" NAME=\"desc", $rec{'id'};
```

continues

LISTING 21.5 CONTINUED

```
    print "\" SIZE =50 VALUE=\"", $rec{'desc'}, "\"></TD>\n";

    # Remove boxes
    print "<TD $bgcolor ALIGN=CENTER>";
    print "<INPUT TYPE=\"checkbox\" NAME=r", $rec{'id'}, "></TD>";

    # end row
    print "</TR>\n";
}

# update all values in case changes were made
sub update_data {
    my $error = 0;              # error checking

    # check to see if showdone is selected;
    if (defined param('showdone')) {
        $showdone = 1;
    } else { $showdone = 0; }

    # get currrent sortby value
    $sortby = param('sortby');

    foreach (@data) {
        my $id = $_->{'id'};    # not the global $id

        # Entries that are marked done cannot be changed (usability
        # assumption).  So if an entry is marked done, and hasn't
        # been changed to not-done, we can skip checking any of the
        # rest of its data.
        if ($_->{'done'} == 1 && defined param('done' . $id)) { next; }

        # All newly done items.
        if (defined param('done' . $id)) {
            $_->{'done'} = 1;
        } else { $_->{'done'} = 0; }

        # dates.  check for wierd date
        if (param('date' . $id) ne $_->{'date'}) {
            $error = check_date(param('date' . $id));
            if ($error) {
                $_->{'date'} = "***" . param('date' . $id);
            } else {
                $_->{'date'} = param('date' . $id);
            }
        }

        # priorities, descriptions, change only if different
        my $thing;
```

```
        foreach $thing ('prior', 'desc') {
            if (param($thing . $id) ne $_->{$thing}) {
               $_->{$thing} = param($thing . $id);
            }
        }
    }
    return $error;
}

# remove items by redoing the @data list
sub remove_selected {
    my @newdata = ();

    foreach (@data) {
        my $id = $_->{'id'};    # also not the global id

        if (!defined param('r' . $id)) {
            push @newdata, $_;  # $_ is the reference
       }
    }
    @data = @newdata;           # get rid of removed items
}

# add a new item. This is only called if check_date has already said OK
sub add_item {
    my %newrec = ();

    $newrec{'desc'} = param('newdesc');
    $newrec{'date'} = param('newdate');
    $newrec{'prior'} = param('newprior');
    $newrec{'done'} = 0;
    $newrec{'id'} = $id++;      # global ID + 1

    push @data, { %newrec };
}

# dates must be in XX/XX/XX format
sub check_date {
    my $date = shift;

    # MM/DD/YYYY, MM and DD can be 0 or 1 char, but YYYY must be four
    # ending whitespace is OK.
    if ($date !~ /^\d{1,2}\/\d{1,2}\/\d{4}\s*$/) {
        return 1;               # error!
    }
   return 0;                   # OK date
}

# rewrite data file
sub write_data {
```

continues

LISTING 21.5 CONTINUED

```
    open(DATA, ">$listdata") or die "Can't open list data: $!.";
    foreach (@data) {
        my %rec = %$_;

        foreach ('desc', 'date','prior','done') { # no ids
            print DATA "$_=$rec{$_}\n";
        }
        print DATA "---\n";
    }
    close(DATA);
}

# I use MM/DD/YY format for dates.  To sort by date you need to
# convert this format back into Perl's seconds-since-1900 format.
# the Time::Local module and the timelocal func do this.
sub date2time {
    my $date = shift;
    if ($date =~ /^\*\*\*/) {   # error formatting, sort to top
        return 0;
    } else {
        my ($m,$d,$y) = split(/\//,$date);
        $m--;           # months start from 0 in perl's time format
        return timelocal(0,0,0,$d,$m,$y);
    }
}
```

Summary

If you had picked up this book without understanding anything about Perl and looked at the script in Listing 21.5, chances are pretty good you might have had a hard time deciphering it—even if you already knew something about programming languages (Perl is funny that way). After 21 days deep into the language and its idiosyncrasies, reading the code in these examples should be easy—or at least less perplexing.

Today, we finished up the week and the book with the usual couple of longer examples (some longer than others). The two scripts we looked at in this lesson, the My Homepage generator and the To Do List application, are both CGI scripts that process data from different sources (or multiple sources) and generate HTML as their output. The second, the To Do List, also generates its own form so that it can process its own data at a later iteration. The former is a good example of cobbling together code from various modules on CPAN and your own glue, as well as being able to customize a generic application. The latter displayed HTML form construction and used a nested data structure to keep track of the data. From these scripts, and the work you've done in the previous 20 chapters, you're now off and running as far as Perl is concerned.

Off you go!

Appendixes

- Perl Functions
- A Survey of Perl Modules
- Setting Up Perl on a UNIX System
- Installing Perl for Windows
- Installing Perl for Macintosh

A

B

C

D

E

APPENDIX A

Perl Functions

This appendix contains a brief reference of all the built-in functions in the Perl language. They are organized in alphabetical order. If you're looking for a function that doesn't exist, there's a good chance that someone has written a module that supports it. For a partial list of modules available for Perl, try Appendix B.

Note that not all the functions in this appendix are supported by all versions of Perl. Day 18, "Perl and the Operating System," contains some background information on which functions may not be available for Windows or Macintosh. For the ultimate list, see the documentation that comes with your Perl port.

For More Information

Further information on any of these functions can be found in the `perlfunc` man page. As with all Perl documentation, you can access this man page through the `man` command on UNIX, the `perldoc` command on UNIX or Windows (`perldoc perlfunc` for the whole thing, or `perldoc -f` for individual functions, or the Shuck application on the Mac).

All the documentation for Perl can also be found on the Web at `http://www.perl.com/CPAN-local/doc/manual/html/pod/`.

In addition to Perl-related man pages, this appendix also frequently refers to other UNIX man pages (mostly because Perl makes frequent use of many UNIX features). UNIX man pages are organized into numbered chapters. When you see an item listed with a number in parentheses after it, it indicates that the item is found in that chapter in the man pages. For example, `fseek(2)` is found in Chapter 2 of the UNIX manual. To look up `fseek` in Chapter 2, you would use the following UNIX command:

```
man 2 fseek
```

Or, on some systems:

```
man -s 2 fseek
```

The command `man man` will give you help on the `man` command itself.

Perl Functions, in Alphabetical Order

Here are the Perl functions, listed alphabetically.

abs

```
abs VALUE
```

Returns the absolute value of `VALUE`. `VALUE` can be a number (like `-7`), or an expression (like `int(5/2)`).

accept

```
accept NEWSOCKET, GENERICSOCKET
```

`accept` is used to accept an incoming socket connection. If the connection is successful, the packed address is returned, otherwise, `FALSE` is returned. Identical to the `accept(2)` system call.

alarm

```
alarm SECONDS
```

The `alarm` function sends a `SIGALRM` to the program after the number of seconds specified in `SECONDS` has elapsed. Only one timer can be running at a time, so if you call this function and a timer is already running, it will be replaced by the more recent call. Calling this function with an argument of 0 will suspend the current timer without starting a new one. If `SECONDS` is not specified, the value in `$_` is used.

A

atan2

```
atan2 Y, X
```

Returns the arctangent of Y/X in the range -p to p. There are functions for the tangent operation in the POSIX and `Math::Trig` modules.

bind

```
bind SOCKET, NAME
```

The `bind` function binds a network address to a socket. `NAME` should contain the packed address for that type of socket. If the `bind` function is successful, it returns `TRUE`, otherwise it returns `FALSE`. Identical to the `bind` system call.

binmode

```
binmode FILEHANDLE
```

`binmode` accepts a filehandle as an argument, and indicates that data should be written to (or read from) the filehandle as binary, as opposed to ASCII, data. It has no effect under UNIX, but is critical under MS-DOS and other archaic platforms. It should be called after a file is opened, but before any I/O is performed on that file.

bless

```
bless REFERENCE, CLASSNAME
```

`bless` is used in object-oriented Perl programming to assign whatever is referenced by `REFERENCE` to the package named by `CLASSNAME`. If `CLASSNAME` is omitted, `REFERENCE` is assigned to the current package. `bless` returns the reference being blessed. For detailed information check out the `perlobj` man page.

caller

```
caller EXPR
caller
```

`caller` returns the context of the current subroutine call. In the scalar context, `caller` returns the package name from which the subroutine was called; in the list context, it returns the package name, filename of the program, and line number from which the call was issued. If `EXPR` is supplied, `caller` also returns extra information used to print a stack trace. `EXPR` indicates how many call frames to go back before the current one. When `EXPR` is supplied, the following list of values is returned:

```
($package, $file, $line, $subname, $hasargs, $wantarray) =
caller(any_func);
```

If called from within the DB package, caller also sets the variable `@DB::args` to the arguments passed to the given stack frame.

chdir

```
chdir EXPR
```

`chdir` accepts an expression as an argument, and attempts to set the current directory to the directory supplied by the expression. If no argument is provided, it attempts to change to the home directory for the current user.

chmod

```
chmod LIST
```

`chmod` is used to change the file permissions for the list of files provided in `LIST`. The first element of `LIST` must be the numerical mode for the files, in octal notation. It should also include the SUID bit. Here's an example of the usage of `chmod`:

```
chmod 0755, @files;
```

Note that the first element of the list is not enclosed within quotation marks, it is a bare number. For more information on file permissions, see the `chmod` man page.

chomp

```
chomp VARIABLE
chomp LIST
chomp
```

`chomp` is a safe version of `chop`, which is described next. It removes any line ending that matches `$/` (the variable that contains the input record separator, usually a newline). If it is called in paragraph mode, it removes all of the trailing newlines from a string.

chop

```
chop VARIABLE
chop LIST
chop
```

`chop` is used to remove the last character from a string. Originally it was designed to make it easy to strip the line feed from the end of a string (when you're editing a file line by line, it often makes sense to remove the line feeds from the lines before you start working on them). The problem with `chop` is that it removes the last character from the string regardless of what it is, so if the string ends with a line feed, great, but if it doesn't then you lose the last character, which may have been meaningful.

A

```
while (<INPUT_FILE>) {
#     Note that in this example, $_ is assumed to be the argument to
#     the chomp function.
     chop;
     push (@names);
}
```

If no argument is supplied to chop, it removes the last character from $_. If a list is supplied, the last character in all the items in the list is removed.

chown

chown LIST

chown is used to set the user and group ownership for files provided in LIST. It returns the number of files that were successfully changed. The first two elements of LIST must be the numerical uid and gid of the user and group which will become the owners of the files. Usually, only the root user can change the owner of files on a system.

chr

chr NUMBER

The chr function returns the character in the ASCII table associated with the number passed to the function. For example; chr(80); returns R. The pack function can be used to convert multiple characters at the same time.

chroot

chroot DIRNAME

The chroot function does the same thing as the chroot system call (see the chroot(2) man page for details). Basically, chroot tells the program that's currently running, as well as all exec calls and subprocesses, to use the directory named in DIRNAME as the new root directory. So, paths starting with / will begin in DIRNAME instead of the actual root directory of the filesystem. Only the root user can use the chroot function.

close

close FILEHANDLE

The close function is used to close a previously opened filehandle (whether it is a file or a pipe). It performs the necessary system-level cleanup operations at the system level, and returns true if all of those operations are successful. Note that all filehandles are closed automatically when a Perl program exits, so you can often get by with not explicitly closing all the filehandles that you open.

closedir

```
closedir DIRHANDLE
```

`closedir` closes a directory opened using the `opendir` function.

connect

```
connect SOCKET, NAME
```

`connect` attempts to connect to a remote socket. `NAME` should contain the packed address appropriate to the type of socket. The function returns `TRUE` if it is successful or `FALSE` if it isn't. Identical to the `connect` system call.

cos

```
cos EXPR
```

Returns the cosine of `EXPR`. To use the inverse cosine operation, you should use the `POSIX::acos()` function, or the `Math::Trig` module.

crypt

```
crypt PLAINTEXT, SALT
```

The `crypt` function is used to encrypt strings in the same way that passwords are stored in a UNIX password file. The function accepts two arguments: the string to be encrypted, and the salt code used to seed the encryption algorithm. The `crypt` function is one-way; there is no known method for decrypting text enciphered using `crypt` (UNIX tests passwords by using `crypt` on the password the user enters and testing it against the encrypted password in `/etc/passwd`).

dbmclose

```
dbmclose HASH
```

`dbmclose` breaks the binding between `HASH` and the DBM file with which it is associated. It has been superseded by the `untie` function.

dbmopen

```
dbmopen HASH, DBNAME, MODE
```

`dbmopen` binds a `dbm`, `ndbm`, `sdbm`, `gdbm`, or Berkeley DB file to a hash. `HASH` is the name of the hash variable to which the database will be bound, and `DBNAME` is the name of the database file, minus the extension. If `DBNAME` doesn't exist, a new file will be created with permissions specified by `MODE`.

This function has been superseded by `tie`.

defined

```
defined EXPR
```

`defined` is used to identify expressions that return the undefined value (as opposed to 0, newline, or other empty return values). It can be used to determine whether a subroutine exists or a scalar variable is defined. If no `EXPR` is given, `defined` checks to see if `$_` is undefined.

delete

```
delete EXPR
```

The `delete` function is used to remove elements from a hash. To delete a member of a hash, you simply pass the name of the hash and the key you wish to remove to the `delete` function. Here's an example:

```
delete $hash{$key};
```

Note that since you're referring to a single member of the hash, you reference the hash variable in the scalar context (using $).

die

```
die LIST
```

`die` accepts a list as its argument. When `die` is called, the program exits returning the value of `$!`, and the list passed to `die` as an argument is printed to standard error. If the list does not end with a newline, the name of the program and the line number where execution halted are appended, along with a newline, to the output of the function.

Here's an example:

```
open (FILE, $file) or die "Can't open $file";
```

will return the following if `$file` can't be opened:

```
Can't open /tmp/file at test_program line 13.
```

do

```
do BLOCK
do SUBROUTINE(LIST)
do EXPR
```

When used with a block of code inside BLOCK, do executes the statements in a block and returns the value of the last statement in the block. If do is used with a loop expression, then BLOCK is executed before the loop condition is tested for the first time.

do SUBROUTINE is a deprecated way to call a subroutine. do EXPR provides a way to run code in another file. EXPR is treated as the filename for a Perl file, and the code inside is executed. Even though you can use do in this way, you should probably use require or use instead, as they are more robust.

dump

```
dump LABEL
```

dump causes Perl to immediately dump core. You can then use the undump program to create a binary that will begin execution by issuing a goto LABEL command.

each

```
each HASH
```

The each function is used to grab values from a hash so that they can be iterated over in a loop. It acts differently depending on whether it is used in the scalar or the list context. Let's look at each.

In the scalar context, the each function returns the key for the next element in the hash. So, you could use it as follows:

```
while ($key = each %hash) {
    $hash{$key}++;
}
```

On the other hand, used in the list context, the each function returns a two-element list that contains the key and the value for the next element in the hash. Let's take a look:

```
while (($key, $value) = each %hash) {
    print "$key = $value\n";
}
```

eof

```
eof FILEHANDLE
eof ()
eof
```

The eof function returns 1 if the next read on FILEHANDLE will return the end of file marker, or if FILEHANDLE is not open. Used without an argument, eof evaluates the last file read. Called with empty parentheses, eof detects the end of the pseudo-file made up

A

of all the files specified on the command line. As the perlfunc man page astutely points out, eof is rarely useful, because Perl returns the undefined value automatically when the end of a file is reached, making it easy to detect file endings without it.

eval

```
eval EXPR
```

eval is used to execute an expression or block of code as though it were a separate Perl program. It is executed within the context of the Perl program that's running, so once the expression within eval finishes executing, all of the variables and other persistent values for the larger program are still defined.

The value returned by an eval is the value of the last expression evaluated. To explicitly return a particular value, you can use a return statement inside the eval. If a syntax or runtime error occurs within the eval statement, or a die statement is executed, the eval statement returns an undefined value, and the variable $@ contains the error message.

Because fatal errors executed within eval statements don't stop execution of the closing program, they can be used to trap errors or run potentially volatile code.

exec

```
exec LIST
```

The exec function executes a system command and never returns, unless the command does not exist. If LIST consists of more than one element, exec uses the system call execvp(3) with the arguments in LIST. If the argument contains a single scalar value, the argument is checked for shell metacharacters. If shell metacharacters exist, the argument is executed through /bin/sh -c; otherwise, the argument is broken into words and passed on to execvp.

exists

```
exists EXPR
```

The exists function is used to check whether a particular key is defined within a hash. Whether a value is defined for that key is not checked by the exists function; it is strictly used to test keys. Here's an example of the usage:

```
if (exists $hash{$key}) { print "Yes."; }
else { print "No.\n"; }
```

exit

`exit EXPR`

The `exit` function evaluates `EXPR` and immediately exits the program. The `die` function is usually a cleaner way to abort execution of a program, because the error information returned can be trapped.

exp

`exp EXPR`

Returns *e* to the power of `EXPR`; if `EXPR` is omitted, then `exp($)` is assumed. For regular exponents, use the ** operator.

fcntl

`fcntl FILEHANDLE, FUNCTION, SCALAR`

Used to emulate the `fcntl(2)` system call. You can `use fcntl;` to obtain the function definitions needed to use this function. See the man page for more information on this function. `fcntl` returns a fatal error if it is not implemented on the platform on which it is called.

fileno

`fileno FILEHANDLE`

`fileno` returns a file descriptor for a given filehandle. A file descriptor is a small integer identifying the file. It can be used to construct bitmaps for use with `select`. If `FILEHANDLE` is not open, it returns `undefined`.

flock

`flock FILEHANDLE, OPERATION`

This function calls the `flock(2)` system call on `FILEHANDLE`. For more information on the operations available, see the `flock(2)` man page. It produces a fatal error on systems that do not support `flock(2)` or some other file locking mechanism.

fork

`fork`

`fork` is used to fork a system call into a separate process. `fork` returns the child PID to the parent process. It is only implemented on UNIX-like platforms. All of the code inside the block will run in a new process.

format

```
format
```

The `format` function is designed to give COBOL programmers a head start in learning Perl. Actually, it provides a method for creating templates for formatted output. For all the details on generating output using `format`, read the `perlform` man page.

formline

```
formline PICTURE, LIST
```

The `formline` function is used internally by formats. It is used to format `LIST` according to `PICTURE`. For more information, see the `perlform` man page.

getc

```
getc FILEHANDLE
```

`getc` returns the next character from `FILEHANDLE`. If `FILEHANDLE` is omitted, `getc` returns the next character from `STDIN`. `getc` does not allow unbuffered input (in other words, if `STDIN` is the console, `getc` does not get the character until the buffer is flushed with a newline).

getlogin

```
getlogin
```

Returns the current login from `/etc/utmp`, if any. If null, you should use `getpwuid()`.

getpeername

```
getpeername SOCKET
```

`getpeername` returns the packed `sockaddr` address of the other end of the `SOCKET` connection.

getpgrp

```
getpgrp PID
```

`getpgrp` returns the process group for the specified process. Supplying a PID of 0 will return the process group for the current process.

getppid

```
getppid
```

`getppid` returns the process ID for the parent process of the current process.

getpriority

```
getpriority WHICH, WHO
```

`getpriority` returns the priority for a process, process group, or user, assuming the system function `getpriority` is implemented on this machine.

getsockname

```
getsockname SOCKET
```

`getsockname` returns the packed `sockaddr` address of this end of the `SOCKET` connection.

getsockopt

```
getsockopt SOCKET, LEVEL, OPTNAME
```

`getsockopt` returns the requested option, or `undefined` in the case of an error.

glob

```
glob EXPR
```

The `glob` function returns the value of `EXPR` with filename expansions, like those that would occur under a shell. If `EXPR` is omitted, `$_` is assumed to be the argument.

gmtime

```
gmtime EXPR
```

`gmtime` converts a time in the format returned by the `time` function (seconds since Jan. 1, 1970, 00:00) to Greenwich standard time (otherwise known as Greenwich Mean Time). The time is returned as a nine element list. The contents of each element are provided in this example:

```
($sec,$min,$hour,$mday,$mon,$year,$wday,$yday,$isdst) = gmtime(time);
```

Note that all of the items are returned in numerical format, and numbers in series (like month and day of the week) begin with 0 rather than 1. This means that months range from 0 to 11. The year returned is the number of years since 1900, not simply the last two digits of the year, thus avoiding the dreaded year 2000 problem. If you use `gmtime` in the scalar context, it returns the time in `ctime(3)` format, like this:

```
Sat Jun  6 01:56:44 1998
```

goto

```
goto LABEL
goto EXPR
goto &NAME
```

The goto function finds the statement labeled with LABEL and continues executing from there. It cannot shift execution to statements within blocks that require initialization, like subroutines or foreach loops. The other two usages of goto are rather arcane. goto EXPR is used to jump to a label that is specified by EXPR, which is scoped dynamically. goto &name substitutes a call to the named subroutine for the currently running subroutine, as though it were the one that was called in the first place.

grep

```
grep EXPR, LIST
grep BLOCK LIST
```

The grep function is used to search lists, and return all the elements in that list matching a particular pattern. grep accepts two arguments, an expression and a list. It returns another list containing each of the elements for which the expression was true. Let's look at an example:

```
@newarray = grep /red/, @oldarray;
```

@newarray will contain a list of all the items in @oldarray that contained the string red. If you call grep within the scalar context, it will return the number of items that matched, instead of a list of items that matched.

hex

```
hex EXPR
```

hex reads EXPR as a hexadecimal string and returns the decimal value. If EXPR is omitted, the function reads $_.

import

```
import CLASSNAME LIST
import CLASSNAME
```

import is not a built-in function; instead, it is implemented by modules that want to export names into another module. The import function is called by the use function when a module is loaded into a Perl program.

index

```
index STR, SUBSTR, POSITION
index STR, SUBSTR
```

index is used to locate a substring within a larger string. It accepts three arguments, one of which is optional. The arguments are the string to search, the substring to search for, and the position where the search should begin (optional). index returns the position in the string where the first occurrence of the substring begins. For example, to find the string `go` within the larger string `bingo`, you could use the following code `index ('bingo', 'go');`. To find the second occurrence of `go` within the string `go or no go`, you could use the optional third argument to start at position 3 in the string like this: `index ('go or no go', 'go', 3);`.

int

```
int EXPR
```

`int` returns the integer portion of a string. Basically, if a string begins with an integer, like `55 MPH`, `int` will return that integer, in this case, `55`. Strings that don't begin with an integer will return 0. If you have Perl warnings turned on, you'll get a warning for any non-numbers in the string.

ioctl

```
ioctl FILEHANDLE, FUNCTION, SCALAR
```

`ioctl` is used to implement the `ioctl(2)` system call. You will probably need to use

```
require "ioctl.ph";
```

in order to import the function definitions for `ioctl`. If it doesn't exist, you will need to create your own function definitions based on the system's `ioctl.h` file.

join

```
join EXPR, LIST
```

The `join` function is the opposite of `split`. It is used to join the elements of a list into a single string. It takes two arguments: an expression and a list. The contents of the expression are used as the delimiter between the elements in the string that is returned.

keys

```
keys HASH
```

The `keys` function returns an array containing all of the keys in the named hash. It is often used to sort the keys in a hash before you iterate over them in a loop. Here's a common example:

```
foreach $key (sort (keys %hash)) {
    print $key, " = ", $value, "\n";
}
```

A

kill

```
kill LIST
```

`kill` is actually used to send a signal to a list of processes, rather than simply killing them. The first argument in `LIST` must be the signal to send; the rest should be the processes that will receive the signal. To kill processes, you would use this code:

```
kill 1, 100, 102, 110;
```

To kill those same processes with extreme prejudice, you would use this code:

```
kill 9, 100, 102, 110;
```

You can supply the signal name inside quotes instead of the signal number if you prefer. See the `signal(5)` man page for more information on signals.

last

```
last LABEL
last
```

The `last` command immediately exits the loop specified by `LABEL`. If no label is specified, the innermost loop exits.

lc

```
lc EXPR
```

The `lc` function converts all the alphabetic characters in a string to lowercase. `lc 'ABC';` returns `abc`. If no expression is provided, the `lc` function acts on `$_`.

lcfirst

```
lcfirst EXPR
```

Returns the value in `EXPR` with the first character lowercased. If `EXPR` is omitted, `$_` is used.

length

```
length EXPR
```

`length` accepts a string as an argument, and an integer containing the length of the string in bytes. For example, `length("dog");` returns 3. If `EXPR` is not supplied, `$_` is used.

link

```
link OLDFILE, NEWFILE
```

Creates a hard (as opposed to symbolic) link from `OLDFILE` to `NEWFILE`. To create a symbolic link, use the `symlink` function.

listen

```
listen SOCKET, QUEUESIZE
```

The `listen` function in Perl performs the same function as the `listen` system call. It returns `TRUE` if it succeeds, `FALSE` if it doesn't.

local

```
local EXPR
```

`local` specifies that the variables listed will be local to the currently executing block, loop, subroutine, `eval {}`, or `do`. If more than one variable is passed to `local`, they should be enclosed in parentheses. To restrict the scope of a variable, though, you should probably use `my` instead.

localtime

```
localtime EXPR
```

The `localtime` function is identical to `gmtime`, except that it returns the time converted to the local time zone instead of Greenwich time.

log

```
log EXPR
```

Returns the logarithm (base *e*) of `EXPR`, or `$_` if `EXPR` is not provided.

lstat

```
lstat FILEHANDLE
lstat EXPR
lstat
```

`lstat` is identical to the `stat` function, except that it stats a symbolic link instead of the file the link points to. If `EXPR` is omitted, `lstat` acts on the value in `$_`.

map

```
map BLOCK LIST
map EXPR, LIST
```

`map` provides an alternative to `foreach` for performing an operation on every element in a list. It can take two forms, and you can perform all of the operations in a block of code on a list like this:

A

```
@backwards_words = map {
   lc;
   reverse;
} @words;
```

The previous example reverses and lowercases each element in the array `@words`. The results of `map` are returned in a list context, which is why I assign them to an array. Note that when each element is processed, it is assigned to the `$_` variable, which is why I can use the functions within the code block without arguments. To perform a single operation on each element of a list, `map` is called like this:

```
@newlist = map(uc, @oldlist);
```

Note that when a single operation is used with `map`, a comma is used to separate the function from the list that is being processed.

mkdir

```
mkdir FILENAME, MODE
```

`mkdir` is used to create a new directory, the name of which is specified in `FILENAME`. You should set the permissions for the directory using `MODE`, which should be specified in standard octal format (as a bare number, not within quotation marks), and should include the SUID bit.

msgctl

```
msgctl ID, CMD, ARG
```

`msgctl` calls the `msgctl(2)` system call. This function is available only on machines supporting System V IPC.

msgget

```
msgget KEY, FLAGS
```

Calls the System V IPC function `msgget` and returns the message queue ID, or `undefined` in the case of an error.

msgrcv

```
msgrcv ID, VAR, SIZE, TYPE, FLAGS
```

Calls the System V ICP function `msgrcv` to receive a message from message queue `ID`, into variable `VAR`, with a maximum size of `SIZE`. Returns `TRUE` if successful or `FALSE` if there's an error.

msgsnd

```
msgsnd ID, MSG, FLAGS
```

Calls the System V IPC function `msgsnd` to send `MSG` to the message queue specified in `ID`. Returns `TRUE` if successful or `FALSE` if there's an error.

my

```
my EXPR
```

`my` is used to scope the listed variables so that they are local to the current block, `eval {}`, subroutine, or imported file. If more than one variable is supplied, they must be placed within parentheses.

next

```
next LABEL
next
```

When the `next` command is encountered within a loop, it skips immediately to the next iteration of that loop.

no

```
no MODULE LIST
```

The `no` module is the opposite of the `use` operator. You can find more information in the `perlobj` man page.

oct

```
oct EXPR
```

`oct` reads `EXPR` as an octal string and returns the decimal value, unless the string starts with `0x`, in which case it is interpreted as a hex value. If `EXPR` is omitted, the function reads `$_`.

open

```
open (FILEHANDLE, EXPR)
```

The `open` function opens the file specified in `EXPR` and assigns it to `FILEHANDLE`. If `EXPR` is omitted, a variable with the same name as `FILEHANDLE` is assumed to contain the name of the file.

By prepending < to the filename, you can open it for input, or by prepending >, you can open it for output. To append data to the output file instead of overwriting it, you should prepend the filename with >>. To open a filehandle using a pipe instead of standard input and output, you can use the pipe character. Placing a | before the program name opens a pipe to that program; placing a | after the filename opens a pipe from the program to your filehandle.

For more information on the `open` function, look at Chapter 15, "Working with Files and I/O."

opendir

```
opendir (DIRHANDLE, EXPR)
```

The `opendir` function opens the directory specified in `EXPR` for input, and assigns it to `DIRHANDLE`. A list of entries in the directory can then be read from the directory handle. Note that the namespace for directory handles does not overlap with that for filehandles.

ord

```
ord EXPR
```

Returns the numeric ASCII value of the first character of `EXPR`. If `EXPR` is omitted, `$_` is used.

pack

```
pack TEMPLATE, LIST
```

`pack` accepts a list of values, packs it into a binary structure, and returns the string containing that structure. The `TEMPLATE` is a list of characters that gives the order and type of the values.

TABLE A.1 `pack` TEMPLATE CHARACTERS

Character	*What It Means*
A	An `ascii` string, will be space padded.
a	An `ascii` string, will be null padded.
b	A bit string (ascending bit order, like `vec()`).
B	A bit string (descending bit order).
h	A hex string (low nybble first).
H	A hex string (high nybble first).
c	A signed char value.
C	An unsigned char value.

continues

TABLE A.1 CONTINUED

s	A signed short value.
S	An unsigned short value. (This "short" is exactly 16 bits, which may differ from what a local C compiler calls "short.")
I	A signed integer value.
I	An unsigned integer value. (This "integer" is at least 32 bits wide. Its exact size depends on what a local C compiler calls "int," and may even be larger than the "long" described in the next item.)
l	A signed long value.
L	An unsigned long value. (This "long" is exactly 32 bits, which may differ from what a local C compiler calls "long.")
n	A short in "network" (big-endian) order.
N	A long in "network" (big-endian) order.
v	A short in "VAX" (little-endian) order.
V	A long in "VAX" (little-endian) order. (These "shorts" and "longs" are exactly 16 bits and exactly 32 bits, respectively.)
f	A single-precision float in the native format.
d	A double-precision float in the native format.
p	A pointer to a null-terminated string.
P	A pointer to a structure (fixed-length string).
u	A uuencoded string.
w	A BER compressed integer. Its bytes represent an unsigned integer in base 128, most significant digit first, with as few digits as possible. Bit eight (the high bit) is set on each byte except the last.
x	A null byte.
X	Back up a byte.
@	Null fill to absolute position.

Each letter can be followed with a number, which is used as the repeat count for that letter. The `unpack` function can be used to extract items stored in a binary structure.

package

```
package NAMESPACE
```

The `package` function declares that all of the variables inside the innermost enclosing block, subroutine, `eval`, or file belong to `NAMESPACE`. For more information, see the `permod` man page.

pipe

```
pipe READHANDLE, WRITEHANDLE
```

pipe opens a pipe from READHANDLE to WRITEHANDLE, like the system call of the same name.

pop

```
pop ARRAY
```

The pop function removes the last item in an array (shortening it by one element) and returns it as a scalar value. Both push (which will be discussed later) and pop are what can be called stack functions. If you imagine an array as a stack of trays in a cafeteria, pop is used to remove the top item from that stack.

pos

```
pos SCALAR
```

Returns the location in SCALAR where the last m//g search left off. If SCALAR is not specified, $_ is used.

print

```
print FILEHANDLE LIST
print LIST
print
```

The print function is used to output the data passed to it in the list context to standard output, or if a filehandle is specified, to that filehandle. If the list of data to print is omitted, then the contents of $_ are printed by default. Note that there shouldn't be a comma between the filehandle and the actual list of data being printed, so to print some data to the filehandle FILE, you would use the following:

```
print FILE $data;
```

Or, to print a list of data, you could do this:

```
print FILE $data, ' ', $more_data, '\n';
```

printf

```
printf FILEHANDLE LIST
printf LIST
```

`printf` is used to format output using the conventions set for the `sprintf` function. Basically, this

```
printf FILEHANDLE FORMAT, LIST;
```

is identical to

```
print FILEHANDLE sprintf(FORMAT, LIST);
```

push

```
push ARRAY, LIST
```

`push` is used to add an element onto the end of an array. When you push a scalar value onto an array, the array is lengthened by one element, and that value is assigned to the last element in the array. Imagining the same stack of trays from the description of the `pop` function, you can envision the `push` function as putting a tray onto the top of the stack. You can also push multiple values onto the array by using a list as the argument to the `push` function.

quotemeta

```
quotemeta EXPR
quotemeta
```

`quotemeta` returns the value of `EXPR`, with all the non-alphanumeric characters escaped using backslashes. Uses `$_` when `EXPR` is omitted.

rand

```
rand EXPR
rand
```

The `rand` function returns a random number between 0 and `EXPR`. If `EXPR` is omitted, the function returns a value between 0 and 1 (not including 1). See `srand` for information on seeding the random number generator.

read

```
read FILEHANDLE, SCALAR, LENGTH, OFFSET
read FILEHANDLE, SCALAR, LENGTH
```

The `read` function is used to read an arbitrary number of bytes of data from a filehandle into a scalar value. It accepts four arguments; filehandle, scalar, length, and offset (offset is optional). The filehandle argument specifies the filehandle from which to read the data. The scalar argument defines the variable to which the data will be assigned. Length specifies how many bytes of data will be read. Offset is used if you want to read the data from a place other than the beginning of the string. Here's an example, which would read 1024 bytes of data from 2048 bytes into the filehandle `FILE` and assign them to the variable `$chunk`:

```
read FILE, $chunk, 1024, 2048;
```

readdir

```
readdir DIRHANDLE
```

`readdir` is used to read entries from a directory that has been opened using the `opendir` function. When used in the scalar context, it returns the next entry in the directory. In the list context, it returns all of the remaining entries in the directory. If all of the entries in the directory have already been read, it returns the `undefined` value.

readlink

```
readlink EXPR
```

The `readlink` function reads the value of a symbolic link. If symbolic links are not implemented on the platform, it returns a fatal error. If `EXPR` is omitted, the value in `$_` is used.

recv

```
recv SOCKET, SCALAR, LEN, FLAGS
```

`recv` is used to receive a message on a socket, using a C `recvfrom`. Receives `LEN` bytes into variable `SCALAR` from `SOCKET`. It returns the address of the sender, unless there's an error, in which case it returns `undefined`. `recv` accepts the same flags as the system call of the same name.

redo

```
redo LABEL
redo
```

`redo` restarts the current loop block, without reevaluating the loop's test condition. If `LABEL` is omitted, `redo` acts on the innermost enclosing block.

ref

```
ref EXPR
```

`ref` returns `TRUE` if `EXPR` is a reference, `FALSE` otherwise. If `EXPR` is omitted, `$_` is used.

rename

`rename OLDNAME, NEWNAME`

The `rename` function changes the name of the file `OLDNAME` to `NEWNAME`.

require

`require EXPR`

`require` is most often used to load an external Perl file into the current program, but more generally speaking, it is used to base some sort of dependency on its argument. If `EXPR` is numeric, that version of Perl is required for the program to run. If no argument is supplied, `$_` is used.

To load a file, you should provide the filename as the argument to `require`. If you provide the filename as a bare word, `.pm` is automatically appended, and `::` will be replaced by `/`, in order to make it easy to load standard modules. The required file must end with a statement that evaluates as true. Customarily, files built to be `required` end with the `1;` statement.

reset

```
reset EXPR
reset
```

`reset` is used to clear global variables or `??` searches and is often used at the beginning of a loop or in the `continue` block at the end of a loop. `reset` clears the values of all the variables beginning with the character provided in `EXPR`. If called with no arguments, reset clears all `??` searches.

return

`return EXPR`

The `return` function suspends execution of an `eval`, subroutine, or `do` file and returns the value of `EXPR`. If no `return` statement is provided, then the value of the last expression evaluated will be returned.

reverse

`reverse LIST`

The `reverse` function accepts a scalar value or a list as its argument. For scalar values, it reverses of the order of the characters in the scalar. For example, `reverse "red";` returns `der`. When a list is passed to `reverse`, the order of the items in the list is reversed. `reverse ("red", "green", "blue");` returns `("blue", "green", "red")`.

A

rewinddir

`rewinddir DIRHANDLE`

`rewinddir` resets the directory handle for a directory opened with `readdir` back to the first entry in that directory.

rmdir

`rmdir FILENAME`

`rmdir` removes the directory specified by `FILENAME`, if it is empty. If the directory is not empty, or the function fails for some other reason, it returns 1. It returns 0 if it is successful. If `FILENAME` is not provided, the value in `$_` is used.

scalar

`scalar EXPR`

Forces the value of `EXPR` to be evaluated in the scalar context, and returns the value of `EXPR`.

seek

`seek FILEHANDLE, OFFSET, WHENCE`

`seek` is used to set the position of `FILEHANDLE`. `WHENCE` can be any of the following values; 0 to set the position to `POSITION`, 1 to add `POSITION` to the current position, and 2 to set it to EOF plus `POSITION` (usually a negative number is used here, for obvious reasons).

seekdir

`seekdir DIRHANDLE, POS`

`seekdir` sets the position of `DIRHANDLE` for the `readdir` function. `POS` must be a value returned by `telldir`.

select

```
select FILEHANDLE
select
```

Called without arguments, `select` returns the currently selected filehandle. When you provide a filehandle (or an expression that returns a filehandle) to `select`, that filehandle is then the default handle to which output will be sent; in other words, it becomes standard output. So, if you will be printing a number of items to a particular filehandle, it may be easier to `select` that filehandle and leave the filehandles out of your `print` statements.

semctl

```
semctl ID, SEMNUM, CMD, ARG
```

`semctl` calls the System V IPC system call `semctl(2)`.

semget

```
semget KEY, NSEMS, SIZE, FLAGS
```

`semget` calls the System V IPC system call `semget(2)` and returns the semaphore ID, or `undefined` if there is an error.

semop

```
semop KEY, OPSTRING
```

Calls the System V IPC system call `semop(2)`, which performs semaphore operations like signaling and waiting.

send

```
send SOCKET, MSG, FLAGS, TO
send SOCKET, MSG, FLAGS
```

The `send` function sends a message over a socket. If the socket is not connected, you must specify an address to send to. The function takes the same flags as the `send` system call and returns the number of characters sent if it is successful, or `undefined` if it fails.

setpgrp

```
setpgrp PID, PGRP
```

`setpgrp` sets the process group for the specified PID. If 0 is supplied as the PID, the process group is set for the current process. Produces a fatal error if `setpgrp(2)` is not supported by the system.

setpriority

```
setpriority WHICH, WHO, PRIORITY
```

Sets the priority for a process, process group, or user. If `setpriority(2)` is not supported, a fatal error occurs.

setsockopt

```
setsockopt SOCKET, LEVEL, OPTNAME, OPTVAL
```

`setsockopt` is used to set the specified option for a socket. If there is an error, `undefined` is returned. Use `undef` for `OPTVAL` to set an option without specifying a value for the option.

shift

```
shift ARRAY
shift
```

The `unshift` function is the opposite of the `shift` function; it removes the first element from an array and returns it as a scalar value. The indexes of all the other elements in the array are decreased by one, and the array winds up one element shorter than it was before. `unshift` is commonly used to process arguments passed to a user-written function. As you know, arguments are passed to functions through the array `@_`. By using commands like `$arg = unshift @_;`, you can easily make use of function arguments without worrying about their indexes.

shmctl

```
shmctl ID, CMD, ARG
```

`shmctl` calls the System V `shmctl(2)` system call.

shmget

```
shmget KEY, SIZE, FLAGS
```

`shmget` calls the System V `shmget(2)` system call.

shmread

```
shmread ID, VAR, POS, SIZE
```

`shmread` calls the System V `shmread(2)` system call.

shmwrite

```
shmwrite ID, STRING, POS, SIZE
```

`shmwrite` calls the System V `shmwrite(2)` system call.

shutdown

```
shutdown SOCKET, HOW
```

`shutdown` closes a socket connection in the manner specified with `HOW`, which uses the same syntax as the `shutdown` system call.

sin

```
sin EXPR
```

Returns the sine of `EXPR`, or of `$_` if no argument is provided.

sleep

```
sleep EXPR
sleep
```

`sleep` causes the program to sleep for `EXPR` seconds, or if `EXPR` is not specified, to sleep indefinitely. `sleep` can be interrupted using the `SIGALRM` signal. It returns the number of seconds actually slept.

socket

```
socket SOCKET, DOMAIN, TYPE, PROTOCOL
```

The `socket` function is used to open a socket attached to filehandle `SOCKET`. `DOMAIN`, `TYPE`, and `PROTOCOL` are specified in the same way that they are specified for the socket system call. You should use `Socket;` to import the `Socket` module before you call the `socket` function in order to import the proper definitions.

socketpair

```
socketpair SOCKET1, SOCKET2, DOMAIN, TYPE, PAIR
```

The `socketpair` function creates a pair of unnamed sockets, in the specified domain, of the specified type. A fatal error occurs if this function is unimplemented; if it is successful, it returns `TRUE`.

sort

```
sort SUBNAME LISt
sort BLOCK LIST
sort LIST
```

The `sort` routine is used to sort the entries in a list and returns the members in the list in the sorted order. There are three ways `sort` can be used; the simplest is to simply invoke `sort` with the list you want to sort as the argument. This returns the list sorted in standard string comparison order.

Another option is to supply a subroutine to compare the items in the list. The subroutine should return an integer less than, equal to, or greater than zero, depending on how the elements of the list should be ordered (the <=> operator, which performs numeric comparisons, and the `cmp` operator, which provides string comparisons, are often used in these subroutines).

While the subroutine method described in the preceding paragraph can be used to sort lists by criteria other than the default, it is more common to simply insert a block of code as the first argument to the function call. You've probably seen the `sort` function used like this:

```
@sortedlist = sort { $a <=> $b } @list;
```

The preceding example sorts `@list` in ascending numerical order and assigns the list returned to the array `@sortedlist`. The items being compared by the `sort` routine are sent to the code block (or subroutine) as `$a` and `$b`, so the preceding block of code compares the two items using the <=> operator. Let's take a look at some other common code blocks used with the `sort` function:

```
# Sort in lexical order (the same as the default sort)
@sortedlist = sort {$a cmp $b } @list;

# Sort in descending lexical order
@sortedlist = sort { $b cmp $a } @list;

# Sort in numerical order
@sortedlist = sort { $a <=> $b } @list;

# Sort in descending numerical order
@sortedlist = sort { $b <=> $a } @list;
```

splice

```
splice ARRAY, OFFSET, LENGTH, LIST
splice ARRAY, OFFSET, LENGTH
splice ARRAY, OFFSET
```

`splice` is the Swiss Army Knife of array functions; it provides a general purpose function for inserting elements into an array, removing elements from an array, or replacing elements in an array with new values. `splice` can be called with up to four arguments, the last two of which are optional. The first argument should be the array you want to splice. The second argument is the offset, the position in the array where the action will take place (to count back from the end of the array, you can use a negative number). The third argument, which is optional, is the number of items you want to remove (if you leave it out, all of the items from the offset to the end of the array will be removed). All of the rest of the arguments are assumed to be a list of items that will be inserted at the offset. That sounds pretty confusing, but an example will make it all clear.

To delete all of the elements in the array after the second element (remember that array indexes begin with 0), you could use the following code:

```
splice(@array, 2);
```

To insert a new scalar value between the second and third elements in an array, without removing anything, you would use:

```
splice(@array, 2, 0, "new value");
```

To replace the second and third elements in an array with three new elements, you could use the following:

```
splice(@array, 2, 2, "red", "green", "blue");
```

You should note that after an array is spliced, all of the elements in the array are reindexed to reflect the changes in the structure. So, in the previous example, all of the indexes for the items after the ones we inserted would be incremented by one since we replaced two items with three.

split

```
split /PATTERN/, EXPR, LIMIT
split /PATTERN/, EXPR
split /PATTERN/
split
```

The `split` function is used to break a string into multiple parts and return those parts as a list. It accepts up to three arguments: a pattern on which to split, the string to split up, and a limit on the number of list items returned (optional). If you leave out the string to be split up, the value stored in `$_` will be used. You can also leave out the pattern on which to split up the string, and Perl will use whitespace as the delimiter. The pattern argument is always a regular expression contained within `//`, so to split the string on commas, you would use `/,/` as the pattern. Let's look at some examples:

```
# Empty pattern splits string into individual characters
@letters = split //, "word";
# A space in the pattern splits the sentence
# into individual words
@words = split / /, "this is a sentence";
# This pattern splits on any white space instead of just
# spaces (same as the default)
@words = split /\s/, "this is a sentence";
# The third argument ensures that only the first two items
# extracted from the string will be returned in the list.
($first, $second) = split /\s/, "this is a sentence", 2;
```

A

sprintf

```
sprintf FORMAT, LIST
```

The Perl `sprintf` function is used to format strings using the conventions established for the C `sprintf` function. Here's a table listing the conversions used with `sprintf`:

TABLE A.2 `sprintf` FORMATS

Format	*What It Represents*
`%%`	A percent sign
`%c`	A character
`%s`	A string
`%d`	A signed integer, in decimal notation
`%u`	An unsigned integer, in decimal notation
`%o`	An unsigned integer, in octal notation
`%x`	An unsigned integer, in hexidecimal notation
`%e`	A floating point number, in scientific notation
`%f`	A floating point number, in fixed decimal notation
`%g`	A floating point number, in `%e` or `%f` notation
`%X`	The same as `%x`, but using capital letters for hexidecimal notation
`%E`	The same as `%e`, but using a capital E
`%G`	The same as `%g`, but using a capital G (if applicable)
`%p`	A pointer, prints the memory location of the Perl value in hexadecimal
`%n`	Stores the number of characters output so far in the next variable in the parameter list

For detailed information on the conventions used with `sprintf`, check out the man page for `printf(3)`.

sqrt

```
sqrt EXPR
```

`sqrt` returns the square root of `EXPR`, or of `$_` if `EXPR` is not supplied.

srand

```
srand EXPR
```

`srand` seeds Perl's random number generator. If you leave off `EXPR`, `srand(time)` is assumed. You should use it only once in your program.

stat

```
stat FILEHANDLE
```

The `stat` function gathers some information on the file specified by `FILEHANDLE` and returns a list containing that information. It can also accept an expression containing a filename instead of an open filehandle. If no argument is provided, the `stat` function uses the value of `$_` as its argument. The data returned by `stat` is in list form and includes:

- The device number of the filesystem
- The file's inode
- The file mode (type and permissions)
- The number of hard links to the file
- The uid and gid of the file's owner
- The device identifier (for special files)
- The size of the file in bytes
- The times since the file was last accessed, and modified and the inode was changed
- The file's block size
- The number of blocks used

Let's take a look at the values returned by `stat`. This is how one might assign the list returned by `stat` to a group of variables.

```
($dev,$inode,$mode,$uid,$gid,$rdev,
$size,$atime,$mtime,$ctime,$blksize,$blocks) = stat $filename;
```

study

```
study SCALAR
study
```

`study` takes extra time to study `SCALAR` (or `$_` if `SCALAR` is omitted), in order to make future pattern matches on the value more efficient. Whether this saves time or not depends on how many pattern matches you plan on making, and the nature of those matches.

substr

```
substr EXPR, OFFSET, LENGTH
substr EXPR, OFFSET
```

substr is used to extract some characters from a string. It accepts three arguments, the last of which is optional. The arguments are the expression from which characters should be extracted (this can be a scalar value, a variable, or a call to another function), the position at which to begin extracting characters and, optionally, the number of characters to extract. So, `substr("foobar", 3, 2);` returns ba. Leaving out the length, like this: `substr("foobar", 3);` returns bar. You can also use a negative offset value, which will count positions from the end of the string instead of the beginning. Here's an example: `substr("foobar", -4, 2);` returns ob.

symlink

```
symlink OLDFILE, NEWFILE
```

The symlink function is used to create a symbolic link from OLDFILE to NEWFILE. symlink produces a fatal error if the system doesn't support symbolic links.

syscall

```
syscall LIST
```

syscall calls the system call specified as the first argument in LIST. The remaining items in LIST are passed to the system call as arguments.

sysopen

```
sysopen FILEHANDLE, FILENAME, MODE
sysopen FILEHANDLE, FILENAME, MODE, PERMS
```

Opens the file specified by FILENAME, associating it with FILEHANDLE. If the file does not exist, it is created.

sysread

```
sysread FILEHANDLE, SCALAR, LENGTH, OFFSET
sysread FILEHANDLE, SCALAR, LENGTH
```

Reads LENGTH bytes from FILEHANDLE into SCALAR using the read(2) system call. Returns the number of bytes read, or undefined if there is an error. OFFSET places the bytes read that many bytes into the string, rather than at the beginning.

sysseek

```
sysseek FILEHANDLE, POSITION, WHENCE
```

Similar to the seek function, except that it uses the lseek(2) system call rather than the fseek(2) call.

system

```
system LIST
```

The `system` function works exactly like `exec LIST`, except that it forks a new process and executes the commands in `LIST` in that process, and then returns.

syswrite

```
syswrite FILEHANDLE, SCALAR, LENGTH, OFFSET
syswrite FILEHANDLE, SCALAR, LENGTH
```

`syswrite` attempts to write `LENGTH` bytes of data from variable `SCALAR` to `FILEHANDLE`, using the `write(2)` system call. It returns the number of bytes written, or `undefined` in the case of an error.

tell

```
tell FILEHANDLE
```

`tell` returns the current position for the specified filehandle or, if no filehandle is specified, for the last file read.

telldir

```
telldir DIRHANDLE
```

`telldir` returns the current position in the specified directory handle.

tie

```
tie VARIABLE, CLASSNAME, LIST
```

`tie` binds a variable to a package class that will provide the implementation for a variable. `VARIABLE` is the name of the variable to be bound, and `CLASSNAME` is the name of the class implementing objects of the correct type. Any additional arguments are passed to the `new` method of the class.

tied

```
tied VARIABLE
```

`tied` returns a reference to the underlying object of `VARIABLE`, if it is tied to a package. If the variable isn't tied, it returns `undefined`.

time

```
time
```

The `time` function returns the number of seconds that have elapsed since the time that the system considers to be the epoch. On most systems, this is 00:00:00 UTC, January 1, 1970; on the MacOs, 00:00:00, January 1, 1904. Most often passed to `localtime` or `gmtime` for formatting.

times

```
times
```

`times` returns a four element array containing the user and system times for the current process, and its children. Here's an example:

```
($user, $system, $cuser, $csystem) = times;
```

truncate

```
truncate FILEHANDLE, LENGTH
truncate EXPR, LENGTH
```

Truncates the file assigned to `FILEHANDLE`, or specified by `EXPR`, to `LENGTH`. If `truncate` isn't implemented on the system, a fatal error occurs.

uc

```
uc EXPR
```

Just as `lc` converts all the letters in a string to lowercase, `uc` converts all the letters in a string to uppercase.

ucfirst

```
ucfirst EXPR
```

Returns `EXPR` with the first character capitalized.

umask

```
umask EXPR
```

`umask` is used to set the default `umask` for the process. It accepts an octal number (not a string of digits). The `umask` function is useful if your program will be creating a number of files. If `EXPR` is omitted, `umask` returns the current `umask`.

undef

```
undef EXPR
```

`undef` is used to eliminate the value of a variable. It can be used on a scalar variable, an entire array, or an entire hash.

unlink

```
unlink (LIST)
```

`unlink` deletes the files passed to it via `LIST`. It returns the number of files it successfully deletes. If no list is passed to `unlink`, it uses `$_` as its argument.

unpack

```
unpack TEMPLATE, EXPR
```

`unpack` is the reverse of `pack`. It accepts a data structure and translates it into a list, based on `TEMPLATE`. The `TEMPLATE` format is the same as that for `pack`.

unshift

```
unshift ARRAY, LIST
```

The `unshift` function inserts a scalar value as the first element in an array, moving the indexes of all of the other items in the array up by one.

utime

```
utime LIST
```

`utime` is the Perl equivalent of the UNIX `touch` command; it sets the access and modification times for a list of files. The first two arguments must contain the numerical access and modification times for the files. All of the arguments after the first two are assumed to be files that should have their access and modification dates changed. The function returns the number of files that were successfully touched.

values

```
values HASH
```

Returns an array containing the `values` for each of the items in a hash, much like `keys` returns an array of the keys in a hash.

vec

```
vec EXPR, OFFSET, BITS
```

`vec` treats a string (specified by `EXPR`) as a vector of unsigned integers and returns the value of the bit field specified by `OFFSET`.

wait

```
wait
```

wait simply waits for a child process to die and then returns the PID of that process.

waitpid

```
waitpid PID, FLAGS
```

The waitpid function waits for a particular child process (specified by PID) to exit, and then returns the process ID of the dead process.

wantarray

```
wantarray
```

wantarray returns TRUE if the context of the subroutine currently being executed requires a list value. If it was called in the scalar or void context, this function returns FALSE. To avoid executing the entire subroutine, you can use a statement like this to make sure that the subroutine was called in the list context:

```
return unless defined wantarray;
```

warn

```
warn LIST
```

warn is used to print a message to standard error without terminating the program. Other than the fact that the program doesn't stop executing, it is just like the die function.

write

```
write FILEHANDLE
```

The write function is used to output data using a template defined with the format function. For more information, check out the perlform man page.

Appendix B

A Survey of Perl Modules

There are literally hundreds of modules that have been developed for use with Perl. Many are available as part of the standard Perl library, part of the Perl distribution itself. Other modules may be bundled with different ports of Perl to make features of a particular platform available to Perl programmers on that platform. Finally, CPAN, the *Comprehensive Perl Archive Network*, serves as a repository for user-developed modules that are of use to the greater developer community. New modules are always being added to CPAN, so any reference covering the selection of Perl modules is dated almost the very moment it has been written. An up-to-date survey of the contents of CPAN can be found at `http://www.perl.com/CPAN/CPAN.html` and in a companion list at `http://www.perl.com/CPAN/modules/00modlist.long.html`.

In the meantime, this appendix covers some of the most popular and most useful Perl modules. For convenience, the modules in this appendix are categorized in the same way that they are categorized on CPAN. If a particular module is not noted as being in the standard library, it is part of CPAN and must be downloaded and installed before it can be used. Once a module is installed on your system, you can use `perldoc` *`MODULE`* or `man` *`MODULE`* to read the documentation for that module.

Please note that this appendix is my no means exhaustive. I've picked out only those modules that are useful, commonly used, or that I found interesting. There are many, many more modules to choose from. See the `perlmod` man page for a complete list of modules in the standard Perl library, and the preceding URLs for the most up-to-date list of CPAN modules.

Note also that not all modules may be available to all platforms; see the documentation that comes with each module to see if it will run on your platform.

Pragmas

Pragmas are modules that provide instructions for Perl to behave at both compile time and runtime. They are imported with the `use` function, like modules. These pragmas are part of the standard Perl library. Additional documentation is available for all the pragmas through man pages (or the `perldoc` system).

`constant`

The `constant` pragma enables you to create constant variables at compile time.

`diagnostics`

The `diagnostics` pragma provides more information in Perl warning messages. It is the same as using the `-w` switch to Perl itself, but can be enabled or disabled for specific parts of a script. The `perldiag` man page contains even further discussion of the warning messages emitted by the `diagnostics` pragma.

`integer`

The `integer` pragma tells Perl to use integer-only arithmetic, which is faster than the alternative, floating-point arithmetic.

`lib`

The `lib` pragma provides more robust methods for including extra directories in `@INC` (the array containing the list of directories to search for libraries and modules).

`overload`

The `overload` pragma allows you to tell Perl how operators should work for your objects.

`sigtrap`

The `sigtrap` pragma allows you to trap and handle Control-Cs sent by the user while a Perl program is running.

`strict`

The `strict` module allows you to disallow symbolic references, global variables, and barewords.

`subs`

The `subs` pragma allows you to predeclare subroutine names.

`vars`

The `vars` pragma allows you to predeclare global variables so that they will be acceptable under the strict pragma.

Basic Perl Modules

These modules, most of which are part of the standard Perl library, provide basic functionality that enables you to extend the Perl language or to affect the way Perl behaves.

`Autoloader`

`Autoloader`, a module for module developers, allows you to load modules on demand, instead of loading them into memory as soon as they are executed. `Autoloader` is part of the standard library.

`B`

`B` is a collection of modules that allow access to the underlying Perl compiler. With these modules, you can create new compiler interfaces, called *backends*, that can translate your Perl code into C, compile your Perl code into platform-independent bytecode, or compile your Perl code into an executable.

`Carp`

The `Carp` module is useful primarily for module developers. `Carp` provides additional error-handling functions similar to `warn` or `die`, except that they report where the subroutine from which they were invoked was called, instead of their location within the subroutine itself. Normally, `warn` and `die` report the line number where they were called. If a script imports a module and then uses that module in such a way as to trigger a `warn` or die, then the location of the error will be somewhere inside the module, not inside the script. Not very useful for debugging. Carp's subroutines to replace warn or die report the location in the enclosing script where the error or warning occurred.

Config

The Config module allows you to access a hash, %Config, which contains the settings for the current Perl installation. Things such as the installation directory, the name of your OS, and support for certain functions are stored here. This module is part of the standard library.

English

The English module enables you to use alternate, spelled out names for some of the cryptic variables in Perl, such as $_, $!, $¦, and the rest. The English module is part of the standard library.

Exporter

Exporter allows you to export variables from one package to another. It is part of the standard library.

Opcode

Opcode is a module for high-level users that enables them to manipulate Perl's internal opcodes. It is part of the standard library.

PodParser

PodParser is a bundle of modules that allows you to manipulate documentation written in the POD (Plain Old Documentation) format. For example, using Pod::Text (one of the modules in the bundle) you can reformat POD documentation as plain text.

Symbol

Symbol is used to manipulate Perl symbols and their names. The Symbol module is part of the standard library.

Tie Modules

The various Tie modules (Tie::Hash, Tie::Scalar, Tie::StdHash, Tie::StdScalar, and Tie::SubstrHash) provide base classes for tied data. All are part of the standard library.

Development Support Modules

These modules are designed to help you write better scripts by providing performance benchmarking and other tools for inspecting your programs.

Benchmark

The `Benchmark` module is used to gauge the performance of your Perl programs, by displaying the amount of CPU time used by a chunk of code. It is part of the standard library.

Devel::DProf

`Devel::DProf` is a profiler for Perl that collects information about the execution time of a program, and its individual subroutines.

ExtUtils

The `ExtUtils` modules are a series of modules to help build and package Perl extensions (`XSUBs`). Many are part of the standard library.

Usage

The `Usage` module allows you to check subroutine arguments for validity. Using this module you can easily check to make sure that subroutine arguments contain a particular value, or that they are of a particular data type.

Operating System Interfaces

Since Perl is more or less platform independent, these modules can be used to add platform-specific functionality if you're using Perl on a particular platform.

AppleII

The `AppleII` module provides block-level access to Apple II disk images.

BSD::Resource

If your operating system supports the `BSD` functions `getrusage()`, `getrlimit()`, `setrlimit()`, `getpriority()`, and/or `setpriority()`, the `BSD::Resource` module enables you to access them through Perl.

BSD::Time

If your operating system supports the BSD gettimeofday() and settimeofday() functions, this module makes them available to your Perl programs.

Env

The Env module makes environment variables available to your Perl program through the %ENV hash. It is part of the standard library.

Fcntl

The Fcntl, or File Control, module provides you with access to low-level system calls for manipulating file descriptors. It is part of the standard library.

Mac Modules

MacPerl contains a number of modules that provide support for Macintosh features through Perl scripts. In addition, CPAN provides other modules for access to other Macintosh features including Mac::Types for access to Macintosh file type information, Mac::Apps::Launch to launch or quit applications, or Mac::Apps::MacPGP to interface with the Mac version of PGP (*Pretty Good Privacy*).

OS2

The OS2 module provides binaries and utilities for the OS2 version of Perl.

POSIX

The POSIX module provides access to the functions that an operating system must implement in order to be POSIX-compliant. It is part of the standard library, but only on POSIX-compliant platforms.

Networking Modules

Networking modules provide interfaces to common (and some not-so-common) network protocols and services. See also “HTML, HTTP, WWW, and CGI-Related Modules.”

IPC::Signal

IPC::Signal provides you with a method of handling operating system signals.

Net::Bind

Net::Bind provides an interface to bind daemon files.

`Net::Cmd`

`Net::Cmd` is a module that contains a set of network commands used by protocols such as SMTP and FTP. It is part of the `libnet` bundle.

`Net::Country`

`Net::Country` maps two-letter Internet country codes to the full country name. For example, it knows that TM stands for Turkmenistan.

`Net::DNS`

`Net::DNS` provides an interface to DNS servers. Any type of DNS query can be executed with this module.

`Net::Domain`

`Net::Domain` allows you to evaluate the current host's hostname and domain.

`Net::FTP`

`Net::FTP` is an interface to FTP, the File Transfer Protocol. It is part of the `libnet` bundle.

`Net::Gen`

`Net::Gen` is a generic sockets interface for Perl. It is bundled with the `Net-ext` bundle.

`Net::Ident`

`Net::Ident` is used to extract the username from the other end of a TCP connection, assuming the remote machine is running `IDENTD`.

`Net::Inet`

`Net::Inet` provides basic services for socket-based communications, and is part of the `Net-ext` bundle.

`Net::Netrc`

`Net::Netrc` provides an interface to `.netrc` files. It is part of the `libnet` bundle.

`Net::NIS`, `Net::NISPlus`

`Net::NIS` provides an interface to Sun's NIS (Network Information Service) and allows multiple computers to share the user account information. `Net::NISPlus` provides an interface to Sun's second generation version of NIS (NIS+).

Net::NNTP

Net::NNTP allows you to communicate through the Network News Transfer Protocol (used by Usenet). Part of the libnet bundle.

Net::Ping

Net::Ping enables you to ping a host, which tells you if the machine is up and how long it takes for your packets to reach it.

Net::POP3

Net::POP3 provides an interface to the POP3 protocol (POP is the Post Office Protocol). You should also see the module Mail::POP3Client. This module is part of the libnet bundle.

Net::SMTP

Net::SMTP provides an interface to the Simple Mail Transfer Protocol, which is the protocol most computers on the Internet use to exchange mail. If you want to send mail from a Perl script, this is the module to use. It is part of the libnet bundle.

Net::SNPP

Net::SNPP is an interface to the Simple Network Pager Protocol. It is part of the libnet bundle.

Net::SSLeay

Net::SSLeay provides an implementation of Netscape's Secure Sockets Layer (SSL) protocol for use in Perl programs.

Net::TCP

Net::TCP allows you to communicate via TCP over sockets. It is part of the Net-ext bundle.

Net::Telnet

Net::Telnet enables you to telnet to another computer and execute commands.

Net::Time

Net::Time enables you to obtain the current time from another computer on the Internet. This module is part of the libnet bundle.

Net::UDP

`Net::UDP` provides for communication using the `UDP` protocol. It is part of the `Net-ext` bundle.

SNMP

`SNMP` is an interface to the Simple Network Management Protocol.

Socket

`Socket` provides additional structures and constants to extend the socket communication functions within Perl. It is part of the standard library.

Data Type Utilities

Data type modules allow you to manipulate data stored in specific data types outside the general types supported by Perl.

Date::DateCalc

`Date::DateCalc` is used to calculate the difference between two dates or to calculate a specified offset from a given date.

Date::Format

`Date::Format` contains some date formatting routines that convert date values to ASCII. Part of the `TimeDate` bundle.

Date::Language

`Date::Language` is used to convert dates into different languages. Part of the `TimeDate` bundle.

Date::Manip

`Date::Manip` is used to manipulate date values; it can calculate differences and offsets, and it can parse dates into UNIX time format. It can also accept dates in a number of formats.

Date::Parse

`Date::Parse` converts dates into UNIX time format. Part of the `TimeDate` bundle.

Math::BigFloat, Math::BigInt

`Math::Bigfloat` and `Math::BigInt` allow arbitrary-length integers and floating-point numbers in Perl. Part of the standard library.

Math::Complex

`Math::Complex` allows processing of complex numbers. Part of the standard library.

Math::Fraction

`Math::Fraction` enables you to handle fractions from within Perl.

Math::Matrix

`Math::Matrix` enables you to perform mathematical operations on matrices from within Perl.

Math::PRSG

`Math::PRSG` provides a more powerful random-number generator than those included with Perl (srand and rand). PRSG stands for Pseudo Random Sequence Generator, it isn't as random as `Math::TrulyRandom`.

Math::Trig

`Math::Trig` provides inverse and hyperbolic trigonometric functions. These are also included in the (bundled) `POSIX` module.

Math::TrulyRandom

`Math::TrulyRandom` generates random numbers from interrupt timing discrepancies.

Ref

The `Ref` module allows you to compare and copy Perl references.

Sort::Versions

`Sort::Versions` allows you to sort version numbers, placing numbers such as 4.1a, 1.1.1, and 4.003_02 in the appropriate order.

Statistics::Descriptive

`Statistics::Descriptive` allows you to perform standard statistical operations such as mean, median, mode, standard deviation, and others.

Time-Modules

The Time-Modules bundle contains the following modules for handling and modifying time and date values: Time::CTime, Time::JulianDay, Time::ParseDate, Time::Timezone, and Time::DaysInMonth.

TimeDate Bundle

The TimeDate bundle is another bundle of modules for converting times and dates, and modifying time and date values. It contains the following modules: Date::Format, Date::Language, Date::Parse, and Time::Zone.

Database-Related Modules

These modules provide interfaces to relational database files as well as DBM-style database files.

AnyDBM_File

AnyDBM_File is used to manipulate files in any of the database manager formats, including Berkeley DBM, GDBM, SDBM, and so forth. It is part of the standard library.

DBD

DBD stands for Database Drivers; it is a package that provides a Perl driver for many popular relational databases. Developed by the Perl DBI initiative, it provides a standard interface to all of the databases that it supports. Right now, there are DBD drivers for Oracle, Sybase, Informix, DB2, Solid, MSQL, MySQL, and ODBC, among others. DBD works by providing the backend driver for the DBI module, which implements the standard database interface.

DBI

DBI (Database Interface) implements a standard interface in Perl for accessing relational database files. By pairing the DBI module with the appropriate DBD driver, you can connect to most popular commercial relational database engines.

DB_File

DB_File provides an interface to Berkeley DB, which is freely available. AnyDBMF_File also provides this functionality.

Msql

The `Msql` module is an interface between Perl and mini SQL, a relational database engine for UNIX systems. This functionality can also be achieved through `DBD/DBI`.

Oraperl

`Oraperl` is a Perl 4 interface to Oracle databases. It has been replaced by `DBI` and the `DBD` driver for Oracle. It is mentioned here because it is still in common use.

Pg

`Pg` is an interface to the freely available Postgres relational database engine.

SDBM_File

`SDBM_File` is an interface to SDBM, the Simple Database Manager, which is part of the standard library. Because SDBM is bundled, you can write portable scripts based on it.

Sybperl

`Sybperl` is a now obsolete interface to Sybase for Perl. It has been replaced by the functionality in `DBI` and `DBD`.

User Interfaces

The user interface modules provide programming interfaces from within Perl to user interface toolkits such as X Windows, curses, and Tk.

Curses

The `Curses` module allows you to create ASCII user interfaces using curses.

Qt

The `Qt` module allows you to utilize the Qt GUI toolkit for X Windows, written by Troll Tech.

Term::AnsiColor

`Term::AnsiColor` allows you to use the escape codes for ANSI color sequences.

Term::Gnuplot

`Term::Gnuplot` allows you to utilize the low-level drawing routines in the Gnuplot system from Perl.

`Tk`

`Tk` is a Perl interface to the Tk graphics toolkit. Tk provides an easy way to create applications from scripting languages (such as Perl). You can read the Perl/Tk FAQ at `http://www.perl.com/CPAN-local/doc/FAQs/tk/`.

`X11::FVWM`

`X11::FVWM` is an interface to the `Fvwm2` (a window manager for X Windows) API.

`X11::Protocol`

`X11::Protocol` provides an interface to the raw X Windows protocol.

File System Modules

These modules provide access to file-system-level facilities that are not supported natively from within Perl.

`Cwd`

`Cwd` provides three functions for determining the current working directory through Perl. It is part of the standard library.

`File::Df`

An implementation of the UNIX `df` command in Perl. It allows you to determine how full your disks are.

`File::Flock`

`File::Flock` is a wrapper for the `flock` system call. The `flock()` system call allows you to lock files so that two processes can't try to write to the same file at the same time, thus preventing data loss. `File::Lock` is also a wrapper for `flock`.

`File::Copy`

`File::Copy` enables you to copy files by name or filehandle from within Perl. It is part of the `File::Tools` bundle.

`File::Lock`

`File::Lock` is a wrapper for the `flock` system call, much like `File::Flock`.

File::Lockf

`File::Lockf` is another file-locking module for Perl. It differs from the others because it uses the `lockf` system call instead of `flock`. It has the advantage of being able to lock files on network mounted drives.

File::Recurse

`File::Recurse` enables you to perform an operation through an entire directory tree. It is part of the `File::Tools` module.

File::Tools

`File::Tools` contains the `File::Copy` and `File::Recurse` modules.

String Processing Modules

There are a number of modules available within CPAN that provide functions for manipulating strings. Before writing any advanced string-processing code, you should check to make sure that someone else hasn't done it already.

Option/Argument Processing

These modules are designed to parse options passed to your programs in common formats; including command-line arguments, and Windows `ini` files.

Getopt::Long

`Getopt::Long` allows you to parse `POSIX` command-line options, with Gnu extensions. It is part of the standard library.

Getopt::Mixed

`Getopt::Mixed` allows you to process Gnu-style command-line options. It contains features of both `Getopt::Mixed` and `Getopt::Std`.

Getopt::Std

`Getopt::Std` enables you to process command-line options in your Perl programs. See the examples on Day 15, "Working with Files and I/O" for details. It is part of the standard library.

IniConf

`IniConf` allows you to read and write Windows `ini` files.

Internationalization and Localization

These modules make it easier to write programs that are designed for other locales.

I18N::Collate

`I18N::Collate` enables you to compare scalar values made up of 8-bit characters based on the current locale.

Locale::Codes

`Locale::Codes` provides access to the complete list of two-letter country codes.

Unicode

The `Unicode` module provides support for Unicode character sets in Perl. This will eventually be part of the core Perl language.

Cryptography, Authentication, and Security

Modules that provide access to common security, cryptography, and authentication algorithms. Some of these modules require that certain system-level libraries are available in order to work.

Authen::Radius

`Authen::Radius` provides an interface to the Radius network authentication protocol.

Crypt::Des

`Crypt::Des` allows you to use the DES block cipher algorithm.

Crypt::Idea

`Crypt::Idea` allows you to use the IDEA block cipher algorithm.

MD5

`MD5` is a message digest algorithm that allows you to create a one-way "thumbnail" of a message that can be used to verify its integrity, created by RSA. The MD5 module allows you to create MD5 thumbnails.

PGP

The `PGP` module is an interface to the Pretty Good Privacy encryption software.

HTML, HTTP, WWW, and CGI-Related Modules

Modules used for Web-related tasks, including CGI and Web client programming.

Apache

The `Apache` Perl modules allow you to write modules for the Apache Web server in Perl. These, in turn, are executed by a Perl interpreter embedded within the Apache `httpd` server. The advantage is that you are saved the overhead of launching the Perl interpreter every time one of these programs is launched.

CGI

The `CGI` module, which is part of the standard library as of version 5.004, makes it easy to create CGI programs that generate, process, and respond to forms. It is an incredibly popular tool for CGI programmers. See Day 16, "Using Perl for CGI Scripting" or *Sams Teach Yourself CGI Programming in a Week* for more details.

libwww

`libwww` is a large bundle of eight separate sets of modules that enable you to create HTTP user agents in Perl, parse and translate HTML, handle MIME encoded content, and more. The bundles it contains are `File`, `Font`, `HTML`, `HTTP`, `LWP`, `MIME`, `URI`, and `WWW`.

Archiving and Compression

This section covers interfaces to common compression algorithms.

Compress

`Compress` provides an interface to the UNIX `zlib` library, which allows you to compress files using standard UNIX (`.Z`) compression.

Convert::BinHex

`Convert::BinHex` allows you to extract the header, data fork, and resource fork from Macintosh files.

Convert::UU

`Convert::UU` allows you to uuencode and uudecode files. Uuencoding is a format often used to translate binary files into an ASCII format.

Image/Bitmap Manipulation

This section lists modules for creating and editing graphics.

GD

GD is a Perl version of the popular gd library for C. It allows you to create and edit GIF images in Perl.

Image::Size

Image::Size is used to determine the size of an image.

Image::Magick

PerlMagick is an interface to the X Windows–based graphic manipulation tool ImageMagick.

Mail and Usenet

These modules provide interfaces to common mail services, and Usenet news.

Mail::POP3Client

Mail::POP3Client is a client-side interface to POP3 mail servers.

News::Newsrc

News::Newsrc allows you to read and manipulate .newsrc files using Perl. newsrc files are used to keep track of the newsgroups that a user reads.

Flow Control Utilities

These modules enable you to take greater control of your program at runtime. Also see the sigtrap pragma.

AtExit

The AtExit module allows you to write code that will be executed when your program exits. Similar functionality exists in END blocks (discussed on Day 13); and in the POSIX module, which also implements an atexit function.

`Religion`

The cleverly named `Religion` module allows you to specify where your Perl programs go when they die, by providing easy access to the `$SIG{__DIE__}` and `$SIG{__WARN__}` functions.

Filehandles and Input/Output

These modules provide additional services for manipulating file input and output in your programs.

`DirHandle`

`DirHandle` enables you to use directory handles as objects. This module is part of the standard library.

`FileCache`

The `FileCache` module allows you to work around limitations placed on the number of file descriptors you can have open at one time. It is part of the standard library.

`FileHandle`

`FileHandle` allows you to treat filehandles as objects. It is part of the standard library.

`IO`

The `IO` module allows you to load the modules `IO::Handle`, `IO::Seekable`, `IO::File`, `IO::Pipe`, and `IO::Socket` at the same time. All of these modules are part of the standard library.

Windows Modules

Windows modules provide functionality specific to the Windows platform. They provide access to Windows-only services, or provide functionality from other platforms to Windows users.

`libwin32`

The `libwin32` bundle is a family of modules that provides access to various features of the Windows platform. They are included with the ActviveState version of Perl for Windows. Many are described on Day 18, "Perl and the Operating System."

Other Modules

This section discusses modules that don't fit under the other categories in CPAN.

Archie

Archie is a service that catalogs the contents of FTP sites. The `Archie` module enables you to generate Archie queries from within Perl.

Business::CreditCard

The `Business::CreditCard` module enables you to check the validity of credit cards and determine the card type from the card number.

CPAN

The `CPAN` module allows you to obtain and install Perl modules from CPAN in an automated manner. It requires the `Net::FTP` module and an Internet connection.

APPENDIX C

Installing Perl on a UNIX System

This appendix explains how to obtain and install Perl for a computer running UNIX. Unlike Windows and the Macintosh, installing Perl on a UNIX computer involves compiling Perl from the source code. Fortunately, thanks to tools like the Configure program and `make`, this process is pretty straightforward. However, it does mean that certain tools should be present on your computer before you get started. This appendix explains which tools are required to install Perl, and where to get them. It also provides step-by-step instructions on performing the installation.

Do You Need to Install Perl?

Unless you're running on a UNIX system where you own the box and you're the only person on it, chances are really good that you don't need to install Perl at all. Perl is so useful to UNIX system administrators that if your system administrator hasn't already installed it, he's an odd UNIX system administrator indeed. From your UNIX system prompt, try this first:

```
% perl -v
```

If you get a message that says `This is perl, version 5.005_02` or some such, you're set. Stop here, and go directly to Day 1 to start working with Perl.

If you get a message that says `perl: command not found`, or if you get the proper version message but it says something like `This is perl, version 4`, then things are going to be tougher. It means that either Perl isn't installed on your system, or Perl is installed but it's an older version (you want to be running a version of Perl 5 or higher for this book; older versions won't work). Or it could mean that Perl is installed but it's not in your search path; you might try looking around in `/usr/bin` or `/usr/local/bin` and seeing if you can find it.

If you still can't find Perl and if you're on a UNIX machine administered by someone else—a system at work, or a public ISP—your next step is to contact the system administrator or support organization for that system and to ask them if they have Perl installed (and if they do, where they put it), or if they've got an old version, to upgrade it. While you can install Perl on a system that you don't have administrator access to, it's generally a better idea for your administrator to do it for you.

And, finally, if you run your own UNIX system—say, a Linux system on a partition of your Windows machine—and you cannot find Perl already installed, then you are your own system administrator, and it's your job to get Perl installed yourself.

Obtaining Perl

To install Perl on your system, you have two choices:

- Download and install a pre-built binary version
- Download, compile, and install the source code version

Getting Binaries

Installing a binary version is the simpler route to installing Perl—you don't need to compile anything, just unpack and go. However, binaries are only available for a very few UNIX platforms, they tend to lag behind the current version of the Perl source code, and there is a danger of viruses or other nasties being hidden in the binary versions if you don't get them from a reputable source. Building the Perl source code is not difficult, and if you use UNIX for any extensive period of time you'll probably end up doing a lot anyhow. Plus, with the source code you'll always end up with the latest and greatest versions. Building Perl from source is the preferred method of getting Perl installed on your system.

If you'd really prefer not to deal with the source, the first place to look for a binary version of Perl is with the vendor of your UNIX system. If you're running Linux, for example, the major Linux support companies such as Red Hat do offer builds of Perl on their FTP sites. Or if your UNIX software came on a CD with a book or in a box from a store, you might check that CD to see if Perl was bundled with that software (although it's likely that any version of Perl bundled on a CD will be several versions behind).

Another place to look, particularly for Solaris and Linux software, is the archive at `http://metalab.unc.edu/pub/`, formerly called Sunsite. Check in `http://metalab.unc.edu/pub/packages/solaris/sparc` for Solaris software, and `http://metalab.unc.edu/pub/Linux` for Linux.

Different companies and sites have different ways of packaging their binaries; you'll need to follow the directions for each site to discover how to install the Perl binaries on your system. You may find that what with tracking down binaries and figuring out how to install them that it was easier to just go the source code route in the first place.

Getting Source (and Related Tools)

To compile and install Perl from the source code, there are several other things you'll need in addition to the Perl code itself: `tar` and `gzip` to unpack the source archive, and a C compiler to compile the source. The Perl installation will also go most smoothly if you have superuser (root) access on the computer on which Perl will be installed. If you're not the system administrator for the computer on which you need to run Perl, you'll probably be better off tracking down the person who is, and asking them to do it.

To expand the Perl archive you'll need `tar` and `gzip`. The `tar` utility is present on almost every UNIX machine. Most UNIX computers also have `gzip` installed, especially if they're running a free version of UNIX such as FreeBSD or Linux. If you don't have these utilities, you'll need to locate them on the Internet, download them, and install them. As with the Perl binaries, it's likely that the vendor of your UNIX system can provide you with access to these tools, or if your UNIX system came on a CD they may have been bundled with that CD. Solaris users can download precompiled `GNUtar` and `gzip` packages from SunSite at `http://metalab.unc.edu/pub/packages/solaris/sparc`.

Second, you'll also need a C compiler. It is likely that the computer you're using will have either `cc` or `gcc` installed (type `cc` or `gcc` at a prompt and see what happens). If you can't locate a C compiler on your system, you should contact your system administrator about locating or installing one. Again, C compilers are almost always installed by default with free UNIX systems, and are also installed with many popular commercial UNIX variants. Solaris users can download precompiled versions of `gcc` at the SunSite URL mentioned above.

Once you're sure that you have all the tools required to successfully install Perl, you can download the Perl source code. The easiest way to get it is to simply point your Web browser at `www.perl.com`, which keeps the latest stable version of Perl at `http://www.perl.com/CPAN/src/stable.tar.gz`.

The `stable.tar.gz` package contains the C source code, which should compile successfully on nearly every UNIX platform. As I write this, that's version 5.005_02, and that's the version that this book covers. If you're feeling really adventurous, you can download the new experimental developer's version of Perl at `http://www.perl.com/CPAN/src/devel.tar.gz`. The developer's version is currently version 5.005_53 (but has most likely changed by the time you read this). You should probably only use it if you already know Perl, know what you're doing, want to check out some of the newer features, and are willing to put up with some odd behavior.

All the `.gz` packages are in binary format, so make sure you download them as binary files. If you download them in text format, they won't decompress (if you use a browser to download them, you don't have to worry about this).

Extracting and Compiling Perl

Once you've successfully downloaded the Perl source code, extract it from its archive. There are two steps required to extract the Perl archive; decompressing it using `gzip`, and expanding the archive using `tar`. To unzip the file, use the following command:

```
gzip -d latest.tar.gz
```

Then, untar the file using this command:

```
tar xvf latest.tar
```

As the `tar` program runs, a list of all the files being extracted from the archive will be printed on the screen. Don't worry about the output. A directory named `perl5.005_02` or something similar will be created, and all of the Perl files will be inside that directory.

Detailed installation instructions can be found in the `README` and `INSTALL` files; I'll summarize the process in the following sections.

Running the Configure Program

Before you install Perl, run the Configure program to set up the compile-time options. First, cd to the Perl directory created when you untarred the archive (usually, `perl` plus a version number, for example, `perl5.005_02`). Then, remove any existing configuration file using

```
rm -f config.sh
```

(There may not be any existing configuration file. Don't worry about it.) Then run the Configure program like this:

```
sh Configure
```

Configure will ask you a lot of questions about the makeup of your system and where things should be installed. If you want to skip most of the questions that Configure will ask you, you can use `sh Configure -d` instead. This will cause Configure to automatically select as many default values as it can, and install Perl in various default locations typical for your platform. These instructions assume you want to run Configure the long way.

C

Note

Before we start, please be aware that Configure is written to configure software for all kinds of complex features of different platforms. Unless you're really very familiar with UNIX systems and with C, a lot of the questions it asks may be really confusing or seem to make no sense. Most every question will have a default value, which you can accept by pressing Return or Enter. Generally you'll do no harm by accepting Configure's default values, so if you don't know what the program is asking, just press Return.

Also, depending on the version of Perl you're installing, some of the questions following may not appear or may appear in a slightly different order. If things start to get confusing, just accept the defaults and you should be fine.

Setting Up

First, Configure makes sure that you have some things necessary for the Perl installation, provides you with some instructions on the installation process (you can read them if you want to, but it's not necessary), and then locates some of the utilities used in the installation process.

To speed up the installation process, Configure guesses which system you're on so that it can set up some default values. Most likely, it'll guess right, so you can just press Enter here and accept the default.

It then makes a guess at which operating system you're using. If the defaults are correct, just press Enter for both the name and version.

Depending on your Perl version, you may be asked if you want to build a threading version of Perl. Unless you know what you're doing, you're better off not building one right now. Threads are experimental. Once you know more about Perl you can go back and recompile it with threads turned on.

Directories and Basic Configuration

The next step, an important one, is to specify under which directory hierarchy Perl will be installed. The default is typically under the `/usr/local` hierarchy; binaries in `/usr/local/bin`, man pages in `/usr/local/man`, and libraries in `/usr/local/lib`. You can change the basic hierarchy where Perl is installed if you choose to do so; for example, to install them under /usr with the system files (`/usr/bin/`, `/usr/lib`, `/usr/man`). Just indicate a prefix here; if you want to customize where you put each part of Perl you'll have an opportunity to do that later on.

The next directory you need to specify is the location for site-specific and architecture dependent Perl libraries. If you've accepted the defaults for the other directory locations, accepting the defaults here are almost certainly okay.

Depending on the version of Perl you're installing, the next question may be whether you want Perl to be binary-compatible with Perl earlier versions. If Perl 5.001 was installed on the machine on which you are currently installing Perl, you'll need to specify where to put the old architecture-dependent library files. For both these questions, the defaults are fine unless you have reason to change them.

Configure then checks for secure `setuid` scripts, and you have a choice of whether to do `setuid` emulation. Chances are good that if you don't know what this means, you don't need it. Accept the default.

The next question is which memory models are supported on the machine; for most, it's none. Accept the default.

Compilers and Libraries

Configure asks you which compiler to use. It figures out which compiler it would prefer to use, and offers you that as the default.

Configure also figures out which directories in which to look for libraries. If you know of other directories to search for shared libraries, add them to the list, and remove any directories that should not be searched from the list. The default will probably work here.

Configure asks for the file extension for shared libraries. If you don't want to use shared libraries, change the default to none. You probably don't want to change it, however.

Next, Configure checks for the presence of some specific libraries on your system. It presents you with a list of shared libraries it will use once it's done. You can add or remove libraries from the list, but the default list will probably work fine.

The Configure program then asks some questions about your compiler. If you don't specifically know a good reason to change the defaults, just go ahead and use them.

One of the compiler questions Configure asks you is where you want to store the Perl binaries. By default the choice is the prefix hierarchy you chose, plus the `bin` directory; for example, `/usr/local/bin`. You have the opportunity to change that here.

Documentation and Networking

After all of the compiler-related questions are finished, Configure asks where you want to place the Perl man files. As with the binaries, the default is the directory prefix plus `man`. You'll only need to change it if you want to put the man page somewhere else on your system. It also asks for the extensions for your man pages; you should accept the default.

Configure then tries to determine your host and domain names. If it guesses right, you can accept the defaults. Otherwise, edit its choices and enter the correct values (the hostname is your fully-qualified Internet name for that particular system (for example, `www.typerl.com`); the domain name is the last part of the address (`typerl.com`).

The next question is your email address. Perl will try to get the right email address here, but it will be specific to the machine on which you are installing Perl. You may need to change it to your general email address. (For example, it will probably select `person@somemachine.somedomain.com`, when what you really want is `person@somedomain.com`.)

Perl also wants the email address for the person who will be responsible for administration of Perl on the machine. If it's not you, enter the email address for the person or group who will be responsible here (be nice).

Other Things

Next, Perl wants the value to place in the shebang line of scripts. The default value is almost certainly correct here, since you've already told Configure where the Perl binaries will be installed. (Don't worry if you don't know what a shebang is; you'll learn about that soon enough. Accept the defaults.)

Then, you need to tell Perl where to place publicly executable scripts. Reasons why you may not want to accept the default are provided by Configure.

Depending on your Perl version, you may be asked for yet more directory pathnames, this time for library files. Once again, the defaults are probably fine.

The next question is whether you want to use the experimental PerlIO abstraction layer instead of `<stdio.h>`. You probably don't.

Configure then checks for the presence of certain system calls, and for other system specific things. It may ask you a few questions along the way. You can probably accept the defaults for all of these. Even if Configure seems to have misgivings (my Linux system triggered a few "WHOA THERE" and "Are you sure" messages), accept the defaults and you'll be fine.

The last questions Configure asks is which Perl extensions you want to load dynamically and statically. You can probably just accept the default, which is to load them all dynamically.

Perl then gives you a chance to edit the configuration file it just built, `config.sh`, manually. You probably don't need to do so; just press Return.

Configure gives you the chance to run `make depend` (go ahead), and then exits.

For detailed instructions on most of the options in the Configure program, you should read the `INSTALL` file in the Perl directory.

Run `make`

The next step after the Configure program generates the `config.sh` file is to type `make` in the Perl directory. `make` will compile all of the Perl binaries and prepare them for installation.

On some systems, the `ar` program is required to build Perl. Unfortunately, for most users, `ar` is not in their path. If the `make` fails because it can't find `ar`, you should do a `man ar`, find out where it is located, and add that directory to your `PATH` environment variable (on Solaris systems, `ar` is in `/usr/ccs/bin`). You should then be able to run `make` again and successfully build Perl. It will take a while for the `make` process to work, so you might want to go do something else while it's working.)

Before you install Perl, you should type `make test` in the Perl directory to make sure everything was built correctly. Once that's finished, you can `make install` to move all of the Perl files to the locations that you specified using Configure.

One last question that might be asked is whether you want to link `/usr/bin/perl` to the location where you actually installed Perl. Many scripts assume that Perl will be located in `/usr/bin/perl`, so if you link your Perl binary to `/usr/bin/perl`, it could save you some work down the road.

Once `make install` is finished, Perl should be installed and ready to go. This time, if you installed Perl in a standard location in your `PATH`, then this time if you type

```
% perl -v
```

you should get a version message (`This is perl, version 5....`), and you're all set and ready to learn Perl.

For More Information

Since you're on UNIX, Perl was written for you. All the core Perl man pages, FAQs, utilities, modules, and documentation were originally written for UNIX, so you should be fine starting right off. The central repository of all things Perl is at `www.perl.com`; start from there and work downward. And, of course, there are always the pointers scattered throughout this book.

APPENDIX D

Installing Perl for Windows

This appendix explains how to obtain and install Perl for the Windows platform, sometimes known as Win32 Perl. Perl for Windows will run on Windows NT or Windows 95/98, although Perl is slightly more robust on Windows NT (I found very little that was different between the two platforms).

With the release of version 5.005 of Perl, Windows support has been incorporated into the core Perl source code tree, and is up to date with the UNIX version. Previously, there had been multiple different versions of Perl for Windows, with each version supporting different features and lagging behind the UNIX platform in different ways. The new merged 5.005 version has made a tremendous difference in stability and support for the Windows platform. If you have installed a previous version of Perl for Windows, I *strongly* suggest you upgrade to the latest version before starting this book.

To install Perl for Windows, you have two choices. You can

- Download the core Perl source code, and compile and build it yourself
- Download a pre-built version of Perl for Windows, sometimes called ActivePerl, from ActiveState

Going the source code route allows you to be up-to-minute with the latest bug fixes, experimental features, and changes, but you must have a modern C++ compiler (Microsoft's Visual C++, Borland C++, and so on) and you must understand how to build large C projects. Windows NT is definitely the better-supported platform for building Perl yourself. You'll also need to download and install the Win32 modules (`libwin32`) yourself in order to get access to various Windows features such as OLE and processes.

The other choice is to download the pre-built binary version of Perl from ActiveState. ActivePerl, as this version is called, contains Perl for Windows, some nice installation scripts, the Win32 Perl modules, PerlScript (an ActiveX scripting engine to replace JavaScript or VBScript inside Internet Explorer), Perl of ISAPI for Perl CGI scripts, and the Perl Package Manager (PPM), which makes installing extra Perl modules much easier.

Because the pre-built ActiveState version of Perl is probably the better choice for most Windows users, this appendix will primarily cover downloading and installing that version. If you'd prefer to build Perl yourself, I've included a section at the end of this appendix ("Downloading the Perl Source Code") to help you get started. The `README` files included with the source can help you get started from there.

Downloading Perl for Windows

The first step in installing Perl for Windows on your computer (either for Windows NT or Windows 95) is to download the installation package from ActiveState's Web site.

ActiveState is a company dedicated to building and supporting Perl and Perl tools on the Windows platform. ActiveState also offers a Perl developer's kit, a GUI-based Perl debugger and a plug-in for NT-based Web serves that improves CGI performance (although none of these packages are part of the core Perl for Windows package).

Get the latest version of Perl for Windows at `http://www.activestate.com/ActivePerl/download.html`. The links at the bottom of the page (under "Download the complete package") allow you to choose which platform (Intel or Alpha) and which download method to use to get the installation package. If you're using a Web browser to do the download, use HTTP.

If you are running Windows 95, you will also need the DCOM package from Microsoft in order to run Perl for Windows (you don't need it if you're running Windows NT or Windows 98). See the page at `http://www.microsoft.com/com/dcom/dcom1_2/default.asp` to get this package, and make sure it's installed before you install Perl for Windows.

Installing Perl for Windows

The Perl installed file you downloaded from ActiveState is a self-extracting zip archive. If you save the file to disk, double-click it to launch it and start the installation process. An installation wizard will launch. You'll need to agree to the Perl license, and read the installation notes (don't worry about what they mean right now). The next screen is the location for where to install Perl. The default location is `C:\Perl`. Choose a different directory, or choose Next to move onto the next screen.

At this step you'll have a choice for which components you want to install. Your choices are

- Perl: The core Perl installation.
- Perl for ISAPI: Only needed if you've got an IIS Web server and you'll be using Perl to develop CGI scripts for it.
- PerlScript: Only needed if you'll be using the PerlScript ActiveX plug-in.
- Online Help and Documentation: Always useful.
- Example Files: Also useful.

Next screen: here are those options you learned about earlier in the installation notes. You may have up to four choices:

- Adding Perl to your path
- Associating `.pl` files with the Perl executable
- Associating `.pl` files with your IIS or WebSite Web servers
- Associating `.plx` files with IIS and Perl for ISAPI

Unless you have compelling reasons not to do these things, you can go ahead and allow all four of these options when they occur.

Next screen: setting up Program Folder icons. Create a new ActivePerl folder, or add one to an existing folder.

The final screen will summarize all the options you've chosen. You can now go back and change your choices, or choose Next to start the actual installation and configuring process.

If you're on Windows 95, the next screen will ask you if you want to change your `autoexec.bat` file to add Perl to your path. This will allow you to run Perl from the command line. Unless you know how to modify the `PATH` variable in the `autoexec.bat` file yourself, and want to do this change on your own, go ahead and let the Perl installer do it for you (this screen will not appear on Windows NT).

After the installer finishes installing the files and configuring Perl for Windows, you can view the release notes or exit (the release notes contain lots of information about what's changed since the last release but probably aren't exceptionally useful if you're installing Perl for the first time). You'll also need to reboot your computer if you're on Windows 95.

And now you're ready to get started with Perl. If you look at the directory `C:\Perl` on your computer (or wherever you chose to install Perl), you'll see several subdirectories:

- `bin`: Contains the executable for Perl and all supporting tools.
- `eg`: Examples. Look at the files in this directory for example scripts various bits of Perl code (most of them are supplied on an as-is basis, and are undocumented, so they won't necessarily be helpful).
- `html`: Online documentation, in HTML format. You can use your favorite browser to read any of these files. Start from the file `index.html`.
- `lib`: Core library files.
- `site`: Additional library files supplied by ActiveState.

Running Perl for Windows

To run Perl for Windows, you'll need to start a command prompt window (a DOS prompt in Windows 95, or a command prompt in Windows NT). At the command line, you can make sure Perl's installed correctly with the `-v` option:

```
c:\> perl -v
```

You'll get a message telling you the version of Perl you're running and some other information about your Perl installation. This verifies that Perl has been installed correctly and that your system can find the Perl executable. From here, you can proceed to Day 1 and start writing Perl scripts.

Downloading the Perl Source Code

If you're looking to live on the cutting edge of Perl for Windows, you'll want to get the Perl source code instead of the binary version. Alternately, if you know something of C code, sometimes having the source around can help you figure out what's going on when your Perl scripts are not behaving the way you'd like them to. In either of these cases, you'll want to download the actual Perl source code as well as, or instead of, the ActiveState version of Perl.

Perl's source code is available at `http://language.perl.com/CPAN/src/`. There are a number of versions in that directory to choose from. The latest stable version is always available as `stable.tar.gz` (as I write this, that's version 5.005_02). Alternatively, the experimental development version is at `devel.tar.gz` (that's version 5.005_53 as I write this, but most likely will have changed by the time you're reading it). This book covers the `stable.tar.gz` version.

Perl source code is stored in UNIX-format `tar` archives, compressed with GNU zip. They are binary files, so download them in binary format. Once you have the archive stored on your system, WinZip can decompress and unarchive the Perl source files just fine.

The file `README.win32` provides detailed documentation for compiling the source into a workable Perl installation.

Getting More Information

Regardless of whether you're using the ActiveState build of Perl for Windows or not, ActiveState's Web site at `www.activestate.com` is a great place to start for help in getting started with Perl for Windows. From there you can find the Perl for Windows FAQ at `http://www.activestate.com/support/faqs/win32` and the various Perl for Windows mailing lists at `http://www.activestate.com/support/mailing_lists.htm`.

ActiveState also offers support for their version of Perl. See `http://www.activestate.com/support/` for details.

And, of course, there are always the standard Perl resources available at `www.perl.com` and pointers scattered throughout this book.

APPENDIX E

Installing Perl for the Macintosh

This appendix describes how to download and install the Perl software on a Macintosh computer. Although Perl is developed primarily on UNIX platform, it is ported to the Macintosh, and MacPerl has most of the features of the newest versions of Perl for UNIX and Windows. In addition, it also has a number of Macintosh-specific features that allow it to take advantage of many of the operating system features provided by the MacOS.

MacPerl requires System 7 or higher in order to run. You can run it on either a PowerPC or 68K Macintosh, although you'll need at least 4 megabytes of RAM and a 68020 or higher.

Downloading MacPerl

The first step in installing MacPerl on your computer is obtaining the installer package. You can find the MacPerl binary package at any number of common Macintosh software sites, but the best place to find it is at `www.perl.com`, specifically

```
http://www.perl.com/CPAN/ports/mac/
```

In that directory you'll see a number of files to choose from with names like `Mac_Perl_520r4_appl.bin`, `Mac_Perl_520r4_bigappl.bin`, or `Mac_Perl_520r4_src.bin`. The numbers refer to the current version (note that the version number may have changed by the time you read this). The `.bin` means its a MacBinary file. The middle parts (`appl`, `bigappl`, `src`, `tool`, and so on) refer to the type of installation package.

> There may also be packages for Perl 4 available in that directory—`Mac_Perl_418_appl.bin`, or some similar version. Don't pick this one. Choose the highest version number that you can. The examples in this book apply to Perl 5, and may not work with an earlier version.

First, you'll need to download the package version with `appl` in the name (`Mac_Perl_520r4_appl.bin`, for example). If you're running on a PowerPC Macintosh, this will have everything you need for the application version of MacPerl: the application, all the libraries, and the documentation.

You may also need some extra packages depending on whether you're using a 68K Mac or whether you're running MPW or not.

If you're running on a 68K Macintosh, the core application will work just fine, but you won't have access to the Mac toolbox libraries or to the GD (GIF graphics) library. To gain access to those extra libraries you'll need a special version of the application package in addition to the core `appl` package: the one with `bigappl` or the one with `appl_cfm68K` in the filenames. What's the difference? The former, `bigappl`, has the libraries compiled into the application itself. It makes for a big application that requires more memory. The latter, `appl_cfm68K`, allows the extra libraries to be dynamically loaded as needed, but in order to use that one you'll also need these files as part of your system (check your system folder):

- CFM-68K Runtime Enabler version 4.0 or higher
- AppleScript Lib version 1.2.2 or higher
- ObjectSupportLib version 1.2 or higher

If you're running MacOS 8 or higher you won't need any of those things, you can use the `appl_cfm68K` version just fine. The easy choice: download both `appl` and `bigappl`.

If you use MPW (Macintosh Programmer's Workshop), there's also an MPW tool available for MacPerl. In addition to the `appl` package, you'll also want the `tool` package (`Mac_Perl_520r4_tool.bin`). If you run MPW on a 68K Mac, you'll need a whole lot of stuff: `appl`, `tool`, your choice of `bigappl` or `appl_cfm68K`, and then `bigtool` as well to make sure you've got all the libraries you need.

There are also two other packages that may be of interest:

- `src`, which contains the MacPerl source code.
- `appl_only`, which is the same as `appl`, without any libraries or documentation.

All the MacPerl installation packages are stored on `www.perl.com` in MacBinary format, and are self-extracting archives. After downloading the file `Mac_Perl_520r4_appl.bin` to your computer, for example, you should end up with application called `Mac_Perl_520r4_appl` (minus the `.bin` extension). If it still has a `.bin` extension, you'll need a tool such as Stuffit or MacBinary II to convert it into an archive that can be double-clicked and launched. These utilities can be acquired at any of the common Mac software repositories (try `www.shareware.com` or `www.download.com`).

Installing MacPerl

Once you've got all the installer files you need downloaded onto your Macintosh, you can install each one in turn. To launch an installer, simply double-click on its icon.

Start with the core MacPerl application regardless of whether you're on a PowerPC or 68K or whether you're using MPW or not. First, read and accept the MacPerl readme. You'll see a standard Macintosh installation dialog, from which you can choose the disk and folder where MacPerl will be installed.

The Easy Install is the easiest solution for installing MacPerl; this will install MacPerl for your platform, as well as all the shared libraries. If you choose Custom Install, you can install a "fat" binary, which will run on both 68K and PowerPC Macintoshes. You'll only need this if you're installing it on a disk that might be used on different machines. You can also choose whether or not to install the shared libraries for MacPerl.

The installation process installs everything into a folder called, amazingly, MacPerl. Inside that folder is

- The MacPerl application
- Folders called `lib` and `ext`, in which all your Perl libraries and extensions are installed

- A folder called `pod`, in which the MacPerl help files are stored
- An application called `Shuck`, with which you can read the pod files
- Many scripts, examples, and README files

Once you have the core installation done, then you can install any other packages you may have downloaded. If you're running on a 68K Mac, install either the `bigappl` or `appl_cfm68K` packages. If you're running MPW, install the `tool` package. And if you're on a 68K Mac running MPW, install `appl` first, then `bigappl` or `appl_cfm68K`, then `tool`, then `bigtool`, in that order.

Starting the MacPerl Application

Once you're done installing everything, you can start MacPerl and begin writing Perl scripts. To start MacPerl, double-click on the MacPerl icon.

For help getting started with MacPerl, you may want to also start the `Shuck` application. `Shuck` provides easy access to all of the MacPerl and Perl documentation, and enables you to read Perl documentation files, like those encapsulated within Perl modules. Check out the options in the Go menu for easy access to the standard MacPerl documentation.

Running MacPerl from Inside MPW

If you're using the Perl MPW tool, I'm assuming you are already familiar with MPW itself. The MPW Perl tool allows you to edit Perl scripts from within MPW and run Perl from the MPW command line. In this respect, it is closer to the original UNIX version of Perl than to an actual Macintosh application.

This book, however, assumes that most readers will be using the application version of MacPerl, and the focus in this book will be on that package.

Getting More Information

As I write this, the current version of MacPerl is 5.2.0r4, which corresponds to the 5.004 version of Perl for UNIX. The 5 part of the MacPerl version refers to the major core Perl version number; the r4 part refers to the minor core Perl version number; and the .2.0 part refers to the minor version number for *MacPerl*, not for Perl itself. Some of the more recent features of Perl may not be available for MacPerl, but for the most part the differences are minor (features in this book that are noted as 5.005 features may not be available for MacPerl).

The official MacPerl home page is at `http://www.iis.ee.ethz.ch/~neeri/macintosh/perl.html`. However, more detailed and up-to-date information about MacPerl can be found in the MacPerl FAQ at `http:www.perl.com/CPAN/doc/FAQs/mac/MacPerlFAQ.html`. The MacPerl pages at Prime Time Freeware, `http://www.ptf.com/macperl/`, also contain a wealth of information.

If you're planning on doing a lot of work with MacPerl, there's a mailing list available. See the page at `http://www.ptf.com/macperl/depts/mlist.html` for information on subscribing or for viewing the archive of posts.

And, of course, there's always the standard Perl resources available at `www.perl.com` and pointers scattered throughout this book.

INDEX

Symbols

A

B

C

D

E

F

G

H

I

J-K

L

M

N

O

P

S

V

W

X-Y-Z

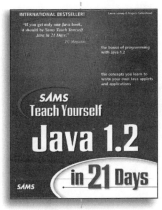